COLD IRON

ALSO BY STINA LEICHT

The Fey and the Fallen
Of Blood and Honey
And Blue Skies From Pain

THE MALORUM GATES
BOOK ONE

COLD IRON

STINA LEICHT

SAGA PRESS

LONDON SYDNEY **NEW YORK** TORONTO NEW DELHI

SAGA PRESS
AN IMPRINT OF SIMON & SCHUSTER, INC.

1230 AVENUE OF THE AMERICAS, NEW YORK, NEW YORK 10020

Text copyright © 2015 by Christina Leicht
Cover illustration copyright © 2015 by Alejandro Colucci

First SAGA PRESS paperback edition July 2015
SAGA PRESS and colophon are trademarks of Simon & Schuster, Inc.
For information about special discounts for bulk purchases, please contact Simon & Schuster Special Sales at 1-866-506-1949 or business@simonandschuster.com.
The Simon & Schuster Speakers Bureau can bring authors to your live event. For more information or to book an event, contact the Simon & Schuster Speakers Bureau at 1-866-248-3049 or visit our website at www.simonspeakers.com.
Also available in a SAGA PRESS hardcover edition
Map illustrations by Robert Lazzaretti
The text for this book is set in Adobe Jenson Pro.
Manufactured in the United States of America
2 4 6 8 10 9 7 5 3 1
CIP data for this book is available from the Library of Congress.
ISBN 978-1-4814-4255-8 (hc)
ISBN 978-1-4814-2777-7 (pbk)
ISBN 978-1-4814-2779-1 (eBook)

To my agent, Barry Goldblatt,
and my editor, Joe Monti,
for believing in me even when I didn't.

And, as always, to Dane Caruthers:
As you wish.

THE CONTINENT OF VÄSTMARKE

KALE

MASSILIA

(see detail map)

Ghost Horse Glacier

DAN

TAHMER

KINGDOM OF YTLAIN

KINGDOM OF ELEDORE

REGNUM OF ACRASIA

N

W — E

S

COLD IRON

⊰ NELS ⊱

ONE

It was late, but Nels couldn't sleep. Worries concerning the morning's journey circled his skull until he grew to hate the look of his bed curtains. Worse, when he had slept, he'd had terrible nightmares. He told himself that prognostication didn't run in his family line and the dreams were meaningless. Nothing seemed to help. The nightmares fomented feelings of nameless dread until the need to flee his bedchamber in search of company was huge.

Captain Karpanen might still be awake, he thought.

A fire in the hearth cast his room in ruddy shadows. Grabbing a thick velvet robe, he crept through his private parlor. Then he exited into the chilly darkness of the outer hallway, the door shutting behind him with a quiet click.

Placing a hand on the cold stone wall, he shuffled into darkness. The sound of his feet against the palace's stately marble floors echoed down the hallway. There were no carpets. They had yet to be replaced—a casualty of one of Nels's pranks. Marble chilled his bare feet until it was painful to walk. His trailing fingers brushed against a painting, almost sending it crashing to the floor, but he caught it and straightened the picture as best he could in the dark. He then resumed his journey. Taking the first left, he spotted warm light pooling at the bottom of the door at the end. He listened before knocking and then entered.

In contrast to the rest of the palace, the captain's sitting room was spare and precise. As usual, it made entering seem like a visit to a foreign country. What furniture there was of Ytlainen make, carved from birch and decorated in intricate geometric patterns. This, in contrast to the current Eledorean fashion of organic curves and swirls. A lone painting graced the wall above the fireplace. It was a landscape depicting an unfamiliar mountain and executed in loose brush strokes. Unlike any work of art Nels had ever seen, it was his favorite. Up close, it appeared to be nothing but flat strokes of color. However, if he viewed it from across the room, the picture took on more depth and reality. Made of soft purples, blues, and greens, it'd taken him an entire afternoon to realize that there was no black pigment in it at all. That in itself was unusual, given that it hung in a soldier's apartments. Nels had always assumed the painting originated from the Kingdom of Ytlain like its owner. Never having been outside of Eledore, let alone the city of Jalokivi, he didn't know for sure.

Nels surreptitiously shut the door behind him. His nose was immediately met with a comforting mix of old incense, warm candle wax, and burning charcoal.

Captain Karpanen paused and then placed a wicked-looking dagger between a beeswax candle and his saber on the birchwood altar table. Several other items were arranged on the table's surface, among them a small, stoppered brown bottle, a black bowl of herbs, and a second ceramic bowl painted dark blue. The ornate blue bowl contained white sand and a single piece of glowing charcoal.

"What are you doing?" Nels asked, eager to put his nightmares behind him.

Karpanen was dressed in a loose, worn evening robe of faded green linen decorated with an ornate Ytlainen pattern. Even the cut of the sleeves was foreign. Nels hadn't seen anyone else in the palace wear anything like it, and he had the impression it was older than he was. The collar of a white silk nightshirt half escaped the frayed robe.

He's not wearing any black, Nels thought. It struck him as a little more than daring. *He's in his own rooms. He can do what he wants, can't he?* In Eledore, the color was used to set soldiers apart. It served as a warning. Soldiers were unclean. *Mother says the Ytlainen don't keep Blood Custom, not like Eledoreans do.*

A small silver medal with the figure of a horse embossed on it hung off a silver chain around Karpanen's neck. His feet were bare, and his long, light brown hair rippled down his back. It looked as though he'd only just freed it of its braid. That was unusual for Karpanen. He was normally exacting and tidy. It gave Nels a bad feeling.

The quiet hiss from the charcoal filled an expectant silence.

Karpanen at last spoke in a cool tone. "Did I say you could enter?"

"I knocked like you asked. But you didn't answer."

"It's late, Nels. I might have been entertaining someone."

Aged fifteen—*almost sixteen*—Nels was annoyed that the captain thought him too young to understand. "You aren't. I listened at the door first. Anyway, I asked Lady Karita months ago if you had a lover, and she said you didn't. You don't even keep an automaton." He'd added that last bit to demonstrate worldliness and then regretted it when he spied a flash of insult in Karpanen's unyielding black eyes. "You've no lover at all. At least, not since you moved into the palace."

The Eledorean royal court was a dangerous place. As crown

prince, Nels had learned early that he couldn't afford ignorance. Therefore, he paid regular bribes in exchange for information.

"Hasn't anyone told you that spying on people is impolite?" Karpanen asked.

"Sure," Nels said with a shrug. "You do. All the time." He gave the captain his most charming smile. "Doesn't stop me, though."

"Too bad," the captain said in a patient tone that bordered on amused.

"No one tells me anything," Nels said. "How else am I to know what's going on?"

"Shouldn't you be asleep?"

Relieved that the offense had been forgiven, Nels relaxed. Of course, the mistake would run over and over in his mind later, and he'd think again and again about what he should've said. He never seemed to learn. Unlike his twin sister, Suvi, he was always saying the wrong thing at the wrong time. Luckily, Karpanen rarely stayed angry with him.

Nels stepped farther into the room. "Is this a soldier's ritual?" There wasn't anyone around to be shocked by his curiosity. Showing off ill-gotten knowledge, he pointed at the contents of the black bowl. "That's sandalwood, isn't it?"

"That would be one of the ingredients." Karpanen sounded almost pleased. His irises changed from hard black to a warm gray.

"And clove oil? That's clove oil." Nels pointed at the little brown bottle. "That's for keeping rust off blades. Oh! I know. This is a cleansing ritual, isn't it?" He'd stolen—*borrowed*—one or two of Karpanen's books on martial practices. Of course, he'd done so one at a time and returned each before Karpanen could notice the loss. "Will you show me how?"

"You know good and well such things are forbidden."

"Show me anyway. Please?" Nels stepped closer to the birchwood altar table with its silver inlay design. "You promised you would one day. I won't tell anyone. I swear."

"I can't. Your mother—"

"Oooooooh! Is that blood?" Nels pointed at the saber lying on the table. He'd heard that there'd been an execution earlier in the day. He didn't know the details. No one of quality spoke openly of blood or death, nor did they associate with those who dealt in them. In any case, the execution wouldn't have involved anyone he knew, other than Karpanen. Karpanen's responsibilities—in addition to watching over the queen and the crown prince—included standing in as royal executioner whenever Nels's father, King Henrik Ilmari, demanded it.

That seemed an odd combination of duties now that Nels thought about it.

"Don't touch that! It's unclean!"

Nels jerked his hand from the blade before it could be slapped, and frowned. "I wasn't going to."

Captain Karpanen sighed, and his eyes lightened to dove gray. "All right. If I show you how to reconsecrate a blade, will you go to bed? Tomorrow will be a long, tiring day, and you need your sleep."

Nels's pride stung. "I'm not a child."

The morning's journey would be his first attempt at independence. Publicly, the intent was to travel south to Gardemeister where the Silmaillia, Saara Korpela, the king's seer and personal healer lived. It was to be a dull holiday excursion—even if it was his first. He'd told everyone he wanted to see the country over which he would one day rule. In reality, his intensions were far more dangerous. *If I'm caught, Uncle Sakari will have me killed. But I have to do something. Now. Before father names Suvi heir in my stead.* Disturbing, persistent questions about the future gnawed at his confidence like rats. *I'm not afraid. I'm not.* Eledorean princes were never afraid. Fear was for the powerless, and he had power. His mother said her side of the family often matured late. She told him she'd had reassurances from the Silmaillia. He didn't have anything to worry about. *I'm a royal prince. I'm not a changeling.*

"Any experienced soldier would know that getting enough sleep can mean the difference between life and death," Karpanen said.

"We're not going into . . . battle."

Karpanen raised an eyebrow in question.

He senses the danger even if you haven't told him the truth, Nels thought. "Fine. I'll go to bed. After."

Karpanen stared him directly in the eyes. The color of his irises had returned to that flinty black. "Do you promise?"

"I swear." Out of habit, Nels made the oath in Acrasian and crossed his heart using his index finger. He understood it was an Acrasian custom. He made a habit of studying foreign languages and cultures. Being able to speak more languages than anyone else made him feel accomplished in spite of his other failings. There were advantages in such information. His father's spies couldn't report what they didn't understand.

Karpanen frowned. "What did you say?"

"I'm sorry," Nels said. "I give you my word, sir." He used formal Eledorean court speech for the oath and had added the "sir" without thinking. His cheeks grew hot, and he looked away. This, after the latest stern talk from the king. Fixing his attention on the altar table, Nels hoped Karpanen didn't notice the slip.

"Stand on the carpet," Karpanen said. "Here. On my left." He paused. "Where are your slippers?"

"I forgot them."

"Aren't you cold?"

Nels nodded.

Karpanen left briefly for his bedchamber and then returned.

Nels noticed a bloodstained rag resting on the table. "What's that?" he asked, pointing at the rag.

"Never mind that." He dropped a pair of old slippers on the floor next to Nels's feet. "Put those on."

Worn brown velvet warmed Nels's frozen feet at once. The slippers were too big, of course. He wiggled his toes, enjoying the feel, nonetheless. "Thanks."

"Be quiet, please. And stop your fidgeting."

"But—"

"Do you want me to teach you or not?" Karpanen asked. "Close your eyes. Focus on your breathing and empty your mind like I taught you."

"Why? Aren't you going to show me how to clean the blade?"

"Don't waste time asking useless questions. What did I tell you about the distinction between what people do and what people say?"

"Actions speak truth even when words lie."

"Exactly. Now be quiet and observe. Empty your mind and then listen carefully. I'll answer your questions afterward."

Nels shut his eyes and breathed in the peaceful atmosphere. The ticking of the mantel clock over the fireplace and the slow ebb-and-flow rhythm of his breaths marked the time. He heard the quiet rustle of silk against linen as Karpanen moved. Nels opened his eyes at once. He didn't want to miss a thing.

Karpanen poured a small amount of herbs onto the charcoal. Thick white smoke rose from the blue bowl. He waved a hand over it, breathing in the scented fumes. He then resumed his former posture, closed his eyes, and raised his hands. Then he spoke in a low voice, almost a whisper. "Great Hasta, White Queen of Crossroads, Horse Mother, Protector of the Weak, Giver of Life, Escort of the Newly Dead, we beg your favor this night." He paused and then bent at the waist with his hands folded in front of his face in prayer.

"Your servant asks your forgiveness, and forgiveness for those I've slain, that they might pass into the next world without the great burden of anger or fear. Bless us, those you have chosen for your rite of life and death. Remove the stains of our inequity, for all are equal in your eyes. Forgive me my rage felt for fallen brothers and sisters. And forgive my pride in my skill as well as my joy in victory. I will remember with respect those I kill, although I remove their life's blood from my blade." He took up the damp, stained cloth and began working at the small amounts of dried crimson on the saber in silence. When he finally finished, he followed this up with a coat of clove oil from the brown bottle, using a clean rag.

Breathing in the spicy mixture of incense smoke and oil, a combination of feelings overcame Nels. He had a sense of the sacred, but he also felt a thrill. *Father would have apoplexy if he knew I was here.*

"Please grant Sir Joonas Pohjonen an easy and safe passage to the next world, Lady Hasta."

Nels blinked as he recognized the name. Sir Pohjonen was a notorious court dandy and a flirt. He was also—*had been*—one of his father's favorite violin players. Nels looked to Karpanen, and the sense of danger intensified.

"Please watch over the loved ones he leaves behind." Karpanen next picked up the wicked-looking dagger, shoved up his sleeve, and sliced the back of a scarred forearm. "I hereby pay the blood-price for their care." He let a few drops of blood fall onto the hot charcoal. It hissed, and the scent of burning blood met the air. He then used the clove oil–soaked cloth to dab the wound clean. When the bleeding stopped, he collected both rags, went to the fireplace, and tossed them into the flames. "Please, Hasta, free your servant and his weapons of all blemish so that he might continue to do your holy work." He turned to the water bowl and rinsed his hands, drying them on a clean white cloth. Then he used the whetstone on both the dagger and the saber. Once they were sharpened to his satisfaction, he gave them a last coat of clove oil before replacing them on the altar. "With this water, please bless your humble servant, Great Hasta." He sprinkled a little on himself, and as if on a whim, Karpanen playfully flicked a bit of water in Nels's face.

Nels was only just able to keep from laughing.

Karpanen resumed a serious demeanor. "Thank you, Lady Hasta." He bowed again with his hands folded in front of his nose. Straightening, he placed another pinch of herbs onto the charcoal and again breathed the smoke. After a few moments of silent prayer, he turned. "All right, Nels. You may ask your questions."

Nels hesitated, not out of a lack of curiosity. There were at least twenty questions burning on his lips. However, there was one in particular he deeply desired to ask. At the same time, he didn't want Karpanen to think him perverted. It wasn't as if Nels had a secret wish to kill. That would be an abomination beyond any he could imagine. It was only that he wanted to know what it was like to be a soldier, and the question was at the heart of what being a soldier was about. He decided to take a chance. "What's it like to kill someone?"

Karpanen blinked and looked away in shame, and Nels felt an overwhelming guilt for having hurt the one person he looked up to and cared for as much as he did his mother and sister.

Stupid! You are a defective, just as they say. How could I ask him that? Nels said out loud, "I'm sorry. I didn't mean—"

"It's time for you to go to bed," Karpanen said without looking at him.

"I do mean it, sir. I'm so sorry."

"Go." Karpanen turned his back on him and ran a hand through his untidy hair. "Now. Please." The hand trembled as he lowered it to his side.

TWO

"Was this the route approved by the Seneschal of the Chamber?" Captain Karpanen asked. "Shouldn't we have taken a left ten miles back? We should be headed east. Not south."

Nels struggled to find an answer that wouldn't be an outright lie. The king had insisted that Nels distance himself from the captain. *You're too dependent upon Karpanen. Everyone knows it. It's unseemly.* But that didn't mean Nels actually wanted to comply with his father's wishes.

I should've left without Karpanen. But Nels knew that would never have happened. The truth was, he hadn't traveled outside the palace without the captain in his life. Of course, if Nels were truthful, and he wasn't always, there'd been another reason for taking Karpanen with him.

Nels was terrified of his Uncle Sakari.

"Why is *he* in charge, sir?" one of the other guardsmen asked Karpanen in a tone just loud enough for Nels to hear. "He isn't old enough to grow a beard. We should turn—"

Karpanen cut off the remainder of the guardsman's words

with a glare. Riding behind Karpanen, Nels didn't actually see it. He didn't need to. He was familiar enough with Karpanen's disapproving stares to know. Chastised, the guardsman in question magically compelled his horse to slow with a word and resumed his place at the rear.

"I asked you a question, young prince," Karpanen said over his shoulder. He used formal court speech, and while the words indicated the utmost respect they still managed to sound like a command.

How does he do that? Nels thought. *And why can't I? I'll never be the leader he is, will I?*

The royal family of Ilmari prided itself on the power of absolute command. All the Ilmaris possessed it in one form or another. The talent had been present in the royal line from the first Ilmari. That unbroken line of power was used to support the divine right of kings. All kainen had talents of one form or another. It was said that the strength of that ability determined one's place in life, and the ability to bend others to your will was what set the upper classes apart from the lower. Even lesser nobility had command of animals. Yet the royal catacombs told a different story. Like much of Eledore's hidden histories, changelings and other defectives supposedly didn't exist in the royal family. However, less than a month before, his father had taken Nels on a private tour beneath the castle. There, he'd seen for himself the quarters where royal changelings lived out the last of their days—buried alive, used for sport. The unspoken message was clear: develop the power of command or vanish in those tombs beneath the palace.

"And now I ask it a second time," Karpanen continued. "Are you certain this is the correct road?"

Heart thudding in his ears, Nels decided to ignore Karpanen. The king did so often enough when underlings asked questions he didn't like. In truth, Nels didn't know how to deal with the complications that a truthful explanation would foster. Summer was almost over. The wind was already perfumed with the scent of dying leaves. With the arrival of fall would come his and his twin sister's sixteenth birthday, and with that would come the official confirmation of their father's successor. Such a thing was unusual, but so was the birth of twins in the Royal House of Hännenen.

More important, there was his father's unspoken warning.

I'm not a changeling. I can't be.

He had no control over when his powers would manifest any more than he could rush the growing of a beard, but he did have the ability to prove himself in other ways. He could best his uncle at one of his games, and he would start with the Province of Hirvi. Uncle Sakari currently served as the protector of Hirvi, but that would end when Nels came of age on his sixteenth birthday. Normally, the crown prince would be eased into the role and kept informed. However, his uncle had repeatedly declined to do so. It was suspicious. Still, Uncle Sakari continued to insist that all was peaceful and profitable in the province, and that there was no need for oversight before the change. The border dispute with Acrasian Regnum was over. In any case, Eledore had nothing to fear from humans—creatures that had more in common with animals than with kainen. That much everyone knew to be true. However, Nels's mother, the queen, had conflicting information. She'd told Nels that reports from Hirvi were being falsified. His mother had been his primary tutor when it came to politics, and she'd taught him that when it came to hidden plots, it was wise to follow the money. There was a reason Sakari didn't want anyone to look too closely at Hirvi. That was obvious, and Nels intended to find out what that reason was. Everything pointed to the city of Merta and her silver mines.

But now, everything is falling apart.

Proving himself was vital. Karpanen's objections weren't.

One more month of being treated like a child. One. Of course, thanks to his father, Nels didn't have a month. He wasn't sure he had one week.

"Well?" Karpanen asked.

What am I to do? He won't give up until I answer. Nels supposed he was lucky the ruse had lasted as long as it had. He hadn't wanted to alert Uncle Sakari. So, he'd chosen an indirect route to Merta. *Should I tell Karpanen our real destination? Can I risk it?* Nels wasn't certain of the other guardsmen. One of them most certainly would be spying for Sakari, and Karpanen would likely insist on returning to Jalokivi. Nonetheless, Nels would not turn back. He couldn't. As long as he was outside the palace, he could buy himself time. He might yet avoid the catacombs. *Can I tell Karpanen?* There was too much at stake, and they still had several days of travel before they reached Merta.

Nels settled on a half-truth. "This journey was organized at Father's request."

The king had suggested a journey but only to rid himself of an annoyance. Angry, Nels had left an inaccurate itinerary with an overwhelmed seneschal. Of course, it wasn't as if the king would notice. *And if I were Suvi, he wouldn't care whether I left Jalokivi or not,* Nels thought. Sometimes, he was envious of his twin sister. Her every move wasn't judged and weighed. She was free to do whatever she wanted. She already had her powers. It wasn't fair. *If Father names Suvi heir designate, what will become of me?*

"Kai? I would see the map. Bring it here." Karpanen muttered another magic-laced word of command to his gelding.

The horse stopped at once, causing Nels to bring Loimuta up short with the reins. Embarrassment heated his cheeks. He hadn't used a verbal command. *The others already think me a defective.*

Kai said, "I don't have the map, sir. I—"

"I have the map," Nels said. "And I'm quite capable of reading it." The plan was to travel south, loop around the end of the Selkäranka Mountains, and then head north to the city of Merta. He squeezed Loimuta's sides with his knees, signaling he wished to continue, and then spoke a useless command word. The horse slowly eased around Karpanen's gelding. "We're exactly where we should be."

Karpanen spat out a word, magically compelling Loimuta to halt. Insulted, Nels turned to face the captain. A cool breeze toyed with the black feather in Karpanen's broad-brimmed black hat. The captain frowned, and his eyes narrowed. Nels's heart slammed even harder inside the cage of his chest. He was only able to hold Karpanen's unyielding black gaze for three heartbeats before looking away.

Remembering the latest reprimand he'd gotten from his father regarding Karpanen, Nels sat taller in the saddle. *I'm in charge. Not him.* He slowed his breathing and once more attempted to face down the captain.

"I know you," Karpanen said, keeping his voice low so that the others wouldn't hear. His gaze was sharp, steady, and yet, there was a hint of compassion. "You're up to something. You have to let me in on it." His horse shifted, restless.

Swallowing a burning lump in his throat, Nels set his jaw. The memory of Sir Joonas Pohjonen's fate was close as Nels struggled with his inadequacy. *Be strong. Firm. The others are watching.* "Do your duties include interpreting my father's wishes in addition to following me about like a nursemaid?"

Captain Karpanen's face registered surprise before it transformed into a mask of professionalism.

Shit, Nels thought. *Now I've done it. I've gone too far.*

Karpanen cleared his throat, then said, "We are at war, young prince."

"The Acrasian quarrel is over. Anyway, that would hardly count as a war," Nels said. "Father says—"

"Listen to me. This area is dangerous," Karpanen said, keeping his voice low. "Acrasian squatters have—"

"Not here. Not this far north. The Acrasian ambassador has assured us that the Regnum has not pressed its interests beyond Greenleaf," Nels said. *It's Uncle Sakari who is up to something, not the Acrasians.*

Captain Karpanen whispered again, "The Acrasian ambassador only tells the king what he wishes to hear."

"That's impossible. Humans aren't mentally capable of such duplicity." Nels felt the blood pound in his temples. Bright spots appeared in his vision until he blinked them away. His stomach did another lurch. He swallowed his nausea as he caught a smirk lodged on the formerly reprimanded guardsman's lips.

"The Acrasian ambassador is entirely under your uncle's thrall," Karpanen whispered. "Listen to me, boy—"

The other guardsman's expression stung Nels. "Release my horse at once," he said as loud as he could.

"I humbly apologize, Your Grace." Captain Karpanen withdrew his influence from Loimuta. Then he shook his head and gave the other guardsmen a short series of hand signals. Resuming the lead, Karpanen's horse broke into a trot.

Nels swallowed the apology wedging itself in his throat. It was unfair to take out his discomfort and frustration on Karpanen, and Nels hated himself for doing it. He admired Karpanen. He was one of Nels's few friends, but the relationship was considered inappropriate and, some said, treasonous. Karpanen was a soldier and a foreigner, no matter he was the queen's cousin. Nels didn't care about taboos or what anyone said. *That is, until now. Now you're worried about what damage he'll do to your position at court. Isn't that right?* Nels wanted to take back the insult more than anything. He wanted to ask Karpanen's advice but couldn't think of how to do so without appearing weak. There was another reason, of course. Nels was afraid of what his father might do to Karpanen if the captain were made a part of the plot.

Father never apologizes, Nels thought. Apparently, that was something kings didn't do, certainly not to servants, and Karpanen was a servant—less than that, really. So were the others. Nels knew he shouldn't care, but he did. He gave Loimuta another hidden signal, shifting his weight forward in the saddle. Disgusted with himself, he didn't bother to cover it with a verbal command. There was no one to notice outside of his personal guards, and they already knew the truth.

Defective. Changeling.

Late maturity isn't unusual in Mother's family line. Mother said so. What if Mother is wrong? What if the Silmaillia lied?

Nels wanted to be sick. Breakfast wasn't sitting well, and even Loimuta's smooth gait was proving a problem. *I won't get sick. I won't show myself for a weakling. Not in front of Karpanen. I won't.* He swallowed the slick lump in the back of his throat, forcing it down. There was something wrong with his eyes, too. All morning, he'd been seeing spots of light come and go—light he was sure wasn't actually there. At least, no one else had reacted as if they'd seen it. He briefly wondered what it meant, and then went back to worrying about his future.

The woods thinned, and half-mown fields appeared on both sides of the path. If the map was accurate, they were nearing a hamlet called Onni. Nels urged Loimuta into a trot, attempting to pass Karpanen. To Nels's annoyance, the captain kept pace, easing to the left. Karpanen issued another series of hand signals. A second Royal Guardsman flanked Nels's right.

Karpanen scowled at the fields and then placed a hand on the hilt of his sword. "Something is wrong."

They'd traveled the few remaining yards to the hamlet's perimeter wall before Nels sensed it, too. He glanced back to the fields. It was late in the season for unharvested crops. *Why would they risk the corn rotting?* An uncertain chill crawled up Nels's spine. At that moment, a hatless woman in patched mercenary black stepped into the middle of the road with a drawn saber. Her long red hair was bound into a ponytail. She held up a hand, barring the way. Nels signaled for Loimuta to stop, barely remembering to speak the command first. The hissing chime of drawn steel gave Nels a start. Sensing the tension, Loimuta stamped in place, and the muscles in the gelding's white neck quivered. Nels kept a wary eye on the mercenary. A male freeholder dressed in green stepped from behind one of the cottages.

"Who are you?" the red-haired mercenary asked.

"Who wishes to know?" Captain Karpanen asked in return.

An archer, also wearing loose-fitting black, settled against the corner of a cottage. Nels counted Onni's buildings, and his unease worsened.

A hamlet of perhaps three families supports two mercenaries?

Captain Karpanen turned to the archer. "Is this the way you greet noble visitors?"

"We are at war, my lord," the red-haired mercenary said. She bowed her head but kept her eyes on Karpanen.

Nels grew impatient with Karpanen's posturing and dismounted. "The war has advanced this far inland?" According to his uncle's agents, the area was peaceful. His mother's contacts indicated otherwise. This was the sort of information Nels needed.

Captain Karpanen cursed, sheathed his blade, and then dismounted. The soles of his black boots slapped hardpacked ground.

Nels dismissed the frowning Karpanen with a gesture. It was time to dispense with pretense. "I'm here to learn the truth." He turned to the red-haired mercenary. "What is your name?"

She stepped closer, examining the falcon emblem stitched on Nels's green velvet traveling coat. The point of her blade lowered, and a surprised look replaced suspicion. "My name is Tarja. Tarja Lassila, Your Highness."

"Tell me. What is going on?" Nels asked.

At that moment, one of the Royal Guardsmen let out a warning cry. Nels felt rather than saw Captain Karpanen throw himself into a protective stance, using his body as a shield. "Get down, Nels!"

A large insect buzzed past Nels's cheek. A crossbow bolt appeared in Tarja's throat. Confused, Nels gaped. Tarja let out a wet choke before collapsing. Then a crushing force drove Nels to the ground. Gasping for air, he registered the hiss of more bolts, thunderclaps, screams, and horse squeals of pain. *Loimuta?* White smoke blotted out the sun. He felt a hard slap. His eyes watered with the sting of the blow. The shivering lights appeared again— this time, the spots grew until they blinded him. He squeezed his eyes shut in spite of all that was happening and bit back frozen panic. *Have I gone blind?* He felt a hand against his left cheek and brushed it away. The sounds of battle stopped almost as soon as they'd started. Peeking out from under his eyelids, he was relieved to discover he could see again, and blinked until his vision shifted into focus. Someone was lying on top of him. He recognized the black braid on the dark blue uniform sleeve.

"Captain, leave off. I'm all right." When no response came, Nels struggled to roll over, but with Karpanen's weight pressing, it was difficult. Muddy stickiness clung to his right cheek. He tasted salty grit. He spit to clear his mouth. *Why doesn't he move?* "Captain Karpanen?"

A pair of scuffed brown boots stopped inches from Nels's nose. He heard deep voices and laughter. It took several moments to register they weren't speaking Eledorean. He strained to look upward. The man standing over him wore peculiar clothes. His features were blunt, and his hair was cropped very short, revealing the rounded tips of his ears. Nels's heart staggered.

They're human. They must be Acrasians.

"You missed one, Lucian," the owner of the brown boots said.

"Is it wearing any black?"

"No," Brown Boots said. "Green."

"Don't pay it any mind. Docile as lambs, they are. It's the ones that wear black you have to worry about." Nels heard footsteps rustle in the dead leaves. "Huh. It looks rich. Maybe it knows where the silver is buried. Georgie said there won't be any markers."

Nels felt the mass trapping him shift. He heard Captain Karpanen groan. Brown Boots stooped and roughly tugged at Karpanen. With the captain's weight gone, Nels was able to sit up. He saw Brown Boots had Captain Karpanen by the hair. Crimson stained the front of Karpanen's uniform coat. There was a round wound in his chest, and Nels could hear wet choking sounds as the captain struggled to breathe. His eyes fluttered open. Blood leaked from his lips. He mouthed one word before Brown Boots's blade caught him under the chin.

Run.

Instead, Nels winced and shut his eyes. A hot splash hit him full in the face. He tasted blood and wiped his face clean. When he saw his crimson-stained hands, everything stopped. At the edges of his vision, the colors of the trees and the ground took on a strange darkness, except for the blood. The blood remained a bright red. He wanted to run as Captain Karpanen had urged, but Nels couldn't get his legs to work. He looked around and found the other three guardsmen were dead. His stomach did another lazy roll. *Captain Karpanen is gone. Do something. Now.*

He can't be. He's my protector.

Brown boots grabbed Nels by his coat collar. Nels's long hair got caught in the Acrasian's grip. Sharp pain slapped back some of the numbness.

"What do I do with this one?" Brown boots asked.

A short Acrasian with graying hair stepped over Captain Karpanen's body. Wiping blood from his knife, he squinted at Nels with pale, unchanging Acrasian eyes. "Leave it for now. Help Paine, Marrek, and Harris round up the others."

Nels was dumped to the ground, getting another mouthful of bloody dirt. Again, his stomach threatened revolt. Brown Boots strode into the hamlet and whistled a jaunty tune. The strange melody echoed off the buildings with a cheerful menace. Nels felt as though he were in a trance. The crash of broken doors and screams held no meaning. No urgency. Such things belonged to a separate existence, one that Nels wasn't yet a part of. He got to his feet and then gazed down at Captain Karpanen's body. *He died for me. He was at my side every day of my life. And I didn't know his full name.*

It wasn't seemly.

What does "seemly" matter now? Nels couldn't look away from the blood, the stillness of the captain's body, the sheen of a polished silver scabbard in the sunlight. *Why didn't Captain Karpanen protect me?* The flash of anger was replaced with shame. *This is my fault. I brought all of them here. I did this. I didn't listen. He was right. This is my fault.* Nels felt a tug on his sleeve.

"Come," Lucian said in badly accented Eledorean.

Nels didn't budge. Lucian muttered something in Acrasian that sounded like a curse and reared back for a slap. Unconcerned, Nels turned to stare at the ruby set in the pommel of Karpanen's saber. Scabbard and blade were half-trapped beneath the captain's leg.

Pick up the sword.

Lucian struck. After an instant's numbness, pain exploded in Nels's jaw. He blinked watering eyes until it faded. His only real connection to the disjointed world was his swelling lip. He explored the bleeding wound with a distracted tongue. *The saber.*

It's forbidden to draw a dead soldier's blade. It wasn't appropriate for someone of his standing to handle weapons of any kind—let alone a blooded saber. Blood was unclean. *Karpanen was my friend. He was supposed to protect me.*

A whisper of anger stirred in the emptiness. *Respect for the dead isn't important. Survival is.*

I'm not a soldier. I'm the crown prince.

Nels felt himself dragged a couple of feet to a cluster of fearful villagers. Others were driven from hiding. Cries of protest mingled with the terrified wailing of small children. An old woman trapped him with a wet stare full of expectation. Anxiety struck home. Captain Karpanen's voice snarled in the back of his mind.

It's your duty to help the people. You are their prince.

Nels squeezed his eyes shut. Although the corners felt sticky and itchy, when he opened them again, his vision cleared. For the first time, he noticed the weapon in Lucian's hands. It resembled a crossbow without the prod—a handheld cannon. Years ago, rumors that the Acrasians had created new, more powerful weapons had filtered into court. It had resulted in a meager debate, but since humans held no magic, such things weren't deemed a threat.

"Hurry up!" Lucian said. "Daylight is burning."

Brown Boots and the other Acrasian humans drove more

freeholders from their homes, shoving the slowest into the dirt. One of the humans was a female with fuzzy brown hair and a nasty burn scar covering half her face. Nels searched the roofs, hopeful for mercenaries, but there were none.

It's your *duty.*

Lucian asked in broken Eledorean, "Where silver is?"

When no one offered an answer, Lucian sighed. "Sil-ver," he said, speaking more slowly as if his audience were stupid and not terrified. Grasping the front of a girl's dress, he shouted into her face and drew a knife. "Silver!"

"Killing her will not produce what you wish. There is no silver here, save this," Nels said in Acrasian. He found himself stepping away from the others, pausing briefly to place a reassuring hand on a freeholder's shoulder. He broke her gaze before it could erode his tenuous resolve. Then he produced a money pouch from inside his coat, tossing it at Lucian's feet. "Take it and go. It is all you will get."

The pouch hit Lucian's black boot with a heavy clank before he snatched it from the ground. "You speak Acrasian?" Lucian asked. "How?"

"One of your missionaries visited the city where I live," Nels said. "She generously offered to teach me your language." In actuality, it had been less an offer and more of a command. *She was under Father's thrall like the Acrasian ambassador was under Uncle's.* He inwardly winced. "Please take the money. Trouble these people no more."

"Who are you, boy?" Lucian asked. His grizzled face with its pale eyes squeezed into a suspicious glare.

"A traveler. Nothing more. Accept the money. It is all I have."

"That's a lie! Everyone knows your kind buries money with their dead," the scarred female said.

Nels frowned. "Why would anyone do that?"

Lucian bounced the leather pouch in his hand. Three slow clinks marked time. "How do we know you're not lying?"

"Search the baggage if you wish. I cannot stop you. As for the rest"—Nels made a sweeping gesture with his arm, showcasing the three cottages and one barn that constituted the whole of Onni— "does this look like a prosperous city to you?"

Someone behind him muttered, "Stinking round ears."

"What did he say?" The scarred female stepped toward the freeholders with a hand on her sword. Her sneering half mouth was now matched with a frown.

"He said please take the money with our compliments." Nels stepped between the freeholders and the scarred human. If she chose to cut him down, there was no Royal Guardsman to stop her. He was trembling, but his voice remained steady. He didn't know how that was possible. "Please take the money and go."

"I don't like any of this," Brown Boots said, pointing at Nels. "And I certainly don't like the look of that kid. He's lying."

"And what do you propose to do about it, Randal?" Lucian said.

Randal grabbed a young woman by the arm and yanked her to him. "She looks like a talker."

A freeholder in the green shirt struggled to force his way through the clinging arms of the other hostages but was held fast. "Raisa!" He turned and caught Nels's gaze. "Your Grace, please. Make them stop."

Again, Lucian squinted as if puzzling over something.

Nels gave his back to Lucian and hissed in Eledorean, "No titles. Not now. Call me Nels. I give you my word that I'll do everything I can. But you have to stay calm." *Stay calm?* It occurred to him that it sounded like something Captain Karpanen would say. The thought made him feel a little stronger.

"What did it say?" Lucian asked.

"Nothing you would wish translated. I have reminded him you are our guests," Nels said, resorting to the formal court tone out of reflex.

"Come on, Lucian," Brown Boots said. "Let's have some fun."

"Honestly, Randal." Lucian sighed. "Do you ever come up with anything original? There's a reason I'm in charge of our little family and you aren't," he said, striding forward. He snatched an elderly male freeholder's shirt front. Before Nels could say a word, Lucian cut the elder's throat.

Again, blood fountained into the dirt. The freeholders screamed and the one in the green shirt fought harder to free himself. Nels felt dizzy. His nausea worsened, and a monstrous headache bloomed behind his left eye. He blinked against the pain, not knowing what to do or say next. He'd never felt so powerless in his life. Captain Karpanen would've fought them. The king would've talked the Acrasians into surrendering. He would've used magic-laced court speech—*domination magic*—to convince the humans to throw themselves on their own daggers. Even Suvi could have compelled them into believing anything she wished, because Acrasians were notoriously weak-willed. However, it was obvious from Lucian's expression that Nels didn't even have enough magical power to misdirect suspicion from a lie.

Make them stop.

Nels knew what the freeholder was asking. He wished he could comply—with his whole being he wished it, but unlike every other kainen of royal blood his age, Nels didn't have the magical talent to control a horse, let alone a human. He used to think the shame of that knowledge would kill him, that the possibility of others discovering his weakness was his worst nightmare. Now he understood his deficiencies could kill others. And that was much, much worse.

"Boy, tell me where the silver is. Now," Lucian said, moving on to Raisa. "Or I will kill her. Am I understood?"

Nels swallowed. *Please. Not this.* "There is no more silver."

Lucian lifted his knife to Raisa's throat. "Don't lie. I don't have the patience for it."

"Please! Don't!"

"Then tell me."

The freeholders moved closer, hesitantly at first. Their hands brushed his arms, back, shoulders. Hesitant and fearful, their voices surrounded him, but he continued to feel distant from them. It felt like a dream. *A nightmare.*

"We implore you . . ."

"Have we done something to offend, Your Highness? Please, save my daughter."

The saber.

"Boy!" Lucian wasn't watching him. The human was intent on Raisa.

Nels acted upon the opportunity. He went to Captain Karpanen's body and grabbed the sword. He didn't think about what he was doing—the consequences. *The aftermath.* All he knew was that he, Nels Gunnar Ari Hännenen, Crown Prince of Eledore and Archduke of Hirvi, had touched the blooded saber of a dead soldier.

Unclean.

Straightening with one hand on the scabbard, the hilt felt oddly warm in his right palm. He shivered. *There'll be no going back after this.* The sword seemed somehow right in his grip and yet, foreign. Not for him.

The people depend upon you. You must do something.

"No, Your Highness!"

There's no other option. Nels eased the curved blade from its scabbard. The hiss of steel sliding free got Lucian's attention. All at once, Nels was inundated with a sense that Captain Karpanen was near, very close—*too close*. In a blink, Nels saw and knew things Captain Karpanen would never have told him. The captain had no family of his own but did in fact have a lover named Laina. Nels blinked back images too private and too jumbled to form coherent patterns. Captain Karpanen was a distant cousin and close friend of the queen and held his commission specifically as Nels's protector at her request. The pair of them, Nels's own mother and Captain Karpanen, had intended to make changes after Nels had assumed the throne, changes that would alter the way Eledore was ruled.

I must set the lad on the right path. It isn't proper, but someone must take a hand, or Nels will be worse than Henrik. Eledore won't last another—

Before Nels had time to register how he felt, the thoughts and images whirled away. Suddenly, he was seeing the captain's death all over again from a more immediate perspective. Karpanen's mind raced along scattered, broken paths. He'd never see Laina again, or the way her face lit up when she smiled. An overpowering sadness combined with the startling beauty of the trees and sky. Nels caught a disturbing vision of himself through Captain Karpanen's eyes. The captain's last thought threatened to shake Nels to the core of his being. He shied from it before it could take full form.

Veli Ari Karpanen, that was his name.

I'm so sorry. Nels's cheeks burned with cold, and he tasted salt from tears.

"Boy!" Lucian's voice snapped Nels back to the present. "Just what do you think you're going to do with that?"

Heeding images from the sword, Nels shifted his grip on the weapon so that it was more secure—thumb parallel to the blade. *That's better.*

Lucian stepped away from Raisa and put out a hand. "Be a good lad. Give me that thing before you cut yourself."

Nels ran at Lucian with a roar. Lucian brought his knife to bear but was too late. Nels swung the saber. The point of the captain's blade bounced off Lucian's ribs and slid to the right, slicing a long, ineffective gash through cloth as it went. Lucian howled and twisted. Nels freed the sword and tried again, jamming the blade into the human's belly using both hands. The sensation of steel sinking into living flesh was more horrible than anything he'd imagined. Cool blood poured onto the ground, coated the blade, splashed on his skin.

It's true. Acrasian blood is colder than Eledorean.

There was an explosion. Nels felt the impact through his feet. Deafened, he hopped backward. The curve of the hilt briefly caught on the man's clothing. Nels automatically jerked the sword free, and the blade slid downward, parting Lucian's belt. The wound gaped wider. Lucian's scream pierced Nels's ears as his hearing recovered. The shriek issuing from the man's throat rose to ever-higher notes of hysteria. Entrails sprang from the cut like a greasy rope, hitting the already blood-soaked ground with a splat. Shocked and nauseated, Nels retreated another step and slipped and fell in the steaming gore. He almost lost the captain's saber.

I've killed Monitoris Lucian, father of five, former carter, Nels thought. Along with his name and family came the knowledge that Onni wasn't the first Eledorean village Lucian had raided. It didn't lessen the terrible sensation of the human's life draining away.

Another explosion parted the smoke-filled air. Sulfur masked the stench of blood and entrails. Struggling to get up, Nels turned toward the sound. One of the humans poured gunpowder into his hand cannon. The uncapped bull's horn rattled and most of the black powder spilled useless onto the ground.

Musket, Nels thought. *The weapon is called a musket.* He got to his knees and then his feet, using his hands to steady himself. He nearly vomited when he saw the ground. Standing, he moved away from Lucian. At the corner of his vision he spied a large freeholder in the green shirt. The young man rushed to Raisa's aid with an Acrasian dagger. Others attacked their captors with bare fists. Sick, Nels watched Lucian vainly hold his guts closed. The human babbled that he was fine, that everything would be all right and then fell over. Beyond him, Green Shirt struggled on the ground with Randal. All the while, voices battled for Nels's attention from within and without. Captain Karpanen. Lucian. The freeholders. The awful stench of death filled his nose and throat. Nels didn't want to breathe it any more and choked.

I don't want to kill anyone else. Please don't make me.

A human slipped in the bloody muck at Nels's feet, dropping his gun. Scrabbling for his sword, the human found the scabbard empty. Nels took the opportunity to kick the musket out of reach. With that, the human scooted backward. A trail of fresh blood was traced in the dirt. Nels looked on, not knowing what else he should do.

"Have mercy! Please! I didn't want to come here," the human said, flinching and holding a hand up to protect his head. "I'll never return. I swear. Just let me live."

"Then leave now and—" Something blunt slammed into Nels's left shoulder, shoving him sideways and back. He turned. It was the woman with the burn scar. Her ugly face was twisted in fury. She held a musket by the barrel.

"Don't you dare hurt my Marrek. Don't you . . ." She stopped before she could finish the sentence. Her anger transformed into confusion and then terror. "It's going to use its demon magic. Look at its eyes."

She dropped her musket and then made a complex motion

with her fingers. Clumsy with terror, she tripped over Marrek. He yelped in pain and jerked his hand from under her boot. She stooped, helping him up—all the while maintaining that meaningless sign. Nels watched them flee into the woods. A bitter laugh bubbled up his throat and died on his lips. It was such a simple thing. The way his irises changed color from their normal black to an unnatural green and then blue. Sometimes, they faded to white when he was frightened. It was the only evidence that he held any magic at all. He didn't even have the ability to control it as Suvi did. *Why couldn't that have frightened Lucian away before anyone died?*

The surviving freeholders gathered into a tight group, inquiring after one another and inventorying their injuries. Nels lurched to Captain Karpanen's body. His knees felt loose, and he swayed like a drunk. The saber tip dragged in the dirt. His head ached, and his guts twisted in terrible knots. He put a hand against a tree to steady himself. He felt empty of everything but misery and agonized whispers so quiet that he couldn't make out words. It was the captain's saber, Nels suddenly understood. He shook his head to clear it. After several deep breaths, he crouched next to Captain Karpanen. The captain lay in the mud, one leg twisted under him, staring upward. The black irises were blank and empty. Nels trembled. For a moment, he saw the trees and sky as Captain Karpanen had last seen them. Nels reached out to tug the captain's leg straight and then paused. *Unclean.*

With a hesitant bloodstained hand, Nels shut Captain Karpanen's eyelids instead.

Don't worry, Nels thought. *There's no chance of me becoming like Father now.* Tears crowded the edges of Nels's burning eyes and traced cool paths down tight, itching cheeks. He sensed movement behind him but didn't have the energy to care. He wiped his face with a stiffening sleeve before a young woman with blond hair and a bloody lump on her forehead sidled into view. She looked terrified until he blinked.

"I am Inari. Raisa's sister. Are you well, Your Grace?"

Your Grace. Suvi would succeed their father now. He, Nels, would become a soldier. *That's better than the palace dungeon, I suppose.*

Inari waited for an answer while unease played on her face.

She's afraid Father will blame them for what I've done. And if something weren't wrong in me, she'd have good reason to fear.

Unclean.

He couldn't open his mouth, so he nodded instead. Inari looked relieved. An old mother moved next to Inari, her hair was a wispy white, and her skin was brown. She stared at Nels for a long time before she spoke.

"I am Marjatta, the elder. We thank you for your great sacrifice and will mourn for you until your family is able." She gave Nels an expectant look. When whatever Marjatta waited for didn't come to pass, she said, "The dead, Your Grace. It is now your place to see to them. Do you need help?"

A soldier buries the dead. Nels blinked at the bodies strewn on the ground. Lucian. Captain Karpanen. The nameless guardsmen. Onni's former guardians. Randal. Three unarmed freeholders.

So many dead.

At least most of the freeholders are safe.

It is your duty to protect them. He winced, but his mouth remained sealed. It was difficult to think around the ache inside his skull.

Marjatta took charge in a soothing but firm tone. "His Highness needs assistance. Dig the graves and light a pyre for the Acrasians. His Highness and the new Guardian will take care of the dead. Erja. Hilma. Find something for winding cloth." When the others were gone, Marjatta moved toward those who remained. "The

Guardians of Onni have passed. Their loss will be felt by all, but their places must now be filled. Who would accept this burden?"

The Green Shirt glanced up. His hands were bloodstained, and he stood near Raisa without touching her. He bent, whispering in her ear, and then waited until she gave him a sorrowful nod.

"I, Armas, must accept," he said.

Raisa huddled deeper into her blanket and stifled another cry. Inari hugged her, pressing Raisa's head to her chest in a motherly gesture. Armas stepped next to Nels, the top of his head level with Nels's shoulder. Armas was stout with muscles forged by hard labor. Nels couldn't help thinking that the freeholder would make a far better soldier than he ever would.

There were no other volunteers.

THREE

The freeholders left to care for the wounded and organize the work details. Nels was relieved to spy Loimuta being led into the barn with the remaining horses. There was a long scratch along the gelding's flank that would need tending. However, he seemed otherwise unharmed. As the young girl led him away, Loimuta jerked the halter out of his handler's grasp. Knowing what would be next, Nels opened his mouth to shout a warning, but he was too late. Loimuta arched his neck and nipped the girl on the shoulder.

"Ouch! Stop it, you big brute," she said.

At fifteen hands, Loimuta wasn't big. *He only thinks he is*, Nels thought. Loimuta lifted a hoof, and the girl dodged his halfhearted kick.

She stared Loimuta in the eyes. "I mean it." Snatching his halter, she then held his head at an uncomfortable angle. "Don't try it again. I don't care who owns you. I'll sell you to a human for his stew."

Nels's lips formed a weak smile. His father had told him that it was childish to form such attachments, because beasts were to be compelled and used, not loved, but Nels had rebelled. Other than his twin sister and Captain Karpanen, Loimuta was the only friend Nels dared to have. Everyone else wanted something. *Loimuta should have an apple tonight.*

Unclean. Nels winced.

I can't touch him. Not until I'm— He felt a gentle tap on his arm and flinched. Captain Karpanen's saber flashed a muddy red in the afternoon light. The sword faded into an apparition of sunlight in Laina's face. Nels shut his eyes and swallowed, but it only blurred Ghost Laina. His head ached with the grief-saturated murmur of the captain's memories.

"Highness, I don't suppose you know the names of your guards' patron deities?" Armas's gentle voice pierced the vision.

I don't even know the guards' *names.* Nels said, "I'm afraid not."

Armas nodded.

Eledoreans practiced many different religions. The Kingdom of Eledore had been formed over centuries as kainen migrated from all over the continent during the Dark Time. Each group brought their gods and goddesses with them. Historically, practitioners of differing beliefs hadn't always agreed with one another. This led to laws stating that individuals were free to practice their religion as they wished, provided those beliefs did not interfere with the practices of another group. No one was exempt from this law, not even the king. Thus, religion was considered a private matter— either kept secret within families and passed from one generation to the next, or individually chosen at a significant life event. Over time, the Commons Church was formed to provide a neutral spiritual meeting space for public events, for those without a specific patron deity, and to support common charity work.

"Perhaps we should start by cleaning that blade," Armas said. "I learned something of the rituals from Tarja. I can show you how. I didn't wish to tell Raisa, but I had thought to take this path before."

Armas's words faded away, and the world took a dizzy tilt to the left. The spots in Nels's vision returned, and his stomach twisted into a hard knot. *I will never see Laina again. She waited so long. I should've bound with her. It isn't as if Mia would've ever have been free.* Nels shook his head and took a slow, deep breath. The back of his mouth felt slick again. He knew what was coming and wasn't sure if he could control his stomach any longer. *I'm not Veli Karpanen. I'm Nels.*

Mia? That's Mother's name.

There are many Mias. It's a common name in Ytlain.

I won't lose control. I won't.

"Are you all right, Highness?" Armas asked.

Nels opened his eyes. Armas's pallid expression was full of concern. For an instant, Nels didn't recognize him. Armas vanished behind another ghostly image, this time of Nels's mother, the queen. She sat in her garden with a face far younger than Nels had ever known. Her hair was the same moon-pale blond as his own, although hers hung around her face in careful ringlets while his fell straight. She placed a protective hand on her swollen belly with a sad smile.

So beautiful. So unhappy. If only she hadn't bound with that flap-dragon. If only her mother hadn't interfered. She loves me yet. I can see it in her eyes. Ideas shifted dizzyingly fast in Nels's mind. Captain Karpanen's last thought solidified and linked with court rumors. Nels slammed his mind closed—his left hand clenched into a fist with the effort, but nothing stopped the echoing whisper laced with a fierce need to protect. *If it is so, there are worse things than dying for your son. Hasta, please. My life's blood for him. Let him live.*

Run, boy!

A devastating mass of terror, love, and longing punched Nels in the gut. Breathing became impossible. The ground no longer seemed to support his feet as certainties were snuffed out like candles. He finally lost control. Luckily, he was quick enough to make it to the privacy of the other side of the tree before retching.

"Highness? Are you all right?"

Nels spat. It took several tries to clear his mouth, but he felt better at once. Stumbling from the pool of vomit, he was afraid of being sick again. He felt something drag, looked down, and understood he was still gripping the saber. *Nels Gunnar Ari Hännenen. Mother gave me one of his names. Goddess, I didn't know.*

I don't want to know.

"What did you say, Highness?" Armas asked.

"The sword," Nels said through his teeth. *You must let go of Karpanen's saber*, he thought. He concentrated on releasing the grip, and the blade finally slipped from his fingers, hitting the ground with a ringing thud. All at once, the haunted echoes died. He was finally able to draw a shuddering breath.

Armas frowned. "Stay here, Highness. I'll get help."

Nels heard Armas run, shouting for Marjatta. *Was Captain Karpanen our father? Surely Mother would have told us. Is that why I've no magic? Can't be. Suvi has magic. So does . . . did Captain Karpanen for that matter.*

Armas returned with a bucket of water and rags. The old woman, Marjatta, followed close behind.

"Were you injured, Your Grace?" Marjatta asked.

Nels shook his head. "The sword." He took another tattered breath. "The sword speaks."

Marjatta frowned.

"We should put it away," Armas said, reaching for the blade lying in the dirt. "It's disrespectful to leave it in the—"

"Do not touch it," Marjatta said.

Armas stopped at once. "Yes, Mother."

"The voice you hear, is it the man who carried this blade?" Marjatta asked.

Nels nodded.

Armas gazed at the saber and a confused line appeared between his brows.

"Armas, fetch me a stool from the barn," Marjatta said.

In the distance, the freeholders dug at the ground, their efforts hammering a dull off-beat rhythm. Nels listened, trying hard to make sense of things that made no sense.

"You're divining the sword's past and strongly so. How long have you been able to scry?" she asked. When he didn't answer, she continued. "It's not my place, I understand, but has no one discussed this with you?"

"It must be the sword. I can't—" Nels shook his head, deeply shamed. "I—I don't have magic."

She squinted at him, judging. "That's not possible. All kainen have magic."

"I don't," Nels whispered and looked away.

"Are you human?"

"No!"

Again, she stared. Then she sighed and said, "That is not a normal sword. It's special, valuable, and very old. Do you see the pattern in the blade?"

Looking closer, Nels noticed the waterlike rippling lines in the steel.

She didn't wait for his answer. "It is believed a soldier's sword absorbs a part of their soul with long use. More so with weapons like that. It is made of water steel." Her stern face softened, but the frown lines around her mouth remained. "No one else must touch it until it is clean of the one who owned it."

Nels nodded again. *How does one clean a saber of a ghost?*

"You understand now why it is forbidden to handle a dead soldier's blade, don't you?" she asked.

He opened his mouth and somehow managed not to choke. "Yes." *But there wasn't any other choice.*

"Good. Now, wipe off the blood and put it away. Do not use it again until it is clean."

Armas arrived freshly washed, carrying a three-legged milking stool. Marjatta perched on it like a noble woman ready to bear witness at court. Her concerned frown never wavered. Nels gritted his teeth and retrieved Captain Karpanen's saber from the mud. To his relief, there was no sound, not a whisper—only the strange warmth from the grip. He wiped the blade with an oiled rag as Marjatta looked on. Several paces away, Armas arranged the dead in a neat row but paused upon reaching the mercenaries. He cut a button from each jacket, his lips moving in prayer.

Armas spied him watching and said, "It is a reminder of those who passed in service, Your Grace. I will sew them to my new coat so that they will not be forgotten. That is the custom."

Nels shuddered. *I don't want to wear a dead man's buttons.* Guilt heated his face.

"Do you wish for me to show you how to properly clean the sword, Highness?" Armas asked.

"Can you free it of the ghost?" Nels asked instead. He didn't want a stranger to demonstrate what he already knew. He didn't want to blur his memory of the rite as Karpanen had taught him.

"We would need a swordmaster to remove a ghost," Armas said. "Tarja only taught me the basic rituals."

He will wonder why I know the ritual. "Then demonstrate what you do know," Nels said.

Armas told him to remove all traces of blood from his face and hands with soap and water first. Doing otherwise would only recontaminate the blade. When that was done, they dumped the dirty water at the base of a birch tree.

"Always use a birch, if you can," Armas said. "Birch trees are guardians of the underworld. A birch will clear the death taint from the water."

Nels blinked, understanding. Only soldiers used birchwood, and now he knew why.

Then Armas demonstrated the first ritual—the Ritual of Contrition, using a fresh bucket of water. Nels rinsed his clean hands three times and recited the prayer with Armas: *With this water, I remember sin. With this water, I declare my sorrow and beg forgiveness. With this water, I cleanse death's stain.* Afterward, he felt refreshed, more himself, that is, until he glanced at the bodies and considered what was ahead.

"What if there is no water?" Nels asked. "What if I'm alone?"

"Then use snow," Armas said. "If you can't conduct a full Ritual of Contrition, close your eyes and imagine doing so. The water isn't what's important, or even the prayer. It's the presence of another soldier. Tarja said confessing the act of killing is at the heart of it. Bearing the weight of death is too much to do alone. So, if you can't perform a full ritual, do so in your mind and confess the sin to your patron god or goddess."

"What if I don't have one?"

"You'll have one soon enough," Armas said. "We all do. For now, you can offer your prayer to the Great Mother." Then he taught Nels a quick blessing using the clove oil from Tarja's pack.

With that done, Nels resumed cleaning Captain Karpanen's blade. He concentrated on transferring the stains from metal to clove oil–soaked cloth. Karpanen's ghost rested quiet. At last, Nels whispered, "With this water, please bless your humble servant, Lady Hasta." Hasta was Ytlainen, and she had been Karpanen's patron, but it felt right as if she were a part of Karpanen he could keep. He sprinkled a little of the water on himself as Karpanen had done back at the palace. The ache of grief pierced Nels's numbness. He swallowed it and then sheathed the saber with a relieved sigh. *Did I do the right thing?* He turned to the freeholders preparing the pyre. Inari handed off dried brush, a fresh bandage on her head. Nels saw how each freeholder interacted with the other. The unspoken emotions communicated in gesture and expression—a tangible connection of love and respect. It occurred to him that he didn't remember seeing such a thing among his family, not openly, and certainly not between his parents. *It is your duty to protect them.*

Nels shrugged off Karpanen's words and went to help with the first shroud.

When the sky faded into darkness, the freeholders brought torches. Still, Marjatta didn't budge from her milking stool. Whenever Nels paused in his work, he spotted her studying him with eyes that reminded him too much of Captain Karpanen. Nels got the impression she worried at some awful judgment. He tried not to think about what it might be. Instead, he focused on how each body should be cleansed, anointed with clove oil, and sewn into a shroud before it was carried to a grave. His apprehension increased with each step of the process explained. He wasn't about to admit it, but he had never used a needle in his life. When Armas finished his demonstration, Nels accepted a second threaded needle with clumsy fingers, instantly dropping it. Armas retrieved it from the mud.

"Please be careful, Your Highness. Needles aren't easy to come by. And they can't be employed for any other purpose once used on a shroud."

Nels nodded. His awkward stitches appeared to amuse Armas, who was too well mannered to comment. By the time they had started on the second shroud, Nels's fingers were bleeding and sore, but he refused to leave the job entirely to Armas. If he did that, neither of them would sleep until well into the next day. The hours dragged. Nels grew accustomed to the stench of fresh death. With each body, he acquired a new respect for Acrasian muskets and was glad the darkness blunted the horror of the violence done. He stepped to the first of the guardsmen and, following Armas's example, cut a button from the jacket. The face was familiar, but that was all. Again, he was reminded of people who had sacrificed everything for his comfort and safety—people he had considered too small to see. Concerned that he would have to report the name of the dead guard, he checked the uniform for identifying marks. His temples were pounding, but he did his best to ignore it.

Is Captain Karpanen our real father? Did Mother lie? Does it count as a lie if you don't declare the truth? He coughed, choking back another lump of pain. Aware that Marjatta was watching, he pressed wet eyes against his filthy sleeve before resuming his search. He tugged open the guardsman's collar and discovered a small silver chain. On the chain was a disc with a name and rank struck into the surface. Nels pulled it free.

"A grave token," Armas said. "It's to cover the price of a coffin. I've never seen one before."

"Shouldn't we provide him a coffin, then?"

"The Commons Church in Gardemeister could supply whatever is needed. They serve, but that would take some time. And I don't know the rituals a wait would involve. I—we can't risk contaminating the living."

Biting his lip, Nels gave it some thought. *And I must leave here before Uncle Sakari finds me.* With that decision made, he took the grave tokens from each body. *I can send someone back to give them the burial they deserve. And if I have the tokens, their families can be informed.* He then studied his inexpert stitching in the torchlight. Standing, he dusted off his aching knees with little success. A painful knot had formed between his shoulder blades, joining the constant headache. His sewing skills had done nothing good for the patched, mismatched fabric. *They deserve better than this.*

"I'm sorry we've but poor quilt tops and horse blankets to offer."

"Your efforts aren't the problem," Nels said, opening and closing his stiff hands in an attempt to stretch out the pain. "Mine are."

A concerned line appeared between Armas's brows. "You're tired, Highness. I can finish this."

Nels shook his head and blinked burning eyes. "This is what I am now. I'd best get used to it." *Was Veli Karpanen my father?* "And please, call me Nels. The bowing and scraping is ludicrous, given the fact I'm covered in the Mother knows what. It's giving me a headache."

Stunned, Armas nodded.

Pinching the bridge of his nose, Nels took up the needle again. When he was done, he helped Armas carry the sixth body to its grave. The freeholders had long since finished digging and retired to their beds. Nels stretched with a yawn, wishing he was home asleep in his own bed. He was cold, his hands were stiff with pain, and the powerful ache continued to throb behind his left eye. He turned to the pyre and saw it was ready to light, its bulk reminding him of a nest of thorns in the torchlight. He returned with Armas to where the last body lay.

Captain Karpanen. Suddenly, Nels was more exhausted than he'd been in his life.

Armas stooped to move Captain Karpanen onto the shroud. Nels held up a wounded hand and noticed his fingers were swollen.

"Please," Nels said. "Let me."

Armas straightened. A question formed on his lips, but he

didn't give it substance. He nodded instead. "I'll see to the humans, then." And with that, he went to place the Acrasian dead on the pyre.

Captain Karpanen was not a small man, and positioning him on the shroud alone wasn't an easy task, but Nels felt he owed the captain that much at least. He bent to place the ghost saber in the dead man's hands.

"Don't," Marjatta said.

Nels started, having forgotten about her. His sore hand trembled as he swept filthy hair from his face. "Why not?"

"Keep the blade, Your Grace. I believe it now holds a part of you. I fear what would happen if it is buried."

Staring at the saber in his hand, coldness washed over Nels at the thought of carrying it the entire journey home. *Captain Karpanen would do so without complaint.* He felt himself nod, lashing the saber to his belt as best he could. Next, he grasped a button on the front of the captain's jacket, paused, and then reached into a coat pocket instead. Nels felt the cool edge of polished wood, knowing exactly what it was—a toy whistle carved long ago for a son who wasn't even aware of the maker's full name. He considered all the times he had cursed Captain Karpanen for interfering, for shielding him from his own reckless selfishness, and saw everything in a different light. As Nels pocketed the whistle, a stray thought entered his mind and stuck. *What will Father say when he sees what I've done? Will he grieve or will he turn away and name me a fool?*

What if he isn't my father?

Stop it.

I shouldn't have come here. Karpanen was right. All I've ever wanted was for Father to look at me the way he does Suvi. Just once. A smothering pain in his chest drove back the numbness. Flames painted shadows as Armas lit the pyre. Nels rubbed burning eyes and then stopped. He bent closer to the captain, comparing angles, studying Captain

Karpanen's dead face for answers, only to find more questions. Careful steps spurred him into tugging the shroud over Karpanen's head before anyone could guess why he had paused. *I wish I had known. If I had, I'd have treated you better.* In his heart, Nels knew it was a lie, and there was no point in lying to the dead. He struggled for a token worthy of Karpanen's sacrifice.

I promise to be the man you hoped I would be.

Nels finished off the last stitches with blurry eyes. Waiting until the seam was done, Armas then took hold of the bottom of the shroud while Nels staggered under the weight of Karpanen's torso. He tripped and nearly fell into the grave. On hands and knees at the edge of the pit, Nels fought for control of his emotions. Armas offered to help him up, but Nels shook his head. Too embarrassed to look him in the face, Nels grabbed the shovel instead and dumped dirt back into the grave with fierce determination. With that, he buried more than Captain Karpanen.

He buried his future.

When he returned home, there would be no more races down the stairs to the grand ballroom with Suvi as they fled frustrated tutors. There would be no more indulgent smiles created on his mother's face with tales of childish rebellion. When he reached the palace at Jalokivi, he would pack the few things he'd be allowed and move into the birchwood-constructed barracks with others of his kind. Forever separate. *Like Captain Karpanen.*

At last he, Nels, had proved his worth.

FOUR

Late the next morning, Nels finished knotting his long, wet hair into a pigtail, folded it into a more manageable length, and bound it with one of Karpanen's black ribbons. It wasn't easy. His fingers were swollen, and he wasn't used to doing it himself. Having slept in the stall with Loimuta, he didn't have access to a mirror, and his hands were painful and clumsy. At least the headache had retreated somewhat. The contents of the bucket were no longer fit to use. So, he set the bucket near the stall gate for emptying. It was then that it occurred to him that there was probably a protocol for this kind of thing, and he may have just contaminated the barn. He slumped. *I should've asked Armas if there was a more appropriate place to bathe.* Sighing, he shrugged on Captain Karpanen's spare coat over his own blue trousers and brown boots. It would have to suffice. Nels glanced up in time to catch Loimuta's incredulous stare.

"Is something wrong?" He knew it was ludicrous to ask, but there were times when he was convinced the gelding understood him. Looking down at the hang of the captain's coat, he answered his own question. "Too big. I know. And I don't hold a rank. But

I've no black. And there's no way to remove the braid without making a mess of the sleeves."

Loimuta returned to his breakfast with what Nels was certain was a derisive snort.

He picked up Karpanen's black sash and found he had to double-wrap it around his waist to prevent it from dragging on the ground. All the Hännenens tended to be tall, but like his magical talent, he hadn't come into his height yet. When he was done, he was glad he didn't have a mirror. He could see enough of himself to feel ridiculous. *What am I thinking? I won't pass for a courier or a Royal Guardsman. Not even from a distance.*

A polite knock on the stall door startled him.

"Coming." Nels opened the stall gate and shut it behind him. He kept his eyes on the barn's hay-littered floor, reluctant to meet the freeholder's eyes. Armas had enough manners not to laugh, but Nels wasn't as sure of anyone else. However, judging by the polished black boots, the one waiting wasn't a freeholder.

An unfamiliar Royal Guardsman bowed, sweeping his broad-brimmed hat in the air between them with a flourish. Nels stared at the top of the man's brown head for two heartbeats before remembering to close his mouth.

"Sergeant Hurme at your service, Your Grace. Half the regiment is scouring the countryside. Your uncle will be most relieved. He—" As he straightened, Sergeant Hurme seemed to take in Nels's clothing at last. His expression drained of color. "Your Grace, did—" He swallowed. "Did you lose your baggage?"

Nels's face burned. *So it begins.* "No."

Sergeant Hurme's gaze drifted to the saber dangling from Nels's hip.

Nels cleared his throat. "Acrasian bandits murdered Captain Karpanen and the others."

Sergeant Hurme gawked. "You killed—"

"I—" Nels cut off the sergeant, unwilling to openly commit to the word "kill." He suppressed a shudder. *What's it like to kill someone?* Well, now he knew, didn't he? He fought yet another urge to be sick. "It was one bandit. But one is all it takes, isn't it?"

"Surely a few freeholders aren't worth—"

"Everyone in the hamlet would've"—*died*—"suffered, if I hadn't. Including me." Nels forced the words between clenched teeth. The pain behind his eyes intensified for a moment. He massaged his temples.

"Is something wrong, Your Grace?"

"I'm—I'm not feeling well."

Sergeant Hurme paused. "Ah, I see." However, his expression demonstrated he didn't. "Perhaps you should eat now, Your Grace. Your uncle will be here soon."

It was as if Loimuta had kicked Nels in the guts. The idea of facing Uncle Sakari while dressed as a baggy clown killed Nels's already-weak appetite. The broader implications came to him in a flash. *You have no protector. And you can't defend yourself, not yet. It would be easy. The captaincy is open. All it would take is one power-hungry Royal Guardsman. Uncle Sakari could blame the Acrasians. No one would say a word. Uncle is too powerful. Nothing stands between him and his ambitions now.*

Nothing but Suvi. A clammy chill settled into Nels's empty stomach. "How many of you are here?"

"Five, Your Grace. The freeholders sent a message to Rehn. We were sent ahead to—"

"When will Uncle Sakari arrive?"

"In a few hours at the most, Your Grace."

"Then we leave in a quarter hour. Inform the others."

"But it will be dark soon."

The pain lurking in Nels's brain reasserted itself, squeezing into a hot ball of agony. He squinted against the pain. Suddenly furious, he strode up to Hurme—not stopping until he'd scuffed the toes of the Sergeant's boots with the tips of his own. "Are you questioning my command?" *If he resists, I've no magic to influence him,* Nels thought, holding the man's gaze. *This is it. Either he does as I say, or I die.*

"No, Your Grace." Sergeant Hurme gulped and looked away.

"Get someone in here to load the baggage and saddle my horse. Now." Nels glanced at the water in the bucket at his feet. "And have someone empty that at the base of a birch tree."

Sergeant Hurme blinked. "Yes, Your Grace." He then scurried out of the barn, nearly falling through the barn doors.

Nels looked on with a measure of surprise until he remembered the violence with which Suvi's magical abilities had first manifested six months ago. Depending upon the specific talent and its strength, the onset of uncontrolled magic could either pass unnoticed or result in something horrific. He'd been in an adjoining classroom with the involuntary Acrasian tutor when Suvi's screams had brought the servants running. He had arrived in time to see a serving girl collapse to the floor in a writhing heap, blood running from her eyes, nose, and mouth. He'd rushed to Suvi to see if she was injured, but their nurse had shooed him out of the room before he could speak or touch his sister. *Suvi had complained of headaches before the accident.*

Headaches. Shit. The thought was followed with an image of Marjatta.

How long have you been able to scry? He swallowed. *Great Mother, please don't let that be my power. Please.* If that was the case, he might as well have no magic at all. He'd be no better than a common peasant. Nonetheless, if his magic truly was manifesting, then he was a danger to everyone around him.

It is your duty to protect them, Captain Karpanen's words whispered in Nels's mind.

I must leave here. Now.

FIVE

Traveling as fast as the horses could stand while avoiding the main roads, Nels and his new escort reached the outskirts of Gardemeister in one day instead of two. Having ridden through the night, they stopped for a short rest at the side of the road around dawn. The journey hadn't done anything good for Nels's headache. He felt terrible. His stomach was still upset—he'd gotten sick twice, and his legs hurt so badly, he could barely walk. At least he was still alive. Ahead, the Angel's Thumb stretched tall next to Grandmother Mountain. Beyond that and just a week's ride away was the forest, a few rivers and then Herraskariano. After that, a journey around the shores of Lake Hedvig would lead to the city of Järvi Satama and finally the capital, Jalokivi. He might make it if he could lose himself in the woods. *Uncle hasn't caught me, not yet. I've been lucky.* His smile died as he turned to the south and spotted the rising column of road dust.

Shit. We're not going to reach Gardemeister, he thought.

If he was going to live, he needed an ally or at least a witness—preferably one who his uncle couldn't manipulate, intimidate, or kill.

The horses were nearly spent. He was running out of options. The fact he was exhausted and sick didn't help. He rubbed sore fingers against his temples once more. Yet again, it did nothing against the pain. He needed a healer, but none among the guard traveling with him had healing talents.

Nels caught Sergeant Hurme's worried expression. As a Royal Guardsman, the sergeant had to be a veteran of more than one family dispute. Nels thought again of Suvi and the serving girl. *Family quarrels aren't the only danger when living among royals.*

Not me. I've more self-control than Suvi. Always did. Mother said so. The sergeant doesn't know that.

On the other hand, are you willing to bet anyone else's life on it?

He looked again at the column of dust. *Aren't I already?* Self-doubt swirled in a quick blast of frustration and anger. *Why did my powers have to assert themselves now? Haven't I enough trouble?*

What if the headache is just a headache?

"I'm sorry I dragged all of you into this," Nels said with a sigh.

Hurme blinked and then his expression softened.

He didn't expect me to consider them, Nels thought. *Before yesterday, I wouldn't have.*

Hurme said, "I see His Grace is getting very close."

It's over, Nels thought with a nod. *There's no point in pushing on. I'll only kill the horses and endanger everyone even more than I already have.* Still, he wasn't ready to admit defeat. "Maybe it isn't him. Maybe it's a mail coach. Maybe—"

Hume looked as though he was going to agree to the lie, stopped himself, and looked away.

Nels's shoulders dropped and the tension in his back loosened a bit. "We'll wait here until they meet us. I'll do everything I can for you. I'll tell Uncle I forced you to come with me."

Hurme raised an incredulous eyebrow as if to point out the

unlikelihood of such a thing. Then he spoke to the woods at the side of the road. "Are you familiar with Saara Korpela, Your Grace?"

"Of course. She's my father's seer and advisor," Nels said. "What does that have to do with anything?"

"Then you probably know the Silmaillia also has an estate less than a mile from here."

"Oh." Nels actually didn't. He thought she lived in the town. Hope took root in despair. "How soon can we leave?"

"Couldn't risk it for another half hour, I'm afraid."

Nels slumped. "Shit."

"You can go on foot. Take Corporal Eriksson with you. His family has a farm a few miles from here. He'll know the way. We'll follow as soon as we can. If your uncle gets here before we can continue, we'll buy you what time we can."

Nels took a deep breath to calm himself. He was trembling and hoped Sergeant Hurme wouldn't notice. *So many have died already.* "I can't. That would mean leaving you to Uncle. Without me here to take responsibility, he might—"

"We understood the risks before we left Onni, even if you didn't." Sergeant Hurme shrugged. "This way, there's a chance something positive will come of it. Whatever happens to us." He turned and shouted orders at Corporal Eriksson.

All at once, the weight of his own actions hit Nels. *I shouldn't have left home. I wish I'd consulted Captain Karpanen. I wish—* But wishes and intentions wouldn't change anything. *People are dying because of me.* "Thank you." It wasn't enough, but it was all he could think of to say.

"Live and remember us," Sergeant Hurme said, and began to turn away.

"I will remember." Nels put out a hand to Hurme. He'd read about the farewell custom in a stolen book belonging to a dead man.

Hurme glanced down, and for a moment, Nels wasn't sure he'd done the right thing. He could feel blood heat his cheeks.

Then Hurme took his hand. "It isn't proper. You've not been initiated. But I appreciate the gesture."

Cheeks still burning, Nels left Loimuta with Sergeant Hurme and followed Corporal Eriksson into the early-morning forest at a run. Panic kept exhaustion and pain at a distance. Nels focused on moving as fast as he could. At this point, the mountain's incline wasn't extreme, and the underbrush wasn't so thick as to slow them down. They'd run for quite a while before he had to stop. He bent over, grabbing his knees.

"How much farther?" he managed to ask between gasps. It was annoying to note that the corporal wasn't even winded.

"Not much, Your Grace. The estate is just over that ridge. If we follow that stream, there will be an easy crossing a few hundred feet from here." Corporal Eriksson looked over his shoulder toward where they'd come from.

"Do you suppose Uncle Sakari has reached them yet?"

Corporal Eriksson shook his head. "We'd have heard something, I'm thinking."

"All right. I'm ready. Let's go."

They continued upward, reaching the crossing in short order. Nels staggered behind Eriksson and made a great deal of noise in the process. Nels no longer cared. His vision narrowed down to the forest floor a few feet ahead. His mouth was dry, he felt dizzy, and the ache in his brain made him want to retch. Still, he pushed onward. It wasn't until he'd thumped face-first into Eriksson's back that he understood the corporal had halted.

Peering beyond Eriksson, Nels spied a girl who might have been a couple of years younger than himself. He wouldn't have called her pretty. She was too odd and angular-looking for that.

Her skirts were patched greens, purples, blues, and browns. Thick blond curls cascaded over her shoulders and down her back. She was all at once graceful and awkward, reminding him of a wild and uncertain colt. At the same time, there was a fierce power behind her eyes that made him uneasy. He watched her irises change from a normal black to a dark green the color of emeralds and back.

"I knew you'd be here," she said with a smile as if she often ran into royal visitors in the woods. "Come on. This way." She whirled, skirts flaring out around her. The fabric caught on a bramble bush, but she didn't give it much thought beyond a short tug. By the ragged state of her skirts, it was clear this was a common practice. He also noticed she was wearing heavy boots instead of slippers. The boots didn't seem to hinder her gracefulness.

Nels scrambled to keep up. "Who are you?"

"I'm Ilta. You're Nels, and he's Petri. There isn't much time. Gran isn't back yet. And we've got to get you inside the house before your uncle gets here."

"How do you know about Uncle Sakari?" Nels asked.

She turned and gave him an impatient look. "Gran is the Silmaillia. And I'm her apprentice, Ilta. Didn't you know?"

"You had a vision about me?" Nels asked, feeling his face heat up yet again. *This little girl has more magical power than I do.*

"We're wasting time," she said. "Can't this wait until we're inside?"

"I guess so."

Ilta whirled again and left. Nels followed as best he could, with Corporal Eriksson assuming the rear. The woods thinned out until Nels found himself in a patch of tall corn. It was part of a vast, well-ordered garden. Corn grew in regimented patches on the outermost edges of the clearing, forming a border. Herbs and roses bloomed in flower beds closer to the house. The house itself rivaled the royal palace in everything but size. It was easy to spot the king's favorite architect's influence in the details on the design of the porch and eaves. The regal three-story structure sported a fashionable tower on the eastern corner, and rows of expensive glass windows reflected the morning sun. A steady breeze bid an eerie welcome with the hundreds of dangling chimes anchored in nearby tree branches. Ilta hadn't paused. He ran to catch up until they came upon a neat circle of person-sized granite stones arranged between the garden and the house. Growing herbs saturated the morning air. He caught the sharp, clean smell of mint. His hands were numb with cold in spite of the captain's floppy coat sleeves. Ilta signaled for them to stop.

That was when he heard the horses.

Ilta motioned for them to get down. "Too late," she whispered. "He's here."

Uncle Sakari's guardsmen rode through the garden without regard to the plants. Their horses were lathered from the long, hard ride. His uncle rode into the dooryard on a tall roan. He was wearing a thick brown leather coat, and his high cheekbones and thick brows were framed by a lush fur collar and matching hat. The resemblance between Nels's uncle and Nels's father ended with the curly hair and straight nose. Where Nels's father was stocky and gruff, Nels's uncle was lean and personable. However, Nels had learned early in life to see underneath the friendly exterior. At the moment, Uncle Sakari's face was far from friendly. It was obvious he'd cruelly forced his mount to continue on beyond her physical capacity to run. The roan mare staggered in her suicidal attempts to please. Her coat was matted with lather.

"Nels!" Uncle Sakari leapt from the saddle and shouted at the house. He had a bundle in his hand. "Stop this pointless game at once!"

The mare fell to her knees and then dropped onto her side, breathing in hoarse gasps. Her eyes rolled, showing their whites, and her hooves continued to spasm as if she were still running. Nels's stomach turned. His mother's warnings took on a new seriousness. He looked away. He couldn't watch the mare kill herself. He wanted to shout to his uncle to command the mare to stop but didn't. There were Ilta and Sergeant Eriksson to consider.

"Nels! Come to me right now!"

The press of domination magic tingled against Nels's skin as it passed through the air. The shock of it caused a quake of cold fear. His uncle had never gone to such depths to control him before.

"This is foolish. I know you're here. The sergeant confessed everything." Uncle Sakari tossed the bundle into the dirt.

Nels saw it was a hand.

"Come to me now, and I may spare your corporal."

Scrambling to his feet, Nels felt Ilta tug at his sleeve.

"Don't," she said.

"I have to," Nels whispered. Every muscle hurt, and the headache was now the worst it'd ever been. Terror spurred his heart into beating ever faster. Pain slammed him with every rapid beat. It was all he could do to step out onto the path leading to the dooryard. "I'm here."

Uncle Sakari said, "You shouldn't have run. It will only make the punishment worse."

Shrugging, Nels moved closer at a measured pace.

His uncle snapped his fingers, and a guardsman that Nels didn't recognize came forward. He pulled at a rope looped around Sergeant Hurme's neck. The three other guardsmen who had helped Nels escape stumbled along behind. Each had their hands tied with a rope that stretched from prisoner to prisoner like a chain. Pale and sweating, Sergeant Hurme hissed in agony as the rope joining him with the others yanked at his wrists. His right arm ended in a stump wrapped in a bloody, dripping rag. Still, he held his head high, and his jaw was set.

"What are you going to do to them?" Nels asked. A knot of dread wrenched his heart.

"You've always seemed a bright-enough boy. It's time you learned a hard lesson," Uncle Sakari said. Another wave of domination magic shoved at the morning air.

"You're not going to-to *kill* me?" Nels wasn't sure why he asked, but he couldn't help hoping.

"Why would I need to do anything so artless and clumsy?" Uncle Sakari shook his head. "Lieutenant, remove their bonds and return their weapons. No. Not the sergeant. Leave him."

Then Uncle Sakari motioned for Sergeant Hurme and the recently freed guardsmen to approach. "Watch, Nels. Watch and learn." Uncle Sakari stared each of the men in the eyes for a long moment. The weight of power in the air became unbearable. Then he said, "Gentlemen, there is a traitor among you. Your sergeant. He went against my orders. He led you into a mistake. Redeem yourselves." He brushed dust from his sleeve. "The first to kill him will be promoted."

There came a clatter of swords being drawn. Sergeant Hurme shouted in defiance once before all three swords pierced his body. One of the men twisted his blade free of the sergeant's chest and then drove it through the sergeant's neck. The blade bit deep before Nels closed his eyes. Someone screamed. It was Ilta.

Corporal Eriksson burst from the garden. "No!" He rushed past Nels and went to Sergeant Hurme.

The sergeant's body lay at Nels's feet. Blood stained the dirt everywhere Nels looked. Bright crimson had splashed on the cooling body of the mare, across Nels's boots, and soaked into the bare earth in a growing puddle. Corporal Eriksson knelt next to the body.

"He didn't deserve this," Corporal Eriksson said.

Uncle Sakari said, "It's time to make a decision, corporal."

Ilta emerged. Her eyes were wild and unfocused. "Please. Don't."

Saara Korpela rode up to the house at a full gallop. She tugged at her reins, bringing her horse up short and dismounted. Her riding clothes were dusty, and she looked exhausted, if furious. She resembled Ilta in that her snowy hair was thick, long, and curly. Where Ilta's features were spare and angular, Saara's were more rounded. "Just what do you think you're doing, traipsing across my land with a damned army?" Saara's question shot through the morning like an Acrasian musket ball. "Get those horses out of my corn!"

Nels's uncle didn't pause. He turned his attention to Saara as if nothing unusual had happened. "I am here to escort His Grace home. As his uncle, it is my duty to see him safely to the palace and return him to his father. The troops are a necessity to assure his safety," Uncle Sakari said. "Much has happened, as you can see. I would not have His Grace risk his life a second time." He motioned to the guardsmen.

Nels moved backward as the soldiers closed. Saara stepped between. She laid a hand on the first guardsman's arm, and he halted as if punched. Then his eyes rolled back, and he dropped to the ground. The second guardsman froze in place.

Uncle Sakari gasped. "What did you—"

"Anyone else want to push me?" Saara asked. Her voice was edged steel. "I was being polite, but I'm done with that. So, let's be clear. I'm perfectly capable of killing the lot of you."

Silence stretched across the dooryard. The fallen guardsman

stirred with a moan. No one else moved. Nels waited and listened to insects, birds, and Ilta's sniffles.

Saara stared at Uncle Sakari in disdain but spoke to Nels. "Take Ilta inside, boy. Get her comfortable, and make her a cup of tea. Stay with her until she drinks all of it, do you hear?"

Nels looked from his uncle to Saara and then to Ilta. Ilta appeared to be in shock. "But—"

"Just get her inside," Saara said. "I need to talk to your uncle. In private."

Nodding, Nels took Ilta by the hand. "Come on." The girl followed him without seeing or resisting. She seemed to be in a trance. When they reached the porch steps, he had to lead her up one step at a time. Saara didn't resume talking until the door clicked shut behind them. Curiosity getting the better of him, Nels stopped there. Her voice carried through the glass panes in the front of the house.

"Don't lie to me. We both know he's not the crown prince any more. What do *you* want with him?"

At the reminder, the ache of disgrace was reborn in Nels's throat. His vision blurred. *So many dead. All my fault. All for nothing.*

"My poor brother will be struck to the floor with grief. Such a tragedy."

"An embarrassment, more like. Which will smart less, you think? A dead son? Or a soldier son with a pulse? It occurs to me that it'd be mighty helpful of the Acrasians to murder him. Damned fine reason to send General Bohinen and the others south, conveniently removing all support for certain weapons proposals," Saara said. "Granting the military power is dangerous, after all."

Proposals? What weapons proposals? Nels frowned.

"Only, he didn't die as planned, did he? How much more power will the military have with a prince in their ranks? Particularly a prince who isn't influenced by your spells."

Nels felt a surge of relief. *Oh.* It was more evidence that he possessed some form of magic—if from his mother's side of the family.

Ilta tugged free, took a deep breath, and then blinked. She seemed to be recovering from her fit. He heard her mutter something he didn't quite understand, but he caught the last of it.

"Don't, Gran," Ilta whispered. "Please don't tell him."

"Why are you saying such things?" Uncle Sakari asked. "We're here to protect Nels. Not—"

"I'm the Silmaillia, not some fool you can spell with court speech. Stay that honeyed wolf's tongue and listen to me."

Ilta laid a hand on Nels's arm. "This isn't for you to hear." Her eyes were still distant, but she seemed more herself.

"I don't care," Nels whispered back, and shrugged her off.

"We should go to the kitchen," Ilta said. "You're supposed to make tea."

"Be quiet." He'd missed his uncle's response.

"That boy's head holds more value than a prop for a crown, you hear me?" Saara asked. "He must live."

Nels felt his mouth fall open.

"What do you mean, old woman?" Uncle Sakari asked, all semblance of civility stripped from his tone.

"Wasn't I plain enough? The Acrasians are on a holy crusade. They won't be reasoned with, charmed, or bought. The humans aren't going to stop until every kainen bearing magic is dead."

"I don't understand what—"

"Let me make it simple for you, then. Kill that boy, and you kill Eledore's future."

Ilta grew more insistent, pulling Nels away from the windows, but again he yanked free.

"Him? He's a defect. My brother should've had him smothered at birth. Twins are an ill omen. Henrik should've counted himself happy with the girl. Better a girl on the throne than a changeling."

Nels curled a fist around old rage and shame. It had been made clear to him in a myriad of small ways, from the time he could first understand, that he owed his life to a foreign midwife—a midwife who'd traveled to Eledore with the queen's retinue.

"Damn you," he gasped through this teeth. *I'm not a changeling.*

"Stop it," Saara said.

For an instant, Nels wondered whether she'd spoken to him or his uncle. He moved closer to the window and heard a sigh.

"Do as I tell you. You may yet have a country to rule when all is done. Ignore my warnings and pay with more than your life. Henrik learned better than to cross the fates. He was a fool to try. You're no different. The only distinction now is the number of people who will pay for your arrogance."

SIX

"Are you warm enough?" Uncle Sakari asked.

Nels nodded, careful not to remove his gaze from the road ahead. He didn't even want to glimpse his uncle's expression. The false smile pinned to Nels's lips locked down his hatred but didn't stop his stomach from rebelling. *I must control myself.* Ilta was watching—he knew it without checking. At the moment, she kept her mare behind Saara's, but if he turned his head just so, he'd catch a glimpse of bright blond curls.

"That coat can't be very warm. You should've accepted my cloak," Uncle Sakari said. He'd been sickeningly attentive for the entire journey to Jalokivi. The reason why rode on a dapple gray mare five feet to Nels's left. Saara sat in the saddle with her chin held high and her eyes fixed to the way ahead and, Nels assumed, the future. He hadn't told her that he'd overheard her predictions. To his knowledge, no one other than Ilta knew. He still didn't understand why Ilta hadn't wanted him to hear. Saara's words gave him hope that everything might be all right after all. He might even be at peace with his new status if it weren't for his uncle, but with each false declaration of concern, Nels's shoulders tightened until the dull tension became a constant ache. *For the moment, I must pretend he is sincere, and that he rescued me without provocation. For the moment, I must pretend I didn't notice Saara check every morsel of food and every cup before it touched my lips.*

For the moment.

The journey home had been a slow one—made even more tedious by his uncle's cloying concerns. An early winter storm had blasted the last of the leaves from the trees and coated the roads in snow and ice. Soon, the mountain roads would be impassable, and the river would freeze solid, isolating the capital for two monotonous months. Normally, that would mean weeks of parties, ice skating, skiing, and other winter amusements, but Nels wouldn't be attending any of the usual social events. Soldiers didn't consort with society, even soldiers of high birth. He took comfort in the fact that there was only a narrow chance of his seeing the royal catacombs. A soldier, like a serf, even one with little magic, was probably considered too useful a resource to discard.

Soldiers have the advantage of being free, at least.

He remembered the myriad of social restrictions and honor codes that Corporal Petri Eriksson had set him to memorizing. *Well, relatively free, anyway.*

The only thing preventing complete misery was Ilta. Her sympathetic smiles and the faces she made behind Uncle Sakari's back had kept Nels from grinding his teeth flat. Curious, he wanted to chat more with her. Unfortunately, no matter how often he arranged to be where she was, Saara would appear, casting an impenetrable barrier of herbal lessons or demands for assistance. He wondered at the reason. *Is it because I'm now a soldier, and Ilta is to be a healer?* The thought set his chest to aching like a bruise. He hadn't heard of any such taboo, but that didn't mean one didn't exist. He hadn't associated with healers before, and he was only just now being taught the confines of a soldier's life.

Over the past few weeks, Corporal Eriksson had begun to rectify that lack. There was a great deal to commit to memory before the initiation—long passages of history about the Old Ones, the appropriate charms, and protections. Thanks to Eriksson's tutelage, Nels now understood why soldiers were required to bury the dead. He also had begun to learn why there was so much fear surrounding blood and death. According to soldiers' lore, the Old Ones didn't walk alone. Still, no one had seen revenants in centuries. Therefore, Nels found it difficult to focus on demons and restless dead. It was hard to believe in such things when he had other, more important concerns. Concerns with the living.

What will Father say?

The stench of sewage and coal smoke reached his nose long before he sighted Jalokivi's granite walls sparkling on the tree-crowned hill. Inns and alehouses lined the road, and ever-larger numbers of common folk retreated from the path as his uncle the Duke, Nels, the Silmaillia, and the Duke's two hundred mounted Royal Guard rode past.

At least the headaches that had plagued him for a week had finally receded. Yet sharp thoughts pricked at the tender insides of Nels's skull. *I'm not even worthy of a healer anymore.* He heard a cough and turned to look behind him. It was Corporal Eriksson. His eyes shot a warning to Nels's right.

"Is something wrong?" Uncle Sakari asked.

Uncle is watching, Nels thought. *You're brooding. Stop it.* For the hundredth time that day, he pushed the fur-trimmed sleeves of his coat up to his elbows. The material crept back over his knuckles with the rhythm of Loimuta's gait. He considered binding the sleeves up but knew what it would look like if he tried. *Leave it be.*

Don't show Uncle that he's getting to you. "Thank you for having the braid removed from Captain Karpanen's coat," Nels said. He tried not to smile when Uncle Sakari twitched at the dead man's name.

"A private's uniform would've been more suitable," Uncle Sakari said. "Imagine. Wearing used soldier's clothes." The air of disgust was apparent when he used the word "soldier." "But there wasn't time to have one made. Your father is very concerned. He was most insistent upon the promptness of your return."

Nels gritted his teeth. *Bad enough that I'm returning in disgrace, but as a private?* It was only another of Uncle's games. *Ignore him.* The anonymity of the uniform proved of some use. There were no outbursts of shock or grief as the column rode past. Reminding himself that Ilta was near, he was able to concentrate on keeping his chin up and his breathing even. By the time they reached the first city gate, Nels's stomach swarmed like an entire unkindness of ravens. He wasn't sure if he was hungry or wanted to be sick. Since they hadn't stopped for lunch, it was probably a combination of both. *What will Father say?*

Is he really my father?

A lieutenant of the Royal Guard approached Uncle Sakari, and after a whispered consultation, the lieutenant moved to the front of the line, muttering orders. Two guardsmen remained behind, and another dashed ahead with what Nels assumed was a message to the palace. As Loimuta's hooves clattered on Jalokivi's narrow, cobbled streets, Nels was overwhelmed by a feeling of unease. It was hard to remember to breathe. The brightly painted buildings, the red, green, yellow, and blue doors and windows that had once seemed cheerful and friendly, only served to hide the city's judging face behind a garish carnival mask.

The Nels who rode through Market Square two months ago is dead. Who am I now?

Changeling. Defect.

The column reached the palace gate, and the lieutenant barked a halt. A guardsman waited at the open portcullis, and Nels recognized the private who had ridden ahead by his auburn hair and square face. The private approached the lieutenant, and the lieutenant, in turn, passed along his message to Uncle Sakari. Risking a glimpse at his uncle, Nels studied the full mouth nestled between the brown moustache and goatee. He couldn't read his uncle's expression. Nels turned away, pushing back the captain's hat and leaning forward to peer through the portcullis, but the courtyard was empty.

"You are to proceed directly to your apartments. We'll supper in my rooms tonight and then discuss—"

Nels's heart stumbled and pitched into his stomach. "We aren't going to see Father?" He winced as his voice cracked. *How could I sound so calm when I killed Lucian and not now?*

"Your audience is scheduled for tomorrow," Uncle Sakari said. His eyes were hard. Cold.

Defect. Changeling, Nels thought, reading his uncle's scorn. "You said Father was concerned."

Uncle Sakari shrugged. "He is aware we have arrived safely and is, therefore, much relieved. He is in the chapter house with the Council of Nobles and cannot be disturbed."

On impulse, Nels kicked Loimuta's sides, urging him through the cluster of Royal Guardsmen.

"What do you think you are you doing?" Uncle Sakari asked.

The lieutenant maneuvered into Loimuta's path, and Loimuta reared, kicking the lieutenant's mount in the chest. Organized lines shattered into a confusion of shrieking horses. The lieutenant's gelding hesitated, and Loimuta bolted past.

"Get that creature under control, you irresponsible—!"

Nels let Loimuta have his head. The horse obliged with a burst of speed Nels hadn't thought the gelding possessed. Loimuta plunged through the portcullis, the hollow clank of his ironshod hooves echoed in the tiny space before they reached the court-yard. He galloped through the courtyard gates—not slowing until they'd reached the arched, iron-fenced west entrance of the cathe-dral. Nels leapt from the saddle onto the steps, not bothering to secure Loimuta's reins.

"Nels! Come back here at once!"

Nels shoved at the main doors with all his might; their pon-derous weight gave way grudgingly. Then he rushed through the nave, past the choir, and through the south transept to the chapter house. Fury and grief blunted the peaceful scent of burning frank-incense, the beautiful vaulted ceilings, rows of white marble pillars and statuary. Startled courtiers, priestesses, priests, and clerks blocked his path until they recognized him. Then they retreated with ashen faces.

"Damn you, boy!"

Upon reaching the passage leading to the chapter house, Nels assumed a more dignified pace. Head high, he forced his way through those loitering there, stomped up the stairs and through the open doorway. His uncle's distant protests were cut off by the slamming of the door. Those trapped inside fell silent—except his father and the short, fat noble he conferred with.

Built by Nels's ancestors, the Great Mother's cathedral was more than five hundred years old, but the chapter house was new. Laid out in an octagon, the small room had yet to inherit an air of the importance from the proceedings occurring within its walls. Half-finished frescos graced eight niches. Four of the stained-glass windows were incomplete. They were temporarily covered with parchment, permitting access to cold drafts and insects. Wooden arches naked of paint formed the vaulted ceiling. The posts were carved with intricate swirls and details. Rows of benches—mere wooden planks balanced on stone steps—bordered the confines of the room. Every bench supported the weight of nobility draped in furs, finery, and, at the moment, disbelief.

Nels felt the door latch turn against the small of his back. Muffled curses seeped through the wood like a bloodstain. He hoped to speak to his father before Uncle Sakari could force the door open, but the king was absorbed in his discussion. Only the top of his dark head was visible. Nels heard a gasp.

To the king's left, the queen's moon-thistle hair shone in graceful ringlets drooping past her shoulders. After Captain Karpanen's revelation, it was reassuring to see that paleness reflected like a mirror, to see the obvious similarities in the line of her nose and the tilt of her eyes. Grief glistened raw on her beautiful face.

"Oh, Nels, darling. What have you done?" his mother asked, covering a sob with a delicate hand.

Involved in their father's discussion, Suvi peeked over the top of the nobleman's bobbing head. Where Nels favored their mother, Suvi took after their father—or had always seemed to. Her unruly brown hair had been tamed into curls, and Nels saw her eyes change from black to a wide white before she caught herself and changed them back.

The portly nobleman turned, and Nels recognized Baron Hiltunen as the man scurried off.

Move. Now. Nels took a deep breath. The scent of raw wood filled his lungs as he traversed the room. The king's face was unreadable. Feeling the weight of every stare, Nels forgot to breathe. He tried not to notice how like Uncle Sakari his father looked with the new moustache and goatee. He tried not to think about the door opening behind him. He focused on getting across the room without tripping—which wasn't easy, since his legs had gone numb. He had imagined many variations of his father's reaction, but none of them had included silence. Time gaped with possibility. When he reached the bench where his family sat, Nels's mind instantly voided all the things he'd thought to say. Instead, he unknotted the braid securing the saber to his side and knelt. Using both hands, he placed the captain's blade at his father's feet.

"Captain Veli Ari Karpanen is gone." Nels paused. "Another will take his place." He followed the form without shaming himself. He was relieved that he'd managed that much properly at least. Still, he didn't have the nerve to look his father in the eye.

He heard his mother choke. His heart slammed in his ears two, three, even six times. Then his father finally shifted in his seat. A loud wooden squeak pierced the air. Standing, he grabbed Nels's shoulders. Nels flinched with the violence of it. His mother sniffed. Nels still couldn't bring himself to look up. The hands gripping him emanated strength, maybe even love. Blood rushed through his veins. The room seemed to swell and fade to the beat of the thundering in his ears. He took a deep breath and braved his father's face.

Black eyes burned with an overwhelming rage. The ground collapsed, and suddenly the only thing keeping Nels upright was the grip of bruising fingers.

King Henrik Ilmari bent close. "You. Are not. My. Son," he whispered between clenched teeth.

⟡ S U V I ⟡

ONE

Masked courtiers danced parallel lines across the royal ballroom floor, mirroring steps across a two-foot divide. Turning, their hands reached across the void. With that, the dancers made their way back to center and linked arms with partners, two by two. A rainbow of silks, feathers, and fine linen spun in tight circles. Wide coat sleeves of heavy brocade, skirts, pocket hoops, and layered petticoats fanned air heavy with the cloying scent of plague herbs. Holding her breath among the dancers, Princess Suvi Natalia Annika Hännenen performed her required role with a smile pinned on her face. This, in spite of wishing to be somewhere else—a somewhere with open skies, tall sails, water, and fresh air, somewhere with smooth wooden planks under her bare feet. *It's been two years*, she thought. *Two very long years since I could freely walk the deck of a ship. Two years since Nels gave up everything and sentenced me to this.*

He wanted a life at court, she reminded herself yet again. *It isn't his fault.*

Unable to employ her fan while dancing, she held her feathered sparrow mask to her face until she reached the outermost edge of the country dance pattern. When she lowered the mask to gulp a few breaths, she sneezed.

"Many blessings, Your Grace," several of the dancers said at once.

"Thank you," she said. The exchange was as practiced and wooden as everything was at court. Her mother had warned her, *Reveal only what you intend to reveal. Watch for weakness in yourself and in others. Be wary of attack. Remember, nothing is what it seems.* These were the seas that Suvi was now doomed to navigate.

At the edge of the dance floor, she caught sight of her father's latest indulgence—a group of performing automatons. The sight of them with their terrified, pleading eyes staring out of serene faces turned Suvi's stomach. At the moment, they were executing a series of awkward tumbling moves. One of them, a human male dressed in old-fashioned motley and bells, sprawled onto the marble floor and crashed into a servant carrying a tray of drinks. Fine crystal and wine exploded on marble. Those watching laughed. The motley automaton jingled as he returned to his tumbling as if nothing had happened, a bloody streak across one cheek.

Suvi inwardly shuddered and turned away. *I'm like they are, trapped by confines over which I've no control.*

Oh, for the Great Mother's sake, stop feeling sorry for yourself. The thought-intruder was Piritta, her lady-in-waiting and her souja—her thought-shield. Dancing nearby, Piritta stayed close enough to dampen anything an opposing thought-reader might overhear.

Suvi would've preferred to rely on self-discipline and not a souja. Unfortunately, she wasn't like her twin brother, Nels. She didn't have the ability to shield herself outside of her magically shielded bedchamber. *I could have you killed for invading my thoughts like this, you know.*

You wouldn't, and we both know it, Piritta thought back. *I'm the only real friend you have.*

That isn't true, Suvi thought back. *There's Nels and Dylan, too.*

And where are they? Piritta asked.

Suvi didn't need to see Piritta's smile. Mentally, Suvi sighed. *They're off living their own lives.*

Oh, shut up and have some fun, Piritta thought. *It's your birthday. Aren't you the least bit excited? All of this is for you.*

Not all of it, Suvi returned. All of the alcoves surrounding the ballroom were draped with deep red velvet curtains. A palace guard was stationed outside each. The little rooms served as spaces for guests to partake of whatever private amusements suited them—whether that was imbibing in alcohol laced with specialized herbs, smoking dreamflower, or indulging in a harmless tryst. *All but Uncle's alcove.* Looking to the heavy white velvet curtains to her right, Suvi caught one of her would-be suitors, Baron Karl Rehn, exiting her uncle's addition to the celebration. Rehn was buttoning his coat, but his shirt was undone beneath. Her blood chilled as the parting curtains revealed a closing door and a brief glimpse of naked automatons chained into place on furniture and walls. Rehn caught her eye and winked. She nodded and forced the corners of her mouth to turn up in return. *Cross Rehn off the list. I'm never seeing that man again.*

Ew, Piritta thought back. Suvi could imagine her wrinkling nose. *I told you something wasn't right about him.*

I didn't like him either, but I didn't take him for one of Uncle Sakari's crowd. Suvi turned back on her dance partner. She thought to Piritta, *You were right again.*

Of course I was, Piritta returned. *It's my duty to be right. Oh, by the way . . . I've some bad news about one of your friends.*

All right, Suvi thought. *Who is it this time?*

Miika Hossi, Piritta thought. *He's gone. Last night. An under-cooked elderberry tart was to blame, I heard.*

Suvi's heart stumbled. *I warned him about Uncle, didn't I?*

Apparently not enough, Piritta thought.

The evening's offering of mourning-ribboned nobles and gentry was larger than the previous month's. Based upon the varying skin tones, clothes, and hairstyles, they represented every province within Eledore as well as some outside of it. A group from the Kingdom of Ytlain—easily spotted by their less colorful clothing and the absence of powdered wigs—clustered near the refreshments, trying hard to hide their horror and disgust at her father's automatons. Waterborne merchants danced among the partygoers as well—her own addition to the guest list. Nonetheless, there were fewer guests in attendance than was usual for such an event.

Another breeze scented with plague herbs refreshed her newest worry. She'd heard the latest outbreak of variola had been restricted to the borderlands, but couldn't be certain whether or not the anemic turnout was a sign that the plague had reached the capital. Such news was kept from her as it was from her father. No one wanted to give the king bad news. It didn't tend to go well for the messenger. *Thousands have died. There aren't enough healers to stem the tide. How can Father and Uncle Sakari pretend nothing is wrong?*

Plot later, Piritta shot back as she whirled past. *Fun now.*

Fine, Suvi thought. *Don't blame me if the kingdom falls.*

Won't happen tonight, Piritta thought. *That's all that matters right now.*

Suvi's dance partner, a young baronet with powdered hair and an ever-so-earnest smile, made an attempt to capture her gaze. He thought himself favored because she had consented to venture with him into one of the ballroom's private alcoves. To her disappointment, he'd proven a pathetic kisser.

"Wouldn't you rather go out for some air?" he asked, linking an arm with hers and then releasing it.

That one is perfectly awful, Piritta thought. *I want to wash, and I'm not even dancing with him. Why in the four winds did you kiss him? Yuck. He looks like a frog, and he dances like an automaton horse with three legs.*

Suvi hid the laugh that burst out of her throat with a cough.

As luck would have it, the baronet had been forced by the next series of steps to turn his back and walk several paces away. It gave Suvi time to recover herself. She avoided his eyes, concentrating on the floor. "I shouldn't leave again. Mother would surely notice," she said. "I don't wish to insult her after she went to so much trouble to arrange this ball." *Damn it, Nels should be here. Mother should've insisted. It's his birthday too*, Suvi thought. *It's his fault I have to spend the evening dodging peacocks.* Since her twin brother had bought his captain's braids eight months before, she had seen less and less of him. Supposedly, his duties had been keeping him from the palace.

Don't be such a baby, Piritta thought. *Surely there's someone you'd like to meet? Oskar Sundqvist is here. Now, he's worth upsetting your father over. Kissing isn't the only thing he's good at. I know from personal experience.*

And have you leering at us the entire time? No, thank you, Suvi thought. But Piritta wasn't the only one Suvi had to worry about.

She whirled in time to the music. Turning, she got a view of her father and Uncle Sakari sitting behind a banquet table chatting. The ubiquitous purple ribbon was knotted above her father's elbow. She fought the urge to roll her eyes. The court assumed the king continued to mourn for his soldier son, but Suvi knew Nels had little to do with it. It was her mother's loss that kept the ribbon on her father's elbow a year after it was proper, and as Suvi grew older, she had come to understand that her mother grieved for someone other than Nels. So it was that the purple ribbon never left her mother's arm. Ever concerned about appearance, her father did the same. Whatever the royal family did, so followed the court—thus, hypocrisy had become virtue throughout the realm. In an effort to cheer Nels, Suvi had jokingly told him to invest in dye merchants, since purple wasn't an easy color to come by. *Too bad he didn't follow my advice*, she thought. However, she'd invested a portion of her allowance, and it'd resulted in a tidy sum—a sum she had, in turn, used to fund her most recent illicit venture. The irony of it all made her potential victory sweeter.

Again, a smile twitched at the corners of her mouth. Keenly aware that her uncle watched, she fixed a flat expression in its place lest he think she was smiling at him. *Does Uncle know what I've done?* Her heart was spurred into a rush of rhythm.

I don't believe so, Piritta thought. *But he's a hard one to read.*

Suvi wrenched herself away from incriminating thoughts. Taking a deep breath, she almost choked. *Stupid plague herbs.* She executed the final curtsey of the dance. Uncle Sakari approached at the edge of her vision. It sent a tiny quake of revulsion and fear through her body. Rapid questions shot through her skull like lightning bolts accompanying a hurricane. *Have I been careful enough? Does he know about the guns?* The edges of the fan bit painfully into her gloved palm as she fought for control. Piritta sent reassuring feelings that slowed Suvi's panic.

Uncle Sakari's presence at the ball was telling. Unlike her father, Uncle Sakari had no patience for art and music. He was more suited for affairs of state. Therefore, Suvi's father allowed Uncle Sakari to deal with the drudgery of the kingdom and invested his time in art, music, automatons, and his pretty castles.

"May I have the honor of this dance?" Uncle Sakari asked. He was wearing a deep Eledorean blue and gold brocade coat with thick gold lace, broad, cuffed sleeves, and matching trousers that stopped at the knee. His stockings were pale yellow, and his dark blue shoes had gold buckles. His powdered wig's long curls were tied at the nape of his neck with a blue silk bow. A gold sash draped from his right shoulder to his left hip displayed his diamond-encrusted badge of office.

Upon catching sight of the competition, the baronet bowed and retreated into the crowd. Nearby, Piritta gave her excuses to her dance partner and left the dance floor. As usual, she kept an expert distance—close enough to shield her charge, yet far enough away to prevent eavesdropping.

"Honestly, a baronet?" Uncle Sakari muttered to Suvi under his breath.

"He has a handsome nose, don't you think?" Suvi asked. "And nice legs."

"He's a graceless buffoon with delusions of grandeur. He trod on your toes twice and scuffed your slippers."

Snatching the excuse not to dance with her uncle, she said, "My feet do feel a touch bruised." She covered a bored yawn with a hand and, at the edge of her vision, registered that her uncle did the same. "I should rest."

"Is something wrong?"

She leaned toward him and spoke without looking directly at him, in part to avoid seeing his face but also to hide another sudden burst of terror jolting her heart. "A slight headache. Nothing more."

"Perhaps I should escort you to your rooms. We can leave the others to enjoy themselves," he said, using a voice that could have soothed the pinfeathers off a hawk.

Careful, Piritta warned.

Suvi concentrated on the white marble floor beneath her feet until the dizziness passed. *Court speech. Again. He's getting desperate,*

Suvi thought. *I'll have to give some ground somewhere soon, or he'll sense my true strength.* She preferred her uncle to underestimate her. It was safer. "Thank you for your concern, but . . . I'm only nearing my moon time," she whispered. Although her mother, a foreigner, had taught her not to be embarrassed by simple bodily functions, it was extremely impolite to bring up such things in Eledorean society. *Eledoreans are so squeamish about blood,* Suvi thought. In any case, it was the truth. She *was* nearing her moon time. Therefore, it was a suitable excuse for her discomfort, and one he couldn't argue with. After a long week of dodging her uncle, she was looking forward to several days of solitude.

Her uncle was uncomfortable. He almost recoiled. "Ah. I see."

"I won't have to sequester myself until tomorrow, of course," Suvi said, enjoying his unease. *Why do Eledoreans fear blood?* Her mother was from Ytlain and had never been able to adequately explain it.

The orchestra launched into a faster-paced Tahmerian reel. Suvi fled the dance floor in search of a chair. Her uncle made pursuit with all the subtlety of a ship of war in the wake of a sloop.

Uncle Sakari said, "Would you care for a tonic?"

Her self-control slipped. A derisive sound escaped her throat. Her uncle's reported penchant for poisoning changed it into a cough. "No. Ah. Thank you."

Two ladies dressed in aqua silk evening gowns rose, bowed. One wore a fashionable patch on her cheek in the shape of a tiny heart. Suvi felt she should know their names but couldn't remember them. Rushed, the pair stood a little too close, and their pocket hoops—wider at the sides than at the front and back—forced them to present themselves at a less-than-graceful angle. Uncle Sakari nodded a dismissal, took over one of their vacated seats, and looped an arm over the back of the empty chair.

"I think I'll have some wine," Suvi said.

"I'll wait here."

She crossed the dance floor to one of the servants carrying a tray of glasses. After giving her uncle's reputation some thought, she selected two crystal goblets instead of one. To his credit, he accepted the wine from her with only a moment's hesitation when she returned. Pleased with her jest but knowing she would pay for it later, she watched him drink the contents before sipping her own wine. Light shimmered through the dark liquid and brought out deep burgundy shades the color of blood.

Blood, blood, blood, Piritta's thoughts cut in. *You are in a mood.*

Uncle Sakari's fingers wrapped around the glass in precise arcs.

Suvi allowed a smile-mask to take over her face, then forced her eyes into what she knew was an unnatural violet. She noticed with a start his were the same shade. "Will you join us for the birthday supper?" she asked.

"I'm honored by the invitation, but I must leave for Ytlain tonight."

Suvi nodded, disguising relief in disappointment. "Ytlain again. I hear Cousin Jenna has reached Binding age. Will you call upon her?"

Newly crowned and currently without an heir, Edvard of Ytlain had made it clear that Sakari would be Edvard's last preference as consort for his sister, risking outright war in doing so.

"Not at this time." Her uncle reflected her smile, but his eyebrows bunched together. The wet shine of his flat eyes was cut off by his eyelids. It made her think of a lighthouse signaling a ship away from the rocks. "Edvard, that damned pirate, has a stranglehold on our shipping lanes again. You'd think he'd have more respect. He thinks that because his first cousin is now our queen, he can do whatever he likes. He should've been taught better."

"What about negotiating an ocean route?"

"What about it?"

"It's the logical option. Why start another conflict we can't afford? We're already fighting the Acrasians—"

Her uncle snorted.

Suvi pressed on. "Cousin Edvard has no power over us. Not when we have other options."

"You're suggesting we negotiate with the Waterborne? Why?"

Suvi thought, *It worked for Grandma Kai and Ytlain. Why shouldn't it work for us? Of course, you damaged our relationship with them, didn't you, Uncle?* "Why not? They would make a powerful ally."

"The Waterborne Nations don't have allies. They have customers. They trade with anyone. What makes you think we can trust them?"

"Waterborne contracts are absolute. They've a reputation for honesty and strict neutrality for good reason. Captains and crew members are magically bound to silence. They can't publicly declare the identities of their clients, much less discuss their interests. They aren't even allowed to trade in client information gained through their travels. Ask a Waterborne what the weather is like in Massilia or Tahmer, and they'll tell you nothing. They may not take sides with individual countries, but they are loyal to themselves and their contracts.

"Eledore has suffered greatly since our connection with them was severed"—Suvi watched her uncle's frown deepen at the allusion to his past blunder. *Careful.* She pressed on, pretending not to notice—"not only in trade but in other areas. Waterborne naturalists have made many advances in the studies of engineering, medicine, mathematics, navigation, and astronomy. Far more than we have in decades."

"The Waterborne are filthy little tradesmen with nothing of their own but what they steal. Where is their country? Their king?" It was obvious from his vehement tone that she'd struck a sore spot. "They don't even have ports of their own—not any they don't rent."

At least, Suvi thought, *none that* you *know of.* Embarrassed, she checked to see if any of her guests were near. "The Waterborne aren't pirates." *Although you employ privateers, don't you, Uncle?* "Even if we don't sign a trade contract with them, think of what we could learn."

"Magical power is that which moves the world. The ability to bend others to your will is everything. No amount of intellectual daydreaming can change that."

"We can gain advantages from such knowledge and conserve magic for better uses." *As Ytlain does,* Suvi thought.

"Ytlain is the power with which we must negotiate, not those— those *merchants.*"

Suvi bit down on a retort. It was pointless to continue. *And when I'm queen, his opinion won't matter, anyway.* "Then I wish you good fortune in your treaties with Cousin Edvard."

An explosion of applause signaled an intermission. The king got up from his chair and a procession formed behind him. Suvi swallowed the last of her wine, gave her uncle a nod, and then assumed her place between her parents.

Uncle Sakari approached her father. "My regrets, Sire, but I cannot further delay my departure. My barge leaves for Mehrinna within the hour."

Her father gave her uncle a distracted smile. "Safe journey."

Uncle Sakari turned, and one eye closed in a mirthless wink. "Be good, Little Sparrow."

Suvi shivered. "Sparrow" was her father's pet name for her, and Uncle Sakari had never used it before. "I will." She gazed across the room and thought again of her plans to combat her uncle for power. *And the Eledorean army.*

I will do what I must for the kingdom.

Poor Nels.

Her uncle abandoned the ballroom, and Suvi followed the others to the banquet hall, staring holes into her Uncle's retreating back as she went.

TWO

The mantel clock had just finished striking midnight when a loud tink against the balcony glass gave Suvi a start. She threw aside the bedcovers and fetched the candle to see who it was. The world's worst hoot owl imitation rose up from the garden and answered her question before she reached the other side of the room. She rushed to throw open the glass-paned balcony doors before he broke a window. Setting the candle on the ledge and then leaning over the railing, she spotted her brother, Nels, below. Free of its regimental pigtail, his hair was as long as hers, easily reaching his hips. With no hat to conceal its distinctive color, it glowed a brilliant white against the darkness of his unbuttoned captain's coat.

How long has it been since I've seen his hair free of a soldier's club? A year?

An army rucksack rested at his feet, and he pointed to a small burlap bag in his raised hand. She nodded, retreating into her rooms, and then searched for a day dress to throw over her silk shift. There was no one to get her into the dress properly, not without waking Piritta, and Suvi wasn't about to take time for stays, pocket hoops, and petticoats. She hoped no one would see her on the stairs and—

Why take the stairs?

Nels's rooms had once been next to hers, and long before, he had made arrangements with a sympathetic gardener to fix a trellis to the palace wall. It was placed so that it could be reached via either balcony. That trellis had been a childhood bridge to night-time escapades from that point forward. She hadn't used it since the day she had turned thirteen and had told Nels she was too sophisticated for such things. Feeling like a carefree child, she jammed her arms into the sleeves of her overdress and flew to the balcony barefoot. She grasped the trellis and hooked her toes into the cool iron bars hidden among the leaves. The spicy green scent of ivy and soft spring air made her feel more awake than she had in months. She used to imagine herself swinging through the rigging of one of her father's ships as she climbed, and the memory made her feel light. It'd been too long since she'd walked a ship's rigging. She missed the lakes almost as much as she missed her brother. She'd gotten halfway down when her foot snagged on the hem of her dress. Catching herself easily, she continued her descent. Below, she heard Nels stifle a laugh.

Go ahead. Snicker, she thought. *I'd like to see you try to navigate an overgrown trellis in skirts.*

Landing safely at the bottom, she slapped him on the shoulder. She almost had to stand on her toes to do it. He was a good six inches taller now. There were hard muscles under his sleeve. He'd filled out, too. All in all, he was less awkward than he used to be, more athletic. He'd made a fine soldier in spite of himself. Rumor had it that he was particularly good with a sword. He'd won two duels that she knew of. It occurred to her that neither of them had gotten the future they'd wanted, and yet she had a feeling they were each more suited to their fates than previously thought. *Maybe everything will be all right for him after all.* "Where were you tonight?"

"Out."

"Fine. Don't tell me." She reached for the bag. "What did you bring?"

He jerked the prize out of reach with a wicked smile. "Who says it's for you?"

"Are you going to tell me you've been throwing rocks at the wrong window? Should I get Piritta?" Suvi gathered her skirts and turned on her heel. "She'll be delighted. Hope you weren't planning on sleeping tonight."

He grabbed her arm and tugged her back from the trellis. "Don't you dare."

"Do you have any idea how long she's wanted to bed you?" Suvi made another playful attempt to escape his grasp. "I'm certain she can spare the energy. I haven't seen Lieutenant Juusten in three weeks."

"Suvi, please. Don't talk like that." He was blushing.

The housekeeper Suvi employed to keep watch over Nels said that there were no lovers in her brother's life—not that he wasn't capable of hiding such things from a mere housekeeper. Nonetheless, Piritta was a sore subject. Suvi didn't understand what held her brother back. She assumed the reasons were sewn to his sleeves, not that it stopped others of his vocation. Rather, it tended to have the opposite effect, and since bedding a soldier was considered daring, there were any number of candidates willing to do so—Piritta included. Whatever his reasons were, it was obvious the matter of Piritta caused Nels discomfort, and it'd been far too long since Suvi had seen him to risk bad feelings. She stopped teasing and put out a hand. "What did you bring for me?"

His shoulders slumped. He handed over the bag with an exaggerated sigh. "Acrasian blood oranges."

She let out a joyful squeak. "Where did you get them?"

"May we retire somewhere more private? Or are you planning on inviting the entire Royal Guard to our birthday picnic?"

"They already know you're here." She hugged the oranges to her chest. "You'd think after ten years, you could get that call right. I know you've heard an owl hoot."

He tugged her away from the palace wall. "If I did it properly, you wouldn't know it was me." He headed for the hedge maze, their childhood hiding place and their traditional meeting spot, but she pulled at his arm. He glanced over his shoulder, confused.

"I don't trust the maze. Not tonight," she said. *Who's to say Uncle Sakari doesn't have someone watching?* And she definitely didn't want to wake Piritta—not now.

"Then where?"

Suvi scanned the garden until she spotted the small boat moored at the river dock. The *Lissa* was an eighteen-footer and technically a sloop, but the mast was designed to collapse so it could double as a rowboat. Hiding the sail made *Lissa* less noticeable. Suvi used her when she wanted to be alone with her thoughts. Water weakened Eledorean magic. Therefore, the chances of being spied upon were less. Her grin spread wide as she tugged her brother toward the dock nestled between the willow trees. "I know just the place."

"Oh, no."

"Oh, yes."

Upon reaching the dock, he slowed and dug in his heels. Her hand slipped through his, and she stumbled. Turning to him, she said, "You won't even have to row, you big baby."

"It leaks."

"She does not," Suvi said, and then lowered her voice. "I need to talk to you. The lake is the safest place."

He stared down at the boat. "No tricks?"

When they were younger, she would've lied, but not now. "No tipping. I promise."

He swallowed once before clumsily stepping from the dock into the boat's prow, nearly flipping it. After the initial graceless scramble, he settled into the bottom of the boat with his ryggsack rather than sitting on the bench. She yanked the dock line free from its slipknot and picked up the oars. Nels frowned up at her, both hands clutching the side. His knuckles were white.

"What did you want to talk about?" he asked.

"Relax, will you? I said no tricks." She gave him her most reassuring smile. "You talk first. Be as quiet as you can. Voices carry across water if you're not careful."

Satisfied that they were far enough from the shore, she dropped anchor and tossed the oars onto the benches. Her shoulders and arms ached, but the warmth in her muscles felt good. With the sailing gear secure, a cozy ten-foot-by-five-foot space was created in the boat's bottom. Nels had taken shelter in the left half, away from sails, line, and swinging oars. She joined him, gathered her skirts, and brought her knees up to her chin.

He waited until the boat stopped rocking, then reached into his pack, handing her a little box tied with a ribbon. "Sorry it's late."

And I was angry about him missing our stupid ball. "The oranges are enough. I don't need anything else."

"Please open it."

She tugged at the ribbon and pried at the lid. A dark bird-shaped pin nested inside, its wings spread in flight.

"It's a cardinal. I couldn't find a sparrow. And I couldn't have one made in time," he said, embarrassed. "The stones aren't real.

They're . . . glass. It's all right if you don't like it, but I thought . . ." His voice trailed off.

Tears blurred her vision, and she could no longer see the pin in her hand. "It's the most beautiful thing I've ever seen." She wiped her face and secured the cardinal to the front of her shift. "Cardinals are related to sparrows, if you believe the Acrasian naturalists." She sniffed and touched the pin. The glass chips were rough against her fingers. "Thank you. I adore it."

"I'm glad." He looked relieved.

"I didn't get you anything."

"That isn't true." After pulling off his boots, Nels stretched out on his back and stared up at the stars. One of his red wool stockings had a hole in the heel.

Why doesn't father give him an allowance? She remembered the gifts he'd brought her with a measure of guilt, having subsisted on a limited allowance herself before becoming crown princess. Her mother had insisted it was good training, and in the end, Suvi had to admit that it had been, but Nels hadn't been given the emotional support she'd had. Their father had cut him off. *What did all this cost Nels?* She silently vowed to do more for him in the future.

"Go on. Eat." Seeming to forget where he was, he propped his feet up on the lip of the boat and wiggled his toes as she dug into the oranges. He then said in Acrasian, "How long has it been since I let you take me out in this thing? Three years? Four?"

"Four." She grinned, wiping at the sticky sweetness burning on her chin with the back of a hand. She found Acrasian too crude, too guttural compared to the graceful flow of Eledorean, but they had used it as their secret language since they were twelve. "Glad you here. You the money got?"

He wrinkled up his face in disgust. "You're out of practice."

She threw an orange peel at him. "You away too long. Talk. I listen."

He pillowed the back of his head with both hands and took a deep breath. "I got the money. Thank you. And we began training with the muskets last week. However, I can only make use of five. One of the six delivered was a matchlock."

"Is difference there?"

"*Is there a difference.* Yes." He rolled his head away from another tossed peel. It fell into his hair. Suvi resisted the urge to pluck it out. They were too old, and they'd been apart for too long for her to mother him anymore.

"Flintlocks are more reliable and don't require a lit match. Battlefield conditions are rarely ideal. It's difficult to keep the damn things from getting wet, going out, or touching off at the wrong time."

She took a moment to translate her next question. "How do you know this?"

"You expect me to lead others into battle and know nothing of what I'm doing?"

She shrugged. "Others do."

"Not me." A determined look appeared on his face, and she knew it for what it was.

Oh, Nels. Do you think Father is going to notice or even care? A sharp pain lodged in her throat, and she stared at the orange pieces in her red-stained hands.

"More muskets, balls, and powder should arrive next week," he said, and paused. "Are you certain you won't get into trouble for this?"

Smuggling Acrasian weapons into the country was illegal. The military was expected to use magic and traditional weapons to combat the enemy. Of course, most wouldn't be in the army if they'd had reliable magical power in the first place. Years into the war against the Acrasians, the nobility's mercenaries had resorted to using whatever weapons they could afford on the front, and Uncle Sakari made a fortune secretly selling weapons to them. Ultimately, Suvi knew that breaking the law wasn't what would matter if they were caught—it was that she'd created her own supplier. If their uncle found out, there would be blood to pay and not all of it common.

Nels thought of my safety first and not what he could gain. She shook her head as if to dislodge the guilt. "He won't find out." They both knew who she meant.

"Good." He turned his face to her. "Thank you. I command as much credibility as a talking goat among the other officers. They sense something is wrong with me, but they don't know. Not for certain." Again, they both knew why. In spite of all of the hints at great power—his ability to withstand command magic, to shield his thoughts, and to scry—Nels never had developed proper magical powers. He looked miserable. "No one listens to me but you."

"Wanted to help," she said. "Need anything else? Horses?"

"Do I need anything else." He paused again. "I don't wish to be ungrateful, but why are you taking this risk?"

There it was. The question she had been dreading. She stuffed an orange slice in her mouth to buy time, but in a nervous reflex, she bit down. Her mouth filled with juice. It slid down her throat before she was ready. Her eyes watered and her throat burned while she tried not to cough. She swallowed tangy juice and cleared her throat while she struggled to think of something to say. He sat up. The boat tilted, and the orange peel fell from his hair. In the moonlight, his eyes blazed a serious pale gray. She could feel her face warm in the intensity of his stare.

He never could restrain the color of his eyes. And she couldn't protect her own thoughts. *Aren't we a pair?*

"You want control of the army," he said in a flat tone. "And you think you can do it through me."

"Oh, Nels." She choked the words past the lump in her throat.

He held up a hand. "Don't worry. I know my place."

"Don't."

He turned his back on her, and gripped the dagger board. She set the remainder of her orange on the bench and dipped her hands in the water, taking care to not jostle the boat. She stared at his back and tried to think of something to say that would salve the sting. After a time, she heard him sigh.

"I'm . . . glad," he said at last.

"What do you mean?" she asked, slipping into Eledorean.

"Someone must stand against Uncle Sakari. It can't be me. I'm not—" He paused, and the tension in his hands vanished. "I'm pleased it will be you. What's your plan?"

"I don't have one," she said in Eledorean.

"Don't lie." He turned. "You know better than to make a move without something in mind. And giving me muskets was no small thing. You know you have my absolute loyalty—"

"Never a doubt," she said in Acrasian.

He shifted closer and tugged up his sleeves. "You can't wait for Father to die before doing something about Uncle. By then, it'll be too late. Uncle has but one head. We have two. Tell me."

"You're not angry?"

He looked down at his hands resting on the dagger board, and she noticed the unfamiliar network of tiny scars vanishing up her twin's sleeves. There were a couple of bigger scars, tracing long, exact lines across the top of his left forearm. Now that she'd been paying attention, she'd noticed similar marks on other soldiers, and she began to wonder what it meant. As close as they'd been while growing up, it was odd to see anything in Nels that she didn't know intimately. She hadn't lied to him. He was the only one in her life whom she dared to trust completely. The old fear of abandonment twitched into a cold knot around her heart. *What else don't I know about him?*

His hair slid over his shoulders as he turned to face her. "I'm not angry. Not really. What choice do you have? To do otherwise would be foolish, and you are not foolish. Not like me."

"Please don't say that."

He looked into her face. "I'm not the best choice. You should start forming an alliance with one of the generals Uncle doesn't control. Sadly, there are only two worth contacting. That would be Field Marshal Kauranen or Brigadier General Bohinen. Colonel Laine would make a good candidate too. Each has taken a stand against Uncle at the councils and managed to keep their seats. None would hesitate to accept backing. Of the three, I'd choose Laine even though you'll have to get him promoted. He's smart. He's come out on top of more than one confrontation with Uncle. Laine is in a good position. The troops love him. He knows what he's doing, and he's more trustworthy than Bohinen. Bohinen is older than the others, and he drinks too much. It'd be too easy to slip him poison and blame age. Kauranen is a good risk too, but she'd be my second choice. I'd recruit her after Laine. The two would make a good team. She didn't buy her shoulder braids like the others. She worked her way through the ranks. That requires courage, intelligence, political shrewdness, and iron will, but she isn't well liked among the troops. She's too new."

"Why not you?"

"You know why. I can't hide my defect forever. That's obvious. And the army will not follow me once it's known that I'm—I can't . . ." He let his voice trail off and shrugged.

Magic; he needs command magic, she thought. "You can't be

influenced or forced with magical power. Your thoughts can't be sensed, either. I need those things from a leader far more than anything else." Still, she'd given the matter long thought. She'd already made a certain decision, but she needed him as an ally. Thus, she needed him to come to the same conclusions she had on his own. *You're manipulating him.*

Is it manipulation or leadership?

Is there a difference? She wanted to believe there was.

"Listen to me. I can't lead the army. You know I can't. Place me in a position of power and my secret will come out at once. If that happens, I'll be useless to you."

He'd be worse than useless. He'd be tortured to death, she thought. An image of her uncle's automatons made her shudder.

"You're my sister. One day you'll be queen. I'll do what I must to protect you. And part of that is knowing I can't be the one to be Grand Marshal for your army."

Feeling a twinge of guilt, she trapped him in a fierce hug, and the boat rocked as the tears she had wanted to cry for months poured out onto the front of his uniform shirt. He was warm and smelled of leather, wool, and soap. She sniffed. "I love you." She honestly meant it.

"I know. I love you, too."

She sat down again. "All right. I'll tell you."

He resumed his reclined position, steadying himself with a hand to the boat's side. He threw the orange peel at her. "In Acrasian."

She groaned.

"You need the practice."

"Visit more often, then," she said in stubborn Eledorean.

He raised an eyebrow.

"I mean it. Promise me you won't wait so long next time."

He smiled and his irises changed from light gray to something much darker. "You missed me?"

"Of course I did, you addle-pate. Seven months is too long." She threw the orange peel back. "I began to think you'd run off with a woman and left me alone with Uncle Sakari."

"Small chance of that." The look on his face said he wished otherwise.

"Oh, there is someone, then? Who? What's she like? I want to meet her."

He folded his arms across his chest and whispered to the sky in Acrasian. "Tell me your plans first and then I may consider it."

She stuck out her tongue.

"I saw that."

"Planning on doing something about it?" She positioned herself for arm wrestling and braced her elbow on the dagger board. "Or are you too rabbit?" she asked in Acrasian and wiggled her fingers.

"Rabbit? Oh. Chicken." He sat up and smiled. "You can't possibly win."

"Try me and see."

He slipped off his uniform coat and rolled up a white sleeve. While he wasn't looking, she smashed a slice of blood orange in her palm.

"You're certain about this?" he asked.

"You talk much." She laughed. "You talk all your enemies to sleep?"

He grasped her hand and then jerked back with a look of disgust. "You brat!"

"Shhhh!" She leaned back with her clean hand over her mouth to stifle the giggles. Then she rinsed her hand in the water a second time. "I win!"

"You cheated!"

"And who taught me how?" She lapsed back into Eledorean.

"I did not!"

"Oh, then that was someone else who dipped his hand in the chamber pot?" It was her turn to wrinkle her nose in disgust. "That was awful."

"I didn't think you'd ever speak to me again after that," he said with a sheepish smile.

"It ruined my favorite dress."

"You had others."

"Hells, I did," she said in Acrasian.

His mouth dropped open. "Where did you learn that word?"

"Wouldn't you like to know?"

He shook his head and sighed. "I should get back."

"What about my plans?"

"You aren't going to tell me what they are."

"I am. Now." She paused and switched to Acrasian. "You say start with Laine?"

"I would. But they each have their strengths. Kauranen is the best tactician. She's intelligent enough to know when tradition is an advantage and when it isn't. Laine is popular. It'd be easier to get control through him once he's been promoted. However, Laine isn't as experienced as Kauranen. It depends upon what you need first. Strategy or control? Eventually, you'll need Bohinen and Näränen, too. If this is to work. But Näränen will be tougher. He's seen Uncle Sakari's bad side. Intimately."

She could see that Nels admired Kauranen. She took a deep breath and gave up on Acrasian. "Make a list."

"Have you decided how you'll get rid of Brigadier General Moilanen?"

Pausing, she considered how much she should tell Nels. Employing a korva to assassinate rivals wasn't unusual at court.

It was only that doing so was morally ambiguous, and she didn't know what Nels would think. "Well . . ."

"I'd be very careful. A korva would be best."

Her mouth dropped open, and she saw his face color.

He looked away. "Dealing in blood is what I do."

"I've already hired a korva." In her shock, she switched back to Eledorean. "Six months ago."

A pleased expression tugged at his lips. "Smart."

"I am plotting to pull the kingdom from Uncle's grasp. He won't give up Eledore easily. And at the very least, not employing a korva to spy on him would be suicide."

"I trust you know what you're doing," he said, putting his hands up in the air.

"Speaking of," she said. "I'd feel better if you employed one, too."

He paused. "Why?"

Korvas wielded a great deal of magical talent—primarily in listening and being fast, silent, and generally unobtrusive to the point of invisibility. They were employed as spies, assassins, and thieves—all occupations that publicly carried heavy punishments, that is, if the korva in question was caught. As a result, korvas outside of the military were expensive and difficult to find, while those serving in the Royal Army were serving out punishment.

Some liked to brag that the Kingdom of Eledore didn't have much of a prison population. That would be because all able-bodied criminals were sentenced to serve in the Royal Army.

"Don't worry. I'll pay for your korva. I'll even send you some recommendations," she said. "Have your choice transferred under your command. The other officers won't think twice. Whatever you are now, you're still a royal. Having a korva in service will have the added benefit of garnering a certain level of respect through fear."

"All right," he said, and then seemed to consider his next words.

"I should transfer to an active unit. One of Kauranen's, if you're planning on using her. She's been ordered to the front. Her brigade leaves next month. That doesn't give us much time."

Suvi nodded. "I know." She hated to think that her plans would put her brother in danger, but there wasn't anything else for it.

"Mother won't like it," he said.

"Leave Mother to me."

"Once you have the army under your influence, what have you planned next?"

She switched back to Acrasian. "Large grant to the Commons Church for plague hospital."

"You would openly defy Father?"

Suvi shook her head. "Secret donation. The Commons Church is beneath Uncle's notice."

"Where will you find enough healers? Most won't risk themselves. The poor don't pay."

Giving up on Acrasian, she kept her voice low. "Saara will convince them to volunteer." Saara was a devout member of the Commons Church. The Silmaillia's lowly ancestry had been quite a shock to the court when she'd been first named all those years ago. However, the Silmaillia wasn't a hereditary title. It was earned via magical talent, and no one had been able to deny that talent. Still, the court hadn't accepted Saara. So, the king had given her an estate far from court on the slopes of Angel's Thumb. "I've spoken with her granddaughter, Ilta, too." At the mention of Ilta's name, Nels looked away, but not before Suvi saw his eyes change. *Ah, so that's the one.*

"Why bother?" he asked.

"No commoners. No crops. No crops. No kingdom."

"Father may not notice a few falcons gone missing here and there, but enough for a hospital?"

"I'll redirect some of Uncle Sakari's financial assets to the hospital," she said. "Start with the money. Always start with the money."

They both said it together. "Mother would."

Suvi paused. The next part would be hardest because it was the most personal. "Another thing . . . the unit in which you choose to serve won't matter. You will be going to the front. Soon. Uncle Sakari is going to have Father commit the entire Royal Army to the war."

"Why? No one but me thinks Acrasia is a threat," Nels said with a frown.

"Cousin Edvard does," Suvi said. "It's why he's distancing Ytlain from Eledore. Uncle thinks Acrasia will be easier to conquer and control than Ytlain. So, he'll commit the army to the war. Plus, there's another reason."

"What other reason?"

Suvi stared at her knees. The moonlight painted the fabric of her pale green dress a muddy gray. She made another attempt at Acrasian, hoping it wouldn't sound as real. "The King's Army are . . . is big. Too difficult to control. War will make army smaller. Remove unwanted . . . persons." She glanced up, hoping he caught the implied warning.

Nels swallowed and then gave out a low whistle. "You have been thinking about this a while."

"Of course." She slapped him on the shoulder. "It important not only to protect kingdom, but to protect you, stupid donkey."

⇥ NELS ⇤

ONE

The river slapped a slow, steady beat against the rented narrowboat tied at the pier. The captain and first mate of the vessel had vanished below decks, taking refuge in the cabin. Thunder grumbled indifferent threats, and the scent of river mud battled the honeysuckles for dominance in the gloom. Moonlit willows, sycamores, and maples squatted on either side of the crude dock, providing excellent cover against the broken hillside. Mr. Almari, the smuggler, wouldn't be home. According to Nels's new korva, Almari had traveled south to Herraskariano and would be gone for a month. Still, Nels couldn't shake a hunch that something wasn't right. He should've sent Lieutenant Reini alone, but he had two reasons for not doing so. The first was that Nels was reluctant to involve others in his plan. Unfortunately, he couldn't handle twenty-five gun crates alone. The second reason was that Reini had come from General Moilanen's brigade, and Moilanen was Uncle Sakari's. Nonetheless, Suvi had recommended Reini, and Nels trusted Suvi's judgment. *For the most part.* So, there Nels was, skulking in shadows—an activity for which he was most certainly not suited.

It would've been better to commit. Take the chance. Give Reini the benefit of a doubt, Nels thought. *This is no way to begin.* It was exactly the sort of error Colonel Pesola would make. *It's too late now.*

Ahead, a disgusted sigh floated backward on stale night air. "There's a pile of leaves over here you could wade through," Lieutenant Reini whispered. "That might make slightly less noise, Your Grace." He had voiced a strong objection to being accompanied and was obviously still angry about being overruled.

"Get on with it, Lieutenant," Nels said. *No wonder Major Lahtela had looked like a cat who'd swallowed a fat mouse when he'd agreed to Reini's transfer.* By reputation, Lieutenant Viktor Reini was one of the best korvas in the entire Royal Eledorean army, if not *the* best. In exchange, Lahtela had demanded an amount that had cost Nels not only the advance Suvi had given him but what amounted to half of his monthly stipend. It still hadn't been enough, and he'd included the promise of a letter of introduction to the newly promoted Field Marshal Laine from Suvi. At the time, Nels thought he would've paid twice that amount to obtain Reini's transfer.

Nels was starting to lose confidence in his investment.

Of course, he knew all along there would be a catch. Soldiers with marketable powers didn't join the Royal Army. They sold themselves as mercenaries to the gentry. Mercenary pay was better, and quality weapons and provisions improved one's chances of survival, but the competition for such posts was intense, and for that reason, Nels had held out hope that he'd been lucky.

Entering the cave, Nels paused until his eyes adjusted to the dim light. Water dripped somewhere ahead, echoing off the smooth, rippled walls. He'd edged a hundred feet down the tunnel before the moonlight gave out and he was forced to feel his way along the wall. He had ordered Reini to wait with the lantern a discreet distance from the entrance. Judging by the absence of light, it was clear they had differing opinions on what that meant.

"You're doing better, even if you do breathe louder than a stampeding herd of elk," Lieutenant Reini whispered. He was close enough that Nels could feel Reini's breath on his ear.

Damn it. This isn't going to work out, is it? Nels thought, and then reconsidered his frustration. *As if you can get through a day without arguing with Major Lindström, you hypocrite.* It was a sign of Reini's great magical talent that Nels hadn't even sensed the use of magic. "Just open the damn lantern before I kill myself."

"Yes, sir, Captain-Highness, sir."

"Cut the crap, Lieutenant, if you plan on retaining the little braid you've got."

"Yes, sir."

Light inundated the passage with a tiny squeak from the hooded lantern, revealing the passage ahead. Nels could now see Lieutenant Reini—an unremarkable six-foot-tall kainen with light brown hair bound into a soldier's club. Shadows cast on Reini's face did not mask the twinkle of humor in his black eyes. If Nels had met Reini under other circumstances, he was certain he'd have liked Reini at once. They shared a similar attitude toward authority, after all.

"The crates are this way," Reini said. "This is going to be like stealing milk from a sleeping cow."

Nels followed Reini, skirting the edge of an underground stream. Shadows cowered from the light. At last, the blackness faded. The lantern's hood was shut, emitting a second squeak. Ahead, a bright circle of moonlight marked the water well behind Almari's house. The curved stone walls of the well were set with a series of iron rings leading to the surface. Looking up, Nels saw limestone and old mortar framing a stormy moonlit sky. Flickers of lightning danced in the gathering clouds.

"I understand Almari does the bulk of his business in smuggled Ytlainen port," Reini whispered. "We should acquire a few casks while we're here."

"Only the muskets, Lieutenant," Nels said. "Anything else is stealing."

"You take the fun out of everything, sir."

"I wouldn't say that," Nels said. "We're here, aren't we?"

Lieutenant Reini paused. "I must say, you aren't entirely what I expected."

"And what did you expect?"

Reini glanced over his shoulder with a sly grin. "A spoiled autocrat with no sense of humor and even less common sense."

"I'd say you're a fair judge of character," Nels whispered. "I'm somewhat short on common sense in particular."

"Ah. I'm right swived, then." Reini moved away from the false water well and then down the passage. He was both graceful and absolutely quiet.

The new passage stretched out for quite a distance before Reini stopped and signaled for silence. He slid farther down the tunnel as it turned left, Nels trailing behind him. After another hundred feet, they came to a ragged tarp covering a doorway on the left. Reini paused again and tilted his head as if listening.

After you, Your Highness, Reini's next gesture said.

Nels pushed the cloth aside and entered a huge cavern with a tall ceiling. It was easy to imagine it'd been hollowed out by centuries of water. Someone had constructed a five-foot-high platform against the far wall. Based on the dampness of the rock floor and the sharp contrast between the top and bottom halves of the supporting posts, Nels assumed it was intended to protect the smuggler's inventory from flooding. *Perhaps the well isn't as fake as all that.*

The platform itself was empty.

Behind him and to the left, a metallic click echoed off the cavern walls—the sound of a pistol hammer locking into place.

"Please be good enough to raise your hands, Your Grace." Almari's gravelly voice came from Nels's right.

So much for the sleeping cow, Nels thought. *Where's Reini? Do they have him, too? How many mercenaries does Almari have with him?* He put his hands in the air. "I only want what I paid for."

"Too bad your shipment was impounded three days ago," Almari said.

The barrel of a gun jabbed into Nels's back, and he staggered forward. *Impounded?*

"I've a new partner," Almari said, not sounding particularly happy about the prospect. "I've you to thank for that."

Is Suvi in danger? "Who?"

"Now, why would I risk my neck as well as the other two thirds of my inventory by answering that question?"

"Perhaps I can make a better offer?" Although Nels couldn't see the pistol, a spot between his shoulder blades itched where he was sure the gun was aimed.

"It's a bit late for that," Almari said. "Turn around."

Turning as ordered, Nels noted that Almari had the grumpy aspect of someone who hadn't slept well in some time. A lone, nervous-looking private aimed two pistols at Nels's chest.

A uniformed private is working for a smuggler? Is he one of Uncle Sakari's? Nels thought. *Has to be, you idiot. Suvi is in trouble.*

Almari cleared his throat. "Now, what am I to do with you?"

Nels searched for Lieutenant Reini, but he was nowhere in sight. Relief briefly loosened the tension in Nels's shoulders and stomach—until it occurred to him that if Reini was half the korva his reputation reported, he must have known Almari and the private were waiting for them. Nels tightened a fist. *If I live through this, Reini is going to wish he never joined the damned army.*

One problem at a time. Court speech rolled off his tongue in a calm timbre, but since there was no domination magic behind the words, they had no effect. "I apologize most profusely for trespassing upon your lands. I don't suppose you might consider settling for a sharp reprimand before sending me on my way?"

"Sharp's a good word," Almari said, drawing a knife. "I like it. The private here can dump you in the river. By the time the fish are through, no one will be the wiser."

Behind Nels's captors, the curtain twitched.

Hopeful that Reini hadn't abandoned him after all, Nels focused on the front of Almari's brown coat. "Won't a missing prince draw unwanted attention?"

Almari laughed. "My partner doesn't seem to think so. I understand you have a reputation for keeping rough company."

The current rough company in question slipped through the curtained doorway without making a sound. Reini's jaw was set at a determined angle, and his fists were clenched. Unaware of Reini's presence, the private stayed as he was. The barrel of his musket trembled.

"Are you confident your new partner can be trusted?" Nels asked, in an attempt to keep Almari and the private distracted.

"It isn't as if I have much choice in the matter," Almari said. "Apparently, you haven't made friends in your new posting. That's fast work. Even for the likes of you."

Nels shrugged. "Soldiers aren't in the business of diplomacy. Neither are smugglers, it seems."

In one fluid motion, Reini stepped behind the private and looped a cord around his neck, jerking him off his feet. The pistols clattered to the stone floor. An instant passed before Nels thought to dive for them. Elbowing Almari out of the way, Nels straightened and then jammed the muzzle of the first pistol into Almari's guts. *Here's hoping the private did a thorough job of ramming the patch.*

The private let out a gag before slumping. Lieutenant Reini lowered the limp form to the floor and stooped, placing a hand on the private's throat.

Nels collected the second gun and said to Almari. "Drop the knife and get against the wall."

Almari tossed the blade in disgust. "I hope you don't think I'd have stained myself with your blood."

"Of course not," Nels said, kicking the knife out of reach. "Although next time, you might want to invest in someone with more enthusiasm to do so for you."

Almari backed up to the cavern wall.

"Sir, I know this man," Reini said. "He's Passi Hesso. I served with him under Major Lahtela. Not closely, mind you. But he's definitely one of Moilanen's."

Maybe Suvi was right about Reini after all. "Is he dead?" Nels asked.

"No, sir. I was careful. And it takes a long time to strangle a man. You got Almari secure?"

"For now," Nels said.

"Bring him here. I'll take care of the rest."

Nels did so.

"Where are my muskets?" Nels asked. "Answer my questions, and I'll send someone to set you free after we're gone. If not . . ." He shrugged. "You're in Herraskariano visiting your aunt. No one's going to think to look for you until it's too late. There'll be no blood if you starve. At least, none I'll see. Technically, I wouldn't even have to bother with cleansing rituals."

"Unnecessary suffering, sir," Reini said. "Although I can leave a trail for the wolves. They won't mind a free meal. Hold on. What am I thinking? It's spring." He snapped his fingers. A fiendish smile stretched across his ordinary mouth, and suddenly, Reini didn't look so commonplace. "How do you feel about bears?"

Almari shuddered. "You wouldn't."

"Oh, trust me, I would," Reini said.

"Major Lahtela. He's the one come calling," Almari said. "Told me that private would see to you. Said there was extra in it if I kept things quiet."

Lahtela came to Almari directly? Damn it. Uncle Sakari is definitely on to us. Swiving hells.

Hang on, Nels thought. *Sakari has been in Ytlain for quite a while. All may not be lost. I don't know how far up the chain this goes. Not yet.* "All right," he said, "get down on the floor." *The guns were impounded. Where are they being stored? And who else knows about what Suvi is up to?*

Reini used the rope to tie Almari and Private Hesso together and then stuffed a rag in Almari's mouth. Nels collected the private's powder horn and ammunition. With that done, Nels headed for the tunnel.

"I had a look outside while you were entertaining our friends," Reini said. "The captain and the mate aren't alone."

Nels frowned. "I thought you said this would be easy."

"Never said that. I believe my exact words were that this was going to be like milking a sleeping cow."

"Exactly," Nels said.

"You don't know much about cows, do you, sir?"

"Next time, inform your superior officer before you let him walk into a trap." Nels knew he should be angry, but they weren't out of danger yet.

"It worked, didn't it?" Reini held open the tarp. "You should've seen your face. Did you honestly think I'd leave you to rot?"

Nels checked either side of the doorway before he stepped through. "Lieutenant, I sincerely hope you aren't too attached to those braids."

"You don't want to demote me yet. Wait until after I tell you how we're going to take care of the ones outside."

"Does it involve me getting my head blown off?"

"No, sir. They're not that effective with guns, not if they're from Lahtela's regiment. And there are only three of them. I'm sure of it."

"Like you were sure where our shipment was being stored?"

"Now, that's hardly fair. It wasn't my fault it was impounded before we got here."

"All right. Tell me your plan."

"Do you know how to swim?"

"No," Nels said.

"That buggers that idea. Your turn."

Nels paused. "We should take the back door to begin with. Once we're there, I'm sure I'll come up with something."

"Good idea, sir."

"Glad you think so," Nels said, pointing to the iron rings anchored to the wall. "Because you're going first. Just in case anyone is up there waiting for us."

Reini glanced up at the night sky through the long, rough tunnel. "Glad you've no hard feelings, sir."

Nels waited until Reini had reached the top and had signaled the clearing above was safe. Looping the musket strap over his shoulder, Nels began the climb. The iron rings felt slick and cold in his hands. Jagged stones and mortar abraded his knuckles. Almost at once, he wished he'd taken the time to remove his boots. They weren't designed for climbing water-well walls. They were infantry boots. The hobnails protruding from the soles functioned to maintain footing on blood-soaked battlefields. Nels had learned a number of lessons in Onni, and among them was that he wanted to stay on his feet in a fight—no matter what he might be treading in or, for that matter, who. His cleats clawed at both wall and iron, and each attempt at inserting his toes in the rungs sent a shower of mortar and stone to the bottom. He shook a boot free of one rung and moved up to the next. The pistols and powder horn thumped heavily against his back and hip. He tried not to think about how far he'd fall if he slipped. By the time he had pulled himself over the well's rim with a sigh of relief, his knuckles were raw and bleeding, and the toes of his infantry boots were thoroughly scratched. He was fairly certain he'd bent or lost at least two hobnails.

Reini signaled to him from the tree line.

When Nels was close enough, Lieutenant Reini whispered, "This way."

The approaching storm signaled warnings from the clouds, painting the scene in alternating color and shadow. One soldier stood ready at the dock, the second paced the long roof of the cabin, and the third stood guard at the cabin door. Each was armed with pistols and swords.

"Damn it all," Nels said. "I should've trusted you to handle Almari on your own. If I had, I would've been here to protect Captain Lumme."

"Or be captured as well."

"Give me some credit, will you?" Nels paused, thinking. "I've only two shots, and I can't be of any use from this distance." As much as he hated the thought of killing their own, he saw no other way around it. "How close do you think we can get before they know we're here?"

"Me? I can steal the boat from under them and be halfway down the river before they notice a thing," Reini said. "You? Well . . . I'm amazed we got this far."

"All right. You go in first. I'll draw their fire and take down as many of them as I can." *And hope none of them is a good shot.* Nels took a deep breath.

"Do try not to shoot me in the process."

"I'll do my best, but I won't make any promises."

"Terrific."

With a deep breath, Nels counted to one hundred. His heart thudded against his chest like a drum. His mouth was dry. He picked his first target—the private standing guard at the dock. Reini had good reason to be nervous. Acrasians didn't rely upon guns for specific targets. They used muskets in ordered groups like a siege weapon. There was a reason for that. Muskets weren't terribly accurate and neither were pistols. They were terribly effective in a unified blast, however.

There are only three of them, Nels thought. *With any luck, Reini will have taken down at least one of them before I'm close enough to engage.* The irony that his own plan actually might involve him getting his head blown off didn't slip past him. He told himself it wouldn't be any different from a pistol duel, which was more about having the courage to stand against fire and less about anyone actually getting shot.

When he was sure Reini had had enough time to get into position, Nels drew his pistols and made for the pier at a run. The downhill slope wasn't steep from his position, and as hoped, the private took precious seconds to register what was happening. Nels made it to the cover provided by the trees at the river bank without mishap. He shouted to draw more attention. The private fired first. The explosion echoed off the surrounding hills. Spent powder smoke enveloped the bank. Nels got the sense that the ball hit something in the trees to his left. He didn't check but kept moving, saving his shots for when he had the best chance of hitting. He ducked under a branch and reached the dock. His infantry boots thudded and clawed the dock planks. The private fired again. This time, Nels felt the wind of the ball's passing against his right cheek. Nels pulled the trigger and felt the heat of the explosion. Powder smoke fogged his line of sight. He tasted grit and sulfur. The private dropped. Nels didn't pause to check the fallen private. He jumped onto the boat deck and pointed his second pistol at the private dashing to the ladder set into the cabin's wall.

"Stop right there," Nels said.

Two hollow thumps and a grunt came from the boat's roof. *Reini*, Nels thought. *Must be.*

The second private slowly turned and then jumped from the ladder to the deck. Landing, he raised a dagger.

Nels's finger twitched against the trigger. Powder smoke hissed. *Misfire! Shi—*

The private slammed into Nels's stomach, forcing the air from his lungs. The back of Nels's head smacked the deck, and he lost his grip on both pistols. The private landed on top of him. Rolling, the private then scrambled to his feet. Nels stood and drew his sword. Twisting, he tried to parry the private's lunge and missed. He felt a dull thump on the shoulder. Giving in to instinct, he dipped his chin down and rammed the top of his forehead into the private's face as hard as he could. He was rewarded with the crunch of breaking bone. The private's eyes rolled back, showing the whites before he dropped. Nels snatched the dagger from the planks and tossed it overboard. He grabbed his pistols at once, jammed them in his belt, and ran to the ladder. With his blade in his teeth, he climbed to the rooftop. He arrived in time to see Reini pitch over the side, pulling a corporal after him.

I hope Reini can swim, Nels thought. He rushed to the roof's edge and scanned the water. Reini broke the surface once with arms flailing before he sank again. *Ah, that would be a no, gods damn it.*

Yanking off his boots and squirming out of his coat, Nels scanned the roof for anything that might float. He spied several wine casks tied off next to the rudder. *That might do.* He chopped the rope binding the barrels together. Dropping his weapons, he grabbed the lightest cask. Then he took four deep breaths, lifted the cask, held it tight, and ran for the roof ledge. One leap and he was over the river.

I swiving hate water, damn it. I really swiving hate—

He hit the surface curled around the cask, landing where he'd last seen Reini go down. The edge of the cask smacked him under the chin and hammered him in the ribs, hard. He tasted blood. Stinging pain clawed his wounded shoulder. None of it was as immediate as the press of water. He had time to wonder if he'd missed Reini completely, when he felt a frantic hand clamp onto his leg. Opening his eyes, he discovered he couldn't see in the murk. The cask began to tug him upward as hoped. Unfortunately, it was no match for Reini's thrashing. Reini clawed Nels's face. Nels was kicked twice. Reini switched to Nels's injured shoulder.

Shit! A sharp bolt of pain burst up Nels's arm and down his spine. The cask slipped and precious air pushed past his lips in agony and frustration. *Reini will kill us both.* His toes brushed against something slimy and hard. *Rock.*

The river isn't deep here.

The fingers digging onto Nels's shoulder and neck lost urgency. He gave up on the cask and swept an arm through the water until he made contact with wet wool. The cask shot upward, scraping his face as it went. His lungs squeezed shut. He fought against an overwhelming urge to breathe—underwater or not. In a last desperate effort, he jumped for the surface. The murk brightened briefly. He heard a muffled rumble and footsteps. A steering pole sliced through the water inches from his nose, startling the last of his air out of him. With one hand, he grabbed at the pole. His head cleared the water, and he gulped air once before sinking again. Reini was heavy. Nels gripped the wet cloth with all his might. He felt it rip. Finally, someone plunged into the river with a splash. Reini was stripped from his grasp. With both hands free, Nels pulled himself up the pole. Cold slapped his face. He swallowed muddy river water and a certain amount of air. He choked. His head slammed into the side of the riverboat. His water-soaked hair blinded him. Then strong hands felt for the top of his head. He was pulled upward and dumped unceremoniously onto the deck. The mate's heavy step drummed away from him and up the ladder.

"That was a very foolish thing you did," the captain said. The wrinkles in his face were set into grim lines that could've been a smile.

Nels spat. "Reini?"

"Didn't manage to drown, it seems. Did a fine job of trying, though."

A coughing fit forced Nels's forehead to the deck. Once it passed, he rolled onto his back. Lightning traveled among the clouds, and a blast of thunder vibrated the deck. As if on cue, fat raindrops smacked his face. He blinked. The sky moved. "We're under way?"

"Couldn't risk staying. Not after all that."

Nels heard someone retching and sat up. He recognized Reini's jacket. The sleeve was torn. Reini—in marginally better shape than his uniform but still whole and alive—lay draped face-first over a large barrel, vomiting up water. Nels stood, staggered once on heavy feet, and felt the captain capture his elbow with an iron grip.

"Don't go pitching over the side again. Can't say as I'll bother fishing you out a second time with what you paid me—not that there'd be much left if I did, by the look of you."

Exhausted, Nels nodded and then crossed the deck. His body

was drenched in river water and dull pain. Chilled rain slapped the crown of his head. Reini slid off the barrel in a heap. Nels weakly tugged a discarded blanket over the lieutenant's shoulders with shaking hands. The barrel did a lazy roll, thumping into the railing. Nels adjusted the blanket so that it covered Reini's back better. After that, he righted the barrel. Then he tugged up his own collar in a futile attempt to protect his neck from the rain.

"You went in after me." Reini's voice was hoarse.

Too weary to stand any longer, Nels sat. His buttocks hit the deck with a teeth-jarring thump. Another bolt of pain shot up his spine. His entire body ached, and it was hard to breathe without angering his ribs.

"Thought you couldn't swim," Reini said.

"I can't," Nels said, staring at Reini through a wet tangle of hair. "My sister joined the navy at fifteen. Was well on her way to an officer's rank before I—" He stopped. He didn't wish to blurt out anything he might regret. "Suvi attempted to teach me to swim, but I couldn't manage. Said my head was made of wood. But she said luckily for me, wood floats."

Reini laughed until tears poured down his face. Nels squinted in mild offense until he recognized the note of hysteria. He turned away. Watching the rain slap the deck boards, he gave Reini time to get control of himself. Throbbing pain in Nels's shoulder kept time with his heart. Several minutes seemed to pass before the laughter finally dissipated.

Reini cleared his throat. "Call me Viktor." He took a long, shuddering breath and held it before letting it out slowly. "You're bleeding, sir."

Nels noted it was the first time Reini had used the word "sir" without an edge of sarcasm. Tugging at his blood-soaked sleeve, Nels peered at the cut underneath through the rent. "I'm fine."

"We should get you to the infirmary when we get back."

Nels shook his head. "The regiment's healer will ask too many questions. I've no wish to land in the disciplinary barracks for dueling any more than I've plans for being hung for smuggling."

"That's good to know, sir." Reini sniffed. "I could manage a field bandage."

"Leave it. It's only a scratch."

TWO

It was very late when the coach stopped in front of the small birchwood-and-stone cottage where Nels kept house. The rain had lost enthusiasm over the journey, slowing to a drizzle. Nels heard the coach driver pull a lever, and the coach step unhinged, clattering open with a bang he could feel through the soles of his boots. His heart suffered a similar jolt when he spied the hooded figure waiting at the front door. He glanced down at his now torn and bloody uniform. Then he grabbed his overcoat and draped it over his shoulders to hide at least some of the damage.

"Who is that?" Viktor asked.

Blond curls spilled from the hood as the small figure ran along the path to the front gate. Nels jumped out of the coach before the door was fully open. He banged his shoulder in the process and winced.

"Thank the Mother," Ilta said, circling his waist with her warm arms and then stretching to kiss his cheek.

"You really shouldn't touch me. I'm tainted." Nels attempted not to glory in her affection too much. *Remember, she's only being nice.*

"Nonsense," she said.

"My turn." Viktor stood on the coach step and threw his arms wide.

Ilta stared at Viktor. "Who are you?"

Nels didn't bother with introductions. It was best if Viktor couldn't name names. "You shouldn't be here. The Narrows is no place for a lady—"

Ilta gasped, shoved the overcoat off his shoulder, and ripped at the blood-blackened wool sticking to the wound. Searing pain penetrated deep into the base of Nels's neck with a spasm, and fresh blood oozed down his arm. He jerked out of her grasp and barely saved his coat from the mud with his good arm.

"Why didn't one of the others bandage this for you?" Ilta asked.

Viktor said, "He wouldn't let me."

"Get inside," Ilta said. "I'll see to it."

"No wonder you didn't want to go to the infirmary." Viktor gave out a low whistle. "You have your own healer. It must be good to be a prince."

Ilta peered at the cut without touching the sleeve. "It's too deep for plasters. It needs stitching. Do you have any mugwort?"

"No," Nels said, giving Viktor a glare. *Go home*, he mouthed.

"I might have mugwort somewhere," said Viktor. "Care to come to my apartments and check?"

"Go home, Lieutenant. That's an order," Nels said, dodging Ilta as she reached for his good arm. "Send for Private Ketola. I need him to run a message." He waited for Viktor to climb back into the coach and then slammed the door. "See you in the morning."

"Yes, sir, Captain-Highness, sir." Viktor leaned out the window. "Tomorrow is a rest day, you know." He mock-whispered, "I hear sleeping late after a good long swive speeds healing."

Nels checked Ilta's face, prepared to apologize, but her gaze was focused somewhere else. He knew that distracted look. She was in one of her trances. She hadn't heard Reini, if she remembered him at all.

"Good night, Viktor," Nels said.

Viktor didn't seem to notice that Ilta couldn't hear him. In Nels's experience, it wasn't all that unusual for others to miss the signs. There had been times when he'd missed them himself.

"And a very good night to you, dear lady." Viktor winked and then waved out the coach window. "Until we meet again."

The coach rattled and splashed down the cobblestones. Relieved, Nels returned his attention to Ilta. Nothing had changed. Afraid to touch her, Nels decided not to lead her out of the rain and merely waited until the trance ended. He wondered what she was doing in the Narrows at this time of night and then began to notice the sorry state of his residence. The poorly tended dooryard looked even more forlorn in the rain, but the darkness did a fair job of hiding the chipped green paint on the door.

I've got to get her out of here, he thought. *Before she's spotted by someone who knows her.*

She blinked and sighed.

"Are you all right?" Nels asked. He made a point of never asking her what she'd seen. Much as he wished he had some form of powerful magic, he didn't envy Ilta. Knowledge of the future seemed more of a maddening burden than a blessing.

She bit her lip and then searched inside her cloak pocket. She found the gold watch she kept with her and checked the time as she always did after one of her spells. "How long was I gone?"

"Not long. Let me get you a coach."

"Did I say or do anything?"

"No."

Looking relieved, she put away the timepiece as well as her anxiety. "Aren't you going to invite me inside?"

He took a deep breath and released it. *If someone finds out, Saara will punish her.* "We both know I can't."

"It's not as if I'll acquire a death taint, you know. I'm a healer." She placed a hand on her hip. "It's ridiculous. As if a battlefield or hospital contains less death energy than a soldier's home. We both deal in life and death."

"Encountering death and causing it are two very different things, and you know it. Why are you here?"

"I wanted to talk to you about your letter. About Acrasian pox-proofing for variola vera."

"I gave you all the information I had. Private Ketola would have the details. You can contact him tomorrow. You shouldn't be here."

"I wanted to make sure you were safe."

"As you can see, I'm home."

"Stop being so stubborn and invite me in." Then she gave him a look that made his stomach flutter.

Committing himself, he pushed past her, and as he did, he caught the faint aroma of winter roses, mint, and rosemary. It sent a delicious shiver down low. He swallowed, forcing away thoughts he shouldn't have and then threw open the door. "After you, Lady Healer."

She retrieved her healer's bag from where it had rested in relative safety on the roofed porch and followed him inside. The lamp that Mrs. Nimonen, the housekeeper, kept lit in the parlor revealed a shabby room of minimal furnishings—a settee, the battered writing desk, a wingback chair, and a small table near the hearth. One rug. No paintings. No decoration outside of the few tokens Suvi had given him. At the first, he hadn't even bothered with a bedstead, sleeping on the floor when he could manage to stagger home from the local alehouse. Mrs. Nimonen, who he suspected was far too efficient a housekeeper for the amount he paid her, had taken charge out of desperation. Two months, one broken nose, an untold number of bruises, and twenty-seven demerits later, he had finally sobered up. Although more than a year had passed since then, he still hadn't bothered to do much with the house. He hadn't seen the point. Watching as Ilta tugged down her hood to survey the furnishings, he suddenly did.

"It's . . . smaller than I imagined," she said.

What were you expecting? It's not like I live in a palace anymore. Forgetting his shoulder, Nels shrugged. He held his breath until the pain faded. "Would you like some tea? Mrs. Nimonen, my housekeeper, is gone for the night. I think I can manage boiling water without burning myself."

Ilta's nervous retort echoed through the empty house. "Point me to the pantry. You'll only get blood in the pot. Anyway, your Mrs. Nimonen is bound to have some mugwort stashed somewhere."

Ilta slipped through the door he indicated, and the sounds of clattering porcelain followed soon after. The cottage was old, and therefore the kitchen was little more than a storage shed with a door to the root cellar. The cooking was done outside in summer and at the hearth in foul weather. He went to the fireplace and stirred the banked coals, then checked the water level in the kettle before swinging it over the heat.

He absolutely avoided thinking about the proximity of his bedstead in the next room. *As if you're in any shape to do anything about it, even if she was interested. Which you damned well know she isn't.*

Ilta returned, balancing a tea pot, biscuits, and other odds and ends on a tray. Her hair threw shadows across her face, masking her expression. "The pot has a crack in it. Did you know that?"

He hadn't noticed. "I've been too busy to replace it."

Setting the tray on the small table next to the hearth, she armed herself with a surgeon's needle and motioned for him to sit. Threading the needle, she spoke without looking away from it. "I'll get started while the water boils. Take off your shirt."

He settled into the upholstered wingback where he took his meals, and began unbuttoning his shirt. *Too bad this is only about my shoulder.*

A knock on the door blasted through the room. Nels ran through a list of possibilities. Had someone seen her enter the house? Was it Saara, come to collect her errant apprentice? Had Major Lahtela sent someone to arrest him?

"Sir? Are you awake?" Private Ketola's soft country accent filtered through the door.

Ketola. You forgot about warning Suvi. Stop thinking with your cock, damn it. He shot Ilta a guilty look and pointed to the back door. She seemed to catch his meaning and left.

"I'm awake." He found Ketola standing on the porch, water-logged tricorne in hand.

Ketola straightened to attention and executed an exact salute. His soggy red curls clung to his face.

"Come in, private. I've a message for the palace."

Ketola hesitated before stepping over the threshold. He scanned the room until he spotted the tea tray set with two cups. Ketola's eyes widened.

Viktor had better not have said a damned thing about Ilta, or I really will have his braid. Nels went to the writing table. The tension knotting the muscles between his shoulder blades aggravated his wounds. He probed the drawer for fresh paper and then sharpened a quill to scratch out a coded warning in Acrasian. "This message is to be delivered to my sister. No one else. Understood?" Ketola knew the drill and could be trusted. Nels had used him to deliver messages to Suvi before. Blotting the page, he folded it neatly into an interlocking square to hide the contents from prying eyes and sealed it with green wax. "Ask if there will be a reply."

"Yes, sir." Ketola nodded and hesitated. "Should I send for a healer?"

"No, thank you. Looks worse than it is." He handed Ketola the folded paper, noting the way the private's coat sagged on his thin frame. Ketola's interest in the tea tray took on another meaning. *Gods, I am tired.* Nels pinched the bridge of his nose to clear his head. "Dispose of the biscuits, will you? Mrs. Nimonen left it. I'm not hungry. And I'm too tired to put the things away."

"Yes, sir."

Ketola stuffed his pockets and left.

Ilta returned and looked meaningfully at the front door. "What was that about?"

"What?"

"You lied to him. You haven't eaten."

"Ketola bound with an Acrasian woman nine years ago. She died last spring. Left him with eight children. Father doesn't pay captains all that well. He pays privates even less. Ketola won't take money. And I'm not one to argue matters of pride."

A warm smile spread over Ilta's face. "You're wonderful."

"Wonderful would be finding him a position with a noble so he could feed his family without selling his ass." Too late, he spied Ilta's shock.

"Do you mean he—"

"To be honest, it's pretty common. Men or women. Often both. Most of the troops don't have an alternative. As long as we're off duty, the Jägerpoliisi look the other way. For the right sort of bribe."

"Oh." She looked away. She somehow managed to look even more uncomfortable.

Then he realized the implication and stammered in panic. "Ah. I don't. Do that. Of course."

Her relieved expression was almost comical. "Oh. I see."

"But after two years of misconduct, I don't have enough personal influence for anything as insignificant as a reference for Ketola. I should've thought about that sooner."

"Don't be so hard on yourself."

"I could ask Suvi to refer him, but I'm new to Kauranen's regiment, and Ketola is one of the few that I know I can trust. Anyway, he isn't the only one having to resort to . . . to—"

"Prostitution. It's all right. I know the word. I'm a healer. Remember?"

"I-I'm enough of a burden on Suvi as it is." He shrugged with his good shoulder. "At least we're headed to an actual war. He won't risk dying in a ridiculous skirmish over a rose bush."

"It wasn't a rose bush." She picked up the needle and thread again. "It was a prize-winning garden."

"What difference does it make?"

"Are you going to sit down and take off that shirt? Or am I going to have to sit you down and do it for you?"

An image of Ilta doing just that seared through Nels's mind quick as a flash of lightning. Blood rushed in his ears and other places. It was accompanied with another quiver of pleasure. Resuming his place in the wingback chair, he painfully hiked his shirt over his head and tossed it onto the floor. With a shock, he registered that the cut in his shoulder was already angry and red.

"This may hurt a little." She glanced up from the wet cloth in her hand. He could have sworn he saw her eyes widen before she glanced away. A corner of her mouth twitched upward. "I-I could remove the pain first if you'd like."

The room suddenly felt close—too warm and charged with

energy. It reminded him of the air on the narrowboat's deck before the storm hit. Unable to trust his tongue, he nodded. She moved closer and laid a cool hand on his bare shoulder. His skin tingled beneath her palm, and his heart raced. Muscles low in his belly tensed. Her eyes closed in concentration. Breathing in the scent of her, he felt the heat born under her hand. It grew more intense until the knot of pain loosened and then faded away. Her lips were near enough to kiss, and her hair brushed against his face like perfumed silk. His hand twitched with a need to plunge into the golden waves. Before he knew it, the glistening strands were sliding through his fingers.

She paused, eyes closed. He licked his lips and swallowed. His heart rammed his breastbone hard enough to bruise. Terrified he'd lose the opportunity, he tilted his head and pressed his mouth to hers. Her lips were warm and wet. She tasted of peppermint. Suddenly, she opened her mouth to his and eased into his lap without breaking the seal. The movement lacked her usual grace and she almost fell. A nervous laugh lodged in his throat and then vaporized when her thigh pressed against him. He twitched, startled. He was certain she'd feel his cock-stand and retreat in disgust. Instead, he felt her mouth curl upward.

"This is nice," she whispered against his lips, and squirmed closer.

A bone in her stays dug painfully into his battered ribs, but he didn't dare move. He was certain if he did, he'd break the spell. "It is." His voice cracked as her hand tickled feather-light down his right side. Pain and desire bonded into a strangely pleasant sensation.

She tore her mouth away and let out a nervous laugh that she seemed to have stolen from him. Staring at him from under half-closed lids, she asked, "Is—is it like you dreamed?"

She knows. She knows, and she doesn't mind.

Rain rushed the windowpanes.

He cleared his throat. "Better." Her eyes were alert, shining in the firelight. "I agree." She unhooked the clasp of her light cloak, and the thin fabric slithered down his shins. "Much better than dreaming."

Before he could ask what she meant, she trapped his mouth again, and he lost himself. After a time, he realized the coals had died and the room had grown chilly. His legs started to prickle with numbness and still he didn't dare dislodge her. When she withdrew to catch her breath, he bent to the base of her neck. The instant his lips made contact, her hips writhed and she moaned. He pictured her fingers tearing at his breeches, plunging under the fabric.

To his surprise, she slid to the floor on her knees. She paused for an instant, her head tilted as if listening. Then she tore at the buttons on his breeches with one hand and thrust the other underneath. Each action was so like what he'd imagined that he was momentarily stunned. Her eyes were closed, and her blind fingers searched deeper until she shyly touched his cock.

He froze, his heart battering his ears. "Ilta?"

For the first time since she'd shed her cloak, she didn't seem to hear him. He thought of her trances. *What if she doesn't know what she's doing?* Cold fear trickled down his back like sleet until she moved to grip his cock, and conscious thought was momentarily obliterated. He wasn't sure how much time passed before he could breathe again. It was almost like drowning. Almost. *Coincidence. Forget it. Let her do what she wants.*

Oh, please, let her want to untie her stays.

As if on cue, she withdrew her hands and tugged her laces free of the top knot. Her shift gaped, and he stared as she revealed her breasts. In an instant, the small, pink nipples were hard points under his thumbs. The skin covering the yielding globes was smooth, firm, softer than he imagined.

That was no coincidence. Stop this. Now.

Part of him thrilled at the idea of finally exerting control over another being. He was immediately ashamed. The need for command magic had been everything for so long—to finally be as his family expected generated tremendous relief and joy. *You can't do this, damn it. This isn't command magic, and even if it was, she's not some dumb animal to be used as you will.* The temptation to ignore his conscience was tremendous. *She's lost in your thoughts. This is no different than rape.* With that thought, everything changed. He pushed her away. She ducked under his arm, tugging at his breeches.

"Stop. You have to stop. Ilta, please! Ilta, wake up, damn it!"

Her head came up with a snap. She blinked in confusion. "Nels?" A hand flew up to her open stays, and then her face, already flushed, turned a deep red. Her eyes filled with tears before she threw herself backward, bumping into the table, knocking the tea tray off the top. The teapot shattered on the hearth tiles.

"Oh, Great Mother. What have I done?" Ilta asked. She fumbled for the watch inside her cloak pocket. "How long was I gone? How long?"

Afraid she would cut herself on broken porcelain, he yanked up his breeches and went to her. She yelped and scuttled away, abandoning the watch. A cannonball of guilt smashed into his gut and for a moment he couldn't breathe.

I did this.

"I-I can't believe I—" She sobbed into her hands.

"It was my fault. I'm so sorry." The shattered look in her eyes crushed his heart. He secured the buttons on his breeches and grabbed his shirt from the floor. "I shouldn't have kissed you."

"I wanted you to kiss me." She hiccupped. "I did. I've wanted it since . . . for so long."

He blinked in surprise and then threw his shirt over his head. *I have to tell her.* He paused. "You weren't acting on your own. I—"

Her eyes went wide, and terror formed ice around his heart.

She'll never speak to you again. Oh, gods, I almost— "Wait! It wasn't like that. Please." But it was, on a certain level, and he knew it. *She knows when you lie.* The knowledge that such a thing was within him was almost too terrible to face. For the first time in his life, Nels was grateful that he'd never had command magic and never would.

She sniffed and stared up at him with dull, wounded eyes. He watched her sitting there in a crumpled half-dressed heap, her arms wrapped around her knees, rocking herself, and fought the urge to fold her in his arms to sooth the hurt away. But he didn't have the right. Not anymore. Not after what he'd done. An overwhelming need to fix what he'd broken, to avenge her pain, curled his hand into a tight fist. He turned his back. "Dress. I won't look."

He heard soft rustling and hated himself for imaging her closing up her shift. Tying her stays. *The swell of her breasts.*

Stop it.

"All right," she said. "You can turn around."

When he did, she seemed calm. More herself. Her lips were pressed into an angry line. She got up from the floor and walked to the ruin on the hearth. "I'm sorry."

"Don't be. It was cracked anyway, remember?" He held his breath.

The line of her lips twitched, revealing no sign he could decipher. "I guess there'll be no tea."

"If you want tea, you'll have tea." Unable to face his guilt any longer, he bolted out the back to the kitchen like a coward. He stood for a moment as if he'd forgotten what he was there for. Once he stopped shaking, he began rooting around in the sideboard and found a jar capable of holding boiling water. Next, he located some cheesecloth and two unmarred tea cups. Balancing them carefully in his hands, he took a deep breath. He expected the worst and hoped for the best. "Not the most elegant tea you've ever had, but it should suffice."

He set the things down on the old wingback chair and retrieved the broom. Then he swept the hearth with energetic strokes. In between chasing down stray porcelain shards and spilled tea grounds, he risked a glance her direction. She was perched on the settee, legs folded under her. The tears were gone, and her face was composed, verging on angry. She watched him with an expression that said she was listening for things that couldn't be heard. He turned his attention to sweeping, keeping his mind very blank.

"You said it was your fault. What did you mean by that?" The question was flat. Cold.

He swung the kettle away from the coals and used his ruined shirttail to lift the kettle's lid. It had boiled dry. He would have to go out to the pump. He considered what he should say, but his mind was as empty as the kettle. Finally, he gave up, knowing that there was no way around it. She had a right to know what happened. Every detail.

But only if she asks.

Coward. "I should've been more careful," he said. "I should've shielded you from my feelings. I knew you were sensitive. I didn't know that could happen. I didn't. But it's no excuse. I'm so sorry."

She glanced down at the floor before confronting him with her eyes again. The mantel clock executed the seconds with cutting ticks while rain drowned the pathetic garden in the dooryard. He was certain she was going to slap him and leave, but she didn't. She stared at him instead. It was much, much worse. Anger sparked in the black of her eyes. He wanted to retreat from it as he'd done with so many things, but didn't. When his endurance had been stretched to its limits, she finally blinked and moved a hand over her skirts, smoothing the folds of fabric. She took a deep breath as if to steady herself for some great decision.

"Did you know my parents sent for Gran the moment they understood what was happening to me?"

Fearful of where the situation was headed but grateful she had spoken at last, he shook his head. Although they had known each other for years, they had spent little of that time alone. Their conversations had been restricted to matters less personal. This was the first time she had spoken at length of her childhood or anything else of importance. It suddenly occurred to him that their relationship was one-sided. That awareness strengthened the shame of what he'd almost done, twisting his heart with fierce self-loathing.

"Gran said I was no more than three or four years old when my powers started to manifest."

He felt his jaw drop.

"I know. For most people . . . most of the time, magic power comes with maturity, but there are exceptions. Some, like myself, are simply born that way."

"Go on."

"So, they sent for Gran as soon as they knew something was wrong. Even so, it was almost too late. I don't remember much. And what I do remember, I couldn't tell you if it really happened—if it was really me, or if it was someone else." She smoothed nonexistent wrinkles from her skirts again. "By the time Gran came for me, they were terrified I'd gone mad. Gran kept me isolated for six years. I saw no one. Not even my parents. Gran said she had to shield me until I could do it for myself. You were the first person my age I'd ever met. Did I tell you that?"

Nels shook his head.

"I'm still learning how to maintain boundaries. Gran says . . ." Her words trailed off and her head tilted, forming a question that her words didn't. "You love me."

He looked her in the eyes and knew the truth. Admitting it wasn't nearly as terrifying as the thought that he may have again ruined something that meant everything to him. *Whatever she says, if she throws it back in my face, I deserve it.* "I love you." He readied himself for the inevitable rejection.

She stared at him for a long time with no expression until she whispered, "I love you, too."

The broom slipped through his numb fingers. He snatched it before it smacked into the mantel. She laughed. The sound wasn't its normal timbre but strong enough, no longer brittle.

He cleared his throat. "I'd best get water for the tea." Snatching the kettle from the hook, he dashed through the front door and outside to the pump. The storm had regrouped. He was drenched before he'd reached his destination. It seemed silly to struggle with the pump when all he really had to do was hold the kettle open in the downpour, but the pump gave his hands something to do. He heard her voice in his mind, repeating what she'd said. *I wanted you to kiss me. I did. I wanted it for so long.*

I don't understand. When the pump had done its job, he dropped the lid back on the kettle and shook his head to remove wet hair and lustful images from his eyes.

What in the world are you doing out here? She's waiting, you fool. I can't. What if something terrible happens?

"Nels?" The door swung open a crack and lamplight sketched a yellow line on the porch planks. "Have you drowned?"

He ran for the steps and then shut the door behind him.

"Let me finish with your shoulder." She took the kettle and exchanged it with a dry cloth for his head. "And stop bounding off like a frightened deer. It's just a few stitches, for the Mother's sake."

"You think I'm afraid of the needle?"

She arched an eyebrow at him. "Would you prefer I thought you're afraid of my loving you?"

"You know I'm not." *I'm afraid of what I might do to you. You are, too. Admit it.*

The arch lingered in her eyebrow. She went to the hearth and touched the clock. She'd managed to light the fire in the time he had been out at the pump. She spoke to the wall. "We need to talk."

He nodded and swallowed. Then he realized she couldn't see him with her back to him. "We do."

"Dry off and change. You're dripping wet. Mrs. Nimonen is going to have a fit when she sees the mud you've tracked all over her floor. And be careful of that cut. Just because it doesn't hurt right now doesn't mean it isn't a problem." She seemed to gain steadiness by assuming her role as healer.

He freed his hair from its ragged queue and let it fall down his back. When he glanced at the hearth, he noticed that not only had she set the fire, but that she had taken the blankets and pillows off his bedstead and arranged them in front of the fireplace. He blinked, and his heart stumbled.

"Don't get any ideas," she said. "You're going to be exhausted when the initial boost of magic wears off. I want you where I can watch you."

"You can't stay here."

"Only until after we talk. Then I promise I'll slip out the back door. No one will see. But . . . no distractions." She turned away again, but not soon enough to hide the flash of anxiety on her face.

She sat next to the blankets and patted the floor. "When you're done. Come. Sit."

He went to his bedchamber and grabbed his civilian breeches off a hook on the wall. He decided not to bother with stockings or a shirt. The shirt would only get stained. It was his last clean and whole one, and his tailor refused to extend credit to soldiers. Having spent almost everything on Reini's transfer, he couldn't have another shirt made until next month, and by then, he might be headed for the front. He reentered the main room to find Ilta hadn't moved from her place on the floor. A basin of steaming water was at her side. The fire backlit her hair with gold.

No distractions, he thought.

"The tea is ready," she said, holding up a cup. "Would you like some?"

"It was for you. I was supposed to make it." He sat next to her and stared into the flames, angry at himself for letting her down yet again.

"At the rate you were going, I'd have had tea in a month." He could hear a smile in her admonishment.

His face burned. "I can't seem to do anything right."

Her hands tenderly stroked his bare shoulder. He blotted out yet another set of searing images. She used a damp cloth to soak the scabs from his shoulder. The coolness of the water brought relief. When he sensed the prick and tug of the needle, he focused on the rain and watched the fire dance. It hissed whenever a stray raindrop ventured down the flue.

She took a breath as if she were about to plunge into deep water and then paused. "Would you like to bind with me for a year?" Her question shattered the quiet calm.

"What?" The needle gouged his upper arm.

"Oh. Sorry," she said, lowering the needle and leaning away from him. "I-I think it would be a good idea. It's the only way Gran will allow me significant time alone with you. And I have to know if I can—if I can be close with people without losing myself completely."

Blood tickled as it traced a line down his bicep. The last stitch had torn free and neither of them had noticed.

"Oh, Goddess, I'm sorry." She snatched up the wet cloth from the basin, wrung it out, and wiped up the fresh blood with a red face.

"After what I did? You want to bind with me?"

She gave him a shy smile. "I guess we both have things to learn about self-control."

The needle stabbed again.

"Now?" he asked.

"I . . . can't right away. Later. In a month or—"

"Yes." He said it although he knew he'd be headed for the front long before then. He didn't want to give her a second chance to retract the offer.

"We can work out the details in a couple of days," she said. "There. Done." She lowered her mouth and bit the thread. Her warm lips pressed against his skin, and her black eyes twinkled. He could've sworn he felt the silky touch of her tongue. It sent another quicksilver bolt of lust through his veins.

"It's going to hurt tomorrow." She withdrew and wrapped a tight bandage around the wound. "You've a bruised rib, but this is the best I can do. It's not a good idea for me to use any more magic on you just now."

He nodded, his eyelids suddenly heavy.

"Why don't you lay down?" She paused. "You can put your head in my lap if you like."

It was the least of what he wanted, but he settled for it and was thankful. He shifted onto his back among the blankets and pillows in front of the fire while her graceful hands eased damp hair from his face.

"Sleep. Don't worry. Everything is going to be all right." She kissed his forehead, and for a moment, his face was sheltered from worry in a cave of spun gold. He looked into her face and firelight glittered stars against the night of her eyes.

I should be soothing her, not the other way around. He struggled to get up from the floor, but his body refused.

THREE

When he woke, his arm was stiff with pain. His ribs, at least, felt fine. He saw that as promised, Ilta had gone. The thought of her warmed his chest. For the first time since he'd become a soldier, he met the morning with a smile on his face. Even the sun seemed to shine brighter. Gathering the blankets and pillows from the floor, he left the room to make his bed. It wasn't long afterward that Mrs. Nimonen entered from the back of the house. She started when she found him at the hearth. It wasn't like him to be up this early on a rest day. He was pouring scalding tea from the jar into his cup and attempting to keep from burning his hands. Distracted, it didn't occur to him to use the towel Ilta had left. He scorched two fingers with a yelp and almost dropped the jar. He set it down on the floor a touch too hard and spilled some of the tea.

"Good morning," Nels said, mopping up the mess with the towel.

"What happened to the teapot?" Mrs. Nimonen asked. A sour frown marred her otherwise pleasant middle-aged face. She finished tying an apron around her waist and smoothed it. "Tell me you didn't pawn it. Or did you lose it in one of your card games?"

He gave her a smile. "I dropped it. Last night. I'll have to buy a new one. Good day for it."

Suspicion crept across her expression. "Did you drop it on your head?"

"No. Why do you ask?"

"I've never seen you this cheerful. In fact, I don't think I've ever seen you smile." She scanned the room. Skepticism deepened the lines around her narrowing eyes. "You've tidied up the place." It was almost an accusation.

"Oh." Nels suddenly noticed the neat stacks of letters on his writing desk. "I suppose I did."

"What happened?"

"Nothing is wrong. Everything is brilliant. Perfect, even."

She crossed the room. Her face set in incredulity as if happy ex–crown princes were omens of ill luck. Stooping, she retrieved a paper-wrapped package resting on the floor. "You're up to no good. I can tell." She placed the flat, rectangular bundle on his writing desk.

"Don't worry. It isn't that I've hired a new housekeeper."

She harrumphed. "I'll get your breakfast, then." The back door closed with an exact thump.

He finished his first cup of tea and then fetched the package with his good hand. He kept his injured arm close to his body. The bundle was heavy, but he could tell from the feel of it that it was a book. Settling into the comfortable old wingback, he spied the red wax seal embossed with a tiny sparrow. *Suvi.* He ripped into the paper and found a leather-bound book. The title, *Tricks and Tools of Mystics, Magicians, and Other Charlatans,* was written in Acrasian. A folded letter was tucked inside. The message was written in swirling Acrasian script: *Not real magic can be as power as real. Acrasian can do. You can do.* Clearly, she wrote Acrasian worse than she spoke it. *More difficult for spies to puzzle it out, I suppose,* he thought. She'd risked much in giving the book to him. Faking magic wasn't unheard-of in Eledore. Any noble who rode practiced it to varying degrees from the time they received their first pony. The demands of riding made the exclusive use of command magic impractical. Still, appearances had to be maintained. The punishment for fraud was severe—particularly if the individual wasn't of noble blood. As a result, the thought of using such tricks to shore up his status hadn't occurred to him. *I'm a royal. No one would question it. Smart. Very smart.*

His smile stretched a touch wider until he spied the small card. Another, separate message was scrawled on its surface.

Do not worry. Major Lahtela sleep from service.

An uneasy shudder crawled up Nels's spine. *Sleep?* It took him a moment to understand. *She means he retired from service. Soldiers don't retire. Royal gardeners retire. Soldiers die. She had him killed.* Nels crushed the card in his good hand and tossed it into the fireplace. It uncurled on hot coals until the edges bloomed with darkness and then caught fire. The words transformed into ash and left behind apprehension-tainted smoke.

⥤ I L T A ⥢

ONE

"Are you sure about this?" Anja Myller asked, holding the sharpened quill Ilta had used to puncture a variola vesicle on a new and otherwise healthy patient.

Anja was wearing an old-fashioned plague mask and robes. In spite of her friendly, familiar voice, the mask's red-lensed eyes and exaggerated "beak" was a thing of nightmares. Ilta thought the costume must be a very effective protection against disease—if your goal was frightening the sick away from the healer.

In the distance, clock tower bells competed with the Commons Church carillon in signaling noon.

"How can you see, let alone breathe, in that thing?" Ilta could smell the lavender, rosemary, and garlic stuffed into the mask's beak from where she was sitting. Designed to cover the powerful stench of dying plague victims, the herb combination was potent enough to overwhelm the much more delicate scents of the hospital's herb garden. "We're outside. There's no possibility of any unpleasant smells making you sick. Can't you take the mask off for a moment?"

The costume was distinctive, and her feelings about that

underlined Ilta's reasons for having chosen the herb garden to meet in the first place. *Gran wouldn't approve, nor would the Healing Council of Elders.* Once more, Ilta glanced in the direction of the overcrowded hospital building on the other side of the thick hedge. "You're more likely to jab me in the eye rather than the arm."

"You would have me expose myself to danger?"

"Variola isn't always fatal. Most of the time it isn't, and you know it," Ilta said.

"It's fatal enough."

"You're powerful. You can't get sick through casual contact. You haven't so far."

Anja gave out a muffled harrumph. "My magic doesn't completely shield me from disease. Unlike you."

"Mine doesn't either—not totally. Otherwise, what would be the point in doing this?"

"That is the question, isn't it? What is the point?"

There are some fates that one shouldn't fight. Isn't that what Gran said? Ilta thought. "Someone has to try—"

"No, they don't. This is a ridiculous Acrasian practice. The strongest among the people will survive this *human* disease. Every being and every thing has a place in the Hallowed Order. The weakest die." Pausing, Anja lowered the sharpened quill and stepped back. "This is unnecessary."

The Hallowed Order was the first thing students of the healing arts were taught, no matter their specific spiritual practice. The highest order had power to affect the lower. Inanimate objects were at the bottom of the Order, followed by plant life, animals, humans, and then kainen at the top. It was believed that the strength of one's magic was what protected one from outside forces, including the magic of others.

"If that's the case, then why bother with healing magic at all?" Ilta asked.

"Don't get smart with me, girl. I can turn my back on this whole affair, you know. Better yet, I can tell the Medical Council—"

"Please don't," Ilta said. "I promise I'm being careful. That's why I'm the best candidate. I'll heal faster. And part of my magical immunity can be transferred to patients who are inoculated with material from my wounds. The logic is sound, and you know it."

There were limits to even the most gifted healer's magic. Sometimes, that power turned in the hands of the healer and harmed the patient. Sometimes, the healer was hurt. It was a known risk. Anja herself wouldn't have argued the point. This was why healing magic was often placed in things of a lesser order: herbs, amulets, potions, bandages, and other items. Healers were taught to avoid direct magic use on patients lest the patient's natural defenses reject the healing power being introduced. Of course, shortcuts could be used by those of greater power. Ilta did so often enough when she was certain her powers were stronger than those of her patient. One didn't always have time to make a lengthy preparation. Gran had taught her as much.

She also taught you that there are some fates that one shouldn't fight, didn't she?

Anja sighed and dropped the quill onto the tray she was holding. "I can't do this. It's against the Healer's Oath."

As Anja was older and inclined toward tradition, including her in the experiment was a gamble at best, but Ilta couldn't think of anyone she trusted as much as her Gran. Ilta couldn't tell her Gran. *Not yet.* Ilta was confident enough in her decision that she felt the risk worthwhile, but if something went wrong and she needed to turn to someone for help, Anja was the best choice. She was not only a friend—and Ilta didn't have many—but Anja was one of the more powerful healers employed at the Commons Hospital. "Too many are dying. We have to find an alternative method. A method that doesn't require magic. There aren't enough healers to deal with this plague."

"All the more reason not to risk yourself."

"This is a sound option. The Acrasians have no healing magic, yet they survive. Nels says the Acrasians invented pox-proofing to prevent deaths from variola vera. Symptoms developed after this type of therapy are far less deadly. I'll be completely safe," Ilta said. It was only partly a lie. Based upon the research that Nels translated for her, a small number of inoculated patients did die, but that number was so much smaller than in naturally occurring cases that inoculation was seeing widespread use. "Best of all, it's a simple method to execute."

"An Acrasian method would have to be."

"Nels says that Acrasian nobles gather in groups on their country estates for inoculation and recover in comfort. They call them Pox Parties."

"Nels says this. Nels says that. He's not a healer. He's a soldier. You're letting your feelings for him cloud your judgment. I can't believe—"

Ilta bit back a retort and ignored Anja's continued protests. She stared down at the newly sprouting frost-kissed grass. *Maybe it was a bad idea to ask for her help, after all.*

Anja finally seemed to run out of energy. She folded her arms across her chest and then said, "Even if the lad is right, you're not an Acrasian."

"Acrasians are no different from kainen. Gran says so."

"The royal court and the teachings of the Hallowed Order disagree."

"The royal court knows nothing outside of centuries-old grudges, half-truths, and myths," Ilta said.

"Have a care—"

"Has anyone other than Nels bothered to study the Acrasians? He says their troops are inoculated. Ours are not. Sickened soldiers cannot protect us from the Regnum. When are we going to break free of outdated thinking? When it's too late, and we've lost the war?"

Anja paused. "Did you have a vision?"

"I can't say. Not yet," Ilta said. That much was truth. However, they were running out of time. Soon, the two of them would be missed. Becoming more frustrated, she continued. "King Henrik acts as if the war isn't happening, let alone an epidemic that kills more than half those exposed to it. There aren't enough living to bury the dead in some parts of the country. It's irresponsible—"

"Shhh!" In her bird mask, Anja awkwardly turned her head to look over her shoulder. "You should be more careful of what you say, girl."

"I'm telling the truth, and you know it."

"I don't care how much you think you love that boy. He's a royal. And royal feuds end messy. Particularly for those who aren't royal."

"Nels is right."

"Silmaillia's apprentice or not, you're not safe from the king. You know the histories. Even the Silmaillia Samsa Rasi lost his head, and he was King Anders's closest friend."

"If King Anders had listened, it would've prevented a famine. Silmaillia Rasi was right to stand up to him."

"Dead right doesn't count, my girl. Even your grandmother has more sense than to push King Henrik too far. Need I remind you that you're only an apprentice? Apprentices can be replaced. Even talented ones."

"I know. I know." Ilta stared at the ground and waited for Anja to finish. It was usually best that way.

"If Saara finds out that I've encouraged you in this—"

"She's not going to, because you're not going to tell her," Ilta said. "And neither am I, until it's too late."

"What makes you think she won't *See* what you've done?"

"We have to know if this works. *I* have to know."

"At the risk of dying in the variola epidemic yourself? Why?"

To save Gran. To keep her from exhausting her powers and killing herself. The nightmare was still fresh, leaving a bad feeling lurking in the back of Ilta's mind. *It was only a dream. A warning. Not a vision. I know the difference.* "I'm not going to die," Ilta said.

However, she had to admit she was frightened. Variola, even when it didn't kill or blind its victims, left terrible scars. *If I'm hideous, will Nels still love me?* Still, all she had to do was think of her Gran.

She cast aside fears and vanity. "I'll be perfectly safe. The variola presented after inoculation is weaker. In a sense, I'll be at less risk of dying than you will be by taking your chances contracting it at its full power. And afterward, I'll be immune just like the others who've survived."

"Have you thought about who will take over for you here while you recover?"

Ilta looked away.

"You haven't, have you?"

"I won't be that sick. A few days. That's all."

"Variola takes two to three weeks to run its course. You know that."

"It won't be the same. Nels said—" Ilta stopped herself when she caught Anja's impatient sigh. "It won't be as bad. I promise." Placing the lancet against her upper arm, Ilta winced as she made a deep enough cut. "This is my responsibility. Not yours. Gran knows how I am when I make up my mind. She'll understand." Her upper arm exposed, she shivered. Winter was still fighting spring for dominance. "Hurry up and stick me with that thing before I lose my nerve."

Anja jabbed the tip of the quill into the fresh wound with a gloved hand. Ilta flinched.

"May the Great Mother have mercy upon us both," Anja said.

"Thank you." Ilta attempted to wrap a fresh bandage around her left arm. Anja took over when she couldn't manage it one-handed.

Letting out another harrumph, Anja asked, "What are you going to do when you start to show symptoms?"

"It won't be so bad. Nels and I are binding for a year. And I thought—"

"A binding? Have you told Saara?"

"Not yet." Ilta was hesitant to discuss it with Gran. Part of the reason why was because she knew if she did that, everything would be more real. Why that was an issue, Ilta wasn't entirely sure. She hadn't exactly had much time to herself for thinking lately—what with one thing and another. *Don't lie to yourself. You know why.* "Is there a problem?"

"He is your first, isn't he?"

That's it. That's the reason. He's the first, and I'm frightened. I've never left home before. In truth, she'd already packed a few things. Her intent was to stay with him that night, but now she wasn't so sure. "Why should that concern Gran?"

Anja nodded. The plague mask gave the action an ominous cast. "It does. Trust me."

"She won't object. She likes him. Not that it matters."

"Oh, it'll matter."

"I can legally bind with whomever I want. I'm seventeen. It's only for a year."

"Saara raised you. To her, you're a daughter, not a granddaughter. You're her little girl."

"Surely she's noticed I've grown up."

"Knowing and understanding aren't the same thing. She'll need time to adjust to the idea. So, you'd best tell her soon."

"All right. I will," Ilta said. *I've only ever been close to three people. Gran, Anja, and Nels. Of those three, Gran is the only one who really knows me.* The thought helped explain some of the trepidation shadowing her excitement. *Gran has meant safety for so long. And Nels—* "Anyway, I thought I'd stay with Nels while I recover."

"You would expose him to variola?"

"He intends to be inoculated, too." Ilta paused, pretending to give the situation more thought. However, there were aspects of her life that she wasn't willing to discuss with Anja in detail. Nels was one of them. Ilta had conflicting feelings. On one hand, she loved him. She wanted to protect him. Part of her motives for moving in with him were selfish. *I will inoculate him tonight. And we can take care of one another. He'll be safe. I'll see to it.*

And if he's ill, he can't leave with his regiment. She inwardly winced, but she couldn't help herself. She hadn't had any visions about him—not yet. She was already dreading the possibility. He was a soldier, and soldiers didn't have a long life expectancy. *I can keep him safe and alive.* She'd considered volunteering for Nels's regiment, except she knew that Gran wouldn't allow it. Ilta was to be the next Silmaillia—not an army healer.

"I'll be there to make certain he's safe. Anyway, he said he wouldn't mind the risk." Ilta knew it was because he felt guilty about what he'd almost done to her. She also knew she was taking advantage of his guilt. *But can I really trust him? And what if Gran dies? I'll be all alone. I'll have no one.* The selfishness at the core of her motivations made her face heat. "I'll protect us both. You know how powerful my magic is. It won't be a problem."

"Isn't he being sent to the war soon?"

"We've weeks before that happens." *But what if Anja is right? What if Gran tries to stop me?* "There isn't time to tell Gran. And anyway, it's only for a little while. I can tell her that I've been asked to help patients living outside the city. Nels and I can be alone to test the inoculation process. Then when Nels goes to war, I can move back in with Gran. I'll tell her about the binding then. That way, I can ease her into the idea. Everything will be fine."

"So, you haven't heard?"

"Heard what? I've been here all day." Afraid she'd lost track of time again, she reached for her pocket watch. She didn't always remember when she had one of her spells.

"Sit still." Anja finished with the bandage, tying it off with a firm jerk, and then faced the hedge keeping them hidden from the hospital.

The wound was already stinging something awful. Ilta pressed the bandage with her fingertips in an attempt to smooth out the pain.

"The Royal Army closed the city by the king's order this morning," Anja said. "Goods are allowed in and out. Other than that, no one but royal messengers are allowed to enter or leave."

"A quarantine makes no sense. Variola is already here."

Anja whispered, "Sickness has nothing to do with it. It's to prevent the common folk from protesting at the palace gates."

"What?"

"People do stupid things when frightened, girl. I've seen this before."

"You're saying the king is afraid?"

Anja seemed to be holding her breath. With the mask on, it was impossible to see her expression, but Ilta had a feeling that she was unsettled, maybe even terrified. "We should get back to work."

Gathering up the quill and the tray holding the bandages and the knife, Ilta said, "I suppose we should." The ache in her arm was now bone-deep. She wondered how bad the pain was going to get and if she would need to numb it in order to prevent anyone from discovering what she'd done to herself.

It will be bad, no doubt, but I can handle it, she thought and followed Anja inside.

TWO

Ilta woke from her nap to an empty room, muffled cries of anger, and the smell of smoke. Outside, glass shattered. An orange glow filtered through the drawn white curtains, casting chaotic patterns that danced on the walls of the hospital's records room. She sat up with a shiver. She'd been sleeping on one of the camp cots prepared for those unable to go home due to the overwhelming numbers of patients. Scheduled naps were practical. All healers were required to catch small amounts of sleep throughout their shifts. She told herself that her reasons for the break had nothing to do with the steady ache in her arm.

The fire in the hearth had gone out, and the cramped room was freezing. Ilta checked the mantel clock above the tiny brick fireplace. It was just past three in the morning. Anja had let her sleep for more than three hours. Ilta frowned.

The quarantine had caused a panic and thus a flood of new patients and concerned relatives. The waiting area had been filled to overflowing with those in need of help. A line had formed in the street, wrapping around the building. The sick were far less of a problem than the healthy. Some came to the hospital to request preemptive treatments and were turned away. Rumors that medical supplies were running short had begun to circulate, and the Royal Army had arrived to restore order. She'd caught a glimpse of Nels dressed in his uniform, talking to several worried town folk in the street. In the crush, she'd only had enough time to catch his eye and give him a wave and a smile. The situation hadn't stabilized until dusk. By then, there was no way she could leave. There was simply too much to do. She'd sent him a message saying that she'd stay the night at the hospital and that she wouldn't be joining him until the next day. She'd then channeled her disappointment into her work.

There wasn't another opportunity for a break until midnight. By the time she'd left for her nap, the frightened crowds had reluctantly surrendered the streets to the army.

I wonder where Gran is.

A loud crash from the other side of the window sent Ilta hunting for her boots. She'd slept fully clothed, only intending to lie down for an hour or so. Slipping her stockinged feet into their snug warmth, she didn't bother with the laces and shuffled over to the window. A mob swelled in the streets below. The manic scene was lit with torches and the bakery across the street's funeral pyre. A Royal Horse regiment battled to control the crowd. She looked on in horror as one of the soldiers drew his sword. It descended in a deadly arc. Someone screamed. The mob let out a roar. Ilta squeezed her eyes shut with a gasp.

Is Nels still out there?

The door behind her flew open with a bang. She whirled around to see who it was. To her relief, it was only Anja. A jumble of bottles, bandages, and other medical supplies filled her arms.

"Get dressed, girl. We're leaving."

"What of the patients?"

Anja rushed across the room, set her burdens down on the writing desk, and then snatched a carpetbag from the floor next to it. She set about filling the bag with the supplies. "Get moving. There's no time for questions. The King's Army have forced the rioters away from the palace. It's only angered the people more. They've started looting. The army are keeping them away from the hospital for now. But that's not going to last."

It occurred to Ilta that she had no way of knowing whether Nels had gotten her message. She didn't even know where he was. *May the Great Mother help him and keep him safe.* Ilta knotted her boot laces and then grabbed her coat. The arm she'd pox-proofed ached even more than ever before. She didn't dare check the inoculation site in front of Anja. Ilta asked, "Where's Gran?"

"She's out back, helping get the patients who can be moved into the wagons. We're heading to the barracks district."

"The Narrows?"

Anja nodded. "We'll be safer there until this is over."

Ilta followed her into the hallway. It was overwhelmed with a confusion of people carrying supplies, books, papers, and patients. Volunteers shoved past in a hurry to gather necessities and flee. Their expressions set in determination, worry, and fear. It all seemed so unreal.

"They're leaving patients behind?" Ilta had to shout to be heard.

"Only the more serious cases. The ones who can't be moved. The whole critical wing."

"We can't do that!"

"There's no time to get them out. Even if there were, moving them would risk killing them."

"Is anyone staying?"

"A few soldiers, maybe. I don't know."

"No healers?" Ilta slowed. The new Commons Hospital was

housed in a repurposed old church building that had been designed in the shape of a small letter *t*. She and Anja were leaving the left wing. As they entered the main building, the congestion became almost impossible to navigate.

"No civilian healers," Anja said. "Soldiers and army healers will suffice until this is over. They can handle it. More so than we can. Come on!"

Ilta stopped where she was. "I'm not leaving."

"Have you gone mad?" Anja turned and tugged at her sleeve. "That mob will rip apart everything and everyone who stands in their way."

"They'd taint themselves with blood?"

"They're frightened. Don't count on such things mattering until long after the fact."

"I won't leave those patients to die! Not when they came to us for help!" Ilta jerked free and made her way toward the ward where the more seriously ill patients were kept.

Anja's ineffective protests were lost in the chaos. Pushing through the crowd while attempting to protect her sore arm, she made her way to the tall double doors separating the critical ward from the rest of the hospital. Outside of a few badly placed bumps and crushed toes, she made the journey in one piece. Gazing through the floor-to-ceiling rows of small glass panes, she saw the ward had been already abandoned. Cabinets and bookcases hung open, their contents having been raided. Sickroom stench was thick in the long, narrow chamber with its two rows of beds shoved against opposite walls. Each bed was occupied as well as all available floor space adequate for sleeping pallets. Locking the doors behind her, she took inventory of the situation. Smoke from the bakery fire had begun to pour in through the open windows. Nearby, Commons Church bells clanged a panicked alert. She rushed to close the sashes and pull the shades, carefully stepping around unconscious and semiconscious patients as she went. Looking out into the night, she spied bucket lines forming in the maelstrom.

"What's happening?" a woman asked. Her voice was weak. It was obvious she could hardly move her mouth to speak due to the pain. The sores usually started in the mouth, making speech difficult. Some healers considered it a blessing. The woman's face was a mass of oozing sores that caked her eyes. Ilta knew at a glance that the poor woman would be blind for the rest of her life.

Ilta threw a window sash with a quick slam. Unsure, she paused. She didn't want to frighten the woman further. *What would be the use in that?* But she didn't want to lie, either. "You aren't alone. Don't be afraid. I won't leave you—not any of you."

"Is that smoke I smell?" the woman's voice gained an edge of hysteria.

"There's a fire across the street. In the bakery. They've already started the bucket lines. We'll be fine." It suddenly occurred to Ilta that the mob wasn't the only problem. *What if the flames reach the hospital? What if the mob sets the building on fire?* She took a deep breath to calm her nerves. *They wouldn't burn down a hospital. Surely, no one would be that cruel.* Suddenly, Anja's remarks came to mind. *People do stupid things when frightened.* A more cynical part of herself filled in the rest. *And people frightened of illness don't risk themselves by entering a hospital.*

No. They'd simply burn it down, wouldn't they? In the confusion, who would know the responsible parties? She swallowed a fresh bout of terror and settled on telling the woman a half-truth. "They'll have everything under control very soon." She counted herself lucky that most of those in the room were too ill to hear, let alone understand that anything was wrong.

She quickly made the rounds to the remaining windows, soothing those she could with quick words as she went. Then she returned to the double doors and peered out of the rows of small glass panes for some sign of what to expect. The hall had emptied but for a few abandoned items lost in the crush in the time it'd taken her to shut the windows. She started with a yelp when she heard a door splinter somewhere in the front of the building. Angry shouts and screams echoed beyond the glass. The harsh command of soldiers punctuated the chaos. Her heart galloped inside her chest.

What if the soldiers can't stop them? She considered her options. *Maybe I can talk to them? What if they don't listen?* She was a sworn healer. It would be against the oath to kill, but she *could* make someone lose consciousness. She'd done it before, but never as a weapon. The thought made her uncomfortable.

Do I stay here and wait? Or do I go see what can be done before they reach the patients? Won't it be too late if they get this far? I'm only one person. All of the commotion was in the front of the building, not the back. So, she headed for the front door. Oil paintings, curtains, and tapestries had been removed from the entry, and the wooden furniture had been moved away from easy reach of the windows. It was a lucky thing that someone had thought to do so. The front doors were broken and splintered. Smoke and the sound of chaos poured through the gaping doorway. A small group of soldiers in the dooryard fought to keep an angry crowd from entering.

"Stay calm! Everything will be fine if you would only go to your homes!" The army lieutenant's formal court speech was laced with command magic. It was helping some. The mob in the hospital dooryard wasn't as frantic as those in the street, but the woman didn't have enough power to do much more than exert mild influence. Under normal circumstances, that would've been enough.

Briefly, Ilta wondered how many times the lieutenant had used her powers and how much longer she would last. Terror gripped Ilta's chest, squeezing everything from her but cold knowledge. Smoke filled her nose, and screams crowded her ears. People on the other side of the black iron fence fled from a slow-trotting cavalry unit. The bucket lines struggling to contain the fire broke in the confusion. Sparks from the flames landed on the roof of a tailor's shop next door. A lone kainen, presumably the tailor in question, splashed water onto the smoking shingles.

I shouldn't be here. I should've evacuated with the others.

But I couldn't abandon the patients. And I won't now. It isn't right. She concentrated on not fleeing to the critical wing. She'd come out to help, and help she would. A handful of soldiers couldn't hold back the mob forever. She didn't know how much use she'd be. She didn't have command magic and therefore couldn't help influence anyone. She was a healer, but she could be one more person to stand in the path of the mob and thus protect the sick. She tasted ash. Panic threatened to take her breath away. It was hard to think beyond the idea that she might die. For a brief instant, she wondered if this was the kind of thing Nels had to deal with every day. She shuddered and wiped slick hands on her skirts. *If he can do it, I can too.* With that, she pushed through the broken doors and into the dooryard. Splinters caught at her skirts, and she tugged them free without care of ripping fabric.

"Please! Do as they say," she said. "Leave this place in peace. You have relatives here. Brothers. Sisters. Parents. Friends. Do not endanger them further. Please! We're doing everything we can. You have to let us!"

"Ilta?! What are you still doing here?"

She heard Nels, but couldn't find him. At that moment, the frightened horde shoved the soldiers several steps backward, and

Ilta with them. Overwhelming terror slammed into her, and she slipped under the crush of others' emotions. Thoughts invaded in a mass so dense that she couldn't separate them into anything coherent. Her perceptions were reduced to an avalanche of feelings. *Panic. Anger. Sorrow. Powerlessness. Frustration.* Pain cut through the confusion and brought her to herself again. The jagged splinters of the broken door clawed at her back and pierced her shoulder. Still, she attempted to throw herself against the crowd. Hands clawed at her, tearing at her sleeves. She was kicked. She tripped and fell. A soldier's boot landed in her side. Agony shot through her body. She screamed.

"Ilta!"

Someone grabbed her by the sore arm and yanked her up. Lost in the pain, her self-control slipped. *Stone. I need stone.* Anchorless, the confusion of the crowd's thoughts slammed into her again. Still, in the turmoil, she understood who had ahold of her. She knew by the steady feel of his thoughts. Instinctually, she fled to Nels—away from chaos and darkness. He was frightened like everyone else, she knew, but he held himself distant from it. She felt shipwrecked—washed up on the only beach for miles. She held onto him with all her might. Her vision was a nauseating mix of both his and hers. She slammed her eyes shut.

Please, she thought. She didn't trust herself to speak. *Make them stop. They have to stop. I can't—*

"Everyone! Stop now!"

Still grasping her arm, Nels stumbled into the other soldiers. He made physical contact with the lieutenant. Suddenly, Ilta felt a powerful jolt wrench her stomach. She tasted tin. And then it was as if someone had pulled a substantial amount of magical energy from her to the point of sharp pain. She lost herself and only managed to stay on her feet because Nels held her.

"I said, stop where you are!" Their words—*no, Nels's*—were charged with a huge surge of command magic. Ilta hadn't felt anything like it before.

Several things happened all at once. Ilta staggered under the vast weight of discharged power. They all did—all but Nels. The crowd fell into a shocked silence and halted their struggles against the soldiers. Nearby, the lieutenant fainted. Ilta felt her lose consciousness in a blink. It was all Ilta could do to keep from blacking out with her.

"Now, please. Be calm," Nels said. His reasoned tone snuffed out the fear and anger. "Let us do what we must. If you've no need for healing, return to your homes. If you need to stay, help put out the fire. Everything will be fine. But you must calm down." He released Ilta's arm and then motioned for the crowd to go.

Magical energy faded away like mist. Ilta swayed on her feet. Suddenly, she felt weaker than she had in her life. She fought an urge to sit. The crowd seemed to let go of the breath they'd been holding, and everything returned to normal. The crowd dispersed in uncertain groups. Some drifted across the street to the flaming bakery. Others left altogether. Ilta watched Nels blink as what he'd done began to sink in.

Both concerned for the lieutenant and unable to stand any longer, Ilta dropped to her knees in the grass. She snatched up the lieutenant's wrist before someone could step on it. The lieutenant's pulse drummed a steady beat against Ilta's fingertips. *Alive. She's alive.* Ilta heard Nels give orders to the soldiers. She got the impression that they complied with renewed respect.

She focused on the lieutenant. She appeared to be in a deep sleep. Ilta slapped her cheeks to wake her, but it didn't have any effect.

I don't know what made me think my powers were greater than his, Ilta thought.

"Are you all right?" Nels asked.

Ilta paused to give herself a casual check. "A little bruised, a few scratches, but I'm fine. I think." The inoculation site hurt even more than before. It had bled through the bandage. Her arm felt swollen. She assumed she'd bumped it or scratched it on the broken doors. *Did the lieutenant simply faint? Or did Nels do something to her? For that matter, what did he do to me?* There were no obvious signs that anything was wrong with the lieutenant. No broken bones. Her breathing was steady as was her heart rate.

"What happened to Harkola?" Nels asked.

"I don't know," Ilta said with a frown. She noted the variola scars on Harkola cheeks. "I think we can move her. Help me get her inside. She'll be safe there. I need the smelling salts."

"All right." Nels stooped to pick up Harkola.

Ilta got to her feet. Swaying, she shoved at the broken door to clear the way for Nels. He draped Harkola over a shoulder and stepped over the battered threshold. Ilta noticed the ease and grace with which he did it. She couldn't help thinking that the awkward boy she used to know was gone.

Do I really know him at all?

The first examination room they came to was a wreck, and so she led him to a second. He gently laid Harkola on the table and stepped back out of the way.

"Do you know what's wrong with her?" There was a shadow of guilt in Nels's question.

Ilta searched the cabinets until she found the brown glass vial she needed. She was thankful that Anja had insisted on inoculating the left arm rather than the right. Everything would've been so much more difficult otherwise. "I'm not sure." Turning, she waved the open bottle under Harkola's nose while avoiding the hated ammonia odor herself. "Maybe she'll remember what happened."

Nels nodded, and just like that, the awkward boy was back. Ilta knew the question foremost in his mind. She could practically see it etched on his face.

To Ilta's relief, Harkola stirred and coughed. "Don't sit up," Ilta said. She asked Nels to wait outside and finished the examination.

Groggy, Harkola had no memory of events beyond that of the crowd gathering in the dooryard. She was exhausted but otherwise fine. Ilta told Harkola to rest, and Harkola slipped immediately into a deep sleep. With that done, Ilta stepped into the hallway and closed the door behind her.

"How is she?" he asked, stopping his pacing.

"She'll need to stay here overnight. I want to be sure nothing else is wrong before I let her return to her barracks house."

"Everyone else evacuated to the Narrows."

"Not everyone, obviously."

"Why didn't you leave?"

Ilta motioned to the critical ward. "Someone had to stay."

"You're bleeding." He touched the back of her left shoulder.

She winced. Glancing down, she saw the inoculation site was red and irritated. Being jostled seemed to have made it much worse. Her whole arm and shoulder were tender and hot to the touch. *It wasn't like that before.* She clamped down on that thought, afraid of what that might mean. "I'll deal with it tomorrow." She didn't have the energy to tend to her own wounds. Above all, she was grateful that Harkola hadn't needed healing magic. Ilta doubted she had enough power left for a simple blessing.

"You should let me bandage it," Nels said. He saw her hesitation and looked away. Shame shrouded his expression.

An uncomfortable silence stretched like taffy between them.

She finally said, "It wasn't your fault."

"It wasn't?" He stared at the wall. "I can't seem to do anything right."

"That isn't true. You stopped that mob."

A stunned smile stretched over his lips. "I didn't imagine it."

"You didn't."

"What does it mean? Is it—is it possible that I used command magic for the first time in my life? It can't be, can it? I'm eighteen."

She paused, thinking. Such a thing had never happened before. It was more likely that his magic had taken an unexpected form—one that had been unlooked-for, previously unknown, and thus missed. At the same time, she saw the joy in his face and couldn't bring herself to destroy it. "I don't know. But I could help you find out during our time together."

His smile grew and then died. "What if it wasn't me? What if it was you?"

"It couldn't have been. I don't have command magic," she said. "Why are you so determined to accept responsibility for the bad things and yet refuse to take credit for the good?"

"I wasn't alone. You were in my mind. I felt it."

She hesitated and then nodded, shamed. "I reached out for the only safety I could. It was you. I'm—I'm sorry."

The smile returned, a specter of its former self. "Don't be."

"I could've hurt you," she said. "I might have."

He shrugged. "You didn't."

"I'm glad."

Another silence was measured by the clock in the entry. Outside, the situation seemed to be stabilizing. The flames from the burning bakery had died back enough that their light no longer brightened the hallway.

Nels's face was painted in careful shadows. "I have to get back to the others."

"All right."

"Are you staying?"

"I am."

He nodded and cleared his throat. "Then I will, too."

She wanted to kiss him, but he turned away before she could. "Thank you."

He looked over his shoulder. "For what?"

"For being there when I needed you."

The smile was resurrected. "I'm happy that I could be." And with that, he went outside.

⚜ SUVI ⚜

ONE

"Didn't expect to see you up here," Dylan said. His teeth flashed white in his dark face. He wore his thick dark brown hair braided into long spirit knots—a Waterborne religious custom. A strong lake breeze blew them around his shoulders. Although smiling at the moment, his face was habitually set into severe lines. This contrast between Dylan's intimidating presence and his warm intelligence inwardly amused Suvi. It made her feel as if she were in on a secret to which others weren't privy.

The kainen of the Waterborne Nations, much like the kainen of Eledore, originated from many different cultures and climates. However, unlike the kainen of Eledore, the Waterborne made no efforts to distinguish a person's worthiness based upon magical power. Rank within Waterborne society was based on one's shipboard role and thus, one's ability to contribute to the survival of the Nations as a whole. Leadership was determined by the crew's vote. Still, the captain of a ship wasn't granted more rights than the crew. As far as Suvi knew, the Waterborne didn't have royalty. Thus, she considered them to be an egalitarian mix of peoples in a sense that even her mother's homeland of Ytlain could never be. Acrasia fascinated her brother Nels because they terrified him. Suvi made a study of the Waterborne because she admired them.

Dylan raised an eyebrow, again asking an unspoken question. She shrugged.

Five years older, Dylan was her closest friend and had been since she'd signed on with the King's Navy when she was twelve. Initially, she'd been warned away from him, of course. He was Waterborne, and Waterborne didn't observe blood custom. So, he bunked with the marines in the hold. There were other reasons she'd been instructed to steer clear of him, she knew, but she befriended him anyway.

She didn't give a shit about other people's stupid prejudices regarding who had sex with whom.

Dylan's smile lifted some of her dark mood. That and the fact that he'd found her first. She had twofold reasons for seeking him out, and she'd been nervous. It'd been months since she'd last seen him. Still, here he was, just as if they'd never been apart. There were very few people with which she felt that comfortable, and she needed to talk to someone she trusted—someone who wasn't Piritta. Suvi loved Piritta, but sometimes she wondered if they'd still be friends if Piritta weren't her souja. In any case, the tension on the ship being what it was of late, it was a relief that Suvi wouldn't have to search for him. It would make warning him without others listening easier, too.

"Hiding from someone, are you?" Dylan asked in a quiet voice. A steady lake breeze tugged at the sheets. The cold wind, cries of birds, thumping rigging, and snapping sails nearly obliterated the question.

"Father," Suvi said. "Who else?"

Balanced on the yard with her back to the mainmast, she took comfort in the rise and fall of the ship. They were sailing south on Dagfinna Lake, on their way to meet her Uncle Sakari's ship, HREMS *Falcon*. Originally, she'd jumped at the chance to get away from the royal court and sail—the one thing that brought her peace and joy. Unfortunately, her happiness was short-lived. So, she'd chose to steal a moment's peace, dressed in a set of Nels's old clothes she'd packed in case a chance of climbing the rigging presented itself. The main topmast was her favorite place to think when she was troubled, and Dylan knew it. If she were completely truthful, she'd lied about her reasons for taking refuge in the rigging, but it was simpler to blame her father. As a rule, his temper ran short. It was even shorter when he was ill, which was why the ship's healer had barricaded himself in the forecastle, the captain had been conferring with his officers for days, and the royal chef was deep in her cups.

Dylan settled on the yard in front of Suvi, his legs dangling as hers did. *Northern Star's* topgallant swelled and snapped with the wind. An eager shiver vibrated through the spar against Suvi's back. She breathed in, listening to wooden creaks, slapping lines, and shouts from the crew below. The acrid stench of hot tar and the hammering from the caulkers floated up from the decks, but the busy noise of those engaged in the constant work required to keep the ship sound was less intrusive so high up. The topmasts were the closest thing to real privacy onboard ship. Still, even this seemed to have little effect on the shadows weighing down her heart.

She laid a hand on polished wood, willing the morning sun to warm her chilled skin. Dylan pretended to check the line binding *Northern Star's* top sail to the yard. A bright red scarf covered the top of his head, and she found herself staring at the beautiful, curled patterns bleached into it.

"Have you ever . . . hurt anyone in a-a fight?" she asked and looked away. She didn't dare look him in the face. Although the effort most Eledoreans made to avoid speaking of death, violence, or blood annoyed her, it didn't make it any less uncomfortable to ask.

"Only when I've had to." Dylan shrugged.

Deeply spiritual, the Waterborne kept different customs—equally valid ones as far as she was concerned. Sadly, Suvi didn't know as much as she would've liked. Even Dylan tended to be closemouthed about certain things. "How do the Waterborne deal with . . . lost lives?" she asked, yielding to internal pressures.

Well known for their water-based magical talents and strict code of honor, the Waterborne were clannish, secretive, and nomadic. Their ships were their homes. Their ultimate loyalty was bound to their families and shipmates. Very few Waterborne opted to live on dry land—let alone serve in foreign navies.

Dylan was one of those few.

"You mean killing," he said, his voice flat.

She nodded.

"Everything and everyone dies. It's part of life. Same as swiving, shitting, and eating."

She felt a corner of her mouth curl upward in spite of herself. Where some people might curb their language in front of her, Dylan never did.

"Why do you ask?" he asked.

"Just curious," she said. She paused to consider whether or not to continue the conversation.

Dylan sat patiently in silence until she resumed speaking.

"Did you do a cleansing ritual afterward?" she asked.

Squinting at the horizon, he said, "There's what your people might call an act of contrition."

"Would you mind me asking what it is?"

Dylan looked her in the eye for a length of ten heartbeats.

Suvi did her best to hold his gaze. For a moment, she wasn't sure whether or not he'd answer her.

"The words are 'May your passage through the deep be swift and true. Let no darkness bind you, and may the Judge of Souls give you your due.' Then if you're wanting to be sure his ghost won't haunt you, make the spirit a gift."

"What kind of gift?"

"Something that shines," he said. "Doesn't have to be valuable. A ghost can't take much into the deep dark but light and memories for warmth." He gave her a questioning look.

She didn't meet his gaze. The wind tugged the loose strands of her hair while she thought of something to distract him from the truth. "I'm afraid Father will be forced to do something about Mother soon. Her . . . headaches . . . are becoming more demanding." When Nels had resigned as heir designate, their mother had withdrawn to her apartments and refused to see anyone. For a year, she had surfaced only when the strictures of government or ceremony dictated otherwise. She claimed to suffer from headaches. Of late, those headaches favored tight breeches, good wine, and expensive horses—not that it mattered to anyone including her father, but the terms of their binding had been permanent and exclusive. Thus, at the very least, the appearance of propriety had to be observed. Substance rarely mattered. Appearances always did. In Suvi's experience, the whole of the Eledorean court was like that. It disgusted her.

Dylan squinted. "Bad, is it?"

She nodded.

"Is that why you asked about—"

"No!" Her head snapped up so fast, her neck popped. "Gods, no."

"Ah, good. Hard to tell with royals sometimes."

"I'm not like that, and you know it," she said. *At least, I didn't used to be.* Something pinched in her chest. *I'll do what I must for the kingdom.*

Is that what Uncle tells himself? She flinched at the thought.

"It'll sort itself out for the best, girl chick. These things do."

Dylan wasn't as old as he pretended, but it amused him to treat her as if she were a little sister. It amused her, too. *Most of the time.*

"I know. I just hope the matter doesn't resolve itself with a headsman's ax," she whispered and glanced up at the platform above.

"Don't worry about Pirnes. He's sleeping off a hangover as usual. I'm covering for him," Dylan said. "He won't hear a thing."

"Lost at cards again?"

"Don't know why I bother," Dylan said. "Should hand over half my pay and avoid the whole thing. I'd get more bunk time."

"Does Pirnes still rub his chin when he has a good hand?"

"Yes."

"And Jokela? Does she still blink when she bluffs?"

"Sure."

"Then why do you keep losing?"

A slow smile spread across his face as he stared out at the glittering expanse of Dagfinna Lake. "Things go smoother when I do. Anyway, I wouldn't have anyone to talk to otherwise."

"Damn, I miss you. I miss this stupid boat, too."

"Ship. For the Sea Mother's sake, have you forgotten the difference already?"

She grinned. "So, how's the *Star*?"

"Shipshape and Mehrinna fashion. Captain's been hanging off the coast like we're tethered," he said. "Ytlainen privateers took three ships on the Sisters last month. And it's not yet summer."

In spite of the years he'd spent in the Eledorean navy, Dylan still used the Waterborne name for the Great Chain Lakes.

We each have our little rebellions, don't we? Suvi thought. "Be careful, will you?"

"No cannonball or splinter has taken me yet."

They sat in silence for a time, each pretending to study the clouds. It was time to ask Dylan the question she dreaded asking. There were multiple reasons for her fear. First, she didn't want to insult Dylan. Over the years that they'd known one another, he'd been reluctant to discuss his past. She didn't understand why but had always respected his wishes. That was about to change. Second, she was afraid of what might happen to him. She was the heir designate. He was known to be her close friend, and her uncle knew of her inability to shield her thoughts. It had been why she'd stayed away from the *Star*, restricting her contact with Dylan to messages that could easily be intercepted. It was also why she hadn't included Dylan in anything political before. Unfortunately, that wasn't an option any longer. Either she included him or her uncle would.

"Will the Waterborne enter the war, do you think?" She brushed her hand along the yard as if soothing the ship and not herself.

She sensed rather than saw Dylan's frown before she looked up.

"Thick-headed, self-righteous bastards or not, the Acrasians are smart enough to leave well enough alone," he said. "The clans won't take sides. Why make enemies when one can secure shipping contracts with both parties and make a killing? Anyway, it isn't their fight." He shrugged. "It's yours."

"What if—what if that wasn't the case any longer? What would you do?"

"What do you mean?"

"The Waterborne have been spying on Eledore. Uncle won't tolerate it—assuming he knows. And I would."

Dylan blinked and tilted his head. "That's not possible."

"You have been away from home for a while."

"It doesn't matter. That isn't something that would ever change."

"Apparently, someone has decided that there's a new policy."

"What have you heard?"

"Those privateers? The Ytlainen.claim they were Acrasians flying an Ytlainen flag. Uncle is looking into it. It's one of the reasons Uncle has been in Ytlain for so long."

"No doubt your uncle is happy. Ytlain will join your war," Dylan said. "But what does any of that have to do with the Waterborne Nations?"

Suvi paused. "Several Waterborne message birds have been intercepted. Message birds from the eastern coast off the port of Mehrinna and destined for Acrasia," she said. "My korva told me."

"Are you sure of him?"

"Yes, I'm sure of *her*."

"No sea lord would risk such a thing. It would endanger every contract—"

"One of the clans has been selling information about Eledore to Acrasia," Suvi said. "She says there's proof."

"That's very serious." Dylan paused, looking out at the horizon again. "Do you know which clan is accused?"

"Jami said the messages originated from someone named Isak Kask," she said. "Kask is your clan, isn't it?"

Dylan's skin went a bit gray.

Suvi blinked. *He knows him.* She hadn't thought that Dylan would.

"And you have proof, you say?" Dylan asked.

"Jami had the messages copied and sent to me before they were destroyed," Suvi said. "I can't imagine that Uncle will be ignorant of the situation for long. It's certain he'll put the pieces together soon enough. And when that happens, the contracts between the Waterborne Nations and Eledore aren't going to survive. You know how Uncle is. Weathermaster or not, you may not be safe. You have to leave. Before he decides you're a person of interest."

Nodding, Dylan stared down at the spar beneath him. He seemed to come to a decision. "May I see your proof?"

"Of course," she said. "Do you have someplace you can go? Do you need money? I can have Jami arrange everything. No one will be the wiser."

Dylan swallowed. "How would you like Sea Lord Kask to owe you a favor?"

She paused. "How big a favor? Big enough to keep you safe?"

"Bigger."

"Big enough to negotiate a favorable supply transport contract?"

"I can't promise, but it would be reasonable to ask for such a thing in exchange."

"You've got to be joking," Suvi said. "Haven't you been exiled?"

"Self-exiled, thank you very much. And if Isak is involved," Dylan said, "well, it may be time for me to go home."

"So, you know Isak Kask?"

"Isak Whitewave of Clan Kask. I do."

"And you think you can do something about this?"

"I'll need to make some inquiries first," Dylan said. "I don't suppose your korva would mind if I borrowed a couple of birds?"

"Not at all." Glancing to her right, she spotted a flicker of white against the water. Like many of the vast lakes that formed the chain of water linking the seven kingdoms, Dagfinna Lake was too huge to see the opposite shore until one was more than halfway across it. Since more than half of Dagfinna was considered Ytlainen territory, it was highly unlikely that the object she'd spotted was anything but a ship.

She pointed. "Is that *Falcon*, you think?"

"You always did have a gull's eye." He stood and squinted, his muscular frame moving with a grace that didn't seem possible. "I count three masts. A frigate. Might be *Falcon*. Might be from Ytlain, too. Can't see what she's flying." He scampered up the standing rigging and pounded on the platform above. "Pirnes! Damn your bones! Wake up! Cast the glass starboard!"

Suvi heard curses followed by the alarm bell. Three sharp clangs—the signal for a friendly ship.

Dylan grinned down at her. "Best get out of those breeks before your father catches sight of you."

She nodded.

On her way to her cabin, Suvi stopped at the rail and whispered, "Major Ander Lahtela, may your passage be swift and true. Let no darkness bind you, and may the Judge give you your due." Then she reached into her pocket and found a gold eagle. It was worth far more than Dylan indicated was necessary, but Lahtela had been Eledorean, not Waterborne. Plus, Suvi hadn't killed the man herself—Jami had done it on her order. So, theoretically it was an offering from them both. She pitched the coin over the side. Gold shimmered in the sunlight for an instant before it vanished.

Royalty didn't have cleansing rituals. She hoped it would be enough.

TWO

Twice the size of *Northern Star*, *Falcon* drew alongside, casting long shadows on the deck. Boarding planks thumped *Star's* rails. Servants scurried across with baggage. The boatswain's call signaled her uncle's arrival and brought one and all to attention on *Star's* decks. Uncle Sakari's stern figure emerged from *Falcon's* chaos dressed in reds and browns. Suvi noted his complexion lacked the sickly pale quality of her father's. Uncle Sakari's stride on the boarding plank was confident and sure. He didn't even look down at the water. The silk ribbons binding his queue whipped in the wind.

"Good to see you," he said, giving her father two slaps on the back with the hug after the ceremonial proprieties had been observed by those of lesser rank. "I'll finally get a decent glass of Islander. All those vineyards and the Ytlainen don't know a damned thing about distilling wine into a good Islander."

With another of the boatswain's whistles, the crew scrambled to their duties while *Falcon's* boarding planks were withdrawn.

"Negotiations were a success, I presume?" her father asked.

"With few exceptions, we got what we wanted," Uncle Sakari said.

Her uncle turned and trapped her in a smothering hug. "Little sparrow! You came to meet me!"

She endured his touch with strictly controlled revulsion. Made of Ytlainen silk, his coat felt slippery and cool against her cheek. He smelled of amber and leather. As much as she liked amber, at that moment, she vowed to never wear it again.

"I've brought you a present," Uncle Sakari said, his eyes changing from brown to a deep green. He fished in his coat pocket and retrieved a carved wooden box.

"Thank you, Uncle. You're very kind." She emphasized the word *uncle* and accepted the gift without touching his hand.

"Aren't you going to ask me what it is?"

"I assume I'll find out when I open the box."

Uncle Sakari touched her father on the shoulder. "Very cautious, this one. Smart. You'd never know she shared the same mother with that—"

"Don't." Her father frowned.

Suvi's mouth tightened, and she clamped her fingers around the box in an effort to keep it from joining the golden eagle at the bottom of the sea.

After dinner, Suvi took refuge in her cabin with Piritta while her father and Uncle Sakari discussed the details of the Ytlainen visit. She picked up the unopened box and lifted the lid as if it might bite her. A tiny glass vial filled with a pale golden-hued oil rested in a bed of cotton. The letter *S* coiled on its glass surface, painted in emerald green—her favorite color. Touching the jeweled stopper, Suvi caught the intoxicating scent of amber, apple blossom, and myrtle.

Piritta gasped. "A courting gift, and there's no mistaking it."

Suvi stopped holding her breath, but the muscles in her stomach cramped. "I don't suppose I could ignore its meaning."

"You could try, but I'm not sure how long the ploy would last. You have had suitors before."

"Yes, but does Uncle know?"

Piritta returned to her embroidery. "As closely as he watches you?" she asked. "Anyway, you haven't exactly been discreet."

"Can I help yearning for one aspect of my life that isn't a state secret or a complete lie?" Suvi sighed. "What am I going to do?"

"A long journey away from court?"

"That isn't a bad idea, although hardly original."

Not looking up from her sewing, Piritta pointed at the door. "Jami's back."

Suvi tiptoed to the door. Putting a finger to her lips, she rested the other hand on the latch and then yanked. A slender, scarred, middle-aged woman dressed in black stood poised to knock. She was wearing a man's coat, breeches, shoes, and stockings tailored to fit her decidedly not-male figure.

"Hello, Jami," Suvi said.

"I do wish you wouldn't do that," Jami said in a cultured accent that would've fit in at court. Long honey-blond hair threaded with silver slipped over her shoulders, and she moved with a feminine grace that belied her masculine clothes.

Suvi stepped aside, making room in the little cabin, and then shut the door. "Were you able to hear anything?" she asked in a whisper.

"I was able to hear enough," Jami said, tugging off her gloves.

Uncle didn't employ a Shield. Kainen magic was unreliable on the lakes, but it worked well enough to make precaution sensible. *Does he think me feeble, or am I meant to know what was said?*

Jami risked more than a headsman's ax by listening in on the king's private councils, and Suvi wouldn't have asked her to do it if she hadn't volunteered. Suvi knew Jami's reasons. Suvi made a point of knowing every one of them well. However, those reasons had nothing to do with Suvi's battle with her uncle, or the rewards Jami was promised, and had everything to do with Jami's own private feud. Jami was different from Piritta. Jami was far more dangerous, and Suvi's mother would've warned her from using Jami, but unlike her mother, Suvi understood the stakes when she decided to take on her uncle in the first place.

"Ytlain has refused to enter the war," Jami said. "However, they will support safe lake passage for our supply lines."

"That isn't much of an offer," Suvi said.

"They want no part of this war," Jami said. "Can you blame them? Five years this has been going on, and no end in sight." She frowned and the crisscross scars on her right cheek deepened.

Suvi let the comment lay. In truth, she agreed.

Jami continued. "You aren't going to like the rest, I'm afraid."

"I'm not Father. And you know it," Suvi said. "Speak."

"Your weathermaster has been sent to the brig," Jami said. "Your father now knows what we know about the Waterborne spy."

"Shit," Suvi said, and toed on her slippers.

Jami arched an eyebrow at the swear word. "No punishment has been assigned. Not yet."

Suvi asked, "Is Father alone?"

Jami said, "He was when I left."

"Jami, stay here. I'll have another job for you when I get back," Suvi said. "Piritta, come with me. I'll need you to shield the conversation, if you can. Do you think that's possible from the passageway?"

Piritta's eyes were tilted like a cat's, and usually it lent a certain feline shrewdness to her face, but not at the moment. "Not through a wall. Not while this ship is in the water and the wind is up."

"All right. Can you tell if anyone is near enough that it would require shielding?"

"Easily, but I won't be able to do much more. Neither will anyone else."

Suvi headed for the door. "A warning is all I require. Knock if there is danger."

Piritta nodded.

When Suvi reached her father's cabin, she motioned for Piritta to wait. Piritta perched on the bench with her embroidery hoop. The Royal Guardsman at the door gave Suvi a short bow of permission before she knocked.

"Damn it all! What in the swiving hells do you want?"

Suvi shouted through the door. "It's me, Father. May I come in?" She heard a small slam. *A book? A cabinet door?* "Are you all right, Father?"

"Enter."

She slid open the cabin door and was struck with a cloud of calming incense so thick, it made her cough.

"The Waterborne have been spying on us! Spying! They've a spy on this boat!" Her father paced the room end to end—a full twenty-five feet. "We've traded with their kind in spite of their terrible manners. But I've done with patience." He paused long enough to comb his hand through his hair. "I'll have him hanged!"

Suvi sat on a chair edge and attempted to be calm. "Are you certain he's the spy?"

"He's Waterborne!"

"Father, please. Calm down." She folded her hands in her lap. "He's innocent."

"Are you arguing with the evidence?"

"You have more than Uncle's accusation?" she asked. "Dylan Kask has served honorably on the *Star* for seven years. I've known him for—"

"Sakari said you'd say that," her father said.

"Please, father. Dylan is a friend," she said. *And that's precisely why he's in danger, and you know it.* "I've known him since I was twelve. He stood up for me when no one else would. He protected me when he didn't have to—when it would've cost him to do so. I trust him. He wouldn't do this."

"What do you know about him?"

"He exiled himself. He left the Waterborne Nations, his family, and his own ship," she said. "What else do I need to know? He's been cut off for seven years, Papa. How does any of this make sense?"

"He's that pirate Sea Lord Kask's son."

Suvi blinked. That, she hadn't known.

"Do you know why he left?" her father asked.

"He's never told me, and I've never asked." She looked away. "He can't be a spy. Why would a sea lord risk his own son in such a venture? Wouldn't it make more sense to use someone easier to deny a connection with? Someone easy to discard if discovered? Anyway, Piritta would've told me if he were a spy."

"You've only employed that souja for three years—"

"She would know. *I* would know."

"He's Waterborne. How do we know that they don't have the ability to—"

"Don't be ridiculous. They're kainen," Suvi said. "Waterborne aren't that different from Eledoreans. Mother says—"

"Your mother isn't Eledorean, either."

"Are you going to tell me that I'm now suspect?" She pushed a bit further. "I'm only half Eledorean myself."

"Don't be ridiculous," her father said. "Stop shifting attention from the real issue."

"Let me handle this."

"You're too young."

"I'm eighteen. And you assumed the rule of Eledore at seventeen," she said. "We need to know what's really going on. We're in a good position. If Dylan Kask is a sea lord's son—"

"He is!"

"Then we can use that to our advantage. We can force Kask to tell us everything."

"You're assuming that the Waterborne have family ties like Eledoreans."

"Stop being stubborn and think," Suvi said. "The Waterborne exist entirely on familial loyalty. Even if that weren't enough proof, every year, they renew that loyalty through magically bound oaths."

"To their ship captains and contracts."

"Their captains and crews aren't like ours, Papa. They aren't hired. They're family. The captains report to the sea lords, and the sea lords run the clans. Family loyalty is the foundation of Waterborne culture. They've no lands. Clan unity is what holds the Waterborne together," she said. "If someone has broken their oath and if Sea Lord Kask does nothing, it will have serious repercussions for the entire clan. Do you know what happens when a clan breaks oath?" She didn't wait for her father to answer. "They're declared renegade and made targets for the Sea Hunt. They're barred from every port where the Waterborne trade. And without a port, they've nowhere to get supplies or repair their ships. Do you know how long a ship can go without fresh water? I do. Trust me. It isn't long. Their assets are free for the taking. Everything except the offending captain and crew. They're put over the side to drown or feed the sharks.

"Sea Lord Kask has more reason to fear this situation than we do."

Her father blinked.

Suvi suppressed a smile. "I want your permission to arrange a meeting. I'll take Dylan Kask with me and use him to negotiate a new treaty. Think of what we can gain. And while I'm there, I can find out what is really going on."

"Absolutely not! I will send someone else!"

"Who? Uncle? We both know that won't work. Why not me?"

"You're heir designate," he said. "I can't send you into a potentially hostile situation. Have you gone mad? What is to stop the Waterborne taking you hostage?"

"You risk Uncle."

"He has command magic to protect himself."

"I do, too," Suvi said, and then used his own prejudices against him. "And unlike the Ytlainen, no Waterborne possesses such a thing."

"Ah."

She let that sink in before pressing her advantage. "We can't hold out much longer against the Acrasians without help. Even Uncle knows it."

"That's not true!"

"Then why did Uncle go to Ytlain?"

Again, her father paused.

"If help isn't coming from Ytlain, then it has to come from another quarter," she said. "Uncle won't stop with Ytlain. He'll go to Massilia and Kaledan next. The Acrasians know this and will put pressure where they can. Wouldn't it be best if help came from somewhere least expected? We wouldn't need the whole of the Waterborne Nations. At least, not at first. We don't have time for that. One exclusive contract with one clan for supplies could bolster our armies against the Acrasians." She didn't mention that the supplies in question would include Acrasian weapons.

"The Acrasians are animals. Humans. A few words, and the mindless creatures do whatever we want."

"Command magic has its limits," she said. "The Acrasians have muskets. Better cannon—"

"Ridiculous toys!"

Suvi's hands clenched. "We should use guns *and* magic. Nels thinks—"

Her father towered over her. "I'm sick to death of his childish fears—"

"Childish?"

"I curse the day your mother gave him my name!"

Nels hasn't used your name since you cut him off. Suvi got to her feet and spoke in her steadiest voice. "Oh? I see, it's far more mature to destroy an entire kingdom because you're too pigheaded to see the real problems? You should listen to someone other than Uncle. An intelligent leader knows better than to ignore good counsel no matter where it comes from. Haven't you told me so yourself?" She was an inch from her father's face. This close, she could see the broken blood vessels in his nose and the glint of silver in his beard. For some reason, it made her uneasy—more so than his anger.

He sucked in his breath, and his skin was turning a brilliant red.

Careful, she thought. "Nels knows more about the Acrasian Regnum than anyone. He's been to their cities. He studies their generals. He knows their strengths—"

Her father made a mocking sound in the back of his throat.

"—and their weaknesses. But fine. Don't listen to him. Listen to me," she said. "We need the Waterborne. You have to let me do this."

"You dare tell me what to do?"

She dropped her glance to the patterned rug. "I only want to help you, Papa." She took a deep breath and let tears well up in her eyes. "It's only that if Nels is to go to war . . ." She let her voice drift off, leaving the sentence hanging.

Her father didn't say anything for a moment, then laid a gentle hand on her shoulder. "My little sparrow, you're like your mother—too soft for the hard decisions."

She kept her eyes on the floor to avoid him spotting her anger. *Mother isn't soft, and I'm not, either. She's like Grandma Kai, who built that Ytlainen navy you're so damned frightened of. How can you have been bound to Mother so long and know so little about her? How can you know so little of me?*

He stepped back. Suvi gave him a pleading look—the one she used on him anytime she wanted anything important. It was a childish manipulation, and she hated herself for resorting to it, but it worked. She could see it in his face.

"Why am I discussing this with you?" he asked, making one last effort. "Stick to doing what you do best. Sail your little boat and be happy."

"I'm eighteen, Papa. I'm ready for this. You wouldn't have named me crown princess otherwise. You need my help."

"I have help. I have Sakari."

She lowered her face and pouted. "Papa, please."

"All right. All right. Enough of that. You can go. And you can take the Waterborne with you as leverage. But you'll have an escort, and you won't leave their safety. Do you hear?" he asked, holding up a hand and turning away.

"Yes, Papa."

"Promise me something in exchange."

"What is it?"

"Have you given much thought to binding?"

A cold shiver crawled up her spine. She'd hoped to avoid the topic for a few more years. It was one of the reasons she'd been so careful not to display any inclination toward long-term lovers since being declared Heir Apparent. She knew what lay ahead if she did. She'd be reduced to a power in name only. Only a male could rule alone. It was how things were done in Eledore. *But not in Ytlain.* Dread tightened the knot in her stomach. She shook her head. "There are so many more important matters."

Her father folded his hands behind his back, nodded, and slowly paced as he did when he wanted to look like he was listening even when he wasn't. She suddenly noticed that his athletic figure had begun to show a paunch. "Why are you so reluctant to talk about marriage?"

She paused, pretending to consider the question. In truth, she'd prepared her answer some time ago—one she knew would appeal to her father's vanity. It was also one that she hoped might breed a certain amount of paranoia in him. "I love you so much, Papa. I don't want anything bad to happen to you."

He whirled, a frown on his face. "I don't understand."

At the same time, she knew the argument would only solidify his idea of her as too sentimental. She took the plunge anyway. "It's only that all this talk of who I'm to marry and who will inherit the kingdom makes me feel like—like we're speaking of your death!"

Deep shock stole over his expression.

"And I—I fear it will only bring it about sooner. I love you, Papa. I don't want you to—to *die*. Please—"

His shock transformed into warmth and indulgence just as she'd hoped. "Little sparrow, what gives you these silly ideas?"

She bit her lip as if reluctant to speak. "Cousin Filip married last fall. And both his parents died a month after." She had chosen her example well. In truth, rumors of an assassin's dart were circulating the Tahmerian court. Some even suggested poisoned soup had been to blame. "What is the rush? There's no need." She looked up to him. "Unless you are feeling ill. You are, aren't you, Papa? Should I get the healer?" Springing up from her chair, she went to the door.

His laughter stopped her. "Sakari told me not to underestimate you," he said between soft chuckles. "It appears he was right."

Shit. She turned and to her relief saw real happiness in her father's face.

"He said you understand more of leadership than I give you credit for." Her father settled on the upholstered bench in front of the long row of windows overlooking the ship's stern. Then he patted the rich blue brocade cushion next to him. "Come, my little sparrow who is no longer so little anymore. Sit."

She sat. He placed an arm around her and drew her to his side with an affectionate squeeze. He hadn't done any such thing since she could remember. Part of her gloried in it, but the more cautious side of her grew wary. "We will speak as equals. You have concerns regarding your uncle," he said. "You think him dangerous? To me?"

"I do, Papa." *Think? I know. And I'm not the only one.*

Her father shook his head. "If that were so, I'd have been dead long ago. I have trusted him since we were boys. He has all the power he could want. He has no need of more."

"If you say so." She thought, *But will he give up that power when you're gone? I doubt it.*

"You're a young woman. The time has come for you to settle down. Have children—"

"All right." *Equals? If I were male would we be having this conversation? Really?* "I don't have to bind permanently. Not yet. I asked Mother if I could try a year's contract once or twice before I settled on someone. She seemed open to the idea, provided it was all right with you. Please, Papa—"

Again, he held up his hand as if to shush her. "I've an option to propose. It's unorthodox but not without precedent."

"Who do you have in mind?"

"What about Sakari?"

"That's disgusting!"

"He is only my half brother. Legally, it's possible."

"I don't care! I won't give the court gossips more fuel. Such a thing would equate to declaring that you aren't my father. What would happen to Mother? I can't!"

"It wouldn't be like that."

"It would!"

"Not if it wasn't a normal binding. It can be declared a political partnership. Executed for the kingdom's sake. He's not interested in anything else. You could take whatever lovers suited you. He would make no claims in that arena. Besides, he has a mistress."

Suvi thought, *And what's to keep him from replacing me with that mistress once you're gone?* "No, Papa!"

"How will it be any different? He can see to the country as he does now. And you can sail your boats."

"If that's the case, why should anything change?"

"My father's name, Ilmari, must continue. And it can. Through him and his heirs."

"I won't do this! I won't!"

"Ytlain has proven too dangerous for closer ties. Massilia's prince is far too old."

"How is a political partnership preferable to a ninety-year-old? At least we would have a chance at uniting two kingdoms under one crown!"

"Massilia's lower nobility would never stand for it."

"You're so sure?"

"I am." He held out his hand, counting down on his fingers. "Henry of Kaledan is too young."

"He's twelve. That didn't stop Grandfather. He was ten."

"Times have changed. It would risk Eledore becoming Kaledan's protectorate. You aren't a king."

"I'm to be a queen. Is there a difference?"

"Suvi, my sweet—"

"Well, is there?"

"We are Eledore, not Ytlain!" He got up and paced across the cabin. "I've allowed your mother too much influence in your education. There are certain proprieties—"

And what makes you think I won't strip down those outdated ideals once I'm in power? On the other hand, is that what this is about? She looked away. *One problem at a time.* "Fine. What of Duke Miguel Isadarr of Tahmer?"

"Have you not heard? He wed an Ytlainen whore last winter."

She paused. A political partnership in lieu of marriage wasn't all that unusual. It'd been done before when royal family lines had drawn too close. Nonetheless, she didn't like the idea of her uncle gaining any more power than he already had. "There are the lesser nobles, Papa. And there's love. I could bind for love."

"Don't be naive."

"I could take your name and not Mother's. Your name could carry on through me." She saw him take in that idea and give it thought.

"You would do that for me?"

She nodded. "It would upset Mother, but Hännenen is only a name, Papa."

His gaze traveled to the landscape painting on the wall opposite. It was a view of the palace in Jalokivi with the mountain range beyond. "There is more to the family of Ilmari than a name, Little Sparrow. Much more. Our traditions have purpose. Our blood has purpose. The royal line of Eledore must remain unbroken. There are reasons for this of which you and your mother are ignorant."

"Yes, Papa." *If you say so*, she thought.

"Perhaps the time has come? A test of the blood." He continued to stare at the painting. "They wait in the dark. There is only one way to be certain."

She opened her mouth to ask what he meant but stopped when she saw his expression. His eyes had faded to a pale gray, and his face seemed blank. Something about it reminded her of the Silmaillia. Suvi didn't think her father had premonitions, but it was possible. She waited to see what he would say next.

He blinked as if waking from a trance, and cleared his throat. "What were we talking about?"

A chill passed through her. She didn't like that brief look of confusion on her father's face. He seemed tired, even old. She didn't like it one bit. "You were talking about Uncle Sakari."

"Ah, yes. Well. All I'm asking for the moment is that you give the matter some consideration. Be polite to him. Humor me." He sat down at her side again. "Do so, and I'll grant you something nice in exchange."

She paused. She didn't like the idea but didn't see a way out of it. "It had better be worth it."

He smiled and touched her chin as if she were ten. The familiar gesture put her at ease once more. "How about a fleet, Little Sparrow?"

Her heart skipped. Although she'd only achieved a lieutenant's stripes before she'd been forced to quit, she'd dreamed her whole life of captaining ships. *A whole fleet?* "Can I decide which ships?"

"You can take your pick. Any you like."

"Even among the nobles?"

"Certainly."

"All right. I'll think about it."

"There's my girl. That wasn't so hard, now, was it?"

She stared at her lap and attempted not to feel she'd been bought. *Perhaps he knows me too well after all.* She told herself that everything had its price. "No, Papa." *I said I'd consider it. I never said I'd agree.*

"That's settled," her father said. He seemed happier, less worried. "Now that that is out of the way, there is something we should tend to before returning home."

"But I thought I'd contact the Waterborne, find a ship, and then leave at once." She didn't want to give her uncle another chance to trap her.

"Not yet. There is something that must be seen to first."

"What about Dylan?"

"What about him?"

"He can't stay in the brig, Father," she said. "It will ruin my chances before I've even started."

"Fine. I will confine him to his quarters until further notice. When we leave the ship, he is to be kept among your retinue and escorted at all times."

"Thank you, Papa."

Her father went to the table and poured himself a glass of wine. "When you leave here, send for the message master. A bird must go to the Silmaillia. She will meet us at the palace. Then we're going to Keeper Mountain."

"Keeper Mountain?" Suvi shuddered. "Whatever for?"

Her father drank the contents of his glass in one swallow and then poured another. The dark red vintage reminded Suvi of blood. "You've a royal duty that must be attended to."

"No one goes there. Isn't it haunted?"

Her father turned to stare at the painting again. "That is the very reason why you must go."

THREE

"Ouch!" Suvi jerked her hand away from the severed blackthorn branch and checked her palm. She pinched out a large thorn with a wince and then resumed helping her father clear away the birch and blackthorn seedlings that had overgrown the cave entrance.

Early-afternoon sun cast inky splotches on the ancient carvings scarring the canyon wall. She turned away and suppressed a shiver. A wind gust ricocheted off the rocky surface, thrashing the forest opposite and making the lush treetops ripple like the surface of a lake in heavy weather. Squinting against flying grit, she imagined the rush of wind through new leaves as the sound of a swell rushing a ship's bow. The soothing image was punctuated with the thud of fine steel meeting its stubborn leafy target. She huddled inside the hood of her fur-trimmed hunting coat while the muscles at the base of her neck pinched. Her palm stung. It was still bleeding, and she wiped fresh blood on the inside of her jacket pocket. She checked an urge to put the wound to her mouth. There was a foul undercurrent in the air, originating from the cave. She didn't recognize the scent.

"I'm not certain this is a fair test," Saara said.

"And why not?" The king paused, sword in the air.

"You damned well know why," Saara said. "Ilta, bring me that bag. I need the mugwort."

"The blood will tell," her father said, returning to his earlier stoicism. "It always does."

"I'm only going through with this under protest," Saara said. "The danger to—"

"Enough!"

Suvi turned, catching Saara's angry expression. Suvi didn't look at her father but kept her eyes on Saara. "Is there something I should be worried about, Papa?"

"Just do as I told you," he said. "And everything will be fine."

Saara frowned.

Every spring, as soon as the roads allow, the Guardian's Ritual must be performed before summer heats the World's Pillar.

Venturing into a dark, haunted cavern without protection seemed foolhardy at best. So Suvi thought, but her father had insisted there were to be no witnesses. So it was that the royal guard, Piritta, Dylan, and the servants had been left at the palace. Suvi had expected a long journey up the mountainside. However, her father had led her, the Silmaillia, and her apprentice, Ilta, to the castle keep, where he stored some of his favorite wines. Located under the palace library, the keep was designed as a haven for royalty during times of war or unrest. And although it was windowless and dank, it had long been one of Suvi's favorite places to read. She'd almost laughed. *All that bluster about wearing warm-enough clothes and sturdy boots.* She'd been surprised when her father showed her the hidden door. Through that, they'd safely made a five-mile journey to Keeper Mountain without the need of an escort. Nonetheless, the ancient tunnel with its mundane cave life would've been uncomfortable enough without knowing what waited for her.

The Guardian's Ritual must be performed before summer heats the World's Pillar.

A strange silence hung over the group. The air felt heavy yet empty. She could hear the far off cry of a bird. Suddenly, what was wrong fell into place. *Where are the usual forest insect noises?*

Keeper Mountain wasn't all that far from the palace. However, there were no roads marring its sides, no farms, nothing. The mountain loomed in the east above the city of Jalokivi, and often Suvi wondered why her ancestors had chosen to build the winter palace so close to such a foreboding place. The summer palace at Järvi Satama was much more beautiful and accessible. Keeper Mountain's brooding slopes gave off a bad feeling even when viewed from the winter palace roof. It was much worse standing on the mountain itself. She felt like an intruder. The peak was rarely free of cloud cover, and so, even on the brightest of days, it seemed an apparition when compared to its sisters and brothers. The court didn't speak of Keeper Mountain. There were no histories told of it, no battles, no adventures on its slopes—at least, none that weren't spoken of at a whisper even in broad daylight.

In the center of the clearing stood a limestone monolith, the World's Pillar. Beyond the Pillar, the rune-scarred mountain face jutted hundreds of feet to the sky. A deep fissure split the wall. On either side of the opening perched the giant stone figure of a gyrfalcon—the symbol of her father's house. One claw raking the air, each raptor stretched wide a fanned wing. Their wingtips over-lapped the top of the arch. The statues were less weathered than the carved prayers and warnings in the old tongue covering the rock walls around and in between. Suvi couldn't read most of what was written, largely because unlike Nels, she was terrible with languages. However, what she could understand sent her hand to the Blessed Mother's circle cast in silver hanging around her neck from a silver chain.

Finished clearing away the brush, her father wiped his blade clean of sap before putting it away. Then he dug around in the pack he'd abandoned at the foot of the pillar until he located a small book. The edges of its pages were yellowed with age.

"We should get started," he said, moving to a position in front of the cave. He reached into a coat pocket for a handkerchief, wiped sweat from his face, and then put the handkerchief away. He opened and closed the book as if checking it. Its cover was made of textured leather polished by what Suvi assumed were hundreds of anxious royal hands. "I pass the Guardianship of Eledore to you, Suvi Natalia Annika, daughter of House Ilmari."

Suvi slowed her breathing. Again, she thought of her new responsibilities, and her unease increased. *Does this mean that Father is giving me a chance to rule without Uncle?*

"Keep the realm safe with the sacrifice of knowledge," her father said, and handed off the little tome.

Checking the cover, she saw that it had no title and the bindings had been repaired multiple times.

Saara set one of the lanterns on the ground with a stern face, then kissed her cheek. "Do as Ilta says, girl. She has been studying for this her whole life. She knows what to do." Straightening, she next laid a hand on Suvi's forehead. "Blessings, Guardian of the Realm, may the Great Mother, Goddess, and Protector of the Earth, the Father, God, and Guardian of the Sky, and all their servants grant you strength."

Suvi remembered to bow her head and then press the book to her heart.

Saara handed the last ornamental lantern to Ilta. She touched the top of Ilta's head and paused. "You're warm. How do you feel?"

"I'm fine, Gran."

Frowning, Saara said, "Are you sick? You feel feverish."

"It's the exertion from the climb. I overdressed."

Saara's frown didn't budge.

"All right, I do feel a little stuffy. Maybe it's a cold." Ilta didn't look her grandmother in the eye.

"You've tired yourself out at the hospital," Saara said. "You've been working too hard."

Ilta nodded. "You're probably right. I just need some rest."

Saara paused. "Perhaps I should go in instead."

"No!" the king said. "We must know if they can work together. You said—"

"There won't be a better opportunity to test them both." Saara nodded and then turned to Ilta. "The moment we're back home, I want to see you in bed."

"Yes, ma'am," Ilta said.

Returning to the ritual, Saara rested her hand on the crown of Ilta's head and said, "Blessings, Lightbearer, Seer, and Healer of the Realm, may the Great Mother, Goddess, and Protector of the Earth, the Father, God, and Guardian of the Sky, and all their servants grant you wisdom."

Ilta curtseyed. "Thank you, Grandmother."

The small ceremony complete, Suvi stretched herself to her full height and faced the black crevice. A bad feeling lodged itself in the back of her mind. Her heart slammed out an executioner's beat against her breastbone. *Would Grandmother Elizabeth cower from a mere cave?* Her mother's mother had been a great admiral and had commanded a fleet that dominated the known lakes— even parts of the ocean. Suvi tilted her chin up, thinking of the first time she'd danced the *Northern Star's* toplines. The dizzy fear of falling clutched her chest as the cave's frigid ceiling swallowed her. Daylight braved a few yards before abandoning them to the dark. Ilta opened her lantern and a warm glow took over the fight, revealing ripples in the walls. Suvi's footsteps echoed down the lonely passage.

"Don't worry. Everything is going to be all right," Ilta said.

"How much experience do you have with this ritual?"

"None. But Gran wouldn't give me this task unless I was ready."

Would that I felt the same about Father, Suvi thought. *Yet another royal secret I knew nothing about until the last. I wonder what else he hasn't told me.* There were moments when she wished she'd been allowed to be a ship's captain. Although every bit as dangerous and unpredictable as court, the lakes didn't lie or vie for power. At the same time, she had to admit to a certain amount of enjoyment in testing her wits against her uncle and others like him. *Political adversaries are challenge enough, but now there are to be demons as well?* She suppressed another shudder. "Have you ever seen one of the Old Ones?"

Ilta shook her head.

"Has Saara?"

"I don't think anyone has. Not in more than two hundred years," Ilta said. "There are stories of them rising from the lakes in recent years, of course. But I'm not sure they should be believed. Everyone knows sailors exaggerate." She paused before her mouth stretched into a rueful half smile. "Present company excepted, of course."

"Oh, I've told my share of fish stories," Suvi said. "Every self-respecting sailor has. I suspect it's listed as a requirement in the Laws of Common." The joke rested uneasy in the anxiety-heavy air, and she trudged another ten paces in silence. She detected an undercurrent of low vibration—the flow of an underground river swelling with melt water. Running a finger along the chilly rock wall, she followed the stone as it curved to the left while the cheerful light of Ilta's lantern burned back the blackness. A low tune drifted up Suvi's throat, and she began to hum—until a sharp rock edge sliced a line into her fingertip.

"What's wrong?" Ilta whispered. Her voice echoed up the passage nonetheless.

Suvi put the injured finger to her mouth and searched for what had cut her. Long grooves etched deep into the rock jolted her into wariness. It was evidence of a creature that had braved the cave and made it its home. *It's only an ordinary bear.*

What if it's still here? What are we to do? Frighten it with a lantern and a ceremonial knife? Taking a second look, she had a sense that the markings were old in spite of their sharpness. She stretched her fingers over the grooves with care and understood by the angles that the creature responsible could not have been a bear, nor any creature whose shape with which she was familiar. A coldness deeper than what seeped out of the rock penetrated her fingers and crept up her arm.

Revenants. Ghosts. Demons. The Old Ones do not know sleep, nor do they walk alone. She jerked her hand away with a shudder.

"Getting harder to think of them as mere legends, isn't it?" Ilta asked in a hushed whisper. The tone of her words said she wished otherwise. Her lantern-shadowed face was an uneasy reminder of bedtime ghost stories.

Clinging to the protective circle of Ilta's lantern light, Suvi followed onward. She tried not to notice the increasing frequency of claw marks on the walls in the ceiling and on the floor—clear evidence of battles past. Annoying traditions began to make sense in ways they hadn't before. Eledore had chosen to forget the Old Ones. Eledore forgot and lived in the shelter of her ignorance, but it was a Royal Guardian's duty to remember.

"Do you know of the hero Kassarina Ilmari?" Ilta asked.

"The first Queen of Eledore," Suvi said, happy of the distraction.

"She's my ancestor through my father's line." She'd been informed of her father's family lineage from birth. Still, she'd known little else other than the name. Like soldiers, women were not held in high regard in Eledore, unlike Ytlain. It was one of the reasons why Suvi had preferred to study stories of her mother's ancestors over her father's.

"She was more than that," Ilta said. "She was also the first Guardian of Eledore. Until one hundred years ago, only female members of the Ilmari family were appointed Guardians. Did you know that?"

"I didn't."

"Grandmother says that Kassarina Ilmari was the first to drive the Old Ones back into the void and bind them there," Ilta said. "An ancient record transcribed by the first Silmaillia describes Kassarina Ilmari's journeys throughout the seven nations. I've read it. Kassarina, the Silmaillia, and representatives from all the nations sealed every crack in the world, every entrance the Old Ones had used to cross over. This was the first. Kainen seeking sanctuary from the Old Ones came to Eledore from all over the world. Eledore used to be a nation of immigrants." Her soothing tone echoed off the walls. "It's the mountains, you see. Stone makes the best barrier."

"Why didn't I know about this?"

Ilta shrugged. "It was Kassarina Ilmari's powerful domination magic that allowed her to complete the task. It was why she was made Queen of Eledore. Did you know that she was originally a weaver in Ytlain? Her family name was Nilssen. She settled here to keep watch over the mountain. She married an Eledorean baron and took his name because she loved the Eledorean people."

"That's not how Father or anyone else tells it. I was told she was a rich widow and that she was given to the Baron by her father."

"Interesting, isn't it? How history changes over time?"

Turning left behind Ilta, Suvi entered a cavern enclosed with watery curtains of rock glistening like melting ice. The feeling of harsh inhospitality intensified.

They reached the end of the oval-shaped cavern and stopped. Like the cave entrance, a crevice split the wall. However, this crack had been sealed with a sickly pale clay and smeared with what looked like old blood. Below the rift was an altar table; in the center of its broad surface lay a small bundle wrapped in badly tanned leather. Feathers and bones had been knotted into the rough twine holding it closed.

It looks like an offering, Suvi thought.

Frowning, Ilta reached for the bundle, but as her finger brushed its surface, she stopped. She shook out her hand with a wince. "It isn't meant for me."

"Who is it for? Father?"

"I think it's intended for you."

"That's nice. But totally unnecessary. I think I'll leave it here."

The vibration seeping through the rock suddenly strengthened. The renewed force of it set Suvi's teeth on edge. It was then she understood the tremor was not an underground river after all. It was the presence of powerful magic. Power gushed out of the sealed crevice, leaving a hard and metallic taste on the back of her tongue. It intensified until the magic in the air was so thick that it choked her. The hairs all along her arms and the back of her neck stiffened, and she coughed with a shudder. "How did"—she found she didn't want to say their name—"did they know it was I who would come and not Father?"

"I don't know. But it's clear they knew."

Suvi reached out and brushed one of the feathers with a fingertip. Its vane clung to her skin like it'd been made of thousands of tiny unpleasant hooks. As if that were the signal sought, the twine parted with a snap, and the wrapping loosened, giving off a musty smell. She leaned closer. Although loath to touch the thing a second time, she gingerly urged the folds open. A toy whistle lay at the center of the package. She recognized the intricate carvings and letters on its surface but had to think of where she'd seen it before. She read her name, spelled out in reverse. It was then she knew they were the mirror image of marks carved into the whistle Nels always kept with him—the toy whistle he had fished out of Captain Veli Ari Karpanen's coat pocket the day he died.

The restless dead walk with the Old Ones. Oh, Mother. Suvi felt the blood drain from her face.

"What is it?" Ilta asked.

"Nothing." Suvi grabbed the whistle before Ilta could get a good look at the thing, jamming it into the drawstring pocket dangling from her waist. The toy created an uneasy weight there. "Shouldn't we start?"

"If you're ready." Ilta tilted her head down and raised her eyebrows. The expression was a replica of the one Saara had given her father.

It gave Suvi a feeling of rightness in spite of the fear shivering up her spine. "Please. Let's. My feet are freezing."

"All right."

Ilta captured her hand with fingers too hot for the chill of the cave.

She is feverish, Suvi thought. But before she could say anything, Suvi felt her palm fill with prickling heat.

"Go on," Ilta said.

Taking a deep breath and closing her eyes, Suvi recited, "In the eight names of the Great Mother and the Father, and by the power of my blood, I command thee to sleep." Her tongue tingled as she concentrated—domination magic empowering the formal court speech. Dropping Ilta's hand, Suvi unsheathed the knife at her hip and ran the silver-laced blade against her palm. Blood welled up almost at once. The edge was so sharp, she hadn't felt the cut. It started to sting as she placed her bleeding palm flat against the wall in the exact place where generations of Ilmari's had done. Unlike the pale clay seal, there was no stain to indicate the place where blood had been shed, only the Mother's circle carved at eye level next to the seal. The odd sensation that the stone drank the blood offered gave her a jolt of terror. Her heart sped up. It took an effort of will to keep her hand pressed against the wall. She counted to seventy and then quickly jerked her hand away.

The circle carving was clean.

She looked into her hand. A thin pale scar traced a line across her palm. Her father had said that would happen and that it would fade until the next year. Remembering she had the rest of the ritual to finish, she took the bloodstained knife and using both hands on the hilt, swept the point through the air in an arc until she pointed it at the ceiling. "In the eight names of the Great Mother and the Father, and by the power of sacred silver, I command thee to sleep."

Although she was following her father's instructions exactly, something didn't feel quite right. She got the sense that the darkness beyond the clay-mended cleft now shoved hungrily against the barrier rather than retreating from it. She could sense when a subject was dominated. There was a palpable connection. Whatever it was on the other side felt slippery. *It's like attempting to dominate Nels.*

Ilta shifted backward.

Suvi concentrated harder on the next set of words, forcing more power into them in the hope that it would help. "By the rocks and earth, I bar thee from this world." She traced the second half of the circle with the point of the blade, directing the knife now to the floor. "By the heat of the sun-warmed earth I bar you from this world." She pointed to her left. "By the rivers and sea I bar you from this world." Reaching the end with some relief, she opened her eyes and moved the blade to her right. She prepared to speak the last part of the ritual. However, she glanced downward, and the words were gone.

Ilta sat shivering on the floor, curled into a defensive ball. Her arms were wrapped tight around her knees. Her head was tilted to one side. She rocked back and forth, staring up toward the white cleft in the wall with a vacant, wide-eyed expression of horror. She whispered one word over and over. "No. No. No."

Suvi scanned the area but no danger revealed itself. A bone-deep chill crawled up from her stomach and settled in her throat. She knelt and gave Ilta a gentle shake. "Ilta, please. You have to wake up."

Ilta opened her mouth and screamed louder than Suvi thought possible. It hurt Suvi's ears. Ilta's cries bounced off the cavern walls. Unsure of what else to do, Suvi shook her again. Suvi wanted to run but couldn't bring herself to leave Ilta alone in the dark, no matter how afraid she was. She didn't trust the cavern. She tried to think of something, anything she could do.

Then Ilta stopped screaming just as abruptly as she'd started. The moment she did, Suvi could have sworn she heard something skitter in the stone ceiling above them.

Is that what they mean when they say something is loud enough to wake the dead? Suvi's mind filled with images of nightmarish creatures with sharp claws bent at unnatural angles. *Wake the dead. Oh, no. Oh, gods.* Suvi had always thought herself brave, but it was at that moment she knew she wasn't. She grabbed the lantern and slipped an arm around Ilta's waist, lifting her. A rock hit the cavern floor. Suvi didn't wait to see where it had come from. She was too terrified to look. She dragged Ilta through the passage as quickly as she could while her back itched with a sense of menacing pursuit. Panic fueled her strength. It wasn't until she spied welcoming daylight that her terror began to fade.

Saara rushed toward them with a swiftness that contradicted her age. "What happened?" she asked, helping ease Ilta to the ground. Ilta let out a small frightened sound. Saara opened Ilta's fist and pressed it to the dirt. "Feel the earth, girl. Touch the warmth of the sun."

"I don't understand. We started the ritual. I looked back, and she was like this." Suvi thought, *Please don't ask me to go back in there.*

Her father frowned. "Started? You didn't finish?"

"I told you you should've sent for Nels in case something went wrong," Saara said. "Well, it's gone wrong."

"That boy is a defect!" Her father stamped his foot. "Tradition dictates one Guardian. One!" He paced. "You know what this means!"

Saara said, "It means nothing of the kind. It means we've need of your son. He's her twin. They shared a womb. It's possible they share their magical talents. Be reasonable, Henrik."

"He is not my son! He has no magic! She is not my daughter, either! She doesn't have the blood to be a Guardian! That whore presented me with another man's—"

Something in Suvi snapped. "Don't talk about Mother like that!"

"Calm yourself, Henrik! We need both your children," Saara said. "Together, they have the power. Stop thinking of Sakari's plots. There are more important things at hand."

Suvi watched her father's face grow red. His hand twitched as if he'd stayed an urge to hit someone. Then he closed his eyes and turned away.

"Give your father the knife." Saara stood up. "Stay with Ilta. The fever is getting worse, and I don't like it. Watch her. See to it she doesn't hurt herself."

Suvi handed off the ceremonial knife without looking at her father. "What might Ilta do?"

"You just see she's comfortable," Saara said, dusting off her skirts. She dug into her pack and brought out a blue glass vial. "Open this and wave it under her nose. Talk until she answers. When she wakes, make her eat something and then drink some water. She'll know what to do after that."

"What if she doesn't wake?" Suvi asked.

Saara frowned. "Then we've got real trouble. Best get to it, girl. Your father and I have bigger things to tend to."

Suvi watched her father enter the cavern with Saara. She didn't think he'd ever looked so small. She waited until they were gone before twisting the stopper off the vial. A strong acidic scent hit her with the force of a blow. She followed Saara's instructions and passed it twice under Ilta's nose. Ilta sat up all at once with a wince and began to shiver.

Replacing the stopper, Suvi asked, "Are you all right?"

Pinching her nose shut, Ilta shook her head. "Oh, gods. I hate smelling salts."

"Saara told me to do it."

Ilta pushed hair away from her face and glanced around her. "What are we doing out here? Where's Gran?" She fumbled in her pockets.

"You collapsed. You're sick. Saara and Father went inside to complete the ritual." Suvi paused. She didn't want to talk about what else had happened until she'd been able to give it thought.

What will Father do to Mother? "Did you have a vision? What did you see?"

The shadow of unease passed over Ilta's face before she located her pocket watch and checked the time. "I don't want to think about it. Not yet." Then she put the watch away, breathed deep, and dug her fingers into the dirt. "Would you mind bringing me Gran's pack? I'm not sure I can stand."

"She said you should have something to eat." The pack felt heavier than it appeared. Suvi thought of Saara carrying the weight up the mountain, and her respect for the older woman was renewed.

Ilta scrounged the contents of the patched carpet bag, producing another blue vial. She checked the label before taking a small sip. "The headaches are the worst."

"You get headaches?"

Ilta nodded. "The visions aren't as bad when I've been able to rest. It's why I can only use a certain amount of healing magic. If I push myself too far, the pain is so awful that light hurts my eyes. I can't do anything until it goes away. Gran says everything has its price."

Suvi gave her the water flask and nodded.

Ilta swallowed and closed her eyes. "The headache should be gone in a little while, I hope."

Looking to the cavern, Suvi said, "How much longer do you think they'll be?"

"I don't know."

Suvi listened to the wind play in the forest. Once again, the lack of background animal sounds was disturbing—only now there were no bird cries, no furtive movements of deer or mice or other small creatures. Only the empty breeze. It was as if the forest was keeping a solemn silence in reverence for a holy place. Except she knew otherwise.

As she waited, the metal taste of the cave's magic began to fade on her tongue. Tension eased from her shoulders but didn't vanish completely.

Ilta's voice shattered the calm. "I saw them."

"Who?"

"The—the Old Ones. They've crossed over. The seal is broken."

Suvi stood up and prepared to go into the cave alone for her father in spite of her terror.

"Not here. Elsewhere. Somewhere in the south. Something is wrong," Ilta said with a shudder. "Oh, Mother. I have to tell you. I have to. But you have to promise not to tell Gran I said anything."

"All right. I promise." Suvi attempted not to show her fear. Ilta seemed upset enough.

"Maybe it won't happen at all. Gran says we see possibilities based upon current circumstances. Something or someone might change everything. You never know."

"What might not happen?" Suvi didn't feel reassured.

Ilta bit her lip. "You can't tell your father what I'm about to say, either."

"I promise. Now tell me."

Taking another deep breath, Ilta whispered, "Your mother should leave Jalokivi now and stay away from the capital until the war is over."

"What? Leave court? Why?"

"She's—she's in danger." Ilta kept her gaze fixed to the ground.

"It isn't Father, is it? Is it something Uncle Sakari is up to? Tell me!"

"It's something else. I—I can't remember the details now. Will you please tell her anyway? I don't think it's too late. It would be best if you stayed away from the palace, too. It'll be this summer, I think."

Suvi paused. "You do remember, don't you?"

"I can't say. I shouldn't. Shit! I hate this!" It was the first time Suvi had ever heard Ilta swear, and it came as a shock. Ilta pounded a fist in the dirt. "Look. I don't know anything for certain. And Gran says it's best not to mention anything until you are. It makes a mess of things. Just . . . please. Take it as a warning. All right?"

"All right. I can arrange to be away from court," Suvi said, and then spied Ilta's expression. "That isn't everything, is it?"

Ilta slumped. "I saw something else."

"What?" Suvi sat back down.

Taking a deep breath, Ilta drew spirals in the dirt. She didn't seem to notice what she was doing. "It's about your brother."

"Is he all right?"

"For now."

"What do you mean?"

Suvi watched the spirals form faster and tighter, almost frantic, then Ilta obliterated them with an angry hand.

"He won't admit it, but he needs you. And you need him." Ilta bit her lip. "Watch over him, will you? I can't—" She choked. Blinking up at the trees, an expression of profound heartbreak stole over her face. "I can't be anywhere near him. Not now."

"What does that mean?" Suvi frowned.

"And . . . tell him to be careful."

⚜ NELS ⚜

ONE

"Would you please limit yourself to trampling one foot or the other?" Nels asked, detecting a slur in his own speech and not caring. "It's the least you could do after dragging me through half the alehouses in Jalokivi."

He hefted Viktor for the third time, trying for better leverage by wedging his shoulder farther under Viktor's arm. Nels stumbled, nearly pitching them both onto the muddy cobblestones. The ravages of variola throughout the rest of the realm didn't seem to have done much to dampen the spirits of residents in the capital city, nor did the doom of impending war. It was long past midnight, but every lamp was lit in nearly every house. The sounds of music and laughter flooded into the night.

Viktor snorted, and Nels got a nose full of sour alcohol-breath. He turned away with a wince.

"'Twould appear you're dragging me at the moment," Viktor said. "Where shall we go next?"

"Your barracks house, to sleep it off."

Viktor stopped or attempted to, but Nels pulled him another laborious step toward home.

"What?" Viktor asked. "With the other half of Jalokivi's fine alehouses unvisited?"

"You've seen them before," Nels said. "I suspect every barman in the city knows you by name."

"Not in a mood for drinking, I see." Viktor held a finger up in the air. "Well, then. We shall visit Helmi. No doubt she's having a nice pre-victory party. Wouldn't you rather wake in the arms of an angel than alone in a smelly barracks house?"

"We leave for the Acrasian border in the morning."

"Exactly." Viktor straightened and then wobbled before Nels caught him.

"You're too drunk to do Helmi any good."

Viktor put a hand to his heart and bowed his head in mock grief. "True. Very true." He looked through the fringe of light brown hair falling into his face. "But you aren't."

"Helmi wouldn't have me even if I were interested—which I'm not."

"She has a v-very generous nature. She might even forfeit the gift price for the Soldier Prince, savior of Eledore."

Nels frowned. "Stop calling me that."

With obvious effort, Viktor withdrew his arm and stood on his own. His brows drew together. "It's that little blond, isn't it?"

Ilta. Her name is Ilta. "You're drunk."

"So are you. Although not as drunk as you should be." Using an accusatory finger, Viktor poked him in the chest. "Damn it all, how long are you going to dangle at the end of that rope?"

"What rope?"

Viktor sighed. Then he made a gesture involving his index finger. "The one that blond has looped around your—"

"We're going back to your barracks house. You're a korva. You have special status. You can be late to formation, and no one will say a word. I can't. Colonel Pesola doesn't much care for me as it is."

"'Pick your battles.' Sound familiar?" Viktor paused. "Hasn't anyone mentioned that one to you before?"

Nels grunted.

"Crashing about like a mad bull can only get you so far in life, you know." Viktor's head dropped, and he swallowed. "Oh, gods."

Afraid his friend was about to be sick, Nels shifted his grip on Viktor and prepared for the worst.

Instead, Viktor said, "I understand your disdain for court, but hobnails really aren't suitable for every occasion."

"Tell me we're not having this conversation again."

"I have it on good authority that women don't much care to have their feet gored during dances," Viktor said. "Might change your luck with—with whatever her name is. Come to think of it, a touch of polish wouldn't be remiss, either. Too bad it won't make you any less noisy."

"I should've left Almari to you. I know. How many times do I have to apologize?"

"One more time, I think. I rather like the sound," Viktor said. "I've a deliciously wicked idea. Let's visit the impound. The docks aren't that far from here."

"No."

"Why not? It would be fun."

"It's too risky. Even if it wasn't, there's no time. We'd have to do it tonight," Nels said, stopping himself. "Correction. *You* would have to do it tonight. If you get caught, Major Lindström will throw me to the wolves. Rabid wolves. In a pit. With a fresh reindeer ham tied around my neck. He said that he might consider throwing in some agitated bees for good measure."

"Me? Caught? Never," Viktor said. "You're the one who should watch himself."

"True. The major *did* say if he receives one more reprimand from Pesola on my behalf—"

"Lindström likes you," Viktor said. "He isn't the one I'd worry about if I were you."

"I wouldn't be so sure."

"It's Colonel Pesola. He's an evil bastard. And *you* are now on his short list for delaying our deployment." Viktor hiccupped. "He was not happy to discover the source of variola in the ranks."

"I followed the chain of command. Can I help it that Major Lindström went straight to the head of Medical Corp? And she decided not to tell him until after it was done?"

"I suspect Pesola doesn't care."

Nels said, "Pesola will thank me later."

"I don't think 'thank' is the word he'd use," Viktor said. "That was some risk you took."

"*We* took. Lindström and I volunteered for inoculation, too." No one had died, and a majority of the troops had recovered with only a few scars. Still, Nels suffered some guilt. Viktor was right. It had been a terrible risk. It didn't help that Nels had been one of the more fortunate ones and had contracted one of the lighter cases.

"Private Ketola is lucky Pesola didn't string him up in spite of the both of you."

"Ketola only did what I told him," Nels said. "What has Pesola to complain about? With all three companies inoculated, there's no chance we'll fall prey to variola on the field. Look at what happened to Major Bohinen."

"Taken by the Acrasians at Södersjö while in his bed."

"What a mess that was."

"He only had his commission because his father is a brigadier general," Viktor said, and lowered his voice. "The troops are saying it's good he was an only child."

Nels pretended he didn't hear that.

"Just the same," Viktor said, and hiccupped again. "Not sure I've seen Pesola that furious. Listen to your korva. It's what you pay me for. I'd watch your back if I were you."

"The most he can do is bust me to lieutenant. I've already lost a kingdom. What's a few bits of braid compared to that?" Nels asked. *Don't lie. You wanted to see major one day. Now you never will.*

Damn it. We needed those muskets.

"Yes. Yes. We've heard that one before. And it's far too depressing a subject for tonight," Viktor said. "I know. Let's go to Helmi's. You won't get caught. I swear it." He placed a hand on his heart. "S-swear."

"Don't make promises you can't keep."

"We'll leave when the clock tower chimes four."

"No."

"I promise not to tell your little blond where you were."

"That doesn't matter." *It's been almost two weeks since I last heard from her. Her last message said she was working at the hospital, but she's left Jalokivi. No one will explain why. They know, but they won't tell me,* Nels thought. *She's changed her mind. Came to her senses at last. But why didn't she tell me first? Why did she leave?* "We're not bound."

"All the more reason to get what you can while you can," Viktor said.

Nels shrugged.

"When was the last time you gave a woman a good swiving?" Viktor asked. "Your right hand doesn't count, even if you do grant it a name like Corporal Kallela does."

"I don't for one instant believe—"

"Calls it Valma, after his first love. Whole regiment knows." Viktor shook his head in disgust. They staggered three more steps toward Viktor's barracks house together. "You write her a letter every day. Does she even answer?"

"Fine. Let's go to Helmi's," Nels said. "Anything is better than listening to you badger me all night."

"Yes!" Due to looking over his shoulder and not watching where he was going, Viktor staggered into a carriage horse. "Begging your pardon, madam." To the driver's confusion, Viktor then doffed his hat and bent into a low, unsteady bow. He glanced up without straightening. "Oh. I do apologize. Sir."

Nels checked the interior of the coach and found it empty. "Are you already engaged?" He asked the driver.

The coachman shook his head.

Yanking Viktor up by his collar, Nels said, "Give the nice coachman the address."

"Why?"

"Because there are many things I'd do for you, but I refuse to carry you all the way to Helmi's bed."

Viktor grinned. "Number sixteen, North Street."

Nels paid and then stuffed Viktor into the coach. Getting him onto the padded bench was another matter, and after several tries, Nels left his friend curled up on the floor. With that done, he rested his boots on the bench opposite and shut gritty eyes. The coach had traveled less than five hundred feet when a snore drifted up from the floorboards. Viktor muttered in his sleep, but the words were lost in the clattering of coach wheels and rattling livery.

How does he do it? Nels thought. Given any opportunity, Viktor could fall asleep no matter the situation—even during a bone-jarring coach ride. In a fit of pique, Nels prodded Viktor. "What did you say?"

"Don't know why you're in a mood. Thought you've been wanting to do something about the Acrasians for years?"

"Not like this. Not war. And not without muskets."

"We have some."

"Not enough for a battle, let alone a war."

"Don't need them. We've magic. Now that all of Eledore is committed to the fight, we'll frighten the Acrasians into the sea."

"We didn't commit to the war all at once. Half our forces have already taken a beating. The rest need training. We need enemy troop reports, proper supplies—"

"They'll run screaming. Everyone says so."

"Not everyone."

"You're paranoid."

Nels stared out the carriage window, watching the revelers while dread bore down on his shoulders. "I was a royal once. If there is one thing I learned, it's that paranoia is what keeps you alive," he whispered to no one in particular.

Viktor resumed his snoring and wouldn't stop, no matter how many times Nels nudged him with the toe of a boot. After a short distance, the coach halted and the coach step clattered open. Nels looked out the window. Clearly, the riots hadn't touched this part of the city. An ornate three-story mansion with stately white columns and gaping windows stared back at him. Rows of lamps outlined the path from gate to porch in the darkness. A woman sang in a cheerful soprano, her voice floating through the open windows. She was accompanied by a pianoforte. Shadowy revelers laughed and chattered within the rectangles of light.

Nels got to the difficult business of levering Viktor's slack body from the floor. Unconscious, his friend seemed to weigh twice as much as usual, and hauling his limp form up the porch steps wasn't going to be fun. For an instant, Nels considered going home.

Helmi's house does have a certain reputation. The ladies employed by the house were reputed to be especially well trained. Some, it was said, had special talents—magical talents, in fact, specific to their craft. He'd never so much as ventured past the front gate in his entire life. *It might be interesting. To look. There's nothing wrong with looking, is there?* He didn't believe he could afford anything beyond that even if he wanted. It said a great deal that Viktor could. *I'll have a drink. Maybe two. Leave Viktor to his fun. Go for a long walk. Collect him, then return to the barracks house.* He shrugged and got to work. To simplify matters, he tossed both of their hats into the dooryard from the coach door. Next, he hopped out and then reached inside, dragging Viktor to the carriage step by the ankles. When Nels yanked him into a sitting position, Viktor's head collided into the edge of the coach door with a hollow *bonk.*

"Good thing you're too drunk to feel that." Nels hefted Viktor over a shoulder and then staggered through the gate. He was then met by one of the ladies of the establishment. Her long hair cascaded down her back and shoulders in frothy black curls. She was short and trim. An infantry tricorne was perched on the crown of her head at a jaunty angle. The front of her gown did a credible job of showcasing plump breasts and a pair of striking legs. Ribbon garters topped her stockings.

She held up the hats. "Did you gentlemen lose something?"

"Ah. Yes. We ... er ... did. Thank you," Nels said.

She bent, getting a closer look at Viktor's face. Nels found himself staring down the front of her stays. Smooth round skin was bathed in moonlight.

It'd be rude to simply drop off Viktor and leave.

"Why, Lieutenant Reini, I do believe you look a bit worse for wear," she said. "I'll get Helmi."

She dashed up the path and vanished into the house. Light

and music spilled onto the porch in equal measures. Nels propped Viktor up against the gate post. Viktor's head bumped against iron—this time with far less force. Viktor didn't even flinch. Nels turned and made arrangements with the coachman to return before dawn. Then he levered his shoulder under Viktor's once more and staggered to the house. Avoiding the lamps along the way, he had lurched as far as the first step when reinforcements arrived—a man twice his size and a beautiful woman with red hair. Both were swathed in very patriotic Eledorean blue.

"My poor Viktor. I wondered when I'd see you tonight." Her voice was deep and sensual.

Viktor's eyes snapped open. "Helmi? Is that you?"

"Here I am, my love." She lifted his chin and gave him a kiss on the now painful-looking lump. "Is my boy having a rough night?"

Viktor said, "The bad captain dropped me on my head. Twice."

She moved to kiss his forehead again, and Viktor moved quickly to meet her lips with his.

"He's yours if you'll have him," Nels said. "Otherwise, he's getting dumped in the dooryard—this time on his ass."

Helmi broke the kiss.

Viktor gave him a reproachful look. "I don't suppose you know someone who can do something about his mood?"

She studied the front of Nels's captain's jacket, and her expression changed. "Why don't we find out?" she asked. "Turo, take the lieutenant to my rooms. I'll join him once his friend is made comfortable."

"See you in the morning." Viktor waved. "Have fun."

"You have until the clock tower chimes four," Nels said. "Then the coach returns to take us home."

Viktor let out a disgusted grunt. "Killjoy."

Turo helped an unsteady Viktor navigate through the open

door and up the broad staircase. Nels paused until the way was clear. The main passage was wide enough to be called a room in its own right. He watched through the cut-glass panes as Turo saved Viktor from pitching over the banister. Holding his breath, Nels waited to speak until they'd reached the top. "Do I owe you something for . . ."

Helmi looped an arm through his and smiled. "Don't ruin a perfectly good evening with sordid details," she said. "The lieutenant and I have an agreement."

"An agreement?"

She tugged him into the main passage and then whispered into his ear, "Viktor told me what you did for him at the river, Captain Hännenen," she said. "Any business arrangements are very much not your concern."

Nels swallowed. "Oh."

Helmi led him through the crowd in the front room, and the sight of his uniform resulted in drunken cheers. Several partygoers, obviously too drunk for propriety, risked slapping him on the back. The half-naked woman at the pianoforte switched to the national anthem. The verses pursued him into an empty drawing room at the back of the house. Helmi deposited him into a cushioned chair.

"To be frank, I expected you much sooner," she said, balancing on the arm.

The house wasn't what he had imagined. For one thing, it wasn't much different from one of his father's apartments at the palace. The furniture was luxurious and expensive with tasteful brocade seats, silk pillows, and gold leaf trim. Landscape paintings and walls of books lined the blue-papered walls. Small, white porcelain sculptures from Ytlain graced strategic places on the shelves. A larger statue carved from marble occupied the corner. The nude subjects— two angels—were entwined in a nearly impossible embrace. Nels recognized the piece as a duplicate of a sculpture from his father's collection. Everything was immaculate, shining, and very much dirt-free.

She watched him take in the room and smiled. "I wasn't always a courtesan, you know," she said. "Now. What would you like?" She leaned forward and traced a light finger along the inside of his thigh that left a burning trail in its wake.

A moment passed before he remembered to breathe. *It's been far too long.* "Whiskey."

"Mika?"

Another large man appeared, dressed in a blue silk coat and breeches that matched the wallpaper. "Yes, Mistress?"

"Get the captain some whiskey. The best we have." She paused. "Bring the bottle."

Mika bowed and left.

"Anything else?" She moved closer until the silk-wrapped side of an ample breast brushed his cheek. Her left hand played with the ribbon that secured his queue. "What kind of company do you . . . fancy?"

Her perfume smelled of roses. He took a deep breath, searching for a suggestion of mint underneath. It instantly dredged up a vivid image of Ilta. He closed his eyes, welcoming the memory of her touch. *She's changed her mind. Am I to wait forever?*

All right. A blond. No. Anything but that. "Brunette."

"Done," she said.

He felt her move away, and his cheek grew cool. Then fingers pressed a whiskey bottle into his hands—by the smell, the bottle was already uncorked. The room executed a slow spin. He hadn't noticed it before when his eyes were open. *Maybe I've had enough. I shouldn't drink any more.*

"Would you like a glass?" she asked.

A glass would've been better but he didn't have much faith in his coordination. He shook his head and then drank from the neck of the bottle. *Two swallows. I don't wish to insult.* Fine alcohol burned down his throat and up the back of his nose, leaving behind a sweet oak taste and a raw feeling of need. *Ilta smells of winter roses and mint.*

Don't think about that right now.

"Hmmm. I should think Ygret will be to your liking. You're definitely her type. She'll be along shortly."

Helmi's warm lips pressed against his cheek. The chair shifted as her weight was removed.

"Good night, dear Captain Hännenen. I trust you'll have a very entertaining evening."

Do I really want to do this? He took a long drink. *Yes. Ilta hasn't come to the house or written. Time to face the truth. She changed her mind. She doesn't want me. Can I blame her? Not after what I almost—*

A floorboard creaked. He sensed soft footfalls. When he opened his eyes again, he expected to see a scantily dressed brunette. Instead, his eyes met with a woman dressed in black. Scars crisscrossed her right cheek—otherwise, she was attractive and confident. The set of her shoulders combined with her black coat sent a warning shiver through Nels's body.

"Ygret?" he asked, already knowing the answer.

Giving him an expression of mild disappointment, she shook her head.

For a sobering moment, he wondered if his uncle had finally sent an assassin to take care of the family disgrace. The marks on her cheek meant she'd been caught once and was powerful enough to warrant a second chance via a wealthy patron. They also meant she'd be utterly ruthless. He reached for the hilt of his saber before remembering he'd left it behind. *Killed in a bawdy house. Ilta will love this. Why now?*

The latest reprimand? The guns? It didn't matter. His uncle wasn't the only one with a good reason to kill him. He decided he was too tired and drunk to care. "What do you want?"

The assassin shrugged. "Your sister wishes a word with you." Her voice was cultured, amused.

Nels set the bottle on the floor next to the chair. The room tilted when he stood up, but he caught himself. *How does Suvi know I'm here?* The answer occurred to him, and then he recognised the woman in the black coat. *She let me see her.* Tightening his jaw, Nels snatched the bottle from the floor. "Lead the way, then."

Suvi's korva shrugged. Nels followed her through the crowded front rooms and out of the bawdy house. On the street, five Royal Guardsmen stood alert next to a gold-trimmed coach.

Suvi charged through the gate. "Why didn't you come to dinner? Mother was disappointed."

"What are you doing here?" Nels asked.

She gave him a disapproving sniff. "You've been drinking."

"It's traditional before going to war."

She looked up at the mansion. "You've taken up with a courtesan?"

"That was the plan."

Suvi wrinkled her nose and whispered, "Why pay? Piritta would—"

"Who I choose to bed is none of your damned business!"

"Oh. I didn't mean to—"

"Of course you didn't." He took a deep breath and let it out slow. "Can we please have this discussion later? Preferably after the war? I've a pressing appointment to keep."

"Why are you angry?" Suvi asked, and then she lowered her voice. "You volunteered for this. I would've selected an administrative—"

"How long have you been spying on me?" He let his anger with Ilta bleed into the question.

Suvi bit her lip.

"That's what I thought." He executed a wobbly turn on his heel. The iron reinforcing his boots scraped the stone path with a sound that set his teeth on edge.

"Don't be upset. Not tonight," Suvi said. A hint of magic prickled in the air.

Unlike anyone else he knew, command magic didn't affect him in the slightest, no matter the strength of the wielder. It was the one useful magical trait that he possessed. *And Suvi knows it.* Fury curled his hands into fists. He stopped but didn't turn around. "What do you want?"

Suvi darted in front of him. "Mother asked me to collect you. She's frightened."

Nels snorted.

"I thought your fight was with Father, not Mother."

"She could've seen me yesterday. Tonight, I'm busy," he said. *She'll say anything to get what she wants.*

"The palace was under quarantine yesterday. It was only lifted today. Why are you being so stubborn?"

His jaw clenched. "Why haven't you gone?"

"Nels, please. Mother has been crying all day. Father has barricaded himself in his apartments. Things are bad at home. You've no idea. Mother needs to see you."

He lifted the bottle and swallowed once. He hoped the wetness in his eyes was due to the sting of the alcohol. "I don't care."

Suvi shoved him. He lost his balance, landing on his butt in the grass. The bottle fell with a dull clank and rolled. He listened to Helmi's fine whiskey pouring into the flowerbed. It took two tries to right the bottle.

Suvi stooped over him and hissed, "You damned idiot! Who do you think pays your debts when you go over your stipend? Who bought you that captaincy so you would have a better chance at surviving? It wasn't Father, and it wasn't me alone, I assure you." She straightened. "Go back into that bawdy house. I'm done."

"Wait, damn you." He struggled to get up from the grass. "I'll go."

There was a long silence.

"Good," Suvi said.

He picked up the bottle, checking its contents against the lamplight.

"Leave it," she said.

"Why should I?"

Suvi exited the gate without looking back. "It's bad enough you smell like an alehouse at dawn and look like you've been sleeping in a pig trough. It would be nice if you weren't unconscious, too."

His cheeks burned as he set the bottle on the step. When he climbed into the coach, his heart suddenly joined the whiskey in his stomach. "Hello, Piritta."

"Hello, Your Grace," Piritta said. She lowered long, dark lashes around her tilted eyes, and her hand strayed to her hair. It was arranged in the same style as Suvi's—just as her dress was the same. As usual, he found it profoundly disturbing.

Sitting opposite Piritta, Suvi slammed her fan on the seat and folded her arms across her chest. She dared him to move it with a glare. Piritta scooted closer to the window and bunched her skirts.

"It would appear that this is the only seat free," Nels said to Piritta. "May I?"

The footman pushed the coach door, and it snapped shut with a certain finality.

Piritta gave Suvi a knowing grin. "Please."

The coach jolted forward, and Nels fell onto the padded bench. He put out a hand to catch himself and found the coach seat unusually warm and yielding. Piritta looked down at the front of her stays. Their eyes met, and she raised an eyebrow.

"Terribly sorry," he said, snatching his hand back as if he'd been scorched.

Piritta's bowed mouth curled upward. "No need for apologies. It was an accident."

Suvi seemed to concentrate on something fascinating on the other side of the window. Only a twitch at the corner of her mouth gave away that she'd seen. Nels folded his arms across his chest and focused on sobering up. The closer they got to the palace, the more difficult it became to keep his eyes open. He now regretted the whiskey in addition to the six pints of ale. The coach bounced and slammed back down on the paving stones. He gripped the upholstery to keep from tumbling into the floor. Fingers brushed his thigh before trapping his knee.

"Are you all right?" Piritta asked.

Nels broke free of Piritta's touch before she could interpret it as encouragement. *She's a souja, and Suvi's souja at that. Allow her close enough, and Suvi will know everything. Suvi will tell Mother. And then I'll never have an instant of privacy again.*

Assuming I had any to begin with.

The coach swayed to a stop in front of the palace, and the footman opened the door. Suvi exited the coach first.

"We'll get you cleaned up. Come on." She turned to Piritta. "Have the kitchen bring coffee to my rooms. And a basin of warm water."

"No need." Concentrating on every step, he stormed past Suvi and headed for his mother's apartments. The cleats on his boots carved angry lines on the entry's marble tiles.

An army of servants scurried about their business. Each stopped with their gaze fixed to the floor the moment he drew near, resuming their duties once he was past. His sister continued fighting with him as if they were alone. The absurdity of it struck him at once. He'd already forgotten what it was like having so many "invisible" people watching and listening. No doubt they were getting an eyeful. He could imagine the stories. *The family disgrace showed up, filthy and stinking of drink.* He clamped down on his emotions with renewed force.

Suvi's footsteps pattered behind him, enraging him all the more.

"How long have you been spying on me?" he asked in a harsh whisper.

She appeared at his elbow. "Why is it important?"

Throwing open the door to the main passage, he went up the steps. He used his anger to keep his legs steady. "That's the sort of thing I expect from Uncle, not you. How can you ask?"

Missing a step, he stumbled and grabbed the banister. He risked a glance over his shoulder. A hurt expression was pinned on Suvi's face.

"I ordered Jami to keep you safe," she said. "Who do you think arranges to get you home when you pass out in the gutter? How do you think you avoided being murdered in the street or robbed since you joined the army? Did you think it was luck?"

He stumbled up the remaining stairs. "Did it ever occur to you that I might have been better off?"

"Don't!"

"Oh, you're right. I have been away too long. I've forgotten what I am." Upon reaching the top of the stairs, he turned. She was one step behind. He leaned in until his nose almost touched hers and whispered, "You only need me because you need someone to use.

Just like Father. Just like Uncle." He reached his mother's apartments and stopped at the door.

"Please." The pain in Suvi's voice wrenched at his anger. "I don't want to part like this. Not now."

He passed a hand through his hair and saw the hand was shaking. It was hard to speak over the emotions trapped in his aching throat. "The truth is, it doesn't matter. No matter how much I wish it did."

"What do you mean?"

"You're all I have left," he whispered loud enough for her to hear.

Her gasp was loud enough to echo down the hallway.

He closed his burning eyes tight, feeling the hurt he'd inflicted. *Damn it*, he thought. *Why are you doing this?*

"Nels—"

"I'm sorry," Nels said.

Grabbing him in a fierce hug, she spoke Acrasian into his jacket. "Apology accepted, you donkey."

He hugged her back. "I believe the word you were looking for is 'ass.'"

"How about 'stupid horse butt'? Maybe 'self-absorbed male chicken'? Or—"

"That will suffice."

"Come back home," she said. "Promise?"

"Promise."

A pox-scarred Royal Guardsman allowed them into the queen's receiving room. Fire popped in the hearth. Nels heard the delicate sound of porcelain chiming against porcelain. Two servants exited through a hidden door to the left. Everything was as he had last seen it years before, except somehow smaller. The matching velvet settees were arranged near the fireplace. The shelves of books were on either side of the window. The same paintings hung on the walls.

His mother's lavender perfume mixed with that of coffee, cinnamon, ginger, cloves, and other spices he couldn't name. It sent him back to his childhood at once.

"Spice cake," he said.

Suvi nodded, a hesitant smile on her lips.

"Nels? Is that you?" His mother's voice was frail.

The sight of her extinguished the last of his already-cooling rage. There were worry lines in her face he didn't remember seeing before. She paused in the entry to her bedchamber dressed in a green Ytlainen silk gown. She clutched a hairbrush in her right hand, and her platinum blond hair hung in loose curls around her hips. Her eyes were red and puffy. The hairbrush clattered to the floor. She covered the distance between them in an instant and gathered him in a desperate hug.

"I didn't think you'd come," she said. "I hoped, but I didn't think it."

"You could've issued an order." He choked out the words.

She touched his face. "It wouldn't have been the same."

A door thumped shut. Suvi was gone.

He hadn't meant to say anything, but his mouth moved. The apology was so quiet he hardly heard it. "I'm sorry."

After a while, she sniffed. "Are you hungry?"

His stomach answered for him.

Smiling, she wiped the wetness from her face and went to the small table where the tea things were arranged. "Sit."

He surprised himself by getting to the settee without staggering. While his mother poured tea, he stared at the fire and tried to sort out the confusion of emotions whirling in his brain. Nothing had resolved itself by the time his mother sat next to him with a plate and a hot teacup. Balancing the cup on the saucer, he slid it onto the small table to his left without upending the plate in his lap.

"So," his mother said, "I'm not sure what a mother is supposed to say the night before her son goes off to die."

"Mother, please."

She smoothed her hand over the arm of the settee. "Promise me you'll be careful."

"I promise."

"I mean it. No more irresponsible risks. No more . . ." She waved a hand at him. "Excess. At least, not unless you know it's safe. You know the histories. The Acrasians hate us."

"We have no love for them, either."

"They destroyed Marren and enslaved thousands of kainen."

"That was fifty years ago. A half century."

"They made slaves of the people. They still do."

"The fate of Acrasians among our kind hasn't been much better. Worse, if you ask me. At least slaves still have their minds."

"They'll do the same to us. Those they don't kill."

"I'll be fine, Mother."

"The border barons haven't had an easy time of it, you know. I understand that if your father hadn't committed to this war when he did, they would've lost the fight."

We will lose anyway. The Acrasians haven't had to be terribly clever in defeating us. A large part of our forces were lost in frivolous skirmishes, he thought. As if that weren't enough, variola had killed more reinforcements than an entire host of incompetent officers. That had been the latest reason Nels had incurred Pesola's wrath. Nels hadn't delayed. He'd had his company poxproofed. With that, his thoughts briefly jumped to Ilta and then shied away.

He knew he should tell his mother that she was right to worry, but he couldn't look her in the face and say the words. That wasn't how these things were done. "It'll be over before you know it."

"That's what I'm afraid of."

The dying reassured the living. Those were the rules, no matter how hard it was—no matter how terrified the dying might be. Dying is something one did alone, and the only comfort was in reassuring the living. "Who would want to kill me, Mother? I'm far too charming."

"Promise me."

Nels sighed, impatient with himself and his doubts. "I'll be careful. I swear."

Her mouth formed a straight line when she pressed her lips together. The worry line etched between her pale brows didn't ease. "Good."

An uncomfortable web of anxiety stretched between them in the silence. He wasn't hungry anymore. Not knowing what else to do, he picked up the fork and took a bite of cake anyway. The taste of cinnamon, cloves, and ginger brought back his appetite with a vengeance.

"Is it good?" she asked.

"I'd forgotten how good." He took another bite and focused on the spongy sweetness on his tongue.

"I remember when you both turned three. You refused to eat anything but cake. It took your nurse two days to dissuade you."

Relieved in the change of subject, Nels took another sip of tea before demolishing the slice of cake.

"What a temper you had. Your sister never gave us that kind of trouble. Always did as she was told."

He made a sound in the back of this throat.

"What?" she asked.

"She isn't perfect, you know. She was only better at getting away with things than I was. Still is."

His mother gave him a distant smile that said he hadn't said anything she didn't already know. He finished the last of the cake and set the plate next to the empty teacup.

"Suvi was free to be what she wanted from the beginning. She didn't have to fight for every inch of self-determination," she said. "I wish you'd had that chance earlier. At least, you have it now. For as long as it lasts."

He prepared himself for her usual speech. She would tell him he was wasting himself. She would say he should do something constructive with his time. She would admonish him for spending his remaining days on gambling and drink. Of course, he hadn't been drunk in months—provided one didn't count his current state. He'd stopped gambling to excess since his promotion, largely due to Major Lindström's influence. His mother damned well knew these things already if Suvi's spies were effective. Remembering the look of Suvi's korva, Nels was certain "effective" was a more-than-fitting term. He prepared himself for yet another tongue-lashing, but his mother didn't launch into her familiar speech. She sat mute and stared at her hands instead. The silence grew ever more uncomfortable.

She finally spoke. "There's something I must show you. Something I want to give you before you leave."

Taking his hand, she led him to a panel on the right side of the fireplace. She pressed the edge of the mantel and the panel slid open. It revealed a tiny room he hadn't seen before. A latticework screen blocked most of the space from view, and votive candles filled the area with warm light. It smelled of musky incense. When she moved the screen, it became clear the place was a private prayer chapel. However, the paintings above the altar shelf didn't portray patron deities. The first was clearly a portrait of himself and Suvi when they were children. Suvi sat clutching a black kitten while he stood in front of one of their father's wolfhounds. It was strange seeing himself in the six-year-old with the pug nose and a juvenile chin set at an arrogant angle. He vaguely remembered sitting for the painting—the tediousness of being still. It was hard to reconcile the boy he was then with the man he was now.

The second painting was of a man wearing an Ytlainen cavalry uniform of green, red, and gold. He held an officer's hat under his arm, and his dark brown hair curled around his shoulders in a style that was no longer fashionable. The face was young and beardless.

"Captain Karpanen," Nels said with a touch of surprise. It wasn't until he compared the faces in the first with the second that he suspected his mother's intent. His knees felt weak.

She traced a tender finger down the golden edge of the frame. "I let no one in here but my maid, and when I die, all this will be burned. Well, this portrait and all that goes with it, in any case." She turned, reaching for the top drawer of the cherrywood tall chest set against the wall under the altar shelf.

In spite of the shock of her discussing her own death, he vomited up a question. "Was Captain Karpanen our father?" *There,* he thought. *It's out. I've asked.* He couldn't move. Karpanen's eyes pinned him in place.

She paused but didn't look up from her search. "As much as I'd like to give you an answer," she said, "I've never answered that question and never will."

"Why?"

She turned. One hand rested on the edge of the drawer. "When I bound with your father, we agreed to follow Ytlainen tradition. His house would carry my name and our binding would be permanent and closed to other relationships. I kept that agreement from the day of the ceremony until he broke it himself five years ago." She returned to sorting through the things in the drawer, didn't find what she wanted, and moved to the drawer below it.

His heart stumbled. "Then he wasn't our father."

"Ari and I met when I bought my first horse. I was fifteen. He was sixteen and already intent on a military career. Things are different in Ytlain. Soldiers aren't deemed shameful or lowly. He was so handsome and a nobleman's son. We used to ride together, you know. I enjoyed racing and fencing. He'd follow as best he could. I was reckless then. As wild as the wind and more beautiful than the moon, he'd say. Mother didn't like him. And when my mother discovered us and forbade me to see him, we met in secret." She looked up at the painting and gave it a sad smile. "I loved him more than I've ever loved anyone. But I had to do what was best for Ytlain. I chose Eledore. And Ari escorted me to Jalokivi and gave me to another man. It broke his heart."

"I don't want to know this."

"But you asked, didn't you?" She straightened. "Didn't it ever occur to you why you were chosen as heir before Suvi, when my name, my line, can only survive through her? Didn't you wonder why we didn't plan on officially presenting you as heir until after your sixteenth birthday?" Her voice was calm, quiet.

"Of course I did. I knew what it meant," he said, feeling his jaw tighten. "The entire court knew."

"Rumor isn't fact," she said. "And as long as I don't declare otherwise—no matter who asks—that is how it will remain. To do otherwise would leave Eledore to Sakari. I've made too many mistakes. He's won his fight with me. Still, I won't grant him that."

Nels staggered backward until he felt the edge of a chair against the back of his knees. He sat with a thump. The room spun; he couldn't breathe. The spice cake and coffee weren't resting quietly.

Her gaze traveled to the painting again. "At least now there's no chance Suvi will marry him. Sakari will have to find another means of securing the throne." She went back to her search. "Ah, there it is," she said, bringing out a delicate silver chain. "As I said before, Ytlain does not share in Eledore's contempt of the military. I have done what I can to urge reform for your sake, but the old families are slow to change. They fear the army will grow and the nobility will dwindle. They fear the army's power and the potential of a commoner rising in the ranks. All sound reasons, I suppose. However, overreaction only causes more harm. It's balance that's needed—a balance in power."

He'd heard those words many times, growing up. His father insisted that Ytlain's monarchy was hampered by a constitution. His mother insisted it was for the betterment of all. Power without limit was easily abused and a danger—no matter the individual or group who wielded it. Her opinions hadn't made much sense until now.

He swallowed the lump rising in this throat.

"Ari wanted to present this to you when you turned twelve, according to Ytlainen custom, but I wouldn't let him," she said. "I was too afraid of what might be read into the act. It's too late. And it isn't my place. But it's what he wanted. I've held it from you too long."

She went to him, leaving the drawer open. He could see its contents, clusters of letters bound with silk ribbons, old clothes, and books. He recognized the dagger lying across the folded clothes. Captain Karpanen had once used it to cut a saddle strap that Nels's spur had tangled on when Nels was ten.

"Does Suvi know?" His throat hurt and voice was hoarse.

His mother didn't look him in the face. "I showed her the portrait this morning."

Stooping, she fiddled with the clasp. A flat silver disk hung off of the chain, and it swung three times before she dropped the chain over his head. She lifted his queue, and cool silver slid around his neck. He touched the disk with a finger, feeling the raised image of a running horse on its surface.

"Wear it close to your skin. And try not to let anyone see it," she said. "She's Hasta, the Ytlainen Horse Goddess. The cavalry honor her above all others. She's yours now. May she watch over you, guide you, and keep you safe."

⧤ ILTA ⧥

ONE

Every inch of Ilta's skin felt woven with threads of shrieking agony. Days were lost in a fog of pain and fever. Vivid nightmares of what was to come—or what might not—laced her sleep with terror. Gran was at her side whenever Ilta surfaced. The knowledge that she was being watched over in her own room and not the Commons Hospital was a comfort. However, she didn't understand why. The journey to the house on Angel's Thumb from the palace was long, too long to take with a sick patient. That knowledge and the worry creasing Gran's brow made Ilta anxious when her mind was clear enough for such things. However, the raw pain in her mouth and throat prevented questions. So, Ilta waited and tried not to think— not that thinking came easy, or sleep. Everything was difficult due to the constant agony. She felt trapped in a half state, never quite asleep and not quite awake. Phantoms haunted her room. Lost, she was unable to discern whether they were real people, dreams, or visions. She hated feeling so disoriented. It reminded her too much of her early childhood, the part she remembered. Her pocket watch was gone. There was no clock on the fireplace mantel. There was nothing with which to anchor herself. So it was that she drifted from one image to the next without context and without a center. She became a creature without self-awareness, language, or restraint. When someone or something hurt her, she struck out even if it only brought more pain. Once, an angry Royal Guardsman shouted a series of questions at her. He grew more and more upset when she couldn't make sense of his words. When she tried to shove him, he roared until Gran ordered him away.

Slowly the pain began to ebb until she came back to herself, and at last the day arrived when she could bear the thought of sitting up. She was alone. Therefore, the process seemed to take forever. Sitting also proved tiring. Unwilling to return to her dreams, she fought the urge to go back to sleep. Was it morning or afternoon? The soft, mournful cries of doves brought her attention to the open window. Sunlight painted the white curtains in warm yellows. A gentle breeze drifted into the room, bringing with it a mixture of pleasant scents from the garden—rosemary, lavender, cherry blossoms, laurel, and roses. Normally, her room was a comfort. She'd counted each and every pineapple on the pink wallpaper and imagined all the possible shapes in the old water stains on the ceiling. None of those things brought solace like they used to. Outside, everything was changing. Inside, she wasn't that little girl who required the safety of solitude. And now she'd lost time she couldn't afford. If only everything would slow down long enough for her to catch up.

Why does everything have to be so confusing?

She thought of Nels. *He's gone now. It's too late. He's off to war, and I didn't get to say good-bye.* Tears gathered force behind her eyes. *Please let him stay safe.* Her throat closed and pain choked her. Wiping away the tears, she dried her fingers on her patched coverlet. That was when she noticed the state of her arms. Three healing variola vesicles were scattered across her left arm and five on the other. Carefully, she pulled back the bedclothes to check her legs and found a few there as well. Each looked like it was healing. That was a good sign. Only one of the sores on her left leg looked particularly bad. At that point, she paused. Her heart jumped, and she bit her lip. She wasn't vain, but she also knew variola tended to leave terrible scars. Taking a deep breath, she gently touched the scabs on her face.

A loud knock gave her a start.

"Ilta? May I come in?"

It took a moment to force the words past her tortured throat. Her voice was hoarse and unfamiliar, and her tongue felt strange in her mouth. "Yes, Gran. Of course. Please." *Why is she still here? Shouldn't she be with her patients? Was I worse off than I thought I'd be? How much healing magic did Gran have to use to keep me stable?*

The key clattered in the lock and then the door swung open. Gran stepped into the bedroom, balancing a tray. "Sitting up, I see. Are you feeling better?"

Why was the door locked? Was I sleepwalking again? She hadn't done that in years. "Much." Once again, Ilta couldn't shake the feeling that something was very wrong.

"Are you hungry?" Gran's question was carefully neutral.

The smell of fresh biscuits and tea made Ilta's mouth water. "Starving."

Gran set the tray down in Ilta's lap with a definitive clink of china and then settled into a chair next to the bed. Ilta tore off a small piece of warm biscuit, soaked it in tea, and then popped it into her mouth rather than biting into it. Her mouth and throat were still tender. Still, she managed a few bites. The tea tasted mildly of cinnamon and cardamom. Both were childhood favorites but stung a bit. Abruptly, the urge to weep hit her like a slap.

Visions she'd had outside the World's Pillar surfaced—images of Gran dying, of a terrible war, of the Old Ones walking free in the night and consuming everything and everyone they came across, of the city of Jalokivi burning. Lastly, there was the vision of Nels in trouble and her being unable to do anything to help. That made her chest ache worst of all. *Don't think about that right now.* Her happiness and confidence in the future had fallen apart so fast. For the first time in her life, she honestly wished she didn't know what was ahead. It was so hard not to tell anyone, so hard not to struggle against the inevitable.

There are some fates that one shouldn't fight. Ilta looked to Gran, sitting next to the bed with her mouth set in a hard line. *Which fates are set? How does one know the difference?* Ilta shook off the bad feeling again and summoned up a cheerfulness she didn't feel. "Now that I'm recovering, you can go back to the Commons Hospital. I'll be fine by myself. And I can join you in a couple of days."

Gran didn't move or speak.

"You're awfully quiet," Ilta said. "What's wrong?"

"We need to talk."

Ilta nodded. "I wanted to ask you about a couple of patients—"

"Finish your tea first."

There came another knock. The voice on the other side of the door was hard and male. Before Ilta could ask who was visiting, Gran got up and answered it.

"What is it, Sergeant Hirvi?"

"A message from the palace, Madam Silmaillia," the sergeant said. "The king shows no symptoms. Neither does the crown princess at this time. However, three others have fallen ill within the palace. Lieutenant Norgen died last night. That's thirty-one total. They're unsure of the answer to your other questions. Communication is . . . difficult."

"I see," Gran said. "I'll be out in a moment. I have a number of recommendations to make. It may help, if His Highness's new healer wouldn't mind."

The king has a new healer? Once again, Ilta checked the room for her pocket watch.

"Yes, Madam Silmaillia. I'll prepare a bird."

When Gran turned around, Ilta glimpsed fear on her features before she composed herself.

"Where is my pocket watch?" Ilta asked.

Gran got up and retrieved it from one of the drawers in the writing desk. "I had to take it from you or you would've smashed it."

"Oh," Ilta said. "Well, anyway, you should go back to the palace. I insist. The king needs you more than I do."

"I can't and neither can you. In fact, you're not to leave this house or its grounds."

"What? Why?"

"You're under arrest."

"Me? Why?"

A sour frown stole across Gran's mouth. She poured fresh tea into a second cup and sipped. "You risked the king's life. Not only his but the crown princess's as well."

Ilta swallowed. "Oh." *I suppose I did.* The weight of what she'd done settled in between her shoulder blades.

"I taught you better than to do a fool thing like that," Gran said. "What were you thinking?"

I was thinking I could save you, Ilta thought. "I don't understand what happened." *Oh, Mother, what if Gran's death is one of those fates that one shouldn't fight?* Her vision blurred. The pain in her throat joined the pain in her heart. She blinked back more tears, but they overwhelmed her resistance. "I shouldn't have been contagious. Not according to the Acrasian medical logs Nels was able to get for me. It'd only been a week since the inoculation. I wasn't even supposed to get ill." She sniffed. "Not yet."

Gran produced a handkerchief and handed it to her. "Tell me what happened. Tell me why you did this to yourself. Now."

"I wanted to prove beyond a doubt that pox-proofing is effective." Ilta gently daubed her cheeks and then carefully blew her nose. Then she told Gran everything about that day in the hospital herb garden.

"Anja should've stopped you."

"I don't understand," Ilta said. "Nels was right. It works."

"You gambled with other people's lives—not just your own!"

"I didn't!" Ilta shook her head. "Nels says the Acrasians—"

"You aren't human. None of us are."

"There's not that much difference between kainen and humans. You've said so yourself!"

"That may be. But there *is* one key difference. Humans don't have magic. We do. Magic, even healing magic, takes a funny turn sometimes. You know that," Gran said. "The more power you have, the more unpredictable it can be."

"I didn't use magic on myself or the—the inoculation. It should've been fine."

"Have some sense," Gran said. "You've not been seriously ill before now. There was a reason for that. And now—" She looked away, and then Ilta understood her grandmother was terrified. "You've forced a disease past your magical defenses. You broke the healer's oath. You did yourself harm. There's no telling what that has done."

"Oh." *The more power*, Ilta thought. She was missing something— something to do with Nels, but it was too hard to think, particularly when it came to Nels.

"Arrogant child! You could've died!" Gran stood up and walked across the room.

"I didn't."

"You're right. *You* didn't. But others have. This isn't over. Not yet."

"Isn't it?"

Her grandmother stared at the wall and didn't say anything.

"Gran?"

Ilta watched Gran's shoulders relax and her head drop a little. "I hope I'm wrong, but the way the sickness took you. The way the rash didn't show until very late. The way you're healing so fast—"

"That's what pox-proofing does. By giving myself a lighter strain of the disease, I build up an immunity. Then we can use material from my healing pustules and treat others. My powers will make it even more effective. That's how it works." Again, there was that long silence. Ilta felt suddenly hollow. Her stomach lurched as if inside an abrupt vacuum. "Isn't it?"

Gran muttered something and then whirled. Ilta couldn't make out the words but once again glimpsed an expression of pure terror on Gran's face before it vanished. "Nothing is certain. We'll wait and see. We'll . . . wait and see."

"If I'm under arrest, fine. I can't leave. But shouldn't you be at the hospital?"

"I told you I can't go into the city. Not now."

"I don't understand."

"We're under quarantine, you and I, and the guards sent to watch over us. They were already exposed at the palace."

It was Ilta's turn to frown. "I don't understand."

"Since you became ill, more than half the people we came in contact with are dead."

"They contracted variola?"

"They contracted something, all right. But I don't believe it was the same variola," Gran said. "Not like we've seen it before, in any case. The rash didn't show. If it shows, it waits until the end."

Ilta's mouth dropped open. "Just like—like me?"

"Like you," Gran said. "This variety of it spread so fast that we're not sure that everyone who'd been exposed has been contained. We can't spread word or send a warning. People are frightened enough as it is. We have to sit this out."

The more power you have, the more unpredictable the result. Oh, Mother. Swallowing the last of her tea, Ilta hid her face. *I wish I hadn't gone to Keeper Mountain. I wish I'd told Gran I was sick.*

"We need to list everyone you came into contact with from the moment you infected yourself with variola," Gran said. She went to the writing desk, selected a quill from those stored in a cup, and began preparing it with the penknife Ilta kept there.

"There's Anja, of course. And you," Ilta said, and then tensed up. "Is Anja all right?"

"She is. And still working in spite of everything. Although I don't know for how long."

"Oh. That's good, I suppose." Ilta bit her lip. "There was everyone at the Commons Hospital, of course."

Gran began writing, stopped, and turned around. She looked thoughtful. "What patients did you have direct contact with?"

"Those in the critical ward, for the most part," Ilta said. "The others are often too frightened to enter the room."

"The critical ward patients died."

Cheeks heating, Ilta began to feel a queasiness that had nothing to do with illness. "No one really expected them to recover. I hoped but . . ." She shrugged.

"That is true," Gran said, and returned her attention to the list. "Of course. There is one fatality that puzzles me."

"Yes?"

"A Lieutenant Kaisa Harkola," Gran said. "Did you know her?"

Ilta struggled to remember. "The name is familiar, but I cannot think why."

"She served in Captain Hännenen's company."

Ilta's heart stumbled and a chill entered her chest. She pulled the quilt closer. "Nels's company?"

"I'm afraid so. The curious thing is, she had already undergone the Acrasian inoculation process."

"How is that possible? I didn't do it."

"Captain Hännenen did," Gran said. "I understand he had himself and his whole company inoculated. Rather successfully, from what I understand. Not a single fatality. That's what puzzles me."

Why didn't he tell me? "Then she should've been immune. What happened?"

"I don't know. That's why I asked you if you knew her."

Lieutenant Kaisa Harkola, Ilta thought, and then it occurred to her where she'd heard the name before. "I met her the night of the riot. The bakery and the tailor shop near the hospital burned to the ground. Remember?"

Gran nodded.

"In order to stop the rioters from entering the hospital building, Nels used command magic," Ilta said.

"But he doesn't have that talent."

"I know. And I wouldn't have believed it, except I was there. I saw—" Ilta swallowed. "He was holding my hand when it happened. It didn't feel like any normal use of magic. I was so tired after. It was as though he'd taken energy from me and then combined it with the lieutenant's command magic. When he spoke, the force of it dominated an entire group of panicked rioters. I meant to ask you about that. Have you ever heard of such a thing?"

"I haven't." Gran frowned. "Was he touching the lieutenant as well?"

"I don't know. Wait. Yes. I think so. I remember feeling her presence. Just not as strongly as Nels's. Why?"

"And the lieutenant died the morning after the riot. Along with every patient in that critical ward. You were resting." Gran abruptly got up and went to the door. She muttered something that Ilta could've sworn sounded like *Twins are an ill omen.*

"Gran? What is it?"

"Stay in bed. Try to sleep. I'll be back as soon as I know something."

TWO

With her brain still healing from the extended bout of fever, it was difficult for Ilta to concentrate on complicated tasks. So, she left the distilling of the latest harvest of medicinal flowers to Gran. Neither of them had uttered their real concerns, because it edged too closely on fears for which there were no easy solutions. In any case, Ilta's energy flagged too easily, and her skin remained sensitive. At least the sores had healed, and the scabs were gone. She was relieved to see that the disease didn't seem to have left many scars, not so far, and none on her face other than the one on her forehead. Although it was near the hairline and easily hidden, it was particularly bad. So, she continued applying the salve Gran gave her and hoped for the best.

In an attempt to distract herself from thinking about all the things making her miserable, she made tea, went for short walks in the garden, and read. Sergeant Hirvi, the brooding guardsman with the black hair and the permanent scowl, followed her wherever she went. Ilta understood why, but it didn't make her comfortable.

That's the point, isn't it? she thought. *Being uncomfortable?* Gran had explained how fortunate she was that the king hadn't had her executed. Apparently, Gran had used all her influence to prevent it. That had been a sobering thought.

Ilta poured boiling water over the latest scoop of tea leaves and replaced the kettle on its hook. Staring at the steeping tea, she allowed herself a little self-pity. *What's the point in knowing the future if you can't stop things like this from happening?* Walking toward the stairs with the fresh teapot, she stopped when Sergeant Hirvi stood in her path.

"The Silmaillia instructed me to give these to you," he said, handing her a bundle of letters tied together with a string. He was looking a little flushed, and he was sweating.

He's feverish. Ilta blinked when she recognized the handwriting on the outsides of the letters and then spotted the broken seals. "Why have these been opened?"

"I thought you understood that you were under arrest," Sergeant Hirvi said.

"But these are deeply personal—"

"When you reply, you will first give your letters to me. Unsealed. I'll read them before they're forwarded," he said, and then turned away.

Ilta thought about protesting but decided against it. "Sergeant?" She hated having to ask. Her face burned. "Has—has Gran read them too?"

She wasn't sure, but she thought his set expression might have softened ever so slightly. "That isn't an aspect of your confinement."

Another wave of guilt nearly choked her. Instead, she nodded and then took Nels's letters up to her room along with her tea. Once there, she perched the hot teapot on the table. She wanted to cry, but she'd already shed so many tears that she wasn't sure she had any left. She tried to think of reasons not to read the letters. To do so would only make the whole situation more awful, she knew. She certainly couldn't answer him. Could she? What could she say?

Dear Nels,

I'm sorry. I've been sick with variola. If I see you while I'm contagious, you'll die. It won't matter if you've been inoculated or not. I don't know when it'll be safe to see you—if it ever will. I know you don't want to hear this, but I'm meant to stay here. Without you. We can't be together. Your power and my magic—it created something horrible, something that will kill everyone it contacts. At least, that's what Gran and I suspect. We don't know for certain, but I won't take the risk.

I made a terrible mistake. And this is the price. Please, go on with your life without me. I'm not the one for you.

I'm not the one for anyone.

But she knew what he'd say. He'd do anything to convince her of the reasons why they should fight against their fates, and she'd had enough of fighting fate. She didn't know if she'd ever have the courage to take such a chance again.

She rested a hand on top of the bundle. She didn't have to count the letters. There was one for every day since she'd left him sleeping in front of the hearth that night. The handwriting on the outside of the last letter was tight and angry.

Her vision blurred and her chest ached. She flipped over the bundle so she didn't have to see his frustration and longing—his self-blame.

Poor Nels. We both made mistakes that night. She now understood aspects of the situation that he didn't. It made her sad that she probably wouldn't ever get the chance to explain. She hadn't told him that night, because she'd already been too frightened. Oh, she had been lost in him, that much was the truth, and he had pushed her a little, and that had terrified her too. However, the situation was . . . complicated. She had wanted him so very much.

Only she hadn't known what to do and had been too embarrassed to ask. So, she did something she shouldn't have. She peeked inside his thoughts while his guard was down. If she were honest with herself, she'd admit that she'd done far more than peek. She'd violated the privacy of his mind. She'd pushed past his defenses. *And if Gran knew what I've done, she'd be livid.*

What is the matter with me? How did everything become such a mess so fast?

Nels thought he was the only one in love and that she'd only recently come to return his feelings, but he was wrong. She'd loved him from the moment she'd first seen him—in a vision a full week before she'd met him in the woods. She'd been fourteen, and for the first time in her life, she hadn't told Gran. Ilta had been afraid that Gran would keep him from her. Gran had kept her from everyone else, after all. Ilta understood the need. Sometimes it was hard enough to keep herself whole, even with Gran. However, Ilta *had* to meet him. That boy. *Nels.* She'd understood what she'd seen in his eyes, the fear and loss. He thought he wasn't like anyone, but he was like her, a little broken and different. Only, he'd had no one to explain what was happening to him or make him understand why. She knew what that was like. *At least for a time, I did,* she thought. It made him vulnerable, and that made her love him all the more.

Again, she smoothed the letters as if soothing him. The paper crinkled. Rough twine scratched her fingertips. She had a sudden urge to hear his voice, to hold something of him tight. Her fingers did the rest. The twine knot came undone and then she'd freed the first letter. With the seal already broken, it fell open, and his words were laid bare. *Words written with those hands.*

She could almost feel his touch—strong and gentle at the same time. His sense of wonder as he explored her skin. It'd been so intense. So wonderful. *So terrifying, too.* She wished he hadn't stopped her. She really had wanted to rip at his clothes. She'd wanted to see him. For an instant, what he wanted hadn't mattered. The selfishness of the thought shamed her.

She remembered the little scars on his knuckles and wrists and the bigger scars on his chest and arms. Each documented events in his life that she couldn't know anything about. She'd sensed he kept them locked away, buried. Not that it would do him any good if she chose to force herself upon him, but it would do more than hurt him. She simply couldn't do that.

Well, not ever again, anyway.

She couldn't have told him without making him laugh, but he was beautiful with his moon-pale hair falling down past his elbows. She was shocked to see that it was almost as long as her own. It was ridiculous, but she wanted nothing more than to brush it for him and listen to him purr. At least, that was how she'd imagined he'd react. She remembered the touch of his skin, the way he'd smelled—dried river water, leather, blood, and sweat. On anyone else, they'd have been ordinary scents, but on him—

She shivered as a flash of her fingertips digging deep inside the front of his trousers burned in her memory. She closed her eyes and recalled the feel of him in her hand and bit her lip.

He stopped himself from hurting me.

Suddenly, she understood how much she could've trusted him. *Far more than he could've trusted me,* she thought, and swallowed yet another bitter lump of guilt. That admission made the loss so much worse.

Why does everything have to be so—so . . . complicated?

She wiped her face dry and started to read.

My Dearest Ilta,
     It's morning, and you've gone. I know you had to go, but

I wish you hadn't. Although it's been only a few hours, it already seems like days. For the first time in years, I'm happy. With you, I could jump from the roof and fly, if I had to. That sounds stupid, doesn't it? Love is too inadequate a word for what I feel.

I'm afraid Mrs. Nimonen will send for Mother. She's convinced I've gone mad. I admit to having some fun at her expense—

The lines blurred. Ilta dropped the letter, threw herself onto her pillow, and sobbed.

⇥ S U V I ⇤

ONE

The HREM *Otter* waited at anchor under the shadow of her larger sister ship, the HREM *Indomitable*. With her sails stowed, the *Otter*'s masts seemed to playfully prod the heavy clouds. Suvi smiled up at the corvette from the longboat, listening as her crew finished the last of the work involved in anchoring the ship. Her chest warmed with pride at how The *Otter* had gracefully skipped and danced through storms while the *Indomitable* had plodded through it all head on, following her sprightlier sister with the will of a bulldog. Suvi had to admit that power was an asset in a frigate. It was what they were made for, after all. But Suvi loved best the feel of a fast ship under her feet—the wind in her hair and ropes in her hands.

And now the smell of the sea. She could understand why Dylan preferred the ocean. It was so much better than the lakes. *Wilder. More free in a way.* Suvi imagined the *Otter* loved it too. She could see it in how the corvette seemed to rest happy on the water, eager for another run.

A warm, idle wind curled waves on the cliff-sheltered bay. The command given, sailors manning oars heaved the *Otter's* longboat from under the *Indomitable's* shadow one powerful, synchronized stroke at a time. Sitting in the bow, Suvi shaded her eyes from the afternoon sun with her right hand, swallowed vague fears, and squinted at the vacant beach. Black sand met clear blue water. A thick forest of tall pines and tangled undergrowth shielded the parts of the island that weren't solid rock, mountain, or empty beach. Imposing cliffs arched against the sky as if barricading the bay. A mountain ridge just beyond the forest blocked the remainder of the island from view. Together, mountains and cliffs created a horseshoe-shaped shield of stone against sea and prying eyes.

Treaty Island, Suvi thought. It wasn't what she'd expected.

More anxiety settled into her already-tense shoulder muscles. Her uncle had been in support of her venture. That alone had given Suvi pause. It was clear he wanted her out of the country for a time, and if it hadn't been for Ilta's warning, Suvi would've devised a reason to stay. However, Dylan's freedom rested in the balance as well as the future of Eledore's relationship with the Waterborne Nations. The full weight of responsibility painfully tightened the muscles in Suvi's shoulders and brought freezing jolts of terror in the middle of the night. Her mother had been unwilling to leave. She'd given the excuse that someone needed to keep an eye on Sakari, which was true enough. However, Suvi knew that her mother employed several korvas for that purpose. Something else was going on at home.

Focus on the problem at hand. Suvi sneaked a sideways glance at Dylan. He sat with a rigid back and a carefully blank expression. She'd done the same herself enough times to recognize it for what it was. Her stomach did yet another uneasy jitter. *What's going to happen to him?*

No doubt, there would be consequences for his return—

consequences he wouldn't like, but she had no idea what those might be, and that worried her. She didn't enjoy entering situations with so many unknowns, particularly when it involved people she cared about. The Sea Lord Kask's acceptance letter to her hadn't provided any clues. It had been cordial, if a bit formal. Since the Waterborne Nations hadn't been open to negotiations with an Ilmari in more than thirty years, some would say that this was an auspicious start. However, the bay was curiously lacking in Waterborne sailing vessels, and angry clouds gathered in the southeast like knotted fists. Something about the storm didn't seem right to Suvi. She double-checked the jagged reef they'd had to navigate through in order to reach the bay. *Is it a trap?* It'd be a simple thing for a weathermaster to smash both the *Otter* and the *Indomitable* on the rocks. Such things had been done before.

In the past.

"The weather will hold until we've gone," Dylan said, fingers trailing in the water as the men and women behind them rowed. His voice was matter-of-fact.

Suvi wished she could be so calm—or at least fake it as well as he was doing. "How do you know?"

A line appeared between Dylan's eyebrows. He closed his eyes and concentrated. "I feel it in the water."

Suvi looked to Jami and Piritta, who were perched with careful poise among the baggage. Suvi whispered to Dylan, "The storm isn't natural."

"I suspect it's only intended as a warning. Of course, if things go bad . . . well . . ." Dylan let the sentence trail off and shrugged.

"You should go back to the *Otter*," Suvi said. "There's no need for you to be among the landing party. I've Jami and Piritta for protection. I'll be safe enough."

Dylan arched an eyebrow at her. "Everything isn't about you,

you know." He leaned forward and whispered, "And it is you who shouldn't be on this boat. You should be careful."

"Are you?" She'd had a lengthy argument with the ship's captain. It seemed the king had given orders about the meeting with Kask taking place on the *Otter* rather than the island, but Suvi had felt it was important to make a show of trust.

"It's not the same thing." Staring at the beach for a long moment, Dylan waited and then said, "It would've come to a challenge sooner or later."

"You didn't say anything about a duel."

"You didn't ask."

"Correct me if I'm wrong, but I believe the words 'piss off, it's none of your damned business' featured heavily in the last discussion."

The bottom of the longboat struck the shore, making a loud scraping noise. A sailor leapt out of the prow and into the water, soaking her clothes up to her knees. She was joined by three others and the boat was dragged farther up a beach composed of tiny, smooth rocks. The sailors stopped tugging, allowing the longboat's passengers to debark. Jami and Suvi were among the first. Dylan and then Piritta, who had to be carried by one of the sailors, followed.

Suvi waded to shore on her own, wetting her tall boots in the warm water. Luckily, her moon time had passed. Skirts and confinement were no longer necessary. She preferred to wear breeches when aboard ship. Regardless, she wore stays underneath her uniform coat—she kept to some conventions while aboard ship, provided she wasn't having to scale ratlines. They weren't regulation, but she liked stays. So, she wore them much to her mother's relief. However, skirts and a pannier were another matter. The idea of having to swim in yards and yards of heavy, waterlogged wool should the worst happen terrified Suvi. There would be no quick means of shedding them, especially since the current dress styles often required Piritta to sew her into them. Still, the occasion required finery. So, Suvi wore her dress uniform, which consisted of a long, dark blue velvet officer's frock coat with cuffs, gold and silver braid, matching dark blue breeches, white stockings, and tall brown boots. She kept the weighty cocked hat with its ridiculous plume of white feathers tucked under her arm.

Breathing in the island's heady perfume of sea spray, pine, and baked sand, she cleared her nose of three weeks' worth of ship's filth. Then she strode up the beach. The crunch of her steps joined the chorus of tiny stones grinding against one another. With the exception of Jami, every party member's footsteps seemed to echo off the cliffs. The marine lieutenant gave his troops a series of silent signals, and two Eledorean marines remained behind to guard the longboat. Suvi stopped twenty feet from the tree line with Dylan on her right and Jami to her left. The korva's scarred face was set in its usual serene mask.

Still, there was no sign of anyone.

What if this was a mistake? Suvi thought. It felt good to have Dylan there. She hadn't seen him in so much finery before and didn't think it a good sign.

Dylan tugged down the formal Waterborne coat of teal-dyed raw silk with green cuffs. His green trousers and deep blue shirt were trimmed in gold thread. The wind tugged at his spirit knots, which were newly adorned with glittering gold and silver jeweled tokens. Even his boots were polished.

"We're at the chart coordinates given. I checked them myself. So, where's Sea Lord Kask?" she asked.

Dylan's left hand rested on the hilt of his cutlass as he scanned the trees. "That storm is his. He isn't far."

"Then where is he?"

"Don't get your feathers ruffled just yet, girl chick," Dylan whispered. "Like as not, this is a test. Eledore isn't known for patience and courtesy. And it *was* your uncle who raided and sank the *Walrus*, after all. Arrogant prick."

"He hasn't changed much," Suvi muttered, and then paused. "That reminds me of something."

"Aye?"

"Try to remember that I'm the marshal of a fleet." She kept her voice low. "Do not refer to me as 'girl chick' in front of anyone again."

Dylan gave out an amused grunt.

If a display of patience was what Sea Lord Kask required, Suvi would give it to him. Unlike her father or her uncle, she was willing to sacrifice a little pride. So, she stood her ground in the humidity while sweat traced an itchy path down her back. The weather was too warm and close for the layers of itching wool. *At least we're standing in the shade,* she thought. The calls of birds and other wildlife drifted back into hearing. Moisture rode the wind gusting off the bay. Midsummer was already a week away. She wondered if this island ever saw a real winter. She suspected not. Staring at the trees, she practiced keeping her mind blank.

A series of snapping twigs jerked her out of her thoughts, and she signaled to the marines. It wasn't long before a lone young woman dressed in blue and green stepped from under the trees. Her light brown hair hung in hip-length spirit knots sparsely threaded with silver charms. Her clothes, made of fine silks, were less formal, and her feet were bare. A large brown dog with short fur kept close. She stopped a few feet from where Suvi stood, made a graceful gesture with her left hand at the dog, and then said something that Suvi didn't understand. The dog, obviously well trained, sat.

Suvi thought it odd that Sea Lord Kask would send a lone

messenger that didn't speak Eledorean to meet an Eledorean diplomatic party. She decided it was some sort of a ploy. *Or a repayment for past insult.*

She turned to Dylan for a translation. "What did she say?"

"Her name is Mirna Spardancer of Kask, little sister of the *Silver Heart*, Second Frigate of the Fleet. She welcomes you to Treaty Island."

"Thank you," Suvi said, and opted to use her mother's name rather than her father's as she had in the previous communication. "I am Lake Marshal Hännenen of the Eledorean Royal Navy." She paused while Dylan completed the introductions. "I've come to meet with Sea Lord Kask. Where is he?" She watched Mirna's face while Dylan translated, hoping to discover some hint of what to expect.

Mirna answered but didn't acknowledge or even look at Dylan. She was no more than fifteen or sixteen, and Suvi got a sense that Mirna's aloofness had more to do with nerves than negativity.

She's not the only one presenting a false front, Suvi thought. *What is Kask up to?*

"She says he waits for us on the other side of the island," Dylan said.

"Why so far?" Suvi asked, blinking in confusion. "Did we drop anchor in the wrong place? Was there a change of plan?"

"We landed where we were meant to land," Dylan said. "We must follow Mirna. Our weapons are permitted as a courtesy. However, we are not to make threats or move to defend ourselves. To do so will result in the revocation of both hospitality and the guarantee of safe passage."

"Do you hear that, Lieutenant Ketola?" Suvi asked. "None of you is to even think about drawing a weapon."

"Yes, sir."

"The same goes for you, Jami," Suvi muttered under her breath. "Twice."

"If you insist," Jami said, not bothering to hide her disgust.

"The terms of the agreement are accepted," Suvi said to Mirna. "Please proceed."

Nodding, Mirna vanished into the brush from which she'd appeared. The dog followed. Jami went in after. Suvi looked to Dylan for reassurance and then did the same. Mirna led them to a path, forcing her way through the underbrush with a quiet grace that almost rivaled Jami's. Suvi stole a moment to dust leaves and twigs from her uniform coat. The surrounding trees were shorter, smaller cousins of the ones from her home. The land itself grew less rocky and became flatter and sandier. The sand itself lightened to a dirty gray and wasn't as black as the beach. Gray-green moss hung down from the branches of the stunted oaks and pines. Unfamiliar insects sang a buzzing chorus in the humidity. Unseen birds chirped. To her left, a tree with broad green leaves and twisted branches displayed large, sweet-smelling white blooms with yellow centers. Suvi again filled her lungs with the combination of fresh pine, ocean, sweet flowers, and warm earth. She waved away a cloud of tiny gnats that had drifted too close to her face.

Mirna stayed where she was until the last of the marines caught up. "You will come," she said in passable Eledorean. "Stay to the trail. Do not leave the path. The island is very dangerous for you."

Suvi nodded and attempted not to show amusement. *Her Eledorean is better than my Acrasian. It's most certainly better than my Ocealandic.* Although it might have been helpful to speak the language of the Waterborne Nations, there were at least five different recorded dialects, and Suvi didn't know which was preferred by Clan Kask. *Not that I couldn't have asked Dylan.*

As if to emphasize the danger, the dog barked at the woods to the right and a loud cat snarl erupted. The sounds frightened a flock of small bright green birds who took flight in a panic. Suvi suppressed a shiver. To their credit, the marines didn't flinch or draw their weapons. Mirna stared into the underbrush and frowned briefly before whispering something Suvi didn't catch. Then Mirna spoke to the dog, ordering it away from the trees.

"Stay to the path," Mirna said as if she needed to repeat herself. "The path is safe." With that, she continued.

Jami took a position between Suvi and the woods where the sound had come from. Suvi focused on the back of Mirna's blue jacket. It'd been embroidered with a beautiful wave pattern that had taken a great deal of skill to execute—more skill than Suvi had ever possessed. They walked for about a mile before the trail began a steady slope upward toward the mountain ridge. Eventually, the grade grew steep enough that Suvi found herself gasping for breath. She sweated through her linen shirt under the wool uniform coat but still refused to loosen the button on her collar. The trail narrowed, and a high black mountain wall emerged from the trees. Mirna finally stopped at a dark fissure barely wide enough to admit one person at a time. Cool air brushed against Suvi's face, providing an instant's pure bliss until she was reminded of the World's Pillar. A surge of fear chilled her to the marrow. For a moment, she wasn't sure she'd be able to enter. She searched the walls for telltale claw marks.

"Is something wrong?" Dylan whispered.

The black stone walls were smooth to the touch. Suvi swallowed and shook her head.

Mirna stopped, reached into a pocket, pulled out a bone whistle, and blew into it. Suvi was reminded of a boatswain's call. The piercing notes echoed down the tunnel, sounding ghostly. A low moan answered, and Suvi shuddered before she understood it had to be the wind. Pocketing the whistle, Mirna waited for a hidden signal before nodding and then entering. The dog bolted ahead with a happy yip. Suvi quickly lost sight of Mirna and Jami when both turned a sharp corner. The fear of embarrassing herself finally spurred Suvi forward. She hadn't gone far before the sweat plastering her shirt to her skin began to chill her. Running to catch up, she was glad of the narrow ribbon of blue sky, the freshening breeze, and the sounds of the singing insects. Every sound echoed. Soon, she spotted several notches carved high into the rock walls that were the source of the wind's low sough. Her shoulder muscles relaxed a bit when a few pebbles landed on the path at her feet. More stones skittered down the left wall, almost hitting Mirna, who continued seemingly unconcerned. Suvi looked up a little higher and thought she spied the toe of a boot protruding from the offending ledge. Glancing backward at Dylan, she saw him shrug in answer to her unspoken question.

The fissure widened, and Suvi was afforded a view of the valley on the other side. The first thing to catch her eye was the ship-crowded bay. Distant sounds of hammering and other evidence of ship repair work drifted up the mountain. She counted sixteen ships of varying sizes, most of which were schooners, but a few were barques. Only two of the vessels carried cannon, and both were heavily armed frigates. Combined, they possessed more than enough firepower to outgun the *Indomitable* and the *Otter*.

Why so many ships? She didn't have long to think about it before the others began the journey down to the buildings below.

Carpeted with thick green grass, this side of the mountain had fewer trees, and the underbrush was nonexistent. The trail grew more defined. Soon it was paved in black stone, eventually evolving into a series of steps leading down to three black stone buildings circled with a protective wall. The buildings stood in a cluster a thousand or so feet from the beach. Suvi recognized a mixture of architectural styles from across the known world. Familiar Eledorean slate roofs with high angles were decorated with stately spires from Tahmer. The bright-colored window glass glittered in shades she knew from Nels's descriptions of Acrasian designs. Kaledan's red-tinted gold graced a dragon-shaped lightning rod from Ytlain that topped the largest building.

They were met at the bottom of the steps by a large group of Waterborne dressed in varying shades of blue and green. Like the island's architecture, their faces and clothing styles seemed borrowed from different parts of the world. Several dogs of various breeds wandered among them, and Mirna's pet ran to meet the others. Standing close to the group of Waterborne, Suvi caught the pleasing scent of foreign perfumes. All were armed but none made threatening moves. Their faces were set in solemn expressions—none giving any indication of how Suvi and her party were to be received. After an exhausting hike across the island, she couldn't help being somewhat irritated.

Remember, Kask has very good reasons to be cautious. Don't give him control. But stay calm.

At the front of the group stood an older man—she assumed he was old, anyway. His spirit knots were bright white against his dark skin. At the same time, his athletic posture didn't indicate age or infirmity.

Mirna didn't halt until she stood directly in front of the white-haired man. Then she nodded a bow and stepped aside.

"I am Sea Lord Kask," the white-haired man said. His voice was deep and warm. He spoke Eledorean with no trace of accent. His eyes were a beautiful pale green and contrasted with the white of his hair and the darkness of his skin. "Welcome, Lake Marshal

Hännenen. I apologize for the lengthy walk. However, I thought it wisest to keep your ship's cannons at a safe distance."

Ah, Uncle. You do make a lasting impression, don't you? Suvi stopped herself mid-shrug. *He did no differently than I'd have done in his place.* Keeping this to herself, she merely said, "No need for apologies. After a week in a tiny ship's cabin, the walk was most enjoyable." She met his eyes with what she hoped was a warm but confident expression. *I'm not my uncle, Mr. Kask. And I am not easily flustered.*

Sea Lord Kask nodded and granted her a small smile in return. Shifting his attention to Dylan, his eyes grew sad and his expression more open. At the same time, Suvi sensed tension. "You have returned."

Dylan answered with calm dignity. "I have, Father."

Kask said, "The conditions under which you're permitted to return have not altered."

"I know," Dylan said.

"Why did you come back?"

"It's been a long time," Dylan said. "Too long. I miss my family. I miss—"

"That's not worth risking your life. Your mother won't be happy about this."

"It's time to—to sort things out."

"I see," Kask said. "Well, I have done what I could to keep your return as . . . quiet as possible."

"What about Darius? Is he—"

"He's fine. Hasn't stopped working toward reconciliation from the first day you left."

"Sounds like him," Dylan said, searching the crowd. "Where is he?"

"He'll arrive tonight with the *Laughing Sea Horse*."

"Isn't that Isak Whitewave's ship?"

"It is," Kask said. "They're ship brothers now."

"Really?"

"Before you get upset, I want you to know that I made it very clear that should anything unusual happen, Isak would be held responsible. It was Darius's choice," Kask said. "I was against it, but he insisted."

"I understand," Dylan said. "Darius was always stubborn."

"Not unlike other persons I could name," Kask said.

Dylan sighed. "I'm sorry. Everything is—is . . . I wish—"

"I know," Kask said. "I do too. In any case, I thought you and Darius would like to reunite with one another privately. Arrangements were made. Unfortunately, I was only able to force Isak to delay the duel until tomorrow night."

"I appreciate that," Dylan said.

Kask asked, "Have you come prepared?"

"I have," Dylan said.

Kask appeared to scan the rest of the Eledorean contingent. "If you have no second, one will be provided."

I hadn't thought of that. Suvi wondered if any of the marines might help Dylan. Then she realized she didn't know what the qualifications for a Waterborne second would be, let alone what would be required of one. What little she knew of dueling she'd learned secondhand from Nels. *I don't even know if a Waterborne duel bears any resemblance to an Eledorean one.*

"I don't think that will be necessary," Dylan said.

Kask asked, "Who, then—"

"I will enter the circle without one," Dylan said.

Kask said. "I can't allow—"

"Yet it is my wish," Dylan said.

"Is it your wish to commit suicide?" Kask asked, frowning.

"No, Father." Dylan held his father's gaze.

The two of them locked wills in silence until Kask finally looked away. "We will discuss this later and in private. There is time yet. And your friends are probably thirsty after such a long walk." Kask signaled to the wall.

A loud whistle sounded, and the iron portcullis lifted. It took Suvi the distance of the courtyard to register that the place wasn't used as a long-term residence. Other than the group who met them at the gate, there were no townspeople. She didn't see evidence of market stalls, and above all, no children. It occurred to her that the entire island might be intended as a place where outsiders were met. Each building was decorated with intricate carvings of swirls and waves and sea creatures—dolphins, whales, fish, and sharks. She recognized some, having visited the port city of Mehrinna's beaches when she was younger, but there were a few animals that she didn't. In particular, a giant creature with multiple arms shaped like slender tree branches or snakes. Its head was bulbous and pointed, the eyes round and flat. The monster was huge in proportion to the stylized ship it clutched. The image gave Suvi a shiver.

They were led up wide, blue-carpeted stairs, and didn't stop until the fifth, topmost floor. There, they entered through a set of tall double doors fashioned from teak. They appeared to have been salvaged from an old ship. Suvi could see where the barnacles had been scraped off.

Kask turned to her. "Lake Marshal Hännenen, you will leave your escort here."

Jami began to protest, but Suvi hushed her with a motion of her hand. "They will remain as you wish." She gave Jami a hard look. Then Suvi followed Kask and Dylan through another set of doors and into a private study. Rows of books lined the walls, yet the room managed to give off a shipboard quality. That was when she understood some of the ships from which the decor had originated weren't all Waterborne.

"I hope my gifts were satisfactory," she said. On Dylan's recommendation, she'd sent a small shipment of ironwood and teak along with her request for council. Waterborne custom dictated such an exchange at the start of business negotiations. It was considered polite. Since all the ironwood forests in Eledore were owned by her family and most of them were managed by her uncle, she felt it was particularly fitting.

"Eledorean teak is quite valuable, but the ironwood is a rarity. It is much appreciated. Thank you." Kask went to the sideboard and poured himself a drink. "Lake Marshal Hännenen, would you like something?"

"No, thank you," Suvi said. She risked rudeness but wanted to keep her wits about her.

Turning to Dylan, Kask asked, "What will you have? Whiskey?"

"Yes," Dylan said.

They then settled into comfortable antique Ytlainen wingback chairs arranged in the middle of the study—she recognized them from the vast amount of decorative scrollwork carved into the legs. It was a style her mother hated. Kask offered her a clay pipe and tobacco, which she refused. He filled one for himself and lit it. After a couple of puffs, he leaned back in his chair. The pleasant scent of good tobacco filled the room. He sipped the amber liquid in his crystal glass. Suvi could smell it from where she sat.

"Well, then. The niceties have been observed. We can get to business," Kask said. "What is so urgent?"

Dylan gave her an encouraging look, and Suvi took a deep breath before taking the plunge. "We have reason to believe that an individual within Clan Kask is selling information about

Eledorean troop movements and shipping routes to the Acrasians."

Kask frowned and set down his glass. "That's impossible."

"I'm afraid we have proof," Suvi said.

Blinking, Kask paused. "Were I to consider what you claim to be even a remote possibility . . . and I'm not saying that I do . . . what kind of proof?"

"Before we get into specifics," Suvi said, taking control. "We will need to discuss compensation."

She watched Kask's frown deepen. "I see," he said.

"Now you understand why I had to come home," Dylan said.

Kask asked, "You bring your friend here to blackmail your clan?"

Dylan said, "That isn't what this is about."

"You've changed," Kask said. "You've been too long among—"

Dylan got up from his chair. "Stop it! Listen to me, please!"

"Why should I? If you betrayed your clan once before—"

"I didn't! I told the truth! Why won't you listen to me?" Dylan stepped to his father's side. The force of his stride thumped the wooden floor through the rug.

Suvi was abruptly reminded of certain confrontations between her father and her brother. The scene was so familiar that she almost laughed.

"Listen?" Kask asked. "Listen? You never gave an explanation. Never made a defense against the charges. You never even accepted Isak's challenge. You never said a word. Instead, you fled like a coward." He stood up. "What am I supposed to think? You just vanished!"

"I—You—I—" Dylan threw his hands up in the air in defeat and frustration. "I couldn't!"

"You couldn't what?" Kask asked.

"Why don't you listen to Lake Marshal Hännenen? She has

the proof that I didn't have." Dylan glanced her direction and then turned away from his father.

Kask's question was quiet. "Who were you protecting?"

Suvi saw the shock on Dylan's face.

"How did you know?" Dylan asked.

"You're my son," Kask said. "You think I don't know you?" He paused and then sat down again. "Well, I used to. Or I . . . thought I did. For the most part."

"I was protecting you," Dylan said. "As I am now."

Kask's eyes narrowed. "You have a funny way of showing it."

"The shipment I was accused of smuggling," Dylan said. "It belonged to Isak."

"Darius said as much," Kask said, "But neither of us understood how—"

"How doesn't matter, Father. The past is the past," Dylan said. "What matters now is, Isak hasn't stopped stealing or dealing in bloodflower."

"That's strictly forbidden. He can't—"

"He wants control of the clan. And he'll do anything to get it. Including betraying the trust of certain Ytlainen clients by spying for the Acrasians and then laying the blame on you."

"That's a very serious charge," Kask said.

"I know," Dylan said. "And I knew I'd need proof. And the only way I could get it to you safely was to have Lake Marshal Hännenen bring it."

"Eledoreans aren't known for their generosity," Kask said. "In exchange for what?"

"I told her you'd be willing to grant a favorable shipping contract as well as safe passage for Eledorean troop transports through Clan Kask waters."

Kask gaped. "Are you mad? I can't do that!"

"You can," Dylan said. "More importantly, you'll want to. The Sea Mother will want the proof. Father, this is bigger than Clan Kask. Isak Whitewave isn't acting alone."

"You think a rival clan is involved?" Kask asked.

"I do," Dylan said.

"All right," Kask said and turned to her. "Let me see what you have, then."

Suvi reached for the case Dylan had been carrying. "I have copies of several intercepted messages." Opening the case, she brought out the twenty messages that she'd gotten from Jami and handed them to Kask.

As she watched, Kask flipped through the messages and read each one twice before setting them aside. Then he finished his drink in one gulp, clamped his pipestem between his teeth, and went to the sideboard. There, he poured himself another. "How many of your people know of this, Lake Marshal Hännenen?"

"This information isn't widely known," Suvi said. "I'm afraid my uncle knows. And he's told my father. My father won't do anything until Uncle clears it first. My uncle is set to discuss the matter with King Edvard of Ytlain. However, Uncle agreed to wait until I'd spoken with you first."

"I see," Kask said, and then swallowed the contents of his second glass.

"She wanted you to know before this became public," Dylan said.

"And why would she want that?" Kask asked. "Tell me, what is it specifically that you want from us, Hännenen?"

At least he gets to the point quickly, Suvi thought. "Only what your son has mentioned—a closer relationship between Clan Kask and Eledore." She needed to be specific. Dylan had told her that she could only negotiate with one clan at a time. The clans existed as a loose confederacy under a regent who commanded only in times of emergency. Unlike Eledore, leadership of the Waterborne Nations wasn't hereditary. The Sea Mother served for a lifetime and then was replaced with a suitable candidate from among the clans. Also unlike Eledore, only women could rule.

Kask raised an eyebrow. "And you have the authority to speak for all of Eledore, Lake Marshal Hännenen?"

"I speak specifically for the Eledorean Royal Navy," Suvi said, inwardly cursing her mistake. "I'm also authorized to offer you a modest ironwood supply, a great deal of teak, as well as several tons of hemp."

"Interesting." Kask paused. "Continue."

Suvi said, "I've taken the liberty of drawing up the proposed quantities, delivery dates, and other details." She accepted the second leather folio from Dylan and gave it to Kask.

Kask didn't move to accept the folio. "Do you have access to Eledorean water steel?"

"What does that have to do with anything?"

"Would you be willing to add a small quantity of water steel to your offer?"

Suvi paused.

Eledore had once been famous for its sword-making, but that had been a hundred years before. Now the blades were treasured, passed from one generation of soldiers to the next, and were almost never seen outside of the country. There were reasons for that. Most were rumored to be haunted by their former bearers. All bore some form of magical mark from their makers—some more than others. Newer blades had been forged since, but none were referred to as water steel, and none were as valued. She wasn't familiar enough with the process of sword-making to understand why. *Perhaps he doesn't understand the difference?*

"You're asking a great deal for someone in your position," Suvi said. She hadn't intended to sound quite so offended, but the question had caught her off guard.

Kask held up a hand. "Don't misunderstand. There is a very good reason why I've asked. A reason that should concern both our interests."

"And?" Suvi did her best not to show unease. She didn't know what her uncle would've done, but her father would've been extremely insulted by Kask's request. It alone would've ended the meeting then and there. *We need Kask. Don't botch this.* Panic emptied her mind until suddenly another, simpler option occurred to her. "If there is a problem the Royal Navy can assist you with, I am willing to consider the matter." *Maybe I won't give you water steel, but I might loan you a few marines armed with it.* She didn't think she could give the Waterborne much in the way of military support—Eledore was at war, after all, but it was an option within her power. The swords weren't.

"Perhaps we should discuss the problem in detail after dinner," Kask said. His expression changed, and he looked weighed down with concern and worry. "It would be ill luck to speak of such matters at the start of a relationship." He finished a third glass of whiskey, and Suvi thought she detected a slight tremor in the hand that lifted the glass.

He's terrified. His reactions took on newer meaning, and she attempted to hide her surprise. She had a bad feeling. *How much did the Waterborne know about water steel? What kind of a problem would force him to take a chance with such a request?* Glancing at Dylan, she could see he was equally tense and distracted—although no one who didn't know him would be able to see it. She assumed it was the impending duel. *Or is it?*

Damn it, she thought. *I really need to talk to him in private.*

"Forgive my manners. The rest of your party is waiting," Kask said. "You are no doubt hungry, and would like to prepare for dinner. I'll have someone show you to your rooms. We should resume this discussion after we eat. Then I've something I must show you."

TWO

Located on the first floor, the dining area was an open room with a high ceiling, and was flanked with rows of tall, glass-paned windows. All the sashes had been thrown open. Thin, white floor-length curtains danced in the sea breeze blowing in from the shore. Suvi had a wonderful view of the sunset over the crowded bay. There were no chairs. The colorful silk cushion she was sitting on felt slick and soft beneath her, and the dinner had been laid out on a fifteen-foot-long teak table. Stroking the worn but polished surface with a fingertip, it was obvious that it too had once been part of a ship. The room was lit with a series of mismatched hanging lamps. Upon entering, she'd examined the brass label on one of them. It listed a ship's name, its country of origin, and the date the ship was taken.

Suvi was seated across from Sea Lord Kask and was impressed with the lavish multicourse meal. Fresh oranges, grapes, lemons, and limes were rarely seen in Eledore, even at her father's table. She had to discipline herself not to gorge on Acrasian blood oranges. A clanswoman acting the role of table servant poured the wine. Suvi waved away the marine stationed at her side who reached for her glass. The red wine tasted fruity and full with a hint of cherry on her tongue. It smelled ever so slightly peppery and the color was a distinctive shade of blood red with a purple tint in the candlelight. She swallowed and smiled as she recognized it.

"The wine is very good," she said. "Better than any of my uncle's vintages by far." Of course, it would be impolite to point out that she knew it as originating from her uncle's vineyard. *How did Kask get it? Through Ytlain?* There were only two vineyards in all of Eledore, her father's and her uncle's. Both were maintained magically because Eledore's climate wasn't suitable for grapes. It was possible her uncle had traded the wine at some point. However, it was highly unlikely that he'd done so with the Waterborne. *What is Kask hinting at? Is this a display of power? An insult?*

Kask nodded, accepting her compliment. "I'll have a cask sent back with you when you go. A gift."

"That's most generous of you," Suvi said.

The second course consisted primarily of meats, fish, sauces, and a few vegetables. Groups of Waterborne bearing trays entered and left the room. The scent of fresh-roasted meat filled the air. Other trays of fish, oysters, and assorted sea creatures arrived. Suvi sampled as much as she could manage. The sauces were heavily spiced and as varied in cultural roots as the surrounding architecture. She tasted dishes she'd never encountered before from lands she'd never heard of, while Kask recited stories of his encounters on the seas—huge storms and waves more vast than buildings, giant sharks capable of sinking ships, and lightning that danced in the rigging. Dylan remained silent, and those serving didn't treat him any differently from the marines. He refused wine, drinking only spice-laced water. Although she'd been careful of the wine, by the end of the meal she was ever so slightly dizzy. She watched as the table was cleared and most of the serving Waterborne left.

Afternoon faded into evening. Hundreds of scented candles and oil lamps were lit. Suvi fought to remain alert. If Kask were anything like her father, he'd choose this moment to solidify the contract—the moment when she was most relaxed.

The room grew quiet. She made out the sound of a ticking clock and distant waves crashing against the beach. The work crews had apparently ceased their toils as the sky was cast in shades of purple, pink, and orange. The weather was perfect if a bit humid. Still, she could almost feel the storm lying in wait on the other side of the island like a wolf pack lurking at the edge of a dying campfire.

Kask's open expression grew shielded and tense. "How much has Dylan told you of the world beyond your shores?"

Suvi stopped herself from smiling at his careful choice of words. Although known for being blunt, even brutally honest, the Waterborne were wary of what they revealed to outsiders. She looked to Dylan first for permission—something her father would've never done—but Dylan trusted her, and she had no intention of breaking trust.

He nodded encouragement but didn't smile.

She said, "Dylan hasn't told me much beyond a few enjoyable fish stories. Like you have tonight."

"Do you know of the Old Ones?" Kask asked.

In a flash, an image of the World's Pillar surfaced in Suvi's mind, and she shuddered. Then it occurred to her that Kask couldn't possibly be talking about the creatures under Keeper Mountain—until she remembered they were speaking in Eledorean and he'd used the appropriate inflection indicating evil. She blinked. "How do you know of the Old Ones?"

Kask paused. "We have heard stories from your soldiers.

Unfortunately, we haven't been able to gather much information. It seems the Old Ones aren't spoken of in passing. They aren't discussed frequently among the Waterborne, either."

"I don't understand," she said. "I'm not certain we're speaking of the same creatures."

"I assure you, we are. Have you had personal contact with them?"

"I haven't. Not personally," Suvi said. "I have visited one of the places where they are said to be trapped." She took a deep breath. "No one has actually seen one in hundreds of years. One of their gates into this world lies buried beneath a mountain I know of within Eledore. There are other such places within each of the seven kingdoms, but I don't know where."

Leaning forward, Kask rested his hands on the table. "The Waterborne are not landless. We have the Mother Islands. Our homeland. I will not tell you where, because it is forbidden."

"I have no need to know, anyway," Suvi said.

Kask seemed somewhat surprised by her response, and again, she thought of her father and her uncle.

"Among our people there are legends of massive creatures that sleep beneath the ocean in the far east," Kask said. "They stink of death and rotting slime and feed from nightmares. It is said they are large enough to eat ships whole. Ships not fortunate enough to be consumed are cast adrift to wander the seas. Their crews linger in a half-living state—their souls stolen from them. Any unfortunate travelers the ghost ships happen upon are boarded, raided, and cannibalized. Legends of ghost ships have existed for centuries. As you say, none have seen the Old Ones or a ghost ship—not within living memory." He took a sip of wine. "Sadly, that is no longer the case."

"You've seen them?" It was Dylan.

"Not myself. No," Kask said without looking up.

"Who?" Dylan asked.

"Three months ago, the *Dolphin* vanished. Not long after that, *Hanna's Storm*, the *Sea Serpent*, the *Ardal Moonchaser*, and *Tess's Star* followed," Kask said.

"Sink it all, that doesn't mean anything," Dylan said. "A storm might have taken them. It's happened before."

"As I thought, myself," Kask said. "Until the *Ardal Moonchaser* returned here from a fishing venture. All her crew had disappeared. All but one. He lived long enough to tell us what happened and then mercifully died."

Dylan's skin took on a gray cast. "What did he say?"

"From what we were able to piece together, it seems the *Dolphin* came upon them in the night. Her sails hung in tatters, and the rigging was a mess."

"Captain Prymm wouldn't have stood for that," Dylan said.

"Exactly," Kask said. "Josiah was able to hide in the hold before they were boarded."

"And he saw one of the Old Ones?" Suvi asked.

"As I said before, I have something to show you." Kask got up from the table. "Please, follow me."

Standing, Suvi understood that the wine had been more potent than she'd thought. Dylan steadied her with a hand to her elbow. Kask didn't appear to notice as he led them down the broad staircase and across the courtyard. A pine-and-lilac-scented breeze pushed her hair away from her face. She tilted her head back and gazed into the night sky, seeking reassurance from the stars. The bad feeling from earlier twisted in her gut. Whatever it was that Kask was going to show her wasn't going to be good.

They arrived at an iron-and-silver reinforced door set into the eastern wall of the third, shorter building. Kask unlocked the door with a key from his pocket. It opened to a set of stairs leading down into darkness. Dylan entered first, then Suvi and Jami. Kask paused to secure the door behind them. Light at the bottom of the steps told Suvi they weren't alone. She followed Dylan, who started down, not stopping until he'd reached a narrow, unfurnished room. She spied another locked door at the end. It suddenly occurred to her that Kask was taking them to a dungeon. The stench of old blood haunted the air. She wanted to ask what they were about to see—anything to break down the fear clouding the atmosphere, but the moment she opened her mouth to speak, she heard a chilling cry. She felt sure the sound couldn't have originated from an animal. Yet it couldn't possibly have come from a person, either. The cross between a howl and a mournful keen echoed up the stairwell. Suvi shivered. Dylan started, and even Jami was affected. She saw her reach inside her shirt and then kiss the medal she kept on the chain around her neck.

Kask unlocked the door, motioned for them to go through, and then re-secured the lock. Two guards had been stationed inside the next room, a dungeon cell. It had a high ceiling and no window. A row of torches kept the cell brightly lit. In the center of the room stood an iron cage. In between the bars, pierced silver coins and tokens hung in floor-to-ceiling-length strands.

A misshapen creature unlike anything she'd seen before cowered in the shadowy corner of the cage, stinking of dust and old gore. The thing appeared malnourished and was about the same height as the average Acrasian—that is, slightly shorter than a kainen. It was clothed in a ragged jacket and loose black-and-white-striped sailor's trousers. Its skin was covered in coarse, spiny fur the color of rotting leaves. It peered at her over a crippled and clawed hand with the shallow black eyes of a shark. Its features were flat and disturbingly nondistinct. A too-wide lipless mouth was set below nose slits, and something about the way it moved reminded her of an insect rather than a mammal.

In a blink the creature changed. First, it became a kainen with dark brown curly hair and a square jaw. "Help me. Please," it said. Its voice was familiar and yet wrong—both sonorous and lisping as if it weren't used to speaking around sharp teeth.

Suvi heard Dylan draw in a quick breath.

"It can't be." *That's Major Ander Lahtela,* Suvi thought. *He's dead! How did he get here?* Without thinking, she reached through the bars.

"Get back!"

Her hand stung as Kask slapped her away from the cage. Almost in the same instant, the creature threw itself at the bars. Silver tokens and coins clinked together like chains. A twisted arm swept through the bars, narrowly missing her. The monster's visage blurred, and it hissed in pain before it became Nels. "Suvi! Please! Get me out of here!"

Stumbling backward, she let out a yelp. "What is that thing?"

"It has many names," Kask said. "The Acrasians call it a malorum. We call it misery-drinker and soulbane. Its bite is quite poisonous, but not always deadly. The venom causes paralysis. More often than not, their victims die due to suffocation. Get enough into a wound, the poison liquefies tissue. Then the soulbane feeds by sucking dry—"

Nauseous, Suvi took another two steps back. "That's revolting."

The soulbane smiled its too-broad smile with her twin brother's mouth. She sensed an undercurrent of malice to its mirth. It opened and closed its jaw. Its teeth met with an audible snap.

"If it is rushed, it will drink a victim dry and leave behind a husk," Kask said.

"Where did you find that thing?" Suvi asked.

"It was hidden on the *Ardal Moonchaser,*" Kask said. "Unfortunately, the boarding crew didn't know it was there until it'd killed six of the crew."

"How does it know what my brother looks like?" Suvi asked.

"Is that how it appears to you?" Kask asked. "It wears a different face for each person who observes it." He turned to look at the thing. Sadness filled his eyes before he blinked. "It senses certain thoughts and targets images that evoke strong emotions. That is why we have to change the guards several times a day. Otherwise, it would lure them to their deaths as it almost did with you."

"Why show me this?" Suvi asked.

"You asked me to explain our need for water steel. Silver can repel them—even kill them over time, but only water steel will kill them outright. Is that not so?"

"I—I'd like to leave now," Suvi said.

"Yes," Kask said. "It is late."

THREE

"You can't sleep either, can you, Suvi?" Dylan asked without turning around. A medium-sized black dog with short hair lay at the edge of the pool on his right. He scratched behind the dog's ears. "This is Jet. She's a good girl. Aren't you, Jettie? The last time I saw her, she was a puppy."

Surprised that Dylan should know her without looking, Suvi sat next to him on the edge of the dueling pool. The sharp brick ledge dug into the back of her thighs. *No, I'm not sleeping. Not after seeing that thing in the dungeon.* She let Jet sniff her hand. "Hello, girl."

Dylan dangled his feet in the water. A perfect duplicate of a clear, star-filled night sky rippled in the pool's surface. Set in the center of an elaborate potted-garden courtyard, the dueling circle was fifty feet in diameter and was no more than a shallow pool, ankle- or knee-deep at the most. The bottom was tiled in complex ceramic mosaic, but she couldn't make out the pattern in the dark. The arena area was furnished with three concentric rings of teak benches—seating for spectators, she assumed. Hundreds of potted plants ranging from huge to small converted the area into a well-mannered forest. Heavy curtains made of rich damask marked entrances and exits and were supported by pairs of fifteen-foot pillars carved from differing shades of stone. There was no ceiling to protect the arena from the elements, only sky.

"At least it's a beautiful night," Suvi said.

Dylan grunted in agreement.

She checked a second time but was fairly certain that they were alone. The odds were good that Jami was near. Suvi didn't know for sure—not that it mattered to her. Suvi listened to the water as little waves slapped the sides of the pool. Running late, the *Sea Horse* wasn't scheduled to arrive for at least another hour. Kask had allowed Dylan and herself access to the dueling ring in order to prepare. Only, there wasn't much preparation going on. Dylan sat at the edge of the water, his face set in a careful expression. As Suvi watched, he leaned forward and let his fingers touch the pool's surface. The water grew cloudy just before tendrils of ice stretched in a sharp-edged halo around his fingertips. Faint crackling tickled the air. Jet sniffed with her nose in the air, got to her feet, and let out a soft bark.

Dylan soothed Jet. "Yes, Jettie. Magic. Good girl. Down."

Jet complied.

"She senses magic?" Suvi asked.

"Cats are kept onboard to control the rats," Dylan said. "Dogs trained to sense magic are kept to inspect shipments and to monitor the weather. I'm not the only weathermaster, you know. And not all the clans have amicable relationships with one another."

"Oh."

He withdrew his hand from the pool and destroyed the watery snowflake with his fist. "This isn't your fight."

"I'm your second."

"You are not," he said. "I'm doing this alone."

"Your father disagrees."

"His opinion doesn't count."

"Oh, I suspect he thinks otherwise. Come to think of it, I do too."

"You don't even know the first thing about a Waterborne duel."

"Could that be because you haven't told me anything? Therefore, my qualifications, or the lack thereof, are entirely your responsibility."

Dylan stared up into the sky and gestured as if to plead with the moon. "I've no time for this. Will you stop arguing with me?"

Suvi unleashed a nervous smile. "What if I don't want to?"

"I'll not back down."

"Well, I'll not either," Suvi said. "How does it feel when a good friend is being a stubborn ass?"

Dylan whirled. The tokens woven into his spirit knots clattered. "This is deadly serious!"

"So I hear."

He let out a frustrated grunt.

"I don't want to add to your problems," she said. "That isn't my intent. But you're not making any sense."

"Conveniently, whether or not you understand isn't a factor." He lowered his voice. "This isn't about you, Your Grace."

"That isn't fair." Suvi frowned and folded her arms across her chest. He'd hit a bit too close to the mark. *Selfish.* "I've never—"

"This entire situation is anything but fair."

"I won't let you commit suicide. I can't. I want to help," Suvi said. "Please, let me."

He sighed and then whispered, "You can't be my second, even if you weren't a crown princess. Even if the sea lord would accept you as my second—"

"He said he would allow it, provided I won't blame Clan Kask if I get hurt."

Dylan's mouth dropped open. "What in the name of the Great Abyss did you do?"

She shrugged. "I conferred with your father while you were off meditating or sleeping. Or worrying. Or whatever it was you were doing earlier."

"You'll be defenseless! And he knows it!"

"Defenseless? Ha!" She looked away. "I've been dodging court plots since I was eight. I have magic. I know how duels work. Nels told me. The second only assures that the fight is fair and acts as a witness. Your father says he won't let you enter the ring without a second. No one else is going to do it. I'm your second."

"I don't believe this." Dylan threw his hands up in the air another time.

"Is it because I'm female?"

Dylan let out a disgusted snort. "The Waterborne don't hold to such stupid ideas."

"Then is it because of Eledorean blood custom?"

Making another derisive sound, he shifted.

"It's not the best alternative, I know. But I won't have to hurt anyone. And my father doesn't have to know I was involved."

"This is not an Eledorean duel," Dylan said, facing her. "Seconds participate in the fight." Pointing at the dueling circle, he then said, "And the duel takes place in seawater."

Suvi's stomach dropped to somewhere around her knees. "Oh." She watched as Dylan got up, paced to the far corner of the arena and back.

"Father knows this," Dylan said. "What in the Abyss was he thinking?"

"What I was thinking. That you needed help."

"You've landed yourself in a great deal of trouble."

"Family habit. Nels *is* my twin brother, you know," she said. "All right. What happens if you don't have a second and your opponent does? Because clearly that's the situation."

Dylan looked away. "Then I must fight them both at the same time."

"Damn it, Dylan!" Suvi said, exasperated. "You've helped me—even when it was dangerous to do so. Who was there for me on my first posting? Who took my side when Lieutenant Mikkola would've had me tossed overboard?"

"That doesn't matter. You don't understand. You're not Waterborne—"

"I owe you this," she said.

Dylan exhaled.

She could see she was wearing him down. He was terrified, not that she blamed him. And although the idea of fighting in a duel made her stomach twist, she knew she couldn't stand by and let Dylan die without attempting to stop it.

"And what of your Eledorean blood taboo?" Dylan asked.

It's nothing but a senseless custom, Suvi thought. *I know that now.* She swallowed revulsion nonetheless. "Will I be required to use a blade or a pistol?"

"This is a magic duel."

"Then I run no risk of staining myself with blood." She let her shoulders drop. "My uncle has demonstrated the boundaries of blood custom in great detail over the years. Trust me." She took a deep breath. "What will you need?"

"The second shields me from whatever Kester might do during the duel."

"Who is Kester?" Suvi asked. "And am I required to kill him? Or can I merely stop him from hurting you?"

"Kester is Isak's brother," Dylan said. "You aren't required to kill him. I simply need you to watch him. Alert me to danger, if you can. Or counter his attacks."

"All right," Suvi said. "If Kester can attack you, can Isak attack me?"

"I very much doubt he'd do that."

"What makes you say that?"

"Because Isak will be more focused on me, if he's smart," Dylan said. "He knows I can expose him. He doesn't know about you or the messages. But he knows I wouldn't be back unless I had some sort of proof."

"How well do you know Isak?" Suvi asked.

"I used to know him very well," Dylan said. "Or so I thought. But he was quite a bit younger then. He was twelve or thirteen when he went to work at one of our warehouses in Acrasia. He always was an ass. His brother is worse. At least, at the time I thought he was. I'm not so sure now. It's been six years."

A door slam signaled that they were no longer alone. The curtains to her right were shoved aside and a young Waterborne with short, Acrasian-styled, blond hair, dark skin, and tilted eyes entered the arena. He appeared to be in his twenties. His ears were pierced like all the Waterborne Suvi had met. He was wearing a long, tailored coat with minimalist decorative stitching that wouldn't have looked out of place in one of Ytlain's more fashionable cities. He also wore thick leather knee-high boots. Everything about him was tidy and refined. It was difficult to imagine him anywhere near a ship as anything but a passenger.

She checked an urge to frown.

He ignored her for the moment and gave Dylan a short bow. "Dylan Kask of the *Sea Dragon*, I presume?"

"I am no longer a member of that crew," Dylan said. "And I haven't been for some time. You know this, Kester. Get to the point."

Kester turned away from Dylan, a sour expression on his face. He then spoke to Suvi, much to her surprise. "I understand you are to be his second?"

Suvi addressed Dylan but kept an eye on Kester. "Well? What do I tell him?"

Dylan gave her a quick nod and turned away.

"I am Lake Marshal Suvi Hännenen of Eledore, and I am Dylan Kask's second."

"And I am Kester Whitewave of Kask, Third Mate of The Laughing Sea Horse, First Frigate of the Fleet." He bent at the waist in a quick bow. "Kask insisted that I meet you here. He stated that you may be unfamiliar with the Waterborne custom of Duello."

"No need to concern yourself." Suvi added an edge of command to her words—just enough power to be a threat. "I learn fast."

Kester seemed unimpressed. "Tradition dictates that I must inquire whether or not an apology is on offer. That is normally your responsibility as the representative of the duel's instigator. However—"

"Instigator?" Dylan asked. "You've got it backward. I didn't ask for this. Isak did."

Kester acted as if he didn't hear. "I take it the answer is no?"

Again, Suvi turned to Dylan. "Are you willing to apologize?"

"I didn't do anything to apologize for!"

Suvi nodded. "Dylan says—"

"It is of no consequence," Kester said, holding up a hand. "I am here to inform you that the instigator's offer is to be declined."

"Then why go through the motions? This is stupid!" Dylan rushed to where Kester stood with clenched fists. "Isak is the one who—"

Kester blinked and placed a hand on the pistol strapped to his waist. Suvi found herself shoving in between them. In two heartbeats, she registered that she might have made a mistake.

Dylan bumped into her with the force of his anger. "Your brother is an oathbreaker and a liar!"

Kester said, "Are you attempting to add a second duel to the first?"

Suvi stopped Dylan's reply with a hand over his mouth. She could feel him trembling under her palm. Forcing calm into her voice as much as possible, she used another boost of command energy to steer the conversation back on course. "Is this fight to be to the first strike or first—"

"For your information, the duel is to the death," Kester said, and sniffed. He executed a third bow and then made for the exit.

Dylan muttered, "Well, that settles that question."

"What question is that?" Suvi asked.

"Kester is still an ass." He waited until the curtain dropped back into place and Kester slammed the door before speaking again. "I almost wish I'd stayed away."

"I should never have told you about those messages."

"If you hadn't, my father would be at Isak's mercy. And when Isak gets what he wants, Darius won't live out the week." Dylan turned his back to her and walked to the pool's edge. "I had to come back. There really wasn't another option. At least I'll see Darius." He took a deep breath. "I don't know how I missed the bells. The *Sea Horse* must have arrived. I haven't seen Darius in years." He looked down at himself. His mood changed and he gave her an odd smile. "Do I look okay?"

Suvi tilted her head. *This Darius is the one who stole your heart, then?* Long having understood Dylan's sexual preferences without being told, she'd wondered why Dylan hadn't taken a lover in all the time she'd known him. *Well . . . how would I know? Given the Eledorean general mind-set in such matters, would he really have chosen to confide in me?* She watched him fuss with his hair and tried not to smile. "Of course. You look fine. If a bit rumpled."

He nodded. It was clear he was too nervous for humor. "I'll see you tomorrow. We'll review the rules of Duello then."

"All right. Good night."

Reaching the exit, he stopped and turned. "Thanks for being my second. I would've asked Darius, but he's never been very good at holding his temper. And Isak knows it. He'd kill Darius just to punish me." Dylan stared at the ground. "It was one of the last threats he made before I went away."

"I don't understand what is going on," Suvi said.

"Isak gave me a choice. I could admit to breaking a contract, accept exile, bring shame on my clan and my father as sea lord, or he could kill me and Darius and dump us overboard. I'd still be blamed, and my clan's name tarnished. I wanted Darius safe. I chose exile."

"But you didn't break the contract?"

"It's not that simple," Dylan said. "Isak betrayed the clan."

Suvi raised an eyebrow. "I wouldn't have thought that a problem. The Nations traffic in stink weed, every variety of dream tea, and Acrasian wormwood cordials. In the name of the Goddess, Clan Kask has been known to sell poisons. Why is bloodflower such a problem?"

Dylan wouldn't meet her gaze. "The reasons have nothing to do with the substance itself. It's how the bloodflower is produced. They use slaves."

"I thought the Seven Kingdoms agreed to outlaw the practice?" *Not that Eledore in any way strictly enforces the intent*, Suvi thought.

"Oh, they did. Technically," Dylan said. "By law, they employ debt-criminals and indentured servants. Only, the contracts are never actually paid off."

"Oh."

"What Massilia publicly claims isn't always what Massilian nobility does."

"That sounds familiar," Suvi said, disgusted. "All right, then. Isak Whitewave is dealing in bloodflower."

"And using those funds to buy more ships and become more powerful in the clan."

"What does that have to do with you?"

"I knew of his plan before he started. However, I thought I could bring charges against him myself. I hated Isak, and I wanted to hurt him. I was stupid. I should've gone to Father at once. I didn't. I thought to gain Isak's trust. I let him involve me in something I shouldn't have. As a result, I gave Isak everything he needed to lay the blame on me."

"So, you were caught with the bloodflower."

Dylan nodded. "Isak said he would take away everything and everyone I ever cared about if I breathed a word of the truth to Father. That was why I broke off from my family like I did. It's why I walked away from Darius, too."

"Oh."

"Tomorrow will see an end to it, at least."

FOUR

Time passed far too fast for Suvi's comfort. She spent most of the next morning exchanging urgent messages with the *Otter's* captain, Elliiya Hansen. Dylan took charge of her afternoon, instructing her in her duties as second. Piritta arrived at dinner along with Suvi's baggage from the *Otter*. When the duel was officially announced, Piritta had fled the table and cried herself into a frenzy. Jami, for her part, hadn't said a word. She'd merely given Suvi a look that would've put one of her father's glares to shame. From then on, Suvi focused on memorizing the rules of the contest.

Suvi listened while Dylan droned on at the dueling circle, bare feet dabbling in the seawater and watching the sky darken. There was so much to learn, and yet she found it difficult to focus. Before she knew it, a clock struck the quarter before midnight. Her stomach fluttered. *Only a quarter of an hour before the fight begins.* The rules were long and complicated. She hoped she'd remember enough of them to keep from making a mistake that would cost Dylan his life. Jami had stayed close. In fact, she was there now, leaning against one of the pillars as if she didn't have a care in the world. Suvi wondered what Jami would do if she, Suvi, were killed? Would she live among the Waterborne? Jami wouldn't be the first Eledorean to do so. Or would she travel to Ytlain? *That, probably. She has family in Ytlain, even if she doesn't care for them much,* Suvi thought. *And then she'll never set foot in Eledore again.*

First to arrive were Dylan's mother and several of his siblings— three of his brothers and two of his sisters. All were older than Dylan. Apparently, he had a total of eleven siblings. The rest were away, tending to unavoidable clan business. Each shared Dylan's broad smile and had inherited either Sea Lord Kask's light green eyes or Dylan's mother's warm brown eyes. Hugs and nervous laughter were exchanged while Suvi stood aside—watching while her chest tightened. Dylan's family was loving and easy with one another. Suvi compared them with her own family, and the tightness of breath gave way to a dull ache. Soon it became too much, and she had to look away.

Darius was the biggest surprise. Tall and handsome, and a little taller than Dylan, Darius had skin of a light brown. His spirit knots were short, only a few inches long, giving him a surprised look that would've seemed comical on anyone else. His eyes were a deep blue so intense that she'd originally thought they'd changed color from black to violet. *But the Waterborne don't have that ability, do they?* she thought. *Only the royal houses of Eledore and Ytlain do.* She thought again about how often kainen from all over the Seven Kingdoms were known to seek asylum among the kainen of the Waterborne Nations. It didn't take much imagination to think a royal bastard or two might have done the same. The inability to practice one's magical talents didn't garner shame among the Waterborne. Thus, it would be a small price to pay for a safe haven.

Dylan's family moved back, allowing space for Darius to greet Dylan. Darius slowly stepped forward, his arms folded across his chest. His arched brows and full mouth were set in a hard line.

"Hello, Dar," Dylan said, shy.

"So," Darius said. "You're back."

"I am."

"What am I supposed to say to you?" Darius asked. His tone was filled with quiet rage.

Dylan blinked. "Well, I was hoping for—"

Darius launched into a tirade. "You paper-skulled, totty-headed, selfish—"

"Don't forget mule-headed," Dylan said.

"Mule-headed ass!" Furious, Darius's shout echoed off the hills. "You left me!"

"I'm sorry," Dylan said. Disappointment welled up in his eyes.

"Nowhere near sorry enough! You broke your promise."

"I thought we worked this out. You said in your letter—"

"You didn't even tell me you were going! Not one word!"

"I couldn't, Dar. Not without—"

"Not a letter!"

"That's not true! I wrote to you! I know you got them. You answered!"

"Months later!"

"I wrote as soon as I could!"

"Shut up! Shut up! I don't want to hear your stupid excuses! I'm so angry with you! I could—I-I could just—" Dar brought up clenched fists. "I hate you! You swiving insufferable barnacle! You left me alone! Alone!"

"But Dar—"

Suvi flinched as Dar flew at Dylan, grabbed him in a tight hug, and cut off his reply with a violent kiss. Dylan staggered under the force of it, almost falling into the pool.

Standing among Dylan's family, Suvi watched their reaction for some sign of how to behave. Dylan's siblings talked quietly among themselves. His mother seemed to be struggling to hide amused approval.

"He deserved that," Dylan's mother whispered. "Every word. And a few more."

Sea Lord Kask cleared his throat. "I told Darius he was welcome to see Dylan earlier. But he refused. He said he couldn't trust himself if there were no witnesses."

"I can't blame him," Dylan's mother said.

"I hate you!" Dar had apparently come up for air.

"No, you don't," Dylan said.

"I do!"

"I said I was sorry."

"Say it some more!"

This time, Dylan kissed Dar.

Suvi looked away.

"All in all, Darius seems to have handled the situation rather well," Dylan's mother said, keeping her voice low.

"Oh, really?" Kask whispered.

"If you'd done the same to me, you wouldn't be walking right now," Dylan's mother said.

"It's early yet," Kask said. "Maybe we should give them some privacy?"

"And miss the fun?" Dylan's younger sister asked. She wore her hair pushed back from her face with a long blue silk scarf tied in a band. She didn't have spirit knots but had her hair styled in a longish mane that caught the lamplight like a soft, curly halo. She spoke to her shorter brother. "Owan, pay up."

"It's not over yet, Joanie," Owan said.

"He's not going to punch him," Joanie said, and held out her hand. "You lose."

"Oh, fine," Owan said.

Joanie pocketed the silver coin.

Dylan's other sister turned to introduce herself. "Hello, Suvi. I'm Moira."

"And I'm Joan."

"Hello," Suvi said.

"Boys," Moira said, rolling her eyes. "Do you have a brother?"

"I do. He's my twin," Suvi said.

"Is your twin as stubborn as Dylan is?" Moira asked.

Suvi said, "Worse."

"Ah, I see," Moira said. She leaned in closer. "Sorry about this. Dar is terrified and has a funny way of expressing it."

"I'll say," Joan said.

"You've known Dar for a while?" Suvi asked.

"Since he was twelve," Moira said. "We're in the same crew now. I try to keep him out of trouble. Doesn't always work."

Finally, Dylan and Darius registered that others were waiting. Dylan finally broke free of the embrace.

Dar said, "I guess I can forgive you."

"Thank you, Dar."

"In a month or so."

"Really?" Dylan asked. "You're going to let me go into a duel thinking you hate me?" He whispered in Dar's ear.

"The whole time?"

Dylan nodded. "I promise."

"Oh, all right. You're forgiven."

Holding Darius's hand, Dylan looked happier than she'd ever seen him. "Lake Marshal Suvi Hännenen of Eledore, I'd like you to meet Darius Teak."

She held out a hand for Dar to shake. "Call me Suvi. Dylan does."

"Dylan wrote to me about you," Dar said with a wicked twinkle in his eye. "Is it true that you once lost a bet and had to dance across the main royal at midnight while stark—"

Dylan cut him off with a playful smack to the back of the head.

Suvi felt her jaw drop and her face heat. "You swore you'd never tell anyone!"

"Drown it, Dar," Dylan said with a rueful smile. "I'm never telling you anything ever again."

"Oh, sure, you are." Darius leaned over and bit Dylan's earlobe. "What did you say?"

Dylan's breath caught. "Great Mother . . ."

"I thought so," Dar said.

Grinning, Suvi said, "Oh, I like him already, Dylan. Really, I do."

A low bell sounded and a short middle-aged woman waded alone and barefoot into the middle of the dueling pool. Her cool, confident, businesslike strides gave her a majestic air. As she was shorter than most, the pool's water level hit her above the knee. Dylan had mentioned that dueling judges weren't allowed to preside over disagreements within their own clans. This prevented personal bias from affecting their rulings. Suvi didn't know of which clan the judge was a member, but it was obvious even to Suvi that she wasn't a local. The refined-looking judge wore loose, calf-length, brightly colored trousers and a red coat decorated with gold braid on the sleeves. She also carried a short, curved blade sheathed at her right side. Her features were more angular and her skin lighter than most within Clan Kask, and her right nostril was pierced with a delicate gold ring. The backs of her hands were tattooed in delicate, beautiful green ink lines. She held her head high and confident as she moved to the pool.

The moment the judge entered the water, the audience assumed their seats in silence. Isak and Kester took positions aligned with the cardinal points of the compass at the edge of the pool.

Darius kissed Dylan on the mouth and then said, "Good luck."

Dylan said, "I love you."

"I love you, too. Even if you did cheat me out of being your second," Darius said. "Now don't just stand there. Kill the worthless bag of shit." Then Darius turned to her and put out a hand. "Watch his back for me."

Taking his hand, Suvi said, "I will. I promise."

Darius leaned in close and whispered, "Watch yourself, too. Kester is deaf in the left ear. Be sure you've got his attention when you use your magic."

Oh, great, Suvi thought. *Why didn't Dylan tell me that before?*

With one last look at Dylan, Darius headed to the benches with Dylan's family.

Dylan took his assigned place at the north compass point, directly across from Isak, and Suvi stood at the western mark at Dylan's right, opposite east and Kester. Taking a deep breath, she did her best to quell the tremor in her limbs. With her shoulders back, chin up, and chest out, she hoped no one would notice she was trembling.

The arena was well lit with rows of brightly burning lanterns strung along the outer walls. More lanterns were bolted to the columns. The viewing benches were packed with anxious clan members of varying ages. The late arrivals resorted to standing at the back. Gazing at the audience, she counted the number of Eledorean marines and came up one short. *That's odd.*

Where is Jami?

"Have the opponents made ready?" the judge asked. Her voice was firm, businesslike.

Suvi returned her attention to the duel and responded as she'd been coached. "I have inspected the site. The initiator is ready." The truth was, Dylan had done the inspection. She hadn't known what to look for, but he'd said it was more important that the inspection was completed and that he officially stated approval through her. With that, she listened to her heart hammering against her breastbone while Kester responded with his own rehearsed script. Dylan seemed calm, but Suvi sensed the anxiety in the set of his shoulders and jaw. Gazing across the dueling pool, she once again studied Dylan's opponent.

Isak was much the same size and muscular build as Dylan. Suvi would've thought him handsome were it not for the scowl. His jaw was square, granting his frown a belligerent edge. His eyes were dark in the lamplight. His left ear was pierced with a gold ring. Like Dylan, he wore spirit knots, but his were shorter—shoulder length—and he didn't have nearly the same number of tokens.

The judge spoke again. "I must ask one more time if an apology and forgiveness can be extended in place of this duel."

Isak spat. "Absolutely not!" His voice was deep.

Nodding, the judge said, "Very well. The bell will be the signal to begin. Good luck, gentlemen and lady." And with that, she waded to the pool's edge and stepped out of the water.

The judge's wet feet slapped the smooth white stone tiles as she made her way to the judge's chair. Suvi focused on returning Kester's stare. Her heart drummed against her chest with all its might. She'd never seen anyone die before. She was sure she didn't want to. Worse, she was certain she wouldn't be able to stand it if it were Dylan. Her palms grew slick with sweat, and her breath came short. She could smell the seawater in the pool. Nervous, she risked a glance at Isak's face and then Dylan's. She dreaded what was to come, yet at the same time, felt an unreasonable impatience to get the matter over with. She thought of a prayer she'd been taught as a child.

Great Mother Stjarrna, Queen of Earth and Sky, watch over us. Grant us your wisdom, and protect us from harm. Give us food, warmth, and shelter. Keep us from winter's cold, and send away those that walk in darkness. So let it be. She was so intent on her prayer that she almost missed the hollow, low bell-ring signaling the duel's start.

Kester stepped into the water, following Isak and Dylan. For her part, Suvi inched closer to the pool but remained outside it. There was no rule stating that she had to be in the water, only that she had to be within the ring. The space remaining was small but it was enough in which to stand, if she were careful. Rough brick abraded her bare toes as she curled and uncurled them on the pool's sharp edge. She expected a flurry of action from Dylan and Isak—some sign of a fight. Instead, they both gracefully assumed a ceremonial pose with their bare feet wide, elbows bent, and hands tucked near their armpits with both palms up. After settling into the stance, they froze in position. Isak glared from across the pool at Dylan, but Dylan closed his eyes as if in intense concentration. That worried her a little, but since no one else seemed to have a problem with it, she waited for some other signal of distress.

The arena grew deadly quiet. No one moved. The audience seemed to hold their breath. When nothing dire happened after what felt like an eternity, Suvi relaxed a little and switched her focus to Kester. He didn't appear to be doing anything either. Sensing her confusion, he gave her a slow, malicious grin. She rolled her eyes in return. Checking on Dylan, she saw that he was fine—at least, so far. She wondered how long they'd stand in the water doing nothing. She recalled Nels's dueling stories. Usually, fights to the death were resolved as rapidly as possible and in as few moves as could be managed. Dueling was exhausting—or so Nels had said—dragging it out left the result to endurance rather than skill. One didn't toy with lives, and dueling was serious business.

Perhaps the Waterborne feel differently? Or maybe Dylan has decided not to fight after all?

She was beginning to wonder if something was wrong when she noticed the wisps of steam drifting up off the pool. Looking closer, she saw the water at Dylan's end of the dueling circle had grown cloudy. A fuzzy white line formed at his feet and was gradually creeping along the pool's bottom toward Isak.

Is that ice? She blinked. The only times she'd witnessed Dylan use magic had been associated with weather—calling up wind for the sails in a dead calm, dispersing fog, or predicting the path of terrible storms. He was powerful. As an outsider living among Eledoreans, he had to be in order to garner respect from the *Northern Star*'s crew as well as the *Otter*'s. However, power didn't mean diversity of skill. In her experience, it usually didn't.

The cloudy water thickened into patches of slush and spread outward in a three-foot radius. The underwater ice line stretched toward Isak, stopping just two feet away from his toes. Meanwhile at Isak's end of the pool, the steam grew increasingly dense and spread out over the top of the water. At the edge, Suvi had the disorienting sensation of feeling the heat with the toes of her right foot and the cold with her left. The temperature difference between one end of the pool and the other was already wide enough that it gave off a fierce hiss as cold fought heat for domination. Salty steam rising from the pool transformed into a swirling thick, chest-high mist. Suvi found it increasingly difficult to see. At the pool's edge, she'd had an advantage in height, but soon even that was lost as the mist rose higher. She sensed shadows where Dylan and Isak stood, but that was all. More importantly, Kester was still in view, but she didn't know how long that would be the case.

From across the pool, Kester made an obscene gesture, and then, just as she'd feared, he ducked into the fog.

I can't see him! What if he can't hear? In a panic, she shouted. "Kester Whitewave!" She put every bit of power she could muster into his name. "Hear the sound of my voice!" There was no response. *I can't do anything to help.*

Suddenly, the air grew heavy with so much static that Suvi could sense it clinging to her hair and clothes. Small flashes appeared in the mist above the pool.

I must do something. I can't leave Dylan to— She blinked. *Above the pool. The mist is above the pool.* The implications began to form options. She glanced at the audience. Dylan's family sat nearby. *It wouldn't be right to bring one of them into it. Particularly not against their will.* That was when she spied Jet. Suvi wasn't sure it would work, but it was better than doing nothing. Dylan's sister Moira held the dog's collar. She appeared to be scanning the mist for some sign of Dylan.

"Jet," Suvi said, lacing the name with command. "Come here."

Jet whined, struggling against Moira's grip.

Suvi tried a second time. "Jet. Come."

Moira released Jet, and the dog sprang to Suvi's feet.

Kneeling, Suvi spoke quietly but kept the power behind her words. "Jet. Pull Kester from the water." She wasn't sure the dog would comprehend who she meant. So, she stared into the dog's black eyes and visualized her intent. "Your friend, Dylan, is in danger. Protect Dylan from the stranger. Pull the stranger out of the pool." Ultimately, it didn't matter which as long as Jet didn't target Dylan. "Understand?"

Jet let out a woof as if in acknowledgment.

"Good girl." Suvi pointed at the pool. "Go."

The dog leapt into the water and was lost in the now thick mist at once. Suvi held her breath. Exclamations came from the crowd mixing with Jet's splashing and playful barking.

Kester's muffled voice erupted from the fog. "What the—" The sound of cracking ice cut him off.

"Shit!" The word was followed with a long string of cursing from several sources—Suvi couldn't tell who in the chaos.

A number of nervous onlookers chuckled. Others protested to the judge. Squinting into the fog, Suvi searched for a sign. The pool was now smothered in mist. There came another series of loud splashes, thumps, and a grunt. The wind freshened. It didn't disperse the fog, only moved it around. Jet finally appeared at the pool's edge, dragging Kester by the collar. He was soaking wet and covered in ice chunks. Kester slapped at the dog, but Jet was relentless. Each time Kester was able to push her away, the dog selected a new target.

"Get away! Let go, drown you! Shoo!" Kester scrambled to his feet.

Jet yanked at Kester's trouser leg, ripping the cloth. Kester cursed, stumbled, and fell into the water again. A loud crack split the air. Two flashes danced in the mist like lightning jumping from cloud to cloud, leaving behind a fresh storm scent. More popping noises followed, and she heard someone other than Kester cry out. Then came another big splash. Warm water washed up onto her toes. She thought to call to Dylan but knew better than to distract him. Jet's barking took on a more urgent tone. In the audience, other dogs joined the chorus. One of them let out a yelp of pain. For a moment, Suvi wondered if it was something she'd done until the warning barks became snarls. Someone behind Suvi shouted. The heavy sound of a body hitting the ground made Suvi turn around. There came another scream—this time it was filled with agony and not merely fear. She turned toward the sound.

The creature from the dungeon crouched over a member of the audience, obviously feeding. One dog's body lay nearby. Two more dogs attacked the monster. Confused screams and shouts erupted as people fled the dueling arena and panic took the reins. The soulbane stood up. Dark liquid oozed from its misshapen mouth as it howled. The cry seemed one part keen and another part low shuddering wail. In response, terror and revulsion shivered up every one of Suvi's nerves. She and several others clutched their ears. Her blood froze. A marine charged the creature, swinging his sword. He missed and was batted into the benches. The soulbane fell upon him in an instant.

Command magic flowed into the word before Suvi even thought about it. "Stop! Don't you touch him!"

The creature paused and then turned to look up at her. She felt a crawling sensation inside her mind as its flat eyes stared into hers. Once again, it changed forms into Major Ander Lahtela.

"You're just like the others," the fake Lahtela said with a strange lisp the real Lahtela never possessed. The creature sniffed the air. "Use us and then throw us away at the first opportunity."

I didn't was her immediate thought. *I'm not.*

The fake Lahtela lurched toward her on uneven legs. "You are like your father. Tyrant. Despot. A true Ilmari."

I'm not, she thought. Her cheeks were burning.

"Like your uncle," the fake Lahtela said. "You don't have the courage for poison. You have your assassin do your killing for you." It shuffled several more steps in her direction. Its stride held an awkward grace like a misshapen spider's—all at once wrong and yet nimble.

"Shut up!" She realized it was only a few feet away now and poised to leap upon her. "Stop!" In her panic, she used twice the amount of magic in the word as she had earlier.

The creature halted. Suvi understood she had a hold on it, but the feel of that control was tenuous, slippery. Just as it had been at the World's Pillar. *It's fighting me*, she thought. *And I don't know how long I can hold it.*

Another gust of wind swept through the arena. Mist from the pool had eased out of the dueling circle. It swirled around her feet. A long series of even brighter flashes went off behind her. She heard ice shatter. A cold, fat raindrop pelted her cheek. Another slapped her on the arm, and another, her nose. Lightning flashed in the sky, and thunder boomed. Again she felt it vibrate the ground. Then the storm let loose. Sleet gushed down upon them, pounding the top of Suvi's head so hard it hurt. She lost concentration. It was only for an instant, but an instant was all it needed. The creature jumped, knocking her to the ground. Its clawed feet and hands jabbed into her chest and hip as it landed on top of her. The back of her head smacked onto stone. Something punched her in the stomach. Stunned, she gasped for air. The creature's prickly touch slid up her leg, and then it tore at her limb with its cold claw-like hands and bit down. A sharp pain ripped a scream out of her throat. Time slowed. Her left leg grew numb.

Suddenly Jami was there. Another of the marines arrived. Both had swords drawn and were trying to force the thing off of her, but it was stronger than it looked.

You don't have long, she thought. She stared at the monster intent on her leg and focused her will. "Stand up. Do it now." Her voice sounded distant and fuzzy in her own ears.

She had time enough to be relieved when the creature followed her instructions before it slipped from her control a second time. It was enough. Jami's sword took the monster's head off at the neck in one swift stroke. Foul gore gushed everywhere. The stench of the creature's blood was worse than anything Suvi had ever smelled before.

"Are you all right, Highness?" Jami asked.

"I can't move," Suvi said, not liking the panic in her voice.

The marine asked, "It bit you?"

Suvi nodded. It was getting difficult to keep her eyes open. "So tired."

The marine backed up, and Jami shifted closer.

"Where is Private Almar?" the marine asked. "How did that thing get loose?"

"Don't go to sleep," Jami said. "You've been poisoned. Hopefully someone here knows what to do."

Suvi licked her lips. Her face felt strange. "My lips are numb." She closed her eyes, but someone shook her.

"Wake up, drown you!" This time it was Dylan. He was bleeding from a cut high on his forehead. A worried-looking Darius was crouched next to him.

Dylan is alive. He must have won. She tried to tell them that she was fine and to leave her alone, but the words came out in a senseless mumble. A part of her knew that she was in trouble. The rest of her didn't care.

"It didn't latch onto her completely." The voice was a woman's. "It only got one poison fang into her."

It took Suvi a moment to recognize the face. *Dylan's sister. Her name is . . . Moira. Yes, Moira.*

Jami said. "Is it too late?"

"I don't think so," Moira said. "If we can keep her breathing for the next hour or so, the venom will wear off."

"You're certain of this?" Jami asked.

"Fairly certain," Moira said. "Get out of my way. Please. I need to slow the bleeding and clean the wound of poison."

Suvi felt a tug, and then a hot bolt of agony shot up her leg. Someone shrieked.

"Suvi, I need you to look at me," Moira said. "Open your eyes. Suvi?"

They were open, Suvi thought, feeling petulant. She stared at Moira.

"That's a good girl," Moira said.

"P-p-princess," Suvi said. The word was strangely difficult to pronounce. Still, she was happy to have been able to force it past her numb lips. "Not g-girl."

Moira smiled. "You're going to be all right," she said. She was holding a surgeon's knife. "Don't worry. Just stay with me. Okay?"

"Don't." Suvi shook her head. It seemed to go on moving back and forth even though she knew it should stop. It felt odd, as if she were drunk. "Don't take my leg." *I can't dance in the rigging on one leg.*

"Your leg will be fine." Moira's smile didn't instill much confidence. "I need to cut the wound to get the poison out."

Staring up at the sky, Suvi attempted to focus on the clouds and not the pain and fear. There wasn't much to see. The sky was a thick haze of gray backlit by a full moon. Someone brought a quilt, and she felt a little better. The next few minutes passed in a warm haze of alternating numbness and searing agony. It was hard to breathe, but every time she stopped, someone shook her until she choked out another breath.

"That's as much as I can do here. Let's get her somewhere where I can see what I'm doing," Moira said. "Darius, get Ivar. He knows more about this than I."

Suvi concentrated on preventing the weight on her chest from smothering her. When she was lifted, gentle as they were, the pain was terrific. She said a quick prayer to Mother Stjarrna and then passed out.

⊰ NELS ⊱

ONE

Colonel Pesola is going to have my skin. Why haven't the damned cannon reached camp yet? Nels urged Loimuta up the mountain in the downpour and cursed the day his infantry company drew artillery escort duty. If there was an unpleasant task on the roster, his company was certain to get the assignment. Nels knew the source for that directive wasn't Major Lindström. Viktor had been right. It was Colonel Pesola. Unfortunately, it was too late to heed Viktor's warning. Nels's only regret was that now his company paid the price of Pesola's grudge too. It was clear that this would be the way of things until Pesola decided otherwise, and Pesola wasn't about to decide otherwise for the foreseeable future.

And this was only the beginning. The Seventh regiment had only progressed as far as the mountains southeast of Herraskariano.

The weather only added to Nels's misery. This was the fourth day in a row of nonstop rain, and after the vanguard's passing, the narrow tree-lined path resembled a swamp more than it did a road. Under ideal conditions, an army could travel twenty to twenty-five miles a day. With the weather as it was, they were lucky to get half that. The artillery was two days behind and likely to be a third by the look of things.

And still it rained.

Having checked on the progress at the front of the artillery line, he'd turned around to make sure of the rest. It wasn't long before he noticed the gap and went to discover what the problem was. He reached the top of the ridge and spied the draft horses straining in the mire. A corporal tugged at the lead mare's headstall. Personnel circled the cannon like panicked bees around an upended hive. Unable to circumvent the obstruction without risking pitching into a ravine, ordnance, baggage wagons, and the remaining troops clogged the road beyond. Nels sighed, gave Loimuta a gentle kick, and plunged into the chaos.

"What's the problem this time?" Nels pushed the brim of his tricorne up with an index finger and leaned forward in the saddle. The heavy weight of the sodden hat shifted. He felt rainwater pour out of the back of his hat and runnel down the shoulders of his foul-weather coat.

"Damned wheel is stuck, sir!" Corporal Kallela said.

Nels searched for Viktor in the bustle of activity and didn't find him. He did, however, notice the dour overlieutenant who always seemed to be watching. *One of Suvi's spies, no doubt. Or would he be one of Uncle Sakari's?* "Underlieutenant Larsson! We need a lever and some brush," Nels said. "Get it under that wheel."

"And where am I to find a lever, sir?" Larsson asked. "We're a bit far from the royal carpentry."

Nels didn't show the jab had hit home. "We're surrounded by an entire forest. Surely a tree will suffice? We've axes aplenty. Now get to it."

"Yes, sir." Larsson's salute could've been replaced with a rude gesture. It carried the same level of respect. She snarled for the carpentry tools to be retrieved from the supply wagons and stomped away in the mud. Moments later, she disappeared behind the tree line with an annoyed flip of soggy brown curls.

Hasta, give me patience, Nels thought.

Extracting draft horses from mud was difficult enough—each cannon and its accompanying materials and gear required the services of thirty-four of the beasts—but excavating a six-thousand-pound howitzer was going to be quite another matter. They didn't have enough troops as it was, with one third of the army deathly ill.

At least my company is safe, Nels thought. *From variola, anyway.* It seemed unreasonable that Pesola could hold it against him. "Private Hanski, inform Colonel Pesola we are delayed. Again."

A variola-scarred private saluted and ran.

Nels hopped off Loimuta, landing in ankle-deep muck. He'd been seven the last time he had actually watched a coachman lever a wheel out of a hole. Such lapses in experience still ambushed him from time to time, giving the troops under his command more ammunition for their contempt. He was all too aware that the fortuitous event at the Commons Hospital had saved him more than any Acrasian illusion ever could. He'd tried over and over to repeat that instance of command magic, to no avail. So it was that he continued to live under the threat of discovery. To his surprise, the pressure was every bit as bad as if he were at court, if not more so. It didn't matter that most of the troops had no useful magical skills themselves, only what his uncle would've referred to as "peasant magic." Nels found it baffling how those who'd suffered so much at the hands of those with unlimited power reinforced the abuse without thought.

A stocky artillery master sergeant named Jarvi forced his way through the chaos and took over managing the placement of the brush. His face was square and obstinate, and his orders came in short barks.

"Can we lighten the load, do you think?" Nels asked.

Master Sergeant Jarvi stomped foliage into the muddy hole and scowled. Mud splashed up on the master sergeant's uniform. "No. And get the swiving hells out of the damned way." He glanced up. "Ah, sorry, Captain."

Nels stepped back, allowing Jarvi the space needed to do his job.

The master sergeant left the wheel and then grabbed a horse's headstall. "Don't just stand there, push, damn you!"

With his career riding on getting the cannon moving, Nels joined the others and wedged himself against the wheel. His body tensed against the weight. Mud sucked at his boots. Cold rainwater oozed down the back of his neck and into his eyes. The gun crept forward, but the wheel slipped, churning leaves and bark into the mud. By the third attempt, Nels's arms felt weak and the muscles in his legs twitched with fatigue. Underlieutenant Larsson and her carpentry detail arrived. Jarvi rammed the makeshift lever into place with expert precision and then ordered everyone back into place. Nels shoved as hard as he could. The cannon inched clear of the mud-filled hole but rocked backward with a splash.

Jarvi's frustrated growl beat against the rain. "Put your backs into it, you Abigails!"

Nels heard a loud squelch, and the howitzer once again came free of the hole. The slimy spokes jerked out of his hands. Six tons of iron gouged the mud, narrowly missing his left boot. He jerked out of the way in time, but in his rush he stumbled backward. Slipping, he landed flat on his backside. Larsson's laugh was abruptly cut off with a grunt.

Heavy raindrops smacked time against the oiled leather of Nels's coat. He counted to ten and retrieved his hat, feeling the muddy ooze drop off the skirts of his coat in clumps as he got to his feet. He knew what they expected, and even a year ago, he'd have given it to them, but not now. Slapping his hat against his thigh to dislodge the last of the sludge, he didn't look up until he was certain of his self-control.

The mountainside behind Larsson had subtly changed. He blinked. Earth and rock slowly shifted. It uprooted a scrubby bush, and he watched it tumble, landing in the road.

"Mudslide!" Nels shoved Larsson from the cannon's path.

Whether it was the sound of his voice or the moving earth, the result was the same—the draft horses panicked, jerking the gun forward. Loimuta let out an angry scream and bolted for the ridge. Terrified, the draft horses followed, dragging the cannon behind. Troops leapt for safety. The cries of kainen and animals were buried in the rumble of moving earth. Nels chased after horses and artillery gun, a lump of dread in his stomach the size of a boulder. With no way to stop the horses, he expected some part of the harness assembly to snap. He topped the ridge with the sole intention of seeing where the cannon would end up, hopefully no worse for wear. The steep incline flattened after a few yards. However, upon reaching the other side of the ridge, the rock in his stomach melted into ice water.

Private Hanski stood in the center of the path.

The horses abruptly slowed, but the cannon didn't. It skidded and slammed into the hindquarters of the rearmost mare and flipped. Before Nels could react, Hanski vanished beneath several tons of iron and writhing animals with a terrified scream. Nels ran to help. Pain-choked shrieks flayed the air. Getting closer, he smelled blood. Horses fought for freedom, lashing out at anything to gain desperate purchase against rattling metal fastenings and the broken harness tongue. Three of the ten were dead, and it looked like two more would have to be put down.

"Hanski? Where are you?" Torn between staying out of danger and missing an important sign, his search was complicated by thrashing hooves the size of his head. He spotted a muddy blue jacket cuff protruding from wreckage and snatched it. "Be alive, damn you." He reached inside the sleeve, and Hanski's hand convulsed, grabbing at Nels's fingers. "I've got you." He peered through the wreckage and shoved at sodden dirt one-handed until Hanski's head was clear.

Hanski moaned. His face was pale against the muck. Dropping the private's hand, Nels began feeling around the twisted harnesses and broken spars. He found Hanski's shoulders and arms, but one leg was half buried under one of the dead horses. Its live harness mate was also partially trapped. The horse squirmed from beneath the hulk, and the body slipped, crushing Hanski to the thigh. The private screamed. A large ironshod hoof slammed against a broken spar near Hanski's head, splintering wood. Checking his pistol first, Nels loaded it and then pressed the barrel against the wounded horse's head. He hoped the powder would catch.

Someone shouted, "No! Don't!"

He pulled the trigger. The pistol's recoil jarred his arm, and burnt gunpowder clouded the air with smoke so heavy, he could taste the grit on his tongue. He felt rather than saw the cannon shift toward the edge.

Can't get Hanski out. Get the horses free first. Nels shoved the hot pistol into his belt and moved to the next pair of tangled horses. He ripped at their harness fastenings, seeking to separate them from the cannon, but the wet metal and leather slithered through his numbed fingers. The smoke started to clear. The howitzer sped up its relentless journey to the edge. He gave up on the buckles and drew a knife. Other troops arrived. He heard their distant warnings, but at that moment, a horse scrambled to its feet. The cannon skidded two yards all at once, knocking Nels down and carrying him with it. He struggled to get up. *Where's Hanski?* A second horse cleared the tangled mess when he spotted the gleam of a harness pin. On instinct, he stretched, reaching for it. The loop at the top felt cold and slick around his finger. He felt gritty mud against his cheek. The cannon tilted.

"It's going to go!"

He rolled out of the way. The artillery gun flipped, pitching over the ledge. Something hard slammed into his back, knocking the breath out of him. He coughed, tasted mud, didn't dare move. When it seemed safe enough, he braved inching toward the now-scarred ledge on his belly, feeling strangely blank. The six-ton howitzer had left behind a wide swath of blood stained and splintered trees. *How are we going to get the swiving thing out of there?*

"Sir? Are you hurt? Sir?"

Nels twisted onto his back, and dull pain throbbed under his right shoulder blade. Master Sergeant Jarvi stared down at him.

Underlieutenant Larsson bent closer, extending a hand. "I thought your job was to get *us* killed," she said.

Nels watched his hand tremble before it touched Larsson's. "Never expect anything of others you aren't willing to do yourself." Standing at last, he asked, "Hanski?"

"Alive. Not sure, but I think his leg is broken," Larsson said.

Stretching, Nels tested his back. Nothing felt out of place, but his muscles protested and the blunt ache gained steady strength with each beat of his heart. *That's going to hurt tomorrow.* "Private, get the healer. Now. Master Sergeant, I'll leave you to figuring out how to get that damned gun out of there. Larsson, find Loimuta."

"Yes, sir!" Larsson said.

Viktor arrived. He was out of breath. "Just what in all the secret names of the Father did you think you were doing?"

"Trying to save us from dragging that cannon to the front ourselves. We may yet, if we lose any more horses," Nels said. "Where have you been?"

Viktor glanced uphill and rubbed his chin. "Looking after your personal baggage. Someone has to. Corporal Mustonen has better things to do."

Nels had observed Viktor while playing cards enough to know that Viktor tended to touch his face when bluffing. *He's lying.* "I don't own anything worth the trouble."

"You can't imagine how much a clean, dry shirt sells for these days, stolen or otherwise." Viktor winked. There was definitely something about his smile that wasn't quite genuine.

"Right, then. We talk about it later," Nels whispered. Then he asked loud enough for others to hear, "What's the damage?"

"Five dead horses. One missing. Other than Hanski, no other injuries. Going to have a deuce of a time digging out," Viktor said. "You sure you're all right?"

Nels ventured a look down into the ravine. "Would you say that was about a two-hundred-and-fifty-foot drop?" Now that the danger was past, the tremor in his hand had spread through his arms and down to his knees, making the ground unstable. *The troops are watching.* He tightened a fist, clamping down on any show of weakness. He didn't want to lose what little regard his fraudulent magic skills had gained. "Other than having a strong need to sit down, I'm fine." He gave Viktor a confident grin—at least, he hoped it was a confident grin.

"Then come away from there. I'd rather not fish you off a mountainside. I have rules about those sorts of things, you know," Viktor said.

Nels shuffled a few steps before Viktor grabbed his elbow. "Rules? What are you, my wet nurse?" Nels whispered.

"Just keep Hanski company while I see what's keeping the healer," Viktor said.

Thankful for a moment to collect himself, Nels collapsed in the mud. The last of the tremors in his legs passed before he noticed Hanski staring. "You'll be fine. Healer will be here soon."

Hanski nodded, wincing. His face was so pale, it was almost blue.

"You swiving bag of glue! Bite me again, and I'll box your damned ears!" Larsson's voice echoed off the mountain.

Nels bit down on the inside of his cheek to stop himself from laughing, then did real damage when Victor reappeared in his usual silent and unexpected way.

"Bad news," Viktor said. "Don't think anyone else is getting through for at least an hour."

"Was afraid of that," Nels said, checking his injured cheek with his tongue. "You're in charge until I get back. Once the way is clear, get Jarvi what he needs to haul that damned cannon out of there." Deciding Larsson had had enough of Loimuta, he put two fingers to his lips and let out a loud whistle.

"What?" Viktor said. "Me?"

Nels got to his feet. His legs were already sore and his back was aching. "Someone has to take care of Hanski. The closest healer available on this side of that mess is commissioned to Colonel Pesola. She's damned well not going to take orders from the likes of you, now, is she?"

Loimuta trotted into view with a ragged-looking Under-lieutenant Larsson limping after.

"Thank you, Lieutenant Larsson." Nels pointed to the ground in front of him. "Loimuta, down."

The gelding snorted and stamped, clearly not pleased with being ordered but willing to play along as usual for the promise of a carrot. The horse knelt down, front legs first.

Viktor gave Loimuta a doubtful look. "Planning on finishing the job on Hanski that cannon started?"

"Loimuta has indulged himself enough, I should think. Haven't you, boy?" Nels gave the horse a soothing pat on the neck before helping Hanski mount.

"If you say so," Viktor said.

As Loimuta righted himself Hanski nearly fell off, grabbing for the reins that Nels had secured in place when he wasn't using them.

"Hold on to the saddle," Nels said, looping his hand through Loimuta's halter. "I've got his head." He led the gelding through the mud. Loimuta thumped him on the shoulder with his nose. "It's good to see you, too," Nels said, and patted Loimuta's cheek.

Once they had rounded the bend, he climbed into the saddle in front of Hanski. Then he shifted his weight back, squeezed his legs against Loimuta's sides, and gave him a short command. The stallion responded with a burst of speed. Nels located the correct tent with little trouble. Several supply crates were stacked near the entrance. A short middle-aged woman lay asleep on the cot. Her hands were neatly folded on her abdomen, and weariness etched a determined line between her brows.

"Kaija Westola?" Nels asked.

She didn't open her eyes or move. Her voice was sharp and pinched at the corners. "What do you want?"

"I've a man with a broken leg."

"The company surgeon is back that way." She waggled her hand in the air toward the ridge. Her eyelids remained shut. "I imagine he'll be here in another hour or so."

"He'll be delayed. I thought—"

"You thought wrong." The line between her brows grew more pronounced. "I'm on retainer as Colonel Pesola's personal healer. I'm not paid to serve the whole damned brigade."

Short on patience, Nels entered the tent. "You do now."

She scowled and sat up. "Who do you—"

"I'm Captain Nels Gunnar Ari *Ilmari* Hännenen." He assumed the haughty tone he used when faking court speech—yet another trick he'd borrowed from the royal horsemaster. Over the past few weeks, he'd discovered that in some ways, people weren't much different from horses. They perceived what they expected, and well, he was an Ilmari, after all. "You'll be paid for your trouble. Get out there."

Kaija Westola glared back, and Nels held her gaze, uncertain whether or not his bluff was going to succeed. She got to her feet, her day dress wrinkled and stained, and her graying hair bound into a fuzzy knot perched on the crown of her head. She was short, and her arms were thin like the bones of a delicate yet belligerent sea bird. She rested both hands on her hips and took a determined step forward; the tip of her pointed nose almost jabbed his solar plexus.

"I don't like you," she said.

He raised an eyebrow. "Is that important?"

"You worthless, bottle-headed, arrogant son of a—"

"Perhaps you can remind me of my many shortcomings later? Private Hanski is in pain." Nels stared down at her.

She looked as though she was going to peck him before she grunted and stamped out of the tent into the rain.

This is going to be a very long day, he thought.

While she patched up Hanski, Nels stationed himself on one of the crates stacked outside the tent and watched when she was too busy to notice. Regardless of her attitude, Westola appeared to be good at her work. The moment she touched Hanski's leg, the lines of pain around his eyes and mouth vanished. She was also stronger than she looked. She set the bone with little trouble and only a small amount of assistance from Nels. When that was done, she gave Hanski a tea to drink. Once the splint was secured in place, Nels paid her two gold falcons.

She stared at the gold in her palm and a strange expression crossed her face. "He should be watched tonight." When Nels didn't appear to take the hint, she sighed. "Wait." She rummaged through a black leather bag. Glass clattered against glass and then she settled on a vial of clear liquid. "If he shows signs of fever, have him drink this and send someone to fetch me."

Whatever he'd attempted to make her think, he wasn't made of gold. "I've only paid you for the—"

"Just do it. No extra charge. Now the two of you get out of here before I have you thrown out."

Nels blinked. "Thank you." Unable to think of anything else to say, he focused on helping Hanski onto Loimuta's back.

Westola leaned against the tentpole. "Been a while since I've dealt with anything more challenging than a headache or gout." She paused and then pulled the tent flap closed.

TWO

Smoky campfires dotted the hills as Nels staggered toward his tent. He couldn't have been more thankful for Master Sergeant Tane Jarvi. As it turned out, Jarvi was not only an excellent gunnery officer but a pyrotechnic. Dry stockings and warm food went a long way when it came to troop morale. As a result, Nels had ordered Jarvi to visit three other companies and ensure that the troops were warm. Nels hoped it might engender a sense of cooperation in an otherwise contentious environment. Comprised as the Royal Army was for the most part of criminals and misfits, an almost total lack of coordination was its biggest failing.

Well, one of them, anyway, Nels thought.

A loud thump in the trees to his left jarred him out of his reverie. It was followed by a muttered curse. He wondered how long Suvi's spy planned to lurk in the brush. Whoever he was, he was no korva. Nels didn't think anyone beside himself could be that noisy while sneaking. He got as far as gripping the tent flap when a joyous shout echoed from across the camp. The chorus of hoots, jeers, and clapping brought him up short. Turning on his heel with a sigh, he headed for the commotion. He didn't need Viktor's ears to find the source—a lean-to constructed of rough logs and a drape. Judging by the shadows cast against the canvas, at least fifteen to twenty soldiers were crammed inside. Lifting the drape, he was met with the smell of unwashed bodies, damp wool, and whiskey. Several faces turned toward him an instant before a number of quick-thinkers made their escape. Corporal Kallela was the first.

Trapped in the center of the group, one of the doomed privates— Private Paiva, in fact—straightened and yelled, "Attention!"

Those not fast enough or sober enough to duck out froze in place. Nels wedged past the cluster of privates and discovered Underlieutenant Larsson at the center. She had the distinct air of someone who was hiding something. An uneasy silence pressed against the canvas walls.

Nels slowly tugged his watch from his coat pocket by its watch chain. "Half past eleven, I see. Underlieutenant Larsson, is there any explanation as to why these troops aren't asleep?"

Larsson looked like she'd swallowed a lemon whole. "Ah, sir. It isn't what you think." She'd positioned herself in front of a barrel, which appeared to have been the group's previous focus.

Nels pushed Larsson aside and spied the dice on top of the water barrel. "Interesting. Do you mind telling me what it is I'm not thinking?"

"We're not gambling, sir." Larsson paused, opened her mouth, and then closed it.

"And why aren't you gambling, Underlieutenant?"

"Because it's against regulations?"

Nels picked up the dice before Larsson could grab them. On a hunch, he tossed them on the barrel three times. They came up seven twice and eleven once. *I'm not the only one in the company who uses tricks, it seems,* he thought as the color in Larsson's face went slightly gray. He turned to the privates. "It's late. And I'd rather be in my bunk, but I pride myself in accommodating my officers. Therefore, I think I shall play for a while."

Larsson dropped her shoulders in obvious relief. "Yes, sir. Just let me get you a fresh set of dice." She reached for the top of the water barrel.

Nels snatched the dice again before she could touch them. "I believe I'll use these."

"What?"

"What's good enough for my officers is good enough for me."

Larsson blinked. He watched the subtle changes in her face as the meaning behind his words sank in.

"Ah. Unenthused," Nels said. "I can't say as I blame you under the circumstances. Tell you what: To make it more interesting, I'll bet double whatever you do."

The privates cheered and clapped Larsson on the back.

"Go on! Give him what for!"

Larsson balanced on a camp cot with the attitude of a condemned prisoner.

"I'll roll first," Nels said. "What will you bet?"

The lean-to filled with excited jeers, and the others exchanged paper notes in a flurry. The audience regained a number of its members as it became apparent that punishment wasn't being dealt out. Larsson brought out a small bundle of folded money and peeled off two paper notes.

"As little as that with these stakes?" Nels asked. "What are you afraid of?" He tossed a ten-falcon note onto the trunk.

There was a gasp.

Nels picked up the dice and threw them onto the makeshift table. They made a hollow thump against the wood. Five white dots came up on the first die, paired with three on the second. "An eight. I wonder if I can do that again." He played the game straight for a few rounds to avoid tipping off the others, but within an hour, he'd taken her for more than two weeks' pay. To Larsson's disgust, he handed out his winnings to those watching.

"I must say, I like these dice," Nels said. "Mind if I keep them?"

Larsson sighed. "No, sir."

"Very generous of you. It seems I've misjudged you, Larsson." Nels stood up. "Walk with me."

Larsson gave him a questioning look but stepped under the canvas flap. It fell back into place behind her. The candles flickered.

"The rest of you, get to your bunks." He exited the tent. Larsson stood waiting for him next to a large oak, a shadow among shadows. There was a worried look on her face.

"It was only a bit of harmless—"

"Don't even start." Nels counted to ten, squeezed a fist in order to gain some control of his temper, and then asked, "Do you know anything of human magic?"

Larsson hesitated, and he thought he detected a flash of guilty unease in her eyes. "Everyone knows humans don't have magic, sir." Her tone was flat.

"It isn't magic as you and I know it. It's trickery, really. Illusion. Fraud," he said, and then paused to let that word and its implications add weight to the conversation. He kept his voice low. "The interesting thing is, when a kainen uses magic, it leaves a certain feeling in the air. I can sense it." That much was true, as much good as it did him. "Human magic, on the other hand . . ." He let his voice trail off. The terrified expression on her face said he had her, all right. When they were far enough from the lean-to, he stopped. "I never want to see that again."

"No, sir. I mean, yes, sir."

"Cheating your platoon? Do you have any idea what they would do if they found out? Do you know what I could do to you?" *I could have you hanged, Larsson. And that's the very least of what I could do.* "We haven't reached the front, not yet. You're new. I assume you've never been in so much as a skirmish?"

Larsson swallowed. "Ah, no, sir."

"I didn't think so. You see, Larsson, soon your life will depend upon your platoon and theirs upon you. I suggest you give the matter long thought," he said. He could see he'd made his point when she glanced at the troops shuffling off to their tents and swallowed.

"In the meantime, you'll do exactly as I tell you," Nels said. "Without question."

"Sir, yes, sir."

"I think you should show more concern for others. We'll start with Loimuta," Nels said. "I want him curried and his hooves cleaned every night. He gets an apple or a carrot once it's done. It comes out of your pay." He paused. "Well, next week's pay."

"Oh, gods, that horse is evil."

He gave her a knowing smile. "That horse is your best friend for the next two weeks. If you can't see to the needs of a damned horse, I'm not trusting you with my troops. I don't care what you paid for those bars. Got it?"

"Yes, sir."

"Go on. Get to your cot."

He returned her salute and watched her walk away, hoping against hope she'd stay out of trouble. When he reached his tent, he was more exhausted than he'd thought possible. Still, he planned to make more progress through the book on Acrasian infantry tactics before sleeping. It was his third time through it, and he'd already memorized half of the text. He knew it wouldn't resolve his questions or lessen his anxiety, but he pored over it anyway on the off chance that he'd find something in it that would stop the night-mares. After two years in the King's Army, he knew wasn't afraid of dying. He lived in a near-constant terror of letting down his troops.

His tent was dark when he reached it. Apparently, Corporal Mustonen had neglected to leave a light for him before retiring. Nels unbuttoned his filthy coat and entered the tent. Sweeping a hand through the air in front of him, he searched for the lamp hanging off the center tentpole. He didn't find it. His skin itched from dried mud and sweat, and he stank. *I'd kill for a bath.* But he was far too tired to bother, and in any case, he didn't want to roust Mustonen out of his well-deserved sleep to fetch and heat water. It'd be cruel.

"Where are my cannon?" The voice was low and hardened with quiet malice.

Nels barked his shin against the end of his cot. *Colonel Pesola.* Icy fingers of fear raked his heart. There were two kinds of people who volunteered for the King's Army. The first group did so because they had little other choice—a short life in the army was a little better than the prospects of starvation or prison. Over the past few weeks, Nels had come to realize that Colonel Pesola fell into the second group. Ultimately, Pesola didn't enjoy killing people as much as he enjoyed hurting them.

"It may be dark in here, but I don't believe that will have affected your hearing. I'm not one to repeat myself, understand," Pesola said. "But given the lateness of the hour, I'll make an excep-tion." He paused as if to give Nels time to focus. "Where are my cannon?" The question was laced with command magic.

"They're here, sir."

"We're one gun short. I counted."

"There was an accident. A mudslide. We were unable to get the howitzer out of the ravine. We spent the whole day—"

Nels was interrupted by three slow, liquid pops in the dark. He hadn't seen Pesola do anything as base as crack his knuckles—except once. During a formal officers' dinner, a clumsy corporal had spilled a glass of Pesola's best port. The corporal had been whipped until she bled. Pesola had an evil reputation among those who served beneath him, which he had earned in every way possible, from Nels's recent observations. Regardless, he often found himself pressing his luck as far as Pesola was concerned. There wasn't a good explanation for it. To do so was dangerous and stupid any way you looked at it, but there it was nonetheless.

Pesola said, "You abandoned your post." *Pop. Pause. Pop.*

"Private Hanski was injured. I left Overlieutenant Reini in charge of—"

"Your orders were 'Get the cannon safely to the front.'" *Pop. Pause. Pop. Pause. Pop.* "Does anything about that sound like 'Escort a foot soldier to a surgeon'? *My* surgeon, I might add."

"Hanski's leg was broken."

"Then he should've been put down. Like the horse." Pesola took in a deep breath. Nels tried not to think of it as a hiss. "Oh, yes, I heard about the horse. Not much gets past me. I've many pairs of eyes. It seems you're an individual that merits a great deal of . . . observation."

Nels thought of the spy. *Not Suvi's. Not mother's. Nor Uncle Sakari's.*

I'm a fool.

"Fine animal, that was. Worth far more than a private too stupid to run from a stampede." *Pop. Pause. Pop.*

Nels's hands formed fists. For the hundredth time since they'd started their journey to the front, he reminded himself that hitting the colonel wasn't worth being hung. As always, it was a close debate. "May I light the lamp, sir?"

"Indulge the captain, Holdon."

A hooded lamp hinge creaked open. Light flooded the tent. Nels held up a hand, blinking against the brightness. Pesola was sitting on the camp cot, and two enlisted soldiers stood at the ready in front of the stacked wooden crates Nels used as both bookshelf and writing desk. Pesola's teeth showed in a bright row like a hungry animal preparing to bite. His eyes were shielded behind spectacles as usual. The glass lenses reflected the lamplight in cold round voids, blank of all emotion save menace.

"Make no mistake, my fine young cock. You've gone too far this time," Pesola said.

Nels swallowed. "Transfer me to another unit."

"Oh, no. I think not." Pesola gave him a predatory smile. "Do you think for one instant I won't put a lash to you?"

The words were out of Nels's mouth before he could stop them. "You wouldn't dare."

Pesola drew in a breath, seeming to savor a particularly fine perfume. "It seems I know a few things you don't. Or is it possible that you haven't quite thought the matter through? You see, I've done some checking. The precariousness of your . . . position wasn't difficult to discover."

Nels bit down a retort that would only make matters worse.

"You appear to be unaware that you and your company are entirely mine to dispose of as I wish," Pesola said. He motioned to the men in front of the bookcase. "Your father wouldn't save you even if he could."

Pesola's men closed on Nels.

"We'll have the irons, Sergeant Holdon. I won't waste the energy compelling him. We'll save that for later. Shall we? Our Captain Hännenen needs a few lessons in humility. As it happens, I'm a fine teacher."

THREE

Disarmed, Nels was led through sleeping troops to an isolated tent on the outermost edge of camp. It stank of old blood and piss. An iron frame had been assembled in the center. The only furnishings other than the iron scaffold were a long folding table with several items arranged on top and a large bucket.

Nels's manacles were briefly unlocked, and his coat and shirt were removed. No explanation was given, and questions—no matter how insistent—were ignored. The irons were replaced on his wrists and the chain between the cuffs was looped onto a hook welded to the top of the iron frame. Nels had to stretch as far as he could and tilt up onto his toes in order for Holdon to attach it. Nels soon discovered that standing with his feet flat on the ground was impossible. Any attempt to do so resulted in the manacles biting painfully deep into his wrists. Holden set the manacle key on the table. Meanwhile, Pesola's corporal filled a steel basin with water and replaced a bloody rag with a fresh cloth. Both moved with the bored air of long-practiced actions. When the preparations were complete, Sergeant Holdon and Pesola's corporal exited.

Pesola didn't show up at any point during the proceedings.

Well, this isn't good, Nels thought. Looking up, he studied how the hook was set into the chain. Cool relief washed over him. *I can get out of this whenever I need to. It's a simple enough trick.*

At that moment, he couldn't have been more thankful for Suvi's last gift. Not all of the information on illusions and escapology had been practical to his situation, but enough of it had been, and he soon discovered that he enjoyed the practice. Before leaving for the front, he'd committed as much as he could to memory and then hid the book in the barracks house. He had a lot to learn yet. Locks and escapology were complicated, but he felt he had enough skill to get free of his current situation. He released the breath he'd been holding, and his heart slowed. *I'll be fine. Another round of pointless saber-rattling from Pesola. That's all.*

Then he spied the bloody cat-o'-nine-tails on the folding table. The whip was arranged near the steel basin and the manacle key. The rest of the table's inventory consisted of a bowl of salt and an ornate silver-framed hourglass with black sand. Pesola's reputation completed the picture. An icy knot formed in Nels's guts as the implications set in.

Don't even think it. I may not have much power or influence, but my father is still the king. Nels hated being afraid. He knew too well the cost of showing fear. He didn't think of himself as a coward— not any longer. However, no one had ever proposed to torture him for the pleasure of it before. He'd had nightmares of such things, of course, thanks to his father's tour of the catacombs beneath the palace. *Pesola doesn't know about that. He won't do it. He wouldn't dare go that far.*

Just in case, hold your tongue. Don't push him. You'll want to. But you have to save some strength for—

At that moment, a callused hand shoved the tent flap aside.

Pesola's corporal entered carrying a folded camp chair. Pesola wasn't far behind.

Nels nearly jumped out of his own skin, and it was followed by an overwhelming surge of rage. "Gods curse you, let me down!" Forgetting the manacles in his fury, he threw himself against his restraints. Something popped, and sharp agony exploded in his shoulder.

Neither man reacted as if they'd heard. Pesola's corporal unfolded the chair, positioned it, and then left. Colonel Pesola sat and then sipped from a steaming cup of what smelled like coffee. He could easily have been in a manor house, enjoying his evening beverage.

"You swiving son of a pox-ridden street whore! I'll rip your throat out!" The pain in Nels's shoulder prevented him from struggling too much. He told himself that the only reason he'd shouted was to make his later acquiescence more believable. It had nothing to do with fear.

Pesola flipped open the book in his lap, and Nels recognized the brown leather cover of the Acrasian tactics manual. "It seems we have the entire evening with which to amuse ourselves." Pesola said in a bored tone and gave the book a small smile. "When I say 'we,' I actually only mean me."

He's gone through my belongings? "I'm killing you the instant I'm free! Do you hear me?"

"Hännenen, do remain silent until I give you permission to speak," Pesola said, using command magic to emphasize his words.

Nels stopped struggling. There was an advantage to allowing Pesola to think command magic affected him, and Nels needed every advantage he could grab. He swallowed.

"Better." Pesola took another slow sip of coffee and again spoke to the open page. "I suspect you have a rather keen interest in my welfare. That is, if you value your mother's life."

Nels narrowed his eyes at Pesola.

"The queen is in a rather precarious position, it seems," Pesola said. "You may speak."

A tremor of icy dread rippled up the nape of Nels's neck. "What do you mean?"

"Ah, polite. Good." Pesola set his tin cup on the ground next to the leg of the camp chair. Then he stood and approached Nels. Pesola didn't stop until he was close—too close as far as Nels was concerned. Pesola reached up and ran a finger along Nels's cheek. "I like that," Pesola said.

Nels fought to keep from showing revulsion. He knew this game. He'd seen it played. Any sign of weakness would make everything so much worse. "What do you know about my mother?"

Pesola's smile was now inches away. Nels could smell the coffee on his breath.

"Let me tell you a story," Pesola said. "It's somewhat sentimental for my tastes, but as it happens, the ending is quite . . . gripping." He grabbed a fistful of Nels's hair and yanked.

The sudden sharp pain brought tears to Nels's eyes.

"It begins with a young gentleman who lost something important. And in his despair, he fell in with the wrong crowd. That part, in and of itself, isn't what's significant," Pesola said, releasing the fistful of hair. Nels's head rocked.

"It's boringly common, I'm afraid," Pesola said. "No, what's significant is that this young gentleman enjoyed risks."

Nels aimed his forehead for Pesola's nose, but Pesola stepped back and the chains brought Nels up short. Agony in Nels's shoulder reminded him to be more careful.

Pesola began a leisurely walk around the iron frame. "What kind of risks, you ask? Mainly, gambling. It seems he was good at it—that is, until his luck ran out. Again, not the most original of stories. Unfortunately, our . . . hero didn't have the sense to quit when he should've. He got in rather . . ."

Something gouged into Nels's bruised back. The unexpected pain was excruciating, and a scream burst free from his mouth.

"Deep," Pesola said. "However, here's where the story gets interesting. You see, his mother took care of the matter for him. The trouble is, she was forced to rescue her son from his creditors—not once but multiple times. And in spite of her lofty title, she didn't always have the funds on hand." He took two steps. "However, she loved her son very much. Very much indeed. Enough to do things—even make agreements with people she probably shouldn't have." Two more steps, and Pesola appeared again to the right. He breathed in, and his teeth flashed a threat on the edge of Nels's vision. "Soon, she might discover that her friends aren't as generous as she thinks. Nor are her secrets as safe from your uncle. Sadly, it seems she used much of her power securing her unfortunate son's safety."

A chill ran through Nels's body. *Oh, Hasta. Why didn't I just die in Onni that day?*

"Permit me to be so bold as to provide an up-to-date summary of the balance of power in Eledore and your place within it, Captain," Pesola said. "Your father favors your uncle. Your mother has no legal means of presenting an opposition, and your sister, your sole means of support, left for the Waterborne kingdoms a month ago and hasn't been heard from since."

"What has any of that to do with you?" *Has something happened to Suvi?*

"Very little. It does, however, factor into our relationship. I own you, bone, muscle, soul, and skin," Pesola said. "Your uncle sends his condolences, by the way."

Nels took two breaths. His heart thundered in his ears loud

enough to blot out all else. He swallowed. *If Uncle intended Pesola to kill me, he'd have done it already.* "What do you want?"

Pesola settled back into the camp chair and stretched out his legs. "Ah. Everything is so much more pleasant when we understand our place, isn't it?" He picked up the Acrasian book and opened it again. "Enjoy learning from your enemies, do you?"

Remaining silent, Nels waited to hear what was next. Pesola closed the book and placed it on the table. Then he got up from the camp chair.

"I believe it's time for your first lesson," Pesola said.

With the rapid grace of a snake, Pesola drew up close again. This time, he punched Nels in the guts with three quick jabs. Air was forced out of Nels's lungs in an instant, and he lost his footing. His full weight was abruptly brought down on his wrists. He would have screamed if he could. As it was, he hung limp on the chain and gasped like a beached fish. Pesola didn't wait for him to recover. Once again he battered Nels's stomach. Nels struggled with all his might not to throw up.

Pesola paused, tilting his head. "What did you say?"

Coughing, Nels fought to reply. "You swiving son of a—" The remainder of his hoarse retort vanished in a fresh and extended burst of pain. The blows rained down on him, and he rapidly lost track of what was happening. Pesola finally stopped. Nels fought to breathe. He tasted blood as it oozed from his nose and mouth. He spit.

That was when he saw Pesola pick up the whip.

FOUR

Nels didn't understand that he'd passed out until a shocking cold force slapped him to the surface. Water ran down his hair and into his eyes. He blinked back water, blood, and tears.

"Don't nap yet," Pesola said. "The discussion was only getting interesting."

Nels's tongue felt too big inside his mouth. His back was a raw agony that his thoughts couldn't escape. It was becoming more and more difficult to breathe. The knowledge that everything should've been far worse didn't help—Pesola had uttered several magic-laden commands that would've intensified the pain.

Stupid. Pushed Pesola too far, Nels thought. *Quiet now. Say nothing. Or you'll not get out of this.* He let his head drop and told himself it was just another tactic—not cowardice. *Save some strength.* What there was to save and for what purpose, he couldn't quite remember.

"I suppose you're right. The conversation has been quite vigorous," Pesola said, dropping the cat-o'-nine-tails on the table. "You have enough to think about for now." He went to the steel basin, rinsed blood from his hands, and then dried them on a cloth resting next to the bowl. "There are other, more urgent matters to attend to for a little while." He reached inside his stained waistcoat pocket, pulled out a watch, and checked the time. Then he flipped the hourglass. "I'll give you an hour to contemplate your situation. I expect you'll see things more reasonably when I return. Because I can make everything so much worse. And I intend to." He put away the watch. "Until then."

Nels listened to Pesola's footsteps until they faded away. Nels's eyelids closed. The urge to sleep was huge. If only he could breathe.

Pesola is insane.

There isn't much time. Do something. Anything.

Sleeping is something. Must conserve energy for—

For what?

He forced his eyes open and scanned the room. *Something important.* He blinked. When nothing on the table triggered the thought he was hoping for, he glanced up.

Oh.

With clumsy movements, he began to work his boots off—one at a time. Toe to heel. As luck would have it, they weren't as well-fitted as they should've been and never had been, since he'd bought them secondhand. The leather was old and worn, and therefore supple. He'd intended to get new ones before leaving Jalokivi for the front but hadn't had the funds. Slipping his boots off without the use of his hands took longer than he would've liked, but he did eventually work them off. When he looked to the hourglass, it was more than half gone. His heart galloped. An image of all that was ahead made the whole situation seem impossible. His back had begun to quiet, settling into a dull menace that kept time with his heart. The idea of waking that pain was almost unbearable. *Don't think about it. Focus on the task at hand.* He'd need his feet and toes. So, he turned his attention to getting his stockings off.

Please, Hasta. Let me have enough strength.

Lifting his legs tortured his back, but he converted the pain to anger and used that to supplement the strength he didn't have. It took several tries, which didn't do his wrists any good either, but he did eventually manage to touch his feet on the top bar. Pausing for breath, his back blazed with fresh agony. He muttered another quick prayer, and then pulled himself up using his wrists until he could hook his legs around the bar. Finally, he hung upside down with his weight completely off his wrists for the first time in what seemed like hours. Naturally, this brought on another round of pain, but the rest was simple. With the chain slack, he disconnected the link from the hook and was free. His hands were throbbing, numb, and tingling. He could barely make fists, but he couldn't wait to recover. Unable to get a good grip on the bar, his hands slipped, and he fell in an agonized heap of clanking chains. He lay on the ground, stunned and shaking with the effort not to scream, praying that Pesola hadn't left anyone outside.

No one came to investigate the noise.

He dragged himself to his feet. Swaying, he staggered to the table and caught himself before he fell a second time. His hands were next to useless. He was grateful that he wouldn't have to attempt anything as complex as picking the manacle locks. Using the key was difficult enough. Dropping it wasn't an option. The idea of stooping over was horrible, and he didn't think he'd have the strength to search for the key in the dirt. His awkward fingers finally did what he wanted. The manacles fell away. He allowed himself a small hiss of triumph, then relocked the empty manacles and replaced the key in the exact position where he'd found it. He consulted the hourglass and estimated that he had less than a quarter of an hour remaining with which to escape. *Provided Pesola didn't lie.*

It took the very last shred of Nels's remaining courage to keep from running out of the tent. Instead, he arranged the irons so that they draped over the iron scaffold.

Let Pesola make of that what he can.

Giving in to fear, Nels shoved on boots and stockings as fast as he could manage. He took the time to slip on his shirt and then grab his coat as well as the Acrasian infantry manual. He didn't bother to button the shirt—his fingers wouldn't have complied if he'd tried. Cold evening air slapped his bare skin. His shirt wouldn't provide much cover and would be a stained ruin in no time, if it wasn't already, but he couldn't bring himself to put on his coat. It'd hurt too much. *No time, anyway.* Staggering like a drunk, he avoided the main path for fear of encountering Pesola. It seemed to take forever, but Nels finally reached the rows of small tents occupied by pairs of enlisted soldiers. Thanks to the darkness, no one paid special attention to him. Outside of the usual earth-shattering snores erupting from Private Horn's dog tent, the camp remained dead quiet. He was thankful for the lateness of the hour. Everyone with any sense was sleeping—anyone who wasn't on sentry duty.

"There you are."

Nels started so violently that Viktor grabbed him by the arm to keep him from falling. Nels let out a short hiss of pain.

"Shut up, Nyberg! Some of us are trying to sleep, damn you."

They both froze in place until the snoring resumed. Nels shuffled onward with Viktor at his side.

"I really wish you wouldn't do that," Nels whispered with swollen lips.

Viktor whispered, "Sorry."

"Shouldn't you be asleep?" Nels asked.

"Corporal Mustonen said Pesola was in your tent when he went to see you settled for the night. After Pesola dismissed him,

Mustonen came looking for me. Somebody has to keep you out of trouble." He paused. "You've been gone for almost two hours."

"That long?" Nels hoped the question sounded casual.

Viktor gave him a long look. "What happened to you?"

Nels decided not to expend the energy on an answer. "How did you find me?"

"It was easy enough," Viktor said. "I listened for the stampeding herd of elk. When I didn't hear any, I settled for the drunken ox."

It took Nels twenty steps to come up with a response. "Thank you." The words barely cleared his bruised lips.

When he didn't rise to the jab, Viktor paused. "You're a mess. Seems I was right to worry."

"Worrying over the state of my clothes is Corporal Mustonen's job. I'll be fine."

"I wasn't talking about your clothes." Viktor touched his arm. "I think you should come with me."

"Why?"

"Because you're in no shape to argue, for one thing," Viktor said. "For another, Mustonen and that surly surgeon you're so fond of are waiting."

Nels stopped. The world tilted. Again, Viktor grabbed him.

"Don't—" Nels flinched.

Viktor wedged his shoulder under Nels's arm. "I've got you. Come on."

"I can walk, damn it." The objection didn't carry much force because he wasn't all that certain he could.

"Sure. If we had all night and I was willing to watch you crawl," Viktor said. "However enjoyable that might be, I think all of us would prefer to get some sleep tonight. In any case, that twice-damned surgeon is probably drinking all of my lovely whiskey and charging me by the hour on top of it all."

Nels felt Viktor begin to steer him away from the lower-ranked officers' area. "Where are we going?"

"Somewhere Pesola isn't going to think of looking for you."

"And where is that?"

"Shut up and trust me," Viktor said with a smile. "This will be brilliant."

"Why do I have a bad feeling about this?"

"Have I ever had a bad idea?"

"I'm too exhausted to make a detailed list," Nels said. "But we could start with stealing those cattle from Lord Ranta."

"Is that humor I detect? You must be feeling better already," Viktor said. They stumbled for a few steps. "It was fun watching Pesola explain how those cows got mixed in with his personal provisions. Wasn't it?"

Nels set his mind to dragging himself the remaining distance. They staggered together for another hundred feet. He couldn't help noticing that even when bearing the weight of a clumsy friend, Viktor made no sound.

"Viktor?"

"Yes?"

"Remind me to drop a bell around your neck tomorrow."

FIVE

Kaija Westola waved away a moth that had strayed too close to her face, with a bored expression. "It's about damned time, Reini," she said in a hushed voice, and then shut the book she'd been reading. "I don't care what you're paying. It won't make up for lost sleep."

She and Corporal Mustonen occupied two camp chairs arranged outside a large, striped tent. Water barrels topped with lanterns were situated next to the chairs, standing in for tables and providing light. The gray- and black-striped tent appeared to be the only one whose occupants weren't asleep. Perched among the ragtag cluster of wagons, threadbare tents, lean-tos, and baggage that comprised the camp, it also appeared far too merry for its dour neighbors. Nels knew where he was at once. Not all families stayed behind when a soldier went to war. Some of them traveled along with the army. Often considered equally unclean as their soldier family members, military families didn't have much reason to remain behind.

"I almost went to bed," Westola said. "Do you have any idea what time it—"

At that moment, Nels's legs decided enough was enough. He tripped and a bolt of searing pain shot through him from neck to toes.

Viktor said, "Can I get some help here?"

Corporal Mustonen rushed to the rescue before Nels finally slipped through Viktor's grip. Nels attempted not to scream his lungs out in the process.

"Get him inside," Westola said, holding the tent flap open. She didn't look remotely shocked when the light within the tent revealed the extent of the damage.

She's seen this before, Nels thought. *Or perhaps it's not as bad as it feels?*

A pretty young woman with long black hair, dressed in an altered sergeant's jacket without the insignia and a pair of tight-fitting trousers, shut the lid of a trunk and straightened. She caught sight of him and gasped. Then she looked away and fled.

On second thought, it is as bad as it feels, Nels bit down on the pain until they finished getting him settled facedown onto a cot.

Viktor suddenly let out a low whistle. "That's impressive."

Westola set about separating his shirt from the wounds. "Pesola made short work of you. Usually, he takes his time. I wonder why he let you go so fast."

Nels ignored Viktor. Laying on his belly, it was easy enough to do. "He didn't. I took my leave."

"You left without his permission?" Westola paused. "How?"

"I have my ways," Nels said.

"He's not going to be happy about that," Westola said.

Unfortunately, that wasn't an aspect of the situation that Nels had thought through. Icy fear formed yet another cold knot in his gut. He did his best to sound cavalier in spite of it. "Is there a reason I should care?"

"If there's anyone else he can blame for your escape," Westola

said. She finished with the shirt and paused again—Nels assumed—
to take inventory of the damage. "You damned well should."

"He didn't leave a guard, if that's what you're asking." Nels gri-
maced when she laid a chilly hand on his shoulder.

"That's good," she said. Her hand warmed and then the pain
slowly eased. "You should be careful of telling anyone where you
were this evening."

*Pesola will punish anyone he can. Westola, Viktor, and Mustonen
will be first on his list. So will whoever owns this tent.* "I should go,"
Nels said, and attempted to get up.

"Lay still, damn you," Westola said, shoving him back down on
the cot. "Or I'll knock you unconscious. I can do it, you know. And
you won't be able to do a damned thing about it."

"Look. You're the one who brought it up. I'm a danger to everyone here," Nels said. "I should get back to my own tent."

"Only to have Pesola whisk you away again before dawn?"
Viktor asked. "Oh no, you don't. You're staying right where you are.
Do you think for an instant I'd let Westola drink the last of my
best whiskey for nothing?"

"That was your best?" Westola asked.

"Just do the job you were hired to do already, will you?" Viktor
settled down on the ground next to the camp cot. His voice belied
the concern etched in his face, but then he ruined the effect and
winked. "Besides, I've got to hear how you managed to get free."

Nels closed his eyes while Westola washed away crusted blood
with warm water. "Magic."

Viktor asked, "That's it? That's all you're going to tell me?"

"Yes," Nels said.

"Swiving bastard," Viktor said.

Comfortable for the first time in hours, Nels smiled. "What
was that, Overlieutenant?"

"I said you're a swiving bastard, *sir*," Viktor said.

"And don't you forget it," Nels mumbled. He was exhausted. He wanted nothing more than to pass out. The tug and pinch of Westola's needle was the only thing keeping him awake. He lay inert, drifting and listening to the hollow clank and splash of water being poured into a tin bath. He smelled soft perfume and burning lamp oil, and did his utmost to avoid thinking of Ilta.

I wonder what she's doing right now.

Stop it.

By the time Westola had finished stitching the wounds in need of it, he was more than half asleep. Mustonen finished filling the bath, prepared a change of clothes, and left. Nels woke with a start when Westola gently shook him.

"I suggest you get cleaned up and then get some rest," Westola said. She looked tired. "You'll not feel any pain for seven or eight hours, if you're careful and don't do anything foolish."

Viktor snorted. "That isn't exactly the plan."

"I know. I know. Just because it doesn't hurt—" Nels sat up.

Westola frowned at him. "I mean it. Do as I say and your back will heal in a day or two," she said, taking the whiskey from Viktor.

"Hey! That's mine," Viktor said.

"You'll scar." Westola ignored Viktor and drank from the neck of the bottle. "There's nothing I can do about that. But you'll be fine otherwise. Push yourself too far, and you'll undo everything. You'll be sleeping on your stomach for a month."

"Yes, ma'am," Nels said, narrowing his eyes at Viktor.

"You're spoiling the fun," Viktor said.

Westola sighed. "And I won't come back to fix the mess you make of yourself, either. You hear me? You're on your own."

"I hear you," Nels said, holding out a hand to her. "You didn't have to do this. Not for me. Thanks."

Westola took it and gave it a gentle shake as if he'd break. Nels attempted not to show amusement.

"You know," she said. "I don't like Pesola any more than the rest of you do."

"Then why do you work for him?" Viktor asked.

Shrugging, Westola started cleaning her surgeon's tools with Viktor's good whiskey. "Why do any of us?"

Because there's no other choice, Nels thought. Westola was very good at her job—better than most healers regulated to the Royal Army. He wondered what transgression she had committed that had forced her into such an assignment. He watched as Viktor offered to pay her, but she held up a hand in refusal.

"Never tell Pesola I had anything to do with this," she said, "and we're even."

Viktor paused and then nodded.

She asked, "What do you plan to do tomorrow, Captain?"

Nels said, "Show up for formation as usual."

"And what will you say?" she asked.

"Nothing," Nels said. "Absolutely nothing. This evening never happened."

She nodded. "You might just live long enough to fight the damned war." She finished packing the last of her medical supplies and tools, and then went off to bed.

Nels watched her go. "She's a much better person than she lets on."

"She fits in with the rest of us, then," Viktor said.

⊰ I L T A ⊱

ONE

If it hadn't been for the visions, Ilta would have dismissed the sporadic flashes on the horizon as lightning. Perched high on Angel's Thumb, Gran's house was remote enough that the thunder of cannon couldn't shatter comfortable illusions, but what was happening upstairs brooked no such self-trickery. Saara Korpela, Eledore's Silmaillia, was dying, and like the war, Ilta was helpless to do anything about it. She had never been more miserable in her whole life. The only good news had arrived with the royal messenger bird that morning along with another bundle of Nels's letters that had been dropped at the gate by the mail coach. The messenger bird brought a pronouncement from the king. Her imprisonment was at an end. The reason why hadn't been because she was forgiven. She was still exiled from the capital and court. The change in her status was because her previous jailer had died, and King Henrik wouldn't be sending another.

A muffled cry drove Ilta inside and up the stairs.

"Gran?" She ran as fast as she could and threw open the bedroom door. "What is it you need?"

The fever had appeared four days ago, and there was still no outward sign of rash. Gran lay huddled in layers of blankets, the fever that was burning away her life painting her face a deep red. Damp curls stuck to her face and neck as she gestured toward the pitcher.

"Water." The once-firm voice was a hoarse whisper.

Ilta carefully perched on the edge of the bedstead and helped Gran hold the glass. The hand resting underneath Ilta's own was too hot, and Ilta considered lowering her grandmother's temperature yet again. She got as far as mentally anchoring herself in preparation when Gran pulled away.

"Don't waste healing energy on the dying," Gran said. "Have you done as I told you?"

Ilta had trouble speaking past the lump in her throat, "I-I've gathered your clothes."

"When I'm gone, burn them. The bedclothes and the feather-bed, too. Same as we did with yours and the sergeant's." Gran fell back on the pillows with a grimace. "Then scrub the floors. Boil everything I touched. Every dish. Every utensil."

"You can't die. Not yet. Please! I can't—" Ilta's words were cut off by Gran's hard frown.

"I daresay you can and you will. Maybe you didn't get in a full apprenticeship, and maybe you've made a few mistakes—"

"I don't want this power. I don't want to be Silmaillia," Ilta said. "Not any more."

"Do you think you're the only one to have regrets? I should've done better by you. I shouldn't have protected you so much. I should've let you be among others more often. It would've better prepared you. I should never have done the things that hurt you in the first place." Her eyelids closed, snuffing out the intensity of her stare. "How was anyone to know?"

"We should've. What's the point in seeing into the future, otherwise?"

"Ironic, isn't it?" Gran swallowed. "Always remember, one can't see in every direction. Sometimes, the gods, the goddesses . . . death . . . life . . . they will all have their way. It is important to remember there is always a bigger power than you."

Ilta nodded and sniffed.

Gran's frown became a small proud smile. "You've got strength in you. More than your parents knew. You'll do."

Ilta said, "Don't talk like that. You're going to recover."

"Don't lie to yourself. You must face the hard things in life," Gran said. "I know Eledorean custom dictates otherwise, but it wasn't always that way. Death may be unpleasant, but it's essential. Every Silmaillia—every healer before you knows this. Dying makes room for new life. Remember the sacred circle. It's a comfort to know I'll sleep beside Jyri again."

Hot tears burned her eyes as Ilta hugged Gran. The old woman's ribs felt brittle as a bird's through the blankets. Ilta told herself that Gran couldn't be this frail creature wasting away on the bed. Gran was strong, a commanding force that even kings reckoned with. "I'll be alone."

"Stop whining, child. Everyone has their time. My time's now. Hanging on longer will only make it worse."

Ilta flinched at the too-familiar words.

"You won't be alone for long. Nels will come." Gran took a deep breath. "How many wounded?"

Ilta blinked away tears and spoke to the wall; the knot of heartbreak in her throat receded as she recalled the vision that had invaded her sleep. "Twelve. Fewer if the snow is early. There'll be others. Many others. But they won't make the trip up the mountain. He won't risk it."

"How soon?" Gran asked.

Ilta sat up, and her grief was overshadowed by thoughts of what was ahead. "Four weeks? Maybe five. It's hard to tell. There are too many influencing factors. The only thing certain is that I'll have to leave this place." She suddenly realized her voice was steady. *Gran's distracting me so I can focus on what I need to do. Oh, Gran, I'll never be as wise and strong as you.*

Gran's expression twisted—the color in her face was leached by pain, and a jolt of terror jerked Ilta to the present. Long moments passed before Gran was able to speak again, but when she did, her voice was steady. "The contagion will have run its course by then, I think. They'll be safe. And it'll give you time to prepare and pack. One last thing." Gran weakly pushed away the blankets. "Bring me the box."

"No. Please," Ilta said. The aching lump returned with a vengeance, threatening to choke her.

Gran's black eyes snapped open. "Do as I say, girl. This is no time for mulishness."

Ilta nodded and ran downstairs to her grandmother's sanctuary. Grabbing the wooden box kept under the altar, she paused. Its shifting contents made small clinking sounds—metal against glass or stone. The box felt strangely light for the weight of responsibility it contained. She returned to the sickroom with a heavy heart and set the small chest on the table next to the bedstead.

"Open it," Gran said.

Ilta swallowed once before pulling the cherrywood lid open by its iron hasp. A lump swathed in a hank of white Ytlainen silk rested on top of cork-stoppered bottles, surgeon's tools, small stones, and charms. She knew what should come next. Everything was happening too fast.

"Give me the knife," Gran said.

Ilta unwrapped the cloth-covered bundle and revealed a

bone-handled knife. The ripple-patterned blade thrummed with power. Although the handle was old, it was much newer than the blade. The blade was ancient and far older than Gran, having belonged to Gran's grandmother's grandmother. Made of fabled water steel, it had been forged by one of the ancient master weaponsmiths. Ilta didn't dare touch the knife directly, keeping the silk between herself and the hilt. Gran sat up straighter with a grunt, putting out a hand for the yellowed handle. She traced a holy sign over the knife, closed her eyes, and silently whispered a blessing. Then she opened her eyes again. Light glinted off the blade's edge as Gran weakly turned the knife widdershins in her hands three times. She paused and uncharacteristic regret softened her expression. "I apologize for the poor ceremony. There should be a priest present. To give his blessing. To represent balance."

Eledore welcomed many different sects from all of the kingdoms, but Ilta and her grandmother were members of the oldest, and the concept of balance was central to their beliefs.

"Then we shouldn't do this now." Ilta's heart hammered at her breastbone. *I don't want to be a Silmaillia. Not now.* She'd been thinking ever since Gran had gotten sick. Maybe the disease was a sign that she, Ilta, wasn't worthy. Maybe she should—

"Don't interrupt." With a deep breath, Gran's face emitted proud warmth. "Do you, Ilta Korpela, swear in the secret names of all the gods and goddesses, making them your witnesses, that you will fulfill this oath according to your ability and judgment?"

Ilta paused. "I do so swear. But I—"

"Do you swear to share your knowledge without thought for selfish gain or profit?"

"We need to talk. I mean it," Ilta said. "I can't do this. Not now."

Gran let the hand holding the knife drop into her lap. "All right. What's wrong?"

"You can't possibly be serious about making me a full-fledged healer, let alone the Silmaillia. Not now. Not after what I've done."

"And why not?"

"I can't be Silmaillia. I'm banished from court."

"It's not King Henrik you'll serve. He won't last out the year. It's Queen Suvi."

Oh. Ilta blinked. "Do you honestly think I can be trusted with the knowledge now?"

"Let me ask you something."

Ilta nodded.

"Will you ever do anything like that again?"

"No! I—"

"Then you've learned," Gran said. "Education in the healing arts doesn't come cheap. Never has. Never will. Anyone who says otherwise is lying."

"But—"

"To hide away what you've learned means that the cost—all those lives lost—was for nothing. If you'd gone into the situation knowing that so many would die and done it anyway, I would agree with you. But you didn't. You made an honest mistake. Now it is up to you to honor those who've paid the price for you learning your lesson. Use your knowledge. Be a better healer and save other lives. None of us are perfect. If only there were time enough to tell you of the mistakes I've made." Gran looked away. "One of them resulted in you being born as you are."

"What are you saying?"

"I'm saying that you were born without the ability to shield yourself, with too much power. And it was my fault."

"That isn't true."

"It is," Gran said. "You might as well know it now."

"How?"

Gran reached for the water glass again, and Ilta helped her with it before it spilled. "In the library." Gran swallowed five times, and Ilta took back the glass. "There's a locked cabinet. Key is in that box. Inside, you'll find my journals. Everything is there. Read them."

"I don't understand."

"You will," Gran said. "There was a reason your parents waited to give you to me until it was clear there was no other choice. It wasn't because they didn't know what was wrong. They had good reasons."

"If you say so."

"We work with energy far more powerful than any kainen has a right to work with. We reach inside other people—inside places that no one was meant to venture. We turn them away from death when death might have its way. There's a price for that power. Balance is more than a word. It's in everything a healer does."

Ilta swallowed.

"You're going to make mistakes," Gran said. "But you'll make good choices, too. You'll save lives. You understand the responsibility now. You understand it better than most who've been practicing half their lives. Don't throw that away. Not now. Not when you'll be needed most."

"So, I have no choice."

"There's always a choice. You can turn away from healing. I'd rather you didn't, but if you'd prefer to not have this responsibility, I'll understand. Nonetheless, refusing won't take away the responsibility you already have—the responsibility for the lives you've already affected. By turning away, you'll affect even more lives. There's no way out of that. You are what you are. At least if you remain a healer, you'll have a chance at equalizing the ledger."

Biting her lip, Ilta asked, "Does it get any easier?"

"In some respects, it only gets harder. Particularly when it comes to those you love. At least you know what's at stake now. Blame disease. Blame war. Blame accidents. Blame the nature of kainen and humans. Blame the gods, if you must. What's done is done. You aren't the first healer to have made such a mistake. You won't be the last. Wisdom doesn't come cheap, either. Nothing does that's of worth."

Ilta took a deep breath. "All right, Gran. I accept the responsibility."

Gently picking up the knife, Gran repeated the ritual from the beginning. This time, Ilta listened to the words and felt more present in the moment.

Finally, Gran asked, "Do you swear to share your knowledge?"

"I do so swear." And the weight of the oath settled onto Ilta's shoulders.

"Do you swear to protect and provide sanctuary to the sick no matter who they might be? No matter who might wish them harm?"

This is really happening. Ilta's stomach quivered, and her mouth was dry. The gloom became a haze smelling of burning oil, poultice herbs, and sickness. The lamp on the table spilled golden light over the bed and the rug on the floor. The bright circle bisected a painting of a younger, happier Gran nestled in the arms of Grandfather Jyri.

Ilta wiped the sweat from her hands onto her skirt, focusing again on the oath before speaking. "I do so swear." *The Threefold Oath. It's done. I'm no longer Gran's apprentice. I'm a healer now.*

A healer who has killed hundreds, maybe even thousands with her arrogance.

Gran closed her eyes and put out her left hand, palm up. Ilta could see the faded spiral scar in the center. "Give me your left hand."

Ilta knew what would come next and couldn't help dreading it. Nonetheless, she laid her hand in Gran's fevered one. Magic weighed in the air as Gran focused. Using the blade, she cut the symbol for life and death into Ilta's palm. Ilta drew in a quick breath against the sharp pain and did her best not to flinch. She understood why her grandmother wasn't using magic to deaden feeling. The pain was a reminder. *Healing cuts two ways.* It was part of the oath and a symbol of the cost.

When she was done, Gran then cut into her own palm, closing off the spiral in two strokes and making it into another symbol entirely—a symbol for completeness and endings. With that, she pressed her left palm against Ilta's left. "We do hereby seal this oath. Blood for blood. Life for life. For the betterment of all. For the best possible outcome. All things in balance." Then she offered Ilta the knife hilt first.

Ilta accepted it, wrapping her injured palm around the bone handle and sensing the heat of her grandmother's fever in it. The knife's grip was slippery in her hand for an instant until her palm tingled. Looking at the knife, the bone grip was no longer a yellowy white. It now was white with a hint of pink.

"I, Saara Roosa Korpela, lay upon you the duty and responsibility of healer and the Silmaillia of the People."

The room blurred as Ilta accepted the charge, rotating the surgeon's ritual knife in the opposite direction—clockwise, the direction of the sun. The lump in Ilta's throat walled off anything she might say. The ache in her chest swelled until it overwhelmed her. Tears spilled down her cheeks. The warmth in knife's hilt didn't dissipate. It remained strangely warm. The blood from her injured palm was gone, and she got the sense that there was more to the blade than Gran had told her.

Great Mother Stjarrna, what am I going to do without Gran?

"One more thing," Gran said. "The World's Pillar."

"Yes, Gran?"

"You must go back before the year ends. Bring them both. The royal twins. You will need both or it will not work. Understand?" Gran's voice was weak. "Don't grieve too much. I had a full life and long. Only wish I were leaving you to easier times." She lay back on the pillows with a grunt; her reserves seemed used up. She turned away, and Ilta heard her mutter something.

"What is it, Gran?"

The words were a whisper. "I love you, granddaughter. May the Great Mother of the Dark and the Great Father of the Light together bless and keep you."

"I love you, too."

And in the time it took for Ilta to draw her next breath, Gran, Saara Roosa Korpela, Silmaillia of the People and advisor to King Henrik of Eledore, was gone.

❦ NELS ❧

ONE

The artillery company Nels and his troops had been assigned to support made camp before dark for a change. Partly, this was due to the fact that they'd finally left the unyielding Selkäranka Mountains behind. The other reason was that there'd been clear skies four days running. Taking advantage of the opportunity to catch up, Field Marshal Kauranen pushed the Sixth Army as fast as it could go. Although tired, Nels's troops were happier than they'd been since leaving the capital and the Sininen River bridge.

The day's journey done, Nels had seen that his soldiers had everything they needed and was now grooming Loimuta. Looking southeast from the camp's horse pickets, he spied the jagged, shadowy, snow-topped ridges of the Dragerhrygg, or the Demon's Spine, and felt a confusing mix of anticipation and dread. When the Dragerhryggs smoothed out into the long stretch of hills leading the city of Virens, the Sixth would at last join the rest of the Eledorean forces. The troops were impatient for a fight. Everyone wanted to reach the front before the war was won, and everyone seemed certain this would be the case—everyone but Nels, it seemed. He couldn't shake the feeling of impending doom. So much so that Viktor had taken to mocking him for it.

Not that that is anything new, Nels thought.

"Captain Hännenen, sir?"

Combing the sweat stains from Loimuta's girth, Nels paused and straightened with only a small amount of pain. His back had healed but was still tender. "Yes?"

He turned and saw it was a corporal he didn't know. Her skin was dark, and her eyes were even darker. Her expression was unreadable. For a moment, Nels panicked—thinking that perhaps that Colonel Pesola hadn't forgotten him after all. Nels's right hand tightened around the currycomb. He could take it with him. It might make a decent weapon. *And then you'd be hanged.* With a long slow breath, he forced himself to switch the currycomb to his left and return her salute.

"Major Lindström would like to speak with you in private as soon as you're available," she said.

Relief relaxed the tension in his fist. "Thank you, corporal. You may inform him I'll be there within the hour."

When the corporal saluted and left, Nels returned to grooming Loimuta. Corporal Mustonen often told him that he should have one of the privates see to the troublesome gelding, but listening to the horse make quiet happy noises was one of small joys Nels had remaining to him. Usually, Nels lingered at the task—taking his time with every detail, but with Lindström waiting, Nels finished as quickly as he could. Then he fed Loimuta the carrot he'd hidden in his coat pocket.

"Sorry, boy. I have to go."

Loimuta thumped him on the shoulder with his forehead.

"I know. I know. I'm sorry. I'll see you tomorrow. Be a good boy."

Loimuta let out a low rumble deep in his throat that sounded like a growl.

"Slip your tether tonight," Nels said, "and there'll be no carrot in the morning."

The horse snorted.

"Don't look at me. I wasn't the one who wandered into the wrong tent. You scared Lieutenant Larsson half to death last night. You're lucky she didn't shoot you." He gave Loimuta's neck one last pat and rushed to his tent. There, he washed face, neck, and hands, and changed into a fresh shirt. He spotted a letter placed on his cot where he'd find it. Recognizing his father's handwriting with a frown, he decided to wait to read it until after he'd seen Major Lindström. He left it where it was, untouched, and headed to the major's tent. It wasn't far—one row back from his own and two tents over. In the time that he'd taken to clean up, the sky had gone completely dark and the temperature had cooled, taking the warm edge off the day. Breathing deep, he felt his tired muscles relax. He was going to sleep well. *Provided Father doesn't have anything awful to say.*

When has he ever not? It then occurred to Nels that the king hadn't written a word to him in years, and a bad feeling tightened a knot in his gut. *It doesn't matter. Not now. Lindström first.*

The major's tent flaps were down, but they weren't tied shut. The glow of the camp lantern painted the white canvas a buttery yellow. Nels stood outside, checking his uniform one last time before knocking on the tentpole centered in the doorway.

"Is that you, Hännenen?" Lindström's voice was calm, maybe even a touch sad.

He isn't angry. That's good. Right? "It is, sir."

"Come in."

Stooping, Nels pushed the tent flap aside and entered. His

nose was met with the scent of fresh-cooked food. He spotted trays loaded with Ytlainen pancakes, lingonberry jam, and a covered dish filled with a savory-smelling soup on the folding table. His stomach reminded him with a loud growl that he hadn't eaten yet. It was then that he noticed that the table had been laid out for two.

Is he expecting someone else?

The major had been relaxing on his camp cot, reading. He closed the book, sat up, and returned Nels's salute. In his late fifties, Lindström had a lean and athletic build. His thick, graying hair was swept back into a queue tied with a black silk ribbon. If there was one matter in which Nels knew himself fortunate, it was in the officer to which he directly reported. Where Pesola was known for his brutality, Lindström had a reputation for fairness and concern for his troops. In addition, something about Lindström reminded Nels of Captain Veli Ari Karpanen. He couldn't have said what it was, but whatever the reason, Nels knew he would do anything for the man. In fact, he had done already—quitting gambling and drinking, for a start.

Well, the gambling, anyway, Nels thought. With the table of food so close, he hoped that whatever it was Lindström wanted to discuss would be quick.

Lindström motioned to the camp chair positioned nearby at the table. "I was about to have some dinner. Care to join me?" Lindström asked. "I have some . . . news, but I thought we should eat first."

"Yes, sir. Thank you, sir."

The major served the pancakes, potatoes with grilled onions, and portions of what turned out to be reindeer meatballs in brown sauce. It was the best meal Nels had had since leaving Jalokivi. Conversation during the meal was polite, if a bit stilted. That was unusual for Lindström. When they were finished eating, the major's corporal cleared the dishes and served the coffee. It wasn't until the corporal also produced a beautiful fruit pie that Nels understood the major probably wanted something from him—something he probably wouldn't be happy about.

Lindström waited until the corporal left. "I've received some news from Jalokivi. Rather bad news for you, I'm afraid."

"Oh?"

"It's about the queen. She's been seriously ill. Variola."

Nels blinked.

"She died. Yesterday," Lindström said. "I'm so sorry."

"Oh." *That's why Father wrote. I should've known,* Nels thought.

"Here. Let me get you some Islander wine." Lindström got up and went to one of his trunks. "No one else knows. There hasn't been any sort of announcement. I felt you should hear it from me first. Because ... well, for obvious reasons, and then there's ... We'll discuss that once you've caught your breath, as it were." He located the bottle he wanted and kicked the trunk lid closed.

Nels sat in silence while Lindström collected glasses and poured the wine. *Why don't I feel anything?* He decided it was shock. He emptied his glass without really tasting the contents. Lindström seemed to be waiting for him to say something, but Nels felt empty. *Blank.*

Lindström filled the wineglass a second time. "Is there anything I can do?"

Shaking his head, Nels swallowed. It was as though someone had yanked the earth from beneath his feet.

"I'd leave you to your grief, but there is an urgent matter we need to discuss," Lindström said.

Nels cleared his throat. "Yes, sir?"

"I understand you speak Acrasian. Is this true?"

"It is." It was a relief to think of anything else for a moment.

"How fluent are you?"

"Quite. But I haven't used Acrasian regularly in a while."

"How long do you think it would take for you to become fluent?"

Nels shrugged. "Not long. I read Acrasian very well. I've been studying Acrasian tactics. Specifically, any paper Lucrosia Marcellus Domitia has written on the subject."

Lindström's eyebrows shot up. "Really?"

"Yes, sir," Nels said. "I thought a knowledge of Acrasian tactics might prove useful."

"Interesting," Lindström said. "If only we had more time . . ."

"More time, sir?"

"I have a new assignment for you. Unfortunately, it involves your temporarily leaving your command."

Oh. The backs of Nels's eyes began to burn, and he felt his fingernails dig into his palms beneath the table.

Lindström continued. "Before you protest, let me explain my decision." He refilled the coffee cups.

Nels left his where it was. Steam drifted off the coffee, executing graceful curls in the tense atmosphere.

"Colonel Sasja Vinter is in charge of the Acrasian prisoners. She's in need of an interpreter to conduct negotiations with the Acrasians for their care. Although I'd prefer not to lose you, ethically, I'm obligated to recommend you for the role. You're the only qualified candidate we have," Major Lindström said. "Now, I'm aware of your history with the Acrasians, but I consider this an opportunity."

"An opportunity?" Nels heard the edge of anger in his question. *First the crown. Now this.*

"Yes," Major Lindström said, lowering his voice. "To get you out from under Pesola's shadow. I'd have you transferred to another company, one not under his authority, but I can't. Everyone with whom I hold any influence is at the front."

"But I—"

"You've done nothing to warrant a transfer. Nothing. I want you to be aware of that fact. I consider you to be one of my best officers."

Nels swallowed his rage. *How can I be this upset over losing my company and yet feel nothing for Mother?* Shame deepened his anger.

"I understand how this must feel after . . . well, after what happened before," Major Lindström said. "But this has nothing to do with your ability to command."

Or lack of it, Nels thought.

"I'm not doing this because I want to. I'm doing it because I have no other choice."

"Is this Pesola's—"

"No. The fact is, I can't protect you from him. Not any longer. Not now that the queen is . . ." Lindström let his sentence drift off unfinished. "Look. Either I get you out of here tonight or something terrible is going to happen. Do you understand?"

"Pesola hasn't forgotten me."

"I'm afraid grudges are Pesola's specialty," Lindström said. "However, he doesn't know about the queen. Not yet. And by the time he finds out, I have every intention of your being safely away."

"I see."

"You *will* have your company back. I'll see to it. But I can't stand by and let him murder you over something he should've thought to do himself."

"Pesola isn't fit to command. You know that, don't you?"

Looking away, Lindström didn't argue the point. "You know I can't answer that question."

"I'll go. Because it's you asking." Nels forced the words past the lump in his throat. "I'm taking Reini with me."

"Of course."

"Where am I to go?"

"You're to report directly to Colonel Vinter of Brigadier General Moilanen's Tenth Regiment, Fifth Infantry." Lindström placed a folded and sealed letter on the table. "Those are your orders. Vinter is in Gardemeister. It's a town located near Angel's Thumb. Do you know where that is?"

Paper crinkled under Nels's numb fingertips. *Didn't Viktor say that Ilta went home to her Gran's place on Angel's Thumb? The thought brought him a small amount of comfort. Maybe she'll see me? Maybe she's been too busy to answer my letters.* "I do."

"Good. Do you have a recommendation for temporary command?"

Nels gave it some thought. "Underlieutenant Kadri Larsson."

Lindström's eyebrows shot up the second time that evening. "Really? Isn't she the one you put on report for gambling?"

"She learned her lesson, sir. Forgive me, but Overlieutenant Rebane is an arrogant hothead. He'll push every boundary at every opportunity. You won't have time for that. He'll do something stupid and self-aggrandizing, *then* think about the consequences for everyone else. Larsson can handle it. She'll follow your lead. She's also clever enough to know when not to do so, and creative enough to do it in such a way that you won't have to notice."

"Interesting," Lindström said. "Well, you would know."

"You asked, sir."

"All right. Send Larsson to see me as soon as possible. I'll handle the details," Lindström said. "Then get packed. You're leaving tonight."

"Yes, sir." Nels got to his feet.

"Oh, and do be quiet about it," Lindström said. "I don't want Pesola to know you're gone until it's too late to do anything about it."

Nels nodded.

"Good luck."

"Thank you, sir." Nels left to pack.

My Dearest Ilta,

I received a bundle of your letters today. These four are the first that have caught up with me. As many times as I've cursed being forced to give up my company, I'm also happy. The journey here brought me closer to you. It also brought your letters. Mind you, I haven't read them, not yet. There hasn't been time, but all four spent the day inside my uniform jacket. Whenever I was certain no one was looking I ran my fingers across them, knowing that the paper and ink had been as near to you as they are to me. I smell them now and imagine I can catch the scent of your hair.

I pray you are all right. I received word you were ill. All this time, I've wondered what happened. Why did you vanish without a word? I would've ridden up the mountain tonight except I've no leave. Not yet. For now, I'm relieved to know you're alive. That's enough. Feel free to send a list of anything you need. Gardemeister isn't that far. I can send supplies or other help. Most of all, please let me know you're safe.

There's an ache inside my chest, and knowing you're only a few miles away only makes it worse. At least I can look up the slopes of Angel's Thumb and imagine you're looking down. The wind that blows through my window is the same that caressed your face not long before. I feel so alone right now. I wish you were here. I want to hear you whisper my name, or laugh. I want to see you smile. Anything. I'd even settle for a frown. Most of all I want to hold you in my arms like I used to. Am I to be permitted to say such things after the mistakes I've made? I must confess that is the biggest reason I haven't opened your letters. All the things I've seen and done, and I'm terrified of a few simple words from you. But there are so many pages folded inside my coat that I have to believe you still love me. You wouldn't have spilled so much ink telling me that you don't. So, now I hold on to hope like I never have before.

A letter from Father arrived last week. Mother has died of variola. It doesn't seem real. I'm not to return home for the funeral as there isn't to be one. Father is too afraid of contracting the plague himself, the coward. I'm so angry. I'm stunned he bothered to write and tell me. Worse, Suvi is missing. She went to negotiate a treaty with the Waterborne Nations, but there have been no message birds in two weeks. Uncle blames the Waterborne. He's been pressing Father to declare war with the Waterborne Nations and make an official statement regarding the succession. I don't know what to do. I'm almost afraid to ask. Have you Seen anything? I've written Suvi but I don't expect an answer.

At least I've my duties to keep my mind off of things. Today was my first day as the 10th Royal Regiment's translator. Colonel Vinter had me running in circles from the moment I arrived early this morning. The state of the Acrasian prisoners is pathetic. Many have died because none of them speak Eledorean, and no one has spoken for them. They can't negotiate for themselves except in the crudest of terms, and the money and supplies for their care have yet to arrive. I can't believe that the Acrasian chain of command would forget their own like this. It's appalling. So, the first thing I did was write to their commanders and beg for food and supplies. It seems strange to be engaged in the business of their welfare. But it's the right thing to do. I know it is. It is what Captain Karpanen would've done.

The situation here is bound to smooth out eventually—at least long enough for me to see you for a few hours.

I must put out the candle now. It's late, and tomorrow will be another long day. Know that as I lay down to sleep I'll stare at the ceiling and think of you. Where are you now? What are you doing? Do you think of me as I do you?

With all my love,

Nels

TWO

"Are you sure you want to go in there, sir? Acrasians stink like dead pigs in high summer. And they use the piss bucket for their drinking water." The private guarding the Acrasian prisoners wrinkled her nose in disgust before glancing over her shoulder. She lowered her voice. "They're animals."

Nels peered through the splintered nine-foot-tall fenced enclosure built for the Acrasian prisoners with a mix of curiosity and dread. In truth, his biggest reasons for studying Acrasians had originated from fear. It wasn't as if he'd not met Acrasians since Onni. However, all but one—Private Ketola's wife, Annaliesa—had been the subjects of command magic. This would mark the first time he'd interacted with an uncontrolled Acrasian over an extended period of time.

They're no different than we are.

In spite of the inclement weather, there was no shelter inside the enclosure other than a four-foot-by-four-foot square of tattered canvas. One end was tied to the fence with rags. The opposite end was stretched out at an angle and anchored to the ground with rocks, forming a rough lean-to tent hardly large enough for one person. He spied a pair of unmoving booted feet sticking out from beneath the canvas shelter and assumed that was the officer. There didn't appear to be any women among them. It struck him as odd. He wasn't sure if that was normal or merely a chance of who'd survived the battle and the journey to Gardemeister. He could smell the prisoners from where he stood. Unable to shave, their faces were covered in unkempt beard growth. Many were ill. Frequent coughing punctuated fetid air. Their uniforms were filthy and their wet hair matted. They huddled in a listless clump on the ground. Nels decided they looked more like starving, beaten dogs than soldiers from the self-proclaimed most feared army in the world. He clamped down on an unwanted flash of empathy.

Captain Karpanen wouldn't be dead but for the Acrasians, Nels thought. Still, he reminded himself that it'd been robbers, not soldiers, who'd killed Karpanen. *There is a distinction.* "When was the last time any of the prisoners ate?"

The private shrugged. "They've been trading with Corporal Ekstrom."

"With what?" Nels asked, noting that she hadn't answered his previous question.

"Acrasian coins, clothes, whatever they have in their packs."

Thunder echoed through the valley. A fresh breeze brought relief from the enclosure's stench. Nels glanced at the sky. Storm clouds bunched in dark and angry knots. It wasn't raining now but would be soon. He turned his attention back to the prisoners. Peering through the splintered wooden poles, he didn't see evidence of any baggage. "They have packs?"

"I don't trade with them, sir. They don't attempt to communicate with me other than to make rude gestures." Again she shrugged. "Corporal Ekstrom says the bald one with the moustache carves things with a chunk of sharpened flint. I hear he's quite good at it."

Nels moved closer to the gate. It'd rained earlier that morning, and the ground was muddy. Inside the enclosure, flies swarmed in clouds. "Open the gate, Private Vangr."

"Yes, sir." Vangr unhooked the keys from her belt and worked the lock. Chains rattled against wood and then she shoved at the gate. It protested with a soggy creak and a clank of chain.

Nels stepped through. A handful of prisoners struggled to their feet. Most stayed as they were in the mud and gave him wary looks. Some appeared too weak to stand. The stench inside the enclosure was a stomach-churning combination of bad cheese, sewage, and a foul sweetness. He could taste it in the back of his throat. Worse, the overpowering stink seemed to penetrate his skull through his nose and mouth, making his eyes water. He was familiar enough with battlefields to know what it meant without seeing the corpse. At his side, Viktor choked and covered his face with a handkerchief. Nels's stomach did a slow roll, and he spat in an effort to clear his mouth. He decided not to venture farther inside—more due to the smell than any possible danger of attack.

He forced himself to ignore the stench and addressed the prisoners in formal Acrasian. "Good morning." He'd parroted the greeting without giving thought to the irony until too late. "My name is Captain Hännenen. Is there one among you who is in charge?"

The prisoners stared back with dull, changeless eyes. None responded, in spite of being addressed in their own language. Finally, an Acrasian corporal with short, greasy light brown hair and dark brown beard stubble looked to the canvas shelter. Nels did the same. From the new angle, it was easy to see that the officer resting beneath it was dead. Black flies crawled all over the open eyes and face unmolested. A dirty, bloodstained bandage was wrapped around his swollen waist.

Gut wound, Nels thought. *That's a slow, painful way to die. Why did they bother transporting him with the others?*

The human corporal got to his feet reluctantly, glanced down at himself, and tugged his loose, dirty uniform coat in a futile attempt to tidy it. If Nels didn't know any better, he'd think the man was readying himself for an execution. Nels felt another twinge of sympathy.

"Since the lieutenant has seen fit to depart this mortal coil . . . I-I suppose that leaves me in charge," the corporal said in an equally formal manner. Unfamiliar with his accent's slow drawl, Nels had to take a moment to translate.

"And your name?" Nels asked.

"Corporal Dayvid Petron." The corporal's voice was steady and low, but he was visibly trembling.

Nels paused again. *He's afraid of magic, of course.* "Thank you, Corporal," he said. "I need a comprehensive list of prisoners so that it may be relayed to your superiors. I will provide you with paper and ink." Education wasn't as common among Acrasians as it was among Eledoreans. "Can you write?"

Corporal Petron's expression grew cold. "My men need water and food. Not a head count."

"I require names in order make arrangements for your care with your leaders. In turn, they will inform your loved ones of your status."

"I understood you the first time, Captain." Corporal Petron lowered his head and shook it. "Don't waste your time. None of us are members of a wealthy gens." He gave a sideways nod toward the body under the makeshift shelter. "Lieutenant Lucrosa was our only chance of getting help. Every one of us was recruited off the streets of Novus Salernum and Archiron. Some by force."

"Oh. I see." Nels swallowed. He couldn't bring himself to tell Petron what they both now knew.

"We can work."

Nels scanned the sorry state of the prisoners. "Work? Corporal, your men can't stand."

Petron straightened. "My father was a farmer. I worked the land from the time I could walk. I've seen your fields. And I observed your people as we marched in. This town doesn't have enough men to work the farms. The coming winter will be a bad one if something isn't done. You need us. Give us food, medical care, clothes, and better shelter. In exchange, we'll work your crops."

He doesn't speak like a farmer. Acrasians placed a great deal of importance on personal wealth, more so than on anything else. Nels wondered how Petron had acquired his education. He grudgingly admired Petron's intelligence and determination. *What if our roles were reversed? What would I do in his place?* "You'll give your parole?"

"Speaking for myself? Yes," Corporal Petron said. "Doubly so, if it means those who can't work will be taken care of. I can't order the men to do the same, but I will ask for volunteers."

Nels examined the other prisoners a bit closer. They were dressed in a mix of uniforms and insignia. *He isn't even from the same unit, and yet he's acting in their behalf.* It went against everything Nels knew about Acrasians. He felt something loosen in his chest. *They've been abandoned to their fate by those in charge, and they know it.* "I'll return with the paperwork."

"How soon?" Petron asked. "Private Landry needs a physician to see to his leg. If something isn't done quickly, he'll die. We need fresh water. We've collected what we can from the rain, but it isn't enough. None of us has eaten in days. We need shelter and blankets. And . . . well . . . the lieutenant is rather ripe."

"I'll be back within an hour," Nels said. "You've my word."

"Thank you, Captain."

Moving toward the gate, Nels heard Petron clear his throat.

"Captain?"

"Yes?" Nels turned.

The dirt didn't hide the open desperation and fear in the corporal's face. "Don't forget us."

"I won't," Nels said. He captured Corporal Petron's gaze in an effort to convey his sincerity. "You're the entire reason I'm here." Then he exited the enclosure.

"You speak their lingo?" Private Vangr asked.

Nels waited for Vangr to secure the gate. "I want that dead officer cleared out of there at once. And those doing so will show the body respect, do you hear me?"

Chastised, Vangr kept her mouth closed and nodded.

"I didn't hear your answer, Private," Nels said.

Vangr snapped to attention. "Yes, sir!"

Nels said, "There will be fresh canteens issued to those prisoners. And from now on, they are to have all the water they need. Am I understood?"

"Yes, sir!"

It isn't much, but it's something. Nels turned his back on her and headed for the inn where the medical corps was headquartered. Their accommodations were located on the farthest, opposite edge of the barracks compound. Gardemeister's military living quarter was small, consisting of a two-block walled-in area. As he passed by the arched gate that signaled the access point between the town and the barracks houses, he couldn't help noticing what Corporal Petron had seen. Nels slowed to a stop. Gardemeister wasn't the thriving town it had been a year or two before. A number of buildings were deserted. The surviving population was composed of old men and women, orphan children, and a few young mothers. He recalled the size of the graveyard between the barracks houses and the enclosure where the Acrasians were being kept. The plague had hit Gardemeister hard, but so had the war.

"What's wrong?" Viktor asked.

Two thunderclaps in quick succession echoed through the mountains, and with that, the rain was released. Nels pulled the collar of his all-weather coat tighter around his neck and angled his tricorne to keep water out of his eyes. "Did you see?" Nels asked.

Viktor glanced over his shoulder and shrugged. "It isn't anything new. Why are you so angry?"

Nels wasn't sure he could explain. "Their own commanders have abandoned them because they lack money. They have no one to care for them."

"They have you."

"I have enough on my hands with Kauranen's Fourth Infantry company."

Viktor gave him a sidelong glance. "I hesitate to bring up a painful subject. But you don't command the Fourth any longer."

Nels sighed and felt his shoulders drop a little.

"I'm sorry."

Turning to gaze back toward the pen where Corporal Petron and his men were being kept, Nels said, "I don't want to care about what happens to them. In a few weeks, we'll be killing men just like them."

"That's war," Viktor said and shrugged. "The only difference is that they are not kainen."

Nels resumed walking. When he reached the Fallen Crow, he threw both hands against painted oak door and shoved. The square bull's-eye panes set in the top half of it rattled in their frames. Entering, he and Viktor were met with hostile stares. The inn's patrons went back to their quiet conversations after a short silence. Nels took a deep breath to calm himself. He spotted the medical corps underlieutenant smoking a clay pipe in the corner and crossed the room with a tightened jaw.

"I need to speak to the medical officer in charge," Nels said.

The underlieutenant reached inside his unbuttoned jacket and produced a pocket watch. "Normally, that would be me. However, I'm not on duty."

"Then who is?"

"It's midday. No one, at the moment."

Nels glanced down at the table. The plate resting on its surface was empty. So was the tea mug next to it. He sat across from the underlieutenant and handed the dirty dishes to Viktor. "You're on duty now."

The underlieutenant opened his mouth to protest. However, after noting Nels's expression and his rank, he swallowed his objection.

"What am I to do with these?" Viktor asked.

"Take them to the kitchen," Nels said, speaking to Viktor while staring at the medical officer.

"Do I look like a barmaid?" Viktor asked.

"Overlieutenant Reini, take the dishes away."

With a barely audible sigh, Viktor left.

"The Acrasian prisoners need a healer to attend them," Nels said.

"Acrasians?" The underlieutenant made a disgusted face. "How much are they paying?"

"They aren't," Nels said. "I'm giving you an order. What is your name?"

"Underlieutenant Olveson."

"Underlieutenant Olveson, would you like to be on report?"

"No, sir."

"Then I suggest you get yourself to the prisoner enclosure," Nels said. "Now."

Resigned, Olveson tapped out his pipe, gathered the worn leather satchel resting on the floor at his feet, and stomped out with a frown. Returning from his trip to the kitchen, Viktor moved aside to let him pass. The door slammed.

"You're going to hear from his captain, you know," Viktor whispered after Olveson was gone.

"I don't care," Nels said.

"You use that expression quite a lot these days. Someone might get the impression you were feeling a little reckless."

"Reckless? Me? When have I ever been reckless?"

"I'd stay healthy during your assignment here if I were you. I don't think the medical corps is going to be doing you any favors for a while."

Dear Nels,

Every day I wait for the sound of the mail coach. The coachman doesn't always stop, but when he does I watch him from under the trees. I tell myself that his brief presence is enough, no matter how lonely I am. I can't risk talking to him. I've no idea how long I'll be contagious. I burned the last of Gran's things today. I hated to do it. It felt as if I was destroying the last of Gran, but I had to. Until now, I never understood how frightening and lonely a quarantine could be.

I have her journals at least. I wouldn't have thought to read them, but she told me to do so. At first it felt like an intrusion, but now . . . It's funny how different she was when she was younger—how much like us. It's almost like having a new friend. It's difficult to imagine Gran as wild and adventurous. Did you know that she used to go out with quite a few men before Grandfather came along? I can't hardly believe it. My Gran was a notorious flirt who loved to dance, and debate the Medical Council, and race horses. I miss her. The house is so empty now. Sometimes I think I hear her walking through the kitchen.

I miss you too. I miss the sound of your voice. I love you. Please stop blaming yourself. If there was anything to forgive, it was forgiven long ago.

I can't tell you how sorry I am to hear about your mother. Oh, Goddess, I'm so very sorry. I'm worried about you. Are you all right? Are you taking care of yourself? No one can make up for such a loss. No one. But for now, please take comfort in knowing that I love you, and I'd be there with you, if I could.

There's so much I should say, but I just can't. I'm afraid you'd hate me, and right now I can't stand the thought. Just please keep writing. Please? Your letters are the highlight of my day. You've always had the ability to make me laugh when I needed it most. Ultimately, I wish I could return the favor. The idea of seeing you smile is everything, but I can't. Not now.

I've done everything I can to catch some glimpse of your sister. I stared at my tea leaves for an hour this morning. Yes, I know. Pathetic, isn't it? I'm sorry. I simply don't have any news. Suvi is someplace I can't see, but I can't help thinking that if she were dead I'd know. That isn't much help, but it's the best I can do for now. You could try writing to your father. He won't accept my counsel, but maybe he'll listen to you? I know you haven't had the best of relationships, but he needs you now more than ever. He's lost without your mother. Can you find it within yourself to forgive him? I don't have to tell you the situation at court isn't good. Your uncle hasn't been idle. I wish there were something more helpful I could do for you both. I *suppose you and I have to wait until your sister gets back. Do try not to worry about her. I think she's fine.*

I so want to hold you and comfort you. I know the Acrasians say the inoculation is protection enough, but the variola that I had, the one that killed Gran, was different. Promise me you'll stay away until I say it's safe? Please? You must not ride up here. It's simply too dangerous. Please. I can't stand the thought of what killed her killing you too. It would tear me apart, and I'd never forgive myself. Please promise to stay away until it's safe. Please. If you love me, do this for me. Please. I'm perfectly safe. Gran's wards keep dangerous animals away, and the garden is doing quite well. You've no need to worry about me. Although, if you can spare the money I could use more writing paper. As you can see, I'm resorting to using the backs of your letters. (I'm sorry.)

I can't believe Gran is gone. Yesterday, I made her favorite anise tea before I remembered. I hate anise. There is no one here to drink it. It's funny how life continues on like nothing important happened—like there's not this gaping hole inside of me. Is that how you feel?

Oh, Goddess above, I miss you. At night, the sky is so deep and bright with stars. Sometimes, I grant myself the luxury of imagining what it'd be like with you at my side, counting them. I must go now. There is so much to do tomorrow, and I must walk this letter to the gate for pickup before I retire.

Love,

Ilta

⚘ SUVI ⚘

ONE

Suvi gazed down upon the foul stains on the stone floor that were all that remained of the four people killed by the soulbane during its attempt at freedom. They'd buried the creature with several Eledorean silver falcons in its ribcage. Without water steel, it was the best way to assure the thing wouldn't rise again.

The dungeon room still stank of death. She gritted her teeth against the slimy lump in the back of her throat. The chilly cell was otherwise the same but for the now-empty cage and a haunted atmosphere. Kask and a number of other Waterborne representatives waited at a short distance, acting as witnesses. Suvi felt tired, weak, and sick. She wanted to go home, but it'd only been a few days since the attack, and she was still recovering. This was the first time she'd been strong enough to stand since the incident. The journey down the stairs to the dungeon had been difficult and painful. Moira had recommended against it, but Suvi felt it was important to see the cell for herself. She had to salvage what she could of the situation, after all. So far, she hadn't heard anything from Kask that sounded like blame. However, that didn't mean this would remain the case forever, given what Jami had told her.

Leaning heavily on the crutch Moira had provided, Suvi winced for reasons outside of the pain in her leg. She whispered, "You're certain it was one of ours that was responsible?"

"Private Grahn came down here while everyone else was attending the duel. He killed the guards and stole the key," Jami said. Her lips made a tight line of anger. "He's lucky that thing got to him before I did."

"Why would he do this?" Suvi asked. "He was a royal marine."

"Not a marine," Jami whispered. "Lieutenant Ketola says Grahn was new to the platoon. A replacement for a private who'd died before we set off. Grahn was a korva. One of your uncle's."

"How do you know?" Suvi asked, keeping her voice low.

"I had my suspicions after examining the body. He had an Ytlainen tattoo in his armpit. It's the sigil of a Ytlainen family known to deal in illegal trade. Your uncle has ties with them. I returned to the *Otter* the instant I recognized it."

Suvi didn't ask why Jami would know such a thing. She didn't need to. It was one of the reasons she'd employed Jami in the first place.

Jami continued. "Unfortunately, I was too late. The *Otter*'s birdmaster was poisoned along with all our message birds. Same with the *Indomitable*. We have Grahn's bunkmate in hand. After some questioning, he admitted that Grahn was reporting to a member of the royal house. And he'd been promised a reward for seeing to the message birds. The birdmaster's log shows Grahn sent and received regular messages to and from the palace in Jalokivi. More so than a mere private could afford, particularly a private from Gardemeister. I searched Grahn's bunk both here and on the ship. I didn't find anything. He was careful."

What am I to do? I can't send any messages home, Suvi thought.

She glanced at Kask. *Great Goddess, this is a mess.* "Let's get back upstairs. I need to sit down."

Kask and his retinue followed as Jami helped her back up the stairs. Suvi tried to use the time it took to think about what should be done. One of her marines was responsible for the deaths of six of Kask's people. Reparations were necessary. Upon reaching her private guest rooms, she invited Kask to remain so that they might discuss the situation, and sent for Dylan. She thought it wouldn't hurt to have his support. It took some time to get settled in the borrowed drawing room. Her leg was agony by the time all was done. She wanted a dose of the medicine Moira had left but knew that a clear head would be required. Suvi waited to speak until after Piritta served the tea.

"I must formally apologize to you, Sea Lord Kask, both as a representative of Eledore's royal family and personally," Suvi said. "It seems one of the men I brought to Treaty Island is responsible for the soulbane's escape. The matter is an internal one. And I am sorry that my problems have so negatively affected you and yours."

Sea Lord Kask nodded but his expression was difficult to read.

Suvi pressed on. "Please understand that there are those in Eledore who wish to prevent a lasting agreement between Eledore and your clan. It is clear that this was an attempt to destroy our progress. And I've no doubt that a successful attempt upon my life would've been blamed upon you and the Waterborne Nations as a whole." She didn't wish to mention her uncle's name. So, she changed course. "I'm so terribly sorry for your losses. Understand that I will do everything in my power to assure that those responsible will be punished."

She didn't believe her father would ever punish her uncle.

However, once she was on the throne, she fully intended to make good upon her word. "I wish to make reparations in addition to the agreements already on the table."

"And what would that be?" Kask asked.

"I understand Isak Whitewave was attempting to finance a takeover of your clan."

"It is of no consequence. Isak Whitewave is dead."

"We both know the situation isn't resolved. Kester Whitewave and whomever his brother Isak was working with are most certainly alive," Suvi said. "Therefore, I propose that Eledore outlaw trade in bloodflower. This will prevent legal transport of bloodflower through the Chain Lakes. Ultimately, it will cut off the continental trade route to Acrasia."

Kask said, "You can do this?"

"I can," Suvi said with full confidence. "My father has no stake in such trade. More importantly, neither does my uncle."

"And the water steel I requested?"

"On that, I must confer with my father. I don't know how many such weapons might be available. We are at war with Acrasia. However, I do agree that it is in both our countries' best interests to provide what assistance we can. I've a possible solution in mind, but I'm afraid the best I can do for now is to promise that the request will be given serious consideration."

"Then that is enough. I accept."

They drank the tea while Piritta put the finishing touches on the agreement. Kask accepted the leather folio with its newly corrected agreement and signed the first treaty between Eledore and a Waterborne clan in over thirty years. Suvi couldn't help smiling.

"With that, I'm afraid I must make preparations to leave as soon as possible," Suvi said.

"Are you certain it's wise?" Kask asked. "Moira says that you need more time to recover. Your wound is serious. You can't afford to relapse."

"The situation at home isn't good," Suvi said. "I need to get back to my father with the signed agreements. Unfortunately, all our message birds were killed. There has been no word of our progress sent for some time. My father is no doubt concerned."

"You have my permission to use one of our couriers. That may buy you some time to heal. None of this will do any good if you die on the journey home."

Suvi blinked and swallowed. The pain was getting bad enough that she was finding it difficult to think. "All right."

TWO

Eleven days after the soulbane attack, HKEL *Otter* departed Treaty Island for the Eledorean port of Rehn. Suvi was anxious to return home. In spite of repeated messages sent both before and after the attack, there hadn't been any news from her father in weeks. She was worried. Unfortunately, there wasn't much she could do with her anxiety. Because of her injured leg, a sea journey meant a lot of time reading. After three days of being confined to her cabin, she'd grown snappish. Piritta had been driven to tears twice. Suvi began to feel like her father. She'd apologized multiple times, and Piritta had accepted, but Suvi still felt awful. Venturing out on deck for much needed air, she hobbled to the quarterdeck's rail. It was early in the evening, and the sky was cluttered with stars. The *Otter* shifted beneath her, and she scrambled to catch herself with the railing. The crutch clattered to the deck. Cursing, she bent and hopped in place until she could retrieve it. She hated the crutch. It annoyed her. In spite of repeated treatments by the ship's healer prior to departing, her leg still ached something terrible. What scared her the most was the idea that it would never heal. In truth, that was the largest part of her impatience.

Once the crutch was retrieved, she settled back into place and closed her eyes. She breathed in sea air laced with heating tar, and reassured herself.

There came a shout from above, and the alarm bell rang the signal for a ship sighting. Suvi searched the horizon, but didn't see anything from her side of the ship.

"Two frigates, sir! Acrasian!"

Suvi's heart froze. *One frigate and a corvette against two frigates?*

"Action stations!"

The bosun's whistle signaled three times. The crew leapt to their assigned places in a flurry of motion. Marine drummers took over the call to action, and the royal marines rushed to the masts and to man the cannons. The explosion of activity vibrated the decks as below partitions were pulled down and stored, ammunition and cannon were readied, and loose objects were secured.

Shit. Shit. Shit, Suvi thought. *We've only the* Indomitable *to protect us.* Sea Lord Kask had sent the *Sea Dragon,* a frigate, as an escort for HKEL *Otter* and HKEL *Indomitable,* but their orders were to see them safely to harbor and assist in case of bad weather. They weren't to participate in a war. "We're nowhere near Acrasian waters. What are they doing here?" she asked, heading for the poop deck as quickly as she could. She paused at the ladder. *Stupid leg.*

"You should get below," Jami said.

Steeling herself for pain, Suvi gripped the rail and began the awkward journey up the ladder. "I'm a sea marshal, damn it! I'm not cowering belowdecks!" She met Captain Hansen at her station near the mizzenmast.

"Two ships of the line. First-class frigates. They were hunting for us," Captain Hansen said, lowering her glass. Her expression was set in grim determination. The scar that bisected her left eyebrow made her look more like a buccaneer and less an Eledorean officer. Her red hair was bound in a tight queue with a black ribbon matching her uniform.

If they're the newer ships, they've one hundred guns each. HREM Indomitable *has ninety, and the HREM* Otter *only has ten.* Suvi asked, "Why are they here?" She looked to their escort, the *Sea Dragon*, off their port bow. Regardless, she knew they were on their own. It wouldn't be long before they separated themselves from the convoy. "What do the Acrasians want?"

"I have my suspicions," Hansen said. Her eyes darted to Suvi with a meaningful squint.

Hansen tended toward the taciturn. However, Suvi read her meaning at once. *You're the heir designate, damn you. Do you think this is an accident?*

"They won't risk sinking us," Suvi said. "They'll want us for a prize."

"They've the weather gage," Hansen said. There was an unspoken question under the statement.

Suvi turned to smile at Dylan's back. "They think they have the advantage over us." He was standing at attention next to Darius. "But we have a weathermaster."

Hansen's right eyebrow arched an instant before she replaced the spyglass to her eye. "We might outrun them. Avoid the entire encounter."

"Do you think they'll meet us with even more strength later?" Suvi asked. She motioned to a lieutenant, and he handed over his spyglass. She peered through the lens. "If they are hunting us, they're certainly not alone."

"My mother had a favorite saying," Hansen said. "It was 'We'll climb that mountain when we get to it.' We must get home as soon as we can. Get back on fresh water."

The sea puts us on the same level as the humans, doesn't it? Suvi thought. *With the exception of Dylan and Darius.*

The Eledorean fleet had one standing order—*When possible, run.* Altercations were considered wasteful and unnecessary. Since magic was unreliable on water, the Eledorean navy wasn't used for war. They were merchant, intelligence, and transport vessels for the most part. Running was the smart thing to do. Thus, speed was prized in an Eledorean ship. The guns were a new addition— Suvi's acknowledgment of her father's concerns before she'd left. It'd taken extra time, but it'd proven wise. However, Suvi had made one more change.

Eledorean ships communicated with one another with birds or signal flags. If the weather was bad, communication between ships was next to impossible without birds. The Waterborne didn't use birds. Therefore, there were none to be had. That meant sub-stantive communication between ships while at sea was going to be a problem. She'd learned Waterborne representatives along the coast communicated with ships using signal lamps. The lamps had been easy enough to acquire. The code system was not. The code was a secret Sea Lord Kask wasn't willing to teach her. Fortunately, devising her own had given her something on which to focus while convalescing.

Time to give the new signal system its first serious test, she thought. "Weathermaster Kask!"

Dylan abandoned his station and saluted. "Yes, sir!"

"We need speed. How much help can you give us?" Suvi asked.

Staring into the night sky, Dylan shrugged. "No clouds. A storm would take too long. Wind is all I can do right now."

"Wind it is, Weathermaster," Suvi said, and turned to Hansen. "It's time for a race. Tell *Indomitable*. And signal *Sea Dragon*. Thank her for her services, but I believe we can take it from here."

"Yes, sir." Hansen turned. "Lieutenant! I want a message to *Indomitable!*"

Suvi passed the spyglass back to its owner. *I hope the Acrasians are as slow in the water as they're reported to be.* She laid a hand on Otter's rail. *All right, my love. It's time to show everyone how well you dance.*

THREE

"Marshal Hännenen?" The question was accompanied with a knock on the cabin door. "It's Underlieutenant Rosberg, Marshal Hännenen?"

Piritta groaned. "Again? What the hell does it take to get any sleep?"

A muffled all-hands call filtered through the cabin walls for the fourth time that night.

What time is it? Suvi reminded herself it was pointless to ask. Like kainen magic, clocks weren't reliable on extended voyages. *How many bells—not the time. I've spent far too much time on dry land.* The interior of the cabin had been blacker than pitch. Now, warm light from the lieutenant's lantern leaked through the crack under the door. Suvi sat up in her hammock and pushed both hands through her hair once she had her balance. She hadn't taken the time to braid it before retiring. Piritta would be an hour brushing out the tangles once things calmed down.

"Orders were to wake you if the Acrasians are spotted, sir." Rosberg's voice was apologetic.

"It's all right, Lieutenant. You're doing your job," Suvi said. "What's happening?"

"The Acrasians have reappeared on our starboard side."

They won't give up, Suvi thought. *That's not a good sign.*

In an attempt to light the oil lamp, Piritta knocked something onto the floor—a teacup, by the sound of shattering porcelain.

"Thank you, Lieutenant," Suvi said, coiling her unruly hair into a knot on top of her head and then feeling for her breeches. There'd be no need for full uniform or even shoes. Chances were this was just another trip onto the deck for another gaze through the glass only to see nothing. "I'm on my way."

"Yes, sir."

Light flooded the cabin. Suvi closed her eyes against it and waited for her sight to adjust before hopping out of her hammock. She bit her lip against the pain in her sore leg and hopped on one foot. "Stay put. No sense in both of us being miserable. I'll be right back."

"Acrasians are evil," Piritta said, collapsing back onto the bunk. "Don't they know enough to pay their calls at a more civilized hour?"

"Perhaps this is a more civilized hour for Acrasia," Suvi said. She pulled on her breeches, tucked in her nightshirt, grabbed the crutch, and limped to the door. "Go back to sleep. One of us should be rested."

A heavy fog had descended sometime since the last alarm. The mist was thick enough to shroud the deck. *Otter's* boards were damp and chilly on her bare toes. She couldn't see more than a couple feet in front of her.

"Where is Weathermaster Kask?" Suvi asked, shrugging into her sea marshal's coat.

"I sent him to his hammock. We don't want to exhaust him," Captain Hansen said. "Not with the Acrasians on our tails."

Suvi nodded and glanced up at the sheets even though she couldn't see a thing. There was enough wind to keep the ship moving, but that was about it. "Glass?"

"Nothing to see. In and out like before." Hansen gave her the spyglass. "I've some bad news."

"What is it?"

"Wasn't one of the original ships," Hansen said. "Name painted on her side was EIMN *Maria Fortuna*."

"She passed close enough to read her name in this?"

Hansen nodded.

"And no one fired?" Suvi asked.

"Too risky," Hansen said. "Might hit one of our own. I assume the Acrasians felt the same."

"Three frigates."

"All of them ships of the line," Hansen said. Her voice was matter-of-fact. "There could be more than three. No way of telling yet."

"Shit." Suvi's leg pained her even more in the clammy air.

"Recommendations?"

"Get us out of here. And wake up Kask," Suvi said. "I want to consult him."

Dylan took the ladder's steps two at a time. He looked gray, worried, and tired. He wasn't alone. Darius remained a respectful distance while Dylan reported to her.

"They're not giving up, I take it?" Dylan asked.

"I'm afraid not," Suvi said. "I don't want to ask but—"

"I can't," Dylan said. "I'm done in. Used all I had to keep us ahead of them."

"Oh."

"But Dar has an idea," Dylan said. He didn't look too happy about it.

"He's a weathermaster too?" Suvi asked, relieved. "That's lucky."

"Ah, no," Darius said, moving forward. "I'm usually in charge of messages."

Suvi frowned. "How is that going to help us?"

"It's how I send messages," Darius said.

"Oh. You're a bird handler?" Suvi asked. "Wait. Waterborne don't use birds."

Darius said, "I use any available sea creature."

Suvi blinked. "I'm sorry. I still don't see how that helps. We're too far from Eledore for another ship to arrive in time. And Clan Kask isn't going to declare war on Acrasia."

Grinning, Darius said, "That wasn't the message I intend to send."

"Enlighten me," Suvi said.

"I can call up something big," Darius said, "and ask it for help."

Suvi turned to Dylan and then back to Darius. "Is that possible?"

"Theoretically it is," Dylan said. He folded his arms across his chest with a grumpy glare at Darius.

"I've never done it before. It might be a bit dangerous," Darius said. "But I think it's worth trying."

"Why? You're not Eledorean," Suvi said.

Darius asked, "What do you think will happen to me and Dylan if the Acrasians board us?"

"What do you think they'll do to our clan? My father signed a contract with Eledore guaranteeing passage through Clan Kask waters," Dylan said. "A contract that is aboard this ship."

"Right," Suvi said. "Darius, what do you need?"

Darius paused. He took a deep breath as if steeling himself. "Reassurance that I won't be lost in the water. And someone to see to it I that don't drown in the process."

"I think we can arrange that. Captain Hansen," Suvi said. "Let's get started."

FOUR

The early morning was chilly and humid, and the wind was slow but steady. Suvi was glad she'd taken a moment to go below and finish dressing. Her injured leg was aching and stiff due to the lack of rest. Piritta had made her drink a bitter-tasting potion for the pain. It had yet to take effect. Leaning over the starboard side, Suvi watched as Darius climbed down the ratlines draped over *Otter*'s side into the ocean. Dylan followed him but scrambled into the waiting longboat instead.

"Shit! The water's like ice," Darius hissed. "Stop rocking the boat. Hold still."

"Yes, sir," Dylan said. "Shall I hold your head under the water for you, too?"

They were keeping their voices low. However, due to the fog and the water's surface, Suvi could easily overhear what was being said.

"Look, do you want me to do this or not?" Darius said, gripping the longboat's side from the water. His short spirit knots and wet clothes gave him the appearance of a surprised otter.

"To be honest? No," Dylan said. "But no one consulted me. Did they?" He didn't take up the oars. He untied the ropes used to lower the boat and let her drift. The cable anchoring the skiff to *Otter* slapped the water as he slowly uncoiled it.

"At least *I* informed you first," Darius said.

"Is that what this is about? Why did you take me back? To punish me for the rest of my life?"

"Maybe a little," Darius said. "Oh, come on. Give me a kiss for luck."

Dylan grunted.

"Don't be like that," Darius said. "It only makes everything more difficult. Please?"

Dylan sighed, leaned over the side, and granted Darius his wish.

"Thanks," Darius said. He looked up to speak to her. "I'll check below first. See if I can get the Acrasians' positions."

"Thank you," Suvi said.

Taking several deep breaths, Darius released the side of the skiff and went under.

Suvi held her breath. She listened for some sign of trouble and was startled when one of the Acrasian ship's bells signaled the top of the hour. It echoed weirdly across the water. *How close are they?* She'd started to worry that Darius had drowned himself when he surfaced. He wiped water from his eyes and face, and then swam to *Otter*'s ratlines.

Suvi whispered, "Did you get something?"

Darius scrambled up the ship's starboard side. When he reached the rail he waved her and Captain Hansen over. "Was only able to communicate with a few fish. They aren't the smartest, but it was enough. I've a good idea of where the Acrasians are." He gave them all the information he was able to get.

With that, Captain Hansen left to talk to the signaler.

"Good luck, Darius," Suvi said. "Thank you."

Darius smiled up at her. "You're welcome." He climbed back down the ratlines and returned to the skiff.

Captain Hansen returned.

Keeping her voice low, Suvi asked Hansen, "Is everything secure?" She shivered and huddled inside her wool sea marshal's coat.

"As secure as we can make it," Captain Hansen said. "If that skiff slips its cable, there'll be no retrieving them. Not in this fog. And if the Acrasians attack while—"

"We still have the weather gage on them," Suvi said. "Yes?"

"We do."

"You were able to signal Commodore Björnstjerna? Does he know the plan?" Suvi asked.

"He acknowledged receipt of the message," Captain Hansen said. "You're taking a big risk with that tactic. The Acrasians will only need to get one good shot down *Indomitable*'s stern—"

"I know," Suvi said. "But *Otter* can't withstand a line of battle, and we both know it. This is the best we can do under the circumstances. Our only advantage is speed."

Again, Captain Hansen nodded. "I'm only registering my misgivings. I didn't say I'd have handled it any differently." She paused. "With the exception of dropping our weathermaster over the side, of course."

"I understand the danger. So do they," Suvi said. "And if we're boarded, more than likely Darius can get a message to *Sea Dragon*, and they can pick them up. They won't be abandoned for long. And at least they won't be taken prisoner by the Acrasians." She'd taken his intent at face value. Still, it was an aspect of the situation that she understood even if neither Dylan nor Darius had mentioned it.

Darius said there must be space between Otter, Indomitable, *and whatever answers his call.*

She watched the skiff vanish into the mist and bit her lip. *Please let them be safe.* She told herself that everything was going to be fine.

Assuming something answers—something Darius can control. She thought of the Acrasian warships and their three hundred guns.

Please let something answer.

Indomitable had already formed a line with *Otter* by moving to the fore. *The Acrasians will bring as many guns to bear as they can. And we must present the least appealing target.* And that was what *Otter* and *Indomitable* were doing, provided Darius's information was correct. If so, then the two lines would form a letter *T.* Still, Captain Hansen had every right to be concerned.

Suvi thought again about Dylan and Darius out on the water. *Alone with whatever creatures he calls.* Unfamiliar with what lived under the ocean, she didn't know what might answer. *Sharks? A whale?* She was caught between wanting Darius to succeed and wanting him to fail. "Don't lose them. You hear?"

"Yes, sir," Captain Hansen said.

Unable to see, Suvi held her breath and listened. The crew didn't have to be told to be quiet. They knew what was at stake. No one moved. Sounds reflected oddly on the mist-covered water. If there were any doubt that the Acrasians were out there, from time to time, one caught the slap of the wind in sails not their own. Sometimes, Acrasian chatter would surface in the fog. When it did, Suvi didn't make much effort to translate. There was no need. It was easy to discern meaning by the tone. Time moved like maple syrup on a winter day. She counted the heartbeats thudding in her ears. The coffee she'd swallowed earlier in a rush had left a sour taste in her mouth.

Movement in the water drew her attention. She rushed to the rail again. Checking the water, she spied a thick russet tentacle as it arched up out of the ocean and slithered alongside *Otter's* hull before vanishing beneath the surface. An image from one of the Waterborne mosaics she'd seen on Treaty Island sprang to mind— the one with the tentacled creature wrestling with the ships. At the time, she'd thought that the scale was impossible. However, if anything, the ratio of ship to sea creature in the image was smaller than the actual. A startled curse came from the mainsail top. A lieutenant standing nearby made a quick blessing sign with his right hand. Several of the crew muttered prayers. A marine officer silenced them with a sharp hiss.

"What in the name of all the gods was that?" Captain Hansen whispered.

"It seems Darius has made a friend," Suvi said, keeping her voice low. "Great Mother help us."

A strange rumbling-bubbling call echoed across the water. It sounded hollow and low.

"Did anyone bother to ask how the beast was to tell the difference between our ships and the enemy's?" Hansen asked.

"I did," Suvi said. "Darius said most sea creatures would be able to taste the difference."

"Would that be before or after eating the ship?" Hansen asked.

Another splash pulled Suvi's gaze to the water. Three tentacles the color of drying blood—each the width of an Eledorean pine tree—surfaced briefly and then sank.

"You know, that was a detail he neglected to mention," Suvi said.

From the fog off the port side, alarm bells sounded. Someone screamed in Acrasian. A loud crack split the air. More screams followed.

"Get ready!" *Get ready? Suvi thought. How do you get ready for a monster emerging from the water?*

There wasn't time to for an answer. An Acrasian frigate's figure-head, a golden eagle, floated into view off of the port side. Another ship took form in the murk to the fore. Many things happened all at once. Two explosions shoved the air against Suvi's ears as the first Acrasian ship's carronade—small cannon mounted in the ship's bow—fired, adding a giant cloud of burning sulfur-laced powder smoke to the mist. She ducked in reflex. Both blasts overshot the deck. She heard a scream as bar shot landed in the fore shrouds. Small gunfire went off—marines shooting from aloft from both Acrasian and Eledorean ships. The position of the Acrasian frigates shot a bolt of frozen terror into her guts.

They've got us! They've formed two columns! We'll be caught in the middle!

Captain Hansen shouted an order to prepare to drop the anchor off the port bow. Sailors bolted up the mainmast shrouds at great risk of falling to sort the sails in anticipation of her next order.

"Port guns, fire at will!"

Otter's marine gun crews answered the attack one by one. To the fore, rapid flashes blinked in the fog and smoke as the *Indomitable's* guns did the same. The deck shuddered under Suvi's feet, and she was deafened. *Otter's* gun crews performed well under pressure. They'd taken into account the roll of the ships, the wind, and the positions of the enemy. The angle on the first three shots was near perfect. Cannonballs, one after the other, tore down the length of the enemy ship perpendicular to *Otter*, leaving behind wakes of destruction as they went. Wood exploded. Sailors, armed and unarmed alike, died. Rigging fouled. Gun crews scrambled to reload.

Suvi knew why Hansen had ordered the anchor to be dropped

but didn't think Hansen would be able to spin *Otter* fast enough to prevent the Acrasians from returning the favor as the first Acrasian ship slid into position between *Otter's* bow and *Indomitable's* stern, and the second eased itself perpendicular to *Otter's* stern. She knew Hansen's maneuver for a last-ditch effort to minimize the damage. A broadside attack at close range was awful enough. Designed to withstand broadside attacks, ships of the line were weakest at bow and stern. Facing broadsides was a standard tactic.

A series of loud wooden cracks and screams from the Acrasian eagle ship followed the hits. Fire bloomed bright orange and yellow in the fog but did nothing for visibility. Shouting, the Acrasian crew rushed to put out the fire. Acrasian carronade roared again. *One. Two.* Wood splinters were sent spinning by the explosions. Suvi registered musket fire thumping the poop deck. Sulfur-infused gunpowder grit filled her nose and mouth. She couldn't help thinking how absurd it was to be standing inactive in the midst of such chaos and destruction. Yet she wouldn't allow herself to hide. To do so would be considered cowardice. She had to take her chances with her crew or lose their faith.

"Again, port side! Fire at will!"

Once again, the deck rumbled under Suvi's feet as *Otter* bore the stress of her guns. For the time being, *Otter* and *Indomitable* held the most advantageous position, but that wouldn't last. They had to pour as much destruction upon the Acrasians as they could while they could. A third set of blasts went off, and cannon after cannon fired one after another. The marines in the rigging shot into the mist. Sails ripped. People fell. Splinters flew. The fog swirled. Cannon fire blossomed even more warm orange-yellow balls of light, resembling a storm.

"Drop anchor! Now!" Captain Hansen roared the order at the top of her lungs.

Sailors clamored secondary orders, passing them to the crew below. All scrambled to obey the captain's instructions. Sails were adjusted for the abrupt course change. From the windlass below-decks came a series of muffled, staccato clanks, and a splash indicated the anchor had dropped.

"Ninety degrees hard to port! Now!" Captain Hansen slapped a hand on a rail. "Hold on!"

Otter responded to the change in course with a low, creaking shudder. The deck tilted under Suvi's feet, and she braced herself with a hand to a nearby rail. She tried not to think of what was happening to Dylan and Darius in their little skiff and failed.

What going to happen to them? Where is Dar's monster?

Tilted as the ship was by the turn, hitting the closest Acrasian ship's decks would be impossible. Therefore, *Otter*'s gun crews waited. Suvi could only watch and pray as the angle of *Otter* slowly veered away from the Acrasian ship. The golden eagle was now pointing at *Otter*'s stern as she slid past, and the angle wasn't the desired ninety degrees. That was good. She also saw that two of the Acrasian frigate's masts were fouled and broken. That was better. Carronade and cannon roared again. *Otter* was struck. The port railing off the stern disintegrated in a cloud of wood splinters and smoke. Bar shot the size of Suvi's body tumbled past. *Close. Too close.* She was knocked off her feet and landed on the deck with a hard thump. Her wounded leg protested. Quickly checking herself, she saw that she was mostly unscathed. She winced, getting to her feet, and then searched for Captain Hansen. Hansen was moving, as were most of the other officers.

The wheel spun on its own. The helmsman was gone.

Limping, Suvi rushed to the wheel and shoved at it with all her might to get the ship back on course. Blood made the huge wheel slick under her palms. She couldn't let the Acrasians retake the column. If that happened, they were sunk. Unfortunately, the ship's wheel required too much strength to budge. The best she could manage was to slow the wheel. She took a chance and stood on one of the rungs to use all her weight. It worked. Pain shot up her leg to her hip and back as she walked from rung to rung. *Otter* resumed her course to port. Suvi continued her awkward progress, focusing on preventing legs, feet, or hands from getting caught in the wheel. Finally, she was joined by a fresh steersman. Once she was sure he had the ship in hand, she hopped down. Gulping for air, she shoved hair from her face. A freshening wind tugged at the mist. Glancing across the water, she spied what was ahead and choked.

The broadside of another Acrasian frigate—twenty-two guns. *Otter*'s bow was angled perfectly for their cannon.

"Enemy frigate dead ahead!"

Suvi heard Hansen swear.

"Slip anchor! Slip anchor! Now, damn it! Now!" Hansen's orders were passed below. Then she gave a fresh course to the new helmsman.

This is it, Suvi thought. *We're sunk.*

The helmsman steered *Otter* for the new Acrasian's bow. However, Suvi knew it would do no good if they didn't slip the anchor fast enough.

Enormous red tentacles shot up out of the water with a huge splash. They wrapped around the third Acrasian ship in an instant. Sails and rigging were ripped from yards, spars, and masts. Two cannon fired before they and their crews were crushed. Blood-tainted spray hit the water. An unearthly roar of rage and pain erupted from the sea monster. It was so loud and deep that Suvi felt it vibrate inside her chest. The Acrasian ship pitched and rolled as the huge monster hauled itself up onto the poop deck in a flash, smashing everything and everyone in a fury-driven rush. Serpentlike arms twisted and snapped the masts. Screams drifted across the water. Suvi's mouth dropped open as the powerful frigate was reduced to little more than a flaming barge. The fire stretched higher into the morning sky, and then just as suddenly, the creature slid into the water. The powder storage caught, and the doomed craft exploded. Suvi flinched and put up a hand as if to protect her face. Chunks of burning ship's timber rained down on the water and nearby ships.

As if blind, the creature's tentacles seemed to feel in the water for a new target. The Acrasian frigate between *Otter* and *Indomitable* was closest. A bloodred tentacle stretched to the Acrasian's stern.

Dylan and Darius. Are they all right? Suvi ran to *Otter*'s stern rail and found where the skiff had been tied off. The cable was stretched tight. *That's a good sign.* She bent down, grabbed the line, and turned to the closest lieutenant—the handsome one with black curly hair. *Noronen?* "Get over here! Help me haul them in!" Together, they worked to pull the longboat to the starboard side.

"Dylan? Darius? Answer me!" Suvi couldn't see the boat—not yet. Around them, the battle progressed. The giant sea beast's roars of pain and rage echoed off the water. Suvi didn't turn to look but concentrated on the task at hand. Her muscles strained against the weight of the boat and those aboard. *Who'd have thought that a skiff would weigh so much?* Again, she was reminded of her shortcomings as a sailor. *Has it been that long? How much have I forgotten?* At last, the prow of the skiff slid into view. Suvi's heart stopped. The boat was swamped—nearly full of water and sinking. Neither Dylan nor Darius were on board.

"I'm so sorry, sir," Lieutenant Noronen said.

"Dylan! Where are you?" Suvi shouted out at the water. Her

thoughts were frozen with panic, sluggish. *They can't be gone. They just can't be.* "Damn it, Dylan! Answer me!"

An explosion from the first Acrasian frigate caught her attention. *Cannon fire.*

"Get down!" Lieutenant Noronen shoved her.

Suvi hit the deck shoulder first, hard. Bar shot caught in the mizzen shrouds. She struggled to get up but a sharp pain in her left shoulder brought her up short.

Lieutenant Noronen asked, "Sir? Are you all right?"

Checking her arm, Suvi didn't find any cuts or punctures. However, she couldn't actually move her arm from the shoulder. The pain was terrific. She'd bitten her tongue. She spit out blood and spoke through clenched teeth. "I don't know. It's my shoulder."

Another round of cannon shot pounded the decks. Noronen felt Suvi's shoulder. She bit down on an urge to scream. Blinking back tears, she noticed the cannon on the opposite side of the second Acrasian frigate were firing. *Who are they shooting at? Indomitable is to starboard, isn't she?* Suvi scanned the mist and found she was right. *It must be the sea monster,* she thought. However, when she looked for the second Acrasian frigate, she found the monster intent on its destruction.

Answering cannon lit up the thinning mist to port.

"Who is that?" Suvi asked.

"*Sea Dragon,* I think," Lieutenant Noronen said.

"It can't be," Suvi said. "The Waterborne aren't at war with the Acrasians. They left us. Didn't they?"

Another round of blasts split the air.

"They must have changed their minds," Noronen said.

Suvi let Noronen help her to her feet. Limping to Captain Hansen's side, Suvi heard the cries from the closest Acrasian ship to port.

"Cease fire! Cease fire!"

Hansen grinned. "The bastards are surrendering."

"Does Darius's friend know that?" Suvi asked. "If not, how are we going to stop it from sinking every Acrasian ship?"

"You know, I should care," Hansen muttered. "But somehow I don't."

FIVE

"Repairs are under way," Captain Hansen said with a hint of pride. "*Otter* may be small, but she's a tough bitch."

"Good," Suvi said. Her left arm was in a temporary sling. She had consoled herself with the knowledge that she hadn't screamed much when the dislocated shoulder joint had been shoved back into place. The pain had settled into a low-grade ache that was simple enough to ignore—provided she remembered not to move it. *At least it gives me something to think about other than my leg.*

The sounds of the repair crews hard at their work drifted through the walls of the captain's cabin. Suvi ran a hand over the casualty report, smoothing it. They'd lost fourteen of the crew. They'd lose more if they didn't get to land soon. The surgeon's healing abilities were hampered by the water. "How soon will *Otter* be ready?"

"We should have the rigging and the new yards sorted within a few hours," Hansen said. "We've a bigger problem."

I sent Dylan to his death. Suvi's good hand trembled as she poured herself a glass of wine. *Just hold together for a bit longer,* she thought. *For now, you have your duty. Fall apart all you like when you're alone. After you've met with the captains.* "What is it?"

"Due to the number of . . . casualties, we can't spare anyone for a prize crew. We're still pulling Acrasian survivors out of the water," Hansen said. "I don't know what we're going to do with all of them. We can't take them home."

It'd required a great deal to convince boat crews that the monster was gone and that it was safe to venture out onto the water—even more so because they were being sent to rescue Acrasians. However, Suvi had enough deaths on her conscience. She blinked back another surge of tears and swallowed the wine in one gulp. *There are too many Acrasians to trust the frigate to a light crew. Our sailors would be outnumbered. Command magic isn't an option on the water. And Acrasians can't be trusted to keep their parole.*

We can't just butcher them. Not after we've fished them out of the water. We can't let them attack us again, either.

"Maybe *Indomitable's* crew is in better shape?" Hansen asked.

There came a knock on the door. "Captain, sir? Commodore Björnstjerna from *Indomitable* is here. And the Waterborne have arrived. Captain Swiftwind of *Sea Dragon* brought the Acrasian captain with him to finalize the terms of surrender with the Sea Marshal."

Hansen looked to Suvi. Suvi nodded.

"We'll meet them on deck," Hansen said.

"Yes, sir."

Suvi checked her uniform one last time in Hansen's mirror. She would need every ounce of presence she could muster to maintain power over the conversation without the use of domination magic. She took a deep breath and headed out the door behind Hansen.

On deck, the mist had been cleared by a fresh breeze and the sky was a deep, cloudless blue. A rather soggy-looking Dylan stepped forward and gave her a salute. Darius wasn't far behind.

"Permission to board, sir," Dylan said, and winked.

Suvi fought an urge to hug him on the spot. "You're alive! Thank the Mother!"

"No thanks to Dar."

"You didn't have to jump in after me," Darius said. "I was fine."

Dylan said, "You were drowning."

"You weren't even watching like you promised. And how would you know?"

"You were quiet," Dylan said. "Unlike now."

"Permission granted," Suvi said, returning the salute. "Both of you." She gave his arm an affectionate squeeze as Dylan passed. Then she returned to business.

The wounded Acrasian captain stood between two Waterborne with a scowl on his face. His golden helmet with its long black feathers was tucked under his arm. Blood stained his uniform coat and trousers. It was obvious he was in pain. His right trouser leg was bloody and torn, and he kept most of his weight on his left leg. She winced a little in sympathy. He was young—no more than five years Suvi's senior—and handsome for an Acrasian. He had straight blond hair and attractive light gray eyes. His sword was still in its scabbard.

"I don't understand why we're bothering with this sham," the Acrasian muttered in his own language. "You only mean to slaughter us."

"Is not . . . intent," Suvi said in flawed Acrasian. She knew her grammar wasn't correct, but the stunned expression on the Acrasian's face served to offset her embarrassment.

The Acrasian blinked and swallowed. He attempted to stand

taller and then turned to Captain Silvan. "I, Captain Bradford of His Imperial Majesty's frigate the *Lion of the North*, do hereby surrender my ship and crew." He drew his small sword and attempted to hand it to Commodore Björnstjerna.

The Waterborne ship's captain, Samuel Swiftwind, translated for those who didn't speak Acrasian.

Björnstjerna shook his head motioned to Suvi.

"I, Sea Marshal Hännenen of Eledore, accept your surrender," Suvi said, allowing Swiftwind to translate.

The Acrasian stared at her and didn't move.

"Is there a problem?" Suvi asked.

"You . . . you're not . . . who I expected," he said.

"You were expecting to meet me?" Suvi asked.

"Yes, I mean, no . . . I—" He cut himself off and resumed a cool demeanor. "I cannot surrender my sword to a mere woman."

"You're far from home. What were you doing out here?" Suvi asked.

After the question was translated, Captain Bradford paused.

"Answer Sea Marshal Hännenen," Swiftwind said.

"I suppose it doesn't matter whether I tell you or not. It will change nothing," Bradford said.

"Go on," Suvi said in Acrasian.

Captain Bradford said, "The Regnum has no intention of tolerating an alliance between the Waterborne and Eledore."

Commodore Björnstjerna asked, "How did they know—"

Suvi held up a hand for silence. She didn't trust that Bradford didn't speak Eledorean. There was no point in translating Björnstjerna's question. It wasn't as if Bradford would answer. "Commodore Björnstjerna, can *Indomitable* spare a prize crew?"

Björnstjerna squinted at Bradford in disgust. "No, sir."

"We can't take her either," Swiftwind said. "She's Acrasian.

Without a notice of dissolution of contract, it would be considered unethical."

"You have a contract with the Acrasians?" Björnstjerna asked.

Of course they do. They've contracts with every nation in the world. Once more, Suvi held up her hand to silence Björnstjerna. The others were staring at her, waiting for an answer. She needed a moment to think. Turning from the delegation, she walked to the ship's rail and gazed over at *Lion.* Groups of prisoners were clumped on her decks. They looked pale and frightened for the most part. Some gave the impression that they were resigned to a fate more terrible than death. Others stared back at her, defiant. Thinking of all those who depended upon her, she avoided their eyes and concentrated on the rigging. Round black wooden blocks threaded with ship's line stared back at her. Each wooden piece had three holes in it, forming a face.

Deadeyes, she thought. *They're called deadeyes because they look like skulls.* And she couldn't help thinking for the first time that they very much resembled their name. It was too easy to imagine their gaping mouths and empty accusatory stares.

I can't have the Acrasians killed. I won't.

I have to stop them dead in the water. But I can't cripple them too much.

The deadeyes continued to stare back at her in mute terror. *Deadeyes.*

She whirled round to face the officer's delegation. "Captain Hansen?"

"Yes, sir?"

"Mr. Bradford shall be our guest," Suvi said. *Piritta may be able to get information from him once we reach land.*

"What?!" Bradford gaped. "You can't do that!"

You do speak Eledorean, Suvi thought. *Got you.*

"Björnstjerna? Cut the deadeyes from their rigging and divide them between *Otter* and *Indomitable*. Rethreading lanyards through the replacements should keep *Lion* busy for a long while."

Hansen let a wicked grin spread across her mouth.

⊰ NELS ⊱

ONE

Nels swung down from Loimuta's saddle and tied the reins to the fence. On the other side of the weathered rails, a group of Acrasian prisoners armed with hoes dug between the turnip plants where a shirtless Corporal Petron and the horse plow hadn't reached. Initially, Nels hadn't had much hope for the agreement between the prisoners and the farmers. The residents of Gardemeister were too familiar with Acrasian raiders. Therefore, it'd been difficult to convince the elders to accept his proposition. There'd been moments when Nels would've preferred to have returned to his company and taken his chances with Pesola. Eventually, the lure of cheap labor finally won out over prejudice. For their part, the Acrasian prisoners had proved to be hard workers—provided their eccentricities were indulged. Their terror of darkness had been a complication due to the days growing shorter. In the end, the tricky negotiations had proved worthwhile. The positive change in the Acrasians over the past couple of weeks was impressive. It was now nearing noon, and the prisoners were almost finished with the day's work. Nels told himself that in spite of not being with his company, he was at least being useful to his sister in a larger sense. The fields and the people were being cared for, and as it happened, the prisoners benefited too.

All but one of them, Nels thought.

He was jerked from his thoughts when Loimuta shook his head and stamped.

"Behave yourself," Nels said to the gelding. He slipped a hand into his jacket pocket and gave Loimuta half the apple he'd stored there. "I mean it. Misbehave, and you won't see the second half of that."

Loimuta made a rumbling sound in the back of his throat, snorted, and then gently took the apple in his teeth. It vanished with a juicy crunch.

"Good boy," Nels said. He patted Loimuta on the neck.

A seven-year-old girl ran to greet him. "Hello, Captain Hännenen." Her light brown hair was knotted into pigtails, and her cheeks were dusted with freckles. Her threadbare dress was too large, and her feet were bare, but something about her reminded him of his sister, Suvi.

"Hello, Elmi," Nels said.

"Can I pet your horse? I'm bored."

"Then shouldn't you be helping?"

"I'm not allowed in the fields while the Acrasians are working. Mother doesn't want me talking to them. I don't know why she's scared. They're too stupid to understand Eledorean," Elmi said. "They smell funny. They look funny, too."

"I suppose they do."

"Mother says they're monsters. Is that so?"

"I don't think so."

"Me neither," Elmi said with all the cynicism her seven years would allow. "Monsters are a lot uglier."

Not all of them, Nels thought.

"Is your horse hungry? I've got some carrot."

"Give it to him if you like," Nels said. "Be careful, though. He bites."

"All horses bite. How else can they eat?" She gave him a sideways glance. "You just got to know how to feed them. Hand flat. Like this. Don't you know that?" She placed a piece of carrot in the center of her palm and fed the treat to Loimuta, who accepted it with a dainty nibble.

If a horse could feign innocence, Loimuta would be the very soul of disguised guilt.

Nels raised his eyebrows. "I see."

"Elmi? Stop bothering the captain. Get over here!"

Elmi wiped a now-damp palm on her dress. "Bye!"

Nels headed for the shady spot at the gate where the private in charge of the prisoners had stationed himself. The private had been sitting and drinking from a bottle that Nels hoped contained water.

Nels returned his salute. "How are the prisoners today?"

"Obedient and quiet, sir." The private's breath proved Nels's hope was for naught.

"I'm here for Corporal Petron," Nels said.

"Yes, sir." The private shouted for the corporal. His annoyed, curse-filled Eledorean order was accompanied by gestures impossible to misinterpret.

Corporal Petron acknowledged the order with a nod. Still, he waited until reaching the end of the row before tying off the plow horse's reins.

Petron's face was sunburned, and his hair stuck to his face in sweaty clumps. He used the shirt draped over the fence to wipe his face and neck. "Yes, Captain?"

"Let's talk," Nels said in Acrasian, and pointed to a water bucket positioned under the shade of a large oak tree.

"You have news about Private Landry," Petron said in a flat tone. His expression was equally emotionless. "It's bad news, then?" He tended to be pessimistic.

In this case, he has reason to be. Nels opened the gate. "After you."

Petron shrugged and then walked through. Nels followed. When Petron got to the bucket, he drank from the ladle. Afterward, he poured more water down his back and washed his face. Nels sat at the foot of the tree, content to let him finish. At last the corporal settled in the grass next to him.

"And?" Petron asked, balancing his forearms on top of his knees. He watched his men working in among the turnips.

"I'm afraid we were too late," Nels said.

"I knew it."

"The surgeon did the best he could to save the leg, but it wasn't possible. If they'd waited any longer, Landry would've died." In fact, it'd taken a sizable bribe to get Landry treated at all, and even then, Nels hadn't trusted the healer in charge. Of course, Viktor had been the one to supply the bribe money, and of course, Nels hadn't exactly told him why he'd needed it.

Petron blinked. "He's alive?"

"Yes," Nels said, confused. "Of course."

"Oh."

It was then that it occurred to Nels that Acrasian medicine, while advanced in some ways, left a lot to be desired in others. "I'm sorry. The surgeon did his best."

Petron nodded, stunned.

"There's something else," Nels said. "A letter. It's addressed to you." He brought out the folded and refolded letter and handed it to Petron.

Nodding, Petron accepted the message but didn't open it. A long, tense moment passed between them. Nels wasn't sure what else to do or say. About the time he was prepared to get up, Petron spoke.

"I thought—I was certain—" He took a deep breath and tried again. "Thank you."

Nels nodded. "How are the new accommodations?"

"An army stable is considerably more comfortable than that animal pen."

"It's temporary. Until I can convince Vinter to put you in the detention barracks."

There was another awkward silence.

"You're different than most of your kind," Petron said.

"I am? I'm almost afraid to ask how."

Petron looked away and the corners of his mouth turned up grudgingly. "It's perhaps best you don't know."

"Fair enough."

Glancing at the letter, Petron asked, "Where are you from?"

"Jalokivi."

"That far north? I figured you for a southerner. Maybe even Ytlain. Although why you'd be serving in the Eledorean army is beyond me."

"Well, I didn't exactly volunteer."

"Neither did I. But it's marginally better than dealing with my father. And the pay is better."

Nels felt a smile spread across his lips. "Why did you think I was from the south?"

"You speak Acrasian," Petron said. "That's unusual for an Eledorean, even those who live along the border. What made you decide to learn?"

Nels lied. "It seemed a good idea."

Petron gave him a long, judging look that told Nels the corporal knew he was lying. "I see." He made a motion toward the letter in his hand. "I assume you read Acrasian as well as you speak it?"

Nels looked away. *We're at war. What else would he expect?* "Better, actually."

"Do you have a family?"

"I don't." Nels resisted an urge to ask the corporal questions whose answers he already knew. In an effort to even out the conversation, he offered up some personal information. "Not yet. I've a . . ." He stopped himself because wasn't sure what to call Ilta in Acrasian. He shrugged. "She doesn't live far from here. But I haven't seen her in months."

"She hasn't visited the bustling metropolis of Gardemeister? Is something wrong with her?"

"Actually, yes. She's under a quarantine. Variola. I think you call it small pox. Everyone else who caught it died. She's living alone up on a mountain, and I can't do anything about it."

"Oh." Petron winced a little.

Suddenly ashamed for having said too much, Nels added, "It's not your fault."

Petron nodded. He seemed to be holding his breath. "I understand you don't have to answer my questions, but I thought I'd ask nonetheless."

"Go on." Nels braced himself for another personal inquiry.

"You've no curfew?" Petron asked.

"We don't. The Eledorean people are happy." *Or would be, but for the war.* Although Nels had ventured as far as the Acrasian border, he'd never been to one of the larger cities. He understood a curfew was imposed in some areas, but hadn't experienced one. He assumed the smaller towns weren't as strictly controlled.

"Have you no malorum?"

"Malorum" was a word that Nels had encountered before, but since the literal translation was "of evil," he'd assumed it meant only that. "We have a few malcontents. Every nation does. But that's what prisons and the army are for."

Confusion sketched a line between Petron's brows. "It's true then? You don't have malorum."

"I don't think I'm understanding your question correctly," Nels said. "Can you try a different word?"

"Malorum are creatures born of nightmares. Demons that live in the darkness and take on different forms. They feed off the living," Petron said. He tugged at a silver chain around his neck. The medal hung off of it had been fashioned from an old Acrasian coin and had clearly spent most of its existence on that chain.

Nels considered what it meant that in spite of nearly starving, the corporal hadn't used it for trade.

"They have one weakness. It's silver."

Oh, Nels thought. "Nothing like that lives in Eledore. Well, not any longer. Not for centuries."

Petron moved closer, apparently eager to hear more. "You found a way to drive away the malorum?"

Uncomfortable with discussing soldier lore that he couldn't even share with Ilta or his sister, Nels hesitated. *No one else speaks Acrasian. Who will know?* "I don't think they were the same creatures. They must not be." He pulled up a blade of grass and picked at it. If he stopped now, he wouldn't know more about Acrasia, and he got the feeling this was important. "I don't know what they are—or were. No one does. No one has seen one in a very long time. We call them the Old Ones. You understand that in Eledore, only soldiers bury the dead?"

Petron said, "I thought that was only a rumor."

"It's the truth," Nels said. "There's a reason for that. The Old

Ones are attracted to blood. They're also known to accompany the dead."

"Accompany the dead?" Petron let out a short laugh. "You Eledoreans do have an interesting interpretation of evil."

"The Old Ones cause the dead to rise from their graves. Soldiers must assure the dead are properly buried. It's part of our sacred duty."

"And what constitutes 'properly buried'?"

"We have our traditions. Rituals." Nels hoped that was answer enough. "Surely, you do too?"

"If they are the same, why do the malorum have so much presence in Acrasia and not here? What's different?"

"That's a good question. Unfortunately, we've spent centuries burying the past. Particularly the notion of death and anyone associated with it," Nels said. "I can't give you an answer."

"Interesting."

"I've traveled into your lands as far as Greenleaf. There was no curfew there, but that was years ago. Has there been a recent change? Are the malorum more frequent than before?"

Surprise flitted across Petron's features before it vanished, leaving no trace. "Eight years ago, the malorum population grew large enough that the emperor declared an emergency. It tore the Regnum apart in ways no one could foresee. Everything nonessential stopped. The people lived in terror. We didn't have enough silver to circulate as currency. The emperor wisely imposed certain mandatory changes. You've seen Acrasian sterling notes?"

Nels nodded.

"The curfew was established, and the Brotherhood of Wardens were charged to hunt the malorum. Let me assure you, our cities are not defenseless at night. Any attacking army would have the city guard, the Watch, and the Brotherhood to contend with as well as the malorum."

"But the malorum roam free after dark?"

"In some areas. They seem to prefer the more-populated places. In any case, they don't venture much farther north than the Kylmapuro River." Petron gave him a sideways glance. "Some have said this is due to a natural aversion of elpharmaceutria. Your kind. Others claim that you're in league with them."

Nels stifled a laugh at the implied question. It wasn't until he noticed Petron was serious that he answered. "I'd venture to say that Eledoreans have a tough time being in league with their neighbors, let alone creatures from outside the world of the living." He got to his feet and dusted off his uniform. "I should get back. Oh, I almost forgot." He reached inside his pocket for the tobacco pouch. "I won this in a card game. I don't smoke, but I thought maybe you or your men might like it."

"Yes, thank you." Petron stood and accepted the pouch. "Thank you for the letter."

He seems less concerned about the message's contents than I'd expect, Nels thought. According to the letter, his pregnant wife has been ill for a long time. *Maybe he doesn't know?* Letter delivery was often unreliable. Still, Nels thought it suspicious.

"And, Captain?"

Turning, Nels asked, "Yes?"

"I'd be careful of how much of Lucrosia Marcellus Domitia's philosophy I'd take to heart."

Nels tried not to show his surprise.

Petron said, "Particularly 'Know your enemy.' Knowledge humanizes them. You aren't human, but I assume you have a similar term. Humanity isn't the easiest concept for soldiers during a war."

TWO

The trumpet had sounded the day's end hours before. Nels rolled over in his bed for what must have been the fiftieth time. He'd retired early because he was exhausted. Regardless, he couldn't get comfortable, and his mind wouldn't rest. Something about Corporal Petron bothered him. *What was the name of the dead Acrasian Lieutenant? Was it Lucrosia?*

He got up, relit the lamp with a long piece of tinder from the banked fire. Then he went to his writing desk and located a copy of the report he'd written a few weeks before, listing the prisoners' names and ranks. When he got to the name of the dead lieutenant, he stopped.

Lucrosia is a common name among Acrasian soldiers, officers in particular. That doesn't mean anything. However, the lieutenant's full name was Lucrosia Marcellus Petreius, and the name Lucrosia Marcellus was significant. It meant that the dead lieutenant did in fact have a connection with the general. If nothing else, it indicated that the lieutenant in question was wealthy enough to purchase a specific relationship with the general's gens. *Or it means what I suspect—that the lieutenant was a relative. Petreius. Petron,* Nels thought.

More and more, Petron's behavior began to form an image Nels wasn't sure he liked. His gaze drifted to the small library of books he'd been able to keep with him in his footlocker. He considered what he knew of Lucrosia Marcellus Domitia's personal life, but the truth was, he didn't know much. *How old is he? Does he have a son?*

Nels had to acknowledge that the general's age had very little to do with whether or not there was a connection. In addition to the buying and selling of family names, Acrasians were known to adopt children—even adults, if it suited them. He told himself that even if Petron was General Lucrosia Marcellus Domitia's son, the coincidence would be unbelievable. *In addition, what reason would he have to lie about his identity?* If he were a famous general's son, he could use that status to return home. The Eledorean army would be more than happy to execute an exchange of prisoners. *It makes no sense.*

The others would treat him with more respect than they do. Petron is a farmer, a peasant. Let it go.

He doesn't speak like a peasant. He doesn't have the hands of a farmer, either.

Or he didn't until now.

Wouldn't Lucrosia Marcellus Domitia's estate have farms on it? Most estates do, don't they? Even Acrasian estates?

You're being ridiculous. Impossible. Major Suorsa will laugh you out of his—

Someone knocked on his door. "Captain Hännenen? Are you awake, sir? Colonel Vinter wishes to see you."

At this hour? Nels checked his pocket watch. It was only nine.

"Captain Hännenen?"

"I hear you," Nels said. "Stop your hammering. I hear you!" He answered the door in his nightshirt.

It was raining. A big, ugly, middle-aged male corporal huddled on the narrow stoop. He saluted. "Corporal Ekstrom, sir. The colonel would meet with you now. Her barracks house."

He returned his salute. "No need to wait. Tell the colonel I'll be there shortly."

"Yes, sir."

The highest-ranking officer in Gardemeister, Colonel Vinter lived in the biggest barracks house in the military compound. The exterior construction was more like that of a noble's than a military officer's. The furnishings inside bordered on opulent. Having resided in Jalokivi's Narrows for the majority of his service, Nels found that odd. He didn't know why Vinter had brought so much with her during a war. Eventually, she would have to travel to the front like all the rest. *Vinter must have a great deal of money to waste*, Nels thought. Of course, there were other possibilities—possibilities that brought Pesola to mind.

He was shown to the colonel's study by Corporal Ekstrom. The large room was made smaller by the shelves and shelves of books that lined the walls. He thought of his own scant library and decided that Vinter couldn't have traveled much in her military career. The house and everything in it spoke of years of residence. Nels had only met the colonel briefly upon his arrival, not long enough to form much of an impression. She was older than his mother and younger than General Kauranen. Her smooth hair was a snowy gray and restricted to a soldier's queue. Her features were square and mannish, and her voice was deep and somehow pleasantly scratchy. Papers were neatly stacked all over the top of her writing desk. She was still dressed in her dark blue and black infantry uniform. The gold braid was spotless. It occurred to him that her uniform had never seen a battlefield. He didn't know why he was surprised.

"Ah, Captain Hännenen. Sit." She returned his salute and motioned to a chair. "We have something important to discuss."

Feeling uneasy, he settled into one of the heavy red velvet upholstered chairs.

"How are the Acrasian prisoners?"

"Well enough, I suppose."

"That was very smart, putting them to work."

"It wasn't my idea," Nels said. "It was Corporal Petron's."

Colonel Vinter didn't appear to listen. She was searching for something. "I sent a report to your colonel, informing him of your excellent performance."

I'll bet he thoroughly loved that. "Thank you."

"He had a suggestion and I've opted to implement it." She retrieved a note from the stacks positioned on the writing desk and scanned it. When she was done, she got up and handed it to him. "These translations need to be completed by tomorrow."

He read the note and blinked. Cold anxiety knotted his guts. "These are infantry commands."

"I know. They're to be translated into Acrasian."

"May I ask why?"

"Your colonel said you dislike authority."

Nels bit down on a reply. *Not all authority. Mainly his.*

"Such attitudes aren't suitable in an officer of the lower ranks. Why isn't relevant to you, Captain. I gave an order."

All right. Maybe more than his. "I understand, sir. I'm not of sufficient rank to know," Nels said. Even more dread chilled his blood. *You know what she'll want next, don't you?* He gambled Vinter wouldn't know enough about Acrasian to understand that what he was about to say was a bold-faced lie. "However, it would help with the translation process if I understood the specific intent. Acrasian is complicated. In Eledorean alone, there are several different verb forms, depending upon intent and status of the speaker in addition to the status of the individual being addressed. In Acrasian, I can think of at least three declarative—"

"Enough," Vinter said. "These are commands which will be given to Acrasian prisoners. Commands *you* will be giving to them. With domination magic."

Nels felt as though the earth had finally been yanked from under him. "What? Why?" *I always knew this day would come. How are you going to fake your way out of this? Assuming you want to comply with such an evil—*

"Don't be stupid," Vinter said. "You've demonstrated that the prisoners can be put to good use. They can't be utilized in a prisoner exchange. The Acrasians won't pay for their care. Posting guards to watch over them costs the army soldiers who would be best sent to fight. Putting the prisoners on the front line is the best use for them. Better that the Acrasians should die than our own soldiers. Think of the lives you'll be saving. *Eledorean* lives."

Oh, gods, Nels thought. "If that's the case, why are you asking me to translate these commands? If I'm to do this myself—"

"Do you think these are the only Acrasian prisoners, Captain?" Vinter asked.

"You can't ask me to—"

"I'm not asking. Your colonel said you'd object—"

"It's immoral! My mother, the queen, worked to pass laws against using command magic in exactly this manner—"

"Laws that the king did not pass."

"I won't do this!"

"Are you refusing an order, Captain? Because if this is the case,

I won't hesitate to have you punished and sent back to your colonel in disgrace."

Nels closed his mouth.

"You have until noon. That is all. You are dismissed." She returned her attention to her work, leaving him to make his way out of the study.

THREE

"What's got your tail tied in a knot now?" Viktor asked over the top of the novel he'd been reading.

Uncertain what to do and unable to think of a way around the situation, Nels had taken the long way home from the meeting with Colonel Vinter. He'd been growing more and more hopeless with each step when he'd spied Viktor relaxing on his own stoop. Viktor sat in the chair with its back tilted against the front of the barracks house. Nels shoved his way through Viktor's front gate and collapsed on the steps in a frustrated heap.

"Don't ask," Nels said.

An open bottle of whiskey rested on the porch at Viktor's feet. Nels grabbed it and took three long drinks.

"Ohhhh," Viktor said, and righted his chair with a wood-creaking thump. "This is going to be good. Did you get a bad letter from the little blond?"

Nels didn't like that Viktor refused to refer to Ilta by her name. Of course, the fact that he hadn't told Viktor her name probably had a great deal more to do with it. "If only it were that simple."

"What is it, then?"

Nels stared at Viktor while whiskey burned away the chill in his guts.

Viktor said, "We both know you'll tell me anyway. I might as well get it out of you while you're sober. It'll take less time for me to puzzle out your drunken rambling."

"The colonel has ordered me to translate some orders into Acrasian."

"That's not surprising. You *are* serving in the capacity of a translator."

"You don't understand," Nels said, taking another swallow. "She wants me to order the prisoners to fight. For *us*. She intends to send them to the front. And she's ordered me to use command magic to do it."

"Oh." Viktor took the bottle from him and sipped from the neck. "I see. That's a problem."

"I can't do it. It's—it's wrong." Nels tried to focus on the half-truth.

"I'm familiar with your stance on command magic. However, if you don't—"

"I'll be stripped of my command." As bad as that would be, Nels knew it wouldn't end there. Once again, the catacombs beneath the palace haunted his thoughts. *I always knew eventually I'd be caught. I'm lucky to have lasted this long.*

"Well, you're not exactly in command now."

"You know what I mean."

"I do." Viktor handed him the bottle, stood up, and went to the door. "Bugger it."

Nels gave him a questioning look.

"I suspect this is going to be a two-bottle night," Viktor said.

FOUR

Nels woke with one of the worst hangovers of his life. The puzzling thing was that he didn't remember drinking enough to warrant it. Sitting up, he found himself on the floor in his own room. Apparently, he hadn't made it to his bed. Considering he didn't remember walking home from Viktor's in the first place, it wasn't too surprising. Someone, he assumed it'd been Viktor, had given him a pillow and tossed a blanket over him.

Daylight filtered through the shabby white curtains.

What time is it? He searched for his pocket watch and discovered he'd forgotten to wind it. His back complained, and he had a painful crick in his neck from sleeping on the floor. The ache in his head worsened with each beat of his heart, and his mouth tasted awful. He felt sluggish. He wanted to go back to bed, but he had to decide what he would do about the translations. He didn't know how late it was, but Colonel Vinter would send someone soon. *What the hells did we drink last night?*

He staggered to the bedroom door. "Viktor!" He grabbed his

head and winced. He reconsidered shouting. "Are you here? Get up! I need to make some coffee. Now. What time is it?"

The house was empty. The coals in the hearth were still banked for the night. Viktor must have gone home. *He couldn't have been in much better shape than I was.* It was a rest day. Viktor had no need to be up early. But for the translations, neither would he. Nels checked the clock on the mantel.

Half past ten, he thought. He decided to get cleaned up, and get to work. He'd turned away when the note on the mantel caught his attention. Unfolding it, he saw it was from Viktor.

> *By now I've resolved your little dilemma. If you don't do anything stupid, they can't blame you. Don't worry about me. That detention barracks is a joke.*
>
> *Sorry about the headache. I wanted to be sure you'd stay put.*
>
> *Do me a favor and burn this. The Jägerpoliisi around here aren't all that bright but even they can read, and I'd rather not have risked my neck for nothing.*
>
> *—V*

Nels tossed the note into the hearth and stirred the coals. He'd gotten dressed when he heard the front gate latch. Peering out the front window, he spotted Corporal Ekstrom and three Royal Jägerpoliisi dressed in blue-and-green uniforms. He didn't wait for them to knock but met them in the dooryard.

"Is there a problem?" Nels asked.

"Captain Hännenen, we have some questions," a Jägerpoliisi with a long mustache said. "Where were you last night?"

Nels couldn't think of a reason not to answer. "I was with Lieutenant Reini. We were drinking. I don't know what time I got home. I didn't think to look. Why?"

"Come with us, please," the Jägerpoliisi said.

"I don't understand," Nels said.

"Overlieutenant Reini is under arrest, and you are wanted for questioning."

"Don't resist, Captain," Corporal Ekstrom said. "They have orders to shoot you if you do."

"All right." Nels put his hands up in the air. "I'll go quietly."

Surrounded by the Jägerpoliisi, he was escorted to the detention barracks. He already had an idea what had happened but he wanted it confirmed.

"What did Reini do?" Nels asked. "Can you tell me?"

Corporal Ekstrom said, "He released the Acrasian prisoners."

Nels stopped. "He did what?!"

A Jägerpoliisi urged him to continue moving with the point of a gun barrel in the back.

"You heard me, Captain," Corporal Ekstrom said. "We are now trying to determine whether or not you ordered him to do so."

"That's easy. I didn't!" Nels dropped his hands and half turned to glare at the Jägerpoliisi.

"So your lieutenant says," Corporal Ekstrom said. "At least your stories seem to match."

"Why would I do such a thing?" Nels asked.

"I'm sure I don't know," Corporal Ekstrom said. "But that is what is to be determined."

"Did Reini say why he did it?" Nels asked.

"He refuses to cooperate. We thought you'd be able to get an answer out of him," Corporal Ekstrom said.

The detention barracks was located near the pens where the Acrasians had been kept. The barracks stable wasn't far. The stench of horse dung was strong. A tall, splintered wooden fence surrounded the barracks, a long redbrick building with no windows.

Nels was led inside and taken to Reini's cell, a small eight-foot-by-eight-foot room with bars for walls. The Jägerpoliisi locked him inside.

Viktor was lying back on the narrow bunk with his hands pillowing his head. He sighed. "I was having a lovely dream about Helmi and her friend Tanja."

"What in the name of all the gods were you thinking?" Nels asked.

"I don't suppose I could ask you to go away?"

"I'm serious!"

"This isn't your problem any more."

Nels leaned in closer. "You're my *korva*. Of course it's my problem. They think I sent you to—"

"I told them you weren't involved."

"Why would they believe that?" Nels asked. "I was with you last night, and I don't exactly remember what we talked about."

"There's a reason for that."

Nels paused. "And that reason would be?"

"I drugged you."

"You did what?!"

Viktor whispered, "Keep your voice down. I don't trust that the Jägerpoliisi don't have great hearing."

"Why would you—"

"I didn't want you involved. I'll tell them I drugged you. They'll find the bottle where I left it and confirm it for themselves. I used something easy to smell, just in case. This way, you'll be sent back to your company. The Acrasians go free. And you don't have to send them to fight against their will."

"There are a couple of problems with your plan."

"Oh, I know," Viktor said. "The first being, you couldn't have commanded the prisoners to fight in the first place."

Nels blinked. "I wouldn't have wanted to—"

Viktor shook his head and lowered his voice even more. "I know. You can't."

"That isn't true."

"Nels, stop it," Viktor said. "The others are idiots." He shrugged. "To be honest, you're not too bad. I still don't know how you managed to pull off that stunt at the hospital in Jalokivi. That said, would I be a very good korva if you could fool me?"

Sighing, Nels pulled up the lone stool and sat. "How long have you known?"

"Since Almari," Viktor said. "Anyone with command magic wouldn't have let that fat bastard get the better of him. No matter how principled they are, no one with the power to keep from being knifed is going to allow themselves to die just because they don't agree with the method used."

"And you didn't tell anyone?"

"It wasn't anyone's business but yours," Viktor said. "If I couldn't keep your secrets, I wouldn't be a korva."

"You still agreed to work for me?"

"With what your sister was paying, why wouldn't I? Anyway, I don't know if you're aware of this," Viktor said, "but you actually care about what happens to your troops. That alone would make you better than most officers. And, well . . . since you do a creditable job of faking magic, who am I to disabuse people of their assumptions? We all have our little flaws." He shrugged. "That said, you couldn't release the Acrasians."

"Why not?"

"Do you have any idea what Vinter would've done to you? It'll make what Pesola did look like a summer holiday."

"Us. What Vinter will do to us."

"Ohhhh, no. You're going back to Major Lindström."

"You think I'll be better off? Are you forgetting Pesola? Please, Viktor. I can't let you—"

Viktor got up and went to the bars. "Hey! Time to let the nice captain go home. We're done here."

"I'm not leaving you."

"You are."

"Stop this. They'll hang you."

"They won't hang me," Viktor said. "I'm a korva. I'm far too valuable to the army to hang."

❧ SUVI ❧

ONE

Stationed on the poop deck, Suvi used a spyglass to scan the horizon for trouble. Others were on watch, but she preferred to look for herself. The afternoon wind harbored a chill, and the seas were growing restless. It was a beautiful day. The sun was high, and the sky was a calm blue with only a few scattered clouds. She breathed in tar-and-sea-salt-laden air, and reveled in *Otter's* graceful speed. They were making swift progress. It'd been a few days since the previous encounter, and things had been quiet, but there was no telling how long that would last. Not only was summer over, but northward progress meant trickier weather. She was of two minds about the change, of course. On one hand, it meant she'd be home soon.

On the other, it meant she'd be home soon.

Piritta had been able to get everything their prisoner knew. With the restriction of the water, it'd taken longer, but that was all. She'd used his fear of kainen magic against him, and in truth, that had done most of the work for her. Thus, Suvi knew the Acrasians had been informed that she would be in the area, but Bradford didn't know the source.

A strong breeze tugged unruly light brown curls from her hastily tied ponytail and blew the strays into her face. Her shoulder was healing. It felt good to be without the sling. However, her left leg reminded her that she'd been standing entirely too long with a cranky pain that shot up through her knee and lodged itself in the back of her skull. She winced and shifted her weight to her right leg. At least she didn't have to use the cane as much any more.

The afternoon watch had been called. There'd been fresh fish for lunch, and her belly was full. That was when she spied a flicker of white on the horizon. She waited until she was certain it was a sail. "Ship to the fore!" She couldn't help a little pride over having spotted it first. She wasn't sure if it was a friendly ship or not. She couldn't make out the flag at the top of the distant mainmast.

A shout from the mainsail topgallant verified her call. It wasn't long before the ship's whistle indicated a sister ship. However, they were still a week or two from the Eledorean port of Mehrinna. Suvi didn't think her messages had had time to reach Jalokivi, not yet. She wasn't expecting an escort. It wasn't like her father to send a ship into the Waterborne Sea—most Eledorean vessels weren't equipped for ocean travel. She gazed through her glass and picked up a few more details.

"Are we sure she's not a Waterborne ship?" she asked Captain Hansen. "I don't recognize her."

Squinting into her own spyglass, Captain Hansen finally said, "She's flying an Eledorean flag. Three masts. Looks like a frigate. She must be new. I don't know her either." Her tone mirrored Suvi's own confusion. "Her paint is fresh. Her construction is Ytlainen. You can tell by her figurehead."

Suvi could make out a carving of the lithe form of a half-nude woman on the frigate's bow. A wreath of flowers crowned her wind-blown hair, and decorative vines draped across the statue's bare breasts. "You're right." Eledorean ships used sculptures of animals or even males, if they had figureheads at all. Eledorean sailors tended to be more traditional in their beliefs and such depictions of women were considered unlucky.

She moved her focus to the main topgallant mast again. There she spied a long, thin banner just below the Eledorean flag and frowned. "She's flying mourning purple." There was only one reason why an Eledorean ship would fly a purple banner with silver trim. *Someone in the royal family died. Is it Father? Uncle? Please don't let it be Nels or Mother. Please let it be Uncle.* She felt a twinge of guilt for wishing such a thing, even upon her uncle.

"Can't read her side. Not yet," Captain Hansen said. "That's interesting. I count twenty-eight guns. Ports are closed."

"She's new," Suvi said. "They're too far from home." Something about the ship bothered her. "I don't like this." *If Father is dead, then would Uncle send a warship?* She had to admit it was a solid possibility. *I'd do it if our roles were reversed.* Her next thought was a quick prayer for her mother and brother. "What are they doing out here?" As she asked, the frigate let fly a new series of signal flags.

Hansen said, "They're requesting to board passengers. We're close enough that they could send a bird. Everything else is aboveboard—on the surface, anyway. I can't think of an excuse to refuse. Can you?"

"Tell them we'll accept the passenger."

"Yes, sir."

"Let's heave to, Captain. And call action stations, but let's do so quietly. I want the marines ready just in case she makes a move we don't like. Inform *Indomitable* to do the same," Suvi said. "We don't want to make trouble where there isn't any."

The frigate indicated she'd be boarding on *Otter's* port side. Hanging aft, *Indomitable* gently moved to port as well. As a precaution, Suvi intended to trap the frigate between *Indomitable's* and *Otter's* guns. She held her breath and inwardly cursed the slow pace of ship movements until it was apparent Captain Björnstjerna received her instructions. As the stranger ship drew nearer, Suvi could finally make out the name *The Winter Rose*. Shadowy kainen on *Rose's* decks went through the motions of preparing to heave to, but it was impossible to make out individual uniforms. Hunting for some sign of trouble or reassurance, she caught a silhouette that gave her a start. *Is that sailor's hair twisted into spirit knots?*

That was when she recognized what had been wrong. *Their ship isn't entirely dependent upon the wind. They've a waterweaver on board, a powerful one too, by the look of it.*

That's a good sign. Right? No Waterborne would serve on one of Uncle's ships. The thought didn't stop the creeping chill raising the small hairs on the back of her neck.

"Maybe you should get below," Hansen said.

"If the message is what I think it is"—Suvi collapsed her spyglass with a quick slap—"we both know it's for me. There's no sense in hiding."

"If you say so, sir."

"I do."

Suvi watched *Rose* draw closer with ever increasing unease. At the last possible instant, *Rose* took a dangerous and normally impossible turn across *Otter's* bow. *Winter Rose's* gun ports opened, and Suvi felt her guts turn to ice water.

No, no, no! Oh, Goddess! You should've known! They've a waterweaver! My fault! "They have us! Call the alarm!" She braced herself on the poop deck rail. *This is my fault! I don't know what I'm doing! I should've let Hansen take—*

The first shot was a solid hit down *Otter's* bow. The bowsprit disintegrated in a cloud of splinters and smoke. Crew members screamed. The nine-pounder stationed at the bow flipped on top of a marine. The rest of her gun crew died in a shower of wood slivers and blood. Bar shot rolled and bounced across the decks. It cut one man in half, took the head off another, slammed into *Otter*'s port rail, and vanished. All at once, another round of bar shot slammed *Otter*. The foremast split with a loud crack just above the fore yard, sending the mast to the deck in a long, tangled arc of ratlines, sails, and shrouds. Marines stationed in the yards fell to their deaths. A cold shard of terror pierced Suvi's heart. The violence with which the *Rose*'s cannon punched the boards sent quakes through the *Otter* that Suvi felt through the souls of her feet. *My fault! My fault!*

Think! Everyone will die if you don't! It was at that moment that she remembered her mother's advice. *A good leader knows when to delegate.*

But dumping responsibility on Hansen would be cowardly!

Hansen knows what to do. You don't.

Winter Rose was now gliding past *Otter*'s starboard side. Suvi was relieved she'd been at least suspicious. "Captain, give the marines the order to fire!"

"Fore guns first! Wait until she's in your sights, blast you! Fire! Fire! Fire!"

Otter's starboard guns hammered *Winter Rose*'s broadside. Caught with *Otter* between itself and *Winter Rose*, *Indomitable* was unable to assist. *Winter Rose* sent another volley into *Otter*'s side as she slipped past. *Otter* rocked violently to port and then starboard. Small fire peppered the boards. A sharp pain in Suvi's weakened leg unbalanced her. She landed hip first on the poop deck with jaw-jarring force and bit her tongue. If she hadn't had a grip on the rail, she'd have been thrown over the side. She saw three of the crew do just that.

Otter righted herself, and *Winter Rose* sailed on. With *Otter*'s foremast destroyed, she couldn't give chase. Suvi scrambled to her feet. The deck was slick with water and gore. Her leg ached but that seemed to be due to the old wound and not because of anything new. She looked to the captain. Hansen's uniform was covered in blood and a splinter protruded from her upper left arm.

"You're bleeding." Suvi pointed to Hansen's arm.

"I don't have time to bleed." Hansen turned to the nearest lieutenant and shouted. "Damage report?" Her voice was calm. *Firm.*

Suvi was shocked at how powerful that was, even without command magic. *I've no healing powers. Even if I did, they probably wouldn't work. The surgeon is below. I need Hansen on her feet. She knows what to do.* Suvi glanced around, searching for a moment of clear thought. She'd watched a healer deal with a similar injury once. *What did he do?* Chaos filled her senses with loud creaking sounds and screams. *Your uniform coat.* She slipped off the coat, rolled it as best she could, and handed it to Hansen. "Tuck this under your arm and press down. The pressure should slow the bleeding until the surgeon gets here."

Hansen only paused for a moment, then accepted the jacket. "Thank you."

It would take some time in the chaos for the second mate to report. In the meantime, *Indomitable* signaled for permission to pursue *Winter Rose.*

"What are your thoughts, Captain?" Suvi asked.

Hansen gave the question some thought before answering. "I'd keep her here, sir. I don't like the looks of *Rose.* She's tricky and fast. I believe in Björnstjerna. He's very good, and he could take her. But if you're the target, *Rose* will be back soon enough. She may even bring friends. We have to be ready to move if she does. Right now, we're dead in the water. We don't know for how long. Worse, we don't know how bad things are below. We don't know how much stress *Otter* can take. I'm not touching the guns until we know the situation. Long story short, we may need *Indomitable* to keep our noses above the water."

"All right, Lieutenant Noronen," Suvi said, "tell Commodore Björnstjerna to stay put. And get a healer up here. Then I want the casualty list."

Of course, they were aboard a ship in the middle of an ocean. There was no guarantee the healer's powers would be reliable, but unlike army surgeons, naval surgeons were trained in how to treat patients without magic. It wasn't nearly as effective. However, it was better than the alternatives.

"Yes, sir."

The second mate arrived. "We got lucky, sir," she said. "Other than the foremast, the damage isn't terrible. All hits were above the waterline. Replacing the bowsprit I can manage, but the foremast we'll have to jury-rig. Repairs are already under way."

Hansen grinned. "Very good, Duiri. Carry on."

Suvi gazed at the wreck left behind by *Winter Rose*'s cannon. "Somehow, I thought the news would be a lot worse."

"Ha! *Otter* is a Mehrinna girl," Hansen said, an edge in her voice. "And Mehrinna girls are harder than ironwood."

With a smile, Suvi recalled that Hansen was also from Mehrinna. "We'll still get home."

"We'll have to go a bit slow and careful. But yes. *Otter* and I will get you home, all right," Hansen said. "I don't care if I have to stand in for the foremast myself and hold her sails up with my teeth."

⊰ NELS ⊱

ONE

With the cool, solid texture of limestone and mortar against his back, Nels inched closer to the end of the farmhouse's front wall. He and his platoons had to reach the barn before those hidden inside understood that they had been spotted. In the distance, Eledorean cannon thundered against the ranks of Acrasians lined up in orderly rows among the waist-high corn, while equally tidy rows of Eledorean infantry advanced. Drums echoed off the hills.

Nels knew his place was artillery support—with the other half of his company. It wasn't here, sneaking around in an attempt to expose an Acrasian ambush. That was the job of a korva, not an infantry captain in hobnail boots.

You've watched Viktor. You've learned a few things. You can do this. In truth, Nels was relieved. Even though Viktor was in trouble, at least he wasn't in the middle of this mess.

Unease had nested in the pit of Nels's stomach since before daybreak. No matter what he did, he couldn't shake the sense that his worst nightmare was about to come true. He knew it was unreasonable, this terror of the Acrasian army, but it was buried deep in his bones. The nightmares hadn't let up from the day he'd packed his ryggsack and left the barracks house in Gardemeister. He told himself over and over that the sense of wrongness wasn't significant. The Royal Eledorean Army had managed to shove the Acrasians as far south and east as the Acrasian city called Virens. Spirits were high. Many felt now that Kauranen's army had at last joined the fight, the end of the war was near. Rumor had it that they outnumbered the Acrasians three to one. Some had already begun celebrating. So much so that the morning's muster had been noticeably depleted and quite a few soldiers had to be put on report.

Nels hadn't been in the mood for celebrations. He'd hardly slept at all the night before, and this morning, the lingering dread was worse than ever. If he weren't certain that he had no useful magic—the incident outside of the Commons Hospital had been a fluke, he was sure of it now—the feeling in his gut might actually mean something. His gaze had kept drifting to the line of hills to the north of Virens. The hills bothered him. He'd recommended sending scouts that direction, but Major Lindström had dismissed the idea. The area had been thoroughly searched by Laine's troops. Lindström had said that if Nels was so certain there was a problem, perhaps he should take a couple of platoons and check the farm at the southern edge of the battlefield himself?

Nels knew he'd used up the last of Lindström's faith with what had happened in Gardemeister. Therefore, he swallowed the last of his pride and kept his mouth shut. If Viktor had been present, Nels would have sent the korva to investigate the hills regardless and then paid the price with Lindström later.

However, Viktor is languishing in a detention barracks. No thanks to me.

At least, I hope he's still in the detention barracks.

There'd been unmistakable signs of enemy troop movement as Nels and his platoons made their way south. He had no idea how many or their most likely location. The one person he relied upon to interpret such information wasn't there.

Signaling to a newly promoted Overlieutenant Larsson, Nels directed his second platoon to circle the farmhouse where the Acrasian troops were hiding. There, Larsson and her platoon would make their way to the back of the barn and quietly set it on fire. Then he signaled Lieutenant Saarinen orders to have his platoon take up a position behind the abandoned wagon in the dooryard. If the private Nels had sent to Lindström hadn't survived the journey back, then an exploding barn would have to serve.

Nels listened to every thump of a wooden musket stock, every clink and clatter as his troops moved into position. With each footfall, each breath, he was certain the element of surprise would be lost.

Make your weaknesses your strengths. It'd been something that Captain Karpanen had taught him long ago. *We can do this. I can do this.*

Horses inside the barn made nervous sounds. He spotted the smoke first. Then the scent of burning wood, hay, and dung. Flames climbed the edge of the barn. It was time to act. He motioned to the first platoon, indicating they should cock their preloaded muskets, and held his breath. With his hand in the air, he waited for the enemy to make a move for safety.

In the distance, trumpets sounded a charge. Cannon fire thundered through the hills. Drums clattered. Horses pounded the earth in the corn fields, and the roar of thousands of soldiers echoed back to Nels's ears. Everything was taking too long. He had an instant's self-doubt before he heard muffled coughing from the barn. Someone kicked open the doors. The heavy wooden things creaked on rusty hinges and slammed against the front wall, making the whole barn shudder. Four squealing horses bolted for freedom.

Everything became sharply focused. Nels glimpsed Acrasian gray uniforms.

They're using the horses for cover. He dropped his hand. The troops stationed behind the wagon fired their muskets. One of the horses was struck in the shoulder. It reared back, knocking an Acrasian into the dirt and trampling him. The Acrasian troops paused to return fire. Then they charged Lieutenant Saarinen's platoon. Nels signaled again. The remainder of the first platoon positioned against the front of the farmhouse made for the barn's dooryard, shouting a war cry. Nels joined them. Startled, half of the Acrasians turned back and retreated to the shelter of the barn. Nels stopped, brought up his musket, and took aim at the first Acrasian to climb the wagon. The bullet took off the top of the Acrasian's skull. He fell over into the dirt on his back in a shower of gore. Musket balls smashed into the wall behind Nels, but the sound was far away like the trumpet calls. To his right, Private Linna let out a small noise. Turning, Nels saw she'd been shot in the throat and the chest. Blood gushed down the front of her uniform. She dropped before he had a chance to think or act.

Thank Hasta that wasn't me. As always, the terrible relief was followed by shame. Nels hated that that was his first thought. It was always his first thought. *Not now. Survive.*

Lieutenant Saarinen ordered another volley into the dooryard. The last of the Acrasians who hadn't taken shelter fell. Smoke poured out of the barn. Coughing came from inside. Larsson's platoon moved toward the barn doors along the sides of the building. Lieutenant Saarinen's platoon reloaded. Nels and the rest made for the barn. An Acrasian stepped out long enough to tug at the barn door. Overlieutenant Larsson clubbed him with her musket. The Acrasian went down with a face full of blood and a flattened nose. A bullet knocked Larsson off her feet. Inside, someone screamed. Their cries became increasingly panicked until a gunshot cut it off. A second Acrasian made an attempt at the big barn door. Throwing himself against it to keep it from swinging shut, Nels spied Corporal Kallela on the opposite side of the doorway. Kallela took aim with a pistol and shot the Acrasian struggling with the door. Then Kallela leapt backward, flattening himself against the barn. He'd lost his tricorne somewhere. His bright red hair stood out against the barn's dull weathered wood.

The corporal grinned and winked.

Nels called to those inside the barn in Acrasian. "Come out with your hands up. You're surrounded."

"You'll only shoot us down, you sorcerous demon."

"Perhaps I should put it this way," Nels said. "You've a choice between us and the fire."

"All we have to do is survive until—"

The farmhouse exploded. The concussion threw Nels against the barn and then down. He reached for his musket and struggled to get up. Large stones from the destroyed walls dropped from the sky, bounced, and rolled. Several punched through the barn walls and roof. Smoke was everywhere. The farmhouse, what was left of it, was in flames, and the wall where he'd hidden was now gone.

Nels swallowed. *If I were still there, I'd have been killed.*

The wagon was in flames. At least two were dead, hit by falling debris. He saw Private Horn peer from under the wagon and snatch up muskets from his fallen comrades. The fire took a firmer hold on the wagon.

Corporal Kallela launched himself at an Acrasian emerging from the barn's doorway. Both rolled across the ground, struggling over a knife blade. Nels got to his feet on the second attempt and drew his saber. He felt unsteady. A cluster of Acrasians exited the barn at a run. There wasn't time to count them. He swung his saber and slashed an Acrasian sergeant across the chest. The Acrasian turned, pointed a pistol at him. Nels's heart stopped. The Acrasian sergeant pulled the trigger. The gun didn't go off. *Misfire.* The Acrasian dropped the weapon and went for his sword. Nels lunged. His saber plunged deep into the Acrasian's belly. A surprised expression spread across the Acrasian's soot-darkened face. His blue eyes were wide. At that moment, Nels was glad he'd trained to keep a barrier between himself, the water steel saber, and those he killed.

He yanked his blade free with a twist. Larsson dropped the last Acrasian with a knife throw.

Nels edged into the burning barn and coughed. Thick smoke made it impossible to see. Flames had spread throughout the building. He didn't think anyone else was inside. If they were, they would've been overcome by the smoke. Finally, the heat drove him back. His coat was smoking, and he thought for certain his hair and eyebrows were singeing.

"Captain? We checked the shed and the outhouse. No one inside," Overlieutenant Larsson said. Blood oozed from a bullet graze on her forehead. "They must've seen us coming. The house was where they were keeping their powder stores. Some of them, anyway. They lit the fuse and . . ." She shrugged.

If I hadn't moved everyone away from the house when I did . . . Nels nodded. "And the bill?"

"We lost Lieutenant Saarinen and Privates Ruutu and Linna. Corporal Kallela was cut bad. Lost a lot of blood. Sergeant Wiberg patched him, but it's deep. Wiberg has limited healing powers, but he won't be able to do much after that. Corporal Kalastaja was shot in the leg. Thigh. The rest is related to the explosion. It tore us up. Private Paiva caught a splinter in the side. Wiberg says it's not too bad. Privates Larsson and Ketola were hit hard too. The rest is small stuff. A few burns and bumps. Wiberg says everyone is good to march, but we'll have to get to a real healer soon."

"We've done all we can here," Nels said. "We bury our dead first. I don't know when we'll be back. Do it quick. Use stones and a dog tent tarp. Got it? Leave the Acrasians where they are. We'll do the rituals later. Get to it, Lieutenant."

"Yes, sir."

By the time they'd finished and had reached the broken fence where they'd originally entered the property, they could see the situation had changed for the worse. Nels felt a chill as all the blood in his body seemed to drain into the earth. The Acrasians had more than quadrupled their forces with an ambush and were attacking from the north and the south as well as the east. The Eledorean armies were pinned. Brigadier General Ahlgren's army and Nels's direct link to the Eledorean forces had been overrun. An overwhelming number of Acrasian troops swarmed the corn fields between themselves and their own troops.

"What are we going to do, Captain?" Corporal Kallela asked.

Nels searched for a safe path to Field Marshal Kauranen's banner. Ahlgren had been the Eledoreans' southernmost flank. Brigadier General Näränen had been next, and now his troops were struggling to keep the Acrasians back while Grand Marshal Valk and Field Marshal Kauranen attempted a fighting retreat. To the north, Laine and Moilanen did their best to provide cover, but the Acrasian trap was closing. Moilanen's lines were collapsing.

"We'll circle to the south. Move behind the Acrasians. Go as far west as we can. Then we'll head north and join with Kauranen," Nels said.

Overlieutenant Larsson said, "Yes, sir."

"Go back and grab all the guns and ammunition you can carry," Nels said. "We'll need it."

TWO

Quietly running through the stone-riddled countryside, Nels fought the feeling he wasn't quite up to the task of getting his troops through the Acrasian lines safely. He told himself over and over that he'd seen worse, but it proved to be a useless litany. Evening was fast approaching. Activity in the battlefield would be winding down, he knew. He tried not to imagine what was going on at that moment and prayed that enough of the Eledorean army had escaped, that he'd been able to warn Major Lindström in time, that they'd done something to help. Nels didn't want to think it was all for nothing.

At least we've managed to successfully avoid discovery.

So far.

Overlieutenant Larsson jogged to his side. She was breathing heavy but seemed otherwise fine. "Captain, we need to stop," she whispered. "Kalastaja has to rest."

Nels glanced over his shoulder. Corporal Kalastaja was being supported by two others. All three were at the rear, struggling to keep up. "We'll find a place to stop, then. It won't be for long. We must get out of here before morning. The Acrasians will be all over these hills, searching for survivors."

"Yes, sir."

They located a suitable area with excellent cover of trees and boulders on the side of a large hill. The moon would rise soon. Nels knew it'd be full. That was both good and bad. It meant they'd have some light, but the same illumination that kept them from breaking ankles on the uneven ground would also give the Acrasians a better chance of spotting them. Tracking would be difficult. The ground was too hard to harbor much of a trace. He counted that as a point in their favor. Short, bushy trees with splintery trunks sprouted in clumps over the surrounding hills. There was a creek below, and uncertain of when they'd next see a water source, he had everyone refill their canteens. Sleeping wouldn't be comfortable among the rocks, but they had a good view of anyone or anything approaching the area.

"You've one hour, Lieutenant," Nels said. "No fire." It would be cold, but they couldn't risk it. "Set a watch. Everyone else sleeps, including you."

Some of the troops were already asleep. Others were whispering among themselves, performing soldiers' rituals required to keep them clear-headed. Nels had Overlieutenant Larsson check on the injured once more before putting her own head down. Sergeant Wiberg was doing the best he could with what little magical power he had. While he didn't have much talent for healing, he could patch fabric. That wouldn't heal anyone near death, but he could create a sturdy bandage, and he had the knowledge to know how best to apply one. So far, it'd been enough to keep the wounded on their feet.

I should sleep too, Nels thought. He sat on a flattened boulder and searched for answers in the smoke-filled valley below.

Where will Kauranen go next?

You're assuming Kauranen survived. What if she's dead like Private Linna? An overwhelming sense of relief washed over him again. *Thank Hasta that wasn't me.* He felt his cheeks heat in the cooling air.

It's normal to think that. You know this. He couldn't afford to indulge in the cleansing rituals with one of the others. Confiding in someone of lesser rank would mean damaging the troops' faith in him, and he didn't have much of that faith to spare. *Think about it later. Take care of the others. You've decisions to make now.* He gazed to the north, beyond the battlefield.

He knew where he wanted to go, but the problem was he couldn't be sure of where Kauranen and the rest of his company would be headed.

We need a real healer. And he knew where to find one. Going anywhere else meant a chance of guessing wrong, and guessing wrong meant condemning his wounded. "Larsson?"

Curled inside her coat on her side on the ground nearby, Over-lieutenant Larsson had her back to him. She sounded half asleep. "Yes, sir?"

"We're going to Gardemeister."

❧ I L T A ❧

ONE

Deep in grief, Ilta hadn't given day-to-day upkeep such as the external wards much thought until she gazed out the front window and spotted the brown bear. It loped toward the apiary in lumbering yet graceful strides.

Her teacup clattered on its saucer. "Oh, shit!"

She abandoned her breakfast at once. Dashing up to her room, she jammed her feet into boots and grabbed her coat. At the front door, she snatched Gran's walking staff from the old butter churn barrel she'd long used to store umbrellas, canes, and walking sticks. Ilta had run out onto the porch before common sense set in.

That is an eight-hundred-pound bear. Am I seriously going to frighten it away with a blackthorn stick? What am I thinking? What if I get seriously hurt? Who is going to help?

No one. Because I'm alone.

And that bear is the least of my worries.

As a chill ran through her, she knew she could no longer afford to feel sorry for herself. *This stops now.*

Shaking with the knowledge of what she'd almost done, she turned around and closed the door. She dropped the walking stick back into its former resting place. Then she got dressed, cleaned up the tea, and finished her breakfast. After that, she located Sergeant Hirvi's weapons. She didn't know how to use a saber or a pistol, but she decided it was time to teach herself. Arranging the necessary components on the table, it became apparent that she didn't have an infinite amount of powder or ammunition. It was also clear that Hirvi regularly cast the bullets himself. She didn't have anyone to show her how to load the thing either, and she had a hunch to do so incorrectly was dangerous. It was then that she decided to leave the guns alone.

Nels will come. Soon, in fact. I saw it. There had been several different variations of that vision, but she knew he was on his way. *I won't be alone for much longer.* She stared out the window and attempted to get an idea of when he'd arrive. She had expected him sooner, but something somewhere had changed. She didn't know what it was. The vision she'd had the night before indicated that he would still show up on her porch with wounded—only there would be more of them. She worried she wouldn't be able to care for them all.

It was time to look after the food stores. *They'll be hungry.* With that done, she'd check her medicine supplies. There were bandages to make and herbs and vegetables to harvest—not to mention the bread to bake. The list brought her back to the apiary. Honey was an important component of wound dressings.

"Asa, Great Mother and Protector of Animals, please send that bear safely to its home," she said out loud. "And while I don't mind sharing your bounty with your creatures, please allow a few of the hives to have survived. I need them. Thank you." With that, Ilta once again put on her coat and ventured into the chilly morning.

What she found both saddened and reassured her. The bear was gone. However, all but two of the hives were destroyed. She went to the shed, gathered the tools she needed, and set about the business of cleaning up the mess. Repairing the combs, she was ambushed by grief for her Gran. However, this time it felt cleaner and less debilitating. Where before Ilta had been angry when day-to-day needs pushed for attention—for everything to go on as if nothing important had happened—carrying on now felt less of a betrayal. She believed that in living and taking take of herself, she was honoring her Gran rather than dismissing her.

Ilta had also reached the point in her Gran's journals with which Gran had been concerned. Ilta's mother, Saana, had fallen gravely ill when she'd been pregnant with Ilta. Gran had chosen not to send for another healer and treated her daughter. During the process, something went wrong. When it looked like both mother and child would be lost, Gran had dared something no healer was permitted to do with a pregnant patient. She'd poured her healing magic directly into Saana, saving her daughter. Ilta had survived too, but unfortunately, she'd also been changed.

"Gran, I think I understand what you meant. It's all right," Ilta whispered from beneath Gran's veiled, wide-brimmed straw hat. "I love you. I miss you, too. Terribly. But I think I'll be okay now."

Finished with her work, Ilta then placed a protective ward on the two remaining hives—bears tended to return to places where they found food.

It was now late afternoon. Sore and hungry, she decided to make something to eat. She couldn't take too much time. It would be dark soon, and she still needed to reset the wards on the edges of the property. If she didn't, she'd have more than one wild visitor. She walked back to the house with more spring in her step than when she'd left it, and prepared her dinner—a thick slice of toast, some cheese, and an apple. She thought of her Gran's journals as she ate. She was almost ready to face the rest of what they contained. At some point, she'd be leaving and would have to decide which volumes she would pack and which would remain behind.

She'd lifted the apple to her lips when a vision ripped away the sunlight.

TWO

Ilta rushed to renew the wards. The vision that had stolen so much precious daylight had also emphasized the need. It was frustrating in the extreme, and if there hadn't been moments when her powers had warned her of an event while it happened—and therefore not allowing her to surface soon enough to experience it for herself— she'd be angry. She checked the sky and cursed. Her pocket watch thumped against her chest where she'd pinned it. There were so many instances she wished she could be normal. Others didn't have to constantly check the date or the hour for fear of losing their sense of continuity. Others didn't have to fear losing their sense of self.

She'd made the circuit, refreshing all but the last ward, when it started to rain. Shivering, she pulled up the hood of her cloak and took the path eastward. She'd left this particular ward last because of its proximity to the Herraskariano road and because of her vision. Each spell was designed to link with the next until a circle of protective magic was formed around the house and its grounds. Normally, Gran kept the road ward separate. It operated as alarm, mail alert, and doorway, allowing individuals in need through and alerting the warder of visitors. It'd amused Gran to give visitors the impression that she'd had a vision foretelling of their arrival even when she hadn't. *It teaches respect,* Gran had said.

Gran had her own sense of humor, Ilta thought with a pang.

Assisting with the wards had been one of Ilta's first magical lessons. She had helped Gran with them once a month ever since. It'd been the reason she'd known the exact moment of Nels's arrival all those years ago. Her visions weren't always clear or exact. It was almost impossible to keep track of time when your mind was persistently invaded by both the past and the future, but there were other ways of compensating.

Her earlier vision had been different. She would have a visitor. *Soon. Tonight.* She wasn't certain he'd be friendly, given the situation at court. Lightning flashed. She counted to twenty before the quiet rumble followed. The main part of the storm hadn't arrived yet.

She found the old hazel in near darkness without expending more energy to magically locate it. She'd have to climb the tree. It was usually her favorite ward for that reason, but it was raining and cold and she was afraid. She wanted to get back to the house for a warm cup of tea. Ideally, she'd finish long before the intruder— *visitor*—showed up. It was possible.

A flash of guilt vaporized the thought. *I'll deal with whatever comes in whatever form it comes to me. No more cheating. Gran would.*

She studied the tree before attempting the climb. The trunk would be wet and slick. She'd have to take off her boots, which would mean her feet would be freezing and dirty by the time she was through. Her left thumb throbbed with a dull ache where she'd repeatedly cut it for the spells.

Let's get this over with, she thought, and sneaked a glance down each end of the steep, furrowed road. There was no one. Of course, she hadn't expected to see him. He'd be hard to spot, even for her.

The climb was an easy one. While one needed to place a ward where it was least likely to be tampered with by the curious, it made no sense to establish a ward where it'd be impossible to reach. The rain slowed to a drizzle. She secured the drawstring bag of supplies around her neck and began to climb. The hazel's trunk was cool and bumpy under the soles of her feet. She reached the bough with little effort. She'd made her way to the branch over the path leading to the house and had the fresh ward in her hands—a bundle of twigs lashed together in the shape of a person—when she heard footsteps. She twitched, almost dropping the fetch. Stopping to listen, she could make out words but couldn't understand them. It took her less than an instant to recognize the texture of the words. Nels had tried to teach her once and failed. *Acrasian. That's Acrasian. There are Acrasians in the area?*

That wasn't who she was expecting at all.

Returning her attention to the task at hand, she retrieved the bottle of consecrating oil from the drawstring bag and then anointed the stick figure. She held the fetch in a trembling right hand and charged it using energy from the hazel tree, adding it to her own. The new ward, no longer intended to serve as a doorway, would hide the path from enemies. It would need more power than it normally held, but she'd designed it with that in mind anyway. She concentrated until the fetch tingled in her hand. Next, she mentally connected it with the others, forming a potent and solid circle. Her skin itched with newly charged power.

The voices from the road fell silent.

Ilta froze. Due to the storm, the remaining light was feeble at best. Rain had gathered on her cloak, dripping from the hood into her face. Unfortunately, she couldn't see the road through the trees, but then, neither could they see her. Carefully, she raised her chilled feet until they were under her cloak, and hugged her knees.

Her back was against the trunk, and she was now in a comfortable and stable position. However, the longer she remained in contact with the ward in her hand, the more her senses would become overwhelmed with information from the entire protective perimeter. She needed to replace the fetch in its former location on the branch. At the same time, she was afraid to move and draw attention to herself. The Acrasians had to be closer than she'd thought to have sensed her magic.

Wait. They're Acrasians. They can't be that sensitive, can they? Once again she wished she could consult with Gran. There was so much she didn't know.

But if Gran were available, you wouldn't be in this fix, would you?

Three birds—*cardinals*—shivered rainwater off their feathers somewhere along the western perimeter. Stragglers, they hadn't joined the others on their way south. A squirrel scampered up the warded yew in the north; she knew the shape of its clawed toes as it passed over the stick-figure carving traced with blood on the trunk. A deer—

Stop it. Focus.

She slowly replaced the ward and almost fell out of the tree at the sight of a young man wearing a black wool uniform coat. *Why didn't I hear him?* He approached with cautious steps. A hissed inquiry came from the road. The young man below her turned, waved the other Acrasian away in an annoyed fashion. Turning back to the path and her, he took another step and paused—a confused expression on his face.

It was one thing to hide what no one knew was present. It was another to make something vanish once its existence was known.

Oh, Great Mother. Oh, shit.

The Acrasian stole toward the hazel with quiet steps. She didn't know what had caught his attention, whether it'd been movement or the feel of fresh magic. Not everyone could sense magical power, but enough could that it was a possibility. *Wait. He's human, not kainen. It had to be movement. Right?* His graceful steps reminded her of a korva. *Not a korva. An assassin.* There was something peculiar about this Acrasian. First, even she knew what an Acrasian soldier's uniform looked like. She'd seen any number of them in visions for years. However, his uniform, and it was obvious that it was a uniform, was different. It was solid black with silver braid. Acrasian uniforms varied somewhat in the details. All military uniforms did. Some had bright red sashes and epaulettes, while others bore yellow, gold, or green detailing, but the primary color for Acrasians was always dark gray, as it was dark blue in Eledore.

The Acrasian reached out for the hazel's trunk as if blind. He glanced up. From this angle, she got a full view of his face. He was a year or two older than she. His hair was dark under the Acrasian tricorne. His eyes were dark too, almost black. Shock showed the whites of his eyes. He muttered something in Acrasian, and at that moment, she knew he'd spotted her.

Her heart thrashed inside her chest. Out of reflex, she lifted her hands in the air so that he could see she wasn't armed. She whispered so that the other Acrasian wouldn't hear. He wouldn't understand, but she did it anyway. "I won't hurt you. See?" Her voice felt hoarse. It'd been so long since she'd spoken to anyone. Her mind whirled. She had to do something, but she didn't think she could hurt him.

A sound from the road drew his attention from her. He turned and looked over his shoulder toward the road. He gasped and went for his pistol. A silent figure darted from the shadows. A long, sharp knife blade sketched a swift horizontal arc, catching the Acrasian under the chin. Blood splattered. The Acrasian dropped to the ground and died, twitching in a swiftly spreading pool of gore.

Ilta swallowed a sick feeling. She hadn't seen such violence since Nels's uncle had invaded Gran's garden.

"You can climb down now. It's safe. All the nasty Wardens are dead. Their friends too." An average-looking kainen of average height and dull brown hair stood over the body in the middle of the road. His uniform was stained with blood. He didn't even glance her direction but was going through the dead Acrasian's pockets.

"What's a Warden?"

"Acrasian assassins. They like to think they can hunt kainen." He gave out a derisive snort. "I came to see if you'd gotten word of the evacuation. Clearly, you haven't."

"What if I don't trust you?"

He laughed, and it reminded her of the first night she'd visited Nels at his barracks house with a sudden pang. "You're Nels's little blond, yes? Named Ilta?"

"Is that any way to address the Silmaillia?"

"You're the Silmaillia's apprentice? *That* Ilta? Ilta Korpela?"

"Yes."

Viktor whistled. "Well, no wonder he never cheated on you," he said. "I thought it was out of an overactive sense of loyalty. Or a spell."

Ilta frowned. "Excuse me?"

"Perhaps you don't remember our first meeting?" He doffed his tricorne with a flourish and gave her a courtly bow with his left leg forward. "Overlieutenant Viktor Reini at your service. I'm a friend of Nels's. I've come to escort you from this place."

Her expected visitor had arrived.

THREE

It'd taken only a small amount of convincing for Viktor to understand that they had to remain at the house. It'd been good to see his genuine relief in the knowledge that Nels was still alive. The news from Virens was bad. Defeated and destroyed, the surviving remnants of the Eledorean army were now fleeing north. The Acrasians were in pursuit. They killed everyone in their path.

"I was tempted to head south and search for Nels," Viktor said, pausing between spoonfuls of hot chicken soup. "But I knew he would want me to make sure you were safe first."

"Thank you." She welcomed the need to guard her mind from his thoughts.

They discussed preparations and packing. It felt good to know that she'd have help. He even offered to show her how to use Sergeant Hirvi's weapons, but she couldn't make up her mind as to whether or not such a thing was counter to her Healer's Oath or not. It was clear not all traditions were worth keeping. On the other hand, the mistakes she'd already made were difficult enough to live with. She ended by telling him she'd think about it.

After they'd eaten, she gave him Sergeant Hirvi's room. Pausing on the steps to her own bed, she turned and gazed back at the main room with its cozy, banked fire. It was wonderful to have another person in the house—even more so that it was a friend of Nels's. She felt a little bit more like herself. She retired for the night in the knowledge that she was safe for the first time since Gran had died.

The next few days passed in a blur of activity. Outside, it stormed and showed no sign of stopping. She attempted not to worry. With Viktor's help, she had the cots, bandages, and tea prepared long before the front door was forced open with a kick. She'd sent Viktor to meet Nels the moment she felt the signal from the wards. The stained glass window in the front door rattled as the door hit the wall.

A lightning flash made three Eledorean soldiers into silhouettes against a brightened night sky as they lurched through the doorway. One was being half carried over the threshold by the other two. Muck and gore masked the sky blue of their uniforms as their muddy boots pounded out ominous drumbeats on Gran's clean floor. Drenching rain formed puddles before Ilta could shut the door, and she caught the reek of old blood and sweat as she hurried past. It took her a moment to recognise Nels.

Rolls of thunder shook the house like a warning.

He was breathing in gasps as he staggered inside. He peered through the wet hair gluing itself to his face and gave her a shy smile that sent a delicious shiver through her. "Hello, Ilta."

She suppressed an urge to hug him that almost broke her heart. "Oh, Nels. I'm so happy you're safe."

"When I heard the Acrasians had sent Warden pack units up the mountain, I thought for certain . . ." Nels didn't finish the sentence. Water dripped down the side of his nose.

"I'm—I'm fine. Lieutenant Reini got here before they did." She opened her arms wide, adopting a happy attitude to smooth over the awkward air. "See? All safe. Now, let's see to your corporal."

"Kalastaja is in bad shape," Nels said. "Wiberg did his best, but he isn't a healer."

Viktor stumbled in beneath the weight of another injured soldier.

"Let's see what I have to work with." Ilta helped Nels lay the shivering and feverish corporal on a cot near the hearth.

Light from the fire gave her a better view of them both. She risked another quick look at Nels. The change in him was a shock. It was more than the filth, the unruly hair, and beard, or the torn and muddy uniform. He was harder somehow. She was glad to see the added confidence but didn't like that he seemed so guarded. She tried not to think about what he'd been through—the rout, the forced march to Gardemeister, getting up the mountain to her. Instead, she focused on her patient.

The wound in the corporal's right thigh gave off a sickly stench when she tugged at the filthy bandage. His skin was hot. She peeled off his blood-stiffened uniform coat and shirt.

Gangrene. That's going to take a lot of energy. Another day, and he'd have been gone. Thank Stjarrna, they got him to me in time.

"There's a tea tin on the hearth," Ilta said. "Use the blue kettle. I'll need the hot water from the big copper one. Cups are in the cupboard."

Nels shook his head. "There are more. I must go back for them. You're—you're sure you're all right?" His question tore the scab staying her misery. *Much as I wish otherwise, I can't be with him. I have to tell him. Letting him think there's hope is cruel.*

But I can't do it now, can I? That would be selfish. She smiled but didn't meet his eyes. *He needs someone to take charge of something, anything to ease this burden.* She pushed back her errant hair and stood tall. When she finally braved his gaze, she saw his irises weren't black. They'd changed color with his moods because he couldn't control it. So, unlike any normal kainen, his eyes tended to be blue or green. However, at the moment, his eyes were hard gray flints.

He's using up everything he has to keep himself together, she thought. A part of her wanted to cry into his chest while he patted her head and told her it would be all right, but she couldn't. "Go. Everything is fine. We'll talk later. We can't—not now. I—I missed you."

"I'm sorry I couldn't get here sooner. I love you."

She paused but couldn't think of a reason not to say it. "I love you too."

With that, he went back outside and left her to her vocation. She selected a knife from the small table where her surgeon's tools were neatly arranged. Then she settled into her work, cutting away the corporal's trouser leg. More patients arrived while she washed blood from his thigh. She attempted to ignore the filling cots for the moment and laid a hand on his wrist and closed her eyes. A warm tingle began in her palm and worked its way up her arm.

Ball only nicked the bone. Infection is the worst of it. The corporal's fever remained high, his heartbeat slow but strong. She concentrated on destroying the last of the gangrene. That was when the confusion of battle blotted out everything and—

The smoke is thick and she is surrounded by the deafening explosions of musket shot and cannon, the knelling of crossed swords and cries of the wounded. Running. Then she hears the jeers from laughing Acrasians and the screams of the dying. No Eledorean standard is to be seen. Foreign flags are waving in their place on the battlefield—a golden eagle flying against a background of gray and red.

A crushing wave of despair and rage overpowered her. With difficulty, she tore herself from Corporal Jori Kalastaja's mind and did what she could to fortify him. As she blinked, the images melted away and became Nels stooping over another of his fallen comrades.

All of this and he lost his mother, too. Oh, Goddess, how terrible this must be for him. Is his sister still alive? She decided to check the auguries when she had the chance.

Viktor arrived with a lieutenant, and together they transferred a wounded private from a makeshift litter to a cot and left. Ilta moved from Corporal Kalastaja's side to her next patient. She recognized him with a start. *Private Ketola. The one who took Nels's message to Suvi that night.* And the full weight of her duty formed in her mind. Nels's troops hadn't had enough supplies or time to tend the wounded. Her patients' injuries were well over a week old and hadn't been properly cleaned. With a glance at her next patient, it was clear the best she could do for Private Paiva was make his last hours comfortable. Worst of all, after she assessed two more patients, she understood she must make a terrible decision. It hadn't occurred to her that she would need to choose who lived or died. She believed such things beyond her. Now two patients required help at once, and it was a close enough thing that she couldn't make an easy determination on who could wait. Gran had always handled those decisions before, making them seem easy. Ilta's thoughts became enmeshed in a thick ooze of terror.

One of them will die, and I must choose which. Oh, Stjarrna, I don't want this.

In her mind she heard her grandmother's voice, hard-edged like steel. *Don't shirk, girl, or you'll lose them both. Time is wasting.*

Ilta decided to first stabilize the straightforward chest injury and leave Private Ketola's more difficult head wound for last. She needed help. If she had someone to handle the simpler tasks, she could save both patients.

If I'm quick enough.

She glanced around the room full of soldiers before taking a deep breath to strengthen her resolve, and motioned for Sergeant Wiberg. "You've been serving as surgeon?"

Wiberg, a sturdy middle-aged kainen with graying hair, nodded.

"Wash up," Ilta said. "I need your help."

Tired, soaked, and cold, Wiberg didn't hesitate. He went straight to the basin and washed his hands. She turned her attention to Private Larsson and the chest wound, and tried to forget about the passing of time. She stole away as much of his pain as she could, dug out musket balls, and stitched with expert motions. The process took longer than she'd hoped, despite asking Wiberg to take over bandaging. She paused to give Private Larsson a boost of healing energy before moving to Private Ketola.

Ketola looked terribly vulnerable in the lamplight. When she touched him, she understood he was on the verge of slipping away. Images of his wife and family swam in Ilta's mind. His wife was gone, but his children were alive when he'd last seen them. However, his family had been following the Eledorean army. They'd been at Virens. *Oh, Goddess.* Ilta took a deep breath to fight off a rush of panic.

Oh, please don't let him die. I didn't choose. I didn't. She selected a clean scalpel and began the fight to save Ketola.

FOUR

It was nearly dawn when she finished the last suture. Her mind was numb, but the muscles in her neck and shoulders were tense knots of pain. She washed her hands in the basin a final time and wiped them dry on a clean apron. Across the room, Overlieutenant Larsson slept with her head resting on the edge of Private Larsson's cot, her hand on top of his chest as if she were monitoring her brother's breathing.

It must be awful to see your own family shot like that.

"You should get some sleep too," Nels said.

Ilta turned, and Nels pressed a warm cup of tea into her hand.

"I don't think I can just yet." She pushed hair out of her eyes again. "Rain's stopped. Would you mind sitting out on the porch with me?" She sipped the tea and warmed her fingers on hot porcelain. She let the cup be the reason she didn't touch Ketola one last time to check his progress. "Tomorrow's going to be another long day, isn't it?"

Nels stared at the sleeping troops and then whispered, "I've hidden the rest of the company in a cave not far from here. These were the most in need. I should go back."

"You need to rest. You've been up all night."

"We were attacked south of Gardemeister. It was my fault. I should've been more careful. I should've seen them. If I had Viktor's ears, I'd have heard them. If I had any power at all—"

"Magical power doesn't fix every problem," Ilta said. For what felt like the hundredth time, she stopped herself from reaching for his hand. "Sometimes it creates more problems than it solves."

"If you say so."

"I do," Ilta said with more frustration than she'd intended to reveal. "It's normal to blame yourself after something like that, but you can't rip yourself apart. Think of what you've accomplished. You got the others here safe, didn't you?"

Nels nodded.

"And that was most of your company?"

"Of the half that was with me at Virens, yes."

She glanced to Viktor, who was sound asleep in a chair by the hearth. He'd taken charge of the hot water for tea and whatever she needed for surgery. It never failed to amaze her how quickly soldiers could drop off. In Viktor's case, she was certain he could sleep standing up.

She lowered her voice even more. "Did you know Viktor has been practically crowing? He seems to think he taught you to be quiet or something."

"I had to abandon a majority of my wounded." A hand curled into a fist. "The Acrasians don't take prisoners."

Remembering Ketola's family, she winced. She didn't know what to say. "I know you did everything you could."

He turned as if avoiding her words. "Front porch?"

Exhausted, she was having trouble keeping up her defenses. Quick images from the minds of her patients threatened to invade her skull. "Yes. Please." She snatched an extra blanket from the sofa and fled after Nels. Cool early morning breathed the post-storm scent of freshly washed air into her face. In a weary daze, she tossed the blanket onto the porch to soak up rain water and sat on the ledge. Nels perched next to her. She stared into the gunmetal sky and swung her feet as she always did when content. Sitting made the standing stones in the dooryard tall enough to block most of the view. Ilta shut her eyes and pretended everything was as it used to be. She drank in the comfortable silence, letting the stress of the evening melt into the beams of the porch, and imagined it flowing into the ground. Then she pulled fresh energy up from the moist earth. When she opened her eyes once more, the sky had acquired a warm orange tinged with blood red in the east.

"I've never seen you at work before," Nels said in a quiet voice. "You're amazing."

Private Ketola.

"You expected otherwise?" she asked, frowning at the sky.

"Not really."

Tick-tick. He was rolling something in the palm of his hand that made the small clicking sound. *Tick-tick.* She leaned over and looked into his palm. He showed her two mushroom-shaped bullets she had cut from Private Paiva's ruined body. She knew Paiva wouldn't see the noon sun but had felt she must try anyway. Gran would've chided her for wasting the energy, but she wasn't hard like Gran had been. She couldn't bring herself to give up on anyone. *Tick-tick.*

Ketola.

Tick-tick. She felt a double cut of grief and guilt. The quiet sound of the ruined musket balls suddenly made her want to weep. *Tick-tick.*

"The Acrasians call it cold iron," he said, staring into his palm. "They're iron-coated lead. Shoots farther. Makes a bigger hole.

Always kills unless you've a healer, and most of the time even then." *Tick*— He wrapped the bullets in a tightened fist and frowned. "I told Father not to underestimate the Acrasians. Why couldn't he have listened for once?" He threw the musket balls at the woods with a growl. The thoughts that followed came with such force, she wondered if he shouted them aloud at first. *My fault. I failed. Again. If I had magic, I could have saved them. He would have listened to me, then. I could have influenced the nobles if I had magic like a proper Ilmari.*

He hopped down from the porch ledge and strode across the dooryard. Turning his back on the witnessing windows, he kicked at a tall weed next to the circle of standing stones. She saw him wipe his face with the back of his hand.

The tea she'd drunk sank in her stomach, hitting the bottom like a stone. She felt more inadequate than ever before, wanting to comfort him but unable to approach. *Let him grieve. He needs it.* It occurred to her that this was the first opportunity he'd had to release any emotions. She didn't have to read his mind to understand. She watched him settle with his back against one of the stones, hiding from the house. She took a sip of cooling tea and watched the sun rise. Later, she would fetch him a fresh cup of tea. In the meantime, she allowed herself to think of things she had been too busy to deal with before. *How much longer can we stay here? Certainly not too long.* If they waited until too late, they'd be trapped.

So tired. She leaned against a porch column and rested her eyes. *Just for a moment.*

When she started awake, the sun was feather-touching the tops of the trees. She went inside to make Nels a cup of chamomile tea. Everyone was still sleeping. She went back outside as quietly as possible, balancing the cup in hand. She'd gotten as far as the stones when she saw Nels was sleeping. She backed up a step. The cup clinked against the saucer.

His eyelids snapped open. He looked up at her with a hand to his pistol.

"It's only me. I brought you this." She offered the tea with one hand. The whites of his eyes were red and the irises were still dark gray. However, they had that smoky quality they took before changing color again. Outwardly he looked calm, but stinging thoughts still buzzed under his skull. She could sense them without trying. She didn't think it was entirely because she was tired, either. He needed rest, more than he'd gotten napping in the wet grass. She considered giving him a little valerian to make him sleep. It felt good to know solutions for simple problems.

He rubbed his eyes and refused the tea with a shake of his head. "I should go. The others will be wondering what happened to us. Although it's more likely they're drinking the whiskey we found hidden in that cave." Nels stood up and gingerly stretched his right arm up in the air with a wince. The other he kept to his side.

There are more wounded waiting in the caves. For a moment, Ilta couldn't breathe. *I used all that energy on Private Paiva, and he's going to die anyway.* She turned to Gran's house—*my house now*— with its three floors, wraparound porch, and tower jutting into the morning sky. *Oh, Gran. Why didn't I think?*

"Thank you," Nels said.

"For what?"

"For letting me be."

If Nels can bear such things, I can too, she thought. "Isn't it my duty to know what my patients need?"

Nels made a futile attempt to brush wet grass from his torn and dirty uniform. There was a saber slash in the left side of his coat. She had been too busy to take notice, or perhaps it was all the grime.

"You're hurt."

He glanced down at his side. "Isn't it my duty to be invincible?"

"Come up to the porch. I'll take care of it. Is it bad?"

"I haven't fallen over yet, have I?"

She didn't know how he managed to make her laugh even when she felt like crying. "The porch. Now. I promise not to let Overlieutenant Larsson witness your mortality. The others are too drugged to care," she said, then ran into the house to grab what was needed. Larsson didn't so much as stir while Ilta gathered supplies.

When she told Nels to remove his shirt, he hesitated.

"What is wrong now?" she asked.

"Nothing."

He shrugged the shirt off, and as he turned around, she saw his back and bit her lip. She'd seen scars like that before, quite often, in fact. The Eledorean army was infamous for beating the troops. She'd once heard an army officer claim that since a majority of the recruits came from Eledore's prisons, there was no other way to maintain discipline. Still, the scars had come as a shock. She hadn't thought anyone would punish Nels in such a manner. Understanding his embarrassment, she pretended she hadn't seen and concentrated on the cut instead. The wound wasn't deep—a narrow gash starting at the lowest left rib and running up his chest to just under the breastbone. Remembering what had happened with the variola, she decided to keep the healing magic to a minimum. She stitched the cut closed without removing the pain first. He held himself still. Once finished, she risked a small healing spell. Sharp pain bloomed behind her eyes, and her head pounded with the beat of her heart.

That's it. I don't have enough power left for anything else today. If the wound had been worse, I could have lost him. The thought was sobering. "Were you planning on waiting for it to fester?" she asked, roughly tying the cloth bandage closed.

"Ouch. Don't tie it so tight."

"I thought you were invincible," she said, and then smacked his hand as he reached for his shirt. "Don't you dare put that filthy thing back on. It stinks."

"I didn't exactly have time to pack a spare during the rout," he said with a shocked look.

"Yet you could save who knows how many bottles of whiskey?"

His expression melted into a wicked smile. "You expect me to drown my sorrows in a clean shirt?"

She sighed. "I'll wash it."

He put a hand on her wrist. "I'll survive without. You need to sleep more than I do. The others will need you tonight," he said. His bravado faded into concern. "You will be able to see to them, won't you? It won't be too much?"

The questions reminded her of her mistake, and she instantly felt horrible. She didn't have the energy to shield herself from Sergeant Jori Kalastaja's dreams or Ketola's images of fishing with his sons or Larsson's worries for her brother. All of it blended with the pain in Ilta's head, and the disorienting combination made her nauseous. She saw Nels get up from the porch in a distant haze and shook her head to clear it. *Careful. Stay present.* "Don't you dare pull those stitches. I'm not sewing you together a second time."

With his shirt in hand and his grimy uniform coat draped over his shoulders, he gave her a formal court bow. "Yes, Silmaillia."

"Do you know what you'll do next? Where we'll go?"

Nels stared at the ground between his feet. His tightened lips indicated he was prepared for an argument. "We'll need to go north. *All* of us."

"I'm ready. Viktor has been helping me pack and prepare the house for the winter. There are things I'd like to save, if I can. We may need them in the future. But I can't take too much with us. Viktor says we'll need to travel fast."

He gazed into her eyes and smiled. "I should've known you'd understand."

Shrugging, she smiled back.

"I've missed you so much."

She winced, and that was all it took. That uneasy wall was between them again. If everything were normal, she'd go to him, put an arm around him, and kiss him. It would smooth everything over. She settled once again on the edge of the porch. *He doesn't need more bad news right now.* She patted the space next to her.

He sat, and she held his hand.

He laid his left on top of hers. "Is it something I've done?"

"It isn't that."

"You've changed your mind? You don't care for me anymore?"

"That isn't it either. I love you with all my heart. You have to know that."

"Then what is it?"

The truth was, she did love him—so much so, her chest hurt. Her eyes began to fill with tears. *I can't do this to him. I just can't. Not now. Can't I at least pretend everything will be all right? Just for a little while? There's too much going on.*

You have to tell him about his mother. That her death was your fault.

I don't know that for certain, do I? Variola is deadly enough. The report could've been wrong. Gran could be wrong.

You have to tell him.

He'll hate me.

"Ilta?"

She sniffed. "It's nothing."

"It's something. You're crying."

"I'm just tired. That's all. And—and it's been a long time since we were alone together."

He shifted closer. He smelled of sweat and grime when he leaned into her. His breath tickled as he whispered into her ear, "May I kiss you?"

She closed her eyes and cursed herself. *I want that so much.* "Please do."

His lips were soft and firm. Beard bristle scraped her mouth. He stank and needed a bath, but so did she. He tasted of the peppermint tea she'd mixed just for him. He'd been drinking it since he arrived. She knew it was his favorite. She knew why, too. Her heart slammed itself against her breastbone in heavy, quick beats. Every inch of her skin felt sensitive. *Ready.* She felt his tongue brush against her teeth. She opened her mouth wider and explored his with her own. She plunged her left hand into his filthy hair. She didn't care about the grime. The foul-smelling uniform jacket slipped off his shoulders. Laying her right hand on his bare chest, she felt the rhythm of his heart, hard and fast. She sensed the edges of his thoughts—the things he desperately wanted to do to her.

Now, that might be interesting.

The intensity of his need was overwhelming, yet he was being so careful not to make a move unless she asked it. That knowledge unbalanced her with a surge of love and attraction. For a second, she tipped on the edge of losing herself.

Stop. Do not invade his thoughts. Do. Not. You're tired. You know what will happen. And you definitely don't want him blaming himself again. She visualized a barrier between her mind and his. It was very difficult to focus on that, given what his mouth was doing to hers.

She opened her eyes and checked the windows. When she was sure no one was watching, she let her right hand drift downward. His moan was trapped by her mouth. She found herself counting the months since the last time she'd taken that tea in the back of her private medicinal cupboard—the tea that Gran said was supposed to prevent pregnancy.

We can't. Not yet. But we can do other things, can't we? She dropped her hand into his lap. Her fingers brushed against the buttons of his trousers.

He broke the kiss at once.

"Oh. I'm sorry," she said. "I—I should've asked first."

"No. I mean, yes." His voice was husky, breathless. "I mean . . . it's not that. You can touch me. Anything. It's all right. I want you to. But . . ." He stopped himself and looked deep into her eyes. "I—I wanted to be sure that you weren't—"

The door swung open, and Viktor Reini exited with a tray. "Time for breakfast."

"Go away," Nels said. "I mean it!"

Viktor paused, blinked. His confusion slid into a wicked grin. "Oh! Right." Setting the tray on the porch, his practically ran back inside.

"What was I asking?" Nels asked.

From within the house, Viktor yanked the curtains closed. His voice was muffled as it traveled through the glass. "Staying very far away now! Larsson, get away from there."

Ilta laughed.

Nels circled an arm around her. "Where were we?"

She wrinkled her nose. "Right at the part where I tell you you need a bath."

Nels made to sniff himself, sighed, and drew away from her in disappointment.

"I've an idea," she said.

"You do?"

"I'm not sure you'll like it."

"Try me."

"It involves . . ." She shifted closer. Her lips brushed his. ". . . water."

He smiled. "Does it?"

"And you removing all those filthy clothes."

"I'm intrigued so far. Anything else?"

"Soap."

Nels slumped. "All right. I'll go."

"Wait. There's a washcloth too."

"I get the idea."

She stopped him with a hand on his shoulder and then whispered in his ear. "And me applying it."

"Oh." He cleared his throat and swallowed. "Look. I don't wish to complicate the matter further, but I . . . er . . . fail to see an aspect of your proposal I might dislike."

"I—I can't get into the water with you. I'm sorry. I need to make certain . . . I have to . . . I just can't yet. I have to take this slow." *Maybe I can be with him? Maybe Gran was wrong? What if I learn how to keep our magic apart?* "Slower than before."

"I'll do whatever you need me to do. Or not." He shrugged. "I love you."

I wish I had half the self-discipline he does. "I love you too."

FIVE

Ilta awoke after one o'clock to a hesitant knock on her bedroom door. She found herself curled at Nels's side with her head on his chest. They'd spent an interesting evening together. She'd set up the tin tub next to the kitchen hearth so she wouldn't have to carry the water far. Afterward, they'd moved to her room. She worried she'd gotten more enjoyment from it than he did, but he didn't complain once, nor did he push her further than she wanted to go.

He's so good with his hands. She shivered a little, remembering.

It took some effort to slide from beneath Nels's arm without disturbing him. Slipping on her day dress over her shift, she stepped into the hallway. An unfamiliar corporal informed her Overlieutenant Larsson was digging a grave for Private Paiva in the little graveyard west of the barn. She thanked him and then went downstairs to grab a cup of tea. All was quiet in the house. Those who were able were outside, helping Larsson. The others were still sleeping. Tea in hand, she took a moment to check on each before going outside herself. She stepped off the porch into warm afternoon sun and glanced up at a perfect blue sky. A cool breeze pushed against her skirts like an affectionate dog. She needed more rest. She was still tired, but her headache had vanished like the storm. She almost felt she could face the rest of her patients. *Almost.*

The lieutenant's reddish-blond hair was bound in a ponytail and there was dirt on the side of her nose.

Ilta paused, watching Larsson stab the shovel into the ground with a vengeance, before walking to the edge of the pit. "I . . . I'm not sure how to tell you this, but . . . we'll need one more grave. I can help you dig after we eat."

There, it's said. I made a decision and Corporal Ketola will die for it.

Fear washed over Larsson's face as she looked up.

But Private Larsson will live.

Ilta bent, placing a comforting hand on the lieutenant's shoulder. "Your little brother should be fine after some rest."

Overlieutenant Larsson nodded. Tears of guilty relief created clean streaks on her dirty face.

Normally, Ilta would have said something about how it wasn't selfish to be glad your loved ones were safe, how everything would be well in spite of what had happened, but everything wasn't going to be well, and she knew it wouldn't be right to give Larsson false hope.

Gran wouldn't. Gran had believed that sometimes it was best to be hard, and that shying away from the truth would only make matters worse. Gran had been right in that.

Ilta tried not to think about how she'd spent her morning. She tried not to think she'd just made a terrible mistake. *I don't care. It's what I want. It's what Nels wants, too. We'll work it out. Together. Nothing else matters.*

She went back inside to prepare a late dinner and left Larsson to her tears. There was much to do before morning.

Ilta had dreamed. She didn't want to tell Nels until after he'd rested. There was a difficult journey ahead. He was wrong. They needed to go east through a mountain pass to catch up with the Eledorean forces, not north. Kauranen had been driven to the eastern side of the Selkäranka mountain range and would be in the city of Merta. The road would be dangerous, but they would reach Field Marshal Kauranen's army without losing anyone else. She was sure of it.

⊰ NELS ⊱

ONE

"The last group evacuating the city is leaving in an hour. Why haven't you packed?" Nels asked.

Several weeks had passed since they'd left Gardemeister and Ilta's home. They'd joined with General Elzbet Kauranen's forces at Merta as hoped, only to find that the bulk of the Eledorean army had been slaughtered at Virens. General Ander Laine's brigade was now the only other surviving unit of substance. Together, Laine and Kauranen had made a desperate choice. Kauranen's forces had been hit hard—Laine's less so. Therefore, Kauranen would accept Laine's wounded and head for the safety of Merta's walls alone. Laine would buy time, leading the Acrasians a merry chase west of the Selkäranka mountains. Ultimately, Laine would make the same journey through the mountain pass that Nels, Viktor, Ilta, and his company had a week before. Should Laine need assistance at the last, Kauranen had decided to halt outside while the wounded were tended inside.

Nels understood why Kauranen had chosen Merta. A mining town created to take advantage of valuable seams rich in silver ore,

Merta was nestled tight against the slopes of the Twins—the two tallest mountains in southern Eledore. The city could only be accessed through its southwestern gate, due to high cliffs and thousand-foot rock walls. Its natural fortifications also meant that commerce was limited by the same restrictions as potential invaders. Thus, Merta had vast storage facilities for grain and other necessities. Water would be no problem. The streams feeding into the Kristallilasi River passed beneath the city. The last of Eledore's forces would survive in relative comfort until spring. The Acrasians, unused to Eledore's winters, wouldn't last a month. By then, Suvi and their father would acquire assistance from Ytlain.

It was a smart plan, a practical plan—so Nels told himself.

The only problem was Laine's brigade.

How long is Kauranen going to wait? What if the Acrasians get here first? And that was why those who could be evacuated were being moved north. After Virens, no one was sure of anything anymore.

The smell of blood, soap, and medicinal herbs crowded the high ceilings of the Commons Church being used as a temporary army infirmary. The scent was as much a presence as the cries of the wounded.

"Didn't you hear me?" Nels asked as quietly as he could. He didn't want to risk yet another fight with Ilta. They'd been living together as a couple since leaving her Grandmother's place. It'd made the journey easier. Now, he wasn't so sure it'd been the smartest idea. "The last group is leaving for Jalokivi soon."

"I heard you the first time."

"Then why are you still here?"

Ilta continued her work on her unconscious patient and didn't glance up at him to reply. "That would be because I'm not leaving."

"We talked about this," Nels said. "You agreed to go."

"As I seem to recall, *we* didn't talk," Ilta said. Her lips pressed into a hard line. "*You* did. And *you* didn't give me a chance to reply, let alone voice an answer. I'm not one of your troops to be ordered about."

"Ilta, please—"

"I'm a healer. I'm needed. *Here*." She paused to motion to the wounded lying on pews, cots, and makeshift surgeon's tables.

Looking around the room and thinking back to Virens, Nels understood how few had survived the journey. It had cost so much to get them there. *Will it be safe enough?* His gut told him no. "I don't want to fight about this."

"Then don't."

"Ilta—"

"You have duties. I have duties too. More wounded are arriving every day," Ilta said, pointing. "Give me that roll of bandages. And do it without getting any dirt on it."

He snatched the rolled linen from the tray and handed it to her. "The Acrasians will be here in a few days."

She glanced up from her work long enough to raise an eyebrow at him. "Do you think I'm unaware of this?"

Westola walked past and paused. Her apron was stained varying shades of crimson and ruddy brown. Her sleeves were rolled up to the elbows. "How does he look?" Her gaze indicated Ilta's patient.

"He'll be fine after some rest," Ilta said. "Tell the Sergeant that Private Idasson can resume his duties tomorrow. I'll be there to assist you with the next patient in a moment."

"No, you won't. You have to pack," Nels said. "Now."

Ilta glared at him. "You're being overprotective. Others take risks. You take risks. Why is it too dangerous for me to stay and not for you or Kaija?"

Westola looked away, clearly not wanting to be involved in a lover's quarrel.

"Westola is an army surgeon. You're not," Nels said.

"I am now," Ilta said.

"We have army surgeons. Maybe not enough, and maybe not any as powerful as you, but we have them. However, *you* are not just a healer. You are the Silmaillia," Nels said. "And your place is with the king."

"He doesn't need me," Ilta said. "I was banished from court. Or have you forgotten?"

"Your grandmother was banished too. I seem to recall Father made a habit of it," Nels said. "Did that stop her from fulfilling her role as Silmaillia? We both know the answer to that question, don't we? Father is a stubborn, thick-headed jackass—"

Westola gaped.

"—at times," Nels continued. "But he does have the ability to change. It's the Silmaillia's responsibility to make sure he does what is right for the people of Eledore. Your grandmother knew that. Father needs you. I know it won't be easy. Working with him never is. If anyone knows it, it's me. But that's your duty. You need to tell him what you've seen. I need you to do it. He won't listen to me. Only you can make sure he doesn't flinch from this. Can't you see that Father and Suvi have far less of a chance at resolving this situation—this war—in a way that we all can survive without you?"

Ilta blinked. "Oh."

"I hate to say this, but your stubborn lout of a boyfriend has a point," Westola ventured.

"He's my binding partner," Ilta said with a slight smile. "And it seems we're well matched after all." She wiped her hands on her bloodstained apron and then untied it at the back. "I'm sorry, Kaija. You'll have to make do without me."

"I thought as much," Westola said. "May the Goddess see you safe to Jalokivi."

TWO

Wiping the sweat from the back of his neck, Nels paused while digging earthworks. Ilta had only been gone for two days, and he missed her already. He gazed south at the woods obscuring the Merta road and the bridges over the Kristallilasi River.

At the same time, he was relieved.

The Acrasian main force will be marching in from the south. We've two days, if the reports are correct.

I shouldn't have waited to send her away. But he'd enjoyed having her close to him. He'd been happy—even when they'd been fighting. It was something he hadn't experienced before. Of course, there'd been a great deal during their short time together that he hadn't experienced before.

You shouldn't have been so selfish. Will she make it to Jalokivi safely? Will the weather hold?

He went back to digging.

"Captain Hännenen, sir?"

Nels turned. "Yes, Private Gusstafson?"

"Hanski says you don't use command magic. Is that true?"

Like a number of others, Private Gerbert Gusstafson had only recently joined his company. Originally, he'd been assigned to one of Colonel Rapp's artillery units. But since many cannon were lost at Virens, he was reassigned to an infantry unit. He wasn't the only one.

Nels noted the number of inquisitive expressions on new faces and understood at once he couldn't brush the question off—not if they were to follow him. These weren't court dandies and noblemen's sons. They were common folk. Some were hardened criminals, more of them than Nels wanted to think about. All had seen hard times and knew that nothing good was ahead. They were searching for any excuse to rebel. The newest troops resented him. The only thing that kept them in check now was the fact that he'd proven himself with the others, but that wasn't quite enough. It didn't help that he was only eighteen years old, and most of those under his command were far older than he was. It didn't matter how far he'd fallen; he was still a prince. Only a prince or a noble could afford to buy a captaincy at eighteen. He hadn't lived as they had. At that moment, Nels knew if he was to lead them without the influence of magic, he had to earn their trust.

Tell them the truth. They'll sense a lie. He scanned their unyielding expressions. *Or as close to it as you can get.* "That is correct," he said. "I won't use magic on my troops."

"Why?" Gusstafson asked. "I mean, how are you going to see us through this shit battle without it? When the fear comes, how are we to hold our ground if you don't remove it? How do I know the others will have my back? I know Oksanen over there. He'll rabbit at the first sound of a Leadbelly's drum. He always does."

"I do not!"

"How do you think you're still alive, you yellow bastard?" Gusstafson asked.

"Enough!" *I am a fraud.* Angry with himself, Nels slammed the mattock into the earth with all his might. The same old fears cropped up. *What if I fail them?* It was then that he spied the trust in Private Hanski's face. And it suddenly occurred to Nels how very different it must be to serve under a normal commander, one who wasn't a—*changeling.* "All right. I'll tell you." He tried to come up with any reason that might make sense to them. He focused on what was different.

"Half of my company were behind the Acrasian lines at Virens. Did the others tell you that? We survived," Nels said. That was something he hadn't allowed himself to take credit for before, and he wasn't so sure he was doing it now. "Do you know why? It's because *I didn't* use magic to motivate my troops. Not once. Instead, I trusted them to do their best as I knew they would. And they did. Because no matter what the other officers have told you, you aren't trash. You've lived through experiences someone like me can only imagine. You have knowledge and understanding that, as your captain, I need to access in order for us all to survive. That means accessing your emotions because you need to be able to think for yourselves. Each of us must depend upon the other, and without your full faculties, you can't access your unique abilities and knowledge. That information might make the difference between the company surviving and the company dying. Simply put, magicked troops are less effective." The moment the words came out of his mouth, he knew them for truth.

He blinked. *Where in the hells did that come from? Never mind that. Finish it.* "I don't know about you, Gusstafson," Nels said. "But I'm in favor of living."

Gusstafson gave him a shocked nod.

"There's another reason. Officers who depend upon magic to motivate their troops end up exhausting themselves. I don't want to have to divide my energies between you and the enemy. You need me to pay attention to what the enemy is doing." Nels returned his blistered hands to the mattock's wooden handle. "Now get back to your work. We've a great deal of digging to finish."

"Yes, sir," Gusstafson said.

The mattock stayed where it was. Nels inwardly cursed. They were watching. But the bastard had buried itself too deep to budge, and so, he had to kick the thing free. He was surprised when none of the others laughed.

Once again, you've managed to fool them. He didn't know whether to be relieved or disgusted. He'd been lucky, and he knew it. Gusstafson hadn't asked the one question he couldn't have answered. *Pretending in order to keep myself alive and out of trouble is one thing. What if I need to command an enemy officer to surrender? I haven't the power.* Just because it hadn't come up yet didn't mean it wouldn't do so in the future. He attacked the ground again and again. *I'm worse than a fraud.*

Images from the past had haunted his dreams. *Please. Make them stop.*

He was tired from digging. The dust was thick in the air. He tasted grit and spat. The sun bore down on him enough to make the nearby spring-fed river inviting. The steady thud of iron against earth was almost soporific. The other men were shirtless in the heat. However, Nels had opted to keep his shirt on. Placing a filthy, blistered hand to his chest where the medal his mother had given him hung from its chain, he attempted to compose a prayer to Hasta. In the short time that he'd owned the medal, he'd found only one small book of formal prayers to the Horse Goddess. Nothing in the text had seemed appropriate. So, he silently made up something.

Please, Hasta. Don't let me fail them. I'll do anything.

He'd had the same fear before every battle and every skirmish. Viktor said everyone with any sense did, but this was different.

He stared at the mountains.

Either Laine would make the final leg of the retreat across the river and up the mountain slope, or he wouldn't. Based upon what Nels had heard from Viktor, they were expecting to be outnumbered two to one. Reports had the Acrasians marching up from the south, the shorter route to Merta from Virens. If Nels still gambled, his money wouldn't be on the Eledorean army holding off the Acrasians if anyone but Kauranen were in charge. She was a wily soul, and Nels believed in her. As bad as everything seemed, if there were a means of living through this mess, Kauranen would be the one to devise it.

But Virens tormented him as much as it did the others— maybe even more so. He'd been behind the lines. He'd seen. They murdered all Eledoreans, even civilians, on sight.

He remembered Corporal Petron and couldn't reconcile the two disparate experiences. There were other things that didn't match up, of course. Petron had said the Brotherhood of Wardens existed to protect Acrasians from malorum. And yet, Viktor had reported seeing them hunting kainen on Angel's Thumb. Had Petron lied about their purpose? Nels didn't get the feeling he had. Nels's hunch was that he was missing something. However, there was no chance of finding out what that something was.

Still, he couldn't help hoping that the corporal and his men had made it back home. Nels didn't know why. Chances were Petron would be part of that vast army marching in from the south.

And here he, Nels, was. *Digging and waiting.* Would he kill the corporal if he saw him again?

If I have to. Nels raised the mattock and let it slam into the dirt. *Let's just hope I don't have to.*

I'd be careful of how much of Lucrosia Marcellus Domitia's philosophy I'd take to heart.

Ultimately, Petron had been right.

"Hännenen! Where in the swiving hells are you?"

Nels flinched before he could stop himself, and the knot of unease in his stomach turned to ice. *It's all right. He's not that angry.* Colonel Pesola's voice hadn't acquired the cold edge that indicated real danger.

"There you are, you lazy, bottle-headed, cocksure bastard! Come here, damned you!"

"Yes, sir." Nels shouldered the mattock and made his way toward Pesola. Nels should've left the thing behind, and if it'd been any other officer, he would have, but he couldn't bring himself to do it. He also made sure to keep his back to the stream and the emerging earthworks. *Coward.*

I'm only being smart.

Pesola stomped through freshly turned dirt while Nels's company labored. He eyed Nels's filthy, sweat-stained shirt. Nels looked away.

"I've a new assignment for you, Captain." Pesola's teeth showed through a nasty smile.

By then, it had to be obvious to the troops Nels wasn't in Pesola's good graces. It'd been apparent that the colonel had hoped Nels and his two platoons had been butchered in the cornfields of Virens. Pesola didn't cope with disappointment well. Unwilling to kill him outright for reasons Nels was unclear on, Pesola had settled for expressing his displeasure in other ways. Thus, Nels had suffered through every shit detail the colonel could devise without complaint. There were moments when Nels wished Pesola would find a new target, but as the captain, Nels felt it was his duty to shield his company. So, he'd weathered the abuse as best he could and kept his anger to himself.

"Yes, sir?" Nels's tone as neutral as he could make it.

"You, Reini, and that artillery master sergeant—whatever his name is. The one with the pyrotechnics—"

"Jarvi, sir. Master Sergeant Jarvi."

The steady, pounding rhythm of iron against earth faltered as a number of soldiers halted their digging.

Pesola glared. He seemed to be in a particularly foul mood after all. "Do not interrupt me, Hännenen. Do so again, and I'll give you another fifty strokes to go with the fifty I already gave you."

The rest of the earthworks crew stopped and gaped.

Nels felt his face heat and his teeth clench. "I apologize, sir."

Pesola sniffed and then made a face as if he'd smelled something unpleasant. "Report to Major Lindström at once."

"Yes, sir." Still, Nels didn't move. The heat in his face didn't dissipate, and neither did the cold rage. "Should I locate Lieutenant Reini and Master Sergeant Jarvi before I do so?"

"Do I need to explain everything to you, Hännenen? Are you that stupid? Or are you drunk?" Pesola waved a hand in front of his face to shoo away a fly. "The rest of you! Get back to work. Or I'll have you entertaining the cat." And then he spun on his heel and left.

Most of the men resumed digging, but someone to Nels's left muttered, "Bastard son of a poxed—"

"Careful, Private Hanski," Nels whispered. He watched Pesola's back until the officer vanished behind a crowd of sweating artillerymen. "You really don't want him to hear you."

"Yes, sir," Hanski said. "No one would be sorry if he ended up with a sword in the back in the middle of battle."

"A stray musket ball is more likely," another private added. His tone contained no humor whatsoever. "Acrasian's aren't known for shooting straight. Things get chaotic in battle. You never know."

"Hanski, Koppola," Nels said. "I never want to hear that kind of talk again. You hear me?"

Both men answered in unison, "Yes, sir."

Not that every damned one of us isn't thinking it, Nels thought. "Where's Jarvi?"

Hanski pointed to the abandoned manor house where General Kauranen had set up temporary headquarters. "Last I saw him, he was there."

"Thank you, Hanski." Nels set down the mattock. "Watch that for me, will you? And if I don't return in an hour, make sure it gets stored where it belongs."

"Yes, sir."

Tracking down Jarvi would be easy. Discovering where Viktor had hidden himself was another matter. Tired as Nels was, he started off at a run. It wouldn't do to give Pesola fresh ammunition—*especially not now*. Pesola wasn't the only one who could end with a convenient musket ball in the back. *What if Pesola decides to pay another call?* That question turned Nels's guts to ice. He told himself that he had his own reasons for rushing, and that Pesola couldn't do anything to him, not now—not with the Acrasians so close. However, the lie was too thin to cover the bigger truth, and in that moment, Nels didn't believe it was possible to hate anyone as much as he hated Pesola.

"Where is Master Sergeant Jarvi?" Nels asked an overwhelmed-looking duty sergeant. Eventually he was directed to a barn where the powder and ammunition were being stored. Nels then left a message for Viktor to report to Major Lindström as soon as possible.

Entering the barn in question, Nels located Jarvi in mid artillery supply inspection. Sunlight filtered through the planks forming the left side of the barn, casting gold dust over stacks of crates, barrels, extra cart wheels, cannon parts, ammunition, and a crew of twenty-four artillery lieutenants. All were performing necessary checks in preparation for the morning's battle.

"Master Sergeant?" Nels asked.

"Yes, sir?"

"You must come with me," Nels said, cutting off Jarvi's protests before they could manifest beyond the frown. "We're both to report to Major Lindström at once per the colonel's order. You'll have to assign the inspection to someone else for now."

Jarvi's mouth opened and closed once, and his bushy gray eyebrows briefly made an angry line before his brain made the connection. "Sergeant Nyman! Take over."

Major Lindström was headquartered in the small library on the first floor of the manor house. When Nels and Jarvi arrived, the major was stooping over a series of hastily drawn maps. He seemed lost in thought and didn't look up at the sound of the closing door. His staff continued to go about their business, making adjustments to the wooden pieces resting on the maps as more information arrived.

Stepping closer with Master Sergeant Jarvi in tow, Nels gave the major a proper salute. "Captain Hännenen reporting, sir."

Major Lindström looked up from his maps and then returned the salute. "Relax, Captain. Has Pesola told you what you're in for?"

"No, sir."

"I thought not." Lindström looked away. A miserable expression flashed across his face.

Nels could only imagine what working directly with the likes of Pesola must cost Lindström on a daily basis.

Major Lindström pointed to the bridges south of Merta on the map. "We've a few problems to resolve before the Acrasians get here."

Beginning to understand, Nels nodded and swallowed. *I can't swim. Of course, Pesola doesn't know that. Or does he? But then, what does it matter?* Nels had given dying a lot of thought since becoming a soldier. He didn't mind the idea of being shot or stabbed—at least, he didn't think so. The prospect of drowning, on the other hand—

"Both bridges must blow at the appropriate time," Lindström said, confirming Nels's hunch.

How deep is the water? Nels had seen the river before, of course, but he hadn't studied it. Artillery batteries didn't tend to move much during a battle, once they were in place, and currently, the cannon were positioned away from the river. *This is another of Pesola's special jobs.* "Yes, sir?" The previous bad feeling in his gut tightened into an even more uncomfortable knot. *This isn't going to be good.*

"The Acrasians don't know we're here, you understand," Lindström said. "The plan is to set the charges off after part of the Acrasian army crosses the bridge. We must cut their larger forces into more manageable pieces. Once they are trapped, our artillery will open fire on them. Do you understand?"

Nels glanced at Jarvi to his left. To his credit, Jarvi showed no signs of catching the deeper meaning behind Lindström's question. *If we survive the initial blast, we'll be blown to bits by our own cannon along with the Acrasians—assuming all goes according to plan.* "Yes, sir."

"I'm sorry, Captain Hännenen. I was . . . ordered to give you this assignment," Lindström said.

This is Pesola's plan for finally murdering me. And he's having Lindström do it for him. Nels decided to have some mercy on the major. "It's all right, sir. I'd have volunteered." *At least Pesola won't be able to hurt me any more. Nor will Uncle be able to use me against Suvi, wherever she is.* Nels clenched a fist. "Was this assignment specifically given to Master Sergeant Jarvi?" He asked the question through a tight jaw. *If I'm to die, why should Jarvi go with me?*

"I included the master sergeant because I thought it prudent," Lindström said. "Jarvi, I understand you're a pyrotechnic?"

"I am, sir."

"Hännenen has no choice in this. However, you do," Lindström said.

Nels turned to Jarvi. "I can do this on my own."

"I volunteer," Jarvi said in the same instant.

Nels raised an eyebrow at Jarvi. *Are you mad?* "Why?"

"Because I can control when the powder goes off. I can rig it to do so from a distance. And I can light the match in the dark without risking exposure," Jarvi said. "I can make this work in ways that you can't, sir."

"I'm not incompetent," Nels said with more anger than he'd intended. "You don't need pyrotechnics to light a damned fuse."

"With respect, sir. You do, if the fuse gets wet. And it's going to be drenched," Jarvi said.

Nels shook his head. "This is suicide!"

"Not if I'm there," Jarvi said. "I can work with smoke, sir. Make more of it in one place and less in another."

"Thank you, Master Sergeant." Lindström seemed happier.

There came a long stream of surprised curses from the corporal assigned to guard the door.

"Lieutenant Reini, are you quite finished playing with my security detail?" Lindström asked.

Viktor entered and gave Lindström a salute. "For now, sir."

"Fair enough." Lindström returned the salute. "Are you prepared for tonight?"

Viktor nodded. "I've never blown up a bridge before. Should be fun."

"Sir, did the colonel order Lieutenant Reini on this assignment, too?" Nels asked.

"He is another of my additions," Lindström said.

"May I object to his being so assigned?" Nels asked.

Lindström folded his arms across his chest. "And what is your objection?"

"He's my company's only korva, sir," Nels said.

"We have six other korvas serving under General Kauranen. Objection denied," Lindström said.

"But sir—"

Major Lindström said, "You're dismissed."

"Yes, sir," Nels said.

"Nice try," Viktor said under his breath. "But I wouldn't miss this for the world."

THREE

"Are you quite finished pouring that gunpowder yet?" Nels asked through chattering teeth. Viktor's bony heels were digging deep into Nels's shoulders. Worse, he had to fight to stay upright in the freezing river's strong current.

Viktor said, "Keep your pants on."

"How is it possible that you've gained weight?" Nels asked, holding Viktor's ankles steady with both hands. "The whole regiment has been on half rations."

"Shut up," Viktor said. "You're ruining my concentration." Nels felt Viktor shift, and then Viktor handed the powder barrel down to Jarvi in Nels's peripheral vision. "Ready for the fuse, Jarvi."

Jarvi waded to shore. "Make sure it's secure and deep inside the hole, sir."

"Hurry up, Jarvi. The captain is cold," Viktor said, and then paused. "On second thought, take your time."

"Shut up," Nels said.

Jarvi passed the fuse cord up to Viktor.

"You're rather noisy for a dead man," Viktor said.

It was a quarter to two the last time Nels had been able to check the pocket watch that was now lying on the river bank along with his boots. He estimated it was long past that time now. It had taken hours to get this far, and this was the first of the two bridges they needed to set with explosives.

Another sharp jab in Nels's shoulder made him wince.

A loud and profane objection came from above. "Stand still, will you? If I fall, I'll bring this whole mess down with me. If I lose the fuse in the water, Pesola will have you shot."

"It'll put me out of my misery. The land of the dead may be cold, but it doesn't smell of dirty feet, does it?"

"Fine. Fine. But Pesola will blame me, too. And I'd like my skin to remain whole, thank you."

Nels said, "Jarvi and I can handle this alone."

"And pass up this wonderful opportunity to be taller than you? Not on your life."

"Oh, swiving hells, when was the last time you washed your stockings?"

"The more you wiggle around, the longer this is going to take," Viktor said.

"You sound like my nurse," Nels said.

"She must have been a wise woman," Viktor said. "The very model of female pulchritude, in fact."

"She was sixty years old, balding, warty, and farted continuously," Nels said. It was a lie, of course, but that wasn't the point. "Come to think of it, you might have something in common after all. In the stench department, at least." Glancing at Jarvi, Nels caught an amused expression tracing a path across the master sergeant's face.

He isn't thinking about the future, Nels thought. *I can do that much.*

"Spoilsport," Viktor said.

"Are you quite done?" Nels asked. "You're killing me."

He felt Viktor's weight shift again. The sound of fuse cord slapping stone indicated that he'd just tossed the remaining fuse length up onto the bridge.

"Yes, yes. Fine. We're done with this side, at least," Viktor said. "Let me down."

"Now?" Nels asked.

"Yes, now," Viktor said.

"Are you quite sure?"

"Damn it—"

Nels hopped backward and then yanked on Viktor's ankles. Unprepared and unbalanced, Viktor fell face first into the freezing water with a shout.

Viktor surfaced and spluttered. Water-darkened brown hair was plastered to his face. "That was the most immature—"

Nels said, "You need a bath anyway."

"So do you," Viktor said, shoving wet hair out of his eyes. "Care to give me a hand?"

"Get yourself out," Nels said, folding his arms across his chest. "I don't trust you for a moment."

Viktor slapped the water, sending a great splash in Nels's direction. "You tried to drown me!"

"In hip-deep water?" Nels asked. "Had I tried, I'd have succeeded."

Jarvi gazed up at the underside of the stone bridge.

Trusting that Viktor was far enough away, Nels risked a look at Viktor's handiwork himself. Ten holes had been chiseled into the mortar across the width of the bridge. Each hole had been filled with gunpowder and set with a loop of fuse like a chain.

"Neatly done, sir," Jarvi said.

Viktor retrieved his hat from the water before it could escape into the deepest part of the river. "Thank you, sergeant."

"Time to see to the other side," Jarvi said, and began to make his way to the bridge with loud, crunching steps up the stony river-bank, leaving them to their childish games. "Water is deeper over there."

"How deep?" Nels asked.

"We'll need a boat," Jarvi said.

"Is there any possibility of this working with only one side finished? This is the side the enemy will be coming from, after all," Nels said.

A doubtful expression settled onto Jarvi's craggy face. "Not reliably."

"Shit," Nels said and sighed. "All right. Let's acquire a swiving boat."

Jarvi jogged up the pebble-strewn riverbank.

"Remind me again as to why I'm the one acting the ladder while Jarvi oversees the work?" Nels asked.

"Because Jarvi knows what the hell he's doing with the explosives, and you don't," Viktor said.

"Then why weren't you holding Jarvi on your shoulders?" Nels asked, wading to shore.

"Because Jarvi isn't tall enough and weighs twice what I do?" Viktor asked. He gathered his boots from the shore and began walking barefoot up the steep incline.

Nels said, "Right."

Viktor asked, "Did you or did you not say something to the effect of 'Viktor, you're better with a chisel than I am'?"

Boots in hand, Nels staggered across the bridge in question, three or so steps behind Viktor. Lifting his face to meet the sun for warmth, Nels attempted to devise a clever retort and failed. His bare feet made wet slapping noises as cold river water runneled out of his soggy clothes, down his legs, and onto the stone surface of the bridge. He remained three steps behind Viktor to keep an eye on him. It was safest. Viktor had a passion for retaliation when it came to practical jokes.

Jarvi was already on the other side, waiting.

"If I'd known the water was going to be that cold, I'd have had you do it," Nels said, enjoying a halfhearted sulk. "My balls have frozen solid."

"Consider it a better excuse for running out on your next courtesan," Viktor said. He cast a crooked smile over his shoulder. "Helmi told me you left her friend unattended."

"Not by choice," Nels said. His teeth were chattering.

"You weren't intimidated, then?" Viktor asked. "Helmi said that she set you up with—"

"For a courtesan, Helmi talks too much," Nels said.

"And your blond doesn't talk at all. And after I made sure you two had all the privacy."

Nels wrung water out of his soggy queue one-handed, sighed, and changed the subject. "Gods, my shoulders are going to hurt tomorrow."

"If Pesola has his way, you'll be too dead to care." Viktor scampered down the opposite bank to the water's edge.

"This is easy enough for you," Nels said. "You're not the one facing another half hour of stinking feet perched under your nose."

"Stop complaining," Viktor said, lifting one bare foot and wiggling muddy toes. "I washed them off for you, didn't I?"

Viktor located a rowboat upstream from the manor house. Nels found an excuse to let Jarvi row back to the bridge with Viktor aboard and then walked the river's length alone. The second set of gunpowder charges proved to be more difficult than the first. In spite of the fact that Jarvi had anchored the boat to the bridge, the vessel wasn't nearly stable enough. Nels held on to the stone arch and kept his eyes firmly closed. Every time he opened them, the boat violently wobbled. He bit down on an urge to vomit. If he got sick, Viktor would never stop teasing him. So, Nels focused with all his might on the stones beneath his palms to prevent tipping and attempted to keep breathing. Uncharacteristically, Viktor had mercy upon him and kept his comments to himself. Nels didn't know if Jarvi could swim or not, but Nels had no wish to find out.

And that was the smaller of the two bridges.

As luck would have it, Jarvi was a powerful swimmer. Nels upended the rowboat twice. With Jarvi there to save Viktor, Nels was able to keep afloat long enough to grab the boat and hold on. The second time it happened, Jarvi had to swim for the oars. Eventually, they got the job done. Relieved, Nels staggered up the riverbank. His shoulders and back were aching, and he was colder than he'd ever been in his life. He lay on the grass next to the bridge, closed his eyes, and attempted to get some control over the shivering.

"I'm starving," Viktor said.

Nels didn't move or open his eyes. "You fetch dinner, then."

"Aren't you hungry?" Viktor asked.

"If I show my face, Pesola is sure to hear I didn't drown. Who knows what new punishment he'll devise? Stale crispbread, cheese, and a bit of soup aren't worth the trouble."

Jarvi's belly let out a loud protest.

"Now that Sergeant Jarvi has said his piece, I'll be back as soon as I can. With food for everyone," Viktor said.

"I'll go, sir," Jarvi said.

"And leave the captain within reach of a body of water? He's likely to throw himself in just by standing next to it," Viktor said.

"Keep it up," Nels said. "You'll go in with me."

"Stay, Jarvi," Viktor said. "I'll go."

Viktor would grab some more supplies while he was at it. Meanwhile, Nels and Jarvi would set up camp low enough on the bank to be out of sight. The plan was to take turns sleeping. No campfire. Soaked through as he was, Nels had a miserable night ahead of him. He'd forgotten to ask Viktor to bring a change of clothes. The shivering was getting worse. He already ached with it. He inched as close as he could to Jarvi's iron kettle of burning coals—pyrotechnics required a source of fire—and rubbed his hands together.

Jarvi dug through his pack and produced some whiskey. He uncorked the bottle and held it out. "For warmth, sir."

Nels accepted the bottle, took several swallows, and then returned it. "Thanks."

"I've a blanket, if you've the need."

"Thank you, but no. I've my own," Nels said. "I'll dry soon enough."

Jarvi nodded and gazed out into the darkening sky. There was a glow to the south. Nels could see it.

"Those are Acrasian campfires, aren't they, sir?"

It was Nels's turn to nod.

"They'll be on us in the morning."

"I suppose they will."

"How do you think we'll do?"

Nels paused. "A lot depends on General Laine, how much of his brigade survived, and whether or not they'll be in shape enough to fight. As for us, I think we can hold." Gazing at the brightly glowing horizon, he did his best to hide his doubts from Jarvi.

"How many would you say are out there?"

Nels drowned a growing sense of unease with the next swallow of whiskey. "I don't know."

"At least we'll be taking a few of them with us."

"Do you have family?"

"I do."

"Are they with the brigade?"

Jarvi shook his head. "My wife is in Jalokivi with my daughters. I didn't want them to risk it. What about you, sir?"

Nels smiled. "We aren't bound yet. Her name is Ilta."

"Is she here, sir?"

"I sent her to Jalokivi. Yesterday."

"Should I come back later? I think I'm going to cry," Viktor said. "And I don't want to get tear stains on my uniform."

Rolling his eyes, Nels said, "That would be about the only stain not on it at the moment." The scent of boiled beef and vegetables made his mouth water.

"Do you want your dinner and dry clothes or not?" Viktor asked, somehow managing to sit down on the riverbank without spilling the contents of either of the two steaming bowls in his hands.

"Hand over the food," Nels said.

"Please?" Viktor asked, giving Jarvi his bowl first.

Nels gave Viktor a toothy grin. "Don't make me wish I had drowned you."

Viktor handed over the bowl, and Nels shoved spoonfuls of salted beef and potatoes in his mouth so fast, he could hardly taste it. Viktor shared out the crispbread and cheese as well.

"Did you bring the whiskey, too?" Nels asked.

"Has the cold affected your brain?" Viktor asked, and then returned to his ryggsack where he'd hidden the crispbread and cheese. Producing three brown bottles, he handed them out. Then he produced the change of clothes.

"Any news?" Nels asked. He crammed several spoonfuls into his mouth at once before shucking the wet shirt.

Viktor glanced at Jarvi, took a long swallow of whiskey, and then answered, "You're not going to like it."

"Jarvi can handle it," Nels said. "I trust him not to panic the others with whatever you say. Spill."

Viktor said, "I shouldn't be telling you, and you damned well know it."

"Sergeant Jarvi," Nels said. "Do you swear by the Great Father that you won't breathe a word of what you're about to hear? No matter what?"

"I do."

"That's enough for me," Nels said. "Talk."

"The Acrasians arrive at dawn," Viktor said. "Two brigades. Almost eleven thousand troops."

Eleven thousand? "We'll number just short of five thousand after Laine arrives."

"So we hope," Viktor said.

"Outnumbered, but not by an extreme," Nels said. "They don't know we're here. We're prepared. It's workable."

"They've also got sixty cannon."

"Traveling that fast?" Nels asked. "How's that possible? They don't have magic—"

"The cannon look lighter. Smaller," Viktor said. "They're a type no one's seen before. Kauranen seems to think they won't be as powerful. But . . . if they're preparing to take on Merta's walls, they'll not do that with peashooters."

"Shit," Nels said, feeling the alcohol fight for a fast path up his throat. He forced it back down with a swallow. It tasted of bile. "Do you know who is at the head of the Acrasian forces?"

"Someone named Lucrosia Marcellus. The second brigade is led by a General Lucrosia Pera. Acrasians sure like the name Lucrosia."

"Lucrosia is one of the five greater gens that run Acrasia," Nels said. "And the Lucrosia control the military."

"I thought the Acrasians had an emperor," Viktor said.

Nels said, "They do."

"What is a gens, sir?" Jarvi asked.

"Think of them as clans, only you buy membership," Nels said, "if you're not born to one. You can also switch gens, if another is more favorable. You can buy anything in Acrasia, provided you have the money." Suddenly, he remembered the Acrasian tactics manual in his ryggsack, and the ground beneath him seemed to fall away. "Viktor. Did you say Lucrosia *Marcellus?*"

"I did," Viktor said.

"Lucrosia Marcellus *Domitia?*"

"I think that was it," Viktor said. "Is there a problem?"

Setting down the half-empty bowl, Nels gripped the grass with his fingers and attempted to keep his dinner from making another appearance. "And Laine? Any news? Is he still being pursued?"

Viktor blinked. "They weren't as of the last report. But none of the korva sent to meet them in the past few days have returned. Kauranen seems to think that this only means they're too rushed and undermanned to get an answer back. They're in bad shape. But they haven't abandoned the artillery, I hear. They probably need every hand they can get. Laine doesn't like relying on message birds. He's notorious for it."

"Damn it," Nels said, looking behind them and to the west. "If Lucrosia Marcellus is here, we'll be attacked from two sides."

"How do you know?" Viktor asked.

"I've been studying him. And trust me, he's been studying us," Nels said. He reached for his ryggsack, fished the tactics manual out, and tossed it on the grass next to Viktor. "The General that wrote that book is camped down that road. And he's their best."

"It's written in Acrasian," Viktor said.

"Of course it is," Nels said.

Viktor stared. "You can read Acrasian?"

"Don't you hear what I'm saying? They intend to pinch Laine between two flanks. From both sides of the mountains. We're sitting in the middle of a swiving trap just like Virens!" Nels staggered to his feet. The steep embankment didn't help his sense of balance nor did the soreness in his calves. "I have to tell Kauranen. Now."

"You can't leave here," Viktor said. "Pesola will have you drawn and quartered. He'll take the time to do it even if the Acrasians are here to watch."

"Shit! Shit! Shit!" Nels staggered up the riverbank to the road.

"Be quiet! And get down, will you?" Viktor hissed. "We aren't the only ones with scouts, you know."

Nels scrambled back down the bank. "Kauranen has to know. Will she listen to you?"

"She'll want to know how I know," Viktor said.

"Shit."

"What if I tell her Prince Nels, the Savior of Eledore, had a vision?" Viktor said.

"Don't be stu—"

"It'll sound more convincing than you read a damned book," Viktor said. "In Acrasian."

"You'd lie to Kauranen?" Nels asked.

"If you're sure," Viktor said.

"I am."

"Then I'd do whatever it takes," Viktor said.

Glancing at Jarvi's taut expression and back to Viktor's, Nels paused. *The Savior of Eledore.* Jarvi didn't know it'd originally been a jibe—a mocking slap at the uppity royal brat who'd fallen low, but Viktor certainly did. Only sixteen, Nels had told his bunkmate about what he'd overheard that day at Saara Korpela's estate. The next day, the whole company knew. There'd been a number of hard lessons that first year; learning to tolerate the taste of whiskey had been the second. Understanding that commoners played the same sorts of brutal games royals did but for lesser stakes was the first.

Viktor got to his feet.

Nels said, "You said I was being paranoid and childish about the Acrasians. Everyone did."

"We should've listened," Viktor said. "I'm listening now." He paused. "If Kauranen won't see me, what do we do?"

Nels knew the real question Viktor was asking but was afraid to utter. *Do we stay and die? Or do we desert while we can?* "Get to Kauranen. Make her listen. Do whatever you have to. She'll figure out something, if anyone can."

Viktor grabbed his whiskey ration from the grass, downed it all at once, and then said, "Don't touch off the fireworks without me. I want to see if Acrasians can fly."

"Before you go," Nels said, "I'd like you to do something for me." He walked with Viktor as far as the woods and gave him a second set of instructions—just in case. Then Nels rejoined Jarvi.

Laine isn't answering, because he's fighting for his life.

Eleven thousand troops to the south. Five thousand more in hot pursuit of Laine in the west. It'll be at least that, based on what I saw at Virens.

We're going to die tomorrow. And if that happens, who will save Jalokivi? What will happen to Father? Where is Suvi? Has she been captured? Or is she staying with the Waterborne? Or is Ilta wrong? What if she's dead?

Jarvi pointed at Nels's abandoned field rations. "You going to eat that?"

FOUR

"Sir?" Jarvi asked in a hushed voice. "Sir, are you awake?"

Nels blinked dry, stinging eyes and sat up. "I am." He wasn't entirely certain that was the truth, but it was a near-enough approximation. The area at the foot of the bridge was very dark. Shivering, he sensed more than saw Jarvi's presence and knew that if he could see, his breath would be forming little clouds. *Thank Hasta and Viktor for the dry clothes.*

"I heard something," Jarvi whispered, and then pointed down to the tree-lined road to the south.

The last vestiges of sleep left Nels with a jolt. "What did you hear, exactly?" He glanced around in search of Viktor. The korva was nowhere in sight, but that didn't mean anything.

"Movement," Jarvi said. "Could be a deer. Could be a scout. For all I know, it's the whole cursed Acrasian army."

"Viktor?" Nels asked.

"Came back a quarter hour ago and then took off down that direction," Jarvi said.

"Why didn't you wake me?"

"He said to let you sleep," Jarvi said. "Said he'd go for one last look and then be right back."

Nels swallowed. The bad feeling grew worse. "And Kauranen? Was he able to make her listen?" To his relief, he saw the shadow-Jarvi nod.

"Said she'd took it well enough, all things considered. Oh, he said that you owe him twenty-five falcons."

"What for this time?"

"He had to bribe Kauranen's corporal. Kauranen was asleep."

"Viktor can wait in line behind my tailor," Nels said, feeling slightly better. *We'll be okay. Kauranen is smart. She'll think of a way out of this*, he thought, and then paused. *Hasta, please let her think of a way out of this.*

Something in the brush at the side of the road let out a grunt.

"Do you think that's Lieutenant Reini?" Jarvi asked.

Nels rolled up his blanket and stuffed it in his ryggsack as quietly as possible. "If it is, then the Acrasians tied an entire string of corpses to his ankles."

Jarvi half crawled to the farthest set of fuses leading to the second bridge. Nels followed suit, taking up a position at the first bridge. Jarvi had charged the powder, fuses, and matches with magic. Nels could sense it in the hemp braid in his hand. He told himself it was impossible for him to ruin it. All he had to do was wade in and light the thing.

A shadow moved close. Nels started, dropping the slow match.

"The Acrasians are on their way," Viktor said, plucking the match from the air before it hit the ground.

Nels whispered a curse. "Damn you, Reini." He could easily imagine Viktor's crooked smile. "How much time do we have, do you think?"

"Oh, about as long as it takes for them to discover their scouts aren't coming back," Viktor said. "An hour. Maybe two. Acrasians aren't the smartest—"

If the Acrasians are so stupid, why are we the ones in the trap? "Isn't that tipping our hand?" Nels asked.

"Not really. They know the brigade is here," Viktor said. "But I think we still have the advantage as far as the bridges are concerned."

"You've been busy."

"It has been rather a long night, I must say. Is Jarvi ready?"

"In position," Nels whispered. "Were you able to get the word to the company?"

Viktor said, "Things go bad, the others will meet us at the crossroads two miles outside of Herraskariano. Then we'll head for Jalokivi together. I didn't tell Pesola, of course."

"No?" Nels attempted to keep the question casual.

"Swive him," Viktor said. "Told Westola everything, though. Not sure she'll wait for the lines to break. That woman can move fast when she sets her mind to it."

Nels thought, *Good. With Ilta gone, we'll have need of a healer.* "And the army families?"

"Most started packing before I finished speaking. A few plan to take their chances in Merta. City is empty for the most part." Viktor shrugged. "They'll have plenty of safe places to hide should the need arise."

"Assuming the Acrasians don't burn it down around them," Nels said. If what Petron said was true, Nels had a hunch the Acrasians would do anything to possess Merta's silver mines. Briefly, he wondered if those in charge had taken that into consideration before evacuating.

Viktor said, "And here I thought a bit of sleep would improve your outlook."

"Take this, will you?" Nels gave Viktor the lit match. "I'm going to talk with Jarvi one last time."

"Let me do it."

"Why?"

Viktor gazed down at Nels's boots. "Do you have to ask? Besides, I'm faster and—" He tilted his head as if listening. "Your friends the Acrasians are early."

FIVE

The morning sun advanced on the horizon as night retreated to a murky gray. Nels could now see what they faced. Every detail of the Acrasian army seemed engineered for intimidation. The troops crowded the Virens Road in precise formations, their gray uniforms only a shade lighter than the early morning sky. The shape of the officers' helmets reminded Nels of ax blades. The army moved with a lethal perfection he'd witnessed only in the most elite units. Rows of gray uniforms stretched as far as he could see. Drummers tapped the rims of their instruments, marking a precise beat. The sharp edges of bayonets raked the sky as the troops marched. Thousands of boots tramped the road in unison and echoed like thunder throughout the valley.

Nels fought both admiration and a visceral need to flee.

Viktor whispered, "Great Mother."

Nels said, "Magic isn't everything."

"Bite your tongue."

"How's Jarvi?"

"Ready. Said to remember to light the fuse and then run."

"Wouldn't do much good to do it the other way around."

"He meant get out of there as fast as you can. Don't play around in the water down there. The quick fuses are short-timed," Viktor said.

Nels nodded. He didn't bother removing his boots and coat but left his ryggsack, watch, and saber with Viktor. Keeping his back to the bridge, Nels quickly made his way to the water's edge. The scent of burning hemp and sulfur mixed with river mold as he took a deep breath and eased into the icy river. Unable to see, he felt for the abrupt drop-off with the soles of his boots as he went. At the ledge, he said a quick prayer to Hasta and took several deep breaths before launching himself toward the bridge support one-handed. He kept his right hand above his head in order to save the slow match from the water. Unfortunately, he misjudged the distance, and his head briefly dropped beneath the river's surface. Panic squeezed his chest for three heartbeats. Then his forward momentum got him to his destination. His left palm slapped cold, slick stone. Gulping for air, he saw he'd managed the journey without soaking the match. He hugged stone and mortar one-handed and anchored himself on the first arch support as best he could in the strong current. He was up to his neck in the water. His teeth once again began to clatter. Squeezing his eyes shut against the cold, he felt the thundering vibration of hundreds of footfalls in the freezing stone against his cheek. The army's passing rumbled in his ears, briefly making him forget his clenching balls.

It was then that he noticed the early morning shadows under the bridge had retreated, taking with them most of the available cover. He stretched to see over his shoulder. The Acrasians marched over the smaller bridge to the east. It occurred to him that all anyone had to do was look down at the waterline, and they would spy him at once. The burning end of the slow match trembled in the darkness. He attempted to steady his hand. His grip on the support slipped, and he almost slid from his precarious underwater perch and lost the match. His heart raced, and his breath came in ragged gasps as his chances of drowning began to rival his chances of being shot. Once again stable, he risked turning his head to face the riverbank and Viktor. Now Nels's left cheek rested against the slimy support. While he waited for Viktor's signal, Nels tried not to think of how many Acrasian troops were crossing—how many would form ranks between them and what remained of the Eledorean army.

Please, Hasta. Don't let them see us.

At last, Viktor signaled that it was time and then waved to Jarvi. Concentrating on not inconveniently drowning, Nels almost missed it. He pulled himself out of the water a few inches, stretched his arm up high, and applied the slow match to the fuse until it caught. Pausing to assure himself it would stay lit, he then abandoned the slow match to the water and dove for shore. The instant his boots touched muddy riverbank, he shot up the beach. Then he grabbed his things from Viktor and headed up the incline at a dead run—or the nearest approximation possible in water-logged boots. Seemingly unaware, the Acrasians formed ranks. Nels and Viktor crested the top of the riverbank. An Acrasian shouted a loud warning. Shots peppered the ground at their feet.

Both bridges exploded.

Nels squeezed his eyes shut against the glare. The blast hurled him face first onto the grass. The sound of the explosion was all at once huge and then just as suddenly gone. He felt the low rumble deep inside his chest and in the earth beneath him. Chunks of debris landed everywhere. An eerie silence blanketed a world of searing heat. Someone grabbed his arm. Rolling onto his side, he saw it was Viktor. A heavy weight on Nels's legs shifted. He looked and saw it was the burned, armless body of an Acrasian soldier. He kicked himself free. Turning back to Viktor, he put out a hand, and Viktor tugged him to his feet. Suddenly, something thumped Nels in the left side—hard, knocking him to the ground. Lying on his cheek, he watched chunks of grass hop like insects. He blinked. *That's gunfire. Move!* Scrambling to his feet, he fought fuzzy-headedness and pain. He risked a glance over his shoulder. Both bridges were smoking ruins. Only a stub of the center support remained, and the spot where he'd lit the fuse was entirely gone. Singed bodies of horses and men choked the bloodstained water littered with burning equipment parts. The earth shuddered with the impact of cannon balls, signaling the arrival of the Eledorean forces.

We did it, Nels thought as he ran.

On the opposite bank, order overcame chaos. The first Acrasian line fired and then dropped to their knees, reloading while the second line emptied their guns. A vast cloud of smoke rolled over the battle like a cresting wave. Soldiers fell dead or wounded. Nels tasted sulfur-laced smoke. Shouting at Viktor, Nels noted how strange and distant his voice sounded to his own ears. Viktor didn't seem to hear him. At the edges of his vision, Nels spied the Eledorean charge. He got the feeling something was wrong, but didn't have time to think about it.

Where is Jarvi?

As if summoned, Jarvi appeared, and with the wave of an arm, a cloud of smoke descended upon them. Nels kept a close eye on both Viktor and Jarvi in the haze. It would be easy to lose his sense of direction as they fled through the confusion. The plan was to keep to the eastern edge of the battle, away from the artillery, and then pray they wouldn't be mistaken for the enemy by their own troops.

Sound slowly drifted back into its proper place, and cannon blasts matched up with flashes of light in the smoke. Nels sensed rather than saw motion to his left and turned. Three Acrasians ran at them with bayonets. Although he knew he would be too late, his hand went to his saber anyway. Viktor whirled, firing his pistol. One of the Acrasians dropped dead. The other two slammed into Nels and Jarvi. Nels twisted away from the bayonet blade. At the same time, he drove his saber into the second Acrasian's neck and shoulder. A musket went off nearby. The bayonet sliced the front of Nels's coat, and he felt a hot line scored across his solar plexus. He heard Jarvi let out a pain-laced grunt in the haze. Warm blood fountained from severed arteries. Nels lost track of time as, all at once, he felt the Acrasian's life ebb away. He'd forgotten to prepare himself. Tensing, he anticipated what would come next.

Private Cole Harrison, an orphan from Novus Salernum. He joined the army to feed his sisters. He was sixteen—

"Answer me, damn it!" Viktor asked, "Nels?"

"Only nobles have gens," Nels said, half-drowned in the dead private's last thoughts. "Their ranks are filled with the poor." He didn't know why that came as a shock. Eledore wasn't that different in that sense. The feeling of watching himself from a distance sapped urgency from the battle. "Magic. No quarter. They're killing us because they're terrified."

"You're hurt! How bad?" Viktor asked.

"You don't understand. They're afraid."

"You're not making any sense," Viktor said. "Did you get hit in the head?"

The hand Nels used to check his side came away covered in blood. He looked down and the distant feeling vanished. "Oh, shit." He paused. "Jarvi? Where's Jarvi?"

"We can't stop here," Viktor said, checking the wound. He swept hair from his forehead. "Bayonet missed, by the look of it. It's only a scratch."

He touched his face. He's lying. The pain was definitely getting worse, but Nels didn't have time for it. "Jarvi!" The smoke was clearing. He didn't take it for a good sign.

"Here, sir!"

Nels went to the sound of Jarvi's voice. Jarvi lay on the ground a few feet to the right. From the look of him, he'd been shot but not badly. Nels helped him up. "Viktor, Jarvi has been hit."

They each got a shoulder under Jarvi's arms, and together they continued east. Jarvi's control over the smoke was fading and so was their cover. Nels caught Viktor's eye.

"It's okay. There's not much farther to go," Viktor said.

Jarvi said, "Too hard to focus."

"You'll be fine," Nels said. "We'll get you to Westola. She'll patch you up."

"They'll see us," Jarvi said. Blood covered half of his face from a slash over his right eyebrow.

Nels said, "Just concentrate on walking. We're on our side of the fight now."

With that, they pushed north. It wasn't long before the trees thinned, and a blood-freezing scream pulled Nels's attention to the left. He had time to register the black-and-blue uniform of the attacker before a saber blade carved a swathe of bark from a tree three inches from his ear. Jarvi dove for the tree trunk as Nels released him.

"We're from the Seventh too, damn you! We're friends!" Viktor shoved at the private rather than stabbing him.

The private roared and charged at Jarvi. Jarvi managed to dodge his clumsy thrust. That's when Nels spotted the private's wide, blank eyes.

"He's been compelled. Jarvi," Nels said. "Look out. Viktor—" *The private isn't going to stop. He can't.*

The private executed yet another graceless attack. Jarvi side-stepped and then hit the private on the back of the head with the pommel of his sword. Nels heard a loud crack. The private went down like a marionette with severed strings.

Jarvi fell to his knees next to the collapsed private. Viktor picked up the private's wrist and checked for a pulse.

"Is he all right?" Nels asked.

Viktor shook his head.

"I killed him," Jarvi said. "He wouldn't listen! I didn't hit him that hard. I—"

Nels leaned against a tree to catch his breath. The cut along his belly stung. His side was throbbing in dull agony. He risked a downward glance and touched the wound. His left side and the lower half of his shirt and coat were dark with blood. Both hung open via a horizontal rent. He found he'd been cut but not disemboweled. *I'm alive.* He felt dizzy and light-headed. *Don't pass out yet. We're not out of danger.* Rough bark scraped his palms. *Guns. Reload your guns.*

"He wouldn't stop. I didn't mean to—"

"He was compelled," Nels said, and began the routine of checking and loading. "Magic. There wasn't anything you could do."

"Why?" Jarvi asked.

Nels remembered his earlier sense of wrongness and had an evil thought. *Please. I don't want to be right this time. Oh, Mother. Oh, Hasta.* "Someone decided to prevent desertion." The back of his throat was slick. The sick feeling in his guts wouldn't go away.

"Like an animal? It's against the Articles of War. Who would do such a thing?" Viktor asked. "Sit, Jarvi. Let me get a bandage on you."

What if it's not merely a squad? What if it's the whole brigade? Nels swallowed the questions. *Please, not my company.* Finished with reloading, he concentrated on keeping watch for another attack while Viktor tended Jarvi.

"Why not withdraw?" Viktor asked. "Or regroup? Commanding someone to fight to the death? It makes no sense!"

It would be easy. The colonel compels his officers—specifically those with the ability to do the same. They in turn command others. There were enough with command magic among the officers to spread the order like a disease. *You only think it's Pesola because you want him to be guilty.* But Nels knew Kauranen would never do such a thing, nor would Lindström. *You don't know that is what has happened. You don't—*

An explosion to the west shook the earth. It was followed by three more.

"What was that?" Viktor asked.

"Artillery. Not ours," Jarvi said between clenched teeth. "Acrasian."

"How do you know?" Viktor asked, tying off the last bandage.

"By the sound. Swiving hells, it's coming from the west," Jarvi said, a sick look on his face. "That other brigade you warned Kauranen about? I think they're here."

With Jarvi patched, Nels and Viktor got him back on his feet, and then headed farther north into the woods. They kept out of sight along the edge of the road until they ran out of cover. Looking west, Nels spied a column of smoke. The manor house was in flames. Neat formations of Acrasians had cut through the Eledorean ranks as if nothing were in their path. Still, the Eledoreans fought. The Acrasians were paying a terrible price, but it wasn't enough to halt the tide. Finally, some of the Eledorean forces broke ranks and ran. The Seventh in their Eledorean blue uniforms were drowning in a sea of gray.

Compelled. Nels doubled over, coughing. White-hot pain blinded him while he attempted to keep from vomiting.

"What do we do?" Viktor asked.

Jarvi stared westward, horrified. "Why isn't the Seventh retreating with the rest?"

Viktor repeated himself, in shock. "What do we do?"

Listening to the sounds of the dying, Nels breathed in gulps. At some point, he'd have to stop and tend to his wounds, or he was going to lose too much blood. He couldn't do it now. The Acrasians would search the woods for survivors soon, and after everything that had just happened, they'd be even less inclined for quarter. *How long do we have? Were any of my troops able to get away? Or were they compelled to kill themselves too?* Nels swallowed another surge of nausea. "We head north. Follow the mountains until we reach the pass. Then head west to the city of Herraskariano. And we hope the others did as I ordered."

Shock flooded Jarvi's expression. "We can't leave them, sir! They need us!"

"The king needs us more," Nels said, hardly believing his own words. He was proposing to desert in order to save the life of a man he hadn't spoken to in two years—a man who hated him and thought of him as dead. And he hadn't just proposed it. He'd *planned* it. Nels's side began to ache. The long burning line the bayonet had carved into his skin was hot to the touch, and his mouth was dry. He reassured himself he was leaving for the sake of his sister. Wherever she was, she was the one who counted now.

I'm a fool. It will make no difference. Nothing I do ever will. "We're all that stands between the Acrasians and Jalokivi now," he said. "Merta is finished. All we'll accomplish by staying is joining the dead." And with that, Nels turned his back on the dying and started the long journey to Herraskariano on foot.

✦ SUVI ✦

ONE

With the foremast jury-rigged, *Otter* was able to continue on her journey home. Suvi imagined the encounter with *Winter Rose* over and over in an attempt to think of what she could've done better. They'd lost sixteen of the crew as well as their prisoner, the Acrasian captain. Each time Suvi thought of the dead, she repeated to herself one of her mother's lessons. *Perfection lacks opportunity for growth. Learn the value of error, especially the errors of others. Do not equate good luck with virtue, and do not indulge in superiority. Above all, remember that the powerful make only one type of mistake—deadly ones. Be careful and be prepared.* She hadn't been prepared. She'd assumed the rank of Sea Marshal, and she only had the experience of a lieutenant, and a low-ranking lieutenant at that.

Be careful. She'd try to remember that in the future.

There'd been no sign of *Winter Rose*. The past week had been spent dodging Acrasian patrols. Doing so drove them ever northward into more dangerous ice-filled seas. In addition to the ice, fall meant storm season. Waterborne avoided the northern sea in winter and fall unless a Waterweaver was among the ship's crew.

For this reason, *Sea Dragon* had passed the role of escort to her sister ship, *Arabella*. That was well enough, but *Otter*'s jury-rigged foremast wouldn't weather a severe winter storm.

So it was that when Suvi heard the call that the Eledorean coast had been spotted, she rushed to the rail with her spyglass and a sense of short-lived relief. The port of Mehrinna nestled between the Selkäranka Mountains and the Greater Sininen River was a beautiful sight, as was the mouth itself of the Greater Sininen River. It would be the last leg of her journey home. The mourning banners fixed to the city walls, on the other hand, were not a welcome sight. Her hopes that *Winter Rose*'s banners had been a meaningless ploy were dashed. Still, the mourning banners were the least of their problems.

"Those are an awful lot of ships," Suvi said, peering through the spyglass.

Wind blew Jami's hair into her face, and she looped the loose strands behind one ear with a frown. "Someone is serious about keeping you away from home."

"I suppose I can't blame Uncle or the Acrasians," Suvi said. "Any idea who the mourning banners are for?" *I need to know.*

Jami paused. Her brows pushed together, forming a frustrated line. Her reply came out in hushed fury. "I don't know."

As long as she'd known Jami, Suvi didn't think she'd ever heard her utter those words. Knowing things that others didn't was Jami's entire purpose for being.

Glaring at the horizon, Jami said, "May I borrow the glass?"

"Certainly," Suvi said.

After several minutes of searching, Jami said, "Oh."

"What is it?" Suvi asked.

At that moment, a lieutenant stepped forward and saluted. "I've a message from Captain Marsh of *Arabella*, sir."

Suvi opened the tiny scroll. It read, *Sea's current will be favorable to you. With your weathermaster's wind, both can see you through. Signal if accept.* "Dylan?"

"Yes, sir."

"How precise can you be with the wind?" Suvi asked.

Dylan's eyes narrowed. "Very. Unfortunately, the more concentrated the force, the more power there is, and the harder it is to control. I can't promise I won't damage our sails."

"Or the foremast," Darius muttered.

"I can't maintain such focus for long, either. Not alone," Dylan said. "It's best if I use my powers to guide weather already present, not force it."

Suvi asked, "Can you blow us through that blockade without granting the Acrasians a favorable wind?"

"It's possible. But once my influence fades, the winds will do as they will. We'll be caught in the gale along with everyone else."

Turning back to face the Acrasian blockade, Suvi considered the plan. "What if a current were to help you?"

Dylan turned to face *Arabella*. "Is that what Marsh offered?"

Suvi nodded.

"The surge is sure to damage the docks," Dylan said.

"That will only make it harder for the Acrasians to land," Suvi said.

"*Arabella* will have to remain behind," Darius said. "Alone. Her waterweaver will be used up. The Acrasians will attack the instant it's obvious they've helped. And it will be obvious. There's no hiding such a thing from any sailor who knows the sea."

Dylan said, "They won't be able to flee until we're through."

Sea Lord Kask has more than earned his water steel. Suvi frowned. "*Arabella* won't stand a chance. Not against all those guns. It's suicide."

Indomitable glided defiant in the water, her sails pregnant with the wind. Suvi thought about all the times she'd dreamed of commanding a navy. Never once did she think about what that really meant. Marines were supposed to take care of the more unpleasant aspects. Everyone knew that. Only, everyone was apparently wrong.

Commodore Björnstjerna. I'm so sorry, Suvi thought. "*Arabella* won't be alone."

"Do you have an answer, sir?" Lieutenant Noronen asked.

"I do. But first I need to contact *Indomitable.* Give me a moment to prepare the message."

"Yes, sir."

Jami said, "Your Grace."

"Yes? You have something to say?" Suvi asked.

"I have bad news," Jami said.

"What is it?" Suvi asked.

"It is regarding the banners on Mehrinna's walls." Jami had used formal court speech. Her normally serene countenance was edged with grief.

Suvi felt as though an icy fist had punched the air out of her lungs. "Father."

Jami slowly shook her head.

"Nels?" *Don't be stupid. He's a soldier. He wouldn't merit royal banners. Think.* Sudden knowledge hit her like a cannonball. Her knees failed her, and she grabbed the rail for support. "It can't be. Not Mother."

"I'm afraid it is," Jami said.

Watching Dylan, it was easy to see he struggled with a need to do the appropriate thing according to Eledorean custom—that is, change the subject—or a need to do something impulsive and Waterborne-ish. "I'm so sorry for your loss," he finally said in Eledorean. Reaching out, he supported her with a hand to her elbow. "She lives now and forever with the Mother."

With a start, Suvi recognized the formal Eledorean response to grief. Of course, she'd offered the same to friends and acquaintances herself on many occasions. However, it'd never occurred to her that anyone would speak them to her. *I'm as bad as everyone else, I suppose.* The cold had transformed into numbness. She was already losing patience with the Eledorean custom of not speaking directly of death. The only acknowledgments allowed were unspoken—the mourning ribbons and badges. Eledoreans preferred to behave as if they were exempt from dying. The euphemisms were as countless as they were endlessly annoying. She didn't know how she would stand the next month as everyone pretended as if the queen had taken an extended holiday. The pretense of immortality that Eledoreans in particular seemed enamored of used to disgust her. *Now that I know what lies beneath Keeper Mountain, it's more difficult to dismiss the aversion. Where is Mother now, I wonder? Is she finally with Captain Karpanen? Is she happy, or is she suffering? Will Karpanen finally be at peace? What has happened to her?*

Suvi thought of the creature that had attacked her, and shuddered.

The restless dead walk with the Old Ones.

Jami spoke to Darius. "Send for Piritta. Now. Her Grace needs to get below."

There are more important things going on. The thought was cold, abrupt, and almost foreign, but Suvi knew it for her own and was horrified. *What's more important than your mother?* Typically, Eledorean women went into grieving and weren't seen for three days and three nights. Then they would reemerge wearing bright colors with smiles pinned on their faces. It was supposed to represent rebirth. It was supposed to be defiance against the long darkness. It was supposed to deny—

If you break now, if you react like a typical woman, no ship's crew will ever follow you again—nor will the kingdom. Suvi blinked. *To follow tradition is to leave the kingdom to Uncle Sakari. Would Mother want that?*

You are a princess. Know when to follow Eledorean tradition and when to break with it. Her mother's words, repeated so often, surfaced in the numbness. *I did not raise you to be a simpering child. You're far too intelligent for that. You must think for yourself—find your own way—if you're to be an example. If you do not, nothing will ever change in Eledore.*

She bit down on grief and panic. "Stop."

Darius turned.

I'm not allowed my grief. Not now. Suvi swallowed her tears. They tasted of salt and bitterness. *I must do what I must. Lives depend upon it.* She breathed in through clenched teeth. "Let Piritta grieve for me. I will remain here."

"What?" Jami asked. The shock on the assassin's face was almost comical.

"Bring me paper, pen, and ink," Suvi said. "I need to compose that message to *Indomitable.*"

The others hesitated.

Lieutenant Noronen said, "You can't possibly mean to—"

"Do as I say," Suvi said. "At once."

Jami whispered, "Think of what the people will say."

"That isn't what matters most right now," Suvi said. "What would you do if tradition dictated one thing and duty demanded another?" She lowered her voice. "You're a korva. *My* korva."

Jami looked away. "I'd do my job."

"I must learn when to follow tradition and when to break with it. All Eledorean women do in one way or another. This is what I have to do. I promise you, I love my mother. I intend her no disrespect. But she was Ytlainen, and she would expect this of me. Please. I need your support. It will be too difficult without it."

Jami blinked and then nodded.

Suvi snatched the paper from Noronen and scribbled out the message to Björnstjerna on the railing. She handed it to Noronen. "Send this. Now."

Lieutenant Noronen spun on his heel and left. Shortly, a striped pennant flag was raised off the aft signal lines. A quarter of an hour passed before *Indomitable* and *Arabella* both indicated acknowledgment.

"Are we ready?" Suvi asked Captain Hansen.

"Yes, sir," Captain Hansen said. "Everything that can be anchored has been. Storm lines are in place."

"Then raise the signal to *Arabella*. Tell her we're ready," Suvi said.

"Yes, sir," Hansen said. "Lieutenant, you heard the Sea Marshal. Get to it. She also ordered the signalmen to prepare to flag the lock. We don't want to go to all the trouble of breaking through the Acrasians' blockade only to wash up against a closed river lock, do we?"

"Yes, sir. I mean, no, sir!"

I'd forgotten about that, Suvi thought. *It would've been a terrible mistake.* She waited until Lieutenant Noronen was gone. "Thank you."

Hansen raised an eyebrow. "I only repeated your orders." She turned to Dylan. "May the gods grant you fortunate winds, weathermaster."

"Thank you, sir." Dylan sat down on the deck next to the aft mast. "So, we're leaving *Indomitable* behind?"

Darius lashed Dylan to the mast and then settled next to his partner.

"*Arabella* can't stand alone against the Acrasians. You said so yourself," Suvi said. "Even if she could, I couldn't allow it. Eledore is at war with the Acrasians, not the Waterborne."

"You should probably find a more secure place to be," Dylan said.

Like below. Mother is dead, after all, Suvi thought, blushing. She knew it wasn't what Dylan meant, but it didn't stop the shame. "Speaking of, I've a question. If you don't mind."

Shrugging, Dylan said, "Shoot."

"Why would *Arabella* choose to sacrifice herself for us?" Suvi asked.

Dylan closed his eyes. "Who is to say it's a sacrifice? Perhaps it is they who should worry."

"The entire Acrasian navy is out there," Suvi said. "The Waterborne are powerful, but you're not that powerful."

Darius asked, "You've never seen an entire Waterborne crew at work, have you?"

"This isn't about Eledore for Marsh. The Acrasians made a mistake. They fired on *Arabella*," Dylan said. "Marsh isn't declaring war. He can't—not for all of the Waterborne Nations. But as a captain of Clan Kask, he is allowed a certain amount of discretion. And Clan Kask officially ceased all business relations with Acrasia weeks ago."

Suvi blinked. *How does he know?* Then it occurred to her that even if Eledorean messages couldn't reach across the sea, the Waterborne had their own methods. "The Acrasians won't acknowledge the distinction."

Dylan said, "I suspect it won't matter. Not today."

"Are you ready?" Darius asked.

Dylan took a deep breath and said, "I am."

Darius took Dylan's hand. "Try not to sink us."

"Try not to drown," Dylan said back.

Suvi lashed herself to the storm line on the poop deck with the other officers. The change in air pressure was abrupt enough to cause her ears to pop. The air smelled as it did just before a heavy storm. The wind slowly increased, and formerly serene clouds bunched and darkened into angry clumps. Someone shouted. Several crew members pointed aft. A great, misshapen wave swelled behind *Otter*. Its narrow crest grew tall, and then the unnatural formation pressed against the ship's stern. The deck tilted under Suvi's feet, and *Otter* gathered speed as wave and wind competed to shove *Otter* at the Acrasians. Faster and faster, the ship sped through the water until the vessel's timbers creaked in protest. Suvi prayed the foremast would hold. The wind howled. *Otter's* sails were strained to the maximum. Someone screamed. One of the aft yards snapped with a loud crack. It plunged into the shrouds. A sailor dropped into the sea. The remaining crew aloft fought sails and rigging to prevent further fouling. *Otter* relentlessly continued her journey toward the intimidating line of Acrasian ships.

Cannon shattered the air, but as Suvi watched, each shot seemed to meet the fierce wind and slow, dropping useless into the water. She looked to Dylan. His eyes were closed and his face was a mask of concentration. At his side, Darius laughed. Suvi couldn't decide if it was out of panic or the thrill of danger. Then all at once, the deck tilted fore at such an extreme angle that Suvi had trouble remaining on her feet. She began to wonder if Marsh's wave would accidentally flip *Otter* end over end.

Otter sprinted through her enemies. Two Acrasian ships were blown far to port and then starboard. Sails ripped to pieces and masts splintered. She could hear the Acrasian sailors' cries. Still *Otter* was propelled forward until Suvi was sure they'd crash into the Acrasians and finally Mehrinna's docks. Then just as suddenly as it'd appeared, the water's force dropped away. It spread outward, and the enemy ships were sent spinning like toys. Some slammed into the docks as the water hit land.

Dylan slumped, and the terrifying wind was free. The Acrasian line was dashed into chaos.

The river lock loomed ahead as the gates slowly opened. Suvi could hardly believe her eyes. She held her breath until the gate closed and the lock chamber began to fill with water. The jury-rigged foremast choose that moment to disintegrate with a huge crash. The crew rushed to prevent further damage. Around them, the storm continued to rage. Protected by the lock's walls, she could only imagine the destruction. She said a quick prayer for *Indomitable* and *Arabella* before fleeing below to mourn for her mother.

⇥ NELS ⇤

ONE

"How many of them are down there? Seventy-five? A hundred?" Gingerly propping himself up on his elbows, Nels gazed at the Acrasian encampment and tried not to show despair.

So far, they'd made fair progress on their journey north, but Westola was struggling to keep the wounded patched together as it was, without encountering rough terrain on top of it. To ease the toll on the troops, Nels had decided to cut back to the road. Walking was less demanding than climbing. He'd told Viktor that they were sure to be ahead of the Acrasian vanguard by now. Viktor had suggested scouting the road first, which had then led to Nels shivering on top of a grassy hill. Once again, Nels wished anyone else were in charge. The troops deserved better.

So much for the road. His wounds ached with the cold. Shivering only made it worse.

He hoped to regroup with the rest of the Eledorean army at Herraskariano before the Acrasians reached it. Unfortunately, the Acrasian scouts below—and he prayed they were only scouts— were camped directly in the center of a bottleneck. The Selkäranka mountains flanked the road to the west, and a steep incline carpeted with a thick ironwood forest crowded the passage to the east. If he had twenty-seven healthy troops, he could— *But I don't. I have twenty-five wounded.* Viktor and Westola were the only two who'd fled Merta unscathed. If they could afford to wait a few days, the scouts would move on, and Westola could get a few more of the troops more solidly on their feet with Sergeant Wiberg's help. But they didn't have any supplies, and winter was on its way.

Time is running out.

Nels could smell the Acrasian campfires from where he was. The scent of roasting meat and baking bread was torture. His mouth watered, and his stomach reminded him that his last meal had been the night before. It'd consisted of raw rabbit and a few nuts Private Ilola had dared to harvest in the woods as they'd fled.

Nels scratched his itching scalp. *I'd give anything for hot food, a healer, a bit of alcohol, a bath, and a soft bed,* he thought. His hand drifted to the bandage strapped around his belly. He suspected the cut was becoming infected. "All right. How bad is the bad news?"

Peering through a collapsible spyglass, Viktor frowned. "It's pretty bad." He handed the glass to Nels and lay down with a disgusted grunt. "I'm beginning to think you're cursed."

Nels looked for himself and felt his guts clench in a cold knot. He winced. About a hundred Acrasians crowded the road. "Shit. Is it the main vanguard, do you think?"

"Cavalry scouts, by the insignia. A lot of them, though. Acrasians don't do anything in half measures, it seems."

"Smaller groups are too easily controlled with command magic," Nels said, remembering Lucrosia Marcellus's notes. "We taught them that."

An Acrasian was playing a violin and singing. The sorrowful strains of a ballad drifted up the hill along with the scent of dinner.

Nels mentally translated the lyrics without effort. *I left my love on a hill far away and came to a distant shore. Silver's song kept her tears from my heart, and here I lie buried, ever more.*

He moved the glass to the horse pickets. *If only we could steal a few horses*, he thought. A flash of long pale mane along with an ill-tempered horse scream drew his eye to the far left. He looked closer. *It can't be.* A stubborn smile drifted onto his lips. *Surely, they'd have shot him and put him in a pot by now.* Nels checked twice to be sure.

Loimuta!

"There's no going the long way around," Viktor said. "If that was your thought. We'll never make it with Corporal Lumme in the shape he's in."

"All right," Nels said, rolling onto his back and scooting down-hill a few feet. His stomach and side were hurting so bad, it was hard to move without flinching. The bandages were filthy. He should have Westola see to his wounds again. However, the others were in dire need of her skills, and although she was teaching Wiberg all she could, Westola was the only real healer they had. She could only be pushed so far. He would do anything to keep the troops on their feet. If that meant he had to do without, he did without. "We need a diversion."

"Any ideas?"

"I'm thinking," Nels said, staring up at the darkening sky. "Got the positions memorized?"

"I do."

"Let's get out of here before I trip over a mountain lion," Nels said.

Viktor turned, as if searching for the obstacle in question. "I don't think there's a mountain lion within miles."

"Leave it to me to find a pride," Nels whispered. "And then bring the entire Acrasian camp down on our heads."

Silent and graceful, Viktor slipped down to the foot of the hillside. "You overestimate your talent for noise."

Nels followed, taking extra care to be as quiet as possible. Naturally, it did little to no good. "All right. What do you want?"

Viktor looked hurt. "What kind of a question is that?"

"You just passed up an opportunity to mock me. You want something. Out with it."

"All right. Fine. We need the horses."

Among other things, Nels thought and glanced over at Viktor in the dark.

Moonlight cast silver on Viktor's shadowy form. Still, it was hard to focus on him—hard not to let his image blend in with the background. Again, Nels swallowed no small amount of envy. *What if I can't get them to Herraskariano in time?*

Viktor didn't look at him. "Corporal Lumme isn't going to make it if we don't get to Herraskariano. Soon. That will make five dead." His voice was flat, matter-of-fact.

"What if"? There is no "what if." I'm a defective. And they're going to die because of it—shit, they have died because of it.

"You have to do something. One more night in the open without food or a fire, and Corporal Lumme won't be the only one. You damned well know it."

Nels couldn't bring himself to face Viktor. It was then that a plan began to form in Nels's brain. Taking a deep breath, he asked, "Do we have any powder at all?"

"If we did, do you think I'd—"

"Jarvi," Nels said. The plan solidified. "We've Master Sergeant Jarvi."

"Private Kulmala is a pyrotechnic too. But that gets us nothing if we've no powder or coal or fire. For that matter, we've only the three guns and no ammunition."

"We won't need guns or powder," Nels said with a broadening smile. "Not if the Acrasians have them."

Viktor halted. "Are you suggesting that Jarvi walks into the middle of their camp and then sets fire to their powder stores? That's suicide."

Nels said, "I'm suggesting that *I* walk into the middle of their camp and *then* Jarvi sets fire to their powder stores when they're focused on me."

Viktor blinked. "You're mad."

"I wouldn't say that." Nels paused. "Well, not entirely." And then he explained why.

TWO

Nels searched for fist-sized stones in the moonlight. Thanks to the forced delay, they'd taken the time to eat. Still, hunger gnawed at his insides in spite of the acorns and walnuts. *At least we have plenty of water.* He closed his eyes and took a deep breath to calm his nerves. The scab on his belly pulled tight. The smell of road dust mixed with sweat and dirt. He was exhausted and uncomfortable. His beard and hair itched. A sharp pain told him his wound had reopened. He told himself again that it wasn't important. Gritting his teeth, he bent and selected a few good-sized stones. He stuffed them in his pockets. A stone wasn't much defense against a musket ball, but since he wasn't planning on getting that close, it beat a saber or an empty gun. When his pockets were full, he made his way to the Acrasian camp. He found a good spot to wait for Viktor's signal. Peering through the underbrush, Nels spied two sentries sitting in the road. They were playing cards with their guns strapped to their backs.

They're not expecting anyone. I don't know whether to be happy or insulted.

A nightingale's song ripped through the quiet. Nels's empty stomach fluttered. Reaching inside his shirt front, he touched the medal there and said a quick prayer for luck. With that, he whistled loud for Loimuta. The gelding's answering call came at once. With that, Nels straightened to his full height and stepped into the middle of the road.

The two Acrasian sentries gaped.

Nels asked in Acrasian, "Care to deal me in?" He whistled again for Loimuta. Chaos erupted in the direction of the horse pickets.

One sentry dropped his cards, scrambled to his feet, and shouted the alarm. His companion stared a moment longer before scrabbling to bring his musket to bear.

Nels aimed the first stone, hitting the shouting sentry on the forehead. "I'll assume that means no?" Then he fished another stone from his pocket and launched it at the second sentry.

The rest of the stones followed the second, keeping the sentries off balance. Nels worked at emptying his pockets until Loimuta arrived. Both sentries were knocked off their feet as the gelding forced his way between them at a canter, stopped, and then reared. Nels grabbed reins and a fistful of mane and then vaulted onto Loimuta's bare back. Behind him, he could hear the sentries struggling to get up. A shot went off, clouding the night air with smoke. He felt the wind of a musket ball's passing against his cheek. Nels gave Loimuta his head and urged him to run. The horse obliged with a full gallop. They'd sprinted a good distance down the road when Nels sensed pursuit. Risking a glance over his shoulder, he counted five or six Acrasian riders. They weren't far behind. Loimuta took the chase as a challenge and answered with a renewed burst of speed.

There was a stream ahead, Nels knew. They had destroyed the bridge on the way north. The water was cold, broad, and deep. He'd found out through personal experience. Viktor had pushed him in afterward in a fit of playful revenge. Nonetheless, Nels trusted Loimuta would easily jump across. The Acrasians' horses would balk—so Nels hoped. *All will be well, provided Loimuta can run the remaining distance without being shot—*

A bright flash brightened the road. The accompanying explosion pressed against his ears. Again, he turned to look. The Acrasians slowed as they understood that they'd been tricked. The leader signaled to the others. All but two turned back to the camp. Nels spurred Loimuta on. Spying the stream in the moonlight, he prepared himself for the jump. Without a saddle, it wasn't going to be comfortable for either of them, but Nels had ridden bareback a great deal when he was younger. He felt Loimuta's muscles bunch beneath him. The horse sailed across in a powerful leap, his hind legs splashing on the muddy bank. Nels heard a shout followed by a loud thump and then a splash. He didn't wait to see if the last Acrasian attempted the stream or not. Nels signaled to Loimuta to turn left and then headed east along the bank. He rode until he didn't hear his pursuers any longer. Then he reined Loimuta to a stop among a group of low-hanging trees. He slid from the gelding's back and, holding his breath, listened. Rushing water signaled the rapids farther downstream.

Loimuta quivered with anticipation and spent energy.

Nels patted his neck and whispered, "You saved us both. I wish I had an apple for you." His stomach let out a loud noise. "I wish I had an apple for myself. As it is, supper will probably consist of acorns and raw rabbit. Again. If we're lucky. Most likely it'll be breakfast before we eat."

Loimuta made a low sound of disapproval as if he would've been happier with the Acrasians.

At least they have food, Nels thought.

Loimuta's snow-white coat practically glowed in the dappled moonlight under the trees.

We're sure to be spotted, Realizing his own hair probably blended into the background about as well as Loimuta did, Nels sighed. Then the splashed river mud on the gelding's flanks suggested a resolution.

Gazing up into the night sky, he listened again. Insects and frogs returned to their chorus over the stream's susurrus. *The Acrasians must have given up. Hasta, I hope so, anyway.* He couldn't afford to wait much longer. The others would be moving camp. He searched for a better place to cross the water and found one. Once on the opposite bank, he applied mud to Loimuta's coat, mane, and tail. For his part, Loimuta did his best to cover Nels too by pushing up against him or shaking like a wet dog at every opportunity. When Nels was finally finished with Loimuta, he then twisted his own hair into a braid and applied more mud. Then he risked making his way north through the woods where those not directly involved in his mad scheme waited.

It took him three hours to find the former makeshift camp. Instead of hungry troops, he discovered Viktor napping against the trunk of a tree. Nearby, a fettered and saddled Acrasian horse nosed the scattered snow for forage.

"You certainly took your time getting back," Viktor said, tilting his hat from his face with an index finger.

"I needed to make sure I wasn't followed."

"Followed? By whom?"

"Two Acrasians chased me all the way to the stream. One of them fell into the water. The second is around here someplace."

"Oh, that. There was only one."

"I counted two."

"The second was me," Viktor said. He got up from the grass

and dusted off his filthy uniform. "Who do you think knocked that Acrasian out of his saddle before he could catch you?"

"Oh." Nels paused. "You let me ride on?"

"You seemed very intent on escaping." Viktor shrugged. "Who am I to argue with royalty?" He smiled. "Nice look. Don't think it'll catch on at the palace, though."

Nels put a hand to his mud-dried hair and face and sighed. "Where is everyone?"

"I sent them ahead," Viktor said. "Along with the supplies. If I didn't know any better, I'd swear Groop, Kurri, and Lassila had once worked together in an unlawful capacity. They were a bit too familiar with how to efficiently rob a camp. With virtually no direction, I might add."

Nels wasn't remotely shocked. "What were you able to get?"

"I suspect we'll never have an accurate inventory. Not that I think it matters. Let's just leave it with 'quite a bit.'" Viktor went to his horse. "We should get out of here."

"You're right. The Acrasians are sure to be searching for us."

"Between Jarvi and Kulmala, the Acrasians will be dealing with the fire until tomorrow night. They aren't going anywhere," Viktor said, unfettering his horse. "I just don't want to miss supper."

THREE

Pesola's eyes widened behind flat, round spectacle lenses. The expression lasted only an instant. Then it was replaced with recognition. His gaze narrowed, and he snapped his teeth together like an agitated predator. His aristocratic features acquired a reddish cast.

Someone neglected to inform you of my arrival, Nels thought. *Someone is getting sloppy. Or did you lose one of your korvas?*

The interior of the tent swelled with the breathless anticipation of forest creatures awaiting the talons of a hawk or the teeth of a wolf. Nels halted a respectful distance from Pesola's breakfast table. Viktor positioned himself at Nels's right. Without Viktor's warning, Nels wouldn't have recognized Pesola right away. Although his uniform was immaculate, Pesola was wigless—no doubt due to lost baggage.

Well, Nels thought. *Isn't that a swiving shame?* No doubt one of the enlisted had paid for that shortcoming with their skin. Nels couldn't help thinking that wigless officers tended to assume a humble quality. It made them seem more vulnerable. *Not Pesola.*

Short-clipped, graying hair stood out in bristles on Pesola's scalp like a bad-tempered wolf's ruff. He dropped his fork and practically snarled. "What are *you* doing here?"

Nels executed a precise salute and held it. "Captain Hännenen, reporting for duty, sir."

"This is intolerable!" Pesola abruptly stood up from his breakfast, upsetting the camp table in the process.

Pesola's corporal darted in. The table remained upright. However, his reflexes weren't fast enough to save the china. Plates, saucer, and cup pitched over, crashing against one another and shattering. Cheese, crispbread, and cold meat scattered into the grass. Spilled tea dripped off the edge of the camp table. Steam rose off the carefully brewed puddle sprawling across the table's surface.

Again, Pesola snapped his teeth together. "You're a disgrace!"

That much was true, Nels had to admit. He'd finally risked the cold and rinsed the mud from his hair, but his uniform was beyond redemption. "I attempted to clean up as best I could before repor—"

"That's no excuse!"

"No, sir," Nels said, conceding the petty victory. Nonetheless, he felt survival mattered more in the midst of a rout. *Careful, Captain Hännenen. The Eledorean army doesn't admit to anything so base as retreat, let alone defeat.* He blinked back an image of magicked troops charging to their deaths against their will.

Others had confirmed Nels's hunch in bits and pieces during the journey to Herraskariano. The Seventh Regiment had committed suicide. Witnesses confirmed that they'd done so against their will. No one knew how much of the regiment had been affected. Nor did any of the survivors seem to know where the order had originated. They only knew that the magically enforced order had flowed down the chain of command. *Was it you, Pesola?*

Nels's hand tightened a fist around the burst of sudden rage. He had every intention of finding out. Although, he didn't know what he'd do when, or if, he did. *Take care. There's more riding on this than your own skin.*

Pesola paced a circle around him and Viktor both. "You are the only ones who survived, I suppose," Pesola said with a sneer.

"The remains of my company are outside, awaiting your orders, sir. Sixty-three total. Although nine are from Laine's brigade." Nels's message to withdraw and regroup had saved his company's lives. Sixty-one out of eighty had walked away from Merta. He had Viktor to thank for that. Nine had died on the march north. Nels hated the idea of giving them over to the likes of Pesola, but it couldn't be helped. *At least, not right now.* Pesola was the highest-ranking officer on the field, at least as far as Nels knew. *That's how it has to be until I report to General Runessen in Jalokivi. After that, we'll see.* "We acquired a few supplies—"

"Shut up!"

"Yes, sir."

Pesola completed his circle, stopping in front of Nels. The action was meant to be intimidating. It did touch on certain memories. However, the effect was diminished by the fury tightening Nels's fists and jaw.

"Fifty-two." Pesola sniffed. "Fifty. Two. That's quite a large number."

"Yes, sir." *Twenty-eight total dead.* Nels could name each one even if he couldn't recall a face to match. He'd made a list of the dead and had planned to visit their families, provided there would be time to make such gestures feasible. *How many troops did you lose, Pesola? Do you even care? Were you the one to give that order?*

"Is there a reason so much of your company survived?" Pesola asked. His voice was calm, but it carried a razor's edge.

Nels recognized it for the warning sign it was. *My troops lived because I didn't allow them to die in order to save your swiving baggage. Is that what you want to know?* "I don't understand the question, sir."

"I'll make an exception regarding my policy of not repeating myself. Just this once, Captain. Out of respect. For your father," Pesola said. His voice honed its edge. "How is it that so much of the Seventh perished at Merta, and yet so few of your company were among them?"

The answer was born from Nels's throat before he had time to stop it. "Perhaps because I didn't command them to fight to the death with magic in order to cover my cowardice. Like you."

Someone gasped.

Pain exploded in Nels's jaw and nose. The blow was so violent that he staggered to keep his feet. Tears blurred his vision. The pain was huge before it finally abated. Still, he somehow managed to keep from crying out. Older wounds joined in his body's list of complaints. His face heated, and he wiped his eyes. Sniffing, he swallowed the taste of blood and shame.

"It was you, wasn't it?" Nels asked, staring down at the grass. He remained stooped. He didn't want to look up. Pesola's face would confirm what Nels already knew, and he didn't know what he'd do. *Not yet. Wait.* He blinked, clearing his vision. It took a moment to register the gore dripping into the grass. Then he daubed at his nose and slowly straightened, resuming attention position. His jaw ached almost as much as his nose did. His lip was swelling. Warm fluid oozed down his chin, but he didn't touch it. He breathed through his mouth. "You gave that order, didn't you? You magicked them. You didn't even let them do it on their own terms."

"Soldiers die," Pesola said. "It's what they do."

"Not like that," Nels said, tilting his chin up. "You sent them to be slaughtered. You used them like animals. All of them. I saw.

They were compelled, not influenced or motivated. *Compelled.* With magic."

Pesola's face was so red, it could've been classified as purple. "Deserter!"

"Not me," Nels said. But the verbal blow had hit home. It was hard not to wince. "I got here as soon as I received word of where to regroup."

In truth, he hadn't been pleased when Viktor had told him it was Pesola camped outside of Herraskariano. Nels had hoped it would be Major Lindström, General Laine, or General Kauranen, but no, it'd been Pesola. The others had died to the last, defending Merta and Eledore.

"Is it true, sir?" The question came from one of the others in the tent.

Pesola ignored the question. "You left your post!"

The shame of the truth hit Nels almost as hard as the blow. He *had* left the battlefield. He *did* leave the others to die. *But I didn't use the lives of thousands to cover my retreat.* It salved the sting somewhat. "My post left me. That was the idea, after all," Nels said. "You ordered me to blow up those bridg—"

"Don't play games with me!"

"Yes, sir." Nels focused on the canvas ceiling just above Pesola's head.

"Is it true?" The question originated from a different corner of the tent—the voice deeper and ever so slightly bolder.

Murmurs filtered through canvas from outside as word was passed from soldier to soldier. The first questioner gathered even more courage. "What the captain said? Is it true?"

"It is," Viktor said. "Captain Hännenen isn't the only one who saw. I did too. As did Master Sergeant Jarvi. Hännenen's entire company, in fact. Ask any of them."

"Who would do such a thing?" someone asked in a low voice.

"Silence!" Pesola's command magic–laced order snapped the air like a whip.

Nels held his breath, dreading what would happen next. He could see the word forming in each soldier's skull as clear as if it had been written in bright crimson ink.

Mutiny.

Nels had to stop it. It was his duty. There had been enough suffering and death through Pesola's actions as it was. Nels couldn't stand by and let what few lives remained be destroyed. He couldn't allow Pesola the excuse.

Pesola turned once more and faced him. "Captain Hännenen, I'm going to ask you a question, and you're going to answer it." The air cracked with the force placed behind the statement. "You will tell the truth. Do you hear me?"

"Yes."

"Yes, what?"

Nels swallowed another mouthful of blood, mucus, and rage. He felt he might choke on it. "Yes, *sir.*"

"Did you order your company to abandon their posts?" Pesola asked.

Pausing, Nels considered exactly how he would answer. *He wants the truth,* he thought. *Let him have the truth.* "No, sir." He paused. "Not specifically."

Pesola frowned. "What were your orders? *Exactly?*"

"I ordered them to defend Merta to the best of their ability," Nels said, and saw Pesola's frown deepen. "However, when the third Acrasian brigade arrived from the west and it became clear that we were overwhelmed, they were to engage in a fighting retreat. They were to leave Merta and head northwest. I told them we would regroup at the coaching inn two miles south of Herraskariano.

Then we would proceed to Jalokivi to defend the king. And that was my plan until I heard you were here."

Letting out a victorious hiss, Pesola leaned forward. "You. *Deserted.* You left the Seventh Regiment to die."

"No, sir. I made a decision based on information others did not have."

"Do not argue with me!" More magic weighed down the air.

Nels felt a muscle in his jaw cramp. *He's right, you know. You did.*

"What's worse is you incited your company to desert as well," Pesola said, making another circle around both Nels and Viktor. "Reini, what do you have to say for yourself?"

Viktor choked. Nels glimpsed his pale expression at the edge of his vision. He hadn't seen raw fear on Viktor's face before.

"Sir?"

"You were with Hännenen, were you not?" Pesola said.

Viktor said, "Yes, sir."

"Why didn't you stop him?" Pesola asked.

"It wasn't my place to question an order, s—"

"Don't lie, Reini! You aren't under Hännenen's command!" Pesola shouted in Viktor's ear. Pesola took a breath as if to calm himself. "I assume you knew about Hännenen's order previous to its execution?"

"Yes, sir."

"Why didn't you report it to me? It is your duty, isn't it?" Pesola again infused his words with command magic. "Answer me, Reini."

Viktor fought against the urge to comply. A doomed expression crossed his face before he opened his mouth to speak.

Nels spoke loud enough to cover Viktor's agonized reply. "He didn't tell you because I compelled him not to tell you, sir."

The response had the desired effect. Pesola changed targets, stepping to Nels's side. Pesola spoke in Nels's ear. "You commanded him not to tell me." His voice was quiet, flat. "I had understood you despised command magic. That you refuse to use it."

Better me than Viktor, Nels thought. "Yes, sir."

"And yet you used it in this instance.

"I did."

"And why is that?" Pesola asked.

Once again, Nels lied. "Because I didn't think it'd be necessary, sir."

"You didn't think it'd be necessary to tell me?"

"I didn't think the retreat would be necessary, sir," Nels said. "Therefore, there was no need to make the report." The logic was weak, but what did it matter? He'd redirected Pesola's wrath from Viktor.

Pesola went to the camp table, picked up the stained linen napkin resting there, and used it to wipe his hands. "Captain Hännenen, you will follow me outside."

"Yes, sir." *What is he going to do?* The next thought shamed Nels with the rapidity of its appearance. *Was the cat lost with the rest of his baggage?* He attempted to come up with anything he could say or do that wouldn't result in the troops being punished for mutiny and/or treason and came up blank. He followed Pesola outside. Dread formed an icy knot in Nels's belly.

Viktor was two steps behind him. "Be careful," he whispered.

Bit late for that, Nels thought.

Pesola's tent emptied. Sensing something important was about to happen, Nels's troops halted whatever it was they'd been doing and gathered, watching.

Having reached a place he deemed appropriate, Pesola stopped in the center of the crowd where all could get a good view. He turned slowly as if taking in the witnesses. He placed a hand on his saber hilt. "Hännenen, I want you to kneel. There." He pointed at the ground inches from the toe of his own boot.

Nels stayed where he was. "Why?"

"I'm executing you for the deserter you are. Now."

"You're going to cut off my head?" Nels asked. Rage still shielded him from all other emotions except the need to stall. *Think, damn you.*

"That's the idea. In fact, I'll be generous. I'll give you a choice. Granted, it's more than you're owed. But I'll gift you the choice nonetheless due to your station," Pesola said, drawing his sword. "Will you kneel on your own? Or do I make you?"

That's it, Nels thought. *Thank Hasta.* "I think you're forgetting something."

"Am I?" Pesola used his sleeve to polish an imaginary stain from the gleaming blade. Seemingly bored, he didn't look up.

"I'm royalty," Nels said, his voice was calm.

"Even royalty aren't exempt from execution for acts of treason. What of it?"

"I've a right to a trial."

"Call it a field court martial, if you wish," Pesola said. "It's been done before." He pointed to one of the others and waved him forward.

Nels recognized the sergeant as he moved into position.

"Sergeant Holdon, disarm Hännenen if he doesn't hand over his sword at once. Then I want you to strip him of his rank. He needs to be made an example. For the others."

Viktor's mouth dropped open.

Nels said, "I've a right to trial by combat."

Pesola paused. "In time of war?"

"The Acrasians aren't here," Nels said. "Not yet. There's time. It's my right."

"I'm afraid he's correct, sir," Holdon said. Nels spied something in his expression. He wasn't sure if it was relief or pity.

"I don't know what you think you'll gain with this," Pesola said. "You're still going to die."

"I'll have my dignity," Nels said. "Unlike the troops you murdered." When he had first fallen to the rank of soldier, his mother had risked scandal and paid a fencing master to train him. She'd said it would help him survive. In the beginning, he hadn't understood her reasoning, but she'd been right after all. He could almost hear his fencing instructor's voice.

Never allow strong emotion to accompany you into a duel, Your Grace. It will kill you just as assuredly as your enemy's blade.

A cold breeze made its way through the clearing. The trees seemed to hiss recriminations among themselves. None of the troops moved. They didn't even breathe. In the distance, an angry falcon shrieked a challenge at an interloper.

Once more Pesola opened his mouth and then closed it. Sheathing his saber with a fierce jerk, he then began unbuttoning his uniform coat. Either his fingers or the coat didn't cooperate. The coat didn't come undone. He yanked at the fabric in frustration, ripping off three buttons. *Pop. Pop. Pop.* "Very well." He threw the coat at Sergeant Holdon as if it had offended him.

It hit Holdon in the face. Holdon scrambled to keep from dropping it.

"Holdon, I'll see to stripping Hännenen of his rank once this farce is complete."

In deliberate contrast to Pesola, Nels took his time. It annoyed Pesola further. Looking down at his hands, Nels was shocked to discover no tremor. He felt more at peace now than he had at any other time.

I've dueled before. This is no different. But it was different. The lives of his troops relied on the outcome, and not only theirs but his father's and his sister's as well. He knew it in his bones, just as he'd known Pesola was responsible for the slaughter of the Seventh.

Viktor reached out for Nels's coat. "You don't have to do this," he whispered.

You would rather I were executed? But Nels knew what Viktor had in mind. The others were poised to rebel. All Nels had to do was to shout the order. *You don't have to do this.* "Actually, I do," Nels whispered back, and fished out two dog-eared letters from his pocket before surrendering the coat to Viktor. With that, Nels handed off the envelopes. "One is for my sister. And if I don't . . . win, will you go to Ilta Korpela, give her the second, and tell her what happened? I suspect she'll know anyway, but—"

"I will," Viktor said.

Nodding, Nels unbuttoned his sleeves. He drew his saber and secured the silver tassel around his wrist.

"You're only delaying the inevitable, you know," Pesola said through clenched teeth. "Are you afraid?"

Nels gave Viktor a confident smile. Keeping his back to Pesola, Nels said, "I confess I am a bit at that. No matter. I'm making you look the fool. I'll take what I can get."

Both Viktor's reaction and Pesola's growl of rage gave Nels the warning he needed to dodge Pesola's charge. Private Johansson wasn't that lucky, however. Pesola slammed into him, stabbing him in the chest in the process. Nels saw Westola run from her place at the campfire to help. Pesola struggled to get his blade free of Johansson. Nels didn't see a means of attacking without risking Westola, Johansson, and a few others besides. Therefore, he waited.

Pesola shouted at Westola. "Leave him, damn you!" Free of Johansson at last, he whirled and faced Nels.

Nels settled into a crouching attack stance—left hand up to his face, palm down, and sword ready in a high guard. His senses were sharp. He felt ready. Pesola mirrored his actions and then shuffled closer before striking. Nels slashed down. His parry caught Pesola's blade. Steel on steel chimed. Pesola pressed his attack with a series of thrusts. Nels gave ground again and again until he was certain of Pesola's overconfidence. At that moment, Nels led in with a swift feint to the belly with a shout. Pesola took the bait. Nels's blade circled around for a strike at Pesola's sword arm. Fabric parted beneath steel. At the same time, Nels felt a dull blow on the shin. He stumbled backward. Getting his footing, he resumed the crouch and waited for signs of another strike.

Pesola's spectacle-framed eyes stared back. "This is pointless."

"Is that so?" Nels asked. "Is that why you're the one who is bleeding?"

Pesola lunged. Again, Nels answered with a parry and a riposte. Pesola ran his blade up against Nels's, and they locked hilts. Nels's knuckles stung. He noticed that Pesola was breathing in gasps.

"Tiring, old man?" Nels asked.

Pesola spat and shoved. Saliva oozing down the side of his face, Nels staggered, but not before getting in a wild slash. It caught Pesola on the cheek.

Halting, Pesola touched the wound. "I've had enough of this."

"You concede the fight?" Viktor asked.

The others seemed poised to join the fray.

"Hännenen, drop your sword," Pesola said. The order prickled the air with power.

"No!" Viktor's protest was joined with the crowd's gasp.

Nels lowered his saber. Pesola didn't wait for more. He charged in. Nels brought up his blade, knocking the threat away with a beat and then a thrust. He knew at that moment that he'd killed Pesola. Nels's mind was flooded with images as details from Pesola's life passed through magicked steel. There were memories of home and family—his father had doted on him while his mother had not. Neither mattered. Pesola genuinely didn't comprehend the existence of others and never truly had. He was what mattered and nothing else. Others were a means of getting what he wanted. Nels also sensed darker thoughts twisting around blood and pain, power and sex. Pesola had murdered women for the pleasure of it. Flashes of agonized screams became confused with more intimate moments.

He had flayed them and then—

Scrambling backward, Nels shuddered in horror and revulsion. He turned his head in case he was going to be sick. *He's a monster. Oh, Hasta, I don't want to know any of that.* He told himself it was no different than the rumors he'd heard at court. That Pesola wasn't an anomaly, but it was one thing to know and another to have seen.

"I commanded you," Pesola said. Shock masked his face.

Nels blinked himself to the present. *The blood. The screams.* He released the breath he'd been holding. His stomach rolled. *Stop this. Now. Wake up. He'll kill you.* Nels focused on the point of Pesola's blade and not—*the blood*—the memories. He forced himself to think only of the duel.

Pesola choked. Nels started at the sound. Pesola dropped his sword and put both hands to the gaping wound in his abdomen. He fell, gasping.

What does it matter? It's time to end it. Still, Nels couldn't stand the thought of what he'd have to endure in the process—the knowledge of a creature like Pesola sullying Captain Karpanen's blade. An unwanted thought sprang to mind. It would take a long time to die from a gut wound. *Pesola likes pain. Then let him enjoy agony.* That is, provided Westola didn't intervene. Nels prayed she wouldn't. *Did she know what Pesola was?*

Searching for Westola, Nels saw she was still at Corporal

Johansson's side. She fussed with the bandage as if it took all her attention.

"How?" It was Pesola.

"You know how, swive you," Nels said. "I won."

Pesola clamped his teeth together—this time in pain, not rage. His teeth were stained crimson. Blood formed bubbles between his teeth. He closed his eyes. "I—I compelled you. How?" He was lying on his side; his face had gone pale. The grass around him was soaked black with gore.

"Oh." Nels wiped his sword's edge clean on a sleeve before sheathing it. Then his hand went to his knife as he stooped closer. The action would have a meaning the others wouldn't miss, nor would Pesola. Everyone would assume it was for the Seventh Regiment, and it was but not all. "I'm immune to command magic. Always was. Royalty, remember?" The last was a lie, of course, but it worked well enough and the others were listening. "Have you made your peace with your gods?"

"You're going to kill *me*?" Pesola smiled and coughed. "With *that*?"

"Yes, I am," Nels said. "I could leave you to die a slow death alone in the cold. I could leave you for the animals to finish off. And you'd deserve it for all you've done. But I won't. Do you know why?"

Pesola let out a sound wedged between a laugh and a choke.

"Because I'm not *you*." Nels didn't wait for Pesola's answer. Nels supposed the colonel had had chance enough to make his peace.

As Nels had hoped, Westola remained where she was. Watching, she didn't flinch. Rather, a small, vengeful smile crossed her face. Nels straightened. The others looked on in silence.

Viktor was the first to move. He produced a handkerchief and handed it off to Nels. In turn, Nels used it to wipe Pesola's blood from the knife. Viktor dropped the handkerchief on Pesola's corpse rather than stuffing it back in his pocket.

Your blood isn't worthy of staining my knife, let alone my sword. It was the worst insult a soldier knew.

"I guess that makes you the new colonel," Viktor said, looking down on Pesola's body.

"I'm not sure it works that way," Nels said. *What are you going to do now? You can't leave him like that. He's—was an officer.*

He flayed them before he—

"There are close to five hundred men here," Viktor said. "And you're the highest-ranking officer."

"Promotion isn't up to me. That's General Näränen's decision."

Viktor said, "Pesola's plan was to winter in Herraskariano."

Of course it was.

Who were you working for, Pesola? "The Acrasians won't stop at Merta or Herraskariano."

Gazing to the southeast, Viktor nodded.

"Tell the others we leave for Jalokivi in the morning," Nels said. "We're going to be there when the Acrasians get there."

"Yes, sir."

Nels had a patrol dump Pesola's body outside of camp. He left it up to them to decide whether or not he was worth burying. The shards of Pesola's memories had cut too deep for Nels to care. There weren't enough rituals to purge the images from his mind.

That night, he woke from nightmares. He heard the calls of the wolves outside of camp and worried if he really was that much different from Pesola after all.

⇥ S U V I ⇤

ONE

Jalokivi's docks were filled to capacity. Had a berth not been reserved for both *Otter* and *Indomitable*, they would've had to drop anchor miles from the capital. Suvi offered a quick prayer for Commodore Björnstjerna and *Arabella* at the sight of *Indomitable*'s empty slip. *I did what I had to do. Clan Kask will send word if they're safe.*

Please let them still be afloat.

Streets and warehouses in the proximity of the wharf were crowded with terrified people. Everything of value was being relocated to more secure facilities within the city walls, if such were available to the owners. The area was overwhelmed with passengers seeking passage out of Eledore via the Chain Lakes.

"And how are you feeling this morning?" Dylan asked Suvi.

Darius dropped his sea bag.

"Dar, please do something about your partner before I smack him," Suvi said, massaging her temples. She was wearing her brightest blue gown for the sake of propriety.

Not far away, Piritta gave orders to the crew assigned to transport the baggage. Jami was already down the gangplank and away.

"Stop tormenting the nice pre-queen," Darius said to Dylan.

"I wasn't the one that drank an entire bottle of wine last night," Dylan said.

"You aren't the one having to face Uncle Sakari this morning, either," Suvi said.

"Point taken," Dylan said.

Darius asked, "Is he really that bad?"

"Do you see the man who is now making his way toward the docks? The one dressed in the most expensive purple velvet?" Suvi asked, turning so that her uncle couldn't see her expression. Jami indicated that Sakari had switched tactics and was making up his financial losses through the treasury. It was an obvious move and one she'd expected. However, she'd counted on being home when that happened. She would have to do something to curb it soon.

"The one with the beard and an expression that could best be described as constipated?" Darius asked.

Suvi covered her mouth.

"Ouch!" Darius massaged his ribs and stepped away from Dylan.

"Stop pointing," Dylan said. "Not only is it obvious, it's rude."

"That would be him," Suvi said, now apparently speaking to the sky.

Giving Dylan a reproachful look, Darius said, "By all the oceans, Suvi. How did you manage to limit yourself to just the one bottle?"

"I realized the ship's stock came from Uncle's vineyard," she said. "Well? What did you two decide?" She'd asked Dylan and Darius the night before if they would like to be her guests at the palace. She wanted to introduce them to her father and formalize negotiations with the Waterborne as soon as possible. Her father would be more open to doing so, she'd explained, if he had a positive personal experience with the Waterborne in question.

"Of course, we'll accept," Dylan said. "We've responsibilities at the embassy to take care of first. And Father will want to know we arrived safely. Send a message when you think it's a good time."

The last of her baggage having been loaded on the waiting carriage, Suvi couldn't delay meeting her uncle any longer. "I will." She turned to Captain Hansen. "Father will hear of your bravery. You and the crew will be rewarded the instant I can arrange it. The harbormaster should provide you with everything you need to finish repairs to *Otter*'s foremast."

The trip up the river had forced ever more creative jury-rigging to keep them moving.

"Yes, sir." Hansen saluted.

"Once the repairs are completed, I want you to move to the farthest Chain Lakes side slip," Suvi said, returning the salute. "And be ready to make for Ytlain when I tell you. It may be impossible to leave if you wait too long."

Captain Hansen nodded before turning her attention to her ship and crew. Suvi grabbed a quick hug from Dylan and Dar and then headed down the gangplank. She did her best to hide any trace of a limp. Her uncle stood on the dock, impatiently fiddling with his cane.

"Where's Father?" Suvi asked.

"That's hardly a greeting for your betrothed," Uncle Sakari said.

"I never accepted," Suvi said. "Where's Father?"

"In his rooms," Uncle Sakari said. "Where he's been hiding for more than a month."

She took the footman's hand as she climbed into the carriage. Once she was settled with Piritta at her side, her uncle followed. The carriage door thumping closed seemed to shut off the last of her good spirits like a prison door.

I know. I know, Suvi thought to Piritta. *Don't be so dramatic.*

Piritta turned to her and raised an eyebrow.

Suvi ignored her. "Where is the Acrasian army? Do we know where they will attack next?"

"It's of no consequence," Uncle Sakari said, shooing the subject away with one hand.

"They've invaded our country. I can't think of anything more important."

"I'd beg to differ," Uncle Sakari said. "When exactly am I to expect an answer to my proposal?"

"How can I think of such things when Mother is gone and my brother is fighting for his life?"

"You've acquired rough manners while you've been away."

"I'm not the one who brought up marriage so soon after Mother—"

"Who are you to bring up propriety?" Uncle Sakari asked. "I heard you didn't even go into confinement. And for your own mother."

"I couldn't," Suvi said, hating the blush heating her cheeks. "Not in the middle of a battle."

"You should've left it to someone else, as is proper."

"And if I'd have done that, I wouldn't be here."

"You're terribly sure of yourself for a little girl," Uncle Sakari said.

"If I'm so little, why would you propose to me?" The words were out before Suvi could stop and consider the consequences. He'd gotten to her, and now he knew he had.

Uncle Sakari's eyes widened. "How dare you—"

Furious with her uncle and herself, Suvi stopped listening and directed her glare out the window. She waited until his diatribe had slowed and then decided to grant him the closest thing to an apology she could stomach. "I'm sorry to have upset you." That much was true. "I'm tired from traveling. And I've much correspondence to catch up on. The Waterborne contracts need finalizing, and there's all that must be done for Father. Grant me another week?" *By then, I should be able to convince Father of your real intentions. And when that happens, I'll be able to reject you openly without serious consequences.*

"All right," he said in a begrudging tone. "Next week." He settled back into the padded seat as the carriage began its journey to the palace with a jerk.

Concentrating on the scenery, Suvi avoided further attempts at conversation. In combination with the coach's loud rattling, it served as a sufficient shield. Now that they were away from the crowded wharf, she was shocked by the sight of empty streets and burned houses. Finally, she couldn't stand not knowing any longer. "What happened?" Whether out of revenge or a real inability to hear her, she had to shout in order to get a response from her uncle.

"Another wave of variola struck while you were away," her uncle said as if it were of little importance. "This is why your father barricaded himself in his apartments." The ghost of a smug smile haunted his lips.

Let him think what he will about my sources. But the truth was, she hadn't known. Jami hadn't informed her. Suvi considered why that may have been. Her korva had been especially distant since the confrontation at Mehrinna. *Is it because she doesn't approve of what I did? Or is it because I angered her?*

The carriage was met by Valterri, the butler, and two others. *So few.* Suvi tried not to display her shock. She greeted the staff as was proper and then headed for her father's apartments. It was hard not to expect to see her mother as she turned each corner.

Her uncle trailed behind. "He won't see you."

"I don't care."

He grabbed her arm just above the elbow and brought her up short.

"You're hurting me," Suvi said. "Let go at once."

"He won't see you because he's terrified."

"I know what he's afraid of," Suvi said. "I've not gotten sick any more than he has."

"He is sick."

That accomplished the one thing that her uncle's grip hadn't. Suvi stopped and asked, "What? When?"

"It isn't variola."

Cold relief washed over her. *Thank the Mother.* "What is it, then?"

"I've no idea. He won't let me in to see him."

"What about Saara? Why hasn't she taken care of him?"

"Saara died of variola, as did the guard we sent with her to confine that granddaughter of hers."

"Ilta? Is Ilta all right?"

"What difference does it make? She exposed the queen to the disease that killed her. The little bitch deserves whatever she gets."

Suvi whirled, resuming her journey to her father's rooms.

"Why bother seeing him? He's incapable, and he knows it. It is up to you and I to save the kingdom."

You dare insult Father? Suvi's hands tightened into fists, and she whispered, "I couldn't disagree more."

"What do you mean?"

Spinning once again to face her uncle, she took a deep breath and then released it. *Get control of yourself. Now.* If there was a time Suvi was happy of Piritta's hovering, it was now. "Do not speak of Father that way. I won't have it. It is up to my father and myself. You aren't a factor. You are not the king."

"I'm his chancellor!"

"I don't give a shit!" She sprinted to her father's door and began knocking. *Oh, Mother, I've lost my temper with him twice in one day. That's going to take weeks to recover from. After I've been so careful.* It'd felt good nonetheless. "Father? It's me, Suvi! I'm here! Father?"

"Go away!" Her father sounded terrible.

"I'm staying right here until you let me in, Papa," Suvi said. "Please!"

She heard him cough. "I don't feel well. Go away!"

"I'm worried about you. Please let me in, Papa. Have you seen a healer?"

Another round of hacking coughs.

"Papa, please. You're scaring me."

"Are you alone?"

"Uncle is here. But I promise not to let him in." Her uncle started to protest, but Suvi cut him off with command magic–laced words. She punched him with everything she had. "He is aware of how much you value your privacy. He will remain outside. He will also shut up. Now." It meant breaking every personal rule she had in regard to her uncle. It meant revealing the extent of her powers, but there came a time when pretense was no longer useful. She'd already revealed her contempt. It was time to demonstrate what power backed up that contempt.

Shock registered on her uncle's face. His mouth opened and closed. Triumph straightened her spine, and she stretched to her full height. She'd finally let him see her for who she really was. A click signaled the unlocking of the door. She pushed it open and relocked it behind her without looking back. Piritta remained in the hallway.

Facing her father at last, she saw he was a ruin of his former self. He hadn't bathed, shaved, or combed his hair in some time. His clothes were wrinkled, and he'd lost a great deal of weight. She went to him at once and hugged him. "Oh, Papa."

"I didn't know how much I needed her until she was gone."

She held him while he sobbed, and for a time, she joined him in his grief. When she had a moment to think, she discovered she wasn't only grieving for her mother. Home wasn't home. Her mother was gone, and her father wasn't even her father anymore. It was obvious she no longer had the luxury of being a child even with her parents— *Parent. Mother is dead.* She sobbed for her mother. She cried for her childhood. She grieved for her world that had fallen apart. *Is this what it means to grow up?*

When it seemed they'd both cried all the tears they could, she released her father and stepped back. "Have you eaten?"

He looked away and shook his head. It wasn't the action of a forceful leader.

The shift in power was disorienting. "We'll see to that first." She searched for the ubiquitous servant but found no one. There wasn't even a guard to provide security.

"I sent them all away," her father said. "It seemed safer."

"Is there anyone in the kitchens?"

Her father gave her a blank look. Now that she was really seeing him, he seemed older, grayer. The events of the past summer had aged him more than the past ten years. Worse, he seemed distracted.

"Papa? Did you hear my question?"

"I sent them all away."

She rang for someone. It took three tries. She'd have gone to the kitchens herself, but she was afraid to leave her father alone lest her uncle get inside the room. At last, she got a response. The emblem on the short, older woman's apron revealed her rank. The royal cook had answered the call herself. Like Suvi's father, she appeared to be in a state of shock.

Suvi asked, "What is your name?"

"Ide Sulin."

"Ide, where are the others?" Suvi used command magic to keep her voice calm and soothing. She knew the answer, but she had to hear it from someone other than her uncle. She didn't want to frighten Ide. Suvi was frightened enough for everyone.

Ide's face crumpled. "Dead. They're all dead. Some of them ran. Much good as it did them."

"But you're here."

"It's my duty." Ide straightened. "Who would feed the king if I left?"

"Thank you," Suvi said. "Thank you so much for staying. You're very brave. It must have been awful. I can't even imagine what it must have been like."

Sniffing, Ide looked down at her hands. They twisted around one another.

"Everything will be all right," Suvi said, not believing it for one moment. "When was the last time my father ate?"

"I took up some food this afternoon. But he wouldn't open the door," Ide said. "I'm so sorry. I did try to make him eat, but—"

"It's all right," Suvi said. "Could you bring up something now? Anything will be fine, even cold meats and crispbread. Whatever you have prepared. Anything at all. Then I'd like for you to get some rest."

"What about you, Your Grace?"

"I can take care of myself," Suvi said.

It took some effort to get her father to eat, but he finally did, and with that, he began to come back to himself. The dark circles under his eyes remained, and the cough didn't get any better. However, Suvi was heartened by even limited progress. An hour later, she left her father to rest in his bedchamber and met with his advisors in the attached private parlor. Of the lot, two were still alive. It became rapidly obvious that not even her uncle had been tending to the basic needs of the country. Luckily, there were those who, like the cook, Ide, had opted to continue with their work regardless. Suvi attempted not to consider what she'd have come home to if they hadn't. She certainly didn't point this out to any of those upon whom she depended.

Civilization is such a fragile thing. She hadn't understood how fragile until then.

She spent the next few days working to pull the ragged ends of the kingdom together, talking to advisors about the status of food supplies, medicine, and war refugees. Her only army commander, a brigadier general named Näränen, gave her what information he had on the surviving remnants of the Eledorean army—primarily that they would use the winter to gather strength in Herraskariano. Admirals discussed the impending Acrasian blockade on Jalokivi and the necessary preparations. She heard Mehrinna had fallen into Acrasian hands shortly after *Otter* had passed through the second river lock. *Indomitable* had sacrificed herself to delay the city's capture long enough for a few to flee. Dylan's windstorm had exacted a high toll on the Acrasian navy. It'd been enough that *Indomitable's* last moments had been effective, but that had been all. *Arabella* had wisely chosen to leave while she could.

Slowly, Suvi got a picture of what she had to work with. She came to realize the seriousness of the situation and that there would be a famine in the spring—provided she couldn't make arrangements with Ytlain or another nation before then. She began to doubt whether Eledore would ever be the same. And yet, she couldn't bring herself to give up. She negotiated assistance from Ytlain, their closest neighbor across the lakes, limiting the tone of her letters to reflect the situation as only a temporary setback. While the Ytlainen weren't willing to commit to a war with the Acrasians themselves, they would be willing to send supplies and other assistance.

Suvi grew confident that she could find a way to make everything work.

Her uncle, for his part, had ceased to pressure her and had apparently given up entirely on the concept of a royal partnership. She shut him out at every opportunity, blaming him for not taking care of the kingdom and her father. She knew she'd won too easily—it wasn't like her uncle to give ground so rapidly, even if she had surprised him. Down deep, she understood that she'd only won the first battle. There was more to come, but she had more than enough to do in the meantime. Based upon the reports from the charity hospital, the new strain of variola was beyond the healers' ability to fight. Either patients died or they didn't contract it at all. Suvi attempted to consult Ilta, sending multiple messenger birds. However, the Silmaillia was nowhere to be found.

"Is she gone?" Suvi asked.

"I've heard rumors that she left Merta for Jalokivi some time ago," Jami said. "But that's all I have. There is nothing new from the front, either."

"Nothing I'm privy to, anyway," Suvi said, dropping a message from the royal harbormaster on top of the stack of letters that required more attention. "Were you able to see General Näränen?"

A sly expression oozed across Jami's scarred face. "I don't think he was happy about it."

Suvi paused. Näränen didn't trust her, not that she could blame him. "What did you do? Exactly?"

"I may have demonstrated that his security detail is lacking."

"You didn't."

"I did."

"I need him to cooperate," Suvi said. "Giving him a fright isn't going to make that easier."

"However, a healthy sense of mortality may mean he'll survive long enough for you to accomplish something together," Jami whispered. "You asked for my trust. I ask for yours. Your uncle isn't idle, you know."

"All right," Suvi said. "What did he say?"

"He accepted your invitation."

"Good," Suvi said. *Hold on. She looks far too self-satisfied.* "You didn't convince him that rejecting the invitation would be an unhealthy idea, did you?"

"I was polite and friendly. I wore a dress," Jami said. "I even smiled."

TWO

Brigadier General Näränen arrived at half past eight. Suvi had him directed to the palace gardens where her father was waiting. Näränen would expect to be seen outside the palace. He was a soldier, after all. The gardens would put him at ease. Suvi's intent was to get her father more involved. It gave him something constructive to focus upon. It also helped integrate them both into the power structure without her uncle. She decided to be late in order to reinforce her father's position as the seat of power—at least, that was the impression Näränen would get. Having never met him, she had to rely on Jami's judgment of Näränen and not her own. It wasn't her preferred method of operation, but she had to start somewhere. With this firmly in mind, she set off for the garden at a quarter to nine. When she and Piritta approached, the king's laughter carried into the hall on a cold breeze through the open doors. Suvi pulled her shawl tighter about her.

Maybe the garden wasn't the best idea, she thought. However, they ran less risk of being spied upon unobserved while meeting in the open.

"I'm relieved to hear you agree, Your Highness," Näränen said in his gravelly voice. The amusement in his tone was apparent.

Her father laughed all the louder.

Good, Suvi thought. *Jami said Näränen was an excellent leader and personable, too.* She entered the garden. Her father and Näränen were seated at a table set with a late evening meal for three. She'd asked Ide to prepare two bottles of her father's favorite wine. It was for a good cause. "I'm glad to see you've started without me."

Piritta drifted to a place next to Valterri a few paces away.

Näränen got up from his seat. "Good evening, Your Grace." He was tall with thick graying hair tied into a neat queue, sideburns, moustache, and a strong chin. His eyes were dark and shone with friendly intelligence.

"Good evening," Suvi said, settling into the empty chair. "Is there enough wine?"

"We've finished the first bottle, I'm afraid," her father said.

Suvi turned to Valterri and signaled for him to bring another. "Then we shouldn't stop there."

Her father nodded. "We'll need it to talk about the war, I'm afraid."

Näränen's friendly face grew serious. "Are you certain you wish to discuss it?"

"Of course," her father said. "I've been a fool. The time for foolishness is long past. Tell me. Everything."

Suvi looked away in an attempt to hide her approval. Näränen hadn't spoken for long when Uncle Sakari barged in with his korva tagging him.

"What is the meaning of this?" Sakari asked.

Biting her lip, Suvi waited for her father to speak first. She watched him turn to Sakari. A series of emotions passed over her father's face. Most were unreadable except the last.

"What did you say, Kar?" her father asked.

Sakari paused. "I—I wasn't aware that General Näränen was here. He shouldn't have disturbed you. You've been unwell."

"Dear Uncle," Suvi said, adding an edge of power to her words. It wasn't enough to force action on anyone's part, but it was enough to ensure she wouldn't be ignored. "I don't think that Father is as helpless as you'd like him to believe."

"Is that what you think?" her father asked, frowning. "That I'm weak?"

"Not at all," Sakari said, blinking. "Only that someone in your condition—"

Her father sat up taller in the chair. "And what is my condition? Do you care to explain?"

Suvi kept her face as blank as she could manage. *Is he really going to do it? Is he really going to stand up to Uncle Sakari?* She'd been waiting for this moment for what seemed her whole life.

"I don't know what young Suvi has been telling you—"

Mistake, Suvi thought.

"Are you implying that I can be manipulated by a nineteen-year-old girl?" her father asked.

Go on, Uncle, Suvi thought. *Embarrass him in front of a* soldier.

"I didn't say that." Sakari held up his hands and bent at the waist. "I apologize. I misjudged—"

"You most certainly did," her father said. "What makes you think you can interrupt a private consultation like this?"

Sakari held his head down, but Suvi could see his jaw tighten. "I presumed—"

"You presumed too much," her father said. "Leave us at once."

"But you need me—"

"Kar, I said leave!"

Suvi started as her father smashed a fist down on the table hard enough to rattle the porcelain.

Näränen kept his gaze firmly on the ground. However, she spotted the slow smile creeping across his face. Sakari bowed even lower, his hands forming tight fists. Suvi didn't need Piritta to tell her what he was feeling.

"Yes, Highness," Sakari said. His voice sounded as if he were choking on something he didn't like. He stepped backward ten paces and then fled.

Suvi wanted to cheer.

Her father turned to Näränen. "Now, then. What were you saying?"

The rest of the audience went smoothly. Her father seemed to be in good spirits throughout. She escorted Näränen to his horse afterward and tried not to show how happy she was. She mentally planned a little victory party with Piritta and Jami as she went. Suvi had reached the front step on her way back to her rooms when she heard her uncle's voice in the courtyard.

"You embarrassed me in front of the king, Näränen," Sakari said, stepping from the shadows. He appeared to make a cursory check for witnesses.

She hid from him in the doorway.

Sakari said, "I absolutely will not tolerate that. Not from the likes of you." He grabbed Näränen's horse by the ear and whispered into it. "General!"

The gelding jerked his head away and reared. Unbalanced, Näränen lost his seat and slammed to the ground in a heap. He didn't move or roll away. He merely lay there gasping for air. The horse, standing on its hind legs, then dropped both front hooves on Näränen's chest and head. Suvi turned away and screamed before she saw the blood.

The sound of his skull being crushed would haunt her for the rest of her life.

⊰ NELS ⊱

ONE

"What in all the hells happened while we were away?" Overlieutenant Sebastian Moller asked, keeping his horse just ahead of Nels's own. Moller, older than either Nels or Viktor, had lost his platoon and therefore had assumed the role of Nels's bodyguard. Nels had hated the idea. So, naturally, Viktor had insisted.

Fighting to keep from showing his growing concern, Nels didn't reply. He couldn't answer the question, anyway. *Father must be all right. I'd have heard something if he wasn't. What about Suvi? Why was she gone so long?* News that the crown princess had returned had swept the countryside. Rumor was short on details, but she'd been attacked and the frigate *Indomitable* sunk.

Is Ilta safe?

Jalokivi was not the robust city he'd left via a parade and cheering hordes mere months before. That city had died and a specter had taken its place. Aside from the overwhelmed harbor areas, the streets were empty. It was market day and not a single merchant stall was open for business. Obviously, there'd been a series of fires and riots. He'd spotted the charred timbers from Palace Road. The reek of decay haunted the mundane city-stench of muck, smoke, and soot. With the army gone, the City Guards should've made up for the lack and buried the dead. Yet they hadn't.

This is the third time we've had to wait for someone to let us through, Nels thought. *Where in the hells are the City Guards?*

Of course, he'd known it would be necessary to send troops to man the walls. He'd planned for that at the start, understanding full well that Uncle Sakari in his arrogance wouldn't have thought to keep much of a force in reserve. At least, Nels hoped so. It would make his life easier. He wasn't about to trust anyone under his uncle's influence with the safety of his father and sister. *Not now. Not when it would be too simple to blame disease or accident.* Once again, he struggled with an urge to hurry. They'd all spied the purple banners flying at Eastgate. Nels told himself that they couldn't possibly be for anyone new. The troops were exhausted and every bit as anxious as Nels was for loved ones. What made his unease worse was that no one had come from the palace to greet them, not so far. Granted, the king never before made an appearance when Nels returned from a campaign. That wasn't unusual.

Where's Suvi? Images of those purple banners fluttering in the breeze sent another surge of icy panic through his veins. He sat up straighter in the saddle and curled his left hand into a fist, clamping down on his fear lest the troops see.

Viktor asked, "Permission to find out what is going on, sir?"

"Let the palace know we're here while you're about it," Nels said.

"Yes, sir." Viktor spurred his horse and was gone.

"Overlieutenant Larsson, get the others to their barracks houses. They'll need some rest." Nels hoped the Narrows had escaped damage, at least. If not, it was going to be interesting finding an appropriate place to bunk. Although, he supposed enough of the city was empty that there would be few to complain wherever they decided to sleep. "Report to me once they're settled. First watch goes to those without families. Got it? I'll be at the palace for an hour. After that, you can reach me at my barracks house." *I should check on Mrs. Nimonen, too.*

"Yes, sir."

Nels urged Loimuta toward the palace, dreading what else he'd discover. Loimuta didn't like the sick smell of Jalokivi any more than he did. The horse vented his own nervousness in small acts of rebellion. Nels patted the gelding on the neck in reassurance but remained wary of Loimuta's tricks until he'd relaxed into an uneasy trot. Moller caught up after a couple hundred feet, and together they reached the palace gates, riding side by side. The sound of iron horseshoes on cobblestone echoed in empty streets. To Nels's relief, both portcullises were raised at the palace gates, and the walls were being patrolled by an appropriate number of Royal Guardsmen. However, the courtyard itself was empty with the exception of the small group waiting at the palace steps. He spied Viktor whispering with Suvi's korva, Jami. With Suvi and Piritta was old Valterri, the royal butler, and someone who Nels was certain was the royal cook. He only knew her because she used to visit with Mrs. Nimonen once a week. It took him a moment to remember her name.

Ide. That's it.

No stablehand arrived to take the horses away. Nels barely had time enough to dismount before Suvi grabbed him in a fierce hug.

"You're alive," she said, burying her face in his filthy uniform coat.

He inwardly winced, thinking of what he must smell like. Returning the hug, he was glad he'd at least had time to take care of all the necessary cleansing rituals the night before. "I am. What's happened? Has Ilta gotten here yet?"

"She's here." Suvi spoke into his shoulder. "Oh, Nels . . . I'm so sorry. Mother is—is . . . gone."

Hearing the news from his sister hit him like a mule kick. "I know. Father wrote."

Hugging him tighter, Suvi said, "Good. I'm glad of that."

"Primarily to inform me that my accounts would be closed."

She released him. "You're joking."

"I wish I were."

"I'll take care of it."

"Don't worry about it," Nels said. "It's not as if any of us have been paid in—"

"Come inside," Suvi said. "We can't talk about this here."

In public. How could I forget? His cheeks burned. "I must report to General Näränen. Tell Father I was here. Or not. It doesn't matter." He turned to Loimuta and prepared to leave. "I'm glad you're safe."

"You can't see Näränen," Suvi said.

"I've a duty to—"

"He's . . ." She lowered her gaze and whispered, "He's . . . dead."

"Then whomever is next in the chain of command."

Suvi shook her head. Guilt hung over her features like a veil. "It was Uncle Sakari. I didn't act fast enough." She looked away. "At least he's been banished. Father finally saw reason."

"That can't be." Nels put out a hand to Loimuta's side for support. "There's no one left?" He felt lost. *I can't be in charge of the entire Eledorean army. I'm only nineteen! I'm a captain! A captain isn't supposed to be in charge!*

"I'm afraid it's true. All of it," Suvi said. "Please come inside. Please."

"And Father?"

"He's in his apartments, resting," Suvi said. "I thought it best."

"He's sick?"

Suvi sighed. "He's not himself. Although he's recovering, I think."

Moller spoke to Overlieutenant Hollen. Then Hollen took Moller's reins, gripped Loimuta's halter, and led both animals away. Loimuta went peacefully enough.

Suvi wrinkled her nose. "You stink."

"I came straight here. I was worried. There wasn't time to—"

"Never mind that," she said, tugging him through the front door. "You're here. That's all that counts." She spoke to Ide. "Can Jenna have a bath ready for my brother? Do we have someone to take care of airing rooms for his guests?"

"Jenna will be happy to do so. I think I can get some help with the rest," Ide said. Then she addressed him. "It's good to have you home again, Your Grace." Then she dashed off to take care of the details.

"You can't let us stay here," Nels said.

"I think I can," Suvi said. "Your old rooms have already been prepared. I thought it'd be easier that way. You won't get lost. Come on. All of you."

Viktor and the others followed. The clanking of military equipment and thump of boots echoed off the flagstones in the main hall. Aside from the missing servants, the dust, and other minor signs of neglect, the palace was the same it'd always been. Nels was welcomed by the familiar scents of burning beeswax and cut flowers.

Valterri shut the doors.

TWO

"I think I've died and gone to the Lands of the Blessed," Nels said, reveling in the warm bath for a moment longer. Once clean, the water was now filthy. He purposely didn't look at what floated on the surface.

On the other side of the room Jenna paused, an upset expression on her face. She was a solemn, skinny girl of seventeen with red hair and freckles sprinkled across her nose and cheeks.

Watch your language, Nels thought. *You've offended the very last maid in the entire palace.* "Ah, thank you, Jenna. For heating the bath."

Jenna nodded. "There's—there are fresh clothes laid out for you, Your Grace." She resumed tucking the bedclothes under the edge of the bedstead.

His wounds had stung like mad when he'd first gotten into the water. The cut across his abdomen looked angry and red. Upon seeing it, Viktor had threatened to send for Westola, but Nels told him it could wait one more night. Westola needed the rest. They all did.

"Will you be requiring anything else?" Jenna asked.

"No. Thank you," Nels said. He kept expecting to see people who were probably dead—his former nurse, his valet, the house-keeper, all the maids who used to stand waiting in the hallways with downcast eyes as he passed. People whose presence he'd been trained not to notice. Now that they were truly gone, it was impossible to ignore their absence. The palace was different. *Empty*. It was downright disconcerting. *Mother is dead*. Except for the initial reaction long before Gardemeister, he'd lodged the information in a compartment within his skull that he couldn't access. Strangely, her death hadn't seemed real until this moment. He wanted to mourn her but found he couldn't. It was as if those feelings were buried too deep. *You're not alone, anyway. You're in the palace. You're always watched in this place.* He didn't have a shield. *Not like Suvi.* Of course, he had better control than she did. Always had. Still, he couldn't count on the contents of his head being his own. *Not here.*

"I'm sorry there's no one to help you dress for supper, Your Grace."

"I've learned quite a bit since I left. I'm sure Lieutenant Reini will be more than happy to assist if I have difficulty remembering how to fasten a button."

"Bugger that," Viktor said from his chair by the fire. "Do it yourself or go naked."

"Dinner will be casual," Nels said. "Suvi won't mind."

Viktor snorted. "But what will the king say?"

"Ah, well," Nels said. "I suppose I can always send for the royal gardener for help."

Jenna coughed.

He's dead, Nels thought. *You idiot! Shit!*

Confusion etched worry lines between her brows and around her eyes. "Your—Your Grace? I'm sorry. The gardener—"

"I apologize," Nels said. "Please don't pay any attention to me."

"Yes, Your Grace." And with that, she rushed out the door.

Mentally cursing himself again, Nels climbed out of the bath and dried off.

Viktor assisted with the fresh bandage but waited until Nels was mostly dressed before saying anything else. "I understand your need to make light of the impossible, but that was going a bit far, even for you."

"I hate this place. I hate what it makes me into." It wasn't only that, Nels knew, but he couldn't bring himself to put his real feelings into words. His mother was dead. His father was apparently in some sort of mental state. His sister was running the country with two council members and a butler. He was in charge of an army that consisted of five hundred and twenty-three soldiers, four cannon, and whatever armaments were fixed to the outer walls of Jalokivi. Most of the city was dead of variola, and the Acrasians were on their way with more troops, ships, and cannon than he'd probably ever seen in his life.

And everyone will expect me *to do something about it.*

"You're terrified," Viktor said. "I am too."

"That's not it at all."

"Sure it is." Viktor gazed into the fire. "I don't have to be a shield to know what you're feeling. Your eyes keep changing from gray to white."

"Shit," Nels said. "I'm sorry."

"Don't worry about it. Jenna doesn't know any better. And I'm the only one in the company who notices such things." Gloom penetrated Viktor's humor, and for a moment, Nels saw just how young Viktor really was.

He's only nineteen. Like me. It stunned Nels to remember that three birthdays had come and gone since he'd left home. *I'll make a mess of this. I make a mess of everything I touch.*

The Acrasians will be here soon. What am I going to do? Throw rocks and sticks at them? We can't even resort to harsh language! No one speaks Acrasian but me!

Viktor continued. "Until now, all of us could pretend nothing mattered—the war, the plague. We could imagine that everything was going to be normal again once we got home. Well, it isn't." He'd scavenged a bottle of whiskey from somewhere. He uncorked it and took a huge swallow from it. "Nothing is the same. And it never will be."

"Give me some of that," Nels said, reaching for the bottle. "I've a bad feeling I'm going to need it tonight."

Viktor didn't move from his perch but stretched out his arm to bridge the gap. "I won't be required to attend dinner, will I?"

Nels crossed the room to retrieve the whiskey. He drank from the bottle and handed it back. "Not unless you want to. Why?"

"I'd—I wish to check on my family. If you're settled."

Oh, Hasta. What's the matter with me? "Go. We'll discuss it tomorrow. I need to meet with Suvi first." *And Father.* "Then I have to think before any decisions are made. We have some time yet."

Viktor stood. "Should I leave the bottle?"

"I can get more. Take it," Nels said. "Go."

"One more thing," Viktor said, snatching a folded letter from the mantel. "I don't think anyone noticed this but me."

Nels accepted it and recognized Ilta's handwriting on the outside. "Thanks." He broke the wax seal and began to read.

My dearest love,

I took the liberty of sending Mrs. N home. I'll be the only guest at your bunkhouse tonight. I hope you don't mind my staying. The Commons Hospital simply isn't an option.

You should stay at the palace for a few days. We both

have work to do, and you need time with your father and sister. I know you're disappointed. I am too, but these talks you will have . . . they're important. Remember you don't have to forgive your father, but for Eledore's sake you do have to listen. Your sister needs you. She can't do what she needs to do without you. Try to see your experiences over the past few years in a positive light. There's an advantage in approaching problems as you do.

I love you. And I'll see you soon.

Ilta

Nels thought, *Advantage? What is she talking about?*

Viktor threw open the door, stopped, and stepped aside. "Good evening, Your Grace."

"Good evening," Suvi said, entering the room.

She was wearing a formal green velvet gown with a purple ribbon stitched onto one sleeve. Spotting that splash of purple, Nels realized he didn't possess any mourning colors. He certainly wasn't wearing any. In fact, were it not for the clean pair of uniform trousers Jenna had somehow scavenged, he wouldn't have been wearing soldier's black, either.

Nels found himself checking for Piritta, but she was nowhere in sight. He folded Ilta's letter and hid it in his pocket. "Am I late for dinner already?"

"We have about an hour," Suvi said. "This came for you." She handed him a sealed message.

Viktor gave him a questioning look.

"Are you still here?" Nels motioned for Viktor to leave and then opened the note. It was from Overlieutenant Larsson, informing him that the Narrows had escaped most of the damage, and that the troops were bunked down for the night. She'd added a note that Mrs. Nimonen would have his barracks house ready for him along with a cold supper. *She's alive. Thank Hasta.*

"What is that about?" Suvi asked.

Nels didn't look up from the report. "You're going to tell me you don't already know?"

"We need to talk."

"I know."

"Before dinner." She paused.

"Do we talk here, in the maze, or will this require the lake?" His uniform jacket was gone. He assumed Jenna had thrown it in the scrap bin or, more likely, burned it. Laid out in its place on the bedstead was an old jacket of his father's. Ramming his arms into it, he discovered it was too big across the middle and the sleeves were too short. *Perfect.* He felt ridiculous. He decided to show up for dinner in shirtsleeves. *Mother isn't here to care, anyway.* "I warn you. This is the only pair of clean uniform trousers I have left. And I've no idea where Jenna found them. So, if you're planning on attempting to drown me, let me change back into my own first."

"This is serious."

"I am being serious."

"Sure you are." She folded her arms across her chest. "Get your boots on. Let's go."

He did as she directed, grabbed the jacket in case he'd have need of it, and then followed her into their father's wing of the palace. Suvi stopped just short of the king's rooms and took a right turn. Not far from there, Piritta stood waiting by a polished black walnut door. Glancing over her shoulder, Suvi placed a finger to her lips. He shrugged in answer. Suvi produced a key, turned the lock, and waited until he entered. Piritta gave him a wave good-bye before shutting the door behind him.

The room's paneling was painted a light gray, and the floor-to-ceiling velvet curtains were deep blue. Books crowded the walls and a large wooden desk was positioned in the center of the room. Once untidy and half-buried in papers, it was now pristine. The rest of the room was furnished with a few padded chairs and end tables. All had been stripped of personal possessions. The only remaining evidence of their previous owner was a lingering scent of pipe smoke and amber cologne.

"This is Uncle Sakari's study," Nels said.

Suvi grinned. "Can you think of a better place to meet?"

"Why isn't Piritta here?"

Suvi shrugged. "She makes you uncomfortable—"

"She doesn't—"

"It's not like she doesn't know. She's a shield, Nels. Anyway, I wanted to talk to you alone," Suvi said. Her grin faded to a faint smile. "And the likelihood of anyone attempting to overhear us in this place is low."

"What in all the hells has been going on here?" He dropped the jacket over the back of an overstuffed chair.

"Sit," she said. "This is going to take a while." And then she began to explain.

With a shudder, Nels soon discovered his twin sister had changed a great deal in the past year.

THREE

A quarter of an hour late for dinner, Nels and Suvi still reached the dining room before their father did. Nels felt even more exhausted than before and yet knew there was no possibility of sleep. *Not tonight. Not after everything Suvi said.* To make matters worse, his emotions were a tangled knot in the hindmost part of his brain. He needed time alone to sort out the frayed ends but knew that was impossible.

Piritta entered the dining room and completed a circuit around the table before Suvi assumed her place.

Especially not in the palace, he repeated to himself. *Not even under these circumstances.*

When he was small, he liked to hide in the deepest, most forgotten cupboards. His nurse fetched him from them time and again, and time and again, she'd asked why he was so determined to cover himself in dust, dirt, and cobwebs. He had never answered her questions. At age three, it was too difficult to verbalize complicated feelings, but he'd always known why. Which in itself was odd when he thought about it. It was ironic that his eyes persistently gave

him away to those who knew him best, yet his twin had the opposite problem.

Suvi sat at the far end of the table, leaving him the seat directly
across from her. It was then that he registered the porcelain had
been laid out for three, not four. Again, he felt as if someone had
gut punched him. All his wadded-up emotions threatened to pour
down his cheeks. *Mother, I'm so sorry I wasn't here. I'm so sorry I never
thanked you for all you did for me. I'm sorry I didn't tell you I loved
you one last time.* His throat closed. A painful lump formed that
he couldn't swallow. Blinking, he again forced his grief from the
surface where it'd be too easily accessed.

Memories of his father's voice surfaced. *Get control of yourself
at once, boy! Don't you cry!*

All three place settings were positioned close, near the head of
the table where his father had always sat.

*The easier for him to lecture me on my many shortcomings, I sup-
pose.* Nels cleared his throat. The pain lodged there budged enough
for him to croak, "After dinner, I'll go back to my quarters in the
Narrows." He couldn't do this. He couldn't stay. No matter what
Ilta thought, there was nothing left in the palace for him. Suvi was
capable of handling things.

"Don't be ridiculous," Suvi said. "Why not?"

"You damned well know why."

"After everything that's happened. After everyone who has"—
she hesitated and then lowered her voice—"died here. Your sleeping in the palace one night isn't going to contaminate the building,"
she said. "At least, no more than it already has been."

He opened his mouth to argue when he heard the black
walnut pocket doors behind him slide open. Taking a cue from
Suvi, he got to his feet and nearly gasped out loud when his father
walked past.

That isn't Father. It can't be.

The change in the king was dramatic. He'd aged twenty years since Nels had seen him last. *Was it really only a year ago?* The king's hair was heavily streaked with gray, and his square shoulders were rounded as if in defeat. The wrinkles in his forehead were drawn deeper, and the skin around his jawline sagged. His eyelids, upper and lower, were puffy as if he hadn't slept in a very long time. He appeared to have shrunk as well. His finery hung off of him in baggy folds.

The king's worn face finally registered Nels's presence. Nels prepared himself for the sharp comment. Instead, he was gratified by a rapid flicker of shock white in his father's eyes.

Suvi resumed her place after their father sat, and replaced her napkin in her lap. "Good evening, Papa. How are you feeling this evening?"

The tone was so like his mother's that Nels blinked. He found he couldn't release the breath he was holding. He dreaded what was to come. His father hadn't spoken to him directly since that day in the chapter house. *Defect. You are not my son.* The hot knot in Nels's throat seeped into his skull, and his eyes stung. *Stop this,* he thought. *Can't you see he isn't worth it?* Nels didn't understand why he was so angry and disappointed—why he felt cheated. The towering figure who had made his childhood a misery had been reduced to a weak old man. There would be no honor in attacking him or facing him down. There was nothing left to fight. Rage flooded Nels's chest and set his teeth against each other. He didn't think he could tolerate staying in the room for an instant longer. His muscles bunched, making ready to flee.

No! I will not run from him. I won't. Not again. Not ever again. Then Nels closed his eyes and bit down on his emotions until the moment passed. All this in the time it took for his father to settle into the ornately carved dining room chair with a prim napkin in his lap.

"I'm well enough," the king said. Even his voice had aged.

"Nels is here, Papa," Suvi said.

"I'm not blind," the king said, his tone neutral. "I'm not feeble, either."

Nels swallowed a retort. It killed his appetite at once.

"Yes, Papa. I know," she said. "I only wanted to—"

The king turned from her and faced him. "You're alive." The king's eyes captured his. No anger or dismissal lurked there—no relief either. His expression, once tired, was now carefully blank, and his eyes were a formidable black.

Searching again for a giant there, Nels found only a phantom. Without the challenge, he wasn't sure how to react. "I am."

His father paused and then asked, "How long do you plan to stay?"

Not certain how much Suvi had told their father, Nels settled on a less personal answer. "The army will winter in Jalokivi." It suddenly occurred to him that he wasn't asking permission. He'd never dared such a thing in his life. *There! How will you react to that, old man?*

Valterri, the butler, lifted the silver cover from the main dish. The scent of roasted meat wafted from the tray.

Nels's mouth watered, and his stomach let out a loud rumble. *How long has it been since I've had a real meal?* Still, the emotions nesting in his gut blunted his appetite.

"Of course, the army should remain," his father said. "You are right in planning to do so."

Nels blinked.

"The fortifications should be sound." His father waited while Valterri laid a meager portion of roasted elk on his plate. "Suvi and I conducted an inspection in preparation for your arrival."

Valterri continued on to Suvi. Dishes and silver chimed as more food was served.

"She tells me there should be sufficient cannon and ammunition to protect the walls from attack until the first snow," his father said.

Any hope of a reply evaporated in Nels's throat. *He's given ground? Twice? Why?* The father he'd left behind was not interested in fortifications or ammunition. Silence stretched across the room like a rope drawn over a canyon. Vigilant for a fresh slight, Nels waited for the signal that the old war between them would resume.

When Suvi was done serving herself, she glanced up at Nels and mouthed, *Well? Go on. Talk to him. Now.*

"I have yet to perform a complete inspection myself, sir," Nels said. Upon hearing his own voice, he understood his words sounded too much like a reproach. "I-it would be helpful to see them first-hand. To know exactly what I have to work with." He felt more awkward than he had in a long time. "No doubt the cannon Suvi commandeered from the navy will make a defense much easier." He spoke to Suvi, since she had taken charge of the navy and its assets. "I hope you didn't confiscate all the navy's guns. They must defend our access to the western Sininen River and—"

Suvi said, "Defend? The majority of our navy consists of merchant vessels. They're not designed for war. Most only have one or two swivel cannon intended to frighten off thieves or wild animals."

"Besides the *Otter*, we have three warships available," the king said.

"Then the warships we do have should be prepared to hold the western docks at all costs. As for the rest . . . those that can't withstand a battle should be prepared for an evacuation. The lakes will be our only retreat should the worst happen." *Who am I fooling? They both know I don't know what I'm doing*, Nels thought. *Your Highness, your army is now in the hands of an incompetent defect. Go on. Say it. Tell me I'm nothing. I know you want to.*

"What about the eastern docks? Shouldn't we stop the Acrasians there?" Suvi asked.

"I'm certain we don't have enough ships to defend both adequately," Nels said. "I'll need to inspect the eastern docks . . ." He shrugged. He didn't wish to argue with Suvi in front of their father.

Valterri appeared at Nels's side and offered him the roasted elk. Nels nodded as Valterri selected a few cuts and replaced the serving fork. Valterri then went to the buffet table, covered the meat, and prepared to make the rounds with the sauce, onions, and carrots. The fragrance of good food filled Nels's nostrils as each dish was served. The scent was almost powerful enough to distract him from the conversation's unspoken landscape.

"Very well. You two should discuss the defenses in detail once your personal inspection is complete. We can address the situation together afterward," his father said. "I should ask this now. You have a better knowledge of the condition of the army. Do you think you have enough troops to defend the walls?"

You can do this, Nels thought. *Pretend you're talking to an officer. It's no different than reporting to Colonel Pesola.* The muscles in his shoulders cramped. His throat felt too tight. He coughed and then took a sip of wine. "We may be short due to a more urgent concern. There are"—*Don't say "dead bodies rotting in the city" even if there are. You're at the dinner table*—"neighborhoods requiring immediate . . . cleansing. To—to prevent further spread of disease." He remembered the empty streets. *How many civilians are left? In the rush of everything Suvi had to say, I forgot to ask.* He blinked back shame. "We won't last a siege without making that a priority."

"It seems the City Guard have been unable to keep up with the problem, sadly. Recruit whomever you can from the City Guard.

The prisons may have a few inmates remaining," his father said, cutting into the meat on his plate and taking a bite. "You also have my permission to use the Royal Guard. Do what you feel you must."

Disconcerted at the show of confidence, Nels nodded. He'd have to ask Suvi how many of the Guard could be made available. As much as he needed the help, it wouldn't be wise to leave the king unprotected.

Protection? Why are you thinking like this?

"Compose a list of requirements for me and send a copy to your sister," his father said. "That should include whatever you need personally. I see you must've lost your baggage."

So it begins. Nels felt his cheeks heat. *Stop reacting as if you're ten.* "Yes, sir. If there is time—"

"I'll provide everything I can. We may be short on certain items. Please bear that in mind," his father said. Exhaustion and defeat had returned to his features. "A great deal has changed since you left."

"We have more than you think. Jalokivi is well designed to withstand a siege," Nels said, once more taking the opposition. "And the Acrasians are southerners. They aren't used to our winters. If we can hold out a month or so and prevent them from acquiring supplies and shelter, they'll be forced to withdraw or freeze to death. I suggested housing as much of the population and supplies that we can within the city walls and then burning out the surrounding farms. It's a standard siege tactic and somewhat expected, but the Acrasians have advanced too rapidly. Their supply trains will be strained to keep up. Which is why we should destroy all possible provisions around Herraskariano, Mehrinna, and every other town or city that the Acrasians haven't taken. The river locks must be destroyed or made nonoperational too—"

"The locks along the Greater and Lesser Sininen Rivers have

already been shut down," Suvi said. "Most can't be operated without magic, anyway."

Nels blinked. He hadn't known that. "Good. Eledore should be as barren as we can make it. Suvi disagrees. She thinks it will anger the common folk."

"The winter will be hard enough without wasting what little we have," Suvi said.

"There is no other choice," Nels said. "We must make use of what few assets we have remaining. Our winter is one of them. If we had enough troops and more time, there are other things I would recommend. Unfortunately, we don't have either."

His father stared. Again, Nels caught that flash of white against black.

Uncomfortable, Nels returned his attention to his plate and took a bite to cover the silence. *Here it comes.* The warm elk meat was tender and moist, and the blackcurrant sauce provided the perfect complement. Savory flavors combined on his tongue—the citrus-pine of juniper berries, pepper, and musky blackcurrant. It was without a doubt the best he'd tasted since the winter holidays. He'd gone hungry enough times to know that hunger accentuated taste. He was overwhelmed with an urge to bolt his food while it was available, in spite of everything. Still, he forced himself to linger over cutting another bite.

His father took a deep breath. It was as if his next words would take a great deal of strength. He glanced at Suvi before he opened his mouth to speak. Nels prepared himself. Then he registered Suvi's nod of approval at the edge of his vision.

"I agree with your recommendation, Nels," his father said. "I—I'm glad you're home."

At that moment, it occurred to Nels that his sister made a formidable diplomat. He checked Suvi's face. Sure enough, she was waiting for his response. She didn't have to mouth anything for him to understand what she would say. *Say something nice in return. Now, damn it. Or you'll regret it.*

"Thank you, sir. It's—it's good to be here." Nels's lie nestled awkwardly in the conversational gap.

"Nels is staying in the palace tonight, Papa. I've had Ide put him in his old rooms."

"I shouldn't. It's unseemly," Nels said, placing his silverware on his plate and using the stiff linen napkin. "Mrs. Nimonen has prepared the barracks house. I've a great deal to do and—"

"No. I—I mean, please. Stay," his father said. "You've only just returned. And it's been too long since you visited."

Visited? Nels thought.

"I'm alone too much these days. With your mother gone . . ." Their father looked away and blinked back what Nels could've sworn were tears. "It'll be . . . good to have you here. If you are finished eating, perhaps we should retire to my study for a pipe and some Islander wine?" He seemed to catch Nels's blank expression. "Ah. Do you . . . smoke? I don't even know."

"No, sir."

His father blinked. "Oh."

Nels caught yet another of his sister's tight-lipped, expectant looks. It was so much like their mother's that he almost smiled. "I meant—I mean, I don't smoke. But yes, sir. I'll stay."

"Thank you," his father said.

Nels didn't think he'd heard his father speak those two words together before in his life, let alone to him. Watching his father get up from his chair, Nels understood that the father that he knew was gone and quite likely wasn't ever coming back. Grief and loss had killed him. The person in front of him was different and needed to be dealt with as such. *Was this what Ilta meant?*

"What of the Islander?" their father asked, getting up. "Do you drink?"

Suvi, in what Nels considered an amazing feat of self-control, covered her mouth. The only sound to escape was a muffled snort that might have passed for a cough to the uninformed.

He can't possibly be ignorant of all the times I was drunk, can he? Mother knew. But then, his mother hadn't cut him off, had she? "I prefer whiskey or wine."

"Oh. All right." The king addressed Valterri. "Do we have anything suitable?"

"Yes, Your Highness. An Islander has already been airing in the study for you. I will decant a bottle of red in case that proves more suitable."

"Thank you very much, Valterri." The king turned to Suvi. "Let's go, then." An edge of relief was evident in his tone. "This room is too . . . empty."

Stunned, Nels followed his sister and their father through the pocket doors. The scent of his father's pipe smoke and aging paper and leather dredged up intense feelings. The royal study with its vaulted ceiling, blue-papered walls, polished cherrywood furniture, and shelves upon shelves of books had been the scene of any number of stern childhood disciplinary talks. Yet even this room seemed somehow diminished.

You don't have to forgive him.

But I do have to find a way to work with him, don't I?

Valterri entered with a silver tray, deposited three crystal goblets and a crystal bottle of red wine on the drinks cabinet, bowed, and left. His steps on the thick Kaledanen carpets were as silent as a korva's. The sound of pouring liquid and the tinkle of crystal punctured the quiet. Suvi took up two filled glasses. Nels accepted one of them from her and ignored the pointed look that accompanied the glass.

"There are a number of things I wish to say to you both," the king said. He took a sip and then wandered over to the table centered under the stained glass window on the west side of the room. "In private."

Nels remembered the window well. It depicted Kassarina Ilmari driving the Old Ones into the mountains. The people of Eledore—refugees from all over the continent differentiated by various skin tones, clothing, and hairstyles—were illustrated behind her. Dressed in plate armor, the stylized figure of Kassarina had no outward indication of her gender. As children, neither he nor Suvi had known that the image was intended to depict an actual event, not until they were older, and for a time, they had argued about whether the knight in the window was male or female. It had been their mother who settled the matter, and it'd been she who'd told them that particular family history, not their father. At first, Nels hadn't known why. Nor had he understood being disappointed that the knight was a woman. Comprehension had come later.

Watching his father gaze out that window made Nels feel sad. The king set his glass down and opened an ornate wooden box on the table. The scent of tobacco wafted up from the container as he loaded his pipe. When that was done, he went to the fireplace and lit the tobacco with a long match from the hearth. After a few puffs, he drifted back to the table and his wine.

"I should have handled . . . our situation differently," their father said. "So much is . . . lost."

"It's all right, Papa," Suvi said.

Their father nodded. He stared out of the colored glass at the shadows and puffed. Nels wasn't sure whether their father had heard Suvi and was acknowledging her or he was confirming his own thoughts. Another long silence weighed in the air, making it difficult to breathe. Their father seemed to be having trouble finding a way to express himself. That too was new. The father Nels remembered would never have been without words. Uncertain and worried, Nels wished he were in his barracks house with his arms around Ilta.

"The new Silmaillia said we cannot hide from the truth," their father finally ventured.

Nels started at his father's mention of Ilta.

The king continued, "Eledore is on the brink of collapse. The truth is that no matter how hard we work, the Eledore that will exist in a year's time won't resemble the Eledore of my youth. My fear is that it won't even resemble the Eledore we knew a year ago— if Eledore survives at all. Too much has been destroyed. There will be no retrieving what is lost. The Acrasian Regnum has cut us too deep. Too much of our lands have been stolen. Too many of our resources are gone. Too many of our people have—have fallen prey to disease and war."

Died, Nels thought. *Father, the word you seek is "dead," not "fallen" or "left." They died. They didn't vanish or pack their things and go. Although, in truth, some had—nobles who had been smart enough to read the signs.*

"We cannot win. The best we can hope for is to stall our ending."

"Oh, Papa," Suvi said.

Turning from the window, their father quieted further protest with a raised hand. "Too many years of inaction have landed us in a situation that simple solutions cannot resolve. I was irresponsible and selfish. I thought that Eledore would always be as it was. I didn't believe that anything I did as far as governing could matter, anyway. So, I turned my attention to private entertainments. I thought great works of art would be my only legacy. Goddess forgive me, I look back at my actions now, and I honestly don't know what I was thinking."

"Then why discuss this?" Suvi asked.

"The truth is . . . I loved your mother, but she never wanted a binding, let alone a marriage," their father said. "However, everything had been arranged, and she was forced to honor the contract. She didn't want me. In the end, I was angry. Insulted. For a long time, I blamed her and tried to destroy anything and everything she cared about in retaliation."

"What's done is done. It isn't important," Suvi said.

"It is," their father said.

"Mother did the best she could, but she wasn't in love with you. She loved Veli Karpanen," Suvi said. "Oh, please. Don't pretend to be shocked, Papa. It's only the three of us. And we shouldn't lie to one another. The country can't afford it. Anyway, Valterri is in the kitchen. And even if he wasn't, I'm certain he's overheard far worse over the years." She closed her eyes as if steeling herself and then opened them.

"It's time for brutal realities," Suvi said. "The world is changing, and we must change with it. Mother saw it before any of us. The future is here. It's now. The old ways of governance won't withstand the onslaught of new knowledge and power. As I see it, this war—this struggle, all the damage—is but a sign that Eledore must fundamentally change in order to live in that future."

Their father nodded. "I—I'm sorry."

Suvi put down her wineglass and went to hug their father. "I know, Papa." Once again, she gave Nels an imploring look. She mouthed the words, *Please, Nels. Help me. I can't do this alone.*

He couldn't decide whether or not he wanted to be sick. Fed up, he downed the last of his glass of wine. *People are dying, and he's feeling sorry for himself? He's the king! He's the one who should be encouraging us, not the other way around!*

It was then that Nels began to understand that there was

nothing godlike about their father—nothing that set him apart from anyone else. He was king due to an accident of birth and nothing more. Studying the man now, Nels suddenly understood the depth of his father's terror. Nels had difficulty caring. However, he did care that Suvi was every bit as frightened, and as much faith as Nels had in her—as intelligent as she was—she didn't have all the answers either. *She can't. She's fallible too.*

She knows we must change, but she doesn't know how to accomplish that from here.

Flexible. We must be flexible. And if there was one thing Nels had learned since leaving the palace, it was a certain mental adaptability.

If Suvi gives up, we are truly lost. This is no different than speaking to your company before a battle. You can do this.

See the advantage in your experiences.

"I think for the first time in my life, I—I understand something. Something Ilta tried to tell me," Nels said. "My . . . magical disadvantage taught me to think and observe in ways others didn't have to. I approach problems from different angles because I couldn't approach them like everyone else. *That* is what you must do—what *we* must do now. We *do* have enough resources if we're creative and intelligent about using them. We *can* survive this war. Maybe not in the way in which we're accustomed, but we *will* live."

He got to his feet. "I'm not giving up. You shouldn't either. As long as we have the capacity to think, we have a chance. I intend to see to it that the Acrasians will face a fight the likes of which they've never before seen. I'll make sure they'll be swiving sorry they ever came to Jalokivi."

FOUR

The rain poured in chilling gusts. A thick fog clung to the wind-sheltered valleys. With all the cloud cover, it was impossible to see much outside the city walls and had been that way for more than two weeks. *A typical Eledorean autumn.* Nels couldn't hear much above the rush of water pounding stone. By the feel of it slapping his foul-weather coat, he could've sworn there was a shard of ice in each drop but decided it was probably only wishful thinking. Every morning he prayed for snow, and every morning it merely rained. He hunched under his tricorne and coat as he trudged along the top of Jalokivi's outmost wall, checking on those stationed at the gatehouses. It was a habit he'd acquired through no fault of the troops. Whereas before he'd lived in fear of letting down his company, now the terror had stretched to even greater proportions. He hadn't slept a whole night through since the day Pesola died. When he did sleep, Nels woke with a bad feeling wedged in the back of his skull.

Wherever Pesola is, he must think himself avenged. "Good morning, Private Kurri, Lassila," Nels said with a nod to the soldiers huddled around the fire basket. He shut the door before the wind could blow out the meager flames. The gatehouse smelled of wet wool, hot iron, and burning coals.

Kurri and Lassila jumped up to offer a salute. "Sir!"

Overlieutenant Larsson turned away from the arrow slit and joined the others in standing at attention. Her tight dark brown curls were black in the dim light.

"At ease," Nels said, returning the salute. "What's it look like, Larsson?"

"Same as yesterday and the day before that and the day before that. Cold soup, sir. Groop is walking the wall. His turn." She shivered and pulled her coat tighter. "Any word?"

"Not yet," Nels said. The Acrasians had taken Mehrinna but had gained very little for their trouble. Nels was happy for that at least. *Please let the snows come early this year.* "I expect the party should begin any day."

She nodded and turned her attention back to the arrow slit. The others made room for him at the fire.

"Got any tea?" Nels asked.

Lassila nodded and fetched a tin cup, cleaned the inside with the tail of his shirt, and then poured. Light from the meager fire cast his darker skin in warm colors.

Nels warmed his gloved palms on hot tin. The tea inside the cup looked to be more water than tea. It tasted worse. *How many times have they reused those leaves?* he thought, and made a note to himself to bring some fresh tea during his next rounds. He had enough. Mrs. Nimonen saw to that through his father, and he supposed his father could spare the extra.

The siege hadn't actually started and there had already been problems with looting and hoarding. He expected it to only get worse. Some items were already in shorter supply—beef, cow's milk, coffee, tea, sugar, Islander wine, silk, cotton—mainly things imported from other countries. At least traditional foods derived from reindeer and goats or fish were plentiful.

For now, the hot water was enough. His first cup had been more than an hour before, and he was chilled to the core of his being. It wasn't even dawn yet. His old boots were soaked through already—they needed new soles. *Autumn. Gods, I hate autumn.* He hated spring, too. They both brought weeks of rain. The only advantage spring had was that summer was on the way. Autumn only meant winter was around the corner. He didn't think he'd ever be warm and dry again. He hated being confined indoors.

Maybe the weather is slowing the Acrasians? He'd expected them to arrive more than a week before.

At least he'd gotten to spend some time with Ilta. She had been working at the charity hospital from early in the morning to late into the evenings. Both exhausted, they hadn't been able to talk much, but sleeping entwined in her arms made up for a great deal— even if they hadn't quite worked up to the actual act of sex. *Yet.* She was afraid of what might happen. In truth, so was he.

An alarm bell rang, the one at the front gate, by the sound. Everyone rushed to the arrow slits. Peering downward into the soggy darkness, Nels couldn't make out a thing. *Are those horses' hooves I hear? Could mean anything.* Someone somewhere called out at the top of their voice. Another series of shouts followed.

"What is it?" Kurri asked in his throaty voice. His family line had originated in the far north, as was evidenced by the bright red hair he pushed out of his eyes. He wore a purple band around his left arm—most did these days. Everyone had lost someone.

Lassila elbowed his friend. "If you'd move, perhaps I could tell you."

"Riders, I think," Overlieutenant Larsson said. "A messenger, maybe? Too many for that. More stragglers from Mehrinna or Herraskariano?"

"We sure could use the help. We're going to be massacred."

"Shut up, Lassila," Overlieutenant Larsson said.

Nels buttoned his coat. "I'll go see."

"I hope it's the Acrasians," Kurri said. "I'm sick to death of all this waiting."

Lassila said, "Speak for yourself. I'll be happy if they never come. They're like locusts."

Careful of the slick stone under his feet, Nels ran down the steps to the main gates. Guttering torches lit the way. He reached his destination just as a messenger was being dispatched. A group of five riders sat atop steaming horses. All five were dressed in Acrasian gray. One carried a horse spear with a strip of soggy white cloth tied to it.

Nels's blood chilled the instant he recognized the markings on their uniform coats. *Well. It seems Kurri got his wish.*

"Colonel Hännenen, sir," Sergeant Gusstafson said. "The message is addressed to you personally. It appears to be from a General Lucrosia Marcellus."

How does he know I'm in charge? An uneasy feeling crawled up Nels's spine. *He hasn't stopped studying us, it seems.* Nels put a hand out for the message.

"Do not attempt your foul magic, demons," one of the Acrasians said, pointing to the white scrap of cloth. "We ride under flag of truce."

"Don't bother, Private," one of the other Acrasians said. "They don't understand Acrasian. You know why we were picked for this duty. So, shut up. We live through this, maybe you'll think twice before you talk back to—"

"You won't be harmed." Nels answered in Acrasian without

thinking. "We know what a white flag means." *Unlike you,* he thought.

"You speak Acrasian?" the Acrasian officer asked.

"I do," Nels said.

"Then you must be Colonel Hännenen. We were informed you would probably be the only one to understand our message," the Acrasian officer said. "They said you'd have a North End accent. Damned if they weren't right."

Nels paused. He tried not to jump to any conclusions regarding Corporal Petron. "And if I am Colonel Hännenen?"

"Then that," the Acrasian officer said with a nod toward the paper, "contains the terms of your surrender. We are to wait for a reply."

Nels cracked the wax seal and read. The message began politely enough. However, it pointed out his utter lack of experience as a military leader and noted the numbers of troops he had at hand as well as the weakness along the west wall. In short, it displayed an alarming amount of knowledge of his situation. It also hinted at what might be done to take advantage of those weaknesses. *I almost wish you were on our side, Marcellus.* In the end, the note demanded an unconditional surrender. The ground under Nels's feet seemed to shift.

He decided to stall. "Your general doesn't mention what is on offer in exchange."

"He said you would inquire about that," the Acrasian officer said. "I was instructed to inform you that your troops, your king, and yourself will be permitted a clean death. And that your sister, Princess Suvi, and the remaining civilian population—strictly those untainted by evil—will be permitted to live."

They know a great deal. Someone is giving them information. Who? He knew at that moment that Corporal Petron couldn't possibly be the source. For a moment, Nels wasn't sure what he'd say. The warmth from the weak tea he'd gulped down minutes before was gone. "What do you mean, 'those not tainted with evil'?"

"Magic." The Acrasian spat the word.

"Ah, I see." *Then, that isn't much of an offer,* Nels thought.

"Your answer?"

This is hopeless. We'll be— Suddenly, Nels remembered a passage from Marcellus's book. *If one can turn one's enemy against themselves through deceit, do so. For an army that believes itself defeated will be defeated.* He almost laughed. *Ah, Marcellus. It all comes down to pretense, does it? Well, I may not have a lot of experience leading an army, but I do have a great deal of practice at fakery.* Nels put on his biggest, brightest smile for the Acrasian officer.

"Your answer?" the Acrasian asked.

Nels tore the message in half and then in quarters. Then he said in perfect Acrasian, "Piss off."

The Acrasian officer blinked. A few of Nels's troops standing nearby let out nervous chuckles. None of them spoke Acrasian, but he supposed it was easy enough to interpret the exchange.

"You heard me. I said piss off," he said. He handed back the pieces. "I don't frighten that easily, Lieutenant. None of us do."

The Acrasian officer's face went red.

Nels turned to the others and spoke in Eledorean. "Raise the portcullis. Let them go back home to their general."

"What was that note, sir?" Sergeant Gusstafson asked.

"General Kauranen would call it a bit of enthusiastic saber-rattling," Nels said. "Everyone, resume your duties. The show is over." He turned his back on the Acrasians and walked away. He decided to pay a visit to Master Sergeant Jarvi. It wasn't likely that Marcellus would use the flaw in the west wall after that note, but it wouldn't do any harm to be prepared.

He gazed up into the graying dawn. The clouds were bunched into angry knots. *Curse the weather.* He needed snow. *Now.* Then he remembered that Suvi had mentioned they had Waterborne visitors. *Aren't they known for weather magic?*

It's time to see a man about a storm, Nels thought.

FIVE

With a tense jaw, Nels waited for his proposal to be declared pathetic and then rejected. Firelight cast mottled patterns across his sister's careful expression. He thought she looked older now, more self-assured. Responsibility was changing her, but he supposed she'd say the same of him. He looked to his father. He appeared to be recovering. There was new color in the king's face, his eyes were alert, and his clothes no longer hung on him like oversized rags. He seemed stronger, too. It was as if a new person had emerged from the ashes of the old one. Nels was happy of it. Then it abruptly occurred to him that the three of them were actually working together for the good of the kingdom.

If only Mother had lived to see this.

Suvi had taken over their uncle's apartments when their father had named her acting chancellor. Although she hadn't done much to alter its appearance, the study was less foreboding. The hearth fire consumed its logs with merry pops and crackles, joining the ticking of the mantel clock in filling the long silence. Tired, Nels fought an urge to collapse into one of the overstuffed chairs and prop his boots up. Resting an elbow on the mantel instead, he stared into the fire in order to seem less concerned with the outcome. He felt bad for approaching his father and sister first. There wasn't time for lengthy debates, but the rapid change in weather would have a heavy effect on the people of Jalokivi and thus the kingdom. In addition, asking anyone to expend the amount of energy required for an out-of-season storm was an imposition. The Waterborne were Suvi's friends, not underlings to be ordered. They were foreign nationals with interests of their own. And while Waterborne were known for weather magic, that didn't necessarily mean Suvi's friends had such power, no more than Eledoreans being known for domination magic meant that Nels himself possessed it. It would be rude to make assumptions, and he couldn't afford rudeness any more than he could afford wasted time.

"You're in luck," Suvi said. "Dylan is a talented weathermaster."

Nels felt his shoulders drop. "Good."

"But he works with water. All Waterborne do."

"We've certainly had enough rain," Nels said.

"And I've never seen Waterborne work magic this far inland," Suvi said. "Still, it might be possible. I have seen Dylan command a storm on land once. But it was on a small island surrounded by the sea."

"We're surrounded by water on three sides. King Einar's Lake to the north and the Greater Sininen river to the south and southwest," Nels said. "Perfect."

"Technically, that's two and a half. Also, river or lake water isn't the same as seawater," Suvi said.

"I wasn't implying that it was," Nels said. "Only that—"

"This is a great deal to ask," their father said. "The treaty hasn't been finalized. I'm uncomfortable relying on allies without a formal agreement in place. What if they make impossible demands later? What if this Dylan harms himself? He's the son of a sea lord. Will Kask blame us and retaliate? Will he abandon us? Or will we then have to fight two wars—"

"Sea Lord Kask isn't like that, Father," Suvi said. "I wouldn't be here if he was."

"We have to think beyond this battle." Their father turned to Suvi. "Can't we last until winter arrives of its own accord? It's only a few weeks. Didn't Nels say that we were in a strong position? There is no siege yet. We should wait."

"Let's not make a decision until we have all the facts, Papa. We should present the idea to Dylan and Darius when they get here," Suvi said.

"I've a very bad feeling," Nels said, his cheeks burning. It was the first time he'd spoken of his hunches in front of anyone other than Viktor. Nels wasn't sure how his father would react. One didn't acquire new talents after puberty any more than one grew a second head.

"You've had a premonition?" his father asked. His eyes became intense, and his brows pressed together. "You?"

"Really?" Suvi scooted to the edge of her chair and leaned forward. "What have you been hiding from us all this time?"

Nels looked away. He hadn't expected that either of them would show this much interest in something so dubious. "It isn't a premonition, exactly."

"Then, what is it?" Suvi asked.

Turning his back on them, Nels wasn't sure he could talk about it. "I don't know. It isn't powerful. It isn't like I had a vision or a dream. Intuition?" Afraid of disappointment and skepticism, he didn't dare look at his sister or his father.

"I don't think that matters," Suvi said.

I knew it, Nels thought. *I shouldn't have said anything.*

"I mean, I don't care what you want to call it. You're the only one who thinks that you don't have power," Suvi said. "Trust yourself. I trust you."

"All right," Nels said, still not turning to face them. "Marcellus knows too much."

"What do you mean?" his father asked.

"The surrender demand," Nels said. "The messenger knew I'd speak Acrasian. With a North End accent, no less. Their information is too specific."

"You believe we've a traitor." Suvi's voice was flat, serious.

Nels nodded. "I do."

"Who?" Suvi asked.

"I'm not sure. Someone who knows us well, certainly," Nels said.

"Uncle Sakari?" Suvi asked.

"No!" Their father got up from his chair and paced the study. "He would never do such a thing. He knows what it would mean. He would never— He's my brother! He has every bit as much to lose as we do if Eledore falls into the hands of the Acrasians!"

Holding his breath, Nels again waited to be dismissed.

"Father," Suvi said. "Don't upset yourself. Please. Sit. We're only discussing possibilities. No one has accused anyone of anything."

Their father returned to his chair. "I won't stand for more talk like that. I know what everyone says about Kar. But he led the kingdom when I couldn't. And he asked for very little in return."

Why ask when you can take whatever you want? Nels thought.

"If he wanted to steal the kingdom from me, he'd have done it long ago."

He didn't? Nels kept his focus on the carpet.

"I know. I know. Let Nels speak," Suvi said. "Stay calm. We're only gathering information. Nothing more. Think. No judgments need to be made right now."

Their father sighed.

Suvi said, "Nels, go on."

"I should consult Ilta before I say anything," Nels said.

"Why isn't she here now?" Suvi asked.

"She's at the Commons Hospital," Nels said. "I think she's still uncomfortable about participating in these councils."

"Hrmph," their father said with a frown. "Saara Korpela made a huge mistake in naming that girl her successor."

Nels said, "No matter what she did—if she actually is to blame, and none of us knows for certain—"

"Nels," Suvi said. "I was there."

"Ilta wouldn't have exposed Father on purpose. She wouldn't. Such a thing would break her Healer's Oath. It was an accident," Nels said. "I should've sent her from Merta sooner. I should've gotten her from Angel's Thumb before Virens. I thought—"

"Stop it. You've nothing to blame yourself for," Suvi said. "The quarantine was necessary. If you'd gone to Angel's Thumb before it was safe, the people of Gardemeister would've caught the new strain of variola. The army units stationed there would've caught it and spread it. We wouldn't have the army. We might not even have you."

"Army? We've hardly enough to man the city walls," Nels said. "The Acrasians have—"

At that moment, there was a knock on the door.

"Enter," Suvi said.

Valterri announced that Suvi's friends were waiting. Everyone remained silent until the butler returned and the Waterborne were shown in.

"Dylan Kask, weathermaster, son of Sea Lord Aodhan Kask of

clan Kask, and Darius Teak, messenger, of clan Kask, formerly the first mate of the *Laughing Sea Horse*," Suvi said, "this is my father, His Majesty King Henrik Ilmari, and my brother, Colonel Nels Hännenen."

Dylan bowed to their father and then offered a hand to Nels. There was something about Dylan that made Nels like him at once. *Perhaps it's the way that he seems so comfortable around Father?*

"Suvi told me a great deal about you," Dylan said.

"She did, did she?" Nels asked.

Dylan said, "Every word was nice."

"Really?" Nels asked. "Then she must have been lying."

"That isn't true," Suvi said.

"Now that all the embarrassing family secrets are out, have a seat," Nels said.

Dylan and Darius settled onto the small sofa next to the hearth.

"Suvi mentioned that you had a proposition for clan Kask?" Dylan asked.

Nels looked to Suvi. "Ah. Not exactly. Not for your clan. For you. I need to ask for your help."

Darius turned to Dylan.

Dylan paused. "All right. What kind of favor do you need this time?"

"Suvi says you're a weathermaster," Nels said.

"I am," Dylan said. "I served on HKEL *Northern Star* for six years. Then I temporarily transferred to HKEL *Sea Otter*. However, I officially resigned from the Eledorean Navy last summer."

"Oh," Nels said. *I hope the navy treats their sailors better than the army treats their soldiers.*

"Eledore granted me asylum when I had nowhere else to go," Dylan said. "So, I'm willing to listen to your request."

"The Acrasians have us cut off," Nels said.

Dylan said, "So I understand."

"I'll be blunt," Nels said. "I was wondering if you could conjure up a snowstorm."

"A blizzard?" Darius asked, outraged.

Placing a hand on Darius's knee, Dylan gestured for Darius to be quiet. "When?"

"Do you think you can?" Nels asked.

"It's not a matter of whether I can," Dylan said. "The question is whether you actually want me to. You do understand what such a thing might do to the city? There's a chance of avalanche this close to the mountains."

"I'm mainly concerned with what it'll do to the Acrasians," Nels said. "We can't let them get too comfortable out there."

"Ah." Dylan smiled as understanding dawned. "I see."

Darius said, "You don't know what it'll do to—"

"Stop worrying so much, Dar," Dylan said. "I've you to help. Don't I?"

"Who said I would help?" Darius asked. "They're asking you to do this, not me."

Dylan said, "It's entirely up to you."

"You haven't asked me, either," Darius said.

"All right," Dylan said, "I'm asking you now."

The two of them stared at one another for a few seconds before Darius laughed.

Dylan said, "We'll do it."

"You don't have to if you don't want to," Suvi said.

"We're trapped here too. Remember?" Dylan asked. "It's not like it'll make Kask's relationship with the Acrasians any worse. And if it means you'll be more likely to deliver the water steel you're offering to Clan Kask . . . well, Father would want me to do this."

"You'll be sick afterward," Darius said.

"As long as I have you to caring for me, it won't be so bad," Dylan said.

"Charmer," Darius said. He spoke to everyone else, "All right. If he's mad enough to agree, I'm in too."

"Thank you," Nels said. "What will you need?"

SIX

"Whose intensely stupid idea was this?" Nels asked in a hushed tone. His breath came out in clouds. The stones under his fingers and toes were slick and icy. He jerked in reflex when a sharp pain in his left hand informed him that he'd cut himself again. The mud below smelled of rotting sewage. Subsequently, broken glass was but one of the hazards of climbing this section of the west wall.

"I believe it was Colonel Hännenen's idea, sir," Viktor whispered, and handed him the fuse cord.

"Ahh. Right," Nels said. "Remind me to tell the colonel that he's an evil swiving bastard."

"Isn't that the definition of 'colonel'?" Viktor asked.

"That explains a few things about Pesola."

"And for the record, you're doing an excellent job."

"As a colonel or with this damned wall?" Nels secured the fuse cord.

"I'll leave that up to you to interpret," Viktor said.

"Thank y— Shit!" Nels resisted the urge to stick the injured digit in his mouth.

"Of course, I'm not certain how well the fuse will light if you soak it in a gallon of blood."

"If Jarvi can set fire to a bridge in a rainstorm while standing in a river, I'm fairly certain a little blood isn't going to be a challenge."

The weather was rapidly getting worse. While it had temporarily stopped raining, the temperature had plummeted the instant the sun had gone down. *Dylan and Darius at their work, thank Hasta,* Nels thought. *At this rate, the snows will hit before the Acrasians are in place. That's what you wanted, right?* His unease was growing rather than fading with the approaching storm. The Acrasians were taking too long, and he didn't like it one bit. Viktor had reported there were only a few companies in place. Either Marcellus had thought to frighten him into surrendering prematurely, or the general was getting overconfident. It seemed Marcellus underestimated him, and Nels was just fine with that. *The longer they wait, the more time we have to prepare a welcome.*

In truth, the Acrasian general's note hadn't revealed much beyond the obvious. The western wall was the only one to which the Acrasian army had access. Jalokivi's eastern side backed against jagged mountains, to the north there was King Einar's Lake, which was said to be bottomless, and the Greater Sininen river hugged the southern wall. Naturally, the western side would be where the Acrasians would look for a flaw in the defenses, and they had found one.

Or whoever had told them of it.

It'd taken most of the night to finish digging, and this was the last of the traps he'd planned. The largest part of the crack was located at the base of the wall. Assuming he'd followed Jarvi's instructions correctly, the explosion at the top would drop rocks and years of the city's garbage on anyone attempting to enter, and fill the breach at the same time. The wall would be shorter, of course.

However, that was why he'd borrowed a couple of cannon from Suvi's ship, the *Otter*. They would provide a nice surprise. It wasn't a bad trap as traps went. He'd designed several over the past few weeks. If the Acrasians entered Jalokivi, his intent was to slow them down enough to give the people a chance at evacuating. *Not much of one but more of a chance than they would've had.*

"That should make Marcellus think twice." Nels replaced the stone and made sure the final loop of fuse cord was hidden and secure. "Are Jarvi and Sirola finished?" His fingers and toes—the ones that hadn't been shredded on broken glass—were going numb.

Viktor turned and signaled to where the pair were working on filling in the trench. After a few seconds, Viktor nodded. "Looks like it."

"Good," Nels said, keeping his voice low. "I'm damned well ready for tea, a fire, and dry feet. My toes are frozen. Do you remember where I left my boots?" His toes weren't the only parts of him that were numb, but as the officer in charge, he was reluctant to bring up the subject.

"You shouldn't be doing this, you know," Viktor said, holding up the boots in question.

"I seem to recall having this conversation before," Nels said. "Anyway, isn't it a bit late to express objections? I'm done." He climbed down, taking care not to cut himself all over again. He got to the bottom without further injury and found a rock to sit on while he stuffed cold feet into warm boots.

"You're not a foot soldier anymore," Viktor said.

"I wasn't in the first place, was I?" Nels checked the cuts on his hands. "Do you think the healer will have time to see me? I don't think I'll be able to write like this."

"You have to be more careful."

"When did you become such a nursemaid?" Nels asked.

Sirola and Jarvi arrived. Jarvi was out of breath.

"Everything is in place, sir," Jarvi said.

"Let's get back inside. I need a beer. The Broken Drum should still have a few barrels left, right, Jarvi?" Nels asked.

Jarvi said, "Maybe?"

"Viktor, make sure the way is clear," Nels said.

"Yes, sir." Viktor headed into the fog.

"How long will this fog last, sir?" Sirola asked.

"As long as we need it to last. For now, until morning," Nels said. "Is something wrong, Sirola?"

"I don't trust Waterborne," Sirola said.

"Why not?" Jarvi asked. "You trust me."

"You're not Waterborne, Sarge," Sirola said.

"My grandmother was," Jarvi said. "On my mother's side."

"Oh," Sirola said.

"Do you have any other opinions about Waterborne you'd like to share?" Jarvi asked.

Nels heard an owl hoot. "Come on. We don't have all night."

"I thought we did, sir," Sirola said.

"Shut up, Private," Jarvi said.

Nels felt something cold brush against his right cheek. Thinking it was an insect—there certainly were enough of them around, due to the sewer at the foot of the west wall—he brushed it away. His hand came away wet. Another big white flake floated past his face, this time to the right. It was followed by three more. Staring up into the night sky, he smiled.

It's snowing, he thought. *Thank the gods.*

SEVEN

Nels was forcefully shaken from bad dreams. He leapt to his feet with a scream.

"Swiving hells!"

Breathing in gulps, Nels recognized the shadowy form and tossed the saber back onto the empty bedstead. Ilta had left for the Commons Hospital sometime in the night. "Viktor? What is it? Why are you here?" The barracks house was very chilly. His bare feet were cold on the floorboards. The coals were still banked for the night. Apparently, Mrs. Nimonen had yet to arrive and stoke the hearth fires for the day.

Viktor said, "You scared the piss out of me."

Nels slumped backward, sitting on the edge of the feather bed, and then rubbed his face. Beard bristle abraded his newly healed palms. At that moment, it occurred to him that the windows were too dark and that Viktor was carrying a lantern. Nels had slept at a bad angle in the night.

Massaging the back of his sore neck with one hand, he asked, "What time is it?"

"Half past two in the morning."

"It's not time for my turn at watch," Nels said. He crawled back under the covers and pulled the pillow over his head. "Go away." It'd been a rough night. The dreams had been worse than ever, and he was worried he wouldn't be able to get back to sleep. Now that he was awake, the anxiety nesting in the back of his skull had grown to the size of Keeper Mountain.

"Get up," Viktor said. "We've got trouble."

Nels sat up at once. "What is it?"

"Something isn't right in the palace."

Jumping to his feet for the second time, Nels snatched his breeches from the hook on the wall. Suddenly, sleep didn't matter. "What something? Tell me!"

"Private Kurri spied a bright red flash. Over the palace," Viktor said. "There was an answering flash above the Acrasian encampment. I sent Kurri along with the rest of his squad to check the palace. No one's reported back yet. Thought you'd want to know. I've a bad feeling about this."

You aren't the only one. Nels tucked in his nightshirt and then dealt with stockings and boots in a rush. "Signal rockets?"

"Signal rockets."

"How long ago was that?"

"More than a quarter of an hour ago. I ordered Corporal Kallela to send word the instant he entered the palace grounds." Viktor's pale, worried face was cast in orange, yellow, and gray. "Sergeant Gusstafson says the Acrasians are moving into position. Is this it?"

"Let's hope not," Nels said. "Roust the regiment. Check the gates. I'll tend to the palace."

"Take Overlieutenant Moller with you. He's waiting outside. For that matter, take a platoon, too. We can spare them for now."

Pausing mid-button, Nels gave Viktor a look. "I think I can manage a walk to the palace on my own."

"And what if the Acrasians have found a way to infiltrate it?"

Nels paused. "All right. Tell Larsson and her platoon to meet us on the corner of Anders Street and Royal."

"Yes, sir."

"And Viktor?"

"Yes?"

"If I don't come back, you're to focus on holding Jalokivi. Got it? I can take care of myself." Nels jammed his arms into his jacket and then his coat.

"I know."

"How's the weather?"

Viktor opened the front door. Overlieutenant Sebastian Moller ceased stomping his feet for warmth and saluted. A thick layer of white carpeted the dooryard and more was pouring from the sky. If the wind were blowing in another direction, there'd have been a two-foot drift blocking the door.

"Your sister's friends really know how to throw a snowstorm," Viktor said.

Nels stepped outside. Between the snow and the darkness, he had trouble seeing the street. "Kurri must have sharp eyes. How did he see anything in all this?"

"The storm intensified while I made my way here," Viktor said.

"Right," Nels said, finishing with the buttons on his coat. "I'll join you at the wall when I'm done. You're in charge until I get there."

"All right," Viktor said.

"The Mother go with you."

"And you, too." And with that, Viktor saluted and vanished into the swirling darkness.

Already shivering, Nels grabbed his hat and then pulled his neck scarf tighter. "Come on, Moller. Let's visit my sister's uninvited guest." Then he set about wading down the street toward the palace with the overlieutenant close behind.

The snow was more than a foot deep in places. The snowdrifts were much higher. Wind gusts burst down the street with enough strength to force Nels to lean into them to keep his balance. He and Moller passed soldiers rousting out for duty while others cleared the street for horses and wagons. Nels was glad of the time he'd had to prepare. He hadn't expected the summoned storm to be quite so powerful. If what they needed hadn't been already in place, the storm would've made things difficult. *And this is only the start. Dylan said it wouldn't reach its peak until tomorrow.* Nels almost felt sorry for the Acrasians. *Almost.*

By the time they'd reached the designated corner, Larsson's platoon was already waiting. Nels's hat was already heavy from accumulated snow. Tilting his head back, he was reassured by the glimpse of a Royal Guardsman's uniform at the top of the palace wall. *They're still at their posts, at least. Maybe Corporal Kallela forgot to check in?* It wasn't likely. Dread knotted Nels's guts as he motioned for the platoon to follow.

A lone Royal Guard was stationed on the other side of the black iron gate. Her eyes darted to the left and then back to him and his accompanying platoon. She bit her lip. Her concerned expression transformed into resolve and resignation.

Viktor was right. Taking off his tricorne, Nels casually beat the snow off of it. "Colonel Hännenen requesting admittance."

"It's late, sir," the guard said. "Ah. No one in the palace is awake at this hour."

"Are you refusing entry?" Nels asked. *I've never been stopped at the gate before. Not like this.*

"Ah, no," the guard said. Again, her eyes flitted to the left.

"Well, open the damned gates, Lieutenant," Nels said. "Now."

The guardsman's hands were shaking as she moved closer and reached through the bars to hand him something. She whispered, "Sir, there are Acr—"

An explosion ended her reply. Several things happened all at once. The side of her head burst open. Deafened, Nels felt warm gobs of flesh splash his face. He tasted blood and sulfur-laden grit. He felt a second musket ball pass too close. In reflex, he dropped to his hands and knees. The troops ducked and drew their weapons. A powder cloud obscured Nels's vision and filled his nose. Spying the dead guard's hand, he scrabbled to retrieve whatever it was she'd been trying to give him. Two of his troops threw themselves at the locked gate to no avail. More shots blossomed orange and yellow. Powder smoke shrouded everything at waist height. However, from the ground he could see the bottom half of Acrasian uniformed soldiers moving toward him and the gate. Again, he gazed at the dead guard's twitching hand. Her palm had fallen open. It took a moment for him to register what he was seeing.

The gate key. May the Great Mother bless her. Nels grabbed it.

One of his troops pulled at his left shoulder. "Sir, we can't get in! We have to get out of here!"

Drawing a pistol, Nels shook off Lieutenant Larsson and fired upward through the bars at the closest Acrasian. The Acrasian dropped. Nels used the key, keeping his head down as much as he could in the process. Then he shoved the gate with all his might. It met resistance in the form of another Acrasian. The Acrasian staggered, caught by the momentum of swinging wrought iron. Another gun went off. Nels felt a hard thump in his left shoulder. Focused on getting to the palace, he didn't check it. There was no time to reload, either. He stuffed the empty pistol back into his belt and got to his feet. "For Eledore!" He didn't wait for the others to follow. Instead, he drew a second pistol and his saber and charged through the gates.

The courtyard was choked with smoke and rifle fire. The bodies of the previous Eledorean patrol littered the ground. In the distance, he heard what he assumed was the first of his and Jarvi's surprises set for the Acrasians. The explosion was huge. It briefly lit up the cloudy courtyard, and he felt the force of it through the soles of his boots. Two Acrasians almost ran into him. Nels killed the first before the Acrasian could shoot him. The second Acrasian missed. One of the other troops took the second Acrasian down while he attempted to reload. Nels kept moving, hoping the powder smoke would provide enough cover. Almost at the palace door, he hoped there wouldn't be another Acrasian reception waiting. He stumbled on the first step and caught himself, slapping his palm against stone. The door's fine brass knob was dented and bent. Nels made one attempt at the knob before resorting to kicking the door in. The main hall was empty. Risking a quick glance over his shoulder, he saw his platoon and Overlieutenant Moller were close behind.

Stepping inside the main hall, Nels yelled, "Suvi?! Father?!" There was no way of knowing where either of them were being held, or even if they were prisoners. It was possible that they'd safely hidden themselves away in the castle keep. It was what a castle keep was for, after all. He decided to take the search one floor at a time, starting with the first-floor library and the keep below it.

Priceless furniture lay overturned in the main hall. The cushions had been gutted. He sneezed. Goose down floated in the air. Valterri wasn't anywhere in sight. *Hiding somewhere safe, I hope, and unhurt*, Nels thought. *No one on the stairs. Good.* He smelled smoke but saw no signs of fire. The immediate danger behind him, his left arm began to throb with dull pain. With his back against the right wall, he provided cover for his troops. They entered the main hall two at a time, each covering their partner. When he was sure it was safe, he took a moment to reload his pistols. Then he edged to the archway leading to the emerald sitting room on the right. He signaled for his platoon to be watchful and to check the room opposite. The last one through the front door was Private Lassila, who then shoved a broken bench against the entrance. Outside, the Acrasians battered the blockage. Lassila placed a pistol muzzle close to the cut lead glass pane and fired, shattering the glass. Flying shards rained down on one and all. Nels was cut, but not too badly, from what he could tell. A cloud of smoke filled the doorway. He shook his head. His ears were ringing.

Peeking into the emerald sitting room, he saw it was empty. He signaled for two of his troops to go in and search. Waiting until the gray room to his left was also clear, he then crossed the main hall. With his back against the wall supporting the grand stairway, he scooted to the pocket doors on the left that led to the first-floor library. The doors were closed. That, in and of itself, wasn't unusual. He laid a gentle hand on one black walnut panel to slide the first half open a crack when the sound of movement brought him up short. He turned and warned the others with a flat hand signal. Two soldiers remained at the front door to defend it. The rest of the platoon arranged itself on either side of the pocket doors. Nels waited until everyone was in place and ready before calling out.

"Suvi? Father? It's Nels. Is that you?"

"Nels! Don't—" It was Suvi.

There was a loud thump. The pocket doors seemed to slam open of their own accord. *Careful. The enemy is hiding on either side, just as we are.* Nels signaled his troops to stay back.

"Colonel Hännenen, I presume?" The words were spoken in Eledorean with a deep, cultured tone and an Acrasian accent.

Formal court speech automatically rolled off Nels's tongue.

"You would appear to have me at a disadvantage." *In more ways than one.* "Who are you?"

"Then permit me to provide an introduction. I am General Lucrosia Marcellus of the Acrasian Regnum. I have your sister and your father prisoner. Are you prepared to surrender? Or must I suffer through another of your crudely charming retorts?"

It was strange hearing an Acrasian affect Eledorean court speech. *Where did you learn it? And more importantly, how did you get inside the palace?* Nels thought.

"Will you stop wasting my time?" Marcellus asked. "Or do I kill your father now?"

"As I see it, you're planning on murdering him anyway," Nels said. "Where is the advantage in surrendering?"

"How about I don't kill your sister as well?"

"That depends; are you planning on shooting me the instant I show myself?"

"I think I'd like to meet the legendary Ghost face to face," Marcellus said.

Nels blinked. "Ghost?"

"Don't sound so humiliated," Marcellus said. "It sounds more formidable in Acrasian."

"Who in all the hells came up with that?"

"My men did. After that skirmish on the road to Herraskariano," Marcellus said.

Nels snorted. "Who'd have thought Acrasians were so easy to impress?"

"Are you coming out or not?" Marcellus asked.

There really wasn't much of an option, as Nels saw it. If he showed himself, he had a chance at a delay and perhaps then an opportunity to come up with a solution. At the least, he'd know what he was up against. If he stayed where he was, it'd end when the Acrasians outside rammed their way into the main hall. *What if they're holding the back door, too? I know I would be.*

One step at a time.

His one advantage was that he knew the palace better than Marcellus did. Nels turned and whispered to Overlieutenant Moller, "There's a servants' entrance at the back of the library. It's a hidden door. They may not have found it. It's connected to a passage that runs between the dining room and the library and then outside to the kitchen. Send Larsson and a squad to the dining room. Have them go through the passage and wait at the secret door. The rest stay here. I'll stall Marcellus and signal the Acrasians' numbers and positions to you, if I can. The instant I step from that doorway, move in. Use smoke grenades for cover. Get in there and take out as many Acrasians as you can. Leave the king and the princess to me. Got it?"

Moller nodded.

"Well?" General Marcellus asked.

"I'm thinking," Nels said. He put away his saber and checked his pistols while Moller conveyed the orders to the others with whispers and hand signals.

"This isn't that difficult a decision," Marcellus said.

"That's easy for you to say. You're not the one being asked to trust an Acrasian."

Marcellus asked, "Excuse me?"

Moller indicated he was done with a nod.

"I would apologize," Nels said, "but holding my father at gunpoint doesn't exactly instill positive thoughts. I'm sure you would feel the same were our roles reversed."

"Let me assure you, our roles would never be reversed," Marcellus said.

"That sounds like a challenge." Nels drew a pistol and then

stepped into the doorway. Hoping the blood soaking his sleeve might account for it, he kept his left hand slack and behind his back and scanned the room. Then he signaled left-handed to Larsson. *Fifteen men. Six on the right. Five on the left. Four in the—*

"Oh. Hello, Uncle," Nels said, doing his best not to show surprise. "Suvi and I thought you might be the source of Marcellus's information."

Uncle Sakari narrowed his eyes. "Don't speak to me, defect."

The troops. They're listening. Nels swallowed and tried not to consider what they'd think if his uncle revealed the truth. "Tell me, Uncle. What do you get out of this? Didn't you have enough already? Or was it because you finally understood that Suvi knew what you were doing? Why should the Acrasians trust you? I have to say, it can't be your taste in entertainment. General Marcellus, I don't suppose you heard about what my uncle did to your last ambassador?"

"I'll see both your hands, Hännenen," Marcellus said. "Now."

Praying Larsson had enough information, Nels raised his left hand with a wince that was only half-faked. Blood pounded in his ears. The pain in his arm gathered strength. New details filtered in. His father's betrayed expression transforming into hope and defiance. The tears and swelling bruises on his sister's face. The hastily stuffed gag in her mouth. The blood smeared across her chin. That worried Nels until he spied the Acrasian soldier on her left. The hand he had clamped on her arm had been badly bitten. Nels almost smiled. His father was gagged, too. *That's interesting.* Then he noticed that the Acrasian soldiers had cotton wool stuffed in their ears.

Smart. Even Marcellus had cotton in one ear. *Not that it would save you. You wouldn't have time to plug your other ear before Uncle had you in his power.*

"Drop the pistol. I want both hands in the air." General Marcellus wasn't as tall as Nels had imagined. His dark brown hair was cropped short, and his eyes were pale. He was wearing a long, dark gray uniform coat over a deep green jacket. Both were layered on top of a yellow waistcoat and a bright red sash. An ornate silver pin marked his rank. His buttons were silver. He stood next to the king. On the other side, an Acrasian soldier had Nels's father at gunpoint. Two more stood on either side of Suvi.

Nels gave his family what hoped was a reassuring look.

"I said, drop the pistol, Hännenen," General Marcellus said.

Nels smiled. "How about I lay it on the ground instead?"

"Just do it. Both pistols. The saber as well."

"All right," Nels said. Keeping his eyes on General Lucrosia, he began placing his weapons on the floor. *How much longer do the troops need?* The servants' entrance to the dining room wasn't hidden. It shouldn't take long to find it. *Unless the Acrasians have troops in the dining room.* His racing heart staggered.

Stop it. You'd have heard something if that were the case. He straightened.

"Kick your weapons toward me," General Marcellus said.

Nels did as ordered. He wasn't enthusiastic about it.

"Now step away from the door," General Marcellus said.

Here's hoping everyone is in position. Nels moved from the doorway.

Moller shouted from the hall, "Larsson!"

A smoke grenade clattered and rolled into the room. The iron ball hit the king in the leg and bounced away. The servants' door slammed open. Larsson and two others fired on the Acrasians from behind. Nels dove for his pistols. Gunfire went off all at once. He was able to reach one pistol before an Acrasian boot caught him in the side. Rolling, he pointed the gun up and fired. Nothing happened. Another round of shots went off. The Acrasian fell. More smoke filled the room. Nels retrieved his second pistol and his saber. Then he covered his nose with the crook of his arm and hunch-walked to his sister and father, who'd taken refuge behind a desk. His father was wounded in the shoulder. Bright crimson stained the teal silk of the loose bed jacket he wore over his nightshirt.

Nels positioned himself on the floor next to Suvi and painfully reloaded both pistols, wary of the battle around them. He spied eight dead on the floor. Five wore Acrasian uniforms. *Where is Uncle Sakari? And Marcellus?*

"Thank the Great Mother, you're still alive," Suvi said. She glanced at him over her shoulder and then continued tugging at her hem. She wasn't making much progress.

"Apparently, I'm good at it." Nels risked peeking inside the drawer where he knew his father kept a penknife. He fished it out and handed it to her.

"They killed Piritta." Suvi accepted the knife and made short work of her silk nightgown's hem. Her expression was hard, determined.

"How?"

"Just do what you have to. There's no point in talking to them." She moved to apply the makeshift bandage to their father's wound. "I've got this."

Nels pulled her hand away. "The blood. Let me. You can't touch—"

"This isn't the time for meaningless taboos," Suvi said.

The king said, "You're my heir. You cannot—"

An Acrasian spotted them and charged. Nels aimed his pistol and fired. The Acrasian dropped but then struggled to get up. Reloading, Nels shot him a second time before he could get closer.

"Father, I love you, but shut up," Suvi said and began to bind their father's wound with white silk. "Mother said, know when to follow tradition and when to ignore it. If this isn't one of those times, I don't know what is. Nels, may I have one of your pistols?"

"What?!"

"Just give me a damned pistol," Suvi said.

"But it's unclean. I used it to kill—"

"Do you *want* us to die?" she asked.

Nels checked the pistol, reloaded it, and handed it to her. He offered her extra shot and powder, but she refused.

"You're staying with us," she said. "I only want the one shot. I won't need more than one. If that. Well, hopefully not even that. I hope."

"We can't stay here," Nels said, peering over the top of the desk. "The Acrasians will break down the front door soon if they haven't already." The smoke was so thick in the room that it was difficult to see and breathe. His eyes stung and his words caught in his throat. He coughed. He wasn't the only one. He checked on the platoon. The fight seemed to be going well. They had the Acrasians out-numbered.

Glass crashed. *A window. They're trying to get fresh air into the room.* Another window shattered. He spied shadows at the openings. "The Acrasians are forcing their way in. I don't know how many are stationed at the back of the house. We can go through the servants' access and take them—"

"The keep," Suvi said, coughing. "We must go down to the keep."

"Right. Good idea. You and Father should go. Once you are both secure, I'll take the platoon down the servants' passage and—"

"You have to go with us," Suvi said. "All of you."

"I can't cower in the keep," Nels said. "I've the city to protect."

"You don't understand," Suvi said. "There's a tunnel under the palace. It leads to Keeper Mountain. If we don't block it off, the Acrasians will blow it up beneath us."

"Oh." *That's how Marcellus got in,* Nels thought. "Wait. Why didn't I know about this?"

"For the Great Mother's sake," Suvi said, "this isn't the—"

An Acrasian leapt up on the desk. Again, Nels fired. Warm blood splattered him in the face. The Acrasian soldier tumbled on top of the king.

Nels shoved the body away. "Father? Are you all right? Father?!"

His father sat up, choking and shuddering. He nodded.

The smoke began to clear. Nels made out the shapes of people but couldn't see their insignia. Another shadowy form approached.

Nels turned, aiming the pistol. "Stop right there!"

"It's me! Larsson, sir! Don't shoot! We've won!"

Lowering his weapon, Nels said, "Report."

"We've two . . ." Larsson gave Suvi and his father a sideways glance.

"Go on," Nels said.

"We've two dead. Three wounded," Larsson said. "The Acrasians are . . . eh . . . gone."

"All of them?" Nels asked. "Where's General Marcellus and my uncle?"

Larsson said, "I never saw your uncle or the general."

"How many Acrasian dead do you count?" Nels asked. *I need to know how many are left.*

"Nine, sir," Larsson said. "We couldn't find the others. Moller thinks they may have fled through the windows."

Another bang and crash caused the building to shudder.

"Tell Private Lassila and the rest to get in here," Nels said. "Then barricade the doors. Gather the wounded. Strip the dead of weapons and powder. And report back to me. We're leaving. Now."

"Yes, sir." Larsson saluted and left.

Suvi helped their father to his feet. He seemed much stronger now that the air was clearing. Nels checked and reloaded his pistols. It wasn't easy with his injured left arm. The pain had finally reached a point where it couldn't be ignored. Finished with the pistols, he decided to risk a look and shed both coat and jacket. The cold drifting in from the broken windows slapped him at once. He tugged at the tear in his sleeve. It was hard to tell at that angle, but he thought the ball had passed through the meat of his upper arm.

"Let me see to that, sir. Mrs. Westola has been teaching me a few things over the past few weeks. Mostly how to judge a wound. I can help," Sergeant Wiberg said. "Looks like you were lucky. It isn't too bad."

"Just get the bleeding stopped," Nels said.

"Yes, sir."

Larsson returned shortly after Wiberg finished and Nels had struggled back into his jacket and coat.

"Let's go," Nels said. "Moller, Kalastaja, and Kulmala, you're with me. We're first. Second squad, you're at the front. When I give the signal, you, Suvi, and Father are next. Then Wiberg, you're with the wounded. First squad, you're last. Lassila and Larsson, you're taking the rear. I want you to bolt the door once we're through. Got it?"

"Yes, sir."

Nels led the way. He found the door to the keep ajar and the lanterns lit in their niches on the way down. The moldy smell coming up from below was more dank than usual. *Must be the rain.*

"I sent Piritta to get the keep prepared," Suvi said, blinking back a fresh set of tears. "I sent her here, and they killed her."

Nels put a finger to his lips, signaling for quiet.

Lantern flames flickered. He felt a cool breeze. Hardly daring to breathe, he inched his way down. There were no sounds from below. The area visible from the steps showed only the familiar rug covering the stone floor and nothing else. Halfway down, Nels put his back against the right wall and signaled for Moller to do the same to the left. Together, they neared the bottom and stopped. With pistols at the ready, Nels slowly made his way to the last step.

The room was empty. A woman lay on the floor dressed in a pale blue silk dressing gown. Dark crimson colored both carpet and silk.

She's lost too much blood, Nels thought. *She's dead.* He told himself he'd been prepared for it. Still, it was one thing to know and another to see.

"Piritta!" Suvi rushed to the body.

Their father said, "Suvi, be careful!"

At the top of the stairs, Larsson slammed the heavy iron door closed, bolted and barred it. "Door is secure, sir."

Nels crossed the room to Piritta's body. He'd seen a great deal of death in his years in the Royal Army. He'd lost friends before, but this was . . . different. Piritta had been his sister's souja. She wasn't a soldier. He'd grown up with her. The situation seemed unreal and distant. It was as if he were watching his sister and Sergeant Wiberg bend over Piritta's body through someone else's eyes. Wiberg recited the Prayer for the Dead Lost in Combat in hushed tones. Suvi held Piritta's head in her lap. Nels half expected Piritta to sit up and push them both away in disgust. At the same time, he had a sense that the body lying on the floor wasn't Piritta any longer. *It couldn't be.* All the years he'd avoided her. All the years she'd made him uncomfortable. *I could've been nice to her. Just once. She would've understood how I felt. She was a souja.* He thought again of everyone and everything he'd lost in the past few months. *Mother.* Guilt and grief lodged huge in his throat.

He turned away from the scene, and when he did, he spotted something he'd never noticed before—an open panel. He grabbed one of the lanterns from its niche and peered inside. Beyond the hidden door, the opening became a twenty-foot-wide tunnel. The ceiling was equally as tall. The smooth walls said it was a naturally formed cave. However, long claw marks stretched several feet at a time. Ancient symbols chiseled into the stone warned away demons and professed the triumph of light. Tree roots pierced the ceiling. It smelled of damp earth, mold, and sweating stone. It was cold, too, far colder than the winter day above. He detected the rush of water in the distance.

"Why is this tunnel here?" he asked with a shudder.

Suvi entered, wielding a second lantern. Piritta's blood stained her clothes. "It leads to a crack in the world. A place where the—"

Their father cleared his throat as if in warning.

"Father, he needs to know," Suvi said.

"These things are secret for a reason," their father said.

"Those reasons are all dead," Suvi said. "We must be practical. I don't even understand why we hid from the truth in the first place. We must be honest with ourselves and our people."

Their father seemed ready to order her into silence. "It isn't right. He isn't—"

Suvi asked, "What happens if something happens to you? What if something happens to us both? Someone has to know what to do. It's too important." She moved farther into the cave. "Come on. I know the way."

Nels paused. *What if the Acrasians break through from upstairs?* "Private Kulmala."

"Yes, sir?"

"You're a pyrotechnic?"

"I have some small power, sir."

"Stay here. Corporal Lumme, second squad supports Kulmala. If the Acrasians break through the door above, I don't care what you have to do to stop them. You blow this end of the tunnel if you can."

"There isn't much powder, sir," Corporal Lumme said. "Not enough to do what you want and leave ammunition for the guns. Kulmala is good enough to light a campfire in the rain, but he's not as powerful as Jarvi."

"Do what you have to do. Just keep the Acrasians from attacking our rear. It's possible the end of this tunnel is being held against us, in which case we'll be back. And we'll have to fight our way back into the palace. But keep the Acrasians off our backs. Whatever it takes. If you do have to blow it," Nels said, "then do so and join us. Got it?"

"Yes, sir," Corporal Lumme said, and turned to his squad. "You heard the colonel. Get on with it." Lumme and his squad went back inside the keep.

"Corporal Mustonen, your squad is with me," Nels said. "Larsson, Moller, let's go."

Moller nodded. "Yes, sir." From his expression, he clearly didn't like the cave any more than Nels did.

Nels said, "All right, Suvi. Where do we go from here?"

Suvi moved to the front of the line, leaving their father with those assigned to guard him. "It's five miles long. This way."

"Five miles?" Nels asked.

"We'll have to keep the noise down," Suvi said. "Sound carries in here."

After a mile, the tunnel narrowed, and continued to do so until it was only ten feet wide. The carvings seemed to stretch the entire length. From the snatches of text that Nels could translate as they rushed past, all were blessings and prayers. Oddly, there were no branches, no alcoves. The cave traced a nearly straight path northwest, following along a fissure. He worried about how much time it would take to reach the end, and the distance between himself and the remainder of his platoon. Behind them, an explosion signaled the arrival of the Acrasians to the rear. Anxiety hit. *How quickly did General Marcellus and Uncle Sakari make the journey? Will we meet Acrasian reinforcements at the other end? Are we trapped? Are the troops holding the city? I've abandoned them. Again. Was it stupid of me to come here? Is Viktor still alive? Ilta! Ilta is at the hospital!*

Eventually, light filtered in, casting the tunnel in dim grays. He set down his lantern lest its light betray their presence, and motioned for Suvi and his father to stay back. Leaving several soldiers to guard them, he led Moller and the rest to the tunnel mouth until the telltale clank of troop movement brought Nels up short.

How many are there? he thought. Looking about him, he searched for any advantage. The tunnel had formed a bottleneck. It would have to do. He signaled for the others to find advantageous positions. Together, they waited in silence for the Acrasians. Nels's heart slammed against his breastbone like a drummer's mallet. His mouth was dry. Still, he felt calm.

He shot the first Acrasian to show himself. The others fired as well. The sound of the gunfire was huge in the small space. The Acrasians fell back, vanishing in the powder smoke. Nels and his troops inched forward in pursuit. Within a few hundred feet, he had an answer to at least one of his questions. There were a little over fifty Acrasians stationed at the end of the tunnel. *A full platoon.* He had half that many to hand, and a few were wounded. They were outnumbered, and they had no way of holding. He signaled a fighting withdrawal. They might be able to keep the Acrasians back at the bottleneck. Desperate for the odds to even out, he counted every Acrasian who fell as they fought. *Three. Four. Five—*

"Second squad is on the way," Moller said.

Nels nodded. *At least we made it to the bottleneck without any more casualties.*

Moller said, "We can hold out, sir. I know we can."

How long will it take Lumme's squad to get here? Nels felt a firm hand on his shoulder.

"You have to stop this," his father said.

"I plan on it," Nels said. "You should get back."

"You don't understand," his father said. "This is where I take over. If you continue the fight, no one will survive. You've done everything you could. I must step in now."

"The Acrasians don't take prisoners," Nels said.

"For what it's worth," his father said. "I'm . . . sorry."

Nels blinked. "For what?"

"I'm proud of you. Your mother was too. I should've believed in you as she did." His father stood with his back to the wall.

Frantically signaling to his own troops, Nels ordered a cease-fire before his father was accidentally hit.

"Kar! Stop this! Now! Do it before I do."

"What do you want, Henrik?" It was Uncle Sakari.

"Let's settle this between the two of us," the king said. "There's no need for further bloodshed."

"All right," Uncle Sakari said. "You first."

"Father, please don't," Nels said.

"I can't risk you or your sister," his father whispered. He turned and shouted, "Tell the Acrasians to lay down their weapons. Once I'm assured it's safe, I'll come out."

"Will you do the same with that whelp's troops?" Uncle Sakari asked.

"Of course I will."

Magic-infused orders were issued. Nels looked on as everyone disarmed. He paused, not sure what to do. *Did they forget that I'd be unaffected?* One look at his father, and Nels knew that wasn't so—at least in his father's case. The king seemed to be saying, *I'm relying on you to protect me.* Nels nodded in acknowledgment and acceptance.

And with that, King Henrik stepped into the middle of the tunnel. "What do you think you'll gain by all this violence?"

"The kingdom," Uncle Sakari said.

"You'll only have destroyed it in the process of acquiring it," the king said.

"I beg to differ," Uncle Sakari said.

"I made mistakes," the king said. "I see that now."

Nels saw his uncle move to the middle of the tunnel. His face was set in a mask of anger and frustration.

"I served you loyally! I did all the things you should have and didn't because you found them unpleasant! I took on all the kingdom's responsibilities while you played with your toys!"

The king nodded. "You're right. I should've paid more attention to my duty. I will now do what I should've all along."

"It's too late."

"It isn't. Not if you help me one last time."

"And why should I do that?" Uncle Sakari asked. "You'll only turn it over to—"

"My rightful heir?"

"That Ytlainen whore influenced you against me. She plotted with that guardsman she cuckolded you with. She would've made Eledore into a protectorate of Ytlain!"

"That isn't true," the king said. "She was my queen. We had our differences, but she only did what she felt was best for the people. She loved Eledore as much as I. Maybe she was right, after all. Maybe it is time for things to change."

"You can't mean to turn the kingdom over to a mere girl!"

The king shook his head. "That mere girl will make a better leader than either of us, Kar. Can't you see that?"

"She isn't even your daughter! Her father was that *guardsman!* A *foreigner!*"

The king paused. "I am her father. I don't care about Karpanen. Suvi is my chosen heir, and you will abide by my wishes. You don't have to do it out of a brother's love. Do it because it's what is best for the kingdom. Because if you don't, Eledore won't survive."

"You're a fool," Uncle Sakari said. "You've always been a fool."

Nels edged closer to his father so that he might get a better view of the situation. He kept his pistols out of sight. There was no point in reminding anyone of his immunity. At the same time, he needed to see the Acrasians. They were unarmed, but that didn't mean they would stay so.

"I'm not the only fool," the king said. "Tell me, what were you planning to do about the Acrasians once Nels, Suvi, and I were gone? Pat them on the head and tell them to go away like nice little automatons? It won't work."

"And why not?"

"Because they outnumber you, Kar. Wake up. Your Acrasian general is far more intelligent than you give him credit for. He plans to kill every Eledorean in this country, including you."

"I've been manipulating dim-witted animals like him all my life." Sakari didn't sound as confident as his words would imply.

"You don't believe me?" the king asked. "All you need do is look into his eyes and ask."

Snow swirled in the cavern entrance, and the sunlight—what little of it filtered through the storm—made the now-docile Acrasians into dim silhouettes. However, Nels's gaze kept drifting back to the general. Something wasn't right about Marcellus.

"All our lives, you've won. You're more intelligent than I am. You're stronger. More athletic. You always have been. So, I retreated into books and art. That's the way it's always been. Hasn't it? But you aren't going to win this time. You can't control your Acrasians without my help," the king said. "Admit it."

Sakari said, "You need me, not the other way around."

"You're wrong."

"You're going to stop me?"

"Actually, I am. I'm going to do something I should've done a long time ago," the king said. "Sakari Ilmari, for the sake of the Eledorean Kingdom, you will bend your knee to me, the rightful king of Eledore."

The tunnel was flooded with an overwhelming amount of magical energy. Nels winced under the weight of it. When he looked up, he saw that Uncle Sakari had dropped to his knees with a stunned expression pinned to his face.

"You will now—"

Pistol fire echoed down the tunnel. Nels gasped as his father was hit and fell. A fresh bloodstain formed in the middle back of the teal silk bed jacket. Suvi screamed.

"Noooo!" Sakari whirled on his knees to face General Marcellus. "You will place that pistol under your chin, now!"

Marcellus stepped into a patch of light. Nels could see that the general had followed orders. However, Nels also registered Marcellus's ploy. Telltale cotton fluff was wedged into his ears.

Time slowed. Nels reached for his own weapons and staggered to his feet. It seemed to take forever. "Uncle, stop! He can't hear—"

The gunshot filled the tunnel. Nels reached his uncle only in time to catch him.

"Time to finally offer up that surrender, boy," Marcellus said, pointing a saber at Nels. "You're beaten."

Suvi said, "Nels, do as he says."

Nels gritted his teeth and lifted his chin. "No." If Marcellus's jibe was meant to get to him, it'd struck home.

"We have to," Suvi said. "He'll kill you."

"You'd best listen to your sister," Marcellus said.

Shadows moved just outside the cave entrance in the swirling snow. There came a shout. Sounds of a scuffle reached the tunnel. Three shots rang out.

Marcellus frowned. "Lucanus? Report!" When the fresh silence wasn't broken with an answer, he shouted for Lucanus again.

"I'm afraid Lucanus isn't available," a familiar female voice answered. "Will I do? Never mind; I'm not a soldier. I am an advisor, however. And I would advise using the word 'surrender' about now."

Nels's jaw dropped. *It can't be.* "Ilta?"

"Suvi? Nels? I knew you'd need reinforcements," Ilta said. "Am I too late?"

EIGHT

"You have a choice, Your Grace," Ilta said, her voice momentarily carrying above the steady fall of snow and strengthening wind.

Suvi said, "It's already been taken care of this year. Remember?"

"Grandmother has passed to the other side," Ilta said. "And now your father has as well. The Old Ones will know. They'll see an opportunity. They won't wait for us to gather strength. We must prove to them that we have the power. Now."

While Nels had collected the last of his platoon and secured the Acrasian prisoners, Ilta had pulled Suvi into a private conversation just outside the cavern. Dressed as she was, in only her silk bed gown and night dress, he noticed Suvi was shivering. So, he sent a corporal with the coat, jacket, and boots from a dead comrade. Nels fully expected her to refuse them. However, to his relief, she didn't. She wouldn't allow him to post a guard nearby. Therefore, he kept Suvi and Ilta in sight. Intent on their arguing, they seemed unaware of anything else. He fought to keep from showing his impatience. If they were to get back inside the city, they'd have to do so before it was too late. With the weather, the walk was going to prove difficult. If it got much worse, he'd risk losing what few troops he had left. Based on the expression on Suvi's face, he didn't have a good feeling about what was to come next.

Overhearing Wiberg's solemn prayers for the newly dead in the background, Nels was reminded of his other duties, and his most recent loss, with a pang. *Father is dead. We're orphans now.*

Not only that, the fragile girl he'd known as Ilta seemed gone, and another more capable woman had taken her place. The new Ilta had more in common with Saara. There were subtle surface differences in her appearance—the small pox scar on her right cheek, the stern expression. Her long hair was bound in tight braids instead of being left in loose curls. Her mouth was set in a determined, narrow line. For the most part, he was glad of the change, and yet, at the same time, he worried that she no longer needed him.

She hasn't spoken more than a few words to you since she arrived. Yet he didn't want to believe his fears were finally realized. So, he tucked away that knowledge for future consideration, provided there would be a future in which to consider it.

"Moller," Nels said.

"Yes, sir?"

"Take inventory," Nels said. "I want to know how much ammunition we have left." He glanced out at the snow. "Also, check how much cold-weather gear we have. Tents. Rope. Supplies, if any. Tell me what we have to work with."

"Yes, sir." Moller turned to the troops and issued orders.

Nels went to Suvi and Ilta. The argument appeared to have slowed to a lull.

Suvi replied loud enough for him to hear, "Nels won't agree."

"Of course he won't," Ilta said. "But you're the queen. He is your soldier. You must command him."

Frowning, Nels approached. "What won't I agree to do?" He

didn't like the flash of guilt that passed over both their faces before they composed themselves.

Ilta turned away from him, unable to hold his gaze. It wrenched his heart.

He thought, *She's seen something—knows something I don't.*

"I've made a decision. And you're not going to like it," Suvi said. "But we—we don't have many options."

"We can dig our way back into the palace. Private Kulmala isn't powerful. So, the rubble can't be that strong of a barrier. It'll take time, but we can do it," Nels said. He was strategizing on his feet, and it felt good. "If we can get a message through to Viktor, he can send a small unit to meet us. We can join the others. We've got Marcellus. We can use him for leverage. And—"

"No," Suvi said.

He paused. Ilta's emotional distance took on new meaning. "Oh." He prepared himself for the news that he was to sacrifice himself and his men to get Suvi somewhere safe. He'd always known this day would come. It was nice that neither of them was comfortable with the idea, but it was his duty, after all.

Suvi glanced to Ilta, but the Silmaillia remained facing the winter storm. Her back was rigid.

"We must leave this place," Suvi said.

"Agreed," Nels said. "We can't shelter here too long. It's only a matter of time before the Acrasians will—"

"We must go up Keeper Mountain," Suvi said.

"In this storm?" Nels asked. "You must be joking."

"The storm ends less than a quarter of a mile from here," Ilta said. "How do you think I was able to get through?"

"Fine," Nels said. "You do whatever it is you need to do. We'll stay. Dig our way back. I'll hold the palace and wait for your return. We'll make a last—"

Suvi said, "You must come with us to Keeper Mountain."

"You can't possibly be serious," Nels said.

"I am," Suvi said.

"You're asking me to abandon Jalokivi," Nels said. "Your people. The civilians. Your army. Five hundred troops. *My* troops. To the Acrasians."

"I'm afraid so," Suvi said.

"And *Ilta* advised this?" Nels said.

"I haven't influenced her decision," Ilta said. "The choice is hers, and hers alone. Either she chooses to remain and Eledore only survives one more season, or she returns to the World's Pillar before it's too late."

"That's a choice?" Nels asked. "That's easy. Pick Eledore. The World's whatever can piss off."

Suvi said, "Nels, please—"

"She can't possibly mean to make you abandon your kingdom," Nels said. "For what?"

"You didn't hear me. Eledore as it was is gone," Ilta said. "If you travel to the World's Pillar now, there's a chance of the kingdom's being reborn. If we do anything else, Eledore won't be the only nation doomed."

Nels turned to Ilta. "How could you even ask this of me? You've finally lost your mind."

Ilta flinched. The jibe had hit her every bit as hard as he knew it would.

Stop this, he thought. *Apologize to her. Now.*

"Nels, please," Suvi said. "You're only making this harder."

He couldn't bring himself to say the words. Too much had happened. "You believe her?"

"She's the Silmaillia," Suvi said. "Of course I believe her."

"Fine. Go," Nels said. "But do it without me. I'm not leaving my troops to die." *Not again.*

"I need you," Suvi said. "I can't perform the ritual without you. Please."

"The hells you can't," Nels said.

"I'm telling you, I can't," Suvi said.

"What kind of ritual is it?" Nels asked. "Is it magical? If so, I've nothing to contribute. Remember?"

"That isn't true," Ilta said. "And you know it."

"I won't do it. I—"

"As your queen," Suvi said, "I hereby command it."

And there it was. The one thing with which he couldn't argue. Nels blinked and then he lowered his voice. "Suvi, please don't do this. You don't know what it'll do to me."

"Are you refusing to obey your queen?" Ilta asked.

Swallowing, Nels turned to look at his platoon. That was it. If he refused his sister, everything was lost. If he followed her wishes—

If I leave them behind, they can take back the palace. Then we can come back and—

Suvi's tone was gentle. "You can leave the others here to dig. If we—" She paused. "When we succeed, we'll need to get back into the palace. You're right. But you must come with me to Keeper Mountain. It's our only real chance at starting over."

Trapped. He stared at his boots. His jaw felt tight. "I will follow orders, *Your Highness.*"

"Nels, please—"

"Do I have time to perform the death rituals for our father?" He met her gaze with a hot glare. The question seemed to hit Suvi like a slap.

She blinked back tears. "How long will it take?"

"I can finish the short-form ritual in a quarter of an hour, Your Highness. The longer—"

"The shorter ritual will have to suffice," Suvi said.

"And the prisoners?" Nels asked. "What do we do with them?" He could make the decision for her, but he was done making things easier.

Suvi paused. "What do you suggest?"

Most of the platoon hadn't brought ryggsacks. There wasn't enough cold-weather gear or other equipment for everyone, but there was enough for a small group to hike up the mountain. It would mean leaving the remainder of the platoon with no supplies. They would need to dig fast. "The prisoners can dig. It'll be easier on the platoon. We have to take Marcellus with us, no matter what," Nels said. "Of course, if Your Highness would rather not bother with—"

Ilta said, "Marcellus should accompany us. He must see the crack in the world."

"Why would he care about such a thing?" Nels asked.

"Nels, just do as you're told," Ilta said, and walked away.

Why is she being so awful? What have I done? Nels bit back a retort by counting to a hundred, or, more accurately, twenty-five. Then he ordered Moller to take charge until he returned. The news that they would take Marcellus with them caused some consternation among the Acrasians.

"You have my word that your general will come to no harm," Nels said.

Marcellus arched an eyebrow. "The word of an Eledorean?"

"I don't have any other kind to give," Nels said.

NINE

Nels forced himself to focus on the rope binding Marcellus's hands behind his back, while Suvi and Ilta went through the things that Ilta had brought for the ritual. Above all, Nels did not look over his shoulder and down at Jalokivi. The last time he'd done so, it'd taken all his will to keep from sprinting down fifteen miles of mountain trails. The Waterborne blizzard now engulfed the city. There was no way of knowing how well Viktor was doing, or if those Nels had left behind had taken back the palace. Flashes of light and low rumbles were the only signs that the battle was continuing. He thought he'd glimpsed the Eledorean flag flying above the main tower, but he wasn't sure.

I've left them to die. I abandoned Viktor.

Nels didn't think he'd ever forgive Suvi or Ilta for what they'd made him do. *There's still a chance. I might get back in time. I might stand with the others.* He wasn't foolish enough to think that his mere presence would change the outcome, but he felt like a coward for leaving—even more so after Merta. "How long is this supposed to take?" he asked no one in particular.

The large, rough stone obelisk that Suvi had called the World's Pillar glistened with a thin layer of snow and ice. The ancient carvings scarring the canyon wall stared back at him accusingly.

"Not long," Ilta said.

The sun was nearing the horizon. He shuddered, sensing a foul undercurrent of rot originating from the cave. The stench of death was everywhere. The clearing was quiet, making each movement or sound the four of them made stand out like a foreign intruder. The feel of powerful magic emanating from the earth beneath his feet set his teeth on edge. He didn't like the place one bit. He'd like it even less in darkness. Of course, no one else seemed to like it either, even Marcellus. It was interesting to see the discomfort in the general's face.

This place is awful enough that an Acrasian can sense it, Nels thought.

Neither Ilta nor Suvi had bothered to inform him of his part in what was ahead. At this point, he didn't care. Then he'd remember the lives being lost, and it was enough to make him wish he could punch someone after all. He felt worse than he had in his entire life. *I'll do whatever it is she demands from me today,* he thought. *And then I'm riding into Jalokivi alone if I must. Let her piece together what remains on her own. I'm finished.*

Savior of Eledore, he thought, ripping at old wounds. *What was Saara thinking?*

"The book," Suvi said. "Oh, Goddess, we don't have the book."

Ilta placed a hand to her belt. "The knife and the lantern are the only magical tools necessary."

"I don't have the ritual memorized," Suvi said.

"You'll remember what you need. It'll be enough. The precise words aren't important," Ilta said. "The intent *is*."

"How do you know?" Suvi asked.

"I know. In any case, I can help with the few words that *are* significant, if your memory fails, but it won't," Ilta said. Facing the cave with its worn statues of gyrfalcons, she took a deep breath. "The blood will tell."

Suvi laughed. "Neither of us is an Ilmari. You know that."

Nels could detect fear in her voice.

Ilta asked, "May I ask you something?"

"Go on," Suvi said. She didn't appear to be looking forward to whatever was in the cave either.

"Do you honestly believe that the Ilmari line is unbroken? That the whole point to this is about royal blood?" Ilta asked, just loud enough for Nels to hear. "That never once in the whole history of the royal Ilmari house did a lover lie about who they'd slept with when? That every child presented to the kingdom as a royal heir was truly that beyond the name? Given the political games played at court for centuries, you honestly believe the truth was told in this one aspect of royal life? Do you really believe your mother was the first to be forced to bind with someone she wasn't in love with?" She let out a short laugh. "Honestly, the stories people in power tell themselves to justify their station."

Nels blinked.

"It's the power that matters," Ilta said. "The power that you and your brother have together. Blood is only to be used as bait. Blood draws the Old Ones. It gets their attention."

"Oh," Suvi said.

Ilta said, "Nels, it's time. Bring Marcellus."

"What did she mean about 'talking blood'?" Marcellus asked in Acrasian. "What will you do with me?"

"I have no plans for you, outside of ransom," Nels said in Acrasian. He wasn't certain who he hated more, himself or the man who'd killed his father and was responsible for the fall of Eledore.

It was cruel to toy with Marcellus's anxiety, but Nels found he couldn't help it. "The bleeding is merely a bonus." He felt ashamed at once. "Let's get this over with."

They passed beneath the stone gyrfalcons' wings, Suvi with the lantern at point and Ilta taking the rear. The disparity between the cavern beneath the palace and the cavern of the World's Pillar hit Nels at once. The World's Pillar was haunted. He knew it in his bones. When they passed a particularly scarred section of stone wall, Nels heard Marcellus whisper.

"What did you say?" Nels asked, keeping his voice low. Whatever slept here was something that he had no interest in waking.

"Powerful malorum walk here," Marcellus said.

Nels recalled the conversation with Corporal Petron. "I suppose they do."

"Then it is true," Marcellus said. "Your kind worship evil."

"What? No!" Nels winced as his objection bounced off the cavern walls.

Suvi stopped and glanced over her shoulder at him.

"Sorry. I wasn't . . ." He shrugged. "Just get on with it." He waited several paces before whispering to Marcellus in Acrasian. "We do not do any such thing."

"Then why are we here, boy?" Marcellus asked.

The cavern tunnel abruptly opened up into a vault with a high ceiling. Nels's head began to ache with the low buzz of overwhelming magical power. The force of it made him stagger. He gagged on the taste of old blood flooding his mouth and nose. Suvi didn't seem to sense it, at least not on the level he did. She didn't stop until she came to what appeared to be a rough altar table. A huge crevice split the wall behind it. Chunks of sickly pale clay smeared with what looked like old gore crusted the edges and were scattered on the ground. Parts of the seal—and it was easy to see that the clay had once been such—were intact but not enough to block the hole. Nels couldn't bring himself to look directly at the blackness. Things moved in the darkness on the other side—things he had no wish to see.

"Gaze upon the crack in the world," Ilta said, pointing. "Translate for the Acrasian."

Nels did so, but he wasn't sure Marcellus heard.

"Now lead the Acrasian there," Ilta said, pointing to a place near the altar. "And bind his legs."

"He's my prisoner," Nels said in Eledorean. "No matter what he's done. I won't harm him. I can't."

"He is only here to bear witness," Ilta said. "He'll be as safe was we are."

"I've some news for you," Nels said, not liking her formal tone. "We're not that safe."

"When you're done, join hands with Suvi and myself in front of the altar."

Nels turned to Marcellus and spoke in Acrasian. "Come on. You might as well get comfortable."

"What is going on?" Marcellus asked. He was making a good effort at hiding his terror.

Nels decided to have a little mercy. "You're here to watch. So, watch." He took up the slack in the rope he'd used to lead Marcellus and then used it to tie the general's feet together.

Ilta and Suvi made room for him between them, and Nels took the place provided. Suvi reached for his hand, but she looked him in the eye before she did. It was the first time she'd dared to do so since demanding that he abandon Jalokivi to the Acrasians.

Her guard dropped. She was his sister again. "I'm so sorry. There really wasn't a choice. Do you see that now?"

He glanced at the crack in the world and paused. Still, he couldn't bring himself to forgive her that easily. *Not yet.*

"I've asked too much, I know," Suvi said.

"You didn't ask," he said.

"I *am* sorry. You're my brother. I love you. If it means anything, I understand how you feel. They're my people, too. All of them—not only the army. All of those who are dying at the hands of the Acrasians now that you aren't there to protect them. You're all the family I have left. And now I've been forced to sacrifice even you." She let out a deep breath. "For the sake of the world."

Her apology hammered at the knot in his chest, and he found himself forgiving her after all, but he couldn't say it. He wouldn't. Too much was in the way. Instead, he took her hand in his and hoped that would be enough. Her skin was cold.

Ilta whispered, "The time has come to shed self-doubt."

"Sure," Nels said.

"You have to understand. We absolutely can't do this without you," Ilta said. "We tried. Last spring."

Nels blinked. "Well, it remains to be seen whether or not you can *with* me," he said. Like Suvi's, Ilta's fingers were chilled. He could feel her tremble.

"You'll see," Ilta said. "Give me your right palm."

Suvi squeezed his hand once before he let go. Ilta took the curved knife she carried and cut a shallow line across the inside of his hand before he had time to tense up.

"Ouch. Did I do something to deserve that?" he asked. The question included more than the physical cut.

He caught the specter of a smile on Ilta's lips. It gave him some hope.

"Just hold Suvi's hand and be quiet." Ilta sounded so much like her old self that he didn't hesitate. After she opened up his left palm she passed the bloodied knife to Suvi.

Suvi directed the blade's point to the ceiling, closed her eyes, and recited in domination magic–laced court speech, "In the eight names of the Great Mother and the Great Father, and by the power of the blood within myself and my brother, I command thee to sleep."

Nels stumbled as a surge of immense power passed from him to his sister through their clasped hands. The breath was forced from his body, and he gasped. Ilta staggered and dropped to one knee. The only thing that kept her from falling was his grip on her hand. He remembered the long-ago riot at the Commons Hospital, and suddenly it all made sense.

"Focus on what Suvi is doing. She needs you," Ilta said. "Help her."

Turning to his sister, Nels watched as she let go of him long enough to slit her palm and place the knife on the altar. Grabbing his hand once more, she pressed her bleeding palm flat against the wall inside the Great Mother's circle carved at eye level next to the open crevice. Nausea twisted Nels's guts. He got the impression that the stone drank his sister's blood. It wanted more, so much more.

It wanted him.

"Nels, please," Ilta said. "She needs you."

He squeezed his eyes shut and concentrated on the power flowing through him. Not all of it was his own. A great deal of it came from Ilta and the earth beneath his feet. A lot of the magic poured into Suvi, but it felt scattered. He could feel her shrinking from agony.

It's too much, he thought. *I'm hurting her.* Without understanding how or why, he gathered up all the power. Instead of aiming it at his sister, he directed it at the crack in the world through Suvi. The earth gave a violent shudder in response. He wondered if they'd all be buried alive in this terrible place. He felt Suvi break contact with the wall. Ilta released his hand.

Without thinking, he forced the excess magical energy back into the earth, where it would do the least harm. He stood alone and blinking, not certain what to do. Then he spoke the words, "In the eight names of the Great Mother and the Great Father, and by the power of sacred silver, I command thee to sleep."

The crack in the world had closed. No more than a hairline seam remained.

"Well," he said. "That wasn't what I expected." And with that, Nels passed out.

TEN

They spent the night in the clearing outside the cave. After the ritual, the area seemed peaceful in the same way that the night felt after a storm has passed. It was a relief. He didn't have enough energy to sit up, much less walk down the mountain. To his great embarrassment, Suvi and Ilta had had to carry him when it was over. Marcellus had followed without a single word.

Lying wrapped in a blanket, Nels watched the campfire cast shadows on the others. Suvi kept getting up and searching the valley below for signs of what was happening. The Waterborne storm still gripped Jalokivi like a fist. Ilta whispered what he assumed were reassurances. As for Marcellus, Nels had the impression that he was still considering what he'd seen. Ilta had untied him in exchange for his promise not to attempt escape. In turn, Suvi gave her word she wouldn't magically compel him to stay.

"May I speak with you?" Marcellus asked in formal Eledorean.

"I'm too exhausted to sleep," Nels answered in Acrasian. The truth was, residual magical energy was still coursing through his system. Every time he closed his eyes to rest, he remembered a new, more intimate aspect of the interior of his sister's mind. Any distraction was welcome. "What do you want?"

"I wish to propose a temporary truce," Marcellus said. "Between my army and yours."

"You're assuming I have an army remaining with which to negotiate," Nels said.

"I give you my word," Marcellus said. "Your people will be allowed to leave and take shelter where they will."

"We aren't leaving. This is our homeland, not yours."

"You've lost the war. This land belongs to the Regnum of Acrasia now."

"You would exile us from Eledore?"

"It is the only way you will be free."

"Free to starve, you mean."

"No, I—" Marcellus paused, frustrated. "I'm trying to grant you the best terms that I can, given the situation. I can't withdraw from Jalokivi. But you and your people can take whatever supplies they need and—"

"And my troops?" Nels asked.

"Those who survive can leave with you. They can take their weapons as well," Marcellus said. "I propose a truce, not surrender."

"I don't understand," Nels said. "You've won. Why would you do this?"

Marcellus glanced at the gyrfalcons guarding the cave. "Your kind can command malorum. And yet, on the brink of destruction, you didn't use them as allies to defeat us. If your people worship evil as they say, then you wouldn't have hesitated. You would've released them, not imprisoned them."

Nels stared. The thought of doing such a thing hadn't even occurred to him.

"I've never been terribly religious," Marcellus said. "I've always left those matters to others. But . . ." He shrugged. "I think the people of Acrasia have been misled."

"You do?" Nels asked.

"My kind couldn't have done what you did in there," Marcellus said, and shuddered. "Do you think . . . would it be possible . . ." He swallowed. "Do you think you and your queen could send all of them back to where they came from? Do you think you could drive the malorum out of Acrasia?"

Nels said, "I think we'd be willing to try."

"Then when I'm questioned as to why I let you go, I'll tell them," Marcellus said. He put out a hand. "I give you my oath."

"The word of an Acrasian?" Nels asked.

Marcellus paused and then drew his dagger.

There was no way Nels could defend himself. He was too weak. *Why did Suvi give him back his weapons?*

"I offer you a blood oath, then," Marcellus said. "I know you believe in those."

"Oh," Nels said. "One moment." He called to Suvi.

"What is it?" she asked, kneeling down next to him. She saw Marcellus's dagger and terror flashed across her face. "I command you—"

"Don't," Nels said before she could finish. "He's offering a truce. He's willing to let everyone go free, but it's not my place to accept."

"Well, tell him I accept before he changes his mind," she said.

"You haven't heard the terms," Nels said.

She said, "Explain so I can accept already. People are dying. We have to get home."

"He's taking the city and turning us out. It's winter," Nels said. "We don't have anywhere to go. We'll freeze to death or starve."

"We can go to Ytlain," Suvi said. "I can't imagine Cousin Edvard will turn us away. Not now."

"Help me up, then," Nels said. "I can't do this lying down."

He reopened the cut in his palm. It stung something awful. When he offered his hand to Marcellus, he repeated a line from the Soldier's Contrition: "What is lost in war cannot be replaced in vengeance."

Confusion clouded Marcellus's face.

Switching back to Acrasian, Nels said, "It's a blessing."

"Ah," Marcellus said, and took his hand. "Very well, then."

"We'll go to the palace in the morning and meet with your army under a flag of truce," Nels said. "Any idea how you're going to convince them that you're not under an Eledorean spell?"

"I'll find a way," Marcellus said. "Are you always this thorough in your pessimism?"

Nels asked, "Wouldn't you be?"

Marcellus seemed to take in the others' faces. "I suppose I would."

⊰ SUVI ⊱

ONE

"Everything is packed, Your Grace," Valterri said, buckling the last trunk. "I'll see that your things get to the coach. The *Otter* is waiting."

Suvi didn't know how the old butler had managed to survive, but she was glad of it. Having him and Ide nearby gave her comfort. *Everything is going to be so different. I won't have any of the things Father had to build with. I'll be starting from nothing.* She paused to say good-bye to the palace, her childhood home, and everything it represented. *Even Kassarina Ilmari, the first Queen of Eledore, had more than I do.* In all the years Suvi had imagined growing up to be like Grandmother Hännenen or the hero of whatever story her mother had told her, Suvi had never thought about what that might really mean. All the best stories, no matter how happy the ending, resulted in the uncertainty of abrupt change and loss. *That's the price of adventure.*

"Ready?" Ilta asked.

"When I read history, everything seemed so preordained," Suvi said. "You don't even consider that there were other options. That everything might not have turned out the way it did."

Ilta nodded. "That's true."

"Did I do the right thing?" Suvi asked. "Did I make the right choice?"

"You made the right choice."

"We'll have nothing," Suvi said.

"The nut must shed its shell in order to grow into a tree."

Suvi gave her a look. "Really? Did you just say that?"

"I'm your advisor. It's my duty to come up with adages, isn't it?"

"Does it have to sound so much like—like a bad poem?"

"I'm new at this." Ilta shrugged and smiled. "Give me time to practice."

"Fair enough."

"Gran said that there are some fates in which it's not wise to meddle. No matter how much you would rather otherwise. It's the Great Circle. Everything is born, grows old, and dies."

"But Eledoreans don't believe in death."

"That was our first mistake. We willfully put off a fate that was not meant to be avoided."

"So, the truth is Eledore is dead?"

"Not dead," Ilta said. "More like . . . sleeping."

Suvi sighed. "We're refugees."

"We have enough to begin again," Ilta said. She stared into the distance. "We'll have help. The way ahead will be difficult, but the people won't starve. Try to think of this as shedding all that we don't need."

"Really?" Suvi asked.

"Grieve first. When you're done, you'll see you have a choice," Ilta said. "To think of all this in a positive light or to think of it negatively. I suspect the first will be more helpful in the long run."

"If you say so."

"We'll be back one day."

"You're sure?"

Ilta paused and then nodded. "We will."

You mean Nels will, Suvi thought.

"You both will," Ilta said. "Together."

Suvi's face grew hot. She'd been reminded again of how little she was able to protect her own thoughts.

"The dead create room for new life." Ilta whispered the phrase as if it were part of a prayer.

"Let's go." Suvi whirled, turning her back on her old rooms and her old life.

Nels and the last of her servants waited outside. They would board *Northern Star* and head southwest toward the Chain Lakes. With Dylan to keep the ice from stopping them, they were free to go. From there, she might even head out to the ocean. She would have her childhood wish—a fleet—and nothing else. *The Water-borne live in much the same way. Why can't we?*

Vast snowdrifts made it easier to pretend the damage from the siege was less. She huddled inside fur-trimmed velvet and nursed the ache in her heart. The air was sharp, crisp, and it pinched her cheeks. Nels stood at attention next to the coach. He looked tired. His uniform was ill used, and yet he'd managed some dignity. His friend Viktor was next to him. A band of Acrasian soldiers clustered around the coach. They'd been sent to escort her to her ship. Marcellus was being generous, allowing her to leave with everything she and her people could carry. She was certain he'd see severe repercussions for it, but it was obvious Ilta's faith in him was well placed.

Reaching out, Nels offered to help her into the coach. She looked back one last time. An Acrasian flag fluttered above the tallest tower, but it wasn't alone. A purple Eledorean banner flew just under it. The sky was a gray and blurry background.

"Dylan says the weather won't wait," Nels said. "Another blizzard will hit before nightfall. It's to be a real beast. He can only hold it back for so long. He must save some of his power to get us to Järvi Satama and the summer palace. We need to get to Ytlain before the Emperor replaces Marcellus."

Suvi nodded. *Three hundred troops and a couple thousand people. That's all we are now. I don't even know how we'll hide them all away.*

The dead create room for new life, she told herself, and turned to face the future.

ACKNOWLEDGMENTS

Once upon a time, I read an essay about the fantasy genre that was printed at the end of Chris Bunch and Allan Cole's Sten Chronicles series. The authors stated that fantasy, unlike science fiction, positively depicts feudalism. The obvious reason why is because J.R.R. Tolkien was British. That thought, in turn, led to the seed question for The Malorum Gates. That is, if Tolkien had been American, what would fantasy look like? I strongly suspect that "more fantasy" was not the goal behind that essay, but I'll thank them for it nonetheless.

The list of resources used for *Cold Iron* is comparatively short. There's a reason for that. I believe that a writer who doesn't take risks is one who doesn't grow in skill. So, this novel stretched a different set of muscles—mainly that of making shit up. That said, *Cold Iron* does have its resources, helpful fairies, guardian angels, and various inspirational influences.

First, I want to thank those who kindly offered their expertise. Chris Levesque answered questions about the military, and Veera Mäkelä kindly provided help with Finnish. Mind you, this book probably still contains bad translations. That's not her fault but mine. Try to keep in mind that Eledore is an imaginary place with imaginary languages that originated from a wide swath of imaginary peoples—much like the United States (only slightly more imaginary.*) I needed some way of demonstrating that Eledore

---

*Ask anyone from Austin to pronounce "Manor," "Guadalupe," "Burnet," or "Manchaca." You'll know what I mean.

had existed for a long time—one of those ways is through the eroding of place names and such. Mind you, if I were as skilled with linguistics as J.R.R. Tolkien, I'd have designed my own language. However, I'm aware of my shortcomings. I'm dyslexic, after all, and hell, I had a tough time with what little Irish I managed to cram into my wooden skull. (And that is very little indeed.) The Finnish learning curve is simply too steep. Mind you, Finnish is definitely worth learning. Like Irish, it's gorgeous.

With that, I should go ahead and thank J.R.R. Tolkien. *The Lord of the Rings* swept me away to Middle Earth, and part of me never came back. Much of my teenage years were spent sketching scenes and characters from his books. (I'm probably one of five people who read *The Silmarillion* three times.) My heart will always live in Middle Earth. And while Tolkien is often (rightly) criticized for his lack of female characters . . . well . . . I'll just start and finish with Eowyn, the first character that showed me I could pick up a sword even though I was female. She told me that my daydreams of being a knight instead of a princess weren't silly. Eowyn, with all her self-doubt, made me understand that in order to be a brave warrior, one had to truly fear. For that reason, she made me feel as if I could do anything. And if someone declared that no man could do something? Well, that restriction sure as hell had no effect upon me because I am a woman. It was the first time I'd seen womanhood demonstrated as an advantage in fantasy. (Sadly, it was also just about the last.) I'd also like to thank George R.R. Martin. My husband handed me a copy of *A Game of Thrones* back in 1998. There is no doubt that it positively inspired me. Martin gave me permission to look outside of the standard epic fantasy medieval framework. He demonstrated that actual history was a very good place to look for fantasy settings, characters, and plots. (Regardless of how "true" you remained with the history.) Another big influence is Sir Terry Pratchett. He is, and always will be, someone I admire. The more I learn about writing, the more his ability to employ humor while conducting a thoughtful discussion on what it means to be human simply takes my breath away. He is, and always will be, one of the greats.

Others I wish to mention are Stephen King, Ray Bradbury, Charles de Lint, Ursula K. Le Guin, Michael Moorcock,[†] Diana Gabaldon, Ellen Kushner, Nisi Shawl, Kari Sperring, Scott Lynch, Mary Robinette Kowal, and Holly Black. All are wonderful writers and well worth your time. I should also list some historical fiction/classic fiction writers whose works helped me wrap my imagination around *Cold Iron*'s technological era: Gabriel Sabatini, Robert Louis Stevenson, Pierre Choderlos de Laclos, Jane Austen, Patrick O'Brian, C. S. Forester, and Bernard Cornwell.

Also? While there are many people who told me I was wasting my time, D&D taught me about world-building and storytelling. I learned a great deal about myself, too. I'm not alone in this. For that reason, I'd like to thank my gaming group—present and past: Thad, Andrew, Valerie, Alex, Andre, Chris, Christian, Alice, Matt, Katie, Leah, Steve, Stephanie, Mo, John, Mandy, Jame, and, of course, my husband, Dane "I've a plan. I need 50 feet of rope and a hobbit." Caruthers.

Thanks must go out to my writing group: Amanda Downum, Fade Manly, Elizabeth Bear, and Skyler White, and my former neighbors, Pat and Fawn, for lending me their front porch. Writing outside isn't the same now that you're not around to share coffee with. (May Seattle make you and little Uli very happy.) Also many thanks to Nisi Shawl, Cynthia Ward, and Mary Robinette for the Writing the Other Workshop.

---

†*Nels does, in fact, get the color of his hair from Elric.*

Bless you, Melissa Tyler. Because.

I want to give a shout-out to Angel Sword of Driftwood, Texas, and Master Swordsmith Daniel Watson for giving me a private tour of his sword forge. A big thank-you to Cherie Priest for taking me around the Civil War battlegrounds in Chattanooga, Tennessee. (Hooray for ghost stories and cannons!) Also, I'd like to mention Moy Yat Kung Fu Studio of Austin (Aaron Vyvial) and Hakkoryu Ken-Nin Dojo of Austin (John Cole).

Some of the nonfiction I used for reference included Lt. Col. Dave Grossman's *On Killing* and *On Combat, Bury My Heart at Wounded Knee* by Dee Brown, *Guns, Germs, and Steel* by Jared Diamond, *Pox Americana* by Elizabeth A. Fenn, *We Were Soldiers Once . . . and Young* by Lt. Gen. Harold G. Moore and Joseph L. Galloway, *War* by Sebastian Junger, *A Rumor of War* by Philip Caputo, and both *Matterhorn* and *What It Is Like to Go to War* by Karl Marlantes.

I am a child of the 1970s. The Vietnam War factored largely in my life during the years when I was first forming my perceptions of the world. Many of the questions in this book are a direct result of what I witnessed. I lived next door to a young man and his wife (sadly I can't remember their names). Not long after they'd moved in, he'd returned from a tour in Vietnam. Captain Karpanen's expression when Nels asks what it's like to kill comes directly from my memory. (Yes, I, like Nels, asked.) In part, this book is for that neighbor and all the others who suffered. Mind you, I'm aware not all of war is about suffering. If it were, we wouldn't read war stories. Certainly, epic fantasy, a genre known for its escapism, wouldn't contain so much war. My belief is that combat—horrifying as it is, not only brings out the very worst in people—it also can bring out the very best. Nonetheless, I much, much prefer peace. I may be a Goth, but I'm also a damned hippie and proud of it.

I'd also like to thank my copyeditor, Richard Shealy. Not only was he a joy to work with, but he laughed at the funny parts. My agent Barry Goldblatt deserves a big THANK-YOU. He knows why. Well . . . outside of the fact that he is amazing, listens to me when I'm being silly, and fought for my welfare even before he was officially my agent. Then there's my editor, Joe Monti. There aren't enough words for the wonderful he is. He plucked me out of the slush pile when he was an agent and snapped me up again when he went back to editing. I remain stunned by that miracle, and I firmly believe that there isn't anyone who understands my work better, outside of myself.

Lastly, there's my husband, Dane. He is, without a doubt, the most wonderful, funny, sexy, patient, and fun man in the world. And since I know a large number of wonderful men, that's saying something.

TURN THE PAGE
FOR A PREVIEW OF
THE NEXT ADVENTURE
FROM THE
MALORUM GATES:

BLACKTHORNE

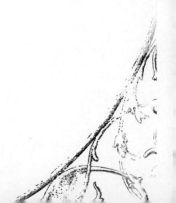

⇥ DRUSUS ⇤

NOVUS SALERNUM
THE REGNUM OF ACRASIA

━━━◦▶◦◀◦━━━

29 AUGUST
THE TWENTY-FIRST YEAR IN THE
SACRED REIGN OF EMPEROR HERMINIUS

"This can't have been a malorum attack," Cadet Warden Fortis Drusus muttered more to himself than to his partner. "It's too messy." Heart pounding in his ears, he gazed at the drying blood on the brick wall while his partner, Tavian, retched.

What a mess, Drusus thought. He fought his own urge to be sick. Focus. Remember your training. Follow procedure and you'll get through this. Show no weakness. Remember Tavian is watching. Glancing at the hunched Tavian, Drusus reconsidered that last thought. Still, this was their first corpse in the field, and Drusus was determined not to give Tavian any opportunities for advancement at his expense. Not like poor Severus.

Drusus's stomach muscles knotted again. Unable to bear the sight any longer, he checked the roofline and alley for trouble. Wiping palms slick with sweat on his uniform trousers, he hoped the beat of his heart was the only thing left to betray him. Otherwise, he felt calm. Too calm, he suspected. He wasn't entirely sure if that was due to the training or the unreality of the situation. He forced himself through the next steps. Making note of the time for the report, he snapped his pocket watch shut with a precise *click*. A quarter to eleven.

At first glance, the victim had appeared to be nothing more significant than a mound of filthy and stained rags. Drusus had been about to return to his rounds when the drying bloodstains had stopped him. He'd gone as far as to signal to Tavian before entering the alley alone when the sight of the disembodied hand had brought him up short. Having only recently graduated from the Academy, he hadn't been sure of himself until that moment. It was a relief to understand that he'd passed the first test.

It's not over yet. Stay aware. There may be malorum nearby, he thought. *Check your partner. Your partner is all you have in the field.* Those words now made sense in ways they hadn't before, and in that instant, he forgave Tavian. Drusus didn't really have a choice because to do otherwise would've ultimately risked his own life.

The stench in the narrow alley was overwhelming. "Tavian? Are you all right?"

Another coughing spasm was the only reply.

Covering nose and mouth with a hand, Drusus risked edging closer to the remains. His gaze drifted from body part to body part as if unable to take in the whole. A small, dead hand cupped a shadow in its palm. The two shortest fingers ended in jagged wounds. A few feet away, a tiny gold earring glittered in the lobe of a delicately pointed ear. The victim, an Eledorean slave girl approximately thirteen to sixteen years of age, judging from the size of the torso and the clothing, had been dragged into the narrow alley where her killer had finished his work.

Drusus looked for but didn't find the assassin's token that might explain the body.

What's next? He glanced again at the reassuring full moon. *Light. We'll need more light. Best get that seen to before Valarius arrives.* He set the hooded lantern he'd been carrying on the filthy paving stones near the remains before wriggling out of his pack. "Tavian?"

Tavian spit and wiped his mouth on the sleeve of his coat. "What?"

Drusus avoided gazing directly at Tavian's weakness in an effort to afford him some dignity. *That could've been me,* Drusus thought. "Do you have your spare lanterns?"

"Of course."

"Get them out." Drusus waited for Tavian to protest. Tavian was of higher social rank. It was his right.

Instead, Tavian straightened, closed his eyes, swallowed, and nodded.

They worked in silence as they unfolded, assembled, lit, and arranged a total of five camp lanterns in a half circle near the body. The lanterns, combined with the oil lamps bolted to the alley's walls and the full moon, accomplished two things: it would make the alley as safe as they could make it and it would provide light for the investigation. Drusus scanned the windows above the drying blood-splashed bricks. No witnesses appeared to lurk behind the small, blank rectangles of glass. He paused while curiosity and ambition tugged him in opposing directions.

We must finish this before the residents wake.

Or would it be better to wait for Valarius?

Tavian straightened, and Drusus caught the pungent scent

of vomit before it was overpowered again by the stench of gore and excrement. Tavian's marks were the highest in the cadet class. Drusus himself hadn't placed nearly as high. It didn't make sense that he, Drusus, was performing well, and Tavian wasn't. *Maybe this is a fluke? Maybe he'll get better with time?* But Drusus knew there was little chance that Tavian would have the luxury of time. If Drusus knew it, Tavian certainly did. That was now obvious. Tavian's face was pale, and his uniform collar was unbuttoned.

His expression bordered on panic. "Drusus?"

"Don't worry." Drusus knew what Tavian would ask, and he was annoyed with himself. *How long have I longed for an advantage over him? And now I'm not going to act on it. I'm sorry, Severus.*

"But I—I was the one that reported— I'm the reason they reassigned Severus."

Drusus blinked. Severus was—had been—Drusus's closest friend. The news that Tavian had been the one to speak to the director wasn't particularly shocking. Drusus had known that for more than a month. What was surprising was that Tavian was now admitting to it. Honesty had been the last thing Drusus had expected from Tavian. That, along with the past month's assignment, altered Drusus's perspective, and he didn't like it.

That's probably why the lieutenant inspector assigned us as partners. Drusus hated feeling manipulated. "I know."

"But now you can—"

"I said, don't worry about it," Drusus said. Revenge wouldn't bring Severus back. Only Severus had that power now, and knowing Severus, that wasn't going to happen any time soon. "Just . . . forget it."

"Thanks," Tavian said. "If I wash out, my father—he won't understand. He'll be angry. Me being a Warden means everything to him. He—"

"Just pull yourself together before Inspector Valarius sees you." Suddenly, it occurred to Drusus that he hadn't followed procedure as well as all that. "Shit."

"What's wrong?"

Drusus rushed to the alley's entrance, reached for the brass whistle hanging from a chain at his neck, and then blew into it with three short bursts. He paused for a count of five and then blew the signal again. *A body has been found. Situation secure.*

With that done, Drusus returned to the alley. He told himself that it was most likely an assassination and not a rogue. But if that's so, where is the token? Blood was everywhere. Assassins weren't this sloppy, not unless there was a message involved. And why would they bother with such a thing when the victim is an Eledorean slave? It then occurred to him that it would require a great deal of work to clean up. It was obvious that Tavian wouldn't be able to handle it, and Drusus didn't want to end up doing all the work himself. If a rogue was to blame, then proper procedure would be to send for the Watch. When the Watch arrived, the cleanup would be their responsibility.

However, Drusus was technically junior to Tavian. He couldn't make the decision. Tavian had to. Drusus said, "Someone should bring Captain Drake from the Watch house. Tell her to come at once. Alone. Tell her it's a special case."

"Are you sure?"

"Sure enough."

Tavian looked away. "You know the rules."

"It's a full moon. We've all this light. It's safe enough. Go on. It'll get you away from here." It would also mean that Tavian would be the one to pay Captain Drake, and Drusus found he was fine with that. Tavian could well afford it, and the Brotherhood would reimburse him anyway. Eventually.

"We'll get into trouble." Tavian wiped his mouth with the back of a hand. The unbuttoned collar of his Academy coat gaped, and the hem was stained with his own vomit. It was clear he didn't want to be anywhere near the body.

"We'll get into trouble if we don't. This isn't a practice," Drusus said. "We're supposed to act as full Wardens. The Watch house isn't far. The Inspectors will have heard my signal. They'll be here soon. I'll be fine." *And you don't want them to see you like this, Tavian.*

"All right." Tavian fixed his collar and combed his fingers through his hair. "How do I look?"

"You'll pass. It's not like the Watch is all that observant."

"And you won't tell anyone I was sick?"

"Are you going to make me swear?" Drusus grabbed a few bits of trash and flung them over the steaming vomit. "There. No one will be the wiser."

"Thanks," Tavian said. "I'll remember this. I will. Oh, I know. My horse?"

"The blood bay?"

"End of the week, she is yours if you want her. I'll talk to Father. It's as good as done. I promise." He then sprinted to the street and was gone.

Maybe Tavian isn't such a bad sort after all, Drusus thought. His mother wouldn't approve of the extra expense a horse would present, but she'd be thrilled with his resulting visits.

Alone with the body, he decided to gather as much information as he could while he had the chance. He patted the pockets of his greatcoat, locating his graphite holder and sketchbook. Then he crouched near the head of the corpse and, taking care to avoid staining his clothing, he gently lifted the remains of the girl's dress with two fingers. The blood-stiffened cloth stuck to a stab wound over the heart. He paused, considering how to proceed. If he forced the fabric free, the action might destroy the signs he sought. He settled for shifting the cloth out of the way. When he did, bloody handprints on the shoulders and neck were revealed. The throat had been cut with a dagger, and the eyes removed. The wounds in and around the eye sockets were thinner than the ones at the neck and in the chest, indicating they had been made with a second, smaller blade.

Malorum never take trophies, he thought. *Neither do assassins.* This wasn't an unpaid debt or an angry lover. He now felt justified in sending Tavian for Captain Drake.

Drusus stuck the graphite holder behind one ear and measured the bloody handprints with a tailor's tape. Then he used his jet-handled dagger to raise stiff cloth from the lower half of the body. Another swell of stench brought tears to his eyes. His stomach rolled, and he turned his head, pausing until his senses adjusted before looking back down. A knife had punctured the stomach and the organs beneath. Based upon the diamond shape of the wounds on the chest and the abdomen, Drusus deduced the blade used was double-edged.

An old crate toppled to the ground. Drusus sprang up, abandoning his sketchbook and drawing his pistol. His heart lodged itself in his throat. He scanned the area again for signs of a malorum. Every detail was sharpened by his terror.

A rat scurried from the garbage, then skirted the bottom of the brick wall. Drusus let out the breath he'd been holding.

"Cadet Drusus, where is Cadet Tavian?"

Drusus whirled to face an older Warden with a solid build and thinning gray hair. Inspector Warden Lucrosa Valarius. Valarius stood in the mouth of the alley and Five Sisters Road with his arms folded across his chest. Valarius's partner appeared at his side.

"I sent Tavian for Watch Captain Drake."

"And why would you do that?" Valarius asked.

"It's a special case, sir," Drusus said, and pointed to the remains.

Valarius's expression remained flat. He nodded to his partner and then stepped into the alley. His partner stationed himself at the mouth of the alley, keeping watch.

"You are not a full Warden, cadet. You've broken regulations, endangering yourself and your partner."

"I know, sir," Drusus said. "But I felt it was—"

"Don't give me excuses." Valarius frowned. "Do you understand how few cadets survive their first year in the field?"

"Yes, sir." Drusus put away the pistol and dagger and waited for Valarius to finish.

"A pistol is very little protection against a malorum." Valarius stooped over the body. "One shot won't stop an adult. It takes silver to bring one down. If I'd been a malorum, you'd be dead about now."

"The moon is full, sir."

"They've been known to risk the light when hungry enough." Valarius paused, looking closer. "Ah. Been at it again, has he?"

"Again? Who?"

Valarius muttered, apparently to himself. "The first was two weeks ago. Near the sector's northern wall."

"What is it?" The second inspector Warden asked in a loud whisper.

Valarius made a few hand signals, explaining the situation to his partner. Drusus understood most of what was said until Valarius turned. *Possible rogue. Watch is on the way. Keep everyone quiet.* "I told the inspector-captain we had a rogue hunter on our hands. You did well to send for Drake."

"Is it really a rogue?" Drusus asked. Rogues were rare. The last one had been caught long before he'd joined the Academy.

Valarius's expression softened. "I wouldn't go repeating that, if you know what's good for you."

"Yes, sir," Drusus said. "What did the inspector-captain do when you told him?"

"My partner and I were assigned cadet training. That's what happened." Valarius hunkered down next to the body. "Interesting. No rogue ever left anything like that before. What do you think it means?" He pointed to Drusus's leather-bound sketchbook. It had landed on the girl's chest, just missing the pungent remains of her stomach.

"Oh. Sorry, sir." Drusus retrieved his sketchbook and then searched for something with which to wipe off the cover.

Valarius asked, "More scribblings? Haven't you been cautioned for that?"

"How is reading signs left on a target any different from tracking?" Drusus asked. "If there are signature differences between hunters, such information could help quickly identify rogues. We could keep records. It would prevent repeated offenses."

"Why bother with all that?" Standing up and dusting off the knees of his breeches, Valarius said, "No rogue has escaped the Brotherhood of Wardens since it was founded."

"But—"

"And neither will this one," Valarius said.

"Nonetheless, the information may prove useful." Drusus suddenly realized he'd forgotten himself. He lowered his gaze. "I'm sorry, sir."

"I can't fault you for enthusiasm," Valarius said. "But there's been talk. You're making people uncomfortable. Take care, or you'll never rise above patrol Warden."

"Who said I wanted otherwise?"

"Trust me. Your purse will."

"It suits you well enough, sir."

Valarius's half smile was a little sad. "Never love an ideal more

than your career, boy. Principled men are rarely happy in this world."
He took a deep breath. "Now it seems we have a bit of a problem. A
rabbit was reported less than a mile from here. We tracked her to
Northbrook Street, but Quintus and Noster are also on her trail.
Bastards will collect the reward, if we're not quick about it. And
I have some hefty debts to pay." Valarius looked up at the night
sky and then scanned the alley. "Can you take care of yourself until
Drake arrives?"

"I think so." *Wouldn't leaving me here alone break regulation?*
Drusus bit back that question lest it antagonize his superior.
Maybe this is a test?

Valarius nodded. "All right. Blow an alarm if anything seems
out of place. You hear? I'd rather lose the reward than a cadet."

"Yes, sir."

"And Drusus?"

"Yes, sir?"

"Inform Tavian he's been issued a verbal caution."

"What for?"

Valarius pointed to the cooling puddle of vomit. "Loyalty to
one's field partner is admirable, but do it again, and you'll both go
on report, understand?"

"Yes, sir," Drusus said.

"I won't put it on record. This time. But do see it doesn't happen
again."

"How did you know it wasn't me?"

Glancing over his shoulder, Valarius said, "Patrol Wardens
survive on their ability to rapidly observe details. I have been in the
field for twenty years, cadet. I would've smelled it on you."

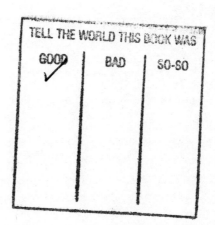

TELL THE WORLD THIS BOOK WAS

GOOD	BAD	SO-SO
✓		

ABOUT THE AUTHOR

STINA LEICHT is a science fiction and fantasy writer living in central Texas. In 2012, she was short-listed for the Crawford Award for her debut novel, *Of Blood and Honey*. Her second novel, a sequel, *And Blue Skies From Pain*, was on the *Locus* Recommended Reading List for 2012. She was a finalist for the John W. Campbell Award for Best New Writer in 2012 and in 2013. She is currently working on book two of the flintlock fantasy series The Malorum Gates, titled *Blackthorne*. She may be found online at csleicht.com and on Twitter at @stinaleicht.

THE
EPIC
TALE
OF
TWO
YOUNG
MEN:

the greatest warrior of his age, and a good-natured con man. Together, they led a rebellion against a tyrannical emperor who had betrayed the gods and his people. These two men were once brothers in arms, but will fidelity and noble goals fall to bitter and tragic actions as they become rival kings battling to rule the seven islands?

This is an epic fantasy novel debut from Ken Liu, one of the most lauded fantasy and science fiction writers of his generation and the winner of the Hugo, Nebula, and World Fantasy Awards.

PRINT AND EBOOK EDITIONS AVAILABLE
SAGAPRESS.COM

What if the *most* beloved
classic stories were true?

Three writers . . . a mysterious atlas . . . and an astonishing
adventure beyond your wildest imagination.

JAMES A. OWEN

DAWN OF
THE DRAGONS

  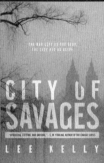